Maxim Jakubowski is a London-based novelist and editor. He was born in the UK and educated in France. Following a career in book publishing, he opened the world-famous Murder One bookshop in London. He now writes full time. He has edited over twenty bestselling erotic anthologies and books on erotic photography, as well as many acclaimed crime collections. His novels include *It's You That I Want to Kiss, Because She Thought She Loved Me* and *On Tenderness Express*, all three recently collected and reprinted in the USA as *Skin in Darkness*. Other books include *Life in the World of Women, The State of Montana, Kiss Me Sadly, Confessions of a Romantic Pornographer* and, recently, *I Was Waiting For You*. In 2006 he published *American Casanova*, a major erotic novel which he edited and on which fifteen of the top erotic writers in the world have collaborated, and his collected erotic short stories as *Fools For Lust*. He compiles two annual acclaimed series for the Mammoth list: *Best New Erotica* and *Best British Crime*. He is a winner of the Anthony and the Karel Awards, a frequent TV and radio broadcaster, a past crime columnist for the *Guardian* newspaper and Literary Director of London's Crime Scene Festival.

D0630958

THE MAMMOTH BOOK OF

Best
New Erotica

Volume 10

Edited and with an introduction
by Maxim Jakubowski

ROBINSON

RUNNING PRESS
PHILADELPHIA · LONDON

Constable & Robinson Ltd
3 The Lanchesters
162 Fulham Palace Road
London W6 9ER
www.constablerobinson.com

First published in the UK by Robinson,
an imprint of Constable & Robinson Ltd., 2011

A copy of the British Library Cataloguing in
Publication data is available from the British Library

UK ISBN: 978-1-84901-365-9

1 3 5 7 9 10 8 6 4 2

First published in the United States in 2011 by Running Press Book Publishers

US Library of Congress number: 2010925956
US ISBN: 978-0-7624-4097-9

Running Press Book Publishers
2300 Chestnut Street
Philadelphia, PA 19103-4371

Visit us on the web!
www.runningpress.com

Printed and bound in the UK

Contents

Acknowledgements

"The Cavern" © 2010 Valerie Grey. Reprinted by permission of the author.

"Honeymoon with Shannon" © 2009 Thom Gautier. First published in Sliptongue.com. Reprinted by permission of the author.

"Being Bobby" © 2009 Donna George Storey. First published in *Clean Sheets*. Reprinted by permission of the author.

"Advanced Corsetry" © 2009 Justine Elyot. First published in *Liaisons*, edited by Lindsay Gordon. Reprinted by permission of the author.

"Royal" © 2009 Adam Berlin. First published in *Clean Sheets*. Reprinted by permission of the author.

"The Strangler Fig" © 2009 J. D. Munro. First published in *Crossed Genres*. Reprinted by permission of the author.

"In the Absence of Motion" © 2009 Peter Baltensperger. First published in *Clean Sheets*. Reprinted by permission of the author.

"On my Knees in Barcelona" © 2009 Kristina Lloyd. First published in *Best Women's Erotica 2010*, edited by Violet Blue. Reprinted by permission of the author.

"Chemistry" © 2009 Velvet Moore. First published in *Clean Sheets*. Reprinted by permission of the author.

"When Lacy LeTush Went Blue, Blue, Blue!" © 2009 Thomas S. Roche. First published in Fishnet.com. Reprinted by permission of the author.

"Blind Tasting" © 2009 EllaRegina. First published in Sliptongue. com. Reprinted by permission of the author.

"Wing Walker" © 2009 Cheyenne Blue. First published in *The Mile High Club*, edited by Rachel Kramer Bussel. Reprinted by permission of the author.

"The Dead End Job" © 2009 Laurence Klavan. First published in Sliptongue.com. Reprinted by permission of the author.

"Perfect Timing" © 2009 Kristina Wright. First published in *Liaisons*, edited by Lindsay Gordon. Reprinted by permission of the author.

"Double Take" © 2009 Madeline Moore. First published in *Ultimate Decadence*, edited by Sarah Berry, Emily Dubberley and Alyson Fixter. Reprinted by permission of the author and Accent Press.

"The Escape" © 2009 Jett Zandersen. First published in *Lucrezia Magazine*. Reprinted by permission of the author.

"Paladins" © 2009 Robert Buckley. First published by *Erotica Readers & Writers Association*. Reprinted by permission of the author.

"Ducks" © 2009 Elizabeth Coldwell. First published in *Oysters & Chocolate*. Reprinted by permission of the author.

"A Cruel Heartless Bitch" © 2009 Severin Rossetti. First published in *Lucrezia Magazine*. Reprinted by permission of the author.

"Pierced" © 2009 Alison Tyler. First published in *BastardLife*. Reprinted by permission of the author.

"The Tinkling of Tiny Silver Bells" © 2009 M. Christian. First published in *Rude Mechanicals*. Reprinted by permission of the author.

"Simon Says" © 2009 Alice Gray. First published by *Erotica Readers & Writers Association*. Reprinted by permission of the author.

"Rain and the Library" © 2009 Kris Saknussemm. First published in Sliptongue.com. Reprinted by permission of the author.

"Park Larks" © 2009 C. Margery Kempe. First published in *Bunnie*. Reprinted by permission of the author.

"She Gleeked Me" © 2010 O'Neil De Noux. Reprinted by permission of the author.

"Slut" © 2009 Charlotte Stein. First published in *Sexy Little Numbers*, edited by Lindsay Gordon. Reprinted by permission of the author.

"Reunion" © 2009 Lisabet Sarai. First published in *Do Not Disturb*, edited by Rachel Kramer Bussel. Reprinted by permission of the author.

"An Inverted Heart. Glowing Ruby Red" © 2010 Mark Ramsden. Reprinted by permission of the author.

"Strippers" © 2009 Greg Jenkins. First published in Sliptongue. com. Reprinted by permission of the author.

"Only When it Rains" © 2009 Rose B. Thorny. First published by *Erotica Readers & Writers Association*. Reprinted by permission of the author.

"Canvas Back" © 2009 Craig J. Sorensen. First published in *The Erotic Woman*. Reprinted by permission of the author.

"The Witch of Jerome Avenue" © 2009 Tsaurah Litzky. First published in *Bitten*, edited by Susie Bright. Reprinted by permission of the author.

"Once More Beneath the Exit Sign" © 2009 Stephen Elliott. First published in *Pleasure Bound*, edited by Alison Tyler. Reprinted by permission of the author.

"Plasticity" © 2009 Salome Wilde. First published in *Clean Sheets*. Reprinted by permission of the author.

"The Spanking Machine" © 2009 Rachel Kramer Bussel. First published in *Bottoms Up*, edited by Rachel Kramer Bussel. Reprinted by permission of the author.

"Raw" © 2009 Adam Berlin. First published in *Clean Sheets*. Reprinted by permission of the author.

"Careful What You Wish For" © 2009 D. L. King. First published in *Swing!*, edited by Jolie du Pré. Reprinted by permission of the author.

"The Communion of Blood and Semen" © 2009 Maxim Jakubowski. First published in *The Sweetest Kiss*, edited by D. L. King. Reprinted by permission of the author.

"The Woman in His Room" © 2009 Saskia Walker. First published in *Girls on Top*, edited by Violet Blue. Reprinted by permission of the author.

"Kiss My Ass" © 2009 Jax Baynard. First published in *Kiss My Ass*, edited by Alison Tyler. Reprinted by permission of the author.

"Ladies Go First" © 2009 Alex Gross. First published in *Clean Sheets*. Reprinted by permission of the author.

"Calendar Girl" © 2009 Angela Caperton. First published in *Peep Show*, edited by Rachel Kramer Bussel. Reprinted by permission of the author.

"The Hamper Affair" © 2009 Mel Bosworth. First published in *Clean Sheets*. Reprinted by permission of the author.

"The Lady and the Unicorn" © 2009 C. Sanchez-Garcia. First published by *Erotica Readers & Writers Association*. Reprinted by permission of the author.

Introduction

Maxim Jakubowski

The swirling tides of erotica continue to sweep in and caress our sensual shores in this new volume of our annual anthology selecting the best erotic stories published during the course of the previous years.

Even though this is technically our tenth volume, we have actually been going for 15 years now as the initial years of our project went unnumbered (respectively the *Mammoth Book of Erotica, New Erotica, International Erotica, Historical Erotica* and *Short Erotic Novels,* for the completists and collectors out there).

As ever, writers the width and breadth of the English-speaking world (and occasionally further afield), continue to fire up their wild imaginations and deliver stories that amaze me, tickle my senses and more and delight readers in myriad ways.

The explosion of erotica writing and publishing marches on, despite the closure of some noted imprints, and 2009 saw a veritable florilege of new anthologies on specific themes (which made my selection tougher in so far as it would have been awkward to feature too many stories about, say, voyeurism, spanking, hotel rooms, vampires, swinging, BDSM, etc. . . .) to which an avalanche of eBooks and further web magazines was added to complicate my editorial choices.

There was truly an embarrassment of sexy possibilities, and I finally read almost 1,800 stories to reach the forty or so featured inside these pages.

A personal sense of satisfaction this year comes from the fact that for the very first time there are almost as many male authors as there are female in the book, a rare occurrence in the world of erotica but one which I feel does better reflect the profile of readers from my own past observations. Sex, in all its manifestations, is an equal opportunity temptation and looking at it from both sides of the gender divide proves a fascinating experience, which reflects real life and not just editorial presumptions. In addition, there are a couple of handfuls of new names, which I hope we will keep on seeing in contents pages, as well as a marked increase in the number of British authors. A milestone year indeed.

So, why waste my time any longer praising the stories and their imaginative variations on a subject too many have always assumed was limited? Jump straight into the book and enjoy the luscious spread of erotic delights that lies in store, and keep your prejudices (and your clothes?) at the door.

Savour, one story at a time!

Maxim Jakubowski

The Cavern

Valerie Grey

I.

The Hotel Arensen sits atop a spacious island planted with formal gardens and hedgerow mazes, tall poplars and tangled strands of ancient oak. One view is more beautiful than the next, and the whole is a symphony of light and form and shadow.

The island is connected to the shore of the lake by a macadam drive; when the sun slants low like this and the water burns red, the hotel and the island appear to be consumed by a lake of fire, attached to the mainland by a road of smoke.

Where the drive connects with the island is a long causeway and at the end of this causeway are the statues of two angels, one on each side of the road; one looks towards the Hotel Arensen, the other looking away, so that one faces the traveller as he enters, and the other faces the guest as he leaves.

Each angel holds a bronze sword, and in the light of the setting sun these swords appear to be aflame, just like the sword wielded by the angel who guarded the entrance to Eden.

When entering the grounds, the one angel keeps the outside world at bay, and on leaving the hotel, the other angel keeps back all that has happened there.

Within the hotel are hallways set with an infinity of doors, marble stairs leading to hidden verandas, and dimly lit corridors set with lush carpets and hung with faded and obscure paintings. There are ballrooms and dining halls, a spa and pools for taking the waters (in ancient times there were Roman baths here), and although the grounds and hotel are impeccably kept, there is a feeling that time has passed this place by; or rather that time has a different meaning here, measured not by the passage of the seasons, but by the continuity of human habitation.

The hotel has assumed a kind of seamless grandeur within the landscape in which it sits, rather like a queen sitting in state over an empty kingdom.

This is the sight that Dominique Béry sees as she alights in front of the hotel from the limousine that has brought her from the station: the marble steps that sweep up to the portico, the parade of Palladian windows gleaming in the dull light, punctuating the ancient façade of the building with a calm and stately rhythm, the ornamental statuary overgrown with spots of ancient moss.

She is slim, with large brown eyes and blonde hair, impeccably dressed in a simple white suit; from her placid appearance there is nothing to suggest that she's a fragile shell, that inside she's still tender and bruised, wounded by the bitter finish of a marriage.

She's brought herself to Hotel Arensen to try to recover the person she used to be; to try to break through the icy scar that has grown around her heart.

She is lost.

She can hide here.

She plans to return to the world fixed, healed.

Right now, she feels her life is like a pretzel, twisted and going nowhere.

The doorman has seen this all before, and takes her bags without a word. She's brought quite a bit of luggage; most guests do. They arrive with the shards of their lives in tow; uncertain as to what to leave behind and what to take with, and so they all bring too much. He leads the way, and Dominique walks to the desk where her key is waiting.

There's an elaborate fountain in the lobby, the waters spilling softly into the pool below with a soothing sound, establishing a kind of tranquility, and Dominique stops to peer into the water. There are flowers within, and fish hang in the stillness. She can see her reflection, and thinks of Michael being there with her and what he would say. She hates the way she automatically invokes his presence whenever she sees or feels something remarkable, but she can't stop it. His absence is like a sore tooth her tongue won't leave alone but has to press at and worry until it hurts again, and then she's satisfied.

"So pleased to have you with us, Ms Béry. I hope you find your room satisfactory," the clerk says as she signs the register. "Dinner is at seven. If there's anything you need, please don't hesitate to call."

Dominique takes her key and follows the handsome young bellman up to the second floor. She stands behind him in the elevator, so she can look at his behind in his tight trousers. It brings a rueful smile:

what she's heard is apparently true. Then down the long, quiet hall, the wheels of the luggage cart squeaking softly as he turns this way and that through the bewildering maze of corridors.

He stops outside room 331 and opens the door, and she walks into a large and spacious room, restored to all its rococo glory, dominated by an antique table and matching canopy bed. On the table an elaborate display of fresh-cut flowers perfumes the air and, as she crosses over to the French doors that overlook the lake and the formal gardens, she stops to run her hand over the ancient wood of the bed, trying to imagine things that had happened there.

Dominique looks at the bellman. He is absurdly handsome in his tight burgundy uniform with yellow piping. His cheeks are pink, his eyes bright with youth and health, but he's no more than a boy, and she hasn't any interest in boys. She imagines that he's quite experienced, working at the Hotel Arensen.

Everyone is here, and everyone's for hire, or so she's heard.

The bellman stands awkwardly, only for a moment.

He opens the French doors.

Dominique steps out on to the small terrace. She hears the call of a peacock and, looking down, sees the group on the shadowy lawn: a cock with three hens.

A flight of little birds bursts from the ivy below her window and scatters into the gloom like an omen. She stands with her hands on the doors, inhaling the scent of the roses in the garden.

Down and to the left, the light in a room is on. The shades are drawn but the drapes are open, and Dominique sees shadows passing by the window in the yellowish light.

She tips the bellman and locks the door behind him. She takes off her jacket and shoes and walks into the bathroom. The floor and walls are of Italian marble, the fixtures harmonious with the eighteenth-century decor, but all apparently new.

An enormous shower, a toilet, a sink and a bidet.

She runs water into the enormous claw-foot tub, pouring in some lilac salts from the collection on the tub's edge. While the bath fills, she unpacks some things, then undresses, carefully hanging up her clothes as if she's aware of the symbolism of the act. She wants to remember this moment of arrival. She wants to remember what she feels like right now, before anything has happened.

She wraps a robe around her and goes back into the bathroom, sits on the edge of the tub and watches the suds accumulate in the steaming water.

She'd tried so hard to make it work. She had assumed from the start that Michael was the one, and even after he'd disappointed her time and again she'd refused to give up hope. In the end it had turned ugly and even degrading, and Dominique had clung to him, terrified of being alone after having given so much of herself.

Her clinging had gained her nothing, and the more she gave, the less she had left of herself. Finally she lost Michael, all she had given, and a great deal more as well. She'd lost parts of herself she didn't think he'd even had access to, parts she had thought were safe.

She takes off her robe and hangs it behind the door, then eases herself into the tub, enjoying the sting of the hot water against her skin. She scrubs the grime of travel from her body and then soaks in the fragrant warmth, trying to think of nothing.

She's lost so much that sometimes the integrity of her body surprises her. It's as if she expects to see a missing limb or vast scar running between her breasts, but no: her body remains surprisingly healthy in spite of all she's been through.

She emerges from the tub and takes a warm towel from the heater and dries herself, then wraps her robe around her body and walks into her sitting room, drying her hair.

From her make-up case she takes three bottles of sleeping pills and puts them on the bedside table, next to the phone, lining them up like soldiers.

Three prescriptions from three different doctors.

No matter how bad things get or what happens to her, she always has these three, more than enough. As long as she has them, every day – every minute – is the result of her decision, and she likes knowing that. She no longer pours them into her hand and fondles them as she once did, toying with the feeling of her own mortality, but still, she thinks of them as her freedom.

She walks over to the flower arrangement on the table and takes a tiger lily blossom in her hands, inhaling the fragrance. She looks at the blossom, so beautiful and yet so blatantly, almost comically sexual, the open and welcoming calyx of the petals, the quivering male anthers dotted with pollen.

She smiles briefly and is aware of it, of how unfamiliar it feels, and she feels encouraged. Maybe this place will work for her. She replaces the flower, then walks out on to the terrace again, into the warm summer night where her eyes are caught by that same lighted window, open now, with a figure in it, sharply silhouetted against the shade.

A man, apparently shirtless, his arms held above his head. He's turned in three-quarters profile, and Dominique can see the dim shadow of another figure behind the shade as well.

Dominique stops towelling her hair and stands transfixed as a woman enters the picture. The woman is wearing a corset, it's obvious from her silhouette, and she's holding a doubled over cord or strap in her hands, bringing her hands together and then pulling them apart with enough force that Dominique can hear the snap from across the way.

She sees the woman bring her arm back, the strap dangling, and bring it down on the man's behind. She hears the slap and sees his body jerk in whatever it is that holds him. Dominique stands as still as a statue as the woman hits him again, and again, and then she slowly backs up into her room and sits down on the bed.

She knows what kind of place this is, of course, and why people come here. The reputation of sex and sexuality hangs heavily over the entire hotel, and the reputation is the reason she came. But the Arensen is also known for its exclusivity and sense of discretion. She hadn't expected to be confronted with such a flagrant and lurid display.

She plugs in her drier and finishes her hair, standing inside her room where she's safe. The clock says seven ten, and she's hungry, but she takes a moment to inspect her room. There's an antique French armoire that holds a courtesy bar and a large television set. The television seems jarringly out of place in this eighteenth-century setting, and she's offended at first, but then she takes the remote control and turns it on.

There is a channel guide atop the set, and she picks it up and looks at it.

Everything is apparently closed circuit.

Channels are grouped together and marked:

Male Escorts
Female Escorts
Dungeon
Exhibitionist
Exhibitionist/Voyeur
Commercial Entertainment

She selects the Male Escorts channel and finds herself watching videos featuring virile young men, all apparently hotel employees – little snatches of them riding horses, or emerging dripping from the lake, strolling through the gardens and smiling for the camera.

She smiles. She wonders if her bellman is in there. Probably, but she's not interested in finding out.

She selects the Exhibitionist channel and find herself staring into a room much like her own, apparently empty, though she can see towels still lying over the back of a chair.

She chooses another Exhibitionist channel and is shocked to see a young man sitting on the side of his bed masturbating. He looks up at the camera with a lascivious leer, his face distorted by his proximity to the wide-angle lens. She quickly changes the channel.

Dominique clicks rapidly through the Exhibitionist channels, and suddenly finds herself looking down at herself in her own room. Her blood runs cold.

"This is room 331," she snaps into the phone, her hand shaking with rage. "Why is there a camera in my room? What's the meaning of this?"

The desk clerk is terribly apologetic. Wasn't madam aware that she'd requested an Exhibitionist room? There it was on her reservation; she's even been charged extra for it. He was looking at her reservation now. The request box had been checked.

"No," she said trying to keep her voice steady. "I'm sorry, but no. There's been some mistake. I want this camera turned off immediately. No. I want it removed. I want it removed or I want a new room."

"At once, madam. I'll have a man sent up immediately. I do so regret the error. Of course you won't be billed for the camera. I'm so terribly sorry. I can't imagine how this happened . . ."

His tone is so contrite and profusely apologetic that Dominique finds herself consoling him. Possibly she had checked that box when she'd filled out her reservation. She'd been quite intoxicated that night. "That's quite all right. Just see that it's turned off. No, there's nothing else. Thank you, that's very considerate. Yes, everything else is quite satisfactory."

She hangs up the phone and, as she does so, she sees the TV screen go blank as her camera is turned off, but now she can't help but wonder.

She aims the remote control at the TV and selects another channel in the Exhibitionist group and finds herself looking down into another empty room. She clicks again and gets yet another empty room, though she can hear voices.

On the third try she finds what she is looking for: a man and a woman making love.

Now that her suspicions are confirmed, her reflex is to turn away and switch it off, but she forces herself to watch. The camera is above and to the right of the foot of the bed, as is the camera in Dominique's room.

She can't see their faces.

The man is between the woman's thighs, his pale ass rising and falling with thrusts so powerful that the woman's legs shake. He's panting, while she gives a little yelp or grunt whenever he thrusts into her.

The camera stares blandly down on them, and though Dominique knows that both of them are aware they're being watched and must even enjoy it, she feels contaminated, as if she's been drawn into their perversion.

But no, it's not the voyeuristic aspects or even the act itself that strikes her as obscene. It's the couple's painful need; a need that makes them eschew their dignity and privacy in exchange for some brief satisfaction. What keeps her watching is her recognition that she shares the same need. It's as if she's watching people suffering from the same disease she knows she has.

It's the woman's hands that seem to hold her attention. With their faces invisible, it's the woman's fingers that seem to be the most human. They spread out and press down urgently on the man's back, or curl into claws to rake his skin.

They leave his body and grab at the sheet, as if she's afraid she'll be swept away, then, in moments of extremity, they reach down as she digs her nails into his buttocks, her knees spreading wide, pulling him into her, beside herself with lust.

Pleasure, pain, love, hatred: Dominique sees them all in the woman's hands.

The hands come up and grab the man's hair, and Dominique sees the woman's face for an instant: a flash of eyes tightly closed and an open, hungry mouth, nothing more.

Both voices rise, his to a low, threatening growl, hers to a shrill and gasping wail that peaks as she throws her head back in a sudden choked silence, a scream locked in her throat. Dominique realizes with a weird thrill that they're both climaxing. Even as she watches, the man's cock must be already jumping inside the woman and spitting out his lust.

The woman's hands ball into fists, then fall back on the bed in helpless surrender as the man's hips lunge at her in angry insistence. It's too much. Dominique can't watch any more. She switches off the TV and puts down the remote. She's breathing deep, her face is flushed.

It's so remarkable what sex does to people: how they need it so much, that terrible intimacy of release in another's arms. With her own ardour quenched and battered by the pain of her break-up, she's been able to look at it more objectively, as an outsider, and it seems so strange. In the past months she's come to realize how hard it is to maintain one's existence in the world, to keep one's ego intact in the face of all that tears at it and attempts to grind it down, and now it seems so strange to see how people fight and contend to give themselves away, to throw themselves at one another and lose themselves in their lover's embrace.

She feels a sudden urge to masturbate that takes her quite by surprise. Since she broke up with Michael she has had no sex, and absolutely no desire for sex. That's why she's come to this place, to try to rekindle that spark, and yet she lives in fear that she might be permanently damaged, that she may have lost the capacity to respond to that kind of intimacy.

She worries that she might be the victim of some form of hysterical frigidity brought about by the trauma of her separation, and that it might be permanent. She's afraid to push herself beyond the level of mild interest she feels now, afraid that she won't respond

She makes herself behave, letting herself feel the subtle tension in her body that she recognizes with welcome relief as the beginnings of sexual arousal. She feels as though some energy within her is being renewed, as if the mainspring of a watch is being wound and tightened. It's a good sign, but it makes her nervous.

She sits at her dressing table and does her face: nothing too elaborate, some eyeliner and shadow, some blush, her lipstick. She brushes her hair and studies herself in the mirror: the large, expressive brown eyes, the fine features. She's lost her girlish sparkle, but perhaps she's gained a degree of depth and maturity.

Michael used to call her his princess for the fineness of her features and the regal way she carried herself, and she wonders now whether her carriage has changed: whether she still walks with her back straight and her head erect. It's something she hasn't even thought to notice before.

It would be easier to stay in tonight, she thinks. She could order in from room service and go to bed early. She wouldn't have to dress, she wouldn't have to see anyone.

She's made a promise to herself and she intends to keep it.

She doesn't have long in the hotel.

II.

She goes to her bag and finds a new package of nylons, opens it, and takes out one of the gauzy stockings. She rolls it up, then inserts her foot and extends her leg, unrolling the stocking as she goes, then running her hands up its length, over her calf, her knee, her thigh, smoothing out the thin fabric. The way it embraces her leg feels good, and the band of material around the top of her thigh feels very erotic. It's good to feel this way again.

She puts on the other stocking, looks through the underthings she's unpacked but doesn't find anything she likes. Impulsively, she pushes them aside and takes out a suspender belt which she fastens around her waist and tugs into place around her hips. She purposely ignores her panties and clips the garters to her stockings, then goes to her closet and selects her black dress; black crêpe, with tiny thin straps that go over her flawless shoulders. It's unlined, but Dominique doesn't hesitate. She leaves her bras in the drawer and slips the dress on over her head, naked beneath it, and looks at herself in the mirror.

The feel of the fabric on her bare nipples and her shaved mound feels very good, very wicked and erotic.

So far, so good.

The dress comes with a black jacket. She puts it on, fastens a gold chain around her neck, and threads the matching earrings through her ears. She puts on her watch and a gold bracelet, takes her bag and checks herself once more. She had hoped she would feel irresistible, but the best she can manage is a kind of stubborn pride and naughtiness. Well, that's close enough. She turns off the lights and exits the room, slipping her key into her purse.

The hotel is bewildering, with hallways that jog and branch off, small sitting rooms that emerge unexpectedly, and stairways that appear in puzzling places, seeming to make no sense. Dominique is quite lost. She was certain she was headed for the main desk, but now she's disorientated and there seems to be no one about to ask for directions.

She hears the murmur of voices and, a few turns later, she's in the lobby again, or rather, a different lobby, and it occurs to her that there must be more than one check-in desk, and she's apparently stumbled upon an alternate.

"Excuse me, but how do I get to the dining room?" she asks the young woman at the desk.

"Which dining room are you looking for?" the girl says. "There are several. The Ladies', the Gentlemen's, the Versailles, the Savoy, the New York Grille, the Tea House."

Dominique holds up her hand and says, "Please. I'm just looking for a place for a quiet meal."

"Is madam alone?"

"Yes."

"If madam would like to choose her own companionship or just dine alone, I'd suggest the Ladies' salon. If you seek to meet some gentlemen looking for companionship, I'd recommend the Gentlemen's room or the New York. Perhaps the Savoy if you're looking for more mature company . . ."

Dominique looks at her in confusion. "I'm sorry. I don't understand."

The girl smiles and slides a brochure across the marble counter. "The Ladies' salon is of course for women. We cater to female tastes there, and hotel escorts are available, or, if you prefer, you may dine alone without being bothered. The Gentlemen's room caters to male tastes, but female patrons often go there to be seen and *socialize*." She gives the word an odd emphasis. "That's where most of the unattached men go to eat."

The girl gives Dominique a knowing smile, but, seeing her confusion, leans over the counter and whispers, "It's very much like a pick-up bar. They'll be all over you there, if that's what you want."

Dominique feels a slight chill run up the back of her neck as the import of what the girl is saying sinks in.

"Other rooms are available too," the girl adds helpfully. "However, you might feel out of place there dining alone. They cater to couples, mostly."

"I see. Yes, I think perhaps the Ladies' salon would be best." She just could not see herself walking into a room filled with leering men, like a piece of meat on a stick thrust into a den of lions. She isn't ready for that.

The girl traces a path on the map with a marker and hands it to her. She picks up the phone and says, "I'll call ahead and tell them to see that you get a good table, Ms . . . ?"

"Béry. And thank you for your help."

The path she takes now avoids the labyrinthine hallways and stays to the main corridors. Dominique has no trouble finding the Ladies' salon, and in fact can't quite understand how she became so turned around before.

She was afraid that the room would be embarrasingly feminine, but that's not the case at all. The room is done in cream, dusky rose and moss green, the fixtures and place settings pure and elegant, the lighting subdued but not dark. There's a mirrored bar set against one wall, and Dominique's somewhat surprised to see that there are some men sitting there, some with women, some alone. Apparently the Ladies' Salon isn't just for women. Despite her misgivings, that lifts her spirits. Although she doesn't want to be stared at by men, neither had she worn this dress for the benefit of women.

A hostess meets Dominique at the entrance and addresses her by name. She leads her to a table towards the edge of the room, hands her a menu and asks her if the table is satisfactory. Dominique nods. From where she sits she can see most of the room, but she herself is unobtrusive.

She studies the menu.

She's ravenous, and everything looks good. A very handsome young waiter comes and takes her order, and it's only after he has gone that Dominique picks up the leather-bound booklet on her table. She had assumed it was a wine list, but looking at it now, she sees it is filled with more pictures of young men, all of them apparently employees of the hotel, and all of them available for a fee.

She turns the pages. She recognizes some from the video she'd seen in her room, but there are many more. Apparently everyone who works in the hotel is indeed available. This one dresses as a cowboy, in boots and leather chaps. Another affects the manner of a rock star. A third dresses like a motorcycle outlaw in leather and chains.

There are princes and businessmen, priests and barbarians and, at the end, a series of pictures of young men who apparently prefer to appear as themselves.

Flipping back towards the front, she finds instructions on how the book is to be used. Forms are available from her waitress upon which she can write her choices. Availability of escorts cannot be guaranteed, so she's urged to make her reservations as early as possible. Fees may be charged to her rooms. Gratuities are customary . . .

She is startled by her waitress bringing the first course, and Dominique's aware that she's been staring at the book. She puts it down and looks at the other women dining around her to see if she's been noticed.

Most of them are alone, but some are in pairs or groups of three or four. How many of them, she wonders, will be asking their waitresses for forms and filling them out?

As she places her napkin in her lap and squeezes lemon over her calamari, she's aware of someone's eyes on her. Looking up, she sees a man at the bar regarding her with calm and open interest, and Dominique finds herself glancing right back at him before she realizes the implications of what she's doing.

The man turns away to let her eat in peace, and she feels a sudden flush of excitement. How could she have stared at him like that? She'd never done anything like that before. It must be this place, something about this place. He's very handsome, distinguished actually, and his maturity is welcome after all the smiling youths she's seen so far.

The calamari are excellent and Dominique eagerly attacks her main course – medallions of veal in Madeira with baby potatoes and fresh peas – keeping one eye on the man at the bar. He's considerably older than she is, and his black hair and beard are flecked with grey. And yet it's impossible to look at his back as he sits at the bar and not think of a man at the height of his powers: knowledgeable and sophisticated. The word "virile" comes to mind, and makes her smile. He's everything that the boys in the catalogue are not and, for the first time since her arrival, Dominique finds her sexual curiosity rising in a personal way. She's not above engaging in a little erotic speculation.

"Ms Béry?"

Again the waitress catches Dominique off guard as she lays down a beautifully arranged tray of cheese, nuts and fruit, accompanied by a cut-glass decanter of wine.

"What's this?" Dominique asks. "I didn't order this."

"Vintage port," the waitress says. "From the gentleman."

Dominique looks up to see the man at the bar looking at her again, nodding in greeting.

Before she can think to say anything, the waitress has poured a glass of port and handed it to her, and there's nothing she can do but take a sip. The wine is thick and rich, its sweetness aged to an earthy maturity, while the alcoholic bouquet hints at the intoxication to come. The sensual complexity of the wine takes her by surprise. She's never had good port before.

She takes another sip.

The man leaves his stool and approaches the table. He stops some distance away, not wanting to impose himself. "It's satisfactory?"

"Yes," she says. "Quite good. Extraordinary. Remarkable." She stops short of thanking him outright, enjoying this slight bit of rudeness on her part, just as she enjoys making him stand there as she takes another sip. After all, she didn't ask for this. She's quite aware this is an opening ploy and she's curious to see how he'll play his hand.

"Allow me," he says.

He takes a knife from the tray and cuts a thin slice of yellow-gold cheese, slides it on to a plate and sets it down before her. "Use your fingers. We don't stand on ceremony here. It's meant to be enjoyed."

Dominique is slightly taken aback by his gesture, but she picks up the piece of cheese and bites into it. It is as firm as flesh at first, then yields to the pressure of her teeth, and her mouth is filled with a rich, sunny flavour, buttery and smooth with an almost citrusy tang.

"The port," he says.

She sips her wine and he smiles as he watches her face.

"Sun in a garden, isn't it? What do you think?"

It's just as he says. The cheese is warm and sunny, the wine cool, fruity and dark; the combination is wonderfully sensual and intimate. But at the same time it's such an obvious pick-up routine that she has to smile, which is just what he expects. His smile in return tells her he knows it's a clumsy approach.

He's very good, perfectly charming, and yet when he looks at her she can see something warm and slightly dangerous in his eyes that brings a welcome flush of heat to her face and chest. She notices that none of the other men have chosen to approach any tables, and she takes that as a compliment.

"Please," she says. "Won't you sit?"

He holds out his hand. "Sheldon Lord," he says. "I hope you're suitably impressed?"

"With your name? Or with the whole presentation? The wine is very good."

"Port," he says. "Vintage port. It was a terribly transparent gesture, I'm afraid. But sincere. Things move very quickly here at the Arensen, and he who hesitates is often lost." He fills her glass and looks at her. "Or she, as the case may be."

Had all this happened only a few hours earlier, Dominique would have laughed in his face, but, sitting here filled with exquisite food and drink, in a room whose beauty seemed to impose its own set of rules, she enjoys his attention and his outrageous flirtation. This is, after all, what the Hotel Arensen is for, and this kind of elaborate attention is something new to her. She never engages in anything like this in her normal life. There's never any time, and normally Dominique prefers to get right to the point. Now, however, she finds his attention both flattering and arousing. She still has doubts about herself, however, about her ability to go through with this.

Sheldon works at the hotel, in some capacity that isn't entirely clear to her, something with event planning, she gathers. He's terribly knowledgeable about the place and often refers to designs and scenes and programmes.

"And how is it that you happen to be in the Ladies' dining room?" she asks him.

"Why not? There's no segregation, nothing like that. Anyone's free to go wherever they please. Most men are put off by the word 'Ladies' and so they stay away. This room is really intended for women who prefer to choose their own partners, free of the kind of pressure they'd feel in one of the mixed rooms. I find such women fascinating to watch." He smiles. "I know, it's terrible. Very voyeuristic, but it fascinates me to observe people exercising their desires. Don't you agree?"

Dominique can only guess what he means. "Perhaps," she says.

"But I hope you don't feel that I'm unduly pressuring you," he says. "I don't want to insert myself where I'm not wanted."

She looks at him and sees a hint of a smile in his steady gaze. He's an intelligent man, and she decides his choice of words was deliberate. She returns his smile and holds out her glass for more wine. "Not at all."

They talk of things of no great consequence, but the words are just an excuse to keep themselves together, like the wine and the cheese. There's no hurry, and yet there's a sense that time is wasting too. Inside Dominique is filled with doubt.

He's everything she's been looking for: older, experienced, and discreet – everything that Michael wasn't – and extremely attractive. And since he works at the hotel, there won't be any strings attached. When they're done, she can just walk away.

Can she do it? Is it really as easy as just saying yes? It's been months since she's thought of being with a man, and she hardly trusts her own feelings any more. She'd be devastated if she failed.

At last the room and the decanter are almost empty, and Dominique is filled with a languorous goodwill. He tries to pay her bill, citing his employee discount, but Dominique won't hear of it and he doesn't insist. He's wise enough to know how things would seem if he paid for her dinner, and so he just signs the tab for the port. She's grateful for his sensitivity.

He will see her back to her room, though, and as they walk from the dining room she notices how the staff acknowledges and defers to him.

Perhaps it's the port, but it seems like she's aware of everything, from the looks of the staff to the rustle of her dress against her naked skin.

He walks her outside on to a vast marble terrace overlooking the water. The lake is dark, the trees darker still, great black shadows blocking the reflection of the stars along the edges of the water. He points out the landscape to her, the various views: the arrangement of the different textures of darkness.

It was all designed to be as beautiful at night as it is in the day, and indeed there is something soothing yet mysterious out there in the darkness. The moon is near full, slashed by thin clouds that cast moving shadows on the lake.

"It's all designed to create a certain aesthetic sense," he says. "Beauty provokes a type of longing in the soul, a desire for intimacy, to join with it. We've worked very hard to achieve that effect here."

III.

The night is warm. The swans are asleep on the far bank, so the surface of the water is mirror smooth. There's nobody about.

Dominique finds herself unaccountably nervous.

She knows what will happen when they reach her room, and it's something she assumed she wanted, but now she wonders whether she'll be up to it, whether her body will respond as it should, or whether she's just going through the motions now because she thinks this is what she needs.

He seems like a lovely man and an interesting and sensitive lover, but what if he's not enough? What if what she really wants is Michael?

"You're worried," he says. "I can feel it. Your wicked past is rising to haunt you, isn't it? A man."

She says, "It's that obvious?"

"A beautiful young woman, alone at the Hotel Arensen. You don't have to be a genius to figure it out. About four or five months ago, I'd say. And now you're wondering if you still have it, if you still have anything left to give."

"Eight months ago," she says. She doesn't comment on the rest of what he's said.

"Eight months ago? It's worse than I thought."

The subject is uncomfortable, so she asks, "Tell me, Mr Lord. Just what is it you do here at the hotel?"

"Sheldon, please," he says. She can see his teeth in the darkness as he smiles. "You're going to hate me. I don't have a regular title, but

I'm a kind of facilitator. I help plan people's activities here, the things they want to do at the hotel."

"Volleyball games? Basket weaving? Things like that?"

He's amused. "People come to us for all sorts of reasons. Most of them are just looking for fun, but some of them come to us with real problems. Sex can be a powerful force for changing people. I facilitate that change."

"Like a therapist?"

"Not exactly. And not a surrogate either, not any more. Those days are behind me. Now I simply recommend therapies, things that might help. Of course, for special cases . . ."

Dominique watches one of the black swans stand up and ruffle its feathers. It beats its wings uneasily, and she can see the moonlight gleaming off the onyx feathers. Then it settles down and tucks its beak under its wing.

The thought that comes to her is an ugly one, but she has to ask.

"Is that why you picked me out? Do I look like someone who needs therapy?"

Again, he is amused. "Of course not. In any case, you'd have to request our services." He's silent for a moment, then asks, "Is that what you want?"

"What if I did? What would you recommend?"

She knows what's going to happen, and at first she hates herself for even inviting it. He puts his hands on her shoulders and turns her to face him and she feels a surge of fear and sudden trepidation. She searches his face but his eyes are impossible to read in the dark. His lips come down on hers in a gentle kiss: tentative, as if he's examining her, and it's not the feel of his lips as much as the sensation of his hands on her shoulders, holding her.

The kiss deepens, and he slides his arms around her back, pressing her against him, and she feels herself press back at him. The feeling of being held is delicious,

She lets herself be kissed, basking in his need for her, letting him take her where she wants to go, and thankfully her body doesn't resist him. She feels again that needful ache between her legs, that fullness in her breasts, and she realizes that she still knows how to respond. Her heart might have forgotten, but her body remembers.

He lets go of her reluctantly, as if he's afraid that he's rumpled her dress, but Dominique is glowing with excitement now, her heart pounding with remembrance.

"Where's your room?" he asks.

She hardly remembers. She has to take the key from her purse and show it to him, and when she does, his eyebrows rise.

"Three thirty-one? But that's an exhibitionist room number. All the threes are for exhibitionists." He looks at her with curiosity.

"It was a mistake. I booked that room by mistake. I had them take the camera out."

He smiles in the dark. "Yes. I don't think that's what you need right now, to be putting on a show for the other guests."

"Is that your professional opinion?"

"No. It's my male opinion." He takes her hand. "Now come with me."

He leads the way across the garden and into a nearly invisible service door at the base of the building. She's hardly paying attention as he finds an elevator, and as they ride to the third floor, he puts his hands around her waist and she willingly wraps her arms around his neck. They kiss, and this time Dominique feels the heat rise into her face as he presses his body against hers.

Her mouth is suddenly hungry, and whatever she does to him, he does again to her, harder and more insistent, so that when she bites his lip, he bites her back, and when she opens her mouth for him, he opens his, and his tongue penetrates her in a lewd and delicious imitation of the sexual act.

His hands rise to find her breasts, and once again it's the feel of his hands on her body that she finds so terribly exciting, even more arousing than these hungry kisses.

The elevator stops and he leads her down a maze of corridors until they stand outside her door. She opens it, and her eyes go immediately to where the camera was. It's gone now, along with its concealing piece of moulding.

He looks about the room, and his eyes fall on the three neatly arranged bottles of pills. He walks over to the bedside table and picks one up, reads the label, then picks up another. She stands there uneasily.

She'd forgotten she'd left them out.

She'd forgotten all about them.

When he looks at her now there is something new in his eyes, something she hadn't expected to see there: a kind of angry lust that makes her weak. She makes herself stand up straight. There's no sense in trying to pretend or make excuses. He knows what they mean.

"It's that bad?" he asks.

"At times."

His eyes soften now and she's relieved she's not going to be lectured or consoled. He's too wise for that. When he takes her in his arms, though, there's a savagery in his touch, a sudden hunger, as if he's afraid now that he might lose her.

One hand goes to the back of her head, holding her in place for his kiss, while the other slides over her back, pressing her close, then down across the small of her back over her bottom, where he opens his hand and grips her tight, squeezing her possessively, so hard that Dominique gasps in surprise.

His sudden hunger thrills her too. He doesn't give her time to worry or think or say yes or no. He's just there, bearing down on her with this furious need, and it's all she can do to keep from being swept away on this cataract of passion. His sudden hunger for her is overwhelming. It's as if she's standing under a waterfall trying to breathe.

Both hands are on her buttocks. He kisses her and bends her back, keeping her hips pressed to his. He gathers up her skirt, lifting it over her bottom till she feels the cool air of the room against her naked ass. Now her decision not to wear anything underneath her dress comes back to haunt her.

What will he think of her now?

His hands find her naked flesh, and if anything it only inflames him more. He grabs both buttocks in his hands and sinks his fingers into her flesh, then pulls them apart. One finger slides down her crack and probes at her anus. Dominique turns her head to the side and gasps for breath, shocked at his boldness.

She clings to his jacket as if she might fall.

He pulls her over to the bed and stands her there, posing her like a doll as he kisses her face, her eyes, her mouth. His kisses are tender now, but still trembling with a restrained hunger. He seems poised on the edge of some terrible violence, and she's almost afraid to move, afraid she might set him off.

He grabs her arms and pushes her elbows back, forcing her breasts to strain against the thin fabric of the dress, and he pulls her against him, crushing her yielding softness against his chest and making her his prisoner.

"I'm going to make you, Dominique," he whispers hotly. "I'm going to make you so good you won't ever think of those pills again. You're more than what your boyfriend thinks, and you're more than you know. That's what I'm going to show you."

He runs his hands up and down her body, from the hardness of her back down to the softness of her ass and Dominique shelters in his arms, her hands against her chest.

"You just leave everything to me," he says. "Understand? You don't have to do anything. You just do as I say."

She already feels overwhelmed and incapable of doing anything. It's exactly what she wants, for someone to take charge of her and do things for her.

He turns her around so her back is to him and unzips her dress. She stands there like a child as he pulls it up over her head, leaving her naked but for her shoes and stockings, her garter belt and jewellery. She should be ashamed to be seen in her nakedness, but already she's taken his advice to heart. She'll do nothing, not even judge herself. She'll let him do as he wishes.

He turns her to face him and steps back, holding her at arm's length so he can have a good look at her. He scans her body up and down, as if confirming what he already knows, and Dominique stands there nervously in her nakedness as he inspects her like a simple commodity. His face seems cold and distant, his inspection almost degrading, until his eyes meet hers again and she sees such a look of heat and desire there that she feels herself begin to swell and grow wet for him. Her pussy, her whole being, feels like a flower opening to the sun under the heat of his eyes.

He goes to the wall switch and turns off the lights. The only illumination is from the moonlight seeping through the French doors. He takes off his jacket and kicks off his shoes; removes his tie and unbuttons his shirt; shrugs off the shirt and lets it fall around his arms as he works on the cuffs. The sight of his chest and the domed muscles of his shoulders makes her breath race.

He's thicker and darker than Michael, and altogether more dangerous. She's so intent on watching him strip that she doesn't even notice her own nakedness.

He pulls off his socks and unbuckles his belt, opens the zipper and lets his pants fall to the floor. Dominique can see his cock tenting his shorts, his beautiful, threatening cock, hard just for her.

When he comes to her and embraces her again, his shaft presses into her lower stomach and she has the strong urge to reach down and feel it, but he grabs her arm and stops her.

"No," he says. "I'm taking charge. I'll tell you *when*. Now, down. *Down*."

He grips her wrists and uses them to force her down to her knees at his feet. There's no real need to force her. She's willing, but his strength excites her: a measure of his hunger. She wants to be used, which is strange, because she's always hated being treated as a sex object, but now his force is exactly what she wants.

She wants to feel the depth of his need for her.

She wants him to make her do things.

He holds her with one hand on her wrist and pulls down his shorts with the other. His cock springs free, standing straight out in rampant eagerness. He's shaved entirely bare, which only makes him look bigger and more magnificent: thick and hard and wreathed in veins, arching upwards defiantly and capped with a straining helmet like a medieval warrior.

Below it, his balls hang ripe and heavy, obscenely potent: stones for a catapult.

Dominique looks up at him from her knees. He looms above her, still holding her wrists in his hands, glaring down like Zeus from Olympus, his hips thrust forwards slightly. Dominique has a brief thought of Michael, of a line she never meant to cross, and then she closes her eyes. She opens her mouth and takes him inside.

He moans, almost a growl, and she feels his hands tighten on her arms, urging her on. She slides her face forwards, feeling the head of his cock rubbing across the roof of her mouth and over her soft palate. She hears him groan again and he shudders, and something inside her smiles with deep relief and satisfaction.

She's never thought of herself as being particularly good at oral sex, but then she'd never really had any way to judge. Michael had tended to lie back and keep quiet, but Sheldon is the exact opposite. She can feel his cock quivering in her mouth, hear his satisfied moans as her lips envelop his shaft, and feel his excitement in the way he grips her arms.

He lets go of her now and reaches down and caresses her face, running his hand over her cheek and then over her lips to feel them stretched around his cock. "Yes," he whispers. "Like that. Show me how you love it."

He begins to move his hips, slowly fucking into her waiting mouth. Dominique puts her hands on his thighs and feels the iron-like rigidity of his muscles. Above her, she can see his stomach trembling with tension, and the realization that she is having such an effect on him arouses her terribly. She begins to bob her head up and down on his cock, sucking as hard as she can.

Already he's panting. Dominique weighs his balls in her hand, feels their heavy potency, and his overwhelming maleness makes her groan herself. She knows where that cock is going, knows there's no way to stop him, and it's such a relief to her. He reaches down and combs his fingers through her hair, pushes it back from her face so he can watch her, then holds her head gently as he begins to fuck her mouth with slow, deep strokes.

The way he uses her excites her; the way he takes control of her and imposes his will leaves her free of any responsibility, free to just experience the feel of him in her mouth. His excitement communicates itself to her, and suddenly she's on fire, sucking his cock, pulling it from her mouth and rubbing it over her cheeks, painting her face with his seeping lubricant. Sheldon thrusts his hips out, wraps her hair in his fists and begins to fuck her mouth with a hard, steady rhythm.

It's a savage way to treat this girl, yet she responds with moans and gasps of her own, thrilled by his violence. His stomach trembles, the big muscles in his thighs stand out like steel cords, and he lets her feel all his animal desire, pure and undiluted. But when he feels himself close to coming – when he feels the muscles tightening in his ass and belly, the fire in his nerves that signal the start of release – he stops, pulls his penis from her open mouth and bends down. He lifts her to her feet before she knows what's happening.

"On the bed," he says.

He pulls her over and pushes her down face first on to the mattress.

Dominique wipes her mouth with her hand, totally confused, on fire for him and feeling her mouth's emptiness throughout her entire body, as if a part of her is missing. Her sudden need makes her weak and unsteady, and she lets him push and pull her around on the bed until he has her as he wants her: head down on the mattress, ass in the air, knees parted.

She remembers the mirror standing against the wall and looks over to see herself. She looks at the woman on the bed, the wicked stockings and garter belt, the breasts hanging down in elongated cones. She is a slut, she realizes, a brazen, shameless slut who's about to be fucked by a total stranger.

Sheldon seems to be capable of reading her mind because he caresses her naked bottom and says, "I want you to forget all about who you are. For tonight I want you to be nothing but a body, pure sensation. All you do is feel."

He pushes her knees together and pulls her hips back so that her puffy lips are compressed into two fleshy buns between her thighs. He holds her knees together, squats down and licks her, a lewd, animal-like swipe of his tongue, totally unexpected. She shudders, and he licks her again, pushing his mouth against her and trying to spear his tongue inside, though with her legs compressed he can only just touch the sensitive nerves at her entrance.

The way he licks her and presses his face against her is obscene, primitive and feral. It's totally unlike what she expected from this worldly and urbane man, but the very wildness of his actions arouses her terribly and brings out her own primal feelings, dirty and deliciously alive.

She sneaks a glance in the mirror again and sees him kneeling on the floor, his face pressed into her ass. One hand caresses her buttocks, pulling them apart and squeezing. His other hand is on his hard, glistening cock, and he's pumping himself, masturbating as he licks and mouths her mons.

He raises his hand and brings it down sharply on her rear, totally unexpected, making Dominique cry out in surprise. No one has ever struck her before, not even in play, and it shocks her, but when she tries to move he pulls her roughly back into place and slaps her bottom again.

"Ow!" she lets out.

"Shush," he warns. "Stay still! I'm not hurting you."

He slaps her again, and Dominique grabs on to the bed cover, not knowing what else to do. It's a violation of all that she believes about love-making, and yet the angry sting of his hand on her flesh satisfies something deep inside her, some need to be owned and possessed, to be punished for her own erotic desires.

Four times he spanks her, and then his hand slides over her ass like a thief returning to the scene of the crime, caressing her, feeling the heat rise to the surface, worshipping her reddened skin. He slaps her twice more and now she makes no protest, feeling his blows as rightful possession.

She feels the mattress sag beneath his weight as he climbs on to the bed.

"I'm going to make you now, my pretty one," he says. "Just like this. Like animals do, back to front. Spread your legs."

She's on fire for him now, wet and aching between her legs, consumed by a wild mixture of shame and raw sexual need. She knows what he meant about forgetting who she is. She doesn't want to think about that, about guilt and remorse and making it good for him or what he'll think about her afterwards. She just wants his hardness inside her and the fierce strength of his lust possessing her.

She spreads her thighs and lifts herself up on her forearms, daring to look back over her shoulder at him . . .

IV.

He doesn't come right into her. Instead he reaches beneath her from behind and presses hard against her labia, as if checking her condition, seeing if she's ready.

His fingers slide between her lips and find her secret flesh, the eager bud of her clitoris, and his touch is almost too much to bear. It's a casual, almost cruel gesture, as if he were checking his bath water, and the callous way he touches her turns her heat into a raging flame. It's so foreign to her to be treated like this, but it inflames her.

He works a finger into her and pumps it in and out mechanically, his other hand on the small of her back. Dominique can feel his eyes on her, and she gasps and covers her head with her hands, lacing her fingers in her hair as if she can hide herself from what he's doing to her.

"Do it!" she hears herself cry. "Love me!"

He only grunts in acknowledgment, and again the mattress rocks as he gets into position. His big cock nudges at her opening, and she grabs the covers and holds on, waiting for his entry.

It's been so long, and she's grown tight, but he's amazingly hard and won't be denied. His hands go to her hips and he grabs the crests of her hip bones and pushes forwards. She feels herself opening up to his onslaught, her stubborn flesh yielding before his irresistible attack.

She calls out to a deity.

"Tight," he says. "You're all closed up, aren't you, Dominique? But we'll open you up, pretty. You'll see. I'll open you up!"

It's like being a virgin again, the same fear of pain, of inadequacy, but now she knows she doesn't have to do anything. It's like he said: he's going to take it from her.

She just has to be there for him and he'll take what he wants.

She cries out as he shoves the entire length into her at last; she feels unused muscles stretch and throb around him. Delicious pain, a thrilling ache as he fills her, till he tightens his grip on her hips and pulls her all the way back, thrusting forwards and impaling her on his rampaging cock, flattening her buttocks against his hard stomach.

Dominique looks into the mirror and sees their image. He's standing tall on his knees and leaning back slightly, his hands on her hips; she's kneeling slavishly before him, ass up, back bowed down as she presses her tits against the bed. All her attention's on his throbbing hardness inside her, on how good he feels, on how sweet it is to be caught on the end of that angry male shaft.

"It's arriving soon," he tells her. "Here it comes, Dominique. Get ready for me."

She doesn't know what he's talking about. Wasn't he already in her balls deep? Her pussy's stretched around the thick base of his cock like an elastic band. She can feel him throbbing inside her. But now he pulls back, increases his grip on her hips, and begins to fuck her, slamming into her, the knobby shaft of his cock bumping over her flesh.

His roughness and selfishness thrill her to the core. He fucks her like she belongs to him, like she has no purpose other than to serve him, and his selfishness sets her free. There's nothing she can do, no way she can reciprocate.

Her only option is to lie there and moan, possessed by his savage lust. It's delicious, liberating, and before she knows what's happening, a little orgasm washes like a wave of fire through her body, summoned by his lust. Her body, her very sensations are no longer hers to control. They belong to him.

He seems to know exactly what she's feeling, for no sooner has she come than he pulls out of her and pushes her over on her back. Dominique's too weak to even try to resist him. She's like a rag doll in his hands and, as soon as he has her on her back, he enters her again with one smooth move of his hips.

He falls on top of her, cradling her head in his hands, and his ass begins to rise and fall, thrusting his prick into her like a battering ram, knocking down all her defences, battering her senseless.

He kisses her, biting and licking her lips like an animal, swallowing her moans and groans into his mouth, and his hips never stop working. Her knees are spread wide, her feet planted weakly on the bed, and her hands grab at the bed cover in a desperate attempt to hold on.

"Take it, Dominique . . . take my big cock and make me come. Can you do it? Can you make me come? Can you make me come in that pretty love cave of yours?"

She wants to. She wants to make it good for him, but he's already moving so fast, fucking her so brutally she can't get any sort of rhythm or purchase on the bed.

She feels herself climbing to another orgasm, her feet and ankles tingling, her face growing hot and flushed.

She turns her head and looks in the mirror and sees herself pressed into the mattress, her knees up and apart and shaking with every bruising thrust of Sheldon's hips. She sees his muscular ass rising and falling, his buttocks clenching as he feeds his cock into her and stirs it around inside.

His shoulders are thick knots of muscle; his face a mask of furious lust and anguish. His violence overwhelms her, thrills her.

He thrusts into her so hard the entire mattress sways beneath her; the whole world rocking to the angry rhythm of his prick inside her.

Sheldon grabs her wrists and pushes them down beside her shoulders, holding her to the bed, holding her immobile while his thundering cock hammers at her cunt, filling her and releasing, filling and releasing. Dominique can't move, can't resist him if she wanted to. She closes her eyes, opens her mouth to his ravishing tongue and gives up; gives up fighting, gives up resisting, and opens herself to him entirely: not just her body, but her heart and soul, letting herself be conquered by his thrusting cock and the tight grip of his hands on her wrists.

She knows then that surrender is triumph, that letting go is security. His wild need proves her worth, and the only way she'll find herself is by giving herself away and, with those thoughts in her mind, she climaxes.

She climaxes with a violence and a thoroughness that she's never felt before, as if her entire soul were washed in brilliant light. For those brief moments she's entirely sexual, nothing but cunt, and she plants her feet on the bed and thrusts her hips up at him hard, enveloping him in her clutching sheath and letting him feel her raging joy.

She has an image of his face above her, his look of furious lust replaced by one of sudden astonishment. His eyes glaze and go sightless, and with a low, feline growl she feels his cock jump inside her, feels his entire body tighten into one tense and trembling mass of muscle, and feels the burning jolt of his ejaculate splash inside her, one gout after another, and each one pushing her higher into a brilliant darkness.

V.

On his left side he faces her, the covers pulled down to his waist, his back to the open French doors so that his right arm and shoulder are lit by moonlight, his face in shadows.

"You're sure?" he asks.

She's on her back, the covers under her chin. She's always cold at night, even in the summer. "Yes. Would there be a problem?"

He lifts himself up on his elbow and looks down at her, reaches out and runs his palm across her breast. "No. No problem. I'd even waive my fee, if that's what you really want to do."

"It is."

"It's not just all fun and games, you know. You'd have to do as I say."

"I don't mind. I want to do it. If it's anything like tonight, I want to do it."

He pulls the covers down and looks into her eyes as his hand caresses her naked breast.

"You have to be with me full time," he says. "So you'll have to extend your stay. I'll take care of your room. I don't want you paying. They won't miss you at work?"

"I don't care about the money," she says. "And they've been after me to take a vacation. They said it would be therapeutic. I don't think anything could be more therapeutic than this."

He lowers his head and his tongue traces circles around her nipple. Dominique closes her eyes and arches her back against his touch. The chills she feels aren't due to the cold.

His hand slips under the sheets and trails down her stomach, detours over her hip and comes to rest against her sex, where she's still wet with the overflow of their passion.

"And you want everything?" he asks.

"Yes. Everything. When can we start?"

He touches her and, despite herself, she gasps and feels her thighs tremble.

"Right now," he says.

VI.

Dominique gets up so early the next morning that the stars are still in the sky. The first thing she thinks of is Sheldon and the night before, and the next thing she thinks of is that he's gone – her bed is empty. The guilt she was prepared to feel is replaced by shame and anger as she remembers her wanton behaviour of last night and wonders whether she's scared him off. Even in this place she embarrasses herself. She feels like she can do nothing right.

She steps out on the balcony. It's very early but already thick clouds are gathering, blown in from the north and tinted red and purple in the east by the rising sun. This may be a cheery place in the summer, but in this season it is grey and foreboding. She hears the dawn call of the peacocks in the garden followed by a woman's distant laughter. It only makes her feel more lonely. She goes inside and goes back to bed.

He comes for her a few hours later, startling her from a dream of Michael, which leaves her with a feeling of nagging unease, as if she's greatly disappointed someone. She transfers this feeling to Sheldon when he enters and tries to beg off their appointment, claiming she's unwell.

"I have things to show you today," he says, unbearably cheerful. "Things most people here never see – the insider's tour. I've arranged for a boat, so dress casual."

He's brought coffee and croissants on a cart, but Dominique has no appetite. It occurs to her that maybe it would have been better if she had scared him off after last night. She can't bear anyone's company in the morning, and sightseeing is the last thing she wants to do today.

She's better after she'd had her coffee and showered. The shower itself is a miracle, hot, over-engineered and lavish with water. She goes through her clothes, wincing at all the romantic dresses and gowns she's brought, as if she'd intended to spend all her time at a ball. She puts on a pair of jeans and a sweater, a pair of athletic shoes.

It's hardly what she thought she'd be wearing when she packed for the Hotel Arensen.

The island upon which the hotel sits is still known as Palace Island and has always been dramatically landscaped and laced with canals, moats, and pools for boating, except at the northern end, where the island rises into sheer cliffs, densely wooded and intentionally left wild. The waters are still and mirror the trees and gardens that line the shore. Swans, black and white, glide upon the surface like clouds. The waterways are especially lovely at night, when little boats, decorated with candles and lanterns, drift about in the darkness like fireflies.

It's to a misty dock on one of these pools that Sheldon brings Dominique in the early afternoon of this grey and forlorn day. He installs her in the prow of a small boat, part canoe, part gondola – short and wide with high and decorated stem and sternposts – and settles himself in with blankets and a paddle. He pushes off and they head for the waters of Lake Arensen that surround the island.

The air is still and a thick mist rises from the water obscuring the towers of the hotel and the tops of the trees – sometimes even the banks themselves – so that they seem to float in a dream world, accompanied only by their own wake on the mirrorlike water. The rose gardens and chrysanthemums they pass are mere smudges of colour in this foggy world of grey and green.

"It's so still," she says.

There are no other boats. The water is the colour of a black mirror.

"Is it always so still?" she asks.

"You've come during the misty season and, while the mists rise, yes, it is still. It's relaxing though, in its way."

"I don't think I've ever been in such a quiet landscape."

"Good. Then this will be a perfect place to talk."

"Talk about what?"

Sheldon pulls in his paddle and lays it across the thwarts. "You," he says.

Dominique knows he's talking about what he said last night, about healing her. "Oh, Sheldon, that was sweet, but you weren't serious? You're going to be my sex therapist?"

"No," he says. "Don't call it that. A sex therapist works on a particular sexual problem. Sex is just the means to the end."

"What's the end?"

"To get you away from him and give you back to yourself. Don't you think that's a worthy goal?"

Dominique looks at him as his eyes scan the shore. Last night he'd seen her in all her naked vulnerability. He'd taken her not against her will, but forcibly, taking what he wanted without asking, and it had been the best thing he could have done. His selfish desire had aroused her more than any gentle consideration would have and had thrilled her, so much so that she was surprised at the lack of shame and remorse she felt today. She'd not only enjoyed last night, but she'd had a most intense orgasm, unusual for her, and quite inexplicable.

The boat barely seems to move. It's a strange shape, unusually wide for a craft so short. The generous beam makes it very stable.

She trails her fingers in the water. "So what do you want to know?"

"About this man, the one who broke your heart. What was his name?"

Dominique brings her hand into the boat and rolls over on her back. The prow of the little boat is an elaborate chair with pillows and cushions. Because of the stillness of the lake, they never become wet.

"Michael," she says. "Just when I was feeling better . . . do we have to, Sheldon?"

"He left you?"

"Yes. He walked out one night, angry. He came back two days later while I was at work and got his things. I couldn't afford the place without him. I had to leave."

"And why did he leave?"

She loathes to talk about it. She says, "We were always fighting."

He asks, "What about?"

Dominique drops her fingers in the still waters again. The smooth movement of the boat leaves barely a ripple. "I don't know. Everything. What do people fight about? It's all so stupid. What we have for dinner at night, where we go on the weekend. Things he said, things I said. I hate to remember those awful words. Words can hurt terribly, don't you think?"

"Mightier than the sword, as they say."

"A knife in the heart," she says.

Sheldon picks up the paddle and strokes them in a new direction. "People don't fight for no reason, Dominique. Either they fight because they're competing for the same thing, or because they hate each other, or because they've exhausted each other. You two didn't hate each other, so I'm going to bet you exhausted yourselves. You were with each other too much. You used each other up."

"Perhaps," she says with a small laugh. She laughs because the truth of his words frightens her.

"It's no joke," Sheldon says. "People exhaust each other all the time. It's the curse of our age, where everyone has to tell everyone everything, be all things to their lovers. Relationships can't stand that. You should always keep something back. Never give everything to anyone. That doesn't do you any good and, believe me, they don't want it. Love's strength comes from mystery. Why do you think falling in love is so much more exciting than being in love?"

Dominique makes a face. "Is that my lesson for today? To just shut up and not talk to men?"

"No."

He drops the subject and peers at the shoreline.

Dominique turns to see that they've changed direction and are heading back to Palace Island, but approaching from the north side, where the island rises into a range of large, heavily wooded hills before plunging down into the lake in a series of precipitous cliffs. This is the wild side of the island, neither cultivated nor landscaped.

"There it is," he says, correcting the boat's motion with his paddle. "No. Today's lesson is about something else. It's about sex, how it's all around you."

"What are you looking for?"

He doesn't answer, just starts taking them in to shore with strong strokes of the paddle. Dominique gets up on her knees and turns around so she can see where they're headed, but all she can see are the ancient willows that dip their leaves into the misty water at the base of the cliffs.

"Watch your head," Sheldon says, and the boat glides under the trailing leaves, strands of willow dragging over Dominique's face and back. She looks up then and is amazed to see a large cave right ahead of them arching over the water.

The opening is partially blocked with an ancient iron water gate. The boat glides in under the overhanging rock and Sheldon backs water to stop them at the very entrance. In the dark twilight he produces a cigarette lighter and lights the kerosene lantern that hangs in the stern.

He passes the lighter to Dominique and tells her to light the bow lantern.

She does, and then gasps as he paddles them into the cave.

The cavern is huge and vast with no walls to be seen. The black waters trail off into the far distance, and stalactites and stalagmites form a forest of columns and stumps that emerge from the water and disappear into the darkness overhead, shadowy shapes painted yellow orange now by the lantern light. The cavern is full of them, and they fade off into the distance in a bewildering maze of pillars and arches.

"What is this, Sheldon? What is this place?"

"You remember Xanadu? 'Where Alph the sacred river ran/ Through caverns measureless to man/Down to a sunless sea.' "

"It rings a bell."

"This is the Cavern. The lake is fed by underground springs, very deep. They formed these caverns. Then, not that long ago by geologic time, the lake broke through and flooded them. The old dukes used this cave to supply the castle in times of war. The castle was replaced by the palace centuries ago, but some of the medieval stonework still remains. The hotel keeps the cave a secret, but they use part of the old landing stage for a wine cellar. That's the dim light you see way up ahead. It's too dangerous down here for the regular guests. Only a few of us even know about it."

The little boat glides along in its dome of yellow light, casting weird shadows on the columns. She cannot see the ceiling, she cannot see the walls. All there is is a forest of strangely shaped columns stretching away on either side as far as she can see, as if the whole island were hollow.

Dominique is spellbound. Speaking in this place seems wrong. They're in a deep and secret place, and the human voice isn't welcome. She looks over the side but sees nothing but her face staring back at her from the ring of lamplight.

The water is a perfect black mirror.

"The water in this cave is very deep," he says. "There are fish down there too, big fish, living at the bottom in the darkness."

The thought of fish there in the black water does something to her, brings up some primitive emotion of fear or reverence, and she unconsciously puts her hand to her chest as if to still her heart.

"They're not dangerous. Some subspecies of catfish, blind and pale white. They won't hurt you."

He paddles on. He tells her, "This is the lesson for today, Dominique."

She looks back at him. "The caverns?"

"Just wait," he says.

VII.

They travel on, keeping the light of the landing stage ahead of them in the distance. The paddle is soundless in the water; the entire cavern is soundless, though Dominique can hear the slow drip of water when they pass certain spots. It is timeless; the deep unimaginable patience of nature, the black water in caves unseen.

Sheldon steers the boat away from the light and behind the shadowy concealment of some fused columns. He takes a rope from the boat's stern and ties it around a stalagmite that emerged from the water, then he turns up the mantles in the lanterns.

The columns flash back at them like thousands of diamonds or shattered mirrors, and Dominique's breath catches in her throat.

"Incredible!"

"They're just quartz," he says. "Quartz and mica. But who would have thought? How lavish nature is with her beauty, isn't she? She just throws it away."

He turns the lanterns down and the sparkle fades. There's no current, and the boat barely moves. Sheldon stands up and joins her in the prow, and now Dominique sees why the boat's shape is so curious. It allows two people to recline together comfortably in the prow and stern.

It's cool down here but not cold, and Sheldon's warmth is quite welcome as he arranges himself behind her and pulls her back against him.

"We'll wait here and let the spirit of this place seep into us. I'm not a religious man, but this is a sacred place. We respond to it on many levels."

They sit in the darkness, in the absolute silence, the only sound the distant drip of water, and Dominique wonders what it is she's supposed to feel: reverence, awe. She's about to speak when Sheldon puts his hands on her breasts and gently pulls her back against him. Dominique holds her breath, afraid to say anything but unsure of what he means to do. His behaviour is shocking but not unwelcome. It's been some time since a man couldn't keep his hands off her and she doesn't object. His human touch is comforting in the silent darkness.

His hands don't move, but Dominique starts to get excited. It's the quiet, the absence of people. She's never felt silence as a presence before, but now it exudes from the very stone and the surface of the water. It makes her want to do things, to yell or scream.

One hand leaves her breast and presses against her cheek, gently turning her face back at him for a kiss, and Dominique feels a surge of excitement before their lips even meet. She opens her mouth to him, eager for his tongue.

His male warmth is wonderful in this cool, dark place, and Dominique feels herself opening for him as if her body is already far ahead of her. His hand slips under her sweater and finds her own warmth and softness and Dominique sighs. She can't remember when a man's hand felt so comforting.

She's ashamed of herself, has been all day; conflicted by her behaviour last night, but now in this underground labyrinth of glistening towers with the black water below and around her, her hunger surfaces to a shocking degree. It's as if the still lifelessness makes their human presence all the more precious and Dominique presses back against him and covers his hand on her breast with her own. There's no one else around. She's never been in a place so totally devoid of humanity and her sensual excitement seems to expand to fill the emptiness like the glow of the little boat's lanterns seeks to fill the darkness.

Sheldon's sitting directly behind her and the feel of his shaft coming to life and pressing against her bottom is terribly exciting. She still worries that her own capacity to respond to a man might have been damaged and it's gratifying to know that it hasn't, but more gratifying is his response to her. His ardour seems greater than her own, and suddenly the memory of last night comes back to her in physical sensations: the memory of his cock inside her and the weight of his body on hers.

Dominique presses back against him. His left hand leaves her breast and travels down between her legs and she groans. She's on fire for him, as if she's been drugged. She raises her knees and lets them fall open.

Behind her, Sheldon chuckles.

"What is it?" she demands. "What's so funny?"

"Nothing. Nothing at all. This place is very magical, isn't it? It invokes feelings of majesty and awe, but finally they all come down to sex, don't they? When words fail us, we always have that."

He uses both hands to open her jeans and his warm hand dips inside. Dominique has to stifle a cry as he finds her and begins to play with her.

"Sheldon! Should you?"

Again, he is amused by her. "I doubt there's another place on earth as private as this," he says.

The boat hardly moves. When Dominique opens her eyes she can see the stone columns stained yellow by the kerosene light, soaring into the darkness. She's in a place of deep beauty and secrecy, and even Sheldon's hand moving between her legs seems to have some extra meaning, summoning up something dark and primal from her depths.

The boat hardly moves. Sheldon is kissing her now, kissing the side of her neck and her face as his hand rubs and massages her breasts and catches her nipples between his fingers. His hand between her legs is busy and coated with her wetness, and Dominique's belly and hips are grinding about as if trying to dispel a sudden empty ache she feels.

His breath is hot on her ear. "I want you to do something for me," he whispers. "I want you to take my cock in your mouth. I want you to suck it, Dominique. I need you to do it."

His words thrill and alarm her. Still, there is something about this place that makes her not only willing, but eager – the closeness, the warmth of him, the darkness and isolation.

"Yes," she says. "Let me."

He arranges her on her knees between his legs as the boat rocks softly. The sound of his zipper is unusually loud, and there is the dull clunk of his belt buckle hitting the seat as he pushed his trousers down. Dominique is on her knees, hungry to taste him. The shame and self-consciousness she feared is totally absent, as if the caverns had made her a different person.

His manhood is soon revealed in the lamplight, and she loses no time in taking it in her hand and running her tongue up and down its length, loving his heat and responsiveness. She opens her mouth and takes him inside.

His gasp of pleasure echoes softly and Dominique is in sensual heaven. His thickness on her tongue, the wild male taste of him. She sucks hungrily, filling her mouth with his virility as he combs his fingers through her hair and stares down at her.

His voice is as soft and insistent as the water that drips in the cavern. "Yes, Dominique. Suck me. Suck my cock." She feels a part of it too, a part of the deep, dark places, a hole in the earth meant to be filled, containing secrets and darkness.

He's so virile, his cock so full of light and life. It's like a torch upon her tongue. Dominique doesn't move. She just leaves his prick sitting in her mouth, the tip edging towards her throat. Her nostrils flare. In the darkness, it's like there's nothing but this: her mouth and his prick. There's all the time in the world.

" 'Male and female made he them'," Sheldon says.

Dominique knows instinctively what he means.

The creation, born from the earth, born in duality.

She feels the hunger for sex as a glow deep within her, deeper than she'd ever imagined, down below the worries and doubts and beyond even the thoughts of love and affection. It's as though they're the only people in the world, male and female, and Dominique feels a thrill at this recognition of her own sexual identity – she's the same as Sheldon, and yet profoundly different, and in that difference lay everything that mattered.

She begins to move her head, feeling his knobby stalk bumping between her lips, and is gratified to feel his fingers tighten in her hair.

"Easy," he says. "Feel me, Dominique. This isn't just for me."

She's done this before of course, but never paid much attention to her own sensations. It was always for Michael, always a matter of finding out what he liked and doing it, but Sheldon is intentionally trying not to respond, to give her no cues and, except for an occasional low moan of appreciation, it's up to her to find her own motivation and derive her own pleasure.

She's aware of the bumps and veined ridges on the shaft of his cock, the way the wide, rounded glans presses against her throat, and the thrilling hardness, the feel of something potent and aggressive pushing at her just above the point where she can swallow him.

On a sudden urge, she pushes her face forwards and feels her throat close in stubborn resistance. She insists, pushing harder, feeling him touch the part of her that makes her want to gag, and she has to back off.

She pulls her head off him, gasping for breath, feeling his cock emerging from her mouth trailing long strings of mucus from the back of her throat, and her sense of shame at her own lasciviousness brings her to a new state of arousal. The boat rocks gently upon the dark water as she repositions herself then slides her head forwards to take his cock again, the head slithering over her tongue and down her throat.

She's determined this time. Something fierce and female possesses her, and she's determined to do this. There's no time for shyness or circumspection; no time to think and worry. Some hunger compels her to take him inside as deep as she possibly can. She wants to swallow him like he's never been swallowed

The blood pounds in her cars as Dominique fights down her gag reflex. The head of his cock is right at the top of her throat and she feels her soft palate close on it in a series of muscular spasms, but still she doesn't stop. She pushes her face farther forwards until the head of his prick is in her gullet.

Tears stream from her eyes as she fights the urge to reject him. She wants him there, deep within, all the way down to her stomach – even farther. Sheldon's groan of harsh pleasure and astonishment echoes off the invisible walls and Dominique has a vision of the fish swimming in the darkness below, blind things in the caves, seeking the dark water.

She becomes aware of Sheldon yelling, pushing at her head, trying to get her off his cock. She coughs as his withdrawing prick sets off her reflex again and chases after him, suddenly missing that throbbing thickness in her throat, but he seems desperate, pushing her away and crying out, "No! Dominique, no!"

He pulls his cock from her lips and she sees it almost glowing in the lamp-lit darkness.

She licks her lips, feels the emptiness in her mouth and the hollowness in her body. She looks up to see Sheldon breathing hard, looking down at her with a look of astonishment on his face, and Dominique gets up on her knees, digs her nails into the bunched muscles of his thighs, and impales herself again on his hard shaft.

It's like diving into deep water.

Again the gag reflex, again the frantic spasm of the ring of muscle in her throat, and again a savage hunger she can't explain forces her head down on him, taking him deep, so deep he's almost a part of her body. The broad, thick head of his cock opens her secret and intimate flesh and holds it open. She feels the tickle of his lubricant burning into her throat, and here she waits.

She waits with the patience of the blind fish in the deep pools, with the patience of the dark cave and the dripping water. She waits as her throat closes on him again and again in a series of peristaltic contractions, milking him, massaging his glans, her very body trying to pull him deeper. She waits with the patience of the female serving her man, and Sheldon groans and throws his head back.

There's no chance of his controlling himself this time. She can tell from his helpless growls and breathless gasps, the spastic shudders of his tightly clenched abdominals. There's no strength in his hand as he touches her, just the feeble palsy of a man at his limit, in the extreme of sensation.

Dominique holds herself there while her ears roar and her throat milks him in a reflex action she can't even control, her lower lip against his balls, her nose digging into his lower stomach. She holds herself there even as she feels his tool jerk in her mouth and he cries out, his head falling back in helpless abandon as his hips thrust against her.

He tries to warn her but he's not in control of himself, and Dominique knows instinctively just what she's doing.

She holds him in her throat and feels him erupt.

Hot, thick gouts of semen hit her in a place where she has few nerves, and yet she can feel the powerful contractions of his cock and the jets of come splattering against the back of her gullet. She can taste it as the aroma wafts up from the sticky pools of his passionate discharge.

He's ejaculating straight into her throat, pouring his seed directly into her body, and she's totally open to him and entirely accepting. She waits till the first two blasts are finished before she pulls her head off his throbbing spear, the thick glans giving her a weird thrill as it passes the portal of her oesophagus.

The come hangs in thick strands from her lips as she holds his slime-covered prick poised at her mouth. The next jet misses and the silvery semen arcs up and lands into the black water.

She can't resist it now and she smothers the head of his cock with her lips, her hand pumping the silky-hard shaft like a demonic machine, demanding his come. She receives the next bolt on the roof of her mouth, and then the rest of his load spills on to her tongue as she swallows greedily.

Sheldon's head rolls back, his fingers tangled in her hair, as he gasps out the last of his savage pleasure.

She drinks him up, with a desperation for his masculine essence that goes beyond the mere sexual. In her life she has denied herself this, has treated the male discharge as something dirty and shameful, but here in the place, surrounded by this feminine darkness, she feeds feverishly at his spurting cock, famished for the taste of his seed, indeed.

Sheldon levers her off his cock forcefully, pushing her until she falls back in the bottom of the boat, her pants still open, her face smeared with semen and saliva, a glazed look of desire on her face. His come was like a drug to her, and she's completely intoxicated, but at the same time his sudden shove brings her back to herself and she looks around in confusion.

"I've never felt anything like that," he tells her. "I was in your belly, Dominique! What happened to you? Where did you learn that?"

She wipes her lip and examines her fingers, looking for any stray drops that might have gotten away. She shudders at her own unexpected depravity. She doesn't know where she learned it or even how she knew she could do it, but inside her is a wild and wilful pride, the pride of a woman in her own sexuality.

After last night's passive performance, she's paid him back in kind and shown him that she's not as helpless and unskilled as he might have thought. And, more importantly, she's taught herself the same thing.

She sits back in the boat and feels the cavern around her like a cloak, tastes his semen in her mouth and still feels him reaching into the darkest part of her body.

The Cavern, she thinks, is a very female place, and she feels a kinship now with the mysterious darkness.

She belongs here.

She *is* the cavern, ready to engulf her lover again, forever.

Honeymoon with Shannon

Thom Gautier

She took my poetry workshop. This was about six years ago. Her name was Shannon. She was only a few years younger than I was but she was several years older than the other students. She was from Ireland but every bit a New Yorker: fluent, talkative, stylish, smart. She was no William Butler Yeats. She could critique poems but she couldn't write a lick of decent verse herself. "It was just an elective, boy," she told me, as she toyed with her cell phone during one of our office conferences. She was a double major in her final semester. Dean's List, thanks to her math skills. "Business law with a minor in real-estate." In the end, I gave her a gentleman's B as a final grade. Later she told me I was a "right shite" for that. "An A minus at least, boy."

She didn't take to calling me "boy" till the term ended; I didn't protest the nickname. Or if I did, I didn't put up a fight.

She had sky blue eyes and a sailor's mouth. One time, when she cursed, I told her she sounded like Tony Soprano trapped inside Lindsay Lohan's body. She vetoed the description. "I don't have a fat man's voice." She was right. Her red hair was long and curly, like some druid fairy out of folklore; she favored Cole Haan leather jackets and Diesel jeans, like a fashionista out of Tribeca. In fact she lived in Tribeca. "Not a bad address for a struggling student," I told her. She stuck her tongue out at me.

Sometimes in my office as we edited one of her Godawful poems our knuckles brushed. Mostly we kept a safe distance. I'd lean back in my chair unbuttoning her blouse with my eyes, imagining planting a kiss near her neckline, my hands cupping and massaging her breasts, suckling her nipples. She would ask me what I was thinking and I answered with cryptic poetic remarks. 'I'm thinking of rain and the color pink.' She would hug her bag so hard that her blouse's neckline would reveal her bra strap. "Rain and the color pink, nice, poet-boy."

She rested her head on her bag and gazed at me with one blue eye peeping through a curtain of red hair. "Don't stare, teacher, that's rude. Tell me what you're thinking, right now. Give me one of your nice Zen lines."

"I'm thinking red waterfalls and hot mornings," I said.

She smiled and kept her head resting on her bag.

As the end of the semester neared, she peppered me with personal questions, waiting for any answer by playing with one of the lace chokers she wore or grabbing the stiletto of her heel.

"I'm divorced," I said, defensively, as if giving testimony before a judge.

"Seeing someone special, then, poet-genius?"

I spiked that question back at her.

She sighed and explained how it was rude to answer a question with a question. "You could say that I am seeing someone," she said, gazing down at her feet.

"Well why don't you say it?"

"Boy, I am not going to say that." She leaned back in her seat, tucked a long strand of hair behind her right ear and looked squarely at me – through me, really – and tugged at the dangling straps of her backpack, clutching the bag's long belts in her pretty white fist. I thought, lucky strap.

She said, "I'm engaged." My heart sank on hearing it. "Don't say anything funny or poetic about it, boy. I have two months of freedom and that's that."

We were already late for class. I tried to play it cool. I'm sure I said something asinine like, "Hey, marriage is a fine thing." She hoisted her backpack on to her shoulder and gave me the finger. I told her that was disrespectful of the teacher and it would not go unpunished. We walked to class together so closely that one of my older female colleagues who passed us in the hall winked at me. As we got to the class I opened the door for her. "Now, respect your teacher," I said and she play-punched me hard in my shoulder as we entered, the other students gaping in bewilderment at our unprofessionalism.

Once the term ended, Shannon and I went out for a beer. At the pub, we talked in circles for a long while, our knees and feet touching the whole time. I told half-truths about my life. Like that my divorce had been "amicable". I was tactful about her private life; but my tact paid off. I found out that her hubby-to-be was twelve years her senior.

And loaded with cash. Her man's daddy had died at his desk at the age of fifty and left him boatloads of insurance pay-off and savings which he then loaded into a successful New York nightclub. Then another club. Which they'd just sold. They were both moving south to open a chain of five nightclubs. The demands of the nightclub business would make a honeymoon for them impossible. They were marrying in Florida. In Orlando.

"Disney World," she said, "to be precise." She repeated that and purposely emphasized the irony of the location, but told me not to make a joke.

I said, "The Magic Kingdom, eh?" When I made mouse ears she gave me the finger. On impulse, I grabbed her middle finger, pulling it so she would move closer, and as her finger slipped out of my grip our faces closed in and we kissed. We kissed and we groped each other so blatantly that the bartender told us to cool it, "Or get lost."

So we got lost.

We spent a half-hour locked in kisses outside on the sidewalk, pressing our hips together, muttering tender obscenities in each others' ears, groping under each other's shirt, taking turns running our index fingers along each other's lower lip, unbuttoning buttons and letting the cold night air ripple over our skin, nibbling each other's neck in full view of a parked patrol car. When we finally let go of each other we waved at the two cops; the officers seemed to blush like schoolboys.

I wished her good night and rode my train home with my face on fire, my cock surging as I recalled my hands on her warm skin, the supple after-tingle of her lips on mine. And most of all that blue-eyed gaze of hers: sharp, hungry, determined.

For two weeks, she phoned me nonstop trying to arrange a rendezvous. I reminded myself that student crushes are just that, and that I would be driving down a dead end – she was going to marry Mr ATM. I hated myself for how much my heart leaped at hearing her voice. My pussyfooting around her requests didn't work. Soon I got tired of resisting. "Why don't you come up here," I suggested.

I met her on the train platform. She was wearing a tight fitting denim jacket over a slate gray halter dress and matching gray sling back heels. We strolled with our arms snaked around each other's back as if we might fall down if we didn't hold tight to prop each other up. She tried to distract us from our own sexual tension by enumerating the property values of the storefronts and buildings we passed.

After dinner, I brought her home to my apartment to "meet my goldfish".

The goldfish was indifferent; I wasn't. When I helped her out of her denim jacket, the sight of her bare arms, lightly freckled and perfumed with talc, made me feel so intensely alive I felt I'd walked into someone else's life.

I led her into my bedroom and I put on Miles Davis' *Sketches of Spain*. She closed her eyes and told me what a sharp interior design eye I have. "For a starving poet, at least."

I knelt down in front of the bed and drew back the slit of her long gray skirt, staring up at her as I raised the fabric over her knees.

She closed her eyes. She asked me for some poetic lines.

"Slate gray like the sea. Scented," I said, "like wave-spray."

She smiled and threw her head back, her long red hair dangling behind her back, her draped hair almost touching the sheets on my bed. I studied her tightly crossed legs. Then I wedged her legs apart, gently, willfully. I quoted the Talking Heads to her. "Dreams walking in broad daylight."

I peeled off her black thong. It was wet, musky-scented. I dangled it from my finger, waiting for her to open her eyes. "Black blindfold removed," I said, dangling the thong with one hand. With my other hand, I slipped a finger along the fleshy nub of her sex. "Black blindfold removed. Now the blind can see."

"You're a right proper tease," she said. "And a right proper genius, in your syrupy way."

I blew her a kiss. She kept her legs apart and closed her eyes again. Like a make believe tattoo artist, I spelled out my initials on her knees, signed my name with my finger around the back of her calves.

She muttered, "Yesyesyes," so sincerely – so musically – that I rewarded her by breathing softly along the inside of her left thigh, puffing warm breaths right on a beauty mark. I grazed my forefinger through her red pubic hair and teased the nub of her sex with the tip of my tongue.

She closed her strong legs around my head and took hold of my free hand on the bed. As I plunged my tongue in further, my nose was tickled by her hairs and by the damp sweetness of her sex as I licked and lapped, my tongue carefully following the pulse of her pussy's pink lips. The harmonious play between my tongue and her sex made me swell in my pants. The leaping jazz bop, the crisp crescendos of Miles Davis' trumpet seemed to be guiding my tongue as I pleasured her.

I let go of her hand and tucked my hands under her thighs and held her ass, squeezing gently as I kissed her clit, then lifting her slightly off the mattress and dragging my pinky finger round back, running my pinky over the brim of her snug hole as my tongue flicked up and down on her clit, down and up and then in. In. And round. Round in ever-tighter ever-more tender tongue-circlings, pausing now and then to let out hot breaths on her. "I see an impatient flower fluttering," I said and I licked her nub deliberately, flicking my tongue at her clit, tickling it with the tip of my tongue back and forth until she'd swollen, supple and pink, like a pistil risen for a honeybee. The sudden pressure of her thighs closed against my head like a vise and forced my mouth against her sex; I was burrowed in her as I licked and kissed and kissed and flicked.

Soon I felt her legs quaking. I licked harder and faster. I felt her loving kicks of joy against my back urging me on; I let my pinky slide inside her snug spot as my tongue stroked her swollen clit so rapidly and so thoroughly my jaw started to ache, and then I heard muffled gasping, then louder shouts lilted by a brogue, "Oh Jesusfuck!" as she roared – and came – wet, violent, salty, her sex shivering warm spasms against my tongue, her voice ringing out so loudly in the room I could no longer hear Miles' trumpet.

I cooked her dinner the next week; she came up on the train.

She brought vanilla and strawberry cupcakes from a boutique bakery in the city and after dinner we played strip poker and undressed. When we got bored with the card game, we smeared and squashed the cupcakes on to each other's chin making fake beards that we licked off.

"Cupcake tits," I said, smearing strawberry icing on the soft underside of her breasts, slathering icing on to her nipples. "Cupcake tits topped by sugar kisses." Then we smeared the melted icing on to our chests, our mouths shaping puckered lips as we lapped every last bit of sugary melt off each other's nipples, even smearing icing up and down our backs, dripping into the clefts of our asses as our sweetened mouths moved lower on each other's body, lapping up love. As her wet mouth closed over my cock, my tongue found her clit wet and swollen. "Sugar pleasures," I said, loudly, and I'm sure, more than once.

We attended to each other's sex so thoroughly and so precisely that it seemed we were in a race to get each other off. I don't remember who came first but I distinctly remember the glaze of her own cum coating her thigh. I remember too how deliberately and dramatically I kissed that glaze, lapping up every drop while she giggled and repeated, "Sugar pleasures, boy, sugar pleasures."

Around three in the morning, we both woke up restless. She said she wanted something but she didn't know what. She crawled on to my stomach and pressed her knees into my chest. "It's not food I want," she said, "that's all I know."

I pulled her out of bed and led her into my bathroom. It was one of my favorite rooms in my otherwise charmless prewar apartment: a cosy bathroom with those old fashioned white pentagon tiles. Like some low-rent prince, I knelt down and slipped her feet back into her navy blue heels and turned her around so she could see herself in the full-length mirror on the bathroom door, her full white breasts flashing in the darkness, even more white and even more full as they gleamed luminously in the glass. I ran a forefinger down her breasts and tickled her nipples. I squeezed each one between my thumb and forefinger. "Buds of some unnamed flower," I said and she jabbed me with her elbow as reward for my waxing poetically.

I planted warm kisses on her nipples. Then I lifted my head and waved at her in the mirror. Her light blue eyes gleamed even in the dark. We both stared into the glass. She blew me a kiss. I rested my head playfully on her shoulder. She stared at my eyes in the mirror and reached back, soft-stroking my cock back to life.

Her lovely fingers hardened me and she leaned forward over the sink, and I entered her, slowly, softly, possessively, squeezing her ass cheeks as she leaned forward, her elbows resting on my porcelain sink, her head raised so she could see her own face in the mirror as I moved in her. The skin below my belly tickled against her smooth cleft.

As we fucked, she matched my motions, slow yet fast, fast and yet slow, working out some delicious dizzying tempo all our own. I ran my hands along her back, across her hips.

I teased the insides of her upper thighs, letting my fingers dance there even as we moved fast and faster, so fast, in fact, that before I could feel the surge burning in my balls she had let out another yelp of "OhJesusfuck," loudly, in that sharp brogue of hers, and she came, flowing over me just as I erupted, erupting in thick spasms, my balls contracting with a force I'd never felt before, as if my body were willing itself to empty all of me into her.

We collapsed clumsily to the cold bathroom floor, our legs akimbo, her high heels scraping against my leg. I propped a towel for a pillow and we dozed off in my bathroom, drifting into deep sleep, waking hours later to the sharp sunlight and the nagging buzz of her cell phone ringing somewhere in my empty bedroom. "That's the bloody Magic Kingdom calling," she said waving her hand around her head as if trying to swat a fly.

On the phone some weeks after those long nights in my place, we finally found time to get together again for coffee in a park. I asked about "the calendar". She said the wedding was in exactly twenty days time and she was feeling bad. "A good-bad, you know?" she said. "But like a right shit too, d'ya know what I mean, boy? Like I ought to be punished even though I know I won't."

At first, I was tone deaf as to her exact point. I thought she should let any guilt go; we hadn't asked anything of each other but fun. Serious fun, but only fun. She explained that it wasn't guilt, exactly, that she was feeling. "Maybe I'm feeling a touch too – well – like this has been very easy. Like getting away with murder, d'ya know what I mean?"

I loved how she contracted a New Yorker's "d'ya know" with her tart accent. I told her I knew exactly what she meant. My cock hardened as I repeated that I knew exactly what she meant, as if suddenly I was not only her lover but her interpreter and protector too. I agreed she was being a bad girl and that yes, she was absolutely getting away with murder lately and that if there was no punishment for her then, "What's to stop every drop-dead gorgeous twenty-eight year old fiancée from going out and getting it on with a hot office buddy or a handsome stranger at a bar?"

She conceded that we were setting a very bad precedent for future fiancées.

"Well, more you than me," I said. "Though the sugar pleasures have been mutual."

She repeated my phrase "sugar pleasures" and play-punched me and told me I ought to be poet.

"There's no money in poetry," I said, "I'm moving into the nightclub business."

"Beware, you'll get bought out, boy," she said.

I sensed from that conversation in the park that she was asking for a kinky and cathartic end to our brief fling so the Saturday before she was to leave for Florida, I rented us a hotel room in the city and booked a table at a fancy restaurant near the East River. Though it was a lie, I told her the place had a strict dress code. "Explain, boy."

"Women must wear little black dresses," I said.

"Go on."

"Sheer black stockings and backless high heels."

"Oh, is that spelled out on their menu, boy? I suppose 'Lingerie required as well'?"

"It's posted on their front door," I said and we laughed.

She said she'd see whether she wanted to conform to the code.

"Dress codes aren't always oppressive," I said. "Besides you said you felt this had been all too easy. So just do it."

"I like your tone, poet," she said. "Keep up that tone, I just might comply."

She showed up at the restaurant in a long black raincoat and a little black dress. Her light skin glowed under her black stockings. She wore hoop earrings and her hair was bunned up and elegantly coiffed, with tendrils spilling round her ears like wisps of red silk. She fixed my white shirt collar and ran an admiring finger down the lapel of my navy blue jacket. "Poet complied with a male dress code too, I see." She teased me by slipping her right hand into my deep trouser pocket and as she probed her right hand around in there she flashed me her other hand, showing off her diamond engagement ring.

The stone in its setting gleamed like a strange crystal star. "So I finally meet the rock," I said. I slung her bag over my shoulder and led her inside, to a round booth, a table draped in ivory cloth and lit by orange scented candles.

We barely poked at our appetizers, our arms snaked round each other, our bodies sparking so much heat that I was sure the tablecloth would catch.

As she stared at me and sipped her wine, I caressed her legs from her ankles and up her calves, my fingers dancing in quick skips across her thighs. I read the lace tops of her stockings as if they were written in Braille.

She held her wineglass and with her free hand compulsively zipped and unzipped and zipped my trousers as if the zipper were her own personal toy. The constant movement over my crotch made my cock stiffen. At one point she poked a finger into my open fly and teased my swelling shaft. "So, I have been reprehensible, huh?" she asked.

"By your own admission, you've been a disgracefully capricious fiancée," I whispered. I reached my arm around her back and squeezed her tightly, warmly to me. The sudden tenderness of our shoulders pressed together made us both feel the moment and our erotic play gave way as we choked up. We coughed. We caught our breath. I realized she was leaving. I toasted the past weeks. "To our pink swims, to midnight coves, to botched poems, to waterfall sketches, to what we have shared." My eyes watered up a little as I held my glass near her but seeing she was so composed pulled me together.

She tapped her glass against mine. She said, "It was what it was, right?"

I assured her that was the only reasonable way to sum it up.

After dessert she rested her head on her hands. "Now, regarding my getting away with murder. My capriciousness. What is poet-boy going to do about that?" she asked, hiding her smile behind the menu as she raised her eyebrows expectantly.

"Oh. You're going to have to get a talking-to." I squeezed her leg and she squealed. The hostess at her podium heard Shannon squeal and smiled over at us.

I slipped my hand under Shannon's skirt and ran my index finger along the scallop-lace border between her panties and her skin. She closed her eyes and winced as I pulled back the fabric and snapped it against her skin. "I want you to put your teacup down. I want you to go to the bathroom and wait inside there for me," I said.

She shrugged and stood up. "Teacher's strange tonight." She tossed her napkin on to my plate. "Well, fair enough. I have to go to the loo anyway."

I grabbed her elbow. "Not the women's. Go into the men's room. Wait. In a stall. Think about how easy it's been for you, these past few weeks with me."

She nodded in disbelief, gave me the finger and sauntered off.

When the wait staff had all vanished from view, I snuck into the men's room.

I stood at a urinal pretending to be going to the bathroom as I waited in the bright fluorescence as two burly men finished their business at the sinks. When the men finally left, I knocked on the last closed stall. "Poet-girl in here?"

I heard a muffled giggle and, through the rank odor, I could smell Shannon's lavender perfume. Her talc.

The latch of the last stall clicked and the door creaked open on as if on its own.

Shannon was crouched on the closed toilet seat, squatted uncomfortably in her shiny black heels with an expression on her face like a cat trapped in a tree. She had one hand over her mouth and was trying to keep from laughing as she held her nose with the other hand. She stepped down off the toilet and straightened her dress, holding her nose again. "This is one stinky joint."

"It's like a confessional," I said rapping my fist against the metal wall. "Now you can rest easy knowing you paid some price for all our fun." I snaked my arm around her and kissed her. I kept an arm secured behind her back, kissing her ear. She teased me by zipping and unzipping my fly again and I reached under her skirt and teased her through her lace panties, feeling her heat build as I ran swift butterfly kisses up and down the nape of her neck. She wriggled and tried to pull my arm away but when I kissed her chin her resistance melted.

She closed her eyes and smiled. She repeated again and again how insane this was. I drew back her panties and let my finger sink into her sex.

"You are a mean teacher," she said. "M-e-a-n."

I unzipped my pants and let my cock out, crudely, like a gesture in some second-rate porno film. She stepped back and stared. "Is that a blowjob request? I don't take requests," she said, staring down at my cock as if she could take it or leave it. "You know me, boy, I prefer life on Easy Street. Giving head is hard work." She chuckled and winked and then shook her head dismissively. Then she grabbed my cock and as she held it she playfully bit my earlobe.

As she kept her hold on me, I lowered myself on to the closed toilet lid and asked her to kneel in front of me.

"Boy, I am not kneeling on this filthy floor." I pulled out sanitary seat liners and strew them in layers on the floor by my feet.

Slowly, moving like a suspicious traveler settling into a strange hotel room, she knelt down on the lined papers on the floor. Holding my cock, she poked out her tongue, looking lost in thought as if she were trying to recall a name. "I'm thinking 'Devil Redhead in the Men's Lod'." she said, "Should I write it as a sonnet?" she asked, speaking into my cock, giggling as she squeezed me harder. Then she licked and lapped my crown, at first gingerly and then aggressively, long licks up my shaft, patiently, thoroughly, a random pace of licks all her own, the way a cat cleans itself at its own pace, in its own sweet time.

Seeing her pink painted fingernails and white fingers cupping my balls nearly made me cum. I held fast to the sides of the bowl and gazed at her, her black high heeled feet tearing at the paper lining on the floor, the almost imperceptible breeze of the paper blowing dust and pubic hairs around in the tile and grouting.

I was sure the loud watery, pocking sound of her tongue lapping as it ran upwards again along my cock could be heard by anyone who came into the bathroom. And the noisy suckling too as she took me in whole, the tearing noise, heels ripping the paper to shreds. As she drew her tight lips upwards, so slowly I felt she'd never let go, I exploded into her warm mouth.

She suckled me until I went soft and then she dribbled, letting my own wad ooze down over my cock.

She stared at my sex intently, only once looking up at my eyes.

Then she stood up, wiped her hands and fingers with tissue paper, fixed her skirt, patted my head.

"Not the cleanest of places. No picnic. But I think I've paid some price, poet-boy, being lured in here."

And then she checked to see that the coast was clear and left me alone in the stall where I lingered, gathering myself together, wondering how she'd gotten the upper hand yet again.

That night, like most of our affair, felt like a surreal, hardcore fairy tale.

After the restaurant, back at the hotel, I gave her a farewell bouquet of lilacs.

The clock was literally ticking over our heads. We didn't talk much. We lay on the bed, hand in hand, surfing TV channels. She nuzzled against my chest and I stroked her hair. She said she was going to miss only one thing about New York.

"The poetry workshop?" I asked.

"Not bloody likely," she said. "Maybe just one meanie of a poet."

She told me she couldn't believe that tawdry encounter in the john was all her punishment for having had "this little illicit madness".

I asked her if she was ready for one last chance to save her soul.

She said in 29 hours she'd be on a plane to Orlando. "If I'm not ready now, when will I be?" I went to the fridge and brought out a bottle of Prosecco and a small white cake I'd bought at the fancy Polish bakery. She asked me what this was. "Your just desserts," I said.

She sat up and beamed. We sat Indian-style on the bed, feeling like kids at a kinky pajama party. I drew a fork out and she asked me where mine was. I informed her that she was eating all this whole cake. "Solo."

"And be a blimp on Monday? Float down the aisle like a bridezilla?" she asked. "I don't think so. Not after tonight's crème brûlée."

I convinced her that as punishments go, a sugary sweet is hardly cruel and unusual and fed her a forkful, watching the icing drip and then plop on to her black skirt, smudging the corners of her lips.

Cake crumbs soon dotted the coverlet around us.

After the second slice she hugged her tummy and said, "No mas, boy."

I cut a third slice and held a forkful near her lips. "Did you give a blowjob in a men's room or was I dreaming that?" I asked, and when she cracked a smile I slipped the cake into her mouth. As I fed her – and overfed her – I felt paternal, fatherly, sadistic. My cock was hard again.

She chewed and giggled and nodded. "I'm going to retch," she said. She chewed, mumbling obscenities and giving me the finger as she ate. "Disgusting."

I removed the cake from the box and kicked the box off the bed, placing the remaining cake near our pillows. I helped her strip down to her bra and stockings.

She slipped my belt off my trousers and wrapped it around her fist and play-punched me in my stomach. Then she fit my belt around her small waist, the buckle dangling. As I lifted her by her haunches she tried to kick free. I lowered her down on the cake and she squirmed, closing her eyes and grinning as her ass crushed the cake. "Boy the icing is bloody cold!"

I told her not to worry. "Help is on the way."

I lay myself down stomach-down on the bed, my head directly in front of her sex. I licked her inner thighs, licking up the flakes of cake and icing, and swirled my sweetened tongue along her sex, flicking my tongue on her cunt until she was wet, warm, wiggling. The icing melted on her skin as I kissed her thighs and dragged the tip of my tongue up her sex and down, in, down, down and then up again, quick strokes with my tongue till her sweetness wet my lips.

I pulled myself up and we lay down in the missionary position, eye to eye, nose to nose, like a couple about to consummate vows.

I entered her slowly, and stayed still inside her, swollen, hot, rigid.

We remained motionless like that, face to face, our hands locked together tenderly savoring something we knew was ending. Ending, that is, until it started, first with her hips moving and then mine, my mouth on her right breast, lapping her nipple, nibbling, lolling my tongue at the soft under-skin of her breasts as my hands cupped her.

She swirled her tongue in my ear and ran her fingers through my hair. I buried my fingers in her mass of red hair, massaging her scalp. I pulled the pins from her hair and let her red hair spill over the pillow and her cheeks. Her hair framed her face so wonderfully she looked like a movie star posed on the cover of *Vanity Fair*.

I told her so and kissed her and lowered my face and kissed her nipples. I nibbled. I dragged the tip of my tongue from her neckline down to the space between her breasts, slathering each nipple again, lifting myself up just enough so that my cock stayed locked in place while I kissed her stomach, my tongue swirling on her warm skin as we rocked like that for what felt like an hour, an hour that ended faster than a millisecond as the two of us came crashing down on each other – into each other – muffling our cries in a kiss, kissing and then licking our chins as we fell, rose and fell and rose again only to fall finally waist deep into the hot running currents between our legs.

The next morning she let me shampoo her hair and I enjoyed lathering the bubbles through her thick wet tresses. We played the *Sketches of Spain* CD loudly and made friendly jokes about our bathroom escapade in the restaurant the night before. Shannon said the night before had definitely not been a case of getting off easily. "I paid the piper in that smelly awful place," she said, shoving me playfully. "And I do feel better now."

We ate breakfast at a local diner and wandered around the city as the sun staggered toward noon.

She educated me about business start-ups. Feasibility studies. Florida's liquor laws. Liability matters that came up when you owned nightclubs. Mr ATM had gone down to Florida weeks ahead to see that the movers didn't destroy their stuff and to get the club renovations finished. I asked her what airline she was taking. She shrugged indifferently. We reminisced about some of the characters in the poetry workshop. She said it felt as though the course had been ten years ago. We agreed that time plays vicious jokes on people. "Personal arcs get tangled up, people meet at the wrong time," she said. "D'ya know what I mean?"

I answered that of course I knew what she meant. I didn't say it but I knew she meant that she needed to marry this man. And I knew, or so I told myself, that I still needed to be on my own, that I needed more time and space to get on my feet after my divorce.

We hugged underneath the FDR Drive and let go without getting weepy. The breeze off the river cooled us some. I hailed a cab for her.

I watched her sling her duffel bag confidently into the taxi and her confidence reassured me that she would be just fine. A double major, a good head on her shoulders, an older, stable businessman for a husband, a new life in sunny climes. We hugged one more time, quickly, and she climbed into the car.

As the cab receded she turned once to wave and then I watched how sun and shadows through the rear windshield cast bright light on and off on her long red hair, and I watched until the car disappeared from view up the highway ramp.

At my apartment the next morning I put a vase of lilacs on my bathroom sink and remembered the first time she'd come over. Clicking my laptop to life, I Googled the mailing address for Disney World's Wedding reception hall. The hit came up as the Magic Kingdom Wedding Castle. As I scrolled down the list I saw the announcement of a Monday wedding "Gary Suggs and Shannon O'Rourke".

I bought a wedding card with a big white cake on the cover and a Starbucks gift card. I crossed out the sappy Hallmark congratulations to a blessed couple on your blessed day. I addressed the card to her and scribbled inside, "With my abiding affection and always in good thoughts, to the girl who had her cake and ate it too. XOXO." Then I slipped the gift card in, licked the envelope slowly, sealed it and paid the postage, handed it over to the Next Day delivery counter.

Outside the post office, I remember thinking it was a balmy summer already and it was only the start of July. Almost like Florida, I thought. She'd worn me out; I needed a nap. And I remember reminding myself that I was free and single, smack down in the middle of my life, and that, even though it was terribly quiet in my life just then, there was no real reason to be down.

Being Bobby

Donna George Storey

It was no ordinary day.

To begin with, Zoe woke up all on her own. Usually it was Bobby who roused her, his hard-on nudging her ass, but it was only six in the morning, and Bobby was still asleep.

Zoe glanced appreciatively at his long, dark curls spilling over the pillow, but she made no move to wake him. She knew the urgent tingling between her legs was less carnal desire than the legacy of last night's beer. She slithered off the bottom of the bed and groped for her underwear in the tangle of clothing on the floor.

College had its advantages. You could spend every night in your boyfriend's bed, and your parents never had a clue. Then again, back home you didn't have to climb down three flights of stairs to go to the bathroom in the freezing January dawn. Teeth chattering, Zoe stepped into her panties and yanked them up over hips. Something was definitely unusual now. Overnight the fabric of her underwear had grown thicker, the fit in the ass snug, and the waistband rode suspiciously high. Zoe smiled. She'd put on Bobby's briefs by mistake. She reached down to take them off.

That's when things began to get very strange indeed.

Instead of hooking themselves under the elastic, her fingers crept lower, as if some invisible hand were guiding them. Before she knew it, she was tracing the front seam, the one that led down to that secret opening, with languid, teasing strokes. Just the other night, Zoe had pulled Bobby's stiff cock through the gap and sucked him. She remembered his red, swollen lollipop poking up from the white cloth and realized, with a grin, that Bobby was always hard when she saw him in his underwear.

Maybe his underpants were enchanted, because she was getting rather turned on herself. She could feel her pussy lips swell, feel a new heat spreading along the crotch of the briefs. Could girls get morning boners?

Touch me.

This was getting even weirder. Could underwear talk?

Go ahead, put your finger inside.

Although she wasn't usually in the habit of taking advice from Bobby's underwear – or anyone else's – Zoe decided it was too early for arguments. Obediently, she snaked her finger under the flap and burrowed through the second opening to greet her clit, already standing at attention. Suddenly she wasn't so cold any more. Knees bent, pelvis tilted forward, she began to strum. The briefs strained against her buttocks, like hands gripping her there. It felt naughty, but exciting, too, to play with herself like some perverted voyeur while she watched Bobby sleep.

He was a very appealing sight. His bare shoulder still had a coppery sheen even in the pewter light of dawn. She loved his skin. To her it tasted of cinnamon, cumin and cloves. Like his gorgeous black ringlets, it was the happy legacy of his adventuring grandfather, a Liberian chieftain's son who stowed away on a steamer bound for New York.

Just then Bobby moaned and shifted, one arm shooting out to embrace the emptiness where Zoe had been sleeping.

She jerked her hand from his underpants. The cold pang of guilt in her stomach reminded her that she really did have to pee. More awake now, she could easily spot her own jeans, bra and blouse in the pile.

But that was what she wore on ordinary days.

Her pulse racing, she pulled on Bobby's sweatshirt and wiggled into his jeans instead. Suddenly the smell of him was all around her, Mediterranean spices and sweat. She could feel the ghost of his body, too, in the looseness of the waistband, the tightness at the hips, the pooling of the denim at her ankles. It wasn't a perfect fit, of course, but it was good enough for a trip to the john.

Stepping into her own shoes – that little glitch in the outfit couldn't be helped – Zoe moved quietly to the door. On the way out she lifted his baseball cap from the dresser and slipped it on her head, brim backwards, the way Bobby wore it.

She shivered and blinked in the harsh light of the stairwell, but by the next floor, she'd found her rhythm, taking two stairs at time. Bobby's clothes were warm now, melting into her skin. Even her flesh and bones felt different, lighter and infinitely at ease, as if the very essence of the universe were pulsing through her veins like liquid sunlight. No one was watching or judging – *hey, man, get a load of those tits*. On ordinary days, Zoe hated the way her breasts jostled when she ran, and she loathed her butt, which remained stubbornly round and full no matter how much she dieted. But this morning she'd somehow escaped the prison of her own body. She was exactly what she wanted to be: long and lean and jazzy, just like Bobby. For once what she looked like was less important than the things her body could do. As she savored each swaggering step, each powerful ripple of muscle in her legs, these words floated into her head: *this must be how boys feel inside*.

Of course, the magic couldn't last forever. The stairs took her straight to the door of the men's bathroom. If she really were Bobby, she could saunter right in, but to get to the ladies' she'd have to follow a long subterranean corridor to the next entryway. The architects who built this dorm a hundred years ago, when the college was all male, probably never dreamed their design would be such a pain in the ass to a young woman creeping down from her boyfriend's bed to answer nature's call. Dead white males – that was another thing about college, everywhere you turned they'd left their mark.

Zoe glanced down the hallway quickly in each direction. All was quiet and cold, deserted as the Siberian tundra.

Go ahead. Do it. No one will see.

Throwing her shoulders back, she strode into the men's room. She half-expected a crash of thunder in divine retribution, but the only sound was a faucet dripping in the far corner and the faint buzz of fluorescent lights.

Zoe paused, sniffing the air. The place reeked of boy, as if the walls had sucked in all the secretions of decades of its inhabitants for posterity: sweat and piss and rivers of milky jism swirling down the shower drains.

She smiled.

Truth be told, this wasn't the first time Zoe had visited the men's room in the fourth entryway of Holder Hall. She'd been here just one month before, but with a proper escort. She and Bobby had stayed on campus for a few days of the Christmas break, supposedly to finish up term papers, but really so they could fuck all day long. One morning Bobby talked her into taking a shower with him. He said guys brought their girlfriends here all the time. He'd come down to brush his teeth or whatever, and he'd spot four feet under a shower curtain, two of them smaller, the toenails painted a tell-tale pink or red. Zoe didn't really need much convincing. She could barely restrain her giggles as she stripped down and slid behind the cheap plastic curtain. At first, they just kissed and rubbed their wet bodies together under the shower spray. Then Bobby took the lead, gliding the white bar of soap over her breasts, moving it in tight circles over her nipples. She leaned against him, reveling in the sensation, an odd combination of cool and rigid, slippery and soft. Then Bobby turned the soap sideways and pushed it up into her cleft, brushing her clit with it, then moving back up over her mons and belly. Only when he had her nearly sobbing with lust did he stop the teasing to press the soap steadily between her labia and pinch her nipple just the way she liked it. Zoe rode the makeshift sex toy, thrusting against the slick, rounded edge, until she came in silent gasps, the hot water lashing her face and chest.

She fell to her knees and gazed up at him, his ringlets wet against his shoulders, his bittersweet chocolate eyes glowing. It was her turn to please him. Greedily she took him in her mouth, her head nodding – *Yes, yes, I'm doing a dirty thing. I'm sucking off a guy in the shower in the men's bathroom.* Bobby's thighs tensed, his cock grew thicker and harder between her lips. She knew it wouldn't be long before he gave her that warning tap on her shoulder. Some guys whined and gave her shit because she didn't like to swallow, but Bobby had always been cool. Yet suddenly, kneeling on the shower stall floor, she felt ready to do something even more wild and daring. She wanted to watch him come, and she wanted to taste it, just a little, before it dissolved in the pulsing spray.

She pulled away and met his eyes.

Come on me, Bobby. Spray me with your jiz.

Of course, she didn't actually say such things out loud. Zoe had never had the nerve to tell a guy the crazy things she dreamed of doing during sex. The words always got all tangled up in her throat.

But Bobby seemed to understand.

He reached down and brushed her cheek with his fingertips. "Do you want me to come on you?" He made the words sound almost romantic.

She bowed her head and nodded, blushing at her own perversity.

Bobby took his dick in his hand and began to pull on it with practiced strokes, aiming it straight at her.

Zoe tilted her head back, lips parted. She knew Bobby masturbated in the shower – what guy didn't? – but it gave her a secret thrill to be here with him, watching and waiting.

Soon Bobby's chest was heaving, his legs shook. The head of his cock was as taut and purple as a plum. The first jet of cream landed on her chest, sizzling into her flesh. The second hit her cheek, hotter than the shower spray. The rest dribbled into his pumping fist. Zoe stared, entranced, but before she had a chance to scoop up any of his gooey, gleaming spunk, the pounding water washed it all away.

No, she wasn't exactly a stranger to this place. She'd had her baptism. Yet, it was different, even dangerous, to come here alone without a native guide. She glanced at the bank of urinals, and shook her head. She wasn't quite ready to take on that challenge.

Instead Zoe marched into the first stall and latched the door. She relieved herself with a luxuriant sigh, her most pressing need finally satisfied. Yet, even after she wiped and zipped, her flesh still throbbed with longing. She had to admit it now: Bobby's clothes were making her very horny. Fortunately, she saw the perfect solution. She could simply go back to the room, slip into bed and do just what Bobby would do. Nudge, nudge – wake up, I want you.

In Bobby's clothes, she could do anything.

Then she heard the footsteps. Heavy, entitled footsteps headed right for the stall door.

Zoe caught her breath as her stomach twisted itself into a pretzel. Had Bobby followed her, mad as hell because she'd stolen not only his clothes but his spirit, too? Or, worse still, was it the custodian, ready to turn her in to the dean? What she'd done might not be quite as weird as if Bobby had put on her panties and bra and flounced into the ladies' room, but she'd still have some serious explaining to do.

The footsteps passed on and stopped by the urinals. There was a cough, then the soothing sound of a waterfall at spring thaw.

Zoe's shoulders sagged in relief. There'd be no angry scene, no disciplinary action. It was just some guy who had to take a pee.

Okay, man, you can skulk here like a pussy or make your move and get out now.

Boldly, Zoe pushed open the stall door and headed for the exit, turning her back to the urinals. She'd heard somewhere that straight guys made it a policy not to check each other out in the men's room. Even if her companion did glance up, dick in hand, there was a decent chance the back of her would pass for male to his bleary morning eye.

And in fact, there was no rough hand on her shoulder, no outraged cry of accusation – *Hey, you don't have a penis, you're not allowed in here.* Zoe bounded up the stairs, laughter bubbling in her chest.

Being Bobby was turning out to be a lot of fun.

Except, unfortunately, it was almost over. Soon she'd have to strip off his potent armor, shrug away the heady legacy of adventure coursing through his blood, and sink down into her own boring skin again.

Back in Bobby's room, Zoe undressed slowly, a gloomy little striptease – jeans, socks, sweatshirt. Yet when it came time to take off the briefs, her hands balked once more. Again she slipped a finger through the secret entry to tickle her needy clit. The other palm cupped its sister protectively. She looked at Bobby, still sleeping innocently on his narrow bed.

She'd always marveled how easily Bobby could spring a woody. Her black minidress had given him a bulge the moment he laid eyes on her, and once he even got a boner from a glimpse of her bare midriff when she reached up to get a book on a high shelf. She'd always wondered how could someone get so turned on just by looking.

Suddenly she knew.

And so she did exactly what Bobby would do. She crawled back into bed, spooned him from behind and pushed her crotch against his firm ass. Reaching around to touch him, she discovered that even without his magic undies, he was already hard.

Bobby mumbled and stretched. "Your hands are fucking freezing."

"I just came back from the bathroom."

He turned and opened his eyes, thick lashes fluttering. "But the rest of you is nice and warm."

His hands cupped her breasts, giving her nipples a quick good-morning tweak, then meandered lower.

Zoe stiffened. She realized, too late, that she should've taken the underwear off before she got in bed. Would Bobby think she was a pervert, a dyke, a gay man in a woman's body? A friend made that joke about another acquaintance and Bobby had grimaced in disgust.

His fingers found the waistband. He paused. "Hey, are these mine?"

"Yeah," she admitted breathlessly. "I couldn't see in the dark, and I put on the wrong ones."

He laughed softly.

Zoe exhaled.

Yet what Bobby did next surprised her. He pulled the covers back and gazed steadily at the extraordinary sight of his girlfriend dressed up in his underwear.

Donna George Storey

A smile dancing on his lips, he reached out to trace her vulva through the cotton.

Zoe gasped, involuntarily parting her thighs as Bobby's finger tunneled through that irresistible opening. Soon she didn't recognize the sounds coming from her lips – shameless moans of pleasure mixed with deep, staccato grunts. Her ass was thrusting so fast in time with his strumming finger, the bedsprings screeched in protest.

Bobby always made her feel good, but it had never quite been this good. As he rubbed, a column of heat arched up into her belly, as if a cock were buried inside her. But it wasn't like a guy's cock, just pressure and motion and heat. It was her cock. She could feel it thicken and throb, feel the hot spunk gather and burn, ready to explode in a fountain of pearly white cream.

In no time at all, she climaxed, arching up off the bed with a bellowing groan.

Afterwards, Bobby wrapped his arms around her as he always did. She was glad she could bury her face in his shoulder to hide her blush. She'd wanted him inside her when she came.

"Wow, you're hot this morning," he breathed. He didn't seem to mind she'd climaxed too soon, like a boy.

Of course, she knew she had the advantage over the typical premature ejaculator. She wouldn't have to work on him with her finger or tongue for god-knows-how-long when all she really wanted to do was go back to sleep. All a girl had to do was lie back and let the guy pump away.

You can do better than that. You take control. Show him what it's like to be you.

Zoe frowned into Bobby's shoulder. Maybe that nagging voice would leave her alone if she finally took his underwear off? Yet, she knew that without those briefs hugging her ass, it would be just another ordinary day.

He's got a soft, pink hole, too, and he'll purr like a kitten when you put your finger inside.

Her fingers prickled. She had to admit the voice hadn't steered her wrong yet. Why not venture farther into the wilderness?

"It's my turn now, Bobby. Lie back and spread your legs." Zoe smiled to soften the command, but the voice – her voice – clearly meant business.

Bobby drew back, eyebrows lifted in surprise. Then, with a wary smile, he rolled on to his back and did as he was told. Zoe crouched between his thighs, licking his cock like an ice cream cone. Her left hand closed around the base, pumping slowly while she teased him with her mouth. Bobby whimpered as she traced quick figure-eights on the sensitive skin right below the head, then groaned when she lapped the swollen knob with the flat of her tongue. Finally she took him all the way into her mouth. Bobby relaxed into the mattress with a sigh.

But this was all familiar ground. Her right hand was itching to embark on its new adventure. First she cupped his balls, then meandered down to the ridge between his legs where her cunt would be, stroking him there until he squirmed and cooed. Her finger crept lower, into the Valley of Darkness.

She advanced slowly, unsure of his response. She'd never done this before, with anyone.

Bobby inched his legs wider. Apparently he was ready for adventure, too.

The terrain grew hotter, faintly moist. When she touched a tender little knoll of flesh just above his asshole, he moaned, a ghostly sound, as if he were melting away. She began to tap him there, like she tapped her own clit. The moans became a song. His cock twitched and pulsed, as hard and smooth as marble between her lips.

Zoe's finger marched onward into the forbidden zone. She traced his secret little mouth with her fingertip. The ring of muscle tensed then pushed open, beckoning her inside. She pulled away, smiling at his groan of disappointment. Quickly moistening her finger with spit, she pushed the tip up through the doorway.

Bobby took her in with a soft "ah" of surrender.

From here on her journey presented a new, physical challenge. Bobby was virgin-tight, like a leather glove two sizes too small, and she didn't want to hurt his tender flesh. She wiggled her fingertip gently to open him, to test if he was ready for more.

Bobby was beyond speech, but his moans were eloquent enough. Now, with each down stroke of her lips on his cock, Zoe pushed in a little deeper, her finger dancing sinuously inside the tight little mini-dress of his asshole.

Bobby's whole body trembled and his cock seemed to swell even thicker, like an over-ripe fruit, strained to bursting. He pawed at her shoulder, the signal to pull off and finish him with her hand.

But Zoe's lips refused to release him, and she realized the rest of her, too, was no longer afraid. She wanted only to have him inside her when he came, just as she was buried inside him. Bobby cried out and his muscles clenched, milking her finger as he shot his spunk into her throat. Instinctively she swallowed it down, so busy in her attentions to his cock and asshole she hardly tasted it. But she did get the chance to savor the last drops: cinnamon, cumin and cloves mixed with sun-drenched meadow grass.

In truth, it wasn't bad at all.

Zoe rose to her knees, eyes sparkling with triumph. And what did Bobby think of the wild things she'd done? She didn't have time to ask because he immediately pulled her down on top of him and whispered into her neck, "You're the best ever."

Lying in his arms, Zoe realized that she must make a queer picture – a curvy girl wearing boy's briefs.

Hey, remember, what you look like is less important than what you do.

Zoe smiled. This time she knew that voice wasn't coming from Bobby's underwear. It was in her head and her flesh, hers to keep.

Advanced Corsetry

Justine Elyot

I fell into this business unintentionally. I started out as an enthusiastic amateur, became a connoisseur and now I am proud to call myself a master – or mistress, I suppose – corsetière. If you ever want to talk busks, fan-lacing, whalebone or the respective merits of under-and-over bust models, I could be your woman.

Of course, should you choose to engage me in conversation on this subject, I must warn you that certain assumptions may be made regarding your personal preferences. These days we get our share of trendy young things surfing the wave of the burlesque revival, but our traditional customer has more personal reasons for favouring this most retro-chic of foundation garments.

Few people are better placed than I to appreciate the allure of the corset: her restrictive embrace, her provocative display of the finer feminine features, her fetishistic cross-lacing. You cannot ever forget you are wearing one; like an insatiable lover, she demands your full attention.

This is why I often find myself measuring and fitting women who want a little more than the traditional ribboned satin or silk. I have requests for custom-made pieces in rubber, latex or leather; others require additional features, such as delicate chains crossing the breasts, or linking the front and back of the garment between the thighs. One customer even emailed me to request that I add a harness-like leather construction connecting the panels, which could run between the thighs and up the cleft of the buttocks, and to which could be attached various phallic objects. I wish she could have summoned the nerve to request this of me face to face; I always had a feeling we may have hit it off.

I thought, then, I had heard every outré suggestion possible: corsets for fetish balls, corsets for waist restriction, corsets for the bedroom, corsets for lovers of Victorian kink.

As it turned out, however, things could, and did, get more decadent still.

My clients had occasionally come with friends, or even lovers; the intention being to canvass an additional opinion on what suited best, or perhaps to add a little titillation to the experience.

The couple I saw on that memorable afternoon were a different proposition entirely.

When I arrived in the small waiting area outside my atelier, she was sitting, hands folded demurely, while he stood scanning the photographs and framed magazine clippings on the wall. At first, there seemed nothing of special note about them, indeed they were rather less showy in their style and fashion taste than many I see. This in itself seems noteworthy in retrospect; at the time I simply cocked an admiring eyebrow at his Italian suit and her immaculate haircut and invited them into my fitting room.

At first I was taken aback when my initial "what can I do for you?" spiel, addressed to the lady, was responded to by the man. He appeared at least twenty years older than her, and for a bizarre moment I wondered if he were her father. It was a relief when he used the words "my wife" in his reply, and I presumed the more exotic dynamic of Dominant and Submissive – a bread-and-butter breed of customer, though I usually only interview one half of the sketch.

Instantly her silence became fascinating to me, and throughout the man's lengthy discourse regarding their wants and tastes, I kept my eye on her. She was somewhere in her twenties, though conservatively dressed for her age in a blouse of ecru silk, the high neck adorned with what is incongruously termed a "pussy-bow". A knee-length tweed skirt and low courts completed the ensemble; hardly the pink-haired rubber-skirted brigade I generally tend to encounter en route to the Fetish Ball.

Her head remained bowed, our eyes never met, and I found myself wondering whether her doggedly maintained silence conveyed weakness or strength.

When the time came for her to have her measurements taken, she stood unbidden and planted herself in the centre of the room, chin up and shoulders back, awaiting instruction.

"You will need to remove your blouse and skirt, Mrs Fox," I told her, affecting intense concentration on my tape measure while she unbuttoned and cast off her outer layers of clothing. I was struck by two things once the clothes were neatly folded: the 1950 styling of her underwear, which was a flesh-coloured bra and girdle with old-fashioned metal suspender snaps; and the understated magnificence of her body, all luscious curves and creamy skin.

"Surely you will need her naked?" said her husband, standing behind her with his arms folded. "To get the true measure of her, I mean."

"I . . . do not usually insist . . ." I told him, though my throat dried at his suggestion. I longed to see what was held in by that severe girdle, cut so tantalizingly high and yet retaining the letter, if not the spirit, of modesty.

"I think in this instance . . ." his voice trailed away, questioningly.

I nodded, caught up in his scheme, made complicit by the slightly menacing smile he flashed in my direction. "If you could just slip out of your underthings for me, Mrs Fox," I said, my voice much lower now.

Even then, she did not look up or speak. Almost casually, she turned to present the clasp of her bra to me. I unhooked it briskly and took it from her, touching her shoulder to indicate that she should face me once more. Beautiful tits, high and firm with strawberry-pink areolae were my reward. I caught myself fidgeting with the tape measure again while she struggled and wriggled out of the tight girdle and, although I am noted for my composure, I found I could not look at her husband for fear of blushing.

Besides, a feast for my eyes was before me; the legs were not model-perfect, but they tapered nicely. The thighs were milky and a well-tended cluster of golden brown fleece curled between and above them. Unusual, I thought, that he doesn't make her shave; I understood it was de rigueur these days.

"Could you raise your arms above your head for me, please."

I moved around behind her, placing one end of my measure in the small of her back, risking a swift glance down at the curve of her arse (perfection) before returning in front to run my smooth tape across her breasts. The coldness of it perked her nipples up more so they stood stiffly, and, without even thinking about it, I pulled the tape a little tauter and rubbed it slightly back and forth. She bit her lip and I had to exhale briefly, watching her rock on the balls of her feet and clench her fists. She felt that. Again, her husband sent that flicker of a smile in my direction, emboldening me.

Keeping the tape firmly held in one hand, I scribbled down her measurements on my deskpad, pulling slightly at her numerated tether while I did so. I had to admire her poise and grace; she did not stumble in the least.

Passing swiftly through the duller terrain of under-bust and waist, I came to another favoured spot – her hips. "Let's keep this smooth – you have just a little pot belly here," I clucked at her, and her husband laughed and said, "Yes, she does, doesn't she." Her cheeks flamed, but she kept her eyes fixed to the floor and made no other response.

"The corset will hold that in for you; nobody will know it is there," I said reassuringly, working hard at keeping my hand steady when I laid my length of plastic-coated fabric across the upper slope of her buttocks. Then I took a measurement I often eschew: the broadest part of her bottom and around the upper thigh. I had to kneel to check the measurement, my nose no more than an inch from her triangle of fuzzy hair, and the smell of her was, for a moment, almost too evocative. I took a lungful of it, to keep and bring out in my bed that night, thinking of other white thighs parted and welcoming, other crimson lips glistening at me. It had been so long.

But I am a professional, and I rolled my tape back up, wrote down my figures and turned to the gentleman, ready to enact business.

He held up a hand. "Don't put your tape away yet," he suggested. "I think we may want something in the way of a garter or stocking top – perhaps you could measure the circumference of her thighs. Just at the very top, perhaps – as high as you can comfortably go."

I stifled a smile. "Certainly, sir. Madam, may I ask you to stand with your feet a little apart." The very tops of her thighs were tightly encircled, just below the crease of her bottom. It was impossible to perform this task without brushing my hand against her muff, and so very easy to rest it gently between the slightly opened lips of her vulva. Good Lord, she was dripping. I pushed my knuckles discreetly upwards, garnering a good coating of her juices, before completing my task. My tape also harvested a little of her lubrication.

It was all I could do not to put my hand to my nose and take a deep breath while I trotted out final arrangements for our fitting at top speed. I wanted them out, door locked, feet up on the desk, skirt hitched, hand inside knickers, post-haste.

For the rest of that week, every spare minute was consumed by thoughts of her. Did she ever speak? What did her voice sound like? In the heat of sex, would she make a noise? Was she silent even at the moment of climax? Had her husband enforced a speaking ban, or was it voluntary? I remembered the humidity between her thighs, the sticky, wanting smell of her. Was she a willing participant in this, or was I her unwitting tormentor?

I hoped to find out the answers to all of these questions, plus more regarding the exact feel and taste of her, at our next meeting – though I expected the latter queries to remain unanswered. I constructed her corset – red satin, with black velvet running the length of the bones – with greater care than I usually expend. How perfectly it would frame her, covering her middle to expose more fully the tempting expanses above and below. I laced the eyelets lovingly, seeing the criss-cross pattern traverse her back from tailbone to bustline in my mind's eye.

The day of our fitting arrived at last; she was again respectably dressed in a boxy Jackie O-inspired skirt suit. When I passed the corset across the desk to her, she fingered it tenderly, catching her breath and shooting me my first eye contact: a cringing gratitude.

"Do you think it will do?" I asked her, smiling.

"I'm sure it will be just right," replied her husband, taking it off her and holding it up in front of him. "Once we've added our little extras."

"Extras?"

"Let's have her try it on first, then we can discuss the adjustments I have in mind."

He left it to me to issue the order to undress. My mind raced while I watched her perfectly polished nails wrestle with the large buttons of her jacket. Adjustments. Extras. Memories of the customized corset the lady had requested by email flashed through my mind. Was something along those lines required here? I rather hoped so.

How obediently she divested herself of her clothes, folding them neatly and piling them on the nearby chair, unsnapping her suspender clips, rolling down her stockings, tackling the hooks and eyes of her front-fastening basque and then standing quietly naked, head bowed as always, hands clasped modestly over her pubic triangle. She was not fully naked, though, for there was a plain silver torque around her neck, which fastened with a tiny chain at the back. Almost like a collar, of a very discreet kind.

She complied patiently with my every request while I settled the corset in under her bust and commenced the task of lacing it.

"How tight do you want it?" I asked, addressing my question unthinkingly to her husband.

"Well, now, I think we decided that we don't want it so tight that her breathing was affected. Tight enough to ensure that she is constantly aware of it, I suppose."

"I understand completely." I pulled hard at the laces, enjoying her gasps, and the first sound to come from her throat – a tiny mewl. "So you have a voice," I said briskly, and she fidgeted uncomfortably. One hand moved to cover her right buttock and I noticed for the first time a tiny mark there, dark red, almost a bruise but not quite.

"Don't cover it, or I shall tell the lady how you came by it," said her husband in a warning tone. "You are to behave yourself for Miss Frost, remember."

Her hand moved away and once more her bare bum was on full display, mark and all. Now that the corset was laced, it swelled and undulated magnificently, crying out for attention.

"Now how's that?" I asked, clapping my hands together with satisfaction at the beautiful picture she made, nude but for her severely cinched waist and silver collar.

"Exquisite," commented her husband. "Almost exactly what we wanted. Give us a twirl, love."

She pirouetted obediently, then struck a number of suggested poses – hands on hips, one leg on a chair, bent at the waist. "Perhaps you would like to photograph her for a private catalogue?" he suggested, and when I demurred he said, "Do you mind if I do?" and took a number of pictures on his mobile phone.

"Almost exactly?" I quoted him when he had finished, holding my notepad and pen in my hand as if ready to dash off a list of new requirements.

"Yes." He lowered his voice. "I have been led to understand that you can provide modifications to order. Is this correct?"

I nodded expressionlessly. "Quite correct. I am discreet and prepared to cater for even the most unusual tastes. If you could tell me what you have in mind . . ."

He produced a piece of crumpled paper from his breast pocket – a blueprint of sorts – and handed it over.

"Fascinating," I commented, looking up at his lovely little submissive, still standing in corset and collar in the centre of the room. "I shall have to think how I can make this work . . . so these . . . ?"

"Chains, linking the top of the corset to her . . . necklet. Crossing the breasts, with a nipple clamp in the centre of each cross. I envisage sterling silver, perhaps even white gold, for the clamps. Would you be able to source something like this?"

"I'm sure I know an outlet or two. And then these straps below . . . ?"

"Yes, thin straps, about a centimetre in width, of black leather, attached to each side of the front panel, crossing her thighs diagonally and meeting in the centre. As you see, they would pass underneath and between her legs, and up the cleft of her arse."

The word "arse" was oddly jarring; perverse as our conversation was, it had the feel of polite dinner party chat.

"Yes, I see, and there are these small metal loops around the . . . anus and the . . . er . . ."

"Yes, they don't have to be metal, though. I will leave that to you. The idea is that a vibrator or dildo can be screwed into each ring and inserted into my wife when she is wearing the corset. The part of the strap that passes between her lips should also have a patch of some reasonably rough or coarse fabric stitched on, which will rub against her clit when she walks. Our aim is that she will be in a state of permanent sexual stimulation, though I would prefer that she cannot quite achieve satisfaction. So the fabric will need to be just a little too rough to be comfortable, and the penetrative objects just long enough to enter, but not so long as to provide relief. What do you think? We can go elsewhere . . ."

"No need for that," I said quietly, though I must admit I had been rendered momentarily speechless by what he had said. Speechless and extremely aroused. I wondered how she felt about it all; she maintained her statuesque pose throughout.

Head bowed, hands clasped.

"I will need to take additional measurements."

"As you wish."

I stood directly in front of my subject, unwinding the tape measure very quickly so she could hear the light swish of it, such an efficient sound.

"Your nipples first, I think. Are they quite hard enough?" I turned to her husband.

"Perhaps they need to be a little harder," he agreed.

The pad of my thumb described a light circle over both tips until her chest began to buck and heave a little. I applied my finishing touch – a firm pinch to each – then wound my tape around the pair, pulling it as hard as I could get away with, looking for a grimace or, better, a sound. I got the grimace; the sound did not come.

"Small but not too small," I noted. "There will be a standardized size of clamps for them."

"Oh, I'm aware of that."

"Now to the matter of the rings. What size of penetrative object were you considering?"

"Big enough to be noticeable. If you could perhaps measure both holes and then order rings for perhaps half a centimetre larger all round. She will need to be stretched a little."

"I understand. Well, shall we start down here? I think, my dear, I will need you to bend over. Could you put your hands on that footstool just there and spread your legs as much as you can. That's . . . just the job, dear."

The whole spread was wide open and willing, from the swollen ruby of her clitoris to the brown bud peeking at me from between her cheeks. I felt like a gourmet at a feast, unsure of which dish to sample first.

I started at the top, or rather, the bottom.

"Perhaps if you use your fingers? To get an idea of what she can comfortably take?"

I acceded to her husband's request, snapping on a pair of thin latex gloves, and took a jar of lubricant he had produced from his trouser pocket. I smeared it liberally around the entrance of her pucker, greasing it up and pressing my thumb against the ring. "Don't clench."

My gloved index finger snaked slowly and surprisingly easily beyond her sphincter. I twisted it around in there for a minute until she began to squirm, then introduced a second finger. She began to whimper a little, so I went for the third, ramming them up as far as I could repeatedly and pressing down on her little red mark with my other hand. "Yes," I said, now having to work at controlling my own breathing. "If I measure the width of these three fingers, that should be sufficient."

I took off the glove and wound the tape around my fingers, enjoying the residual warmth from the invasion of her most private space. I thought about putting a fresh pair of gloves on for the next part of my measuring mission, but the prospect of all that hot, wet, yielding flesh against mine was too much to resist.

One finger was sucked into the tight, slick cave of her cunt; two were better, scissoring and prodding at the sides, feeling for the bump of her g-spot, finding it and rubbing it. And then, yes, she definitely moaned; her walls quivered, and I added a third finger. I could feel the suction; she was pulling me in and I was tempted to stay, but I realized that this was not on today's agenda, so I pulled out with a luscious squelch and added the figures to the list.

"She's extremely receptive," I remarked to her husband.

"She's a slut," he said, and the smallest of sighs escaped his wife's lips.

That night I thought about Ruby for the first time in years.

I thought about how she had loved to be on display, how she would contrive to show off her suspenders even in polite company, how she would goad me into meting out discipline, how she would beg to be shared.

And that had been the sticking point. I had been unable to share her.

Mr Fox, it seemed, had no such scruple. Sharing his wife would be my first taste of that particular brand of honey in almost a decade. But was she like Ruby, or was she just doing it to please her husband? Perhaps I should just take her gushing pussy as a silent consent. Yes, perhaps I would do that.

Production of the Foxs' custom corset was a complicated job, involving much research and negotiation with some of the BDSM toy suppliers, but I looked upon it as a labour of lust.

When I was eventually able to stroke the leather nether harness, poking a finger or two through its rings, I called my deviant couple to invite them for a final fitting. On the mannequin, the contraption looked devilishly wicked and alluring and I could not seem to stop experimenting with tightening and adjusting its fixtures. The two specially made dildoes – thick, but not quite long enough to go far – stood on my desk like sentinels, ready to greet her when she walked through the door.

She saw them straightaway, flinched and then turned to the mannequin.

With her eyes, she asked her husband's permission to touch and examine her new garment, and she stood before it, running her elegant fingers over the smooth silk and the expensive leather; moving closer in to gape at the shining silver nipple clamps.

"You've done a wonderful job," commented Mr Fox. "My wife will get a lot of pleasure from this. And so will I."

Mention of his wife's pleasure struck me instantly as a subtle green light. I smiled at him and nodded. "The pleasure was all mine. I do enjoy these projects."

"Good. Should we move on to the fitting?"

Without having to be asked, my model tugged at the ties of her wrap dress until it fell open, exposing her bra. She slipped off the skyscraper heels she was wearing, but her husband shook his head, and she put them back on again. She had only to shrug off the dress, unclip her bra and step out of her knickers today, and it was scant minutes before she stood in front of us in nothing but hold-up stockings, high heels and that silver collar.

Having removed the corset from the mannequin, I prepared to transfer it to Mrs Fox – a complex operation, involving much unlacing and unclipping. First I tied the main body of the corset tightly, but not too tightly, reining her in until the required hourglass was moulded. The straps at the front hung down between her thighs, but I left them there and began work on the thin chains that were to cross her breasts.

I clipped each chain to her collar, so that silver Xs adorned the pert little tits, then I went to work on attaching the nipple clamps. One notch, then two; the nipples crimsoned and stood out like tiny beacons. How lickable they looked, and the discomfort indicated by her gritted teeth was not putting me off in the least.

Nonetheless, it was time to move downwards, to fix the leather straps, passing them down between her thighs to hook them up at the base of her spine.

"Open your legs; this needs to pass between your pussy lips," I told her, keeping my voice dispassionate. I manipulated the strap until it sat inside her labia, pressing directly against her clitoris. I lined up the ring with her vaginal entrance, then pulled the strap upwards between her bottom cheeks, performing the same alignment exercise over her hidden rosette.

"Is that tight enough, do you think?" I asked Mr Fox, tensing the strap as much as I could.

"That seems just about right," he opined. "Let me check." He pinched and felt his way around the new features, nodding approval as he did so. "She certainly won't be able to forget she is wearing it. Even less so when the extras are added."

"Shall we try them out?"

"Oh, yes, I think so."

I picked up the thicker of the dildoes, relaxed the strap enough to screw it into place in its ring and then ordered Mrs Fox to bend over on the desk with her legs as wide as possible.

"Is she wet enough to take this straight in?" I wondered aloud.

"Why don't you test her with a finger?" suggested her husband.

I took him up on it, giving her clit a good workout before pushing two fingers into the soaked void. She was wet enough all right, wiggling her bum frantically and trying to pull me in further. Oh no, she was not getting that yet.

"She's saturated," I laughed to Mr Fox. "I don't often see a customer as satisfied as this!"

He laughed back at me. "Not satisfied yet. Not until permission is granted, at least."

"I quite understand. Now let's stretch that dripping little quim, shall we?" I pushed the dildo inside in one swift move; her hips rotated, desperate to suck it in further, but she would get no more than the four inches of smooth black silicone.

Now I was too involved in my work to think about donning gloves; I affixed the anal plug to its ring and lubricated her clenching and unclenching arsehole with some of the copious juices of her pussy. I took my time with this operation, keeping the cheeks spread wide while I worked, talking to her in a low voice as one would to a skittish horse, for she was trying to hump the dildo in her cunt like a woman possessed.

"Keep it nice and relaxed, dear," I whispered. "It will stretch you, and you will feel it, but it won't fill you; no, you mustn't have that satisfaction without your husband's permission, must you, my dear? I do wonder where you will be wearing this lovely thing; I'm sure no amount of cover-up would hide the obvious fact that your holes are filled and your nipples as swollen as overripe cherries. I expect you'll draw quite a lot of attention, wherever you go. I like those heels, my dear; they do thrust out your bum quite helpfully – look how ready you are now. Now keep still, dear girl, and don't tense those muscles."

I pushed the dildo against the tight little pucker, easing it in, keeping a tight hold of her spread cheeks in case she panicked, though I suspected she was well used to this method of penetration. She took it without protest, grunting quietly and rocking back and forth, until it was fully seated.

All that remained for me to do was to tighten the straps so that neither dildo could possibly be dislodged and leave her to accustom herself to the sensation.

"Well, that's . . . very nice," said Mr Fox, and I had to agree with him. The slightly protuberant flange of the anal dildo separated her cheeks pleasingly, and her pussy lips swelled out at either side of the invasive strap. Now I was tempted to take up Mr Fox's offer of a photography session, but he interrupted my train of thought, ordering his lady to, "Walk across the room for us. No tottering on those heels."

Mrs Fox straightened, straining to keep her posture dignified and refined, but from the moment she took her first waddling step, it was obvious that dignity and refinement would not characterize her gait in this garment. Unable to close her thighs, and highly conscious of her penetrated bottom hole, she had to bow her legs slightly in order to get anywhere. Keeping her head down, she shuffled across the room, working hard at keeping upright on those vertiginous five inch heels, coming to a halt at the full-length mirror.

"Lovely. Now get on your hands and knees and crawl back."

She dropped to all fours and began to creep towards us. Oh Lord, I had never seen anything so exquisite than this beautiful, silent, submissive woman in her depraved garb, crawling in my direction, embodying all my sublimated fantasies together.

"Would you excuse me for a moment?" Mr Fox picked the strangest moment to leave the room, just as his wife had arrived at my feet.

"Oh . . ." I glanced after him, mildly consternated, then turned my attention to the woman on the floor. Without looking up at me, she crouched over and kissed the toe of each of my patent leather court shoes.

Then she spoke.

"Mistress," she said. Her voice was low, almost a groan.

"I beg your pardon?"

"Please forgive me," she murmured, her lips still so close that her breath misted the shiny shoes. "I have not been quite . . . honest with you."

I reached down and hauled her into a standing position by the elbow. "What do you mean?" I snapped, horrible visions of myself and her in the Sunday scandal rags springing into my head.

"No, no, there's no harm done, I hope!" she beseeched. "I'm sorry; let me tell you the truth and I hope you can forgive me. Please?"

I nodded and went to sit behind my desk, indicating that she should remain standing. When my mind was at rest, then so could her body be.

"I . . . the thing is . . . I've spent months wondering how to set up a meeting like this. I've thought and thought about it, but I'm quite shy . . ."

She looked at me questioningly.

"Go on," I said.

"That man – Mr Fox, or whatever – is not my husband. He's a friend of mine. He agreed to do this for me. The thing is, you've probably forgotten, but I came in once with a girlfriend. She wanted a rubber one. I just . . . I suppose I became a little bit obsessed with you. Your manner, it's very mistressish, you know, and I really like that . . . I longed to come in and get fitted myself, but I was just too shy. I couldn't face it. I fantasized about it all the time though, discussed it with my friends on the net until they got quite sick of hearing about it. It was me that emailed you about the corset design, thinking at least if I had the corset . . . but it wasn't the same. I knew I had to come in myself, but there was no way I could ask for this on my own behalf. Ralph agreed to help me. I know him quite well, from the internet and a couple of parties. I was pretty sure I could trust him."

She stopped for a second, her darkly lipsticked mouth half-open, as if it had run out of steam.

"You wanted me to dominate you while fitting a corset?" I asked for clarification.

"Oh yes. And afterwards, of course. But I do love corsets. The fabrics, the restraint, the frills and finishing touches. They are so erotic to me."

I half-smiled at her. "Well, I certainly agree with you there."

I stood up and positioned myself in front of her. Even on her heels she was a few inches shorter than me. I wrenched up her chin and put my lips against her ear. "I don't know your name, little girl, but I do know your game, and it's an exceptionally dangerous one."

She moaned, pushing her face against me, trying to divert my lips on to hers. I wouldn't have it.

"What about your friend Ralph? Do you want to involve him in this game now?"

"I want him to watch. He wants to watch," she half-sobbed, her body gyrating again in an effort to get some pleasure from its stubby shortened intruders.

"Where is he now?"

"He said he'd wait by the stairs."

"Then you'd better go and fetch him."

I released her chin and turned her towards the door, setting her on her way with a stinging slap to her bum.

Off she waddled, returning five minutes later with her mildly embarrassed-looking friend.

"Ah, you're back," I said. "I have a favour to ask of you. In my desk drawer you will find a selection of full-length dildoes. I would like you to replace those in Miss here's harness with two larger examples.

Then, while she is busy using her tongue to satisfy me, I want you to make sure that she is feeling the full benefit of the replacements. Do you think you can do that?"

"I'm sure I can," he said smoothly, rummaging in the drawer while my little admirer stood trembling with arousal at the side of the desk.

"Good. Bend over then, girl, and wait for him to saddle you up."

I watched while the shorter objects were removed and long, thick rubber intruders took their place. She whimpered a little when the anal plug was halfway in, but Ralph was not one to allow that kind of thing to put him off, and he slid it slowly to the hilt, tightening the strap in place once more. Now she was barely able to walk at all, but, at my command, she knelt in front of me.

I leant back against the desk, steadying myself. I did not want that imposter Ralph to get a good eyeful of my cunt, so this would require some delicacy.

"Now I want you to push my skirt up just enough so that your tongue is able to reach my quim. Can you do that?"

"I'll try, ma'am," she said, pushing her head under the tweed and up to my stocking tops. I rarely wear knickers when I am corseted myself, so she had no obstructions to encounter. The rumpled skirt rested on top of her head, and there was no way Ralph could see anything forbidden to him.

"Good girl," I crooned. "Now, Ralph, get down on your knees behind her and work that arse and pussy hard. Come on then, girl, get to it." I reached down and tweaked a clamped nipple; she squealed and her tongue darted out, hitting the spot perfectly.

What a hungry little mouth she had, devouring my liquid heat, running the tip of her tongue around my clit in luxurious circles, waiting for it to swell to unbearable proportions before sliding her lips over and breathing on it, lapping at it, sucking on it. Tiny yelps issued from her throat, vibrating over my whole sex, in time with Ralph's diligent pull-and-pushing on the deep-set dildoes.

"You can't imagine what you look like, can you, you little trollop? Kneeling here being fucked in both holes while you eat pussy as if your life depended on it. I don't think I've ever seen a slut to compare with you. I'd love to introduce you to my friends."

A long, starved moan buzzed between my thighs; I signalled Ralph to slow down. I didn't want her coming just yet. Noticing the man's bulging trousers, I gave him permission to masturbate, pulling her head closer to my crotch, mashing her mouth up against my clit, using my other hand to twiddle with her sore little nipples.

"Next time you pull a stunt like this, young lady, I'll spank your arse for you," I promised her. She sighed, her tongue in a frenzy now, her bottom wiggling furiously, while her whole body worked at relieving itself on the twin phalluses.

The three peaks came in rapid series, one rising as another fell. First Ralph roared and splashed his seed all over her bum and thighs, then, as it dripped downwards, she caught the perfect configuration of dildo and nerve-ending and howled on to my clit, triggering my own explosion.

For a few minutes, the three of us were slumped together like felled skittles, panting and enjoying the stars that circled our heads.

Ralph was first to tuck himself in and button himself up, leaving my naughty little customer to fall sideways. I wiped my thighs with a tissue and patted down my skirt, thinking that now was the time for private catalogue photography.

She was flushed and sweating; her mouth glistening with my spendings; her bottom and thighs sticky with Ralph's spunk. Her cheeks were still rudely thrust apart by the large dildo, and the strap still cut into the middle of her cunt lips. Her nipples were more like cherry stones than cherries now and one high heeled shoe hung off her heel. She looked a mess; a gorgeous dirty feast of a mess.

"We need photographs," I told Ralph, and he nodded.

Her name, it turned out, was Jess. Her modelling and catalogue work for me is much admired in corsetry circles these days. And if you gain my trust, and ask me very, very respectfully, I might just show you my private collection.

Royal

Adam Berlin

I opened the door to my building, on the way out to have some drinks, and there she was, sitting on the stairs. I saw the back of her first. Her hair, more gold than blonde, fell halfway down her back, the backs of her arms were thin and graceful, and her posture was perfect. I'm a jaded man, but I have to admit she stopped me. Of course I knew, even as I stopped, how easy it was to be beautiful from the back. Chances were this woman on my stoop wouldn't live up. I'd walk down the stairs, take a glance at her face, confirm that her features were not as perfectly proportioned, her skin not as smooth, her mouth not as mysterious and her eyes not as mesmerizing as I'd hoped, and then I'd walk on and get my first drink and my second and my third and soon pretty much everyone would be pretty much beautiful.

So I walked down the steps. I glanced at her face. And I stopped again. She had the kind of quiet beauty I dreamed about. Models, movie stars and high-class hookers roamed Manhattan's streets, especially at night, but their beauty was obvious. You saw them and you knew what they did. This woman, sitting quietly, looking across the street with eyes so far away she could have been gazing at the other side of the world, was different.

If I'd already downed my third or fourth drink, I would have spoken to her immediately. I would have worked to get her up the stairs and into my bed, to open her up and fuck her, and in fucking her she would lose some of her beauty and then I wouldn't fall in love. I preferred my day-to-days steady and slightly numb. And I preferred my nights full of easy highs that had nothing to do with love. I'd drink, live my pretend-adventure, wake with a hangover in some stranger's bed and sneak out. The early morning Yoo-Hoos I sipped while walking to the nearest subway coated my stomach. And like the birds chirping optimistically about the sun's imminent rise,

I felt good in these pre-dawn moments. My cock comfortably sore. My balls unloaded. My body mighty and ready to sleep at the same time. I'd get through my day and when the urge hit me again a day or two later, sometimes three, I'd go out again. I hadn't had any drinks. I was sober. And sober, I was less aggressive. But I knew if I walked on, I would never again see this quiet beauty sitting on my steps. Maybe it was the night. I felt drunk sometimes even before I had my first drink. Maybe it was how jaded I was, hoping to prove her less than she was. If she spoke and she was stupid or vapid or just too normal, her aura would disappear. Maybe it was the way her eyes moved from whatever horizon she was looking at to my eyes. She looked at me for a long time and, not being one to lose a staring contest, I looked at her for a long time too.

"It's anatomical," I said.

"What is?" she said and I liked her voice. It was quiet and calm. Two words spoken, one question, but she sounded like she had all the time in the world. And she had the faintest accent, refined, almost regal.

"My eyes," I said. "I don't need to blink. I can look at something for hours without blinking."

"At something?" she said.

"Or someone."

"And you can look for hours?"

"If I have to."

"Well," she said and smiled and then she blinked slowly, not because she had to but because blinking went so well with her smile.

"Are you waiting for someone?"

"No," she said. "I'm simply tired. I've just arrived to New York City and feel quite jet-lagged. I thought I'd sit for a few moments before I walked on."

"Europe?" I said.

"Yes. Though you'll never guess the country."

I looked at my watch. "So it's around two in the morning for you."

"Exactly. And I didn't sleep well on the flight."

"I'm going to get a drink. Would you like to come along? A little alcohol might help you with your jet lag."

Without a word she stood and, just like that, took my arm, her hand around my bicep and we walked down the street.

We drank. I had my usual gin on the rocks. It was summer and in summer I drank gin. She drank Sauvignon Blanc. It felt like a movie. It was just us, the leading man and woman. Everyone else in the bar was an out-of-focus extra. Her laugh was pure. Her eyes were clear. Her voice was crisp on the consonants and round on the vowels. Her hand, when she touched my arm, was warm. We talked. Not biographies. We just talked. And when we looked at each other, not blinking, it wasn't a game. I didn't ask her to come back to my apartment. She just took my arm when we left the bar and that's where we went.

We didn't fuck. That had never happened to me before, not in all my years in New York City and I'd moved to Manhattan when I was seventeen, a small-town high school kid looking for big-city action. When I took a woman to my place, which I almost never did, or when a woman took me to her place, the sleepovers were never about sleep. Only in the hardest cases, when the woman was hesitant, first-date or first-meet morality tempering her lust, did I have to use the *Let's just sleep together* line. But every time, as I walked the stairs to her apartment, watching her ass move, or took the elevator up to her apartment, watching her finger press the button, I always smiled. Sleeping together sounded innocent enough, but it was a euphemism so obvious it always went corrupt. Sometimes it took some work, but by dawn just sleeping together meant my cock was inside her.

With this woman, it was different. She was upstairs, in my room, but we only kissed. We kissed like I had never kissed. Her mouth was soft and firm, her tongue rapid-fire one moment, slow and sensual the next, and the way she kissed made me kiss differently. I wasn't just kissing her to move to the next place, the way I kissed others, routine foreplay to fast-forward the one night stand. I could imagine kissing this woman for hours. I could imagine not growing tired of her kiss. We kissed and we kissed and I didn't know where my mouth ended and hers began, didn't know if that was my lip or her lip, my tongue or her tongue. But when I moved my hand over her shoulder, to her breast, smoothing my palm across her nipple, she took my wrist in her hand and moved my hand back to her shoulder.

"It's not time," she said and I didn't feel the need to push.

Time stopped beyond the cliché. Then she moved her mouth from mine and looked at me.

"I have to sleep," she said. "And I have to sleep alone. I'd like to sleep with you, of course, but tonight I have to sleep alone."

"You have to?"

"Yes," she said and I left it at that.

Chivalrously I offered my bed and said I'd sleep on the couch. She excused herself to the bathroom to wash up. I grabbed a spare comforter from the closet and threw it on the couch.

She was still in the bathroom. I went into my bedroom to get a pair of boxers to sleep in. I needed to do laundry and it was my last pair of clean boxers and there it was, where I hid it, and that's when I got the thought. Maybe it was fate. I lifted my last pair of boxers and saw its head peeking out from under a sock in the back of the drawer. Maybe it wasn't fate. I'd never been in this position before, not in this apartment, not in this city, not ever, and so I got the thought. My last sort-of girlfriend had given me her dildo, saying she didn't need it now that she'd met me. She wanted me to have her favorite dildo as a sign of eternal gratitude for making her come like a porn star. I'd grown tired of her by the time she gave me her special gift, so tired I didn't bother correcting her. She wasn't the porn star. I was the porn star. I was the one making her come.

Making the golden-haired beauty in my bathroom come was what I wanted. I wanted to see her perfect mouth open in orgasm. I wanted to feel her perfect hands holding my biceps as I moved my cock inside her. I wanted her perfect legs wrapped around my waist. And most of all I wanted her perfect eyes, eyes that could look and linger, to look at me, look through me, while I was fucking her and then, something I had never really wanted before, I wanted her eyes to stay on my eyes after we were done. I was a jaded man, but I wanted her and not just to fuck. I would sleep on the couch if that's what it took. But I had to know, had to know now, that she was as sexual as her kiss, that she could keep up with me and keep me fulfilled for more than a night and then, maybe, I could fall. Like the fairytale I'd heard so many times as a kid, I took the dildo from my drawer and, as if it were the pea to the puzzle, put it under my mattress.

I went back to the couch. I was the opposite of tired.

She came out of the bathroom, her face freshly washed, and she kissed me once more. "Thank you for tonight," she said. "I'll see you in the morning."

"I hope so."

"And thank you for letting me stay over. I had a room reserved and my family arrives tomorrow, but I'm glad I'm here. It feels real to me here. It feels like a home."

"This place is nothing like a home," I said. "I live like a Spartan. There's nothing here."

"You don't have much, but what you do have is yours."

She looked around my living room and I followed her eyes. To the piece of driftwood propped up in the corner of the room. To the prints on the wall, blurred black-and-whites of cityscapes. To the single photograph of me standing in front of the high-end auto shop where I worked, mock-squinting like some B-movie tough guy. I was wearing my usual jeans and an oil-stained T-shirt, looking too blue-collar for Manhattan.

"Good night," she said again and she smiled and blinked and walked into my bedroom and closed the door.

I lay down on the couch. My eyes stayed open and I thought of her.

The city's night noises went through their pattern. At midnight, the moan of a garbage truck's compactor. At one, the drunken chatter of students moving bar to bar. At two, a homeless person sifting trash. At three, a cursing drunk, angry at himself, angry at the world. At four it was mostly quiet, just the intermittent sounds of cabs taking their fares home. My eyes were still open. And then I heard a new noise, or a louder version of a noise I'd heard when we'd kissed. She was moaning, a low, steady moan. I got off the couch. Perhaps the pea was working. I had to see.

I cracked the door and looked in. My eyes were already adjusted to the darkness and the streetlight across the street, shining through the blinds, helped show me all I needed to see. She was on her stomach, pressing into the bed, her pussy grinding exactly into the place where I'd put the dildo under the mattress. Pressing and pressing and moaning. My cock was hard while I watched her.

The morning sounds started. Newspaper trucks arriving at five. Early-morning risers walking to the subway at six. I shifted on the couch, shifted again, thought of her in my bedroom, thought of how she'd looked and how she'd sounded. My cock had been hard all night. I waited and finally the bedroom door opened. I closed my eyes and listened to her bare feet on the floor. Then I felt her sit down at my legs. I opened my eyes and she was looking at me.

"How did you sleep?" I said.

"I don't know. I had dreams all night. The dreams were so real I feel like I didn't sleep at all."

"Good dreams?"

"Wonderful dreams," she said. "And you were in them."

"Really?" I said.

"You were perfect," she said and she smiled.

She was wearing one of my T-shirts. That's all. Her bare legs looked long and lean. I moved my hand from under the comforter and touched her leg. Her skin was smoother than any skin I'd touched. I moved my hand up her thigh and she didn't stop me. I moved my fingers over her pussy. She was completely shaved and the skin was smoother still. And then I put a finger inside her. The smoothest skin of all. I worked my fingers in and out and I heard the sounds I'd heard. I put my fingers in her mouth and her lips and tongue that had been on my lips and tongue the night before sucked and licked my fingers. She was pushing her mouth into my fingers, thrusting her hips forward on the couch. I sat up. I stood up. I lifted her up. I carried her to my bed. I took off her shirt and spread her before me and she was the most beautiful woman I'd ever seen. From the back. From the front. With her legs open in front of me, her pussy open, her mouth open, her eyes open. I took off my boxers and put my cock inside her and she took me in. It was perfect. She was perfect. I moved slowly. Just the head first. In and out. I watched her eyes. Then more of my cock. In and out. Then all of my cock and she thrust forward, her legs wrapping around me, tight, her moans louder now and I moved hard and harder and watched her the whole time. Her face flushed. Her teeth flashed. Her eyes stayed open.

"Come in me," she said.

"Is it safe?"

"It is. Come in me. I want to feel you. I dreamed you came in me last night and I want to feel you now."

I hunkered down, pressed into her. I closed my eyes and moved inside her for myself but I wasn't thinking of anyone else, only her, and I saw her in my bed, pressing herself into the sheets, pressing herself into the place where I'd hid the dildo under the mattress and that's when I came.

We were side by side.

We were looking at the ceiling.

I listened to her breaths, now slow, rested.

"I didn't sleep either," I said.

"Were you dreaming of me like I was dreaming of you?"

"I was waiting for you," I said.

"I'm here."

"Stay here," I said.

She moved her fingers over my chest.

"Stay," I said again.

"I can't."

"Why not?"

"Tonight I'll be at the Ritz Carlton staying in the penthouse suite. That's where we stay when we come to New York City. But even if I'm there, I'll be wishing I were here."

"Then be here."

"I can't. My parents have official business to attend to and I have to go where they go."

"You work for your parents?"

"I belong to them. My father is a head of state and my mother is considered royalty where I come from. I'm their daughter."

"You're a princess?"

She didn't blink.

So the fairytale, at least that part of the fairytale, was true.

"No wonder," I said.

"No wonder what?"

"No wonder you didn't sleep well last night. It was the mattress. You must be used to sleeping on the softest mattresses in the world."

We stayed there looking at the ceiling.

"Royalty," I said.

"In a way," she said and her fingers stopped moving over my chest.

"In a way I am royalty," she said. "And so were you. You were a perfect prince."

"A perfect prince. I like the sound of that."

"A perfect prince for one night."

"For one night?"

"Yes," she said. "One night. Isn't that how you do it?"

"How do you know?"

"I feel it."

I didn't ask if it was like feeling a dildo at the bottom of a bed. As soon as we met, she'd held my eyes for as long as I held hers and that had made her my princess.

"You lived up," I said.

She smiled. She got out of bed. She still looked beautiful to me. She took my T-shirt from the floor, folded it, placed it on the bed.

"I saw you from behind sitting on my steps and then I saw you from the front and you lived up. And you lived up every moment after that."

"That's why we'll say good-bye now," she said. "So we'll never falter. You never want to see the fairytale a year later."

"Or even a week later," I said. "Or even a day."

"Yes," she said. "Or even a day."

She dressed.

I dressed.

We went down.

We kissed at the door. A final kiss. A fairytale kiss.

She walked down the stairs and I watched her, from behind, move into her day.

The Strangler Fig

J. D. Munro

We'd never spoken until today, except for the day she named me long ago in a backstage hallway. She had crouched to tie her shoe, and roadies bumped the black-haired backup singer as if she didn't exist. Only I saw her. I snapped her: *click*. Her head snapped up at the sound. *Click*, she mimicked the camera's voice, a voice I throw. She worked an air shutter. I shuddered, newly baptized as Click.

Then, when I developed into her shadow, I became Click the Tick. I was in two places at once. I followed her career, and flashed it ahead of her at the same time. With my photos, I made Kiara, and she made me.

Click the Tick, her tongue castanets. Click the Tick, her fingers snap. Click the Tick, her heels on tile. Not only do I cling tight; I measure time, her second hand. I count.

But we don't talk to each other. One does not expect conversation from one's deity. One expects lightning bolts. And Kiara delivered, turning me with one syllable from ordinary Thomas, nerd with a telephoto, to Click: best of the celluloid infantry. A man worthy enough to have a nickname. Loners are never called anything but what's on their birth certificates, called out in medical waiting rooms and at airport gates. Until they become unhinged and acquire a pet name. Unabomber. Killer Clown. Jack the Ripper. When they see their new moniker hit the papers, they know they've become somebody, important enough for re-christening.

I can't forgive her when she disappears like this. Every year, the same time, up in a puff of smoke. Before she vanishes, she starts to cover herself up like a virgin fundamentalist, and her voice starts to crack. I could never pinpoint the date's significance – not her birthday, not the solstice, not the anniversary of her Mexican grandmother's death – but I've learned that tomorrow marks the beginning of the annual Huichol pilgrimage to Xapa, the Tree That

Rains. The villagers have begun to file out in droves, heading for the peyote ceremony to get fried in the name of extinct gods.

Before her annual evanescence, Kiara refuses interviews or performances, claiming laryngitis. She hides behind sunglasses, scarves, and baggy dresses; the baby bump rumors start. She takes a new lover. Then she goes underground, untraceable. She re-emerges a few weeks later looking fresh and young, bikini-clad and gorgeous, her voice sliding up and down the range of a piano as easily as hands do. The rags crow that she's gone under the knife. These know-it-alls know *nada*. I know every crease of her flesh better than my own (no one wants to look at me, including myself). I am her microscope. No knife, no injection, but . . . something.

Flawless, like last year around this time, at the gala benefit – for cancer, or animals, or animals with cancer, who gives a rip, we just care about the gowns and games – *Mi ácaro*, my tick, she mouthed silently to me and blew a kiss. Then turned away, into the microphones of the yakking interviewers.

But I don't hear. I only see. Freeze-frames parade through my head, as if I look at a contact sheet instead of at the chaotic mob. First: her sandaled toes peek out through the cracked-open limo door. No nail color, ever. We glimpse her long, sepia leg – no stockings, always bare skin, one of her trademarks. Then: a pause. We intuit the whole of her, complete entity in the dark and cool interior. We stare, yearning, as funereal congregations gaze upon the coffin, knowing what's inside. We sense the pearled and powdered beauty beneath the mahogany slab.

Then comes the heel, ankle, calf, nudging open high skirt slit, my life's meaning thrust through a stage curtain. So like her tongue through her lips, taking her time, teasing. Then knee, thigh. A hand. A twist at her waist, unseen. Then Kiara. We receive the whole of her, but we never get enough. Not even with the backless dress, tease of drapery and miracle of architecture cascading from threads at her shoulders, offering us the entirety of her spine. Each vertebra, count them, fulcrum of her grace. The wisp of cloth waterfalls beneath her sacrum, sacred seat of her soul, god-made indentation for a man's palm to guide her – but no man will. This she proffers to us, so much more profound a revelation than pedestrian cleavage heaving along the catwalk.

Amidst the perfume and hairspray and sweat, her natural fragrance shimmers: nutmeg and mango and oak-barreled whiskey. Chocolate and chili. All simmered into the essence of her skin.

Most paps don't work the red carpet. After all, the paparazzi get top dollar for the shots of stars with their clothes off, not their makeup on. We want the wrinkle, the wart, not the de la Renta. But Click'll get the candid of her that everyone wants (Kiara checking, over her shoulder in the limo's reflection, the transition from skin to silk just at the swell of her tailbone, a mere millisecond). All the other hacks with single lens reflex stand in the same place, with the same equipment. But blind.

Just a few weeks before that, I caught her on an icicled balcony in the middle of godforsaken nowhere, 1,000 mm and F2.8 all the way through, grainy but solid gold, unmistakably her despite the sunglasses, *ushanka*, and white mink coat swaddling her up past her chin. The tabloid editors say *Christ, Click, how'd you know? How'd you get the shot?*

She'd sprinkled none of her usual clues for me to follow. She cuddled with a new lover (cropped out), descendant of some Svalbardian prince, or so he claimed. His Highness soon disappeared, though his absence never hit the US papers – we don't care much for the fate of jaundiced, bottom-runged nobility. An alleged accident on the way to his hunting lodge. It seems that his Stolichnaya-fond majesty had always been careless near crevasses. Poor out-of-the-frame prince, wedged into his gorge of snow like a pallid lemon slice. Shaken like an ice cube, his dentures chatter and clatter in that great martini glass in the sky. But who knows if that's really how he met his maker, since the body was never found?

Then Kiara lost me again, as I knew she would. I'm sure she, too, was shaken when the photo hit the checkout stands, and she realized I'd tracked her without the calculated hints she left for me throughout the rest of the year. I'd sniffed her out despite no phone bills left in her garbage, listing calls to her next destination. She knew I'd cropped out the only evidence that paired her with the wan prince.

Along with the digital shots I take for the pimps who sell my work to the highest bidder, I shoot film – high and low speed, 35 mm and 4×5, color and b/w, long and short exposures – for my experiments. I pondered Prince Icechip's frozen image under my Agfa Lupe. Why him? Anodyne, disinherited scion, won't be missed. No thorough inquiry. Lost himself *on the rocks*. A shrug, case closed. Still, a poor specimen. Kiara has slipped, skittering over the edge with an elbow called *time* at her back.

She resurfaced in LA for the gala, once again looking as if she'd bedded Father Time, nudging back his hands. So gentle, turning over this mythic, snoring bed partner without waking him, so that he doesn't know he's rolled back the clock in his sleep. Dark in her new tan, even her eyes seemed darker, the whites tinted, like her image had steeped too long in fixer bath. Stiletto-heeled starlets, starving over salads and suffering under the knife, clutch skinny soy lattes by her poolside, begging for her secret. She confesses with that impish, ever modest smile, that she's blessed by her genetics. A little relaxation, a little *amarosa*, and food of the soul, a recipe passed down from her ancestors – and here she pauses over her enchilada, smothered in mólé, the traditional dark sauce that Latina grandmothers take three days to make with a hundred secret ingredients – all work wonders for an overworked girl. She could say *goddess*. Say *star*. But she says *girl*, as if she were still a waitress in Cleveland who had need of a surname and a phone book listing.

She knows I'm there, watching through my telephoto, her shadow at noontime, underfoot but unseen.

But not today. She doesn't know I've finally tracked her to this filthy Mexican town. So this is where she goes when she ditches me every year.

I wait in the cemetery, City of the Dead. *La Ciudad de los Muertos*, I say out loud, killing the time, but I make a hash of it, as usual. I cannot master my own tongue, much less her adopted one. The words are clear in my head, but they tumble out of my mouth like scree down a talus of shale, all clatter and squawk.

My telephoto points across the small bay to her house, perched on a rock outcropping at the north end. Behind me, the graveyard's haphazard, angled headstones look as if they crept from the mounded earth, not as if human hands lodged them there. The jungle creeps nearly to the ocean here, and the strange trees that lurk around the graves creak and groan as the branches rub together. Strangler Figs, requiring sacrificial host trees of a different species to wrap themselves around. I had asked my hotel proprietress about the peculiar, tentacled trunks. The host tree eventually dies, mummified in the arms of the Strangler.

The Stranglers' dry leaves whisper in the sibilant wind. Crones chattering, clicking their tongues, tsk tsking. They scuff their gnarled toes, shy and tall ladies wallflowered behind me, waiting to be asked to dance. They skulk and scuttle. But when I turn to face them, they haven't moved. Their canopy blends together, like schoolgirls holding hands overhead, singing "Ring Around the Rosy". A massive Strangler towers over the others, most likely the mother of all the other trees, sending out vines that snake down doomed host trees; the aerial roots encircle the helpless tree and fuse together to become daughter Stranglers. I lean against a coarse, latticed trunk; my hand comes away sticky with a dark pus. Wasps cluster around the bitter fruit.

Hummingbirds levitate near low bushes, pollinating as they suck up oleander dew that would kill a man three thousand times their size, *click click clicking*, mocking me as I wait for her. Even before dawn like this, the hot pumice air grinds me down. A dry scraping hasps at my ankle, a skeletal caress. The roots form into fleshless hands, winding around my Achilles heel and up my shin.

I start awake, kicking. I must have dozed standing-up, leaning against a Strangler. A small branch snags my sleeve, and another scratches down my collar. A prehistoric-looking beast, the size of a newborn baby, crawls over my foot. It hisses at me, frantic pulse visible in its corded neck, then thrashes away through the underbrush. Just an iguana, mistaking me for a tree in my khakis and camo vest. I swipe at the prickles left by its thick hide and move to the tideline, washing him away with the sting of salt water.

It makes its ungainly way up the shore of Moth Bay, Bahia de Polilla. I follow it in my viewfinder until it disappears beneath the sudden onyx of her skirts close in my sights.

Covered up like a Biblical virgin, all Jackie O shades and glimmering veils and robes, she's still somehow ripe with curves and supple secrets under the shapeless drapery. She moves between me and the burial ground and rasps, "*Ácaro*," the first word she's said out loud to me since that fateful day backstage two decades ago. Her voice seems abraded by incinerated bones, as brittle as the papery husk of dead moth's wings. Nothing like her usual velvet butterfly voice. She mimes pulling a swollen acarid from her scalp and flicking it away. But she can't get rid of me so easily. Such careless removal leaves the tick partly embedded and contaminates the host. Ticks require gasoline and fire. Only hellish conflagration removes us.

I snap her: *click*. She grabs my camera. I don't resist her. We're never this close, and I smell her skin, though I've barely noticed the dank, whale breath smell of this Mexican town that the few off-season tourists gripe about. Fingers under their noses, they flee north, where the sand is infested with fleas, but they prefer bites to this unholy stench.

Sucking waves lick at our feet, leaving green-tinged foam on the hissing sand. Seaweed litters the dingy shore in gnat-plagued mounds. A crow-like bird caws on the sodden mass, a masticated-looking clump. Three turkey buzzards peck at a fish carcass – the fishermen here gut their dorado and *huachinango* immediately and dump the carrion on the sand. The buzzards pause to look up at her, then return to their grisly work. Their beaks *click click click* on dorsal bone.

The smell of her overpowers the ocean brine and decomposing sea plants, the fetid jungle and mulching cemetery. But instead of wanting to pinch my nose, I yearn to chew her odor like cud. Beneath the yeast of her lurks a spice that tingles on the tongue.

She pops open the catch and yanks out the film, then shoves it all back at me. Her fingers brush my hands. I'm never privileged to touch her. But I've seen the goose bumps that rise on her lovers' skin. Hers isn't the warm maggot touch I would expect in this tropical germ whorehouse, but is the icy touch of a princess asleep for centuries on her crystal pallet. My sense of her is always only of sight. So today, with smell and touch, I'm satiated, as with the sex I only have with her photo collage and my own hand, a découpage tryst.

"You shouldn't have followed me here." Her voice grates like a rusted lock.

I don't mind that she's destroyed my morning's work. It's not like I could sell these photos of her looking like a war widow, unrecognizable in her weeds. I stuff the exposed negs into the darkness of my bag, where I'll save them for my experiments later.

She whirls around and creeps back up the inlet, returning to her *casa* on the jagged bluff. The thatch-roofed, adobe manor lords it over the tiny, high peninsula of cragged black rock. She moves slowly, as if she aches. Her black form climbs the steps, past the terraced gardens, past the pool, past the large palapa with its umbrellas and lounge chairs (where her latest man-boy, whom she ignores, dozes).

I follow her with the telephoto, one eye shut to all around me, the other eye open only to her in the crosshairs. She looks like a scarab, an injured beetle that continues to limp along, making its crushed way toward its final destination despite being one of eight legs away from death. She crests the top step and passes behind the cratered walls surrounding the house. Rows of arches form the walls – like skeletal eye sockets stacked in catacombs. The skulled arches are too small for a man but let in the breeze. And mosquitoes. And celluloid, an almost impossible shot from daylight into darkness. Almost.

Dingy stucco, grimed with dust and time, slathers the strange walls. A domed and thatched roof rises behind it. Support beams at haphazard intervals thrust up through the dark straw and pierce the sky, hinting of heads speared on dungeon gates.

As she disappears, she doesn't even glance my way. I am shut out, like a lens cap blotting my sight of her. I imagine her standing in the mottled darkness of her temple that I was never meant to see. If I could manage a complete picture of her behind this bank of blank eyes, I imagine it would look much like the pieced-together collage of her on my bedroom wall. But instead of being assembled from chopped-up film squares, she would be dissected by these gaping ovals.

The malicious sun breaks behind me and washes her out.

Her boy stirs; she's called to him. He lifts his designer sunglasses.

Kiara's voice. How could a planet, a nation, a man, help but fall under its spell? She flirts with octaves as she toys with lovers like this palomino colt, foolish braying boy with his golden skin, sun-bleached hair, and nothing between his mule ears.

Sad to think that – unlike the Stradivarius, whose song remains ever beautiful through the centuries, deepening with time into mournful eloquence – the human voice must weaken and falter, soundtrack to the lines and sags that must eventually mar our skin. Unlike the strings of that fabled instrument, our vocal cords cannot be replaced. Not an ageless instrument composed of wood, but mortal, with sinews and synapses that rot and atrophy.

The boy, dressed in a skimpy Speedo that doesn't bother with his rump, stands up and crosses over to the pocked wall. Straight-spined, no shame or hard work to weigh him down, he left a trail of brags about his famous mistress, all too easy to follow. Who knows how old this preening donkey is? Twenty? Thirty? Hard to tell now that I've passed forty and then some, and she's not far behind me though she still looks just beyond jailbait. Youth all looks the same to me now, bland, like this new crop of bare-bellied hoochie girl singers who can't touch Kiara's talent or beauty; you can't tell them apart except for the Kool-Aid streaks in their hair that I want to yank. So easy for me to pollute their images with the shots I manufacture, their disgrace smeared across the checkout stands.

The boy, this spoiled pony, kneels in front of the cat-holed wall. Kiara's panicked, grown careless to allow his unbridled mouth. He reaches through an opening, his scapula flexing as his arm disappears up to his shoulder. The other hand reaches between his own legs. I know he paws under the folds of her shrouds as she stands on the other side. Thinking he fondles a creature who looks like the poster in his gym locker. She hasn't wholly given herself to him, yet. She makes them all wait, until they have little sense left when the time comes. Their last glimpse of her must paralyse them.

This little display is for me. *Not you*, she's saying to me. *Never you.*

I cap the telephoto; she sees my eye blink closed.

The boy's hand drops free. Even from here, I see his fingers rise to his nose, see the snap of his head, turning away, the hand snapping in the other direction away from his face.

Put it in your mouth, I say out loud, but he kneels beside the pool and splashes it in the water, then dries it on a towel, rubbing until it's well past dry.

Developing film has been almost impossible in this sun-drenched town. Dust, salt-laden air, and Cancer's Tropic light all leach through door seams and window cracks, infiltrating even inner rooms, like the ants and cockroaches. I can't darken even the back bedroom or bathroom, but I manage to stuff myself into a closet and feed the negs into the metal roller. I cap the lid on the canister and move my wrists, not rapid like a bartender's, but smooth like a dancer's, to agitate the developer evenly over the film. The solution is not one I purchase over a counter, but my own concocted recipe. It's taken a great deal of experimentation and patience to perfect the formula.

I've done this so often that I don't need a timer's beep to let me know when to rinse and fix. Trapped in darkness with the fumes, I don't need a red light to illuminate my task. The rattle of coat hangers at my back startles me, as if a cold hand taps me on the shoulder. I snap on the light, unsurprised by what I can already make out in the celluloid coils. Her image isn't there, of course, no residual ghost of her in her Bride of the Dead costume. Even the murky dawn light flashed her out, like a nuclear bomb would disintegrate a real person.

But the others are there. Auras of faces, mouths open, all of them, a hideous Munch canvas of tortured souls in each tiny square. I can see them even in miniature like this, though at first it was only in large blowups that I recognized the pixel-masses for what they were. Some of them I've come to recognize. Like old friends, they're there whenever I take such a picture. There: a jaundiced smudge that coalesces into an ignoble desperate for a tipple. Her new palomino pony will be here soon (but not soon enough for me), oh so surprised, faint at first behind the others, but staining deeper with time. The distorted shapes and splotches gel into discernible features. If I overlay an old shot of a lover's face (irrelevant mugs cropped out but saved, as I hoard everything she touches), I make a perfect match. Of course they've followed her here, too. They are always with her. Like me.

You might call me a stalker – obsessed, dangerous – except that it's my job to follow her. She is my life's blood, my income, my career.

Not psychotic. Symbiotic. She needs me as well. My lens raises her to mythic heights of beauty. She is my creation.

There are many of my kind, a dime a dozen making their bread and butter exposing the cellulite and transgressions of gods who should be perfect. The business of our pack is to smear the unbesmirched. To mar what is sacred.

But there is only one Kiara, posed on her holy pedestal. My eidolon. Only one of my kind can destroy her, burn her image, and turn her to ash in the public mind's eye. But she knows I never will. To smash my idol would be to destroy myself.

On my bedroom wall back home I had assembled her graven image. Craven, distorted collage: breast, hipbone, elbow, knuckle, snapshots in skewed angles captured through windows and doors. I staple gunned pieces of her to the plaster. It took me years to acquire the surreal whole, every inch of her, nude, life-size. Four walls: front, back, both her sides. I see her through a fly's eyes, compound images multiplied densely and divided into myriad squares – right side up, of course. I studied it as I fell asleep and awoke. Not my bedroom, but my laboratory, my own psyche pinned to the plaster.

In the hazy state of half-sleep, I started to see things.

Another face. Not hers.

Then: another.

My own jealousy, I thought, of the men who'd been inside her, while I'm perennially outside, always her surface: skin, curl of hair, lay of a dress. To touch her nostril or earlobe would be enough, but they've been inside the chalice of her. Don't say the vulgar word you're thinking, the clinical word. This she does not have. What she has is holy.

If I stood back and looked, as at a museum painting, they weren't there. Only as I looked away, or fell asleep, did I see them. Like the Rorschach images burned into the eyelids when you close your eyes after staring into the sun. Like the green flash as the sun sets on the horizon that you're never sure you've actually seen. Glaring magenta screams behind my Kiara.

I began to test new methods. Infrared lenses. Sun filters at dusk. Noontime ASA film at midnight. A flash at noon. Millisecond or

32-minute exposures. Pinpoint cameras and coated lenses. Dodging and push processing. Half-developing negatives. Reciprocity effects and reticulation. I've never tried completely exposing the film like this, leaving not a trace of her latent image. But the trapped lovers remain, unwilling ghosts nattering at her back. More clear than I've ever seen them.

Maybe it's this place and not the process. The graveyard sulked behind her.

Long ago, I gave her a photo of herself. A gift left outside her dressing room, shared with other nameless backup singers, a black and white she could use to promote herself, still plain Kara Grealy. I included a caption: *Kara's Chiaroscuro. Love, Click.* I heard her asking someone for a dictionary. I gave her the negative, too, one of the few no-nos in my line of work. I'd like that negative back, because I know what I'd see behind her: nothing. Just my Kiara. No stains.

Then she disappeared. *Poof.* I hit the bottle. She reemerged a year later as simply Kiara. So you see, I named her, too. Exotic creature, her own fabulous tapestry woven from the frayed threads of her mixed and murky lineage. Her name needed no further appellation. Like Jesus. Mary. Lucifer.

She was suddenly fluent in the language of the Mexican grandmother she now claimed – a woman she'd never met, a country she'd never visited, until summoned to her deathbed, or so goes her most famous ballad. I dried myself out, bought a Spanish translation dictionary, hired a tutor, worked diligently, but words don't roll easy on my tongue. Some I can manage. Photo: *foto.* Film: *membrana.* Naked: *en carne.* Same as meat: *carne,* my line of business. *Sin tu,* without you, a sin. But I stumble over words. Speech is not my method of communicating. I lip read better than I talk. I smell a false trail more easily than I can recite the Pledge of Allegiance.

Like the mólé of her adopted country, she took a hundred separate ingredients and used her secret, inherited recipe, boiling them down into one dish – her new identity. I backed it all up. I documented her made-up truths, turned her lies into reality. The fame that had eluded her until then exploded like a supernova.

Year by year, she's grown darker – though her skin is still smooth and unlined – easily explained by sun worship, though modern actresses have given up this pagan ritual in our cancer-riddled times. But I know that she draws her curtains to *el sol* and casts her devotion to the moon. Her skin can only be the pigment of her grandmother calling from the distant past.

I want to be part of the fabric. Not apart.

Not what I am, a bedbug on the linen, despised irritant.

Not what I am, always witness, never in the frame.

Not what I am, one of the mongrel pack who chase her, like the hundreds of stray dogs that crowd the pitted streets of Moth Bay. All descended from just a few lost pets long ago, the hotel proprietress, a transplanted gringo, told me. Like the townspeople themselves, all descended from just two ancestors: a Huichol priestess and the first Catholic priest to land on this shore, a man of the cloth who disrobed to lie with her. I see hints of Kiara when I look at the villagers. They won't talk to me, even when I stutter out an *hola* at the *mercado*. Secretive, as tight knit as the jungle trees. They say it was the women who saved the town from slaughter when the conquerors invaded. The white men simply disappeared, one by one.

The Moth Bay dogs ceaselessly hump each other, copulating though they're nothing but sacks of ribs and mange, as if they had no choice but to mate, a last ditch effort at immortality. A spastic, robotic rutting lacking in joy – like me and my hand and my photo collage. The proprietress warned me the townsfolk will set out poisoned meat tonight, as they do every year at this time, a ritual cleansing before the pilgrimage and influx of tourists. Tomorrow, before dawn, a noose of dead dogs will be tossed into the ocean. Tied tail to neck, in a distended necklace of bloated corpses, surreal killick that anchors this town to a medieval notion of purging its incestuous plague. The lariat of carrion will rock gently beneath the surface, so easy to tangle an ankle and be sucked down to doom. The water will turn filthy with jellyfish, feeding on the swollen bait. But no matter what the town does to eradicate the dogs, the proprietress says, they return and multiply, a virus. They reincarnate themselves, refusing to be exterminated.

Like them, we paparazzi exist on the margins, fighting each other over scraps of humanity. We're punched and kicked, flipped off, wished dead. The masses spit on us but buy the snaps we take, starving for more. We hound the perimeters, hated, but without us, the fiction falls apart.

The spool of film crackles in my hand. I stumble from the closet and bump into Malele, the maid's toddler. She follows me everywhere. Malele's dress is dirty, her upper lip encrusted with dried snot. Her mother trails me through the house, sweeping after me, making me uneasy. She leaves cleanliness in her wake, silent except for the *flap flap* of her rubber slippers and the *swish swish* of her broom.

Malele and I have been teaching each other the names of colors. We point to the deadly oleander: *pink*. To the sleeping grass that snaps its leaves shut when touched: *verde*. To the prickly *guanabana* fruit that looks like an angry blowfish: *green*. To the bumblebee drowned in the pool: *negro*. To the poisonous angel's trumpet flower: *amarillo*. We argue over the ocean's color: *Azul*, she says. No, not blue, gray. To my hair: *blanco*. It turned white overnight, when I saw the faces – not from horror, but with terror that we would grow further apart as I aged while Kiara remained unchanged. A gecko *click, click, clicks* at us: *brown*. Malcle stomps upon it with her bare foot. It scampers away, leaving its tail, and she runs after it. I pick up the gecko tail and carry it outside, flinging it on to the sand, where the rich insect life will make short work of it. The gecko will grow another tail, a nifty trick of rebirth.

A hammock stretches itself between two coconut trees. Erosion of the beach has exposed the skirted black roots of the trees, shameful like a widow's slip showing. A bulbous, black termite nest hangs in one, a malignant tumor. The termites' tunneled tracks scar the tree from the inside out, an old man's raised and scabbed veins, but the termites shy from light and won't cross the whitewashed trunks. I shed my many-pocketed vest and lie in the hammock. She'll know I'm no longer watching, the third eye closed. A skinny horse nearby strips a banana tree of its leaves, its grinding molars audible even over the constant, hammering waves. The harsh sun blotches the back of my eyelids. Inside the coconut trunk, the termites' busy drone lulls me into siesta.

Kiara approaches me on the beach, scarab skirts crackling around her. A mantilla, flowing from a tortoise shell comb, falls over her shoulders. She peels back her webbed veil, peels back the skin of her lovely face, revealing a travesty of decay. My Canon has captured the slivered hints of her deterioration just before her annual donning of full vestments. Her nose, earlobe, the corner of her lips: rotting like a leper.

She climbs into the hammock and tucks the gecko tail behind her ear, a flower that grows reptilian limbs. The ocean froths behind her, beating its fists against the pebbles and shells, which chatter and clatter with each grasping wave. Her long nails tap, a beetling *click click click*. Castanets of my soul. Scrape scratch tease the inside of my skin, palms and shins inflamed with her inside me. She crouches over me, her back to me, astride me, so graceful the hammock doesn't rock. I pry the comb from her scalp and run the mantis-limb prongs through her hair. She tips her head back, her black hair brushing my chest, scampering ants tickling. Her wet hair drips. Dark water stains my nipples, leaves tracks down my belly, pools in my navel. Her hair oozes, pungent unguent, an urgent seeping. Smell of damp mulch, a gold-bearing alluvial soil. Black secretion, amnion seething, leaching weeping coils in my fist, dripping ink tattooing my hide. Black dye. *No*, Malele points, shrieking. *Roja. Sangre* drips down my cheek. I poke out my tongue to lick, to taste the brine of her, but feel a tickling instead.

I thrash awake, nearly tossing myself from the hammock, and pluck a dying termite from my lips. Termites live only one day, long enough to mate and destroy. It's nearly sunset, and my fingers cramp around the cold black lens that I'm never without. A moth *click click clicks* against a porch light, hurling itself against the impostor moon.

Seaweed pops and sizzles, cooked by the sun and now cooling. While I've slept, I've lost my shade. My pasty skin is now red – outlined by the white shape of the camera on my chest – my body too used to scuttling in the night, covered by vests and baggy pants, layered with pockets and pouches – to hide things in, to hide myself behind, to secrete. I'm sure the hammock ropes indent my back like a chessboard.

I am a game board. Play me.

Kiara moves down the beach, real now, still in her nun's garb. Beside her, the flaxen pony frolics in white briefs (aptly named in his case). He ignores her, running to retrieve a child's ball and dancing in the waves. With them, an old woman. They creep toward the graveyard. The green strobe flashes as the sun sets.

I will not follow. I'm tired.

When I was young, I chased butterflies. Caught them in nets, spread and pinned them, displayed them in boxes. Good practice for what I do now – study, capture, still the moving subject, frame. Only to find they were all just moths, every last one of them common pests. Their identity mattered, though their outward beauty hadn't changed. Like a candid of a has-been or of a beautiful nobody – worthless. Now here I am, burned out in the cloying heat of Moth Bay. Poetic justice. Full circle. God has a sense of humor.

A rusted pickup jounces along the hard-crusted beach. Its tires pass over a dead gull fanned out in the sand, pressing feathers and bones beneath tread marks, leaving a trace of shocked shape. The creaking, squeaking truck crawls past, crunching the seaweed. *Camarones! Camarones!* An old man in the pickup bed squawks through a loud speaker that amplifies and strangles his words. Translucent and veined shrimp dangle from strings stretched across a high bed frame. They dance with the lurching truck, synchronized like sickly chorus girls lifting their skirts, spindly legs tapping together. Their exoskeletons brush each other, *click click click*. Dust and flies chase their ghostly, fetal bodies, but each heaving bounce keeps them from settling, skittish. The old man gives me the once over, leering recognition in his eyes. A look that all of the townspeople seem to give me.

Tough day for business. Besides the stench, no one can swim because of the dark tide, an influx of toxic seaweed. Like the riptides, no signs announce the danger, no newspaper articles, no lifeguards. But there is Kiara, a dark silhouette, unmistakable to me, cleaving the dark water, a kelpie drawing the unaware to their own doom. Lemmings, the early tourists will dive in if they see another swimmer, assuming their safety.

She seals her way back to her promontory. She thinks I'll pace her on the beach, like the iguana paralleling her on the sand, its flailing gait leaving thrashed tracks. But I sit tight.

She climbs out of the water up on to the rocks at her crown of land. Even at dusk I see that she's lost her nun's habit and is naked, her lithe body haloed in the crepuscular light. She emits her own corona. She disappears behind the apertured wall.

I heave myself out of my webbed cradle and turn the other way and walk South towards the City of the Dead. I leave my camera in the rope net.

I'm used to working at night, but the darkness here is complete; no refracting neon brightens the sky like a hippie god. *La luna*, gorged on light, hoists its full belly over the top of the towering Strangler Figs and washes the jungle in a pale glow. The arms of the enveloping Stranglers shroud the slivered ghosts of the host trees.

I touch the smooth bark of a host sapling no higher than myself but with much better posture. A gust rattles its bleached leaves, sending a shudder down its shimmering, golden trunk. Quite a lovely tree, really. Just behind it, a Strangler Fig reaches with murderous arms to hug its trembling limbs. Long roots have just begun to unfurl themselves from the canopy to coil around its outflung branches, grafting themselves around the slender trunk and knotting themselves together in a callused embrace.

I break off a branch of the palomino sapling with a vicious snap. Dark sap flows from the wound. I taste it, bitter, and feel a mercury shock in my veins, a paprika tingle on my lips, a rancid-meat nausea in my belly. The over-arching canopy stirs, setting off a dry whispering of leaves. A bird caterwauls.

"The sap dries up too soon," she says from behind me. I'm not surprised that she's there; I smelled her, her earlier scent of rotting mulch now gone beneath her usual complex myrrh. Her familiar velvet voice violins down my spine, with no trace of her earlier clawed tones. "They're not strong enough to survive." She points to an anemic stalk nearby that's caught in the maws of a giant Strangler Fig. Wooden bangles *click, click, click* on her smooth arm. Gone are her vestments. Dark nipples tinge her white halter top, as does the triangle of dark hair beneath her tiny, white shorts. She looks younger than the day I first saw her.

The thick Strangler hide wraps itself around the pallid host tree and soon will completely shroud the pus-colored torso and all of its blanched leaves, joining itself down the middle in a long scar. "This one can't take the heat. A transplant too used to the cold."

"Maybe he just needs a vodka martini." I emphasize the *he*. She smiles at me, not startled that I'm flitting near the truth. She wants me to know. She must. She wanted me to follow this time.

She places her hand reverently on the Strangler. "*Graçias, abuela,*" she murmurs. She strokes a knobby protuberance on the sallow trunk in the Strangler's grasp. The tree crackles, leaking out a meager black sap that she catches in a clay bowl. She licks her finger, and the clock of her face ticks backwards.

I would stand here forever, voluntarily, to feed her needs, to be inside her like that. No, I would kneel.

"I can give you what they can't," I say, too close to begging. I have what they lack: patience, endurance, persistence, desire. A knack for camouflage and standing still. And no other need but her.

"A daughter," she says. "But it requires a strong will. As the years pass, it takes more and more to sustain me. These have no stamina. To have a child, it would take an exceptionally hardy—"

I interrupt her, afraid she'll say *specimen*, not *man*. "There's truth in the power of a man who chooses his fate willingly for the one he loves." I don't use the word *sacrifice*, for I have nothing to lose.

"Yes."

She's known all along it would be me.

We are moral equals. Or should I say immoral equals. Stopping at nothing to freeze time. We belong together.

She points to a tombstone wedged into the rooted knees of the largest Strangler Fig. There's no sign of its original host tree, long since sealed completely within its massive trunk. "My great-grandmother," she says. "*Bisabuela*." She's looking at the tree, not at the grave.

She steps toward me. She takes another lick of the black sap from her bowl, and then she kisses me, tasting of acrid electricity. My knees almost buckle, but I hold myself up as she backs me toward the *bisabuela* tree. She slides her shorts down and presses against me, reaching for my fly.

Out of nowhere the iguana appears at my feet, its thick hide identical to the tree's bark, and it winds its way around my ankles; I can't distinguish between its tail and the roots.

"Grandmother looked just like me on the day she passed over and passed on the gift. Though some call it a curse. My own mother refused it. Fled to a new country. These souls, they're hollow, but heavy. I'm tired, too, Click." Her bracelets echo my name as her hand slides up and down, a friction, a fissure broken open.

I'm naked. Inside her. I can't tell where the tree behind me ends and Kiara, enveloping me, begins.

To be like this, always.

I picture the relief.

I stand in one place, for all eternity, welcomed into the bosom of her family, waiting for her to come to me for her sustenance, knowing someday I'll be wrapped in her arms forever. No longer scurrying after her, a rat sniffing her scraps. My boughs forever extend out to her in eternal welcome. My obvolute fingers caress her as she strokes me. She needs me as never before, to nourish her. Me, the key ingredient to her mólé – spectral treacle. She stands with her chattering sisters, the *azul* beach framed behind her. Tourists spy her under the protective canopy. *Look!* they cry. *Kiara!* Kiara, who had retired and gone underground in search of peace, quiet, family.

She graciously poses for them, still looking like a girl of twenty, standing against a tree, a babe cradled in her arms. The infant looks up at the swaying branches as at a cooing father. The tourists snap her picture.

Click.

There I am. At last.

I'm in the frame.

Like the others, my mouth will be open. Not in horror, but in joy.

In the Absence of Motion

Peter Baltensperger

Bernard fell in love with the statue the moment he saw her at the back of the park. He had just moved into a new neighborhood on the outskirts of the city and was just starting to explore the area around the apartment building. He was following a small stream running along the edge of a field when he came to a secluded park surrounded by old trees. Walking along the path leading into the park between the trees, he immediately noticed the statue at the back. Without a moment's hesitation, he walked across the grass until he stood right in front of her.

He had had several statues in the past, in different places where he lived, but this one was without doubt the most beautiful of them all. Sculpted from white, white stone, she stood on a low pedestal in front of a semi-circle of trees resembling guardians, wise old men. Endowed with a perfect body with just the right amount of lines and curves in all the right places, she was the epitome of femininity, an artistic treasure in an otherwise quite ordinary setting.

She had her arms lifted and her hands folded behind her head, her head titled slightly forward so that she was looking directly at him from her enigmatic stone eyes. He couldn't take his eyes off her, the finely chiseled features of her face, her perfectly shaped breasts, her molded waist, her slender legs. Her pubic area was a mere suggestion where her thighs came together, a virginal understatement that suited her perfectly. He couldn't believe his luck to have found such a beautiful statue in an obscure place like this, and quite by accident at that.

He loved statues of all kinds, but this one all the more so because of her unique bearing, the solemn guardians behind her, the calming stillness of her environment. Statues never moved, regardless of what he did. They simply stood there, looking at him without complaints, without telling him what to do, without expecting anything from him, faithful and trusting lovers every one of them.

Although still a virgin at twenty-six, he had heard and read and seen more than enough about women and their relationships with men to render him permanently suspicious and distrustful of them. Yet despite all his misgivings about the female sex and any kind of contact or relationship with them, he still dreamed of maybe someday meeting a woman whom he could trust like a statue, who would accept him without reservations for who he was the way the statues did, a woman he could love absolutely and would love him the same way in return.

So far, he hadn't been able to find anybody even remotely like that, and so he kept dreaming and indulging in his penchant for statues wherever and whenever he could. His new love was still standing on her pedestal, patiently waiting, her charisma devoid of any kind of urgency, her stony gaze unchanged. He rejoiced in her presence, utterly content just to stand before her and admire her.

Yet the more he lost himself in her beauty, the more he saw her as not just a lifeless statue and the more aroused he became. He glanced furtively around the park, but there was nobody else. Keeping his eyes fixed on hers, he pulled down the zipper of his pants, his hands trembling with anticipation, pulled his penis out into the evening air, and rubbed it into an erection for her to see. The look on her face told him that she approved, accepted him for himself.

Holding his erection in his hand, he walked up to her and stepped on the pedestal to stand in front of her. He put his arm around her slender waist, took her perfect breast in his hand, her hard nipple pressing against his palm, and rubbed himself to a thundering orgasm against her pubic mound. He gasped with pleasure, moaned against her smooth stone skin. He thought he could feel her shudder ever so slightly, could feel her eyes on him, could feel her stone-cold body warm in his embrace. He pressed himself against her until the rush of excitement began to abate, then detached himself from her and stepped off the pedestal.

Arranging his trousers and straightening his clothes, he found a bench from where he could observe her for a while longer while he caught his breath and managed to get his body to relax. She was his now. He no longer had to worry about her because she would always be there for him and he would always be able to go to her again. He decided to name her Esmeralda, his precious stone, to mark the momentous occasion.

Back in his apartment, his life-size, anatomically correct doll with the flexible limbs was waiting for him in her shocking pink negligée.

She was sitting on the couch in the living room where he kept her when he was at work during the day and when he had supper and watched TV in the evening. He had only acquired her a couple of years ago when he felt that his trysts with the statues weren't quite fulfilling him any more. For one thing, he couldn't always get to them, especially during the cold weather and when he was occupied with other things. It also started to bother him that as much as he enjoyed his relationships with the statues, he still always found himself alone in his apartment at the end of the day.

When he came across the doll in one of the specialty shops, he felt she was the perfect addition to his statues. She was in every way the same in that she never complained or demanded or criticized and was always there when he needed her. Only now he had a statue of his own he could keep in his apartment, share his evenings, dress her in whatever clothes he decided to buy for her, and take her to bed with him to keep him company during the night. He named her Lydia because he liked the name and he thought it suited her quite well.

The only problem was that her skin was a rosy flesh color and he had come to like the whiteness of the statues. In an effort to make her more statue-like, he scrubbed her repeatedly with bleach and in the end managed to lighten her skin considerably. She still wasn't statue-white, by any means, but it was enough for her to fit in.

Lydia knew about the statues, but she didn't mind at all because in the end he always came back to her and she was his main companion. Besides, she was much warmer than the outdoor statues. Her breasts were soft and pliable, and her pussy molded true to life and fully functioning to provide him with pleasures the statues simply couldn't supply. She didn't have any problems with the arrangements.

Bernard told her about Esmeralda as soon as he came home. He sat down on the couch beside her, put his arm around her shoulders and a hand on her warm breast and told her all about his excursion, his discovery, his encounter. Lydia didn't mind at all. She didn't say that she didn't mind, but the expression on her face seemed to indicate that she was quite all right with his new arrangement just as she had been with his previous liaisons, as long as he always came back to her and didn't neglect her too much. He definitely wasn't planning on doing that.

Having settled that to his satisfaction, he turned on the TV, took her into his arms, and watched a couple of shows with her until it was time to go to bed. He carried her into the bedroom, pulled off her negligée, and sat her on the bed so she could watch him get undressed. Then he climbed on the bed, pulled her down beside him, and put his arms around her. It was much more like having a woman with him than when he was with the statues, even though he would never have dreamed of giving them up. They were his first and greatest love, and would always be.

Yet, he had to admit, it was much more comfortable and more arousing being with Lydia. He could squeeze her breasts to his heart's content, he could bite her nipples if he felt so inclined, he could manipulate her body in any way he felt like, and she never complained or criticized anything he did. What he enjoyed most about her, and missed most in the statues, was that she had a perfectly molded pussy with a tuft of real hair he could caress with his fingers, and a tight, life-like vagina that perfectly accommodated his full erection.

Even though he was quite tired after his excursion, he played with her breasts for a while so as not to disappoint her. Then he climbed on top of her, penetrated her, and started to work himself up to another orgasm. It took him quite a while, but Lydia didn't mind at all. She just kept lying there on the bed with her legs spread and let him pump her for as long as he needed to. He finally did have another orgasm, much to his relief. He moaned and groaned for a while to let her know how much he enjoyed the act. Then he climbed off her again, took her back into his arms, and went to sleep.

He kept going back to Esmeralda whenever his schedule and the weather afforded him the luxury of a visit. At the same time, he made sure that he paid enough attention to Lydia and spent enough time with her as well. Visiting Esmeralda with her perfect body and her beautiful surroundings again stirred up, for some inscrutable reason he couldn't quite figure out, his fantasies about having a real woman for a companion. Despite his excellent relationship with his new statue, he kept wishing increasingly more often that he could have a woman in whom he could trust and with whom he could play real-life statue games.

And then, one nondescript chilly November evening when he couldn't go in the park, he decided to visit one of the neighborhood bars he had started to frequent to have a couple of drinks to warm himself and just to be among people for a while. He was sitting at a small table near the bar nursing a Bourbon when he glanced around the room and saw a woman sitting alone at a table not very far from his own. She wasn't exactly pretty, rather plain, in fact, and wore rather plain, loose clothes that didn't do much to improve her appearance. Her face was framed by light blond, almost white, curly hair, and she looked quite skinny and rather pale, emaciated, almost, it seemed to him. Yet there was something about her that attracted him to her in a strange, perplexing kind of way and he found himself glancing in her direction more and more frequently.

What probably struck him the most about her was that she never seemed to move. She was sitting at her table with her legs crossed, one arm in her lap and the other on the tabletop. Her hand was holding a piña colada, her watery blue eyes staring expressionlessly out into the crowd. Every now and then, she would lift the glass, take a sip of her drink, and put it down again. Other than that, he didn't see her move at all.

Bernard watched her for a while and considered his options, weighed his chances. He had never approached a woman before with what he obviously had in mind, and he wasn't sure if he could, and if he could handle the highly probable rejection. Yet the more he looked at her, the more he felt he should do something and the more he convinced himself that it would be all right.

The woman seemed to be getting near the bottom of her drink, so he finally picked up his glass, rose from his table, and walked over to her.

"Is it all right if I join you?" he asked, his voice shaking with uncertainty.

The woman slowly turned her head and ever so slowly looked up at him, scrutinizing him, appraising him. He shuddered, wondering what he had done.

"I suppose that would be all right," the woman said to his surprise and relief. She gestured to a chair across from her.

Bernard sat down and extended his hand. "I'm Bernard," he introduced himself.

"Valerie," the woman replied. She put a limp, pale hand into his and he held it for a moment before letting it go again.

"Would you like another drink?" he asked

"I think I could use another one," she said.

"Not feeling very well?" Bernard asked, thinking of her pale complexion, her emaciated look.

"I'm fine," Valerie replied. "I could just use another drink, that's all. I was going to order another one myself if you hadn't come along."

They finished their respective drinks, called the waitress to bring them two more, and settled back in their chairs. Valerie wasn't the most talkative woman and he had to carry most of the conversation, but she listened attentively to everything he said and responded appropriately albeit briefly to his remarks. The second drinks loosened them up a bit and he was gradually warming up to her.

The feeling that there was something different and special about her and that he was oddly attracted to her was getting progressively stronger, perhaps from the drink, although he didn't think so. The longer he sat across from her and the longer they talked, the more he knew that he wanted to know her better, that there were possibilities, promises. He noticed that she hadn't moved again since their mutual introduction, except that she was now looking at him instead of staring at the crowd.

Valerie finished her drink and put her glass down on the table. "Time to go," she said. "It's getting late."

Bernard screwed up his courage and asked her if he could take her home.

"That's what I meant," Valerie replied, her face expressionless, her watery blue eyes focused on his.

Bernard felt a surge of relief. Everything was progressing without any problems, although he still wasn't quite sure what this woman was all about. But then, he had only had contact with statues and a doll all those years and simply didn't know what to expect or what to do.

He did know enough to pay for the drinks, hold out his hand when she started to get up from her chair, and help her with her jacket. Then he guided her through the crowd and out of the bar with his hand on her elbow.

"I just live a short distance from here," Valerie announced when they stepped out into the chilly November night. "We can walk."

Bernard tentatively put his arm around her waist. Valerie didn't protest, but snuggled up to him instead. He was delighted. It only took a few minutes to get to her apartment, as she had said. She unlocked the door and motioned him inside, then led the way straight to her bedroom at the back.

She turned on the lamps on the night tables, took off her jacket, and stood by the bed, looking expectantly at him.

"Could I ask you something?" Bernard asked, his voice trembling again with insecurity. He really had to get a hold of himself, he thought, but Valerie didn't seem to notice, or just didn't mind.

"You can always ask," she said, her eyes still looking at him without even a touch of emotion.

"I wanted to ask," he began, cleared his throat, started again. "I wanted to ask if you wouldn't mind keeping perfectly still."

"No problem," Valerie replied, to his relief. "I don't particularly like having to do anything."

"Really?" he asked, surprised by her answer.

"Really," she said. He noticed that she hadn't moved an inch from her spot by the bed, not even her head.

Bernard was feeling better and better about everything. He reached out and started to undo her blouse and she never moved at all, not even when he pulled the blouse down over her shoulders. So far, so good. He stepped behind her and undid the clasps of her bra, pulled it down over her arms, and reached around her to take her breasts into his hands. They weren't very big, but they definitely felt very nice. It was the first time he had ever touched a woman's breasts, and the sensation sent shivers of pleasure and delight through his body.

Valerie never made a single sound, just stood there motionlessly the way he had asked her to. He proceeded to undo her skirt and pull it down over her legs. She didn't even lift her feet to step out of it. He knelt down on the floor, lifted one foot after the other, and pulled her skirt from underneath. Then he took hold of her panties and pulled them down the way he had done with her skirt, lifting her feet again to pull the panties from underneath them as well.

She stood quietly before him, the first naked woman in his life, her pale skin looking almost white in the light of the bedside lamps. He looked at her for a while the way he looked at the statues, reveling in her pure femininity, admiring her shape and her curves, her quaint breasts, her barely concealed pussy between her slightly parted legs.

Then he quickly undressed himself, took Valerie by the shoulders, and lowered her on to the bed. He rolled her towards the middle to make room for himself beside her.

Spending quite a long time playing with her breasts, he delighted in the unique experience of touching real-life, soft, pliable breasts with his virgin hands. Valerie kept lying on the bed without moving once, without saying a word, without any suggestions or complaints.

Bernard was in heaven. In all his fantasies, he had never pictured anything like this with a real woman. This was so much better than what he was able to do with his doll, and infinitely better than his encounters with the statues. This was real: real, warm, living flesh, trembling ever so slightly under his hands, responding to his touch, making him feel fuzzy and exceedingly pleased.

He let go of one of the breasts and moved his freed hand down Valerie's body until he reached her pussy with the light blond fluff. For the first time, he felt a woman's genitals, felt the warmth and the freely flowing juices, felt the puffiness of the lips, the protruding clit. It was an incredible experience, especially since he didn't have to worry at all about any of the things he had always fussed about.

Valerie was a perfect statue, a perfect doll. She lay absolutely still, never made a sound or said a word, and just let him do whatever he wanted to do. Emboldened, he knelt beside her and spread her legs apart, then climbed on top of her and buried his by now throbbing and pulsatingly eager penis in the unbelievably wonderful, warm, soft, pliable cave.

He half expected Valerie to react in some way, but she didn't, to his great delight. She still didn't move or do anything when he started to move in and out of her, took hold of her breasts with both hands, and pumped himself to a glorious, earth-shattering, way beyond wonderful, exhilarating and fantastic orgasm inside a real life, receptive, lubricated vagina.

He stayed on top of her motionless body, gasping and moaning with pleasure and unconcealed delight until he was able to catch his breath, and then rolled off her again. She still hadn't moved at all. He wondered what the experience had been like for her since she hadn't given him any indication at all.

"Did you have an orgasm, too?" he asked, wanting to make sure the whole encounter hadn't just been for his benefit as it was with the statues and the doll.

"Of course, I did," Valerie replied matter-of-factly. "I always do."

"I'm glad," Bernard said. "I was worried that maybe you didn't."

"You don't have to worry about me," Valerie said. "I know how to look after myself. Was what I was doing all right for you?"

"More than all right," Bernard enthused. "It was absolutely perfect. You were absolutely perfect."

"Good," Valerie said. "I was sure that's what you wanted."

They lay quietly side by side for a while, enjoying the soothing afterglow of their union, lost in their own thoughts.

"Do you think we could do this again?" Bernard finally broke the silence.

"Of course, we will," Valerie said without hesitation. "Next time, your turn!"

On My Knees in Barcelona

Kristina Lloyd

This happened before the Olympics, a summer when the nights were so hot the city couldn't sleep and everyone grew angry and crazy. Zero tolerance was just a rumor, so whores, thieves and smackheads skulked in narrow streets and everyone avoided the docks. I only went to Bar Anise in the hope they'd give me some ice. Had I known what kind of bar it was, I might have stayed away.

It was nearly 2:00 a.m. and I was standing on my dinky balcony, feeling pretty zonked. The fuse had gone in my fan and the air in my apartment felt thick enough to slice. In the street below, a globe lamp hung like a moon on a bracket, adding a sheen of pearl to the facade of Bar Anise. I held a damp cloth to the back of my neck, arms resting on metal too hot to touch during the day. Earlier, the cloth had contained fast-melting ice and my mind returned to the cold rivulets trickling over my shoulders, collarbone and breasts. Like a tongue, I'd thought, the tongue of a lover making whoopee with my skin. How long had it been now? Oh, too many months to count.

Six floors below, footsteps echoed in the dark street. I watched a guy in a white T-shirt stride along with a sense of purpose unsuited to the hour. When he suddenly looked up I was unnerved, feeling a rupture of that odd balance where my balcony is at once part of the street and part of my home. It was as if he'd barged in on my privacy.

I turned away, embarrassed to have been caught watching, then glanced back to see him enter Bar Anise. A relic from another age, the bar's exterior glowed with low-watt tones of honey and oak, its door closed, its windows pasted with faded posters, that globe lamp fuzzed with a halo of white light. As the guy pushed the door, I half expected the structure to wobble like a stage set.

How come I'd never been in before? Generally speaking, I socialized in Barcelona's hipper bars along Las Ramblas, in Plaça Reial or Barri Gòtic, and I only ventured into local bars to buy late-night beers or water. They were down-at-heel joints with Formica tabletops, fruit machines and a TV tuned permanently to the lotto draw. I fancied Bar Anise was different but I'd never set foot inside. Oh, sure, I was curious but the place seemed to exist in a world of its own. It may as well have had NO ENTRY on its door.

At 2:00 a.m., however, it was the only bar open.

I wiped the damp cloth over my face, reminding myself I was lucky to be single and sleeping alone. Along my street, shabby ironwork balconies were cluttered with blushing geraniums, cramped little washing lines, green roller blinds and even a bird in a cage three buildings to my right. In these Spanish homes, behind the old lace at the windows, the occupants probably slept two to a bed, sticky bodies wrestling with hot, tangled sheets. Yes, in this heat, I was lucky to be single. Some ice to see me through the night would be welcome though. Unfortunately, my ice compartment was empty so I had to ask myself: how badly did I want it?

My sandals were noisy in the deserted street, ringing off walls and metal shutters. I hesitated before the door of Bar Anise, disconcerted by the sense of stillness beyond. A sign in Catalan proclaimed the bar open but was it really? And if so, was it open to the likes of me? In those months, I was working as a subeditor on a weekly expat newspaper called *Gander*. Prior to that, I'd spent three years teaching English in Seville until I'd tired of both the work and a boyfriend who'd kept the fingernails long on his right hand so he could simultaneously learn Spanish guitar and repulse me. Sometimes, I felt at home in that foreign land but when I stood on the threshold of Bar Anise, I felt I'd just arrived from Mars.

I considered quitting, then recalled those tongues of molten ice trailing across my skin. Taking a deep breath, I entered. Cigarette smoke hung in the yellowing light and a ceiling fan turned sluggishly as if enervated by the heat. Half a dozen men sat alone at separate tables, smoking, reading or staring into space. No one paid me any notice and I was grateful. I took it to be one of those places where everyone is a stranger, even people who've been drinking side by side for years.

When I approached the counter with my empty jug, a customer seated there cast me a look of lazy appraisal. He wore a white T-shirt and I took him to be the guy I'd seen from my balcony. Big nosed with dark hair feathering across his forehead, his wrinkles added interest to a strong, angular face. But irrespective of rugged charm, middle-aged men who believe they're entitled to leer unsettle my confidence. I was self-conscious in asking for ice and when my request was met with a frown, I stumbled in repeating myself. The bartender wiped the counter with a cloth, apparently loath to serve me. Behind him, among shelves gleaming with bottles and glasses, a mirrored Coca-Cola clock said quarter past two. The clock's red logo gave me that old jolt of jarring familiarity, making me feel I was on territory at once homely and strange.

"I have money," I said.

With that, the bartender disappeared into an adjoining room, a curtain of plastic strips clattering lightly as he passed. I waited, wondering if the drinkers could see the ice tonguing my skin; if they could see me at night, water coursing over my flesh; if they could see how I tried to kill the heat of my longing, failing as the ice melted away and I climaxed once again.

I felt they could and it troubled me. On the counter, a wedge of tortilla sat forlornly under a plastic dome. I could hear the bartender on the phone in the adjoining room. All this for some ice? When he returned with my jug blissfully full, I asked how much I owed him. Before he could reply, Big Nose interrupted, addressing the bartender in Catalan, a language I wasn't yet familiar with. The bartender poured a large brandy, then set it in front of me.

"Gratis," he said.

Unwilling to risk offence, I accepted the drink while trying to convince myself it left me under no obligation. So bloody English of me. Why couldn't I decline the brandy, pay for the ice conventionally and leave?

"*Graçias*," I said, turning to the customer, but I didn't smile.

He nodded, lips tilting in wry amusement. The brandy was rough, its heat scorching my throat and blazing inside my chest. The nape of my neck was wet with sweat, my hair damp. I was concerned about the ice melting in my jug and wished I could sip the ice water. The ceiling fan clicked faintly. Nobody spoke and I was relieved. It could simply be this guy was silently extending the hand of friendship. If so, I would silently shake it then shoot off home. The brandy was difficult to drink though, fire when I wanted ice.

"*Ay, qué calor*," said my new friend at length.

"*Si, qué calor*," I replied.

Hot weather. I sipped my brandy. I could feel him watching and his passive interest bugged me. After a couple more minutes, wanting to escape his gaze, I asked for the *lavabos* and was directed down a flight of rickety stairs. I descended toward a basement with scruffy, dark crimson walls, toilets at the far end and a swinging door with a small, dirty window lined with wire mesh. Halfway down the stairs, movement below caught my eye. I paused, looking over my shoulder at the corridor behind me. Beyond an open door was a guy on a chair and a woman on her knees, her head bobbing in his lap. I clutched the banister, immobilized by fear and a sudden, pornographic lust.

My cunt swelled and swelled, blood throbbing there. Oh, Christ, what a picture. The guy's mouth was slack, his head tipped back, as the woman, her chestnut curls fanning over his thighs, dipped up and down, up and down. Had they heard me? Hell, I hoped not. I needed to watch. Until that moment, I hadn't known how much I wanted cock; hadn't known how much I'd missed it since dumping the guitarist; hadn't known that stab of raging desire. Because while I could fuck myself with cock-shaped objects (cool as a cucumber), nothing could ever come close to the overwhelming sensations of a deep, dark, blinding mouthful. I stared, hardly daring to breathe.

The guy was young and lean, a tumble of ink black curls giving him an air of flamenco passion. Transfixed, I watched him grow fiercer, pulling the woman on to him, his fingers snarled in her hair as his pelvis rocked either to meet or defeat her. In her kneeling position, the woman kicked at the floor, squealing in muffled protest, her hands flapping. My yearning for cock was knocked for six by a second wave, a shocking urge to be claimed and used in a myriad of filthy ways.

My cunt flared to a cushiony mass of need, so sensitive I fancied I could feel the warp and weft of cotton in my underwear. I wanted to be where she was, at the mercy of a wild stranger who regarded me as nothing but an object for his pleasure, insignificant and disposable. I wanted to be all body and no mind, a thing made of cunt, mouth and ass, wide open and ready to receive.

Face aflame, I turned, intending to hurry back to the bar. I would put it from my thoughts, pretend nothing had happened, pretend I hadn't seen either the couple or the grubby depths of my desire. Was this because I hadn't had sex for so long? Was I craving the basest sort of action as compensation for those months of lack? Feeling shaky, I clasped the banister, mouth dry as a bone.

My stomach somersaulted. To my horror, at the head of the stairs stood the big-nosed guy from the bar. He grinned, descending in slow, swaggering steps. Panicking, I glanced down to the room. The guy in the chair was looking right at me, smirking as he slammed the woman's head between his thighs. My knees turned wobbly while blood pumped in my ears, roaring like seashells and high fever.

Big Nose was at my side, his forehead gleaming with a film of sweat. He tipped his eyebrows at me. "*Cuatro miles pesetas,*" he said.

Outrage spiked my fear. Four thousand pesetas! He thought I was a whore, thought I would blow him for a nasty brandy and a handful of notes!

"*Déjame paso!*" I snapped, attempting to sidestep him. He mirrored me, blocking my path. I grew more afraid then, trapped between these two randy *cucarachas*, and yet my groin was pulsing as hard as my heart.

"*Cuatro miles,*" he repeated, nodding toward the basement room. Then in Spanish he added, "Take it, go on. It is a good price. You know you want it."

And I understood at once that I was to pay; that I was the punter not the whore. I didn't know whether to be more or less insulted. I stared at him, incredulous. He actually thought I was so desperate for cock I would pay to suck off a stranger in a sleazy, backstreet bar!

"Move," I said, no longer bothering to speak his language. Despite being on a lower step, I tried shouldering him out of the way but with swift skill, he jostled me backward. I cried out to realize I was now sandwiched between him and the wall, his chest pressing against my breasts, my arms trapped in his hands. For several seconds we stood there, our breaths shallow and tense.

"*No me molestes,*" I said, a Berlitz phrase I'd never had to use before.

The guy laughed and with good reason. My demand sounded so pitifully insincere I may as well have said, "Molest me." He crooked a finger, resting it in the hollow of my throat, and I turned aside, looking past him to the room below. The woman was watching us. She wiped the back of her hand across her mouth and laughed, white teeth flashing. I was relieved to see she wasn't in trouble but, more than that, I was relieved to see I wasn't the only woman keen on skirting so close to danger.

I turned to face Big Nose with renewed bravery but he trailed his bent finger up my neck. My skin tingled to his touch, tiny shivers of pleasure rippling through my body's heat. I tried defying him, tried steeling myself against his advances, but I caught the sadistic brightness in his bitter chocolate eyes and I melted a little more. I pressed my head back to the wall.

"*No me molestes,*" I repeated, my voice soft and tremulous.

He laughed quietly, his breath tickling my face. I wanted him to touch me in horrible ways, to stick his hand between my thighs or paw my breasts. But he didn't. He just reiterated his price. When I didn't reply, he ground his crotch against me, rubbing his hard-on above the swell of my pubis. The pressure of him there distilled to my cunt, making my lips part and pout.

"*Qué barato!*" he said. A good price.

The basement was hot as hell. Sweat prickled on my back, cotton clinging damply. He knew he was turning me on and every rock of his body was sweet torture, twisting me with what I didn't want to want.

In Spanish, I said, "I just came for ice. I need to go home now. Release me, please."

"You will not sleep," he replied. "It's too hot."

"I have ice."

"You don't want ice," he said. "You want cock."

I felt the color rise in my face. He placed his hands either side of my head, caging me loosely in his arms, his biceps forming swarthy little hillocks on the edges of my vision. A waft of sweat, earthy and masculine, surged into my senses and I wanted to bury my nose in his armpits and inhale him.

"There's cock here," he continued. "Take it, *guapa*. We are not expensive. Take what you want then go home."

His eyes were such a deep brown I could barely distinguish pupil from iris.

"I don't have much money on me," I said.

He chuckled and I flushed deeper to realize I'd betrayed myself.

"Then go get some money," he said. "There's a cash machine—"

"No," I murmured.

"Yes, stop resisting yourself. Do you agree it is a fair price?"

"I don't know," I whispered, and I genuinely didn't. It seemed an amount I'd pay without too many qualms. But fair, good? There was no market value for this; it flew in the face of the usual sexism dictating the flow of supply and demand: women give, men get. Without a scarcity of clean men with hard cocks, why would I pay? And what in the world would prompt a cock-drought? Guys were always up for it. But here and now in the early hours in Bar Anise, they'd changed the world, creating both a need and a scarcity. Demand outstripped supply. A fair price? The thud in my pussy insisted it was a bargain.

I swallowed. "I have money in my *piso*," I said, deeply ashamed. "I live across the street."

He stepped back. "*Vete!*" he said, gesturing up the stairs.

I wasted no time, striding through the bar, head held high. At that point, I was unsure if I would return. I thought I might come to my senses but the night was sultry and weighted with the city, its heat wrapping me in strange enchantments where Bar Anise's subterranean secrets seduced me away from the prosaic. The man's voice echoed in my mind: Stop resisting yourself.

Gone was the Barcelona I knew where the metro whisked me to work, sunshine poured on mosaic lizards, plane trees shimmered and cathedral spires and scaffolding stabbed a flat blue sky. Instead, lust conspired with magic and menace to lead me as if in a dream to collect money from my apartment and scurry back to the bar.

Stop resisting yourself.

I downed the brandy still awaiting me on the counter and crept downstairs, my sordid hunger flaring at the wine-dark walls and scents of sweat and semen lingering in the shadows. All I'm doing, I told myself, is buying sex much as men have done for centuries. Nonetheless, I felt myself less an empowered consumer and more a desperate, greedy slut, a woman shameless enough to slake her desire in this masculine habitat of beer, cigarettes and sullen, perceptible misogyny. But I liked that these guys probably didn't much care for me except as an object to fuck. The feeling was mutual.

No one was about in the basement so, nervously, I entered the room I'd seen earlier, an underused storeroom with drums of olive oil lined against a wall, boxes under a large wooden table and four towers of orange chairs stacked in a corner. Big Nose was sitting spread-legged on a reversed chair, arms folded on its back. Behind him on the table sat his flamenco-looking friend, one leg swinging back and forth. My heart was going nineteen to the dozen.

"Who takes the money?" I asked.

Big Nose held out a hand. Feigning confidence, I gave him the notes. Stretching, he passed them to Flamenco who bundled them into his jeans pocket as if he were the pimp. There was a brief exchange in Catalan and I understood only that it was about money and that Big Nose was called Jordi.

"*Graçias,*" said Flamenco, relaxing his posture to suggest his work was done.

Jordi stood and spun the chair to face me. Still standing, he said, "On your knees."

I glanced at Flamenco who was making no moves to leave. "It's not a floor show," I said.

Jordi grabbed my face with a broad hand, forcing me to meet his gaze. He squeezed my cheeks. "On your fucking knees."

His nastiness sent shards of arousal to my groin. I felt bullied and debased, even more so because of our audience, and it was everything I wanted but would never have dared ask for. I fell to my knees, the scuffed hardwood floor briefly cooling my skin. Ahead of me, the fly of Jordi's jeans undulated over his boner, the faded denim at his crotch reminding me how much of a stranger he was, the rhythms of a life unknown imprinted on fabric concealing the cock I was about to blow. With a clink of metal, he unbuckled and unzipped, rummaging to release his erection.

My heart gave a kick of joy at the sight of his hard-on raging up from the wiry thicket of his pubes. I'd forgotten how obscenely aggressive hard cocks are and his was a brutish beauty, the color suffusing the head with such intensity I fancied it might seep through his skin to stain the air with a blood violet hue. He gripped himself, fingers thick around his girth, the sea blue vein on his underside peeping as he gently jerked.

"It's a good price, no?" he said.

Doing my best to forget about Flamenco, I opened my mouth to take Jordi but he stilled me with a hand on my forehead. "It's a good price," he repeated sternly.

His balls were tucked up tight and they lifted as he worked his shaft.

"*Si, sí, claro,*" I replied.

He clasped my head and drew me sharply on to his cock. The sudden fullness of my mouth made me splutter and he held me there, forcing me to inhale his humidity and that smell I'd forgotten, the smell of men, a smell reminiscent of depths and of things discarded, of dark oceans, forest floors, dereliction, old tires and knives left out in the sun.

"*Así me gusta, nena,*" he said approvingly as I withdrew to his tip.

He held my head, adding a slight pressure as I began slurping back and forth, making it seem as if he were the one leading. Perhaps he was. That seemed at odds with me being the paying customer but I enjoyed him taking the upper hand, so perhaps the incongruity was superficial.

"*Qué bonita,*" said Flamenco. How pretty.

Those watching eyes inflamed a shame that fueled my lust. I swallowed Jordi as deep as I could, my appetite provoking him to greater force. He began fucking my face, driving into my instinctive resistance, making me whimper and cough as my saliva spilled and my eyes watered. I felt sluttish and used, at the mercy of these callous brutes, and it was bliss. My swollen cunt was so fat and rich it barely seemed to have room between my thighs.

"Hey, Àngel," said Jordi, addressing his friend. "Why don't you give her a free fuck? You would like this, *nena*? *Es gratis!*"

He withdrew from my mouth to let me speak.

"*Sí, sí, fóllame!*" I croaked, gazing up at Jordi through a veil of tears. He sat heavily in the chair, lowering my head to his height. I dropped on to all fours, engulfing his length again while hoping the free fuck would be as hot and rough as the free brandy.

I heard Àngel cross the room. Àngel. What a perfect, preternatural name for this other-worldly scenario. Taking position behind me, Àngel flipped up my skirt and yanked down my underwear. I groaned around Jordi's cock and his answering groan echoed in my ears. I heard Àngel unzip and I shuffled my knees wider, groaning again when he teased me by slotting his cock to the length of my folds. He sawed to and fro, the upward strain of his erection pressing into my wetness and making me ache for penetration.

Àngel spoke to Jordi in Catalan, tight hard words muttered under his breath. Jordi replied, throaty and urgent. With a sound like an expletive, Àngel slammed into me, hissing as he lodged himself high. He was meaty and solid and he clasped my hips, gripping hard as he began driving into my hole. Every thrust jolted my body, jerking me forward on to Jordi's lap. I felt skewered all the way through, my mouth and cunt both stuffed to capacity. The two men worked together, fucking, pushing, grunting and groaning. Occasionally they exchanged words I didn't understand and once or twice there was amusement and faint laughter.

They had me. They well and truly had me. And when Àngel reached for my clit, I knew I was lost. My climax raced closer and I bleated with nearness. Àngel hissed in Catalan. Jordi growled.

"*Sigue, sigue*," he said. He grabbed fistfuls of my hair, his cock swelling to its absolute limit in my mouth. I was a rag doll between the two men, so close to coming my limbs seemed to have lost their bones. With a hoarse cry, Jordi came, flooding my mouth with his bitter silk, and the sound of his release tipped me over the edge. I came hard, disoriented and dizzy as pleasure clutched and stars exploded in my mind.

Moments later, my body began to drop with exhaustion but there was no letup from Àngel. He kept fucking me like there was no tomorrow and my pulpy walls, swollen with sensitivity, clung to his thrusts. I held Jordi in my mouth, gasping on his dwindling erection until Àngel's hammering became so frenzied I fancied he wanted to destroy me. He peaked with a long, low groan, wedging himself deep, and I moaned around Jordi's cock, wishing I could melt clean away.

The three of us held still until Jordi stroked my hair, a tender gesture that took me by surprise. Àngel caressed my buttocks. For a minute or two, we rested in silence and, in those moments, I felt we shared a tacit understanding and mutual respect. We had all got what we wanted and were grateful.

But I didn't want to stay. I had nothing to say to them, nor them to me. Conversation would have made us awkward and I wanted to leave it there, pure and perfect, a moment out of time devoted entirely to pleasure. Àngel slipped away and I tidied myself up. Jordi asked how I was. I told him I was fine just as Àngel returned with my jug, full to the brim with ice. There was no one in the bar when I left and all the lights were off. Jordi unlocked the door so I could leave.

"*Graçias,*" I said.

"*De nada,*" he replied with a smile. "*Y graçias.*"

Back in my apartment, I tipped half the ice into a freezer bag, stashed it in my ice compartment, and took the remaining ice to bed. I thought I would do my usual routine of rubbing cubes over my skin to cool me into sleep but I must have crashed out at once. In the morning, my jug contained only water and my mind was a fog of lust and filth. Where had I been? What had I done? Did that actually happen?

I slipped on a T-shirt, rolled up my shutter and stepped out on to my balcony. It was early morning but already the heat pulsed like the midday sun. I rubbed my eyes. Below, the street was coming to life, the baker's window lined with breads and pastries, people heading to work, a woman on a Vespa turning left. I could see a couple of bars were open but not Bar Anise. It looked as if it hadn't been open for years, its facade concealed by chipboard, graffiti and tatty fly posters. Of course. Hadn't it always been derelict, just another dump waiting to be spruced up before the Olympics?

Drowsily, I padded to the kitchen. Had it been a dream then, just a crazy dream brought on by the heat? I withdrew the bag of ice from my fridge and went back to bed. I had another hour before work. I broke the ice into the jug, scooped up a handful and cupped it to my skin. Just a dream, I told myself, and I lay back on the pillows, wondering if the heat would transport me to Bar Anise on nights to come.

I smeared the ice over my skin, savoring the trickle of water melting on to my stomach. I murmured softly, imagining the touch was the lick of a lover. Just a dream. Words floated to me as if from a great distance. Stop resisting yourself. And I slid an ice cube up my neck then sucked it into my mouth, closing my eyes as I twirled my tongue around the cube, ice when I wanted fire.

Chemistry

Velvet Moore

The smell of science makes me horny.

I narrowly resisted shoving my hands down my pants and rubbing myself to oblivion during my niece's science fair. My stomach dips with pleasure every time someone lights a match. Each July I'm aroused by the vapors of the noise-making, novelty fireworks called "snappers". Little do tricksters know that when they crack one on the pavement at my feet, I shiver out of excitement, not fear.

Smell is the sense tied most closely to human memory. So when I sense any use of potassium chlorate, a white, crystalline compound well-stocked in science laboratories and often used for combustion, I remember how it felt to have the fire of orgasm sizzle its way through my body and melt a liquid path down my legs. The chemical's odor singes my nostrils and flashes me back to the feel of a chilly, marble countertop pressed against my back, to the press of fingers digging into my supple thighs, to the slick pressure of rounded glass slipping in and out.

And it's what I remember most about him.

Most scientists that I've met fit the typical stereotypes. Most would rather analyse your genes than pry off your jeans. Yet I suspected that Michael Harrison was capable of much more than shedding me of my pants. With wavy black hair, broad shoulders and Clark Kent glasses, I believed that stripped of his unassuming attire, he would have something surprising and heroically powerful bulging underneath.

I understood this the first time I shook his hand and caught the scent of chemicals trapped in his clothes and seared into his skin, a smell faint and tangy and far too interesting to be cologne. Like the smell of your body after a lengthy swim in a freshly chlorinated pool. I imagined that if I should run my tongue along his perky nipples, my tongue would sizzle as though touched to the tip of a battery.

We needed a scientist to impress the hospital donors with a tour of the lab. I planned to find an excuse to use him.

I spent the following week visiting the lab to get a sense of his work. His area of interest was biochemistry and I was certainly interested in his chemistry. I came to notice how his hands flexed tightly, fighting against the latex gloves each time he cupped a beaker full of liquid. I watched as he gradually pushed the tip of the lengthy pipette into the stickiness of the gel and ejected its contents. I'd secretly graze my hand across my chest as he pinched and lifted the bell jar by its perky, nipple-like top and used the glassware to create a vacuum.

He stood beside me as an orator while his lab staff performed an experiment in front of eager donors. "Molten potassium chlorate is a strong oxidizing agent that reacts violently with sugar," he explained.

A lab student added a plump, red Gummi Bear to the white liquid bubbling in a test tube over an open flame. In an instant, the candy ignited, sparking and steaming with the power of an electrical fire and screaming like a train whistle. The sudden pop of energy startled me and I jumped in reaction as though I had been smacked sharply across the ass with a ruler.

Instantly, his hand splayed across my lower back to calm me, a touch that managed to still my nerves and wet my panties. Quicker than the smoke from the candied combustion, he cleared himself from me and attended diligently to the prospective donors. He ought to have looked like a pauper among princes, he in a rumpled white lab coat and tattered tennis shoes, specked among designer suits and patent leather pumps. Yet they clung to his every word, enraptured by the mystifying language of science. As he led the group further into the lab I heard him begin to boast about the facility's latest microarray technology. Good boy, I thought. He had obeyed my coaching and was hitting all of the major speaking points.

After the event, I congratulated him and mentioned that if he felt the need, we could debrief. He told me that he would be working late and that if I stopped by, we would review things.

I agreed.

That evening, I found him bowed over a polarizing light microscope, his pert little ass hidden by the draping of his white lab coat. He stopped upon noticing my arrival.

"I'm just examining some potassium chlorate," he said. "Want to take a look?"

I shifted toward the microscope resting on the waist-high table and bent to peer in the lens. Magnetized, the crystalline powder was transformed into jagged cubes of translucent hues, like miniature icecaps in Technicolor. Although lacking scientific training, I could appreciate beauty enough to admire the hidden complexity of a seemingly simple form.

"It's beautiful," I said.

"Yes, it is," he said, then smoothed the fingers of one hand down my lower back and around the curve of my rear.

I didn't move, and he continued, "I've been meaning to tell you how much I appreciate the short skirts." His fingers continued their downward path and crept between the slit of my skirt. Two fingertips moved forward to slowly stroke the crease of my panties, which rested against my inner thigh. I felt the material soak with a sudden urgency. Unnerved by the speed of the situation, I stood straight and stepped aside. His hands trailed out of their reach.

"You think I didn't notice that you've been dressing for me?" he asked, as he moved closer, trapping me between his body and the chest-high countertop of the lab bench, now pressed against my spine. "Safety is important in a lab; that's why it's necessary to wear long pants and flat shoes. I'm glad you choose to live a little dangerously."

I blushed and averted my gaze downward as he called me out.

"Do you know much about potassium chlorate?" he asked.

I squinted as I retook his gaze and shook my head no, undoubtedly revealing my confusion, if not disappointment, by the sudden topic shift.

"It's a fairly common compound, yet incredibly powerful. What's so amazing about it is that it looks unassuming, but when combined with something sweet, it releases a surprising amount of energy." With that, he closed the remaining distance between our bodies and, reaching with one hand, slowly grazed the pad of his thumb across my smooth lower lip. The touch tingled lips above and below my waist.

I watched as he lifted his hand to his mouth and tasted his thumb where my mouth had just been. "I found something sweet . . . I think we should experiment."

His hot mouth crushed against mine and I swiftly slid my tongue between his slick lips to pry them open. When his tongue pressed back with equal force, my breath caught and my folds swelled. Eager for pressure, I shoved my hips forward and ground my pelvis against the strong plane of his body. He grabbed my hands, now tangled in his hair, loosened my grip and lowered them to rest against the lab bench ledge. Like a fallen angel, I stood with arms spread wide awaiting his command. His nimble fingers made quick work of my shirt's buttons and my bra and he encircled my right breast with his slick mouth.

As he feasted to the right, he pinched my left nipple, pausing only to roll it between his fingers like a fine cigar. The groans that escaped his muffled mouth made me raw with want. Then he suddenly pulled back. I reached out to draw him back in but he again pressed my hands down. I was eager to see the lengthy muscle that had so eagerly been pushed against my aching middle, but he lowered to his knees without disrobing. He gripped the fronts of my thighs beneath my skirt and spread my legs further. He pushed the skirt up around my waist, tucking the bottom into the waistband to keep it put. Down slipped my soaked panties as he pried them down my legs and tossed them aside. A hand cupped possessively at my swollen sex, his palm spreading my lips, pressing against my throbbing clit, fingers toying along the crease of my rear.

He met my eyes and showed a sly smile.

Removing his hand from my body, he reached into the deep pocket of his white lab coat, and then pulled out a glass test tube. I gripped the lab bench a little tighter. The slender cylinder slipped easily on to his middle finger. His sly expression disappeared and a look of intense concentration took its place as he leaned forward and leisurely ran the weighty tip of his tongue from the bottom of my soaked sex to the tip of my throbbing clit, making sure to increase pressure during his ascent.

I felt his tongue flick vigorously over my clit while he slipped into me with his glass shrouded finger. The tube glided easily along my slick folds and its rounded tip bumped against all the right places. The combination of his tongue and the tool shot jagged, electric currents destined for between my legs, causing me to twitch, my legs to wobble, my heart to race, my breath to become shallow, moans to escape, my head to roll back, my hands to tighten their grip, and my mind cloud with the sharp thrill of sexual release. Fingers of his free hand gripped my ass when the height of my orgasm hit, causing me to groan out an "oh god" that echoed throughout the lab and I pushed his mouth away to abate the overwhelming intensity. He slipped out of me, lifted from his knees and stood silently, watching as my body calmed. Once my breath had slowed I raised my head, attempting to fight the post-peak weariness. Wanting to please him and willing for more, I grabbed the waistband of his pants, unbuttoned and unzipped them and pushed them down and off his sturdy legs. Next, I headed for the buttons of his collared shirt and painstakingly attempted to undo them all.

Sensing my lingering fatigue, he assisted and then finally removed his boxers, letting his solid shaft stand free. He stood there mostly naked, draped in his lab coat, like a Central Park flasher with a PhD.

Reaching out, I coiled his cock in my hand and he groaned when I began tugging my tightened grip. With equal force he clenched the wrist of my offending hand and pulled me off. Taking advantage of my surprise and of his hold, he spun me around and pressed me forward against the lab bench so that its edge that once pushed along my spine now settled against my abs. Like a yogi in a bow of submission, I stretched my arms forward to steady myself, carelessly pushing aside bottles, scales and other miscellaneous laboratory equipment. I was poised for sexual satisfaction, not for scientific measurement.

He yanked at my hips and I shuffled to a wider stance. His knuckles bumped along my crease as his hand guided his powerful cock inside me, slipping in deeply easily and filling me like a man should, and in a way that glass could never match. "Oh, shit, you're tight," he said with a groan. I clenched around him for added effect.

The pumping started easily at first, long and steady, allowing my faded excitement to bubble back to the surface, like a beaker over low heat. In this eased pace, I was able to press my pelvis forward enough to knock my clit against the brass handle of the drawer beneath me. The pressing of his hips repeatedly shoved his cock in and out of me and the handle against my center, bringing it to a sensitive, plump peak. With my female firearm triggered, I felt myself grow wetter with every intrusion; his pleasured moans serving as a catalyst to my excitement. Now edgy with pleasure and eager for speed, I shoved my ass toward him, drawing him in deeper and signaling my desire. His pace quickened and he pummeled my soaking pussy with plunged force. The sound of my ass smacking against his skin and the flaps of his coat ticking against the bench added to the rising symphony of our sex.

My shallow breathing accelerated and the electricity that resonated between my thighs prickled swiftly to my limbs signaling my oncoming climax. I pulled his hand from my hip and used his fist to bite back the intensity. But the taste of his coppery skin coupled with his pumping overwhelmed me; my body shuddered as I came with electric force. He pulled his hand from my mouth, yanked my body up from my sprawled pose and with rapid fire released his hot cum into me.

We leaned together as our breathing calmed and the heat of bodies cooled together. I turned and switched my resting place from his chest to the countertop and looked upon him with a glazed gaze.

He gradually buttoned his lab coat and once completely cloaked, he advanced with equal lethargy.

"What did you learn from our little experiment?" he asked, using a finger to draw lazy, yet tantalizing figure eights around my belly button.

I grabbed the wrist of the wandering hand, cupped his palm against my breast and responded, "It's all about chemistry."

When Lacy LeTush Went Blue, Blue, Blue!

Thomas S. Roche

". . . Two three four five six seven eight – *Fuck me! God damn it!*"

Lacy threw her feather boa across the stage, drop-kicked her baton and slammed down the bowling pin. She collapsed dejectedly into the wooden chair she'd just been trying to hump, and cursed some more, loudly, her voice echoing through the cavernous environs of the Chimera Theatre. She kicked the ancient cassette boom box with her marabou-clad right foot and Cab Calloway stopped abruptly as the cord yanked from the wall. Good riddance, Cab: hi-de-ho indeed, fucker.

It really shouldn't be that difficult, Lacy told herself. She danced in front of an audience four nights and one afternoon a week under the nom-de-hump Amber Lust. "Amber" did not shimmy in an old historical theater like the Chimera, of course, but at The Mustang out on Highway 35. Nor did she work it in front of a well-dressed crowd of San Esteban's screamingest queers and howlingest hipsters swilling highballs and cosmopolitans while yowling, "Woo-woo-woo-Take it off!" but, rather, in front of an ill-washed crowd of mustachioed truckers glugging Bud and Jack Daniels and screaming "Show us your pussy!" She also did the Stang's particular brand of dance minus the feather boa, the rhinestone headdress, the choker, the hot pink bustier and matching satin skirt and the fishnet stay-ups and the fan or the tinsel-trailing baton and the mask and the peignoir and the bowling pins. Instead, she started out in a black string bikini, Sally's-issue because that was the way they did things at the Stang, black because after her first six shifts she'd begged and pleaded with Bobo not to make her wear neon pink any more. It was kinda hard to striptease when all you had to lose was your top. At the ultra-sleazy Stang, county liquor laws required her to retain the bottoms throughout the performance. But exuding the kind of smoldering sensuality that reduced men to cash-waving lunatics had come naturally to Lacy ever since she started at the Stang late last year; maybe she was just a natural exhibitionist. Whether it was natural or cultivated, there was no question that the moister she was when she finished a show, the more cash she had stuffed in her G-string.

Easy as pie – so why couldn't she pull it off with vintage lingerie and improbable props? She was a dancer, a professional dancer – had been for months. Shouldn't this all come naturally to her?

That was maybe the problem – it actually kinda did come naturally, which was where the chair-humping came in. Every time she got up onstage at the Chimera, she did one of two things. Either she stuck to the routine as prescribed and approved by the powers that be, and ended up looking like a white guy from Albuquerque. Or she went with her instincts, and careened from campy innocence directly into X-rated material, strictly *verboten* for Happy Henderson's Ba-Ba-Bazoomba Revue, "Where the tease is queen!" as Hap put it. Well, that son of a bitch should know.

Hap, famous for running his dance revue like a well-oiled military machine of unhappy hoofers, had already warned Lacy multiple times about the humping, the nipple-pinching, the thigh-stroking, and that dirty little thing she was always doing with her tongue, not to mention when that one time she spanked herself. Then, of course, there was the popping out of her top – could she be blamed if her nipples didn't like spirit gum? Time was, girls with D-cups got cut a little friggin' slack. But Hap was not an understanding guy when it came to Lacy's problems with her renegade sisters, or anything else. She was one wardrobe malfunction away from being cut loose. Happy Henderson had told Lacy in no uncertain terms that if she didn't lose the stripper moves and keep her nipples to herself, he was going to bounce her from Friday's lineup, and "you and your tassels can look for another revue, *Miss* Le fucking Tush!"

In a college town like San Esteban, finding another place to perform would be no small order. The coastal enclave of culture held one historic theater (the Chimera) and one skanky little gay bar (the Pumping Station). San E. could only support about one and a half burlesque troupes. Happy's was the one, and the Courtney Capricious Burlesque Ordeal on Tuesday nights over at the Station was the half, being entirely too well named for its own good. Their shows usually descended into amyl-huffing karaoke orgies and loogie-catching contests between female stiltwalkers wearing nothing but Nine Inch Nails tattoos, frightwigs and Groucho noses.

The girls of the Ordeal seemed to have more fun than those of the tightly scripted Bazoomba Revue, but God damn it, fun wasn't what burlesque was about! Lacy wanted a paying gig in the thriving San Francisco burlesque revival scene, and trolling around with dildo-juggling punk girls wouldn't fast-track her any more than humping the brass pole at the Stang. If she couldn't land a performance job down in San Francisco, after finals she'd be stuck moving back to her parents' place in Concord and then on to grad school in friggin' Palo Alto – and, Lord have mercy, nobody sane wanted that.

Besides, as much of a bitch as Happy was, there was something special about performing for the Revue. The Ba-Ba-Bazoomba Revue traced its lineage back in an unbroken line to Pinky Perry's Ra-Ra-Revue, the raunchy burlesque troupe that operated out of the Chimera when it was a speakeasy – though the term "speakeasy" implied a level of covertness that really wasn't necessary in this town back then. At that time, San Esteban was a major staging point for shipments of illegal liquor coming down the coast to San Francisco and points south. It was also destination for sophisticates from San Francisco, who would drive up the then challenging coastal roads heading North to enjoy a weekend in a lawless town of drink and debauchery. The local cops were in the pocket of the Syndicate. The mayor and city council were on the payroll. This was way before the University came to town in the sixties, of course – San Esteban was just a sleepy coastal burg before the Syndicate showed up and made it a party town.

In this environment, a number of off-color theaters had thrived along Main Street to cater to the stream of visitors from SF. Chief among them was Pinky Perry's Chimera Theater, where drink was served openly and even the Treasury agents looked the other way. Six nights a week, Pinky Perry, née Pino Perelman, could be found greeting guests and wandering through the crowd drinking imported Canadian whisky from a coffee mug, while his guests drank from cocktail glasses. This affectation was in mockery of the coffee cups the other joints served in, as if to drive home the point that Pinky Perry, like everyone in San Esteban's close-knit underworld, was well above the law.

The end of Prohibition had called a halt to the corruption and vice that accompanied the liquor trade in San Esteban as elsewhere, but Perry had soldiered on, reinventing the Chimera as a movie theater and thereafter as kind of a half-assed strip club. But he'd never given up his dreams of burlesque glory for the Chimera. In fact, Pinky Perry had died in this very theater, in 1963 at the age of sixty, during the inaugural performance of the Ba-Ba Revue Revival – swilling Canadian whisky from his coffee mug, an affection he'd continued even 30 years after the repeal of the Volstead act. Reportedly Perry's last words were "Take it off!"

It had been a sadly abortive revival, given that Perry's sudden death left the troupe leaderless and led to the sale of the Chimera at auction the next year. The Chimera had even been featured on an episode of the Explorations Channel's *Ghostlovers* a few years back. The story went that Pinky's ghost haunted the Chimera because in that final performance he'd died before he got to see the reveal. Plenty of the other dancers in Hap's revue were pretty freaky about the ghost thing, which was why Lacy'd kept her own sightings to herself – weird faces in the windows, knocking sounds in the dressing room, the faint sound of cheering. Lacy'd always had a tendency to see things, and she tried never to take it that seriously – ever since her family had lived in the old house on Holliday Lane in Perdido, up in the Sierras. Her mom, an inveterate hippie, regarded Lacy as a "sensitive", but Lacy figured it was mostly bullshit –

Wait a minute, had she left the door open? She could hear enthusiastic clapping from the balcony. She peered into the spots, most of which she'd turned on for the practice, and saw a shadowy form outlined against them.

"Gorgeous!" came the voice. "Absolutely gorgeous! I especially liked the chair-schtupping, dollface. Sometimes they say we're goin' too blue, but I got one thing to say to that, people – ain't no such thing as too blue Va-va-va-voom, miss, you're a *tsatskeh* if I ever saw one, if you don't mind my saying. *A maidel mit a klaidel.*"

"Excuse me?"

"You look good, toots," he clarified. "I never saw a girl stiffen my *shvantz* so fast to Cab Calloway before!"

"Hey!" shouted Lacy.

"Sorry," the guy said. "Sometimes I go blue myself, a little! No offense meant."

"Do I know you?" She was in deep shit: Hap had been exceedingly reluctant about letting her practice in the theater after hours; he'd made her swear up and down she wouldn't forget to lock the stage door. Now some freaky old homeless dude had wandered in.

"Do you know me?" The old guy laughed. "Sorry, Jane Russell, in this case introductions aren't in order. I know it's a little rude, but maybe you could give your routine another little run-through for me? Without stopping at that thing you did with, you know, with the spanking . . . that was gorgeous. It did things to me. It's like I said, blue is a beautiful color."

"Oh yeah?" said Lacy. "Wish you'd talk to Happy Henderson."

"Henderson? I talked to him, I talked to him. The man's a *nishtikeit*! He doesn't know a roll from a rimshot. Please, Miss – what was your name again?"

"The name's Lacy LeTush," Lacy said. It was dorky, but that was the order of the day with burlesque names. She'd stuck with her real first name but figured "LeTush" was more mellifluous than "Litchfield", a name she'd gotten teased about her whole life, as if "Lacy" wasn't bad enough. "And you are—"

"I'm gonna ask your indulgence," the guy interrupted. "Just for a few minutes, I hope you won't mind if I go nameless. And I'm gonna ask you a favor – please, would you run through it again? And this time no stopping at the chair part – or the spanking. I love that. Especially toward the end. Just let those things *move*, beautiful."

"Toward the end?" Lacy squinted into the lights.

"Sorry, guess I gotta spell it out. When you're – you know, *en déshabillé*. After the big reveal, gorgeous." There was a pleased chuckle that managed to sound obscene and charming. "You're not wearing any pasties."

"No shit," said Lacy, adjusting the bustier self-consciously. Spirit gum wasn't her idea of a Saturday afternoon. "I'm not wearing a G-string either." She never did at practice. Who the hell wanted gold lamé crawling up her ass if it wasn't absolutely necessary?

"Yeah," the guy chuckled. "Yeah, I gotta say, I never got used to the smooth look – but on you, it's – va-va-voom. You mind my saying?"

"Not particularly," said Lacy. "It's that obvious?"

"Obvious? You're falling out of that skirt, *tsatskeh*. And trust me on this one, it suits you. You should kinda let it go for a minute. You'll shock the schmucks, but you'll get your headlines."

"Listen, no offense, but you're kinda freaking me out, mister. It's creepy having you watch me."

"Please, miss," the guy said. "Lacy LeTush, you're the most beautiful woman who ever walked on that stage. I love you, I love your legs, I love your hair. I love everything about you. I even love your Taiwan orchid tattos. I've been waiting forty-five years to see you lose the skirt and do that chair like it was Burt Lancaster. Will you indulge me a little?"

It took a second for the guy's words to sink in; a weird creepy little chill ran from the tattoos in the small of Lacy's back up to the back of her head, like a mentholated tidal wave had just exploded through her.

"How do you know they're Taiwan orchids?"

"I've been up here a while," the guy said guiltily. "I heard you telling the blonde girl the other Thursday."

"Jeez. Um, creepy much!?" said Lacy.

"Sorry, I probably shoulda said something sooner. I know it's unorthodox, but I'm not trying to be a cad. Now will you do an old man a favor, Lacy? I'm begging you, Lacy LeTush – you're the queen of the Chimera tonight, would you grant a little bump and grind to your one loyal subject? And, Lacy LeTush . . . I'm on my knees up here, I mean, I know you can't see it because of the lights, but trust me, I'm on my knees, I'm begging, I'm pleading: Lacy LeTush, go blue, blue, blue!"

Lacy swallowed hard; this was getting a way too weird for comfort, and she was well beyond punchy. Between studying and practice, there'd been little sleep and vast amounts of coffee in the last fourteen days – plus, she was still a little hung over from the last night's after-party, where she'd drowned her Hap-related sorrows in half a dozen vodka tonics and a shared joint of the local skunkweed. She'd had more than her share of strange experiences in her life, most recently in the town's purportedly haunted house on Redwood Highway during a midnight Halloween tour when she thought for a second that a face reflected in a window made an obscene gesture at her – and she did not plan for today's dance practice to make it two. She was not going to let some weird old dude freak her out by wandering in and being creepy . . . besides, he seemed nice enough. What she was doing was, essentially, giving him a free Stang show. But wasn't that already what she did every Friday and Saturday at the Chimera, and in those cases for the sole profit of Happy Henderson, who was by everyone's reckoning a serious son-of-a-bitch?

"All right, mister," Lacy said. "But I want to hear some howling."

"Miss, I guaran-damn-tee you that you will hear some howling."

Lacy retrieved her boom box and set it up again; she was about to rewind Cab Calloway when she paused, frowned, and scampered to her bag. She pulled out her MP3 player and plugged the cord in to the AUX outlet on the boom box. She paged through a dozen songs and found the one she wanted. She kicked the baton and the fan and the silver mask and the bowling pins off the stage – on this she was going new-school. She took one last glance to make sure that her girls were safely ensconced, pasty-free, in the bustier; that wouldn't last, but what the hell. She stretched her foot out toward the MP3 player and pressed the PLAY button with her toe, in a move she'd perfected through months of solo dance practice.

"Playing something special, are we, Lacy?"

"You better believe it," she said nastily, as the music started with blaring horns and a screaming electric guitar. It was Lacy's favorite band, the Bindlestiffs, playing "Drink, Rob, and Fuck", a violent punk homage to corruption in 1920s-era Chicago. She figured it suited the situation.

Lacy started dancing with a savagery that she usually reserved for slow nights at The Mustang. It never failed to liven things up.

This particular MP3 of "Drink, Rob, and Fuck" was a live recording, so she could hear the roaring of the crowd with each crooned boneheaded obscenity: "Big Al C he rules the street/but I just wanna lick your feet/bathtub gin goes down the hatch/you got a license for that snatch?" Lacy pulled a nasty twirl and went shimmying across the stage with her body undulating viciously; at the back edge, she pulled a scissor-move and started climbing up the curtains like they were a stripper-pole, popping out of her bustier, nipples erect and pointing like pistols. Hap would be having a heart-attack about now if he could see her. She did an inverted twirl and came down in a flying pirouette; executing a perfect landing, she brought the filmy peignoir across her chest in a coquettish conceal; she figured fuck the peignoir, fuck the bustier; the skirt was a tearaway, so she cast it at the balcony, though it didn't make it far. Lacy was down on her hands and knees wearing nothing but fishnet stockings and marabou-fluffed heels. She spun on to her back, scissored up and writhed her way to the chair. *Never got used to the smooth look, eh? Here, pal, get a faceful.* She started working the chair obscenely, pumping her body in time with the violent music; had she pulled this particular move at The Mustang, she would promptly have been buried under $5 bills and just as promptly been fired for spreading her legs without a G-string. Even with bikini bottoms she would have been pushing the envelope here; obscene pelvic thrusts were as fun to make as they were pleasing to the audience, but too many of them and you sometimes ran afoul of the local cops, so the manager Bobo kept a close eye on things.

But her pelvic thrusts had nothing on what she was about to do; in each dance, she found a moment when she knew Bobo wasn't watching and dipped her hand down into her bikini bottoms and brought it up with a *see-how-wet-I-am?* look; that always brought a cascade of bills and a guarantee of a dozen well-paid lap dances when she came off the stage. She figured if the weird old guy wanted blue, that was as blue as it got, so she slid her hand sensuously down her belly and tucked it between her spread legs, staring up at the balcony and screaming along with the lyrics: "*Drink and rob and fuck like hell!*"

She gave Creepy Old Dude the little tongue-swirl that so completely addled Happy Henderson, then slipped her middle finger into her mouth, and – Whoa, she actually *was* wet, which she hadn't really been expecting but it was kind of nice. She did it again, slowly, sensuously, down her belly and up over her tits and into her mouth, wetter this time. She could hear a steady wave of howls erupting all around her; funny, she didn't remember any howling on this particular live recording.

She stood, spun with the chair, leaned over and spanked herself hard in time with the music as she ground her crotch toward the chair, pumping, writhing, undulating. It wasn't ballet, but – damn! She was enjoying herself. More howling erupted; when she spun around for final round of chair-humping, she got dizzy, smelled liquor, and could have sworn . . .

Lacy backed off and abandoned the chair, hearing it crash over the edge of the stage. She ran to her MP3 player and hit STOP. She looked around, her eyes dazzled by the lights; for a second, she had this creepy feeling like the theater was full, like the howls were coming not from the boom box but – then it was all gone. The sounds echoing through the theatre as in a single instant the power went out. It was the goddamn fuse box again; this old theater had wiring from hell. The lights died in a few long seconds with a hot orange fading glow.

Lacy stood there dizzy in the dark, trying to get her bearings.

But it sounded, as the soft echoes pulse, like the cheers and howls from the MP3 player died even more slowly than they should have, while up in the balcony, she could hear the sound of her lone spectator stomping his feet, clapping, howling, wolfwhistling. "Bravo! Bravo! Bravo! Lacy! Lacy! Lacy! Lacy LeTush, bravo!" The voice faded slowly into the cavernous black of the ancient theater. Then everything went dark and quiet and the black closed in around her. Lacy felt her heart pounding.

"Hello?" she called out. All she could hear was her own nervous panting. "Hello? Creepy old dude?"

She didn't get an answer.

Lacy groped around for her clothes. She had never before put on a pair of sweat pants and a T-shirt so fast. She hit Main Street running for her car, and didn't even check to make sure the door of the Chimera was locked.

Lacy tried not to freak out; hey, she was sleep-deprived, and sometimes that makes things weird.

She did think hard about her routine, however, and about what a huge pain in the ass Happy Henderson was. In the end, she decided that the screaming control queen could bloody well go fuck himself.

And for all the warnings he'd given Lacy, Hap was distracted enough that night that he didn't even notice when she slipped Armando the DJ a burned disk of "Drink, Rob and Fuck" to replace "Minnie the Moocher". She handed it over along with a $20 bill, and told Armando to blame it all on her when Hap hit the roof.

"With pleasure," said Armando, and put the disc in the stack. "It's always good for a laugh when Hap freaks out."

Oh, she'd wear a G-string, all right – no point in *completely* shocking the straights. But pasties? She'd call it a wardrobe malfunction. If she spun her boobies just right, maybe she could make her pasties hit Happy Henderson in the face when they flew off at the first chorus of "Drink, Rob and Fuck".

Maybe the old man was right: she'd get her headlines, and Hap Henderson would get to hit the roof, which he seemed to love. He'd fire her, and the incident would enter the long burlesque history of the Chimera in some infinitesimal way; she'd be stuck working the Stang and spending Tuesday nights riding a unicycle while having naked ketchup fights on stage to the strains of fourth-rate punk bands. At the moment, that actually didn't sound so bad.

Maybe she'd even come up with a new routine. The Courtney Capricious Burlesque Ordeal could really use a little pole-dancing.

She'd worry about that in the morning. Right now, Lacy LeTush had some pasties to loosen.

Blind Tasting

EllaRegina

They called themselves the Montridge Eight, after the metropolitan
area suburb in which they lived, a 39-minute commute to the
city, and though the name sounded like an underground terrorist
group from the 1960s, their most incendiary efforts had involved
turning on a Viking stove or lighting a Weber grill. A four-couple
gourmet cooking club, the Montridge Eight met once a month,
their homes revolving as venue, to travel the world gastronomically,
one country and cuisine at a time. Creative professionals all,
they were detail-oriented: an evening's theme would extend well
beyond the food, to the decor, the wine, the music, sometimes
even to the furniture.

The Greens, the Blacks, the Grays, the Whites: a box of crayons
– an odd one since the Blacks were not, the Whites were light brown
and the Greens and Grays beige variations. They were the epitome
of sophistication and urbane modern living. The men had long been
vasectomized, completely relieving their marriages of pregnancy
scares and latex fluid barriers. The couples were close and getting
closer. The Montridge Eight gatherings elicited flirtatious behavior
that grew stronger over the years. It began with one foot finding
another under the table, or venturing further, toes slowly massaging
a crotch. Hands would sneak inside waistbands from behind. Soon,
parlor games were incorporated: first dirty Mad Libs – "Name
of Person in Room" particularly revealing – then adult Charades,
followed sequentially by Twister, strip tease, Strip Poker and Spin-
the-Bottle. The Blacks, who lived in a former firehouse, offered
their pole for dancing when they hosted, a mirrored ball on the high
ceiling throwing sparkles over the dimmed space as each woman
spun around the shiny brass upright, inspired by the thumping disco
groans of Donna Summer and company. With each installment of
the cooking club the Montridge Eight became increasingly daring

and experimental. Perhaps it was the Cabernet, or the Pinot Grigio, or the Riesling, or the Rioja.

Although beyond familiar, the Greens, Blacks, Grays, and Whites – a living version of the board game Clue – decided from the onset that during these occasions they would refer to each other, including their own spouses, as Monsieur or Madame, evoking old black and white movies where the husband called the wife "Mother", lending the evenings a certain frisson of staged formality – an interesting counterpoint to the sub-table footsie and miscellaneous lusty doings – often inspiring unscripted postprandial role-playing once the couples were back in their own bedrooms:

"Would you do it to me in the Library with the Lead Pipe, Monsieur Gray?"

"Most assuredly, Madame Gray. My very large one. Where shall I put it?"

Across Montridge's verdant tree-lined streets, a parallel scene was unfolding at the Green house:

"In the Billiard Room, on the table, with the Rope, Madame Green?"

"Of course, Monsieur Green. A hog-tie is definitely in order," she replied, spreading her excited legs as Monsieur Green undid his perfectly slip-knotted neckwear, anxious to truss Madame's limbs, rigid cock pointed towards her from an unbuttoned fly.

The February get-together, at the White home, followed a Brazilian theme, it being a Saturday coinciding with Carnival in Rio de Janeiro. Invitations were e-mailed to everyone separately. In those sent to each Madame, a curious request was made. After noting her specific menu contribution – assigned from wine, hors d'oeuvre, side dish and dessert categories; the hosts would provide cocktails, the main course, and coffee – it was stated:

> *If not already hairless in your nether regions, a full Brazilian waxing should be undergone the day before the Montridge Eight event. Do not expose those waxed parts to the Monsieur, let him feel them, nor explain why. Note: if skin sensitivity precludes the application of hot wax a cream depilatory may be used.*
>
> *No perfume or scented body lotion.*

The Monsieurs received similar directives to eliminate any existing hair from navel to knees, by whatever means necessary, the day of the meeting. Monsieur Black was asked to shave off his goatee and, if queried by Madame Black, to say that he just felt like a change. The playing field was to be leveled, literally mowed. Fingernails were to be neatly trimmed.

All e-mails gave the same cryptic proclamatory ending:

The evening will conclude with a Blind Tasting.
On February 21st the Montridge Eight will travel further than they have ever gone.

The Whites – the Monsieur, a film producer; the Madame an architect – lived in a house of Madame White's design – a sprawling one-storey of stone and glass. A central hall was flanked by sixteen interconnected corridor-like rooms that could be walked through, from one to the next, with the exception of a guest bath and five sleeping chambers – rectangular beads on a string, each painted a different vivid color. Traversing their floor plan was crossing a rainbow. The Whites joked that their home simply reflected that they were people of color, but the spatial effect was more than ironic – the palette had a cumulative beguiling influence.

The group ambled through the house, giddily drinking *Caipirinhas*, the Monsieurs in cashmere sweaters and wool suits; the Mesdames wearing flowing crêpe and clingy silk, tottering on stilettos and kitten heels – they could be quadruplets or a ballerina quartet, so similarly sized, shaped and toned from weight-lifting, tennis and Pilates. The Monsieurs also had comparable physiques – athletic well-tended bodies the result of running, swimming, and biking. Even their cocks shared a resemblance, formidable every one, this mutually and tacitly observed in the pool club locker room.

Monsieur White's custom audio mix played everywhere, emanating from speakers hidden behind walls: "The Girl from Ipanema" bossa nova charmed the ballroom; a samba romanced the conservatory; and Carmen Miranda belted out a frenetic *Tico Tico* from an unseen Copacabana in the lounge. Other rooms featured Brazilian jazz or indigenous music – whistles, flutes, horns, rattles and drums imitating the sounds of the Amazon rainforest. The entire house was animated.

Plasma HD TVs descended from ceilings in almost every room, volume muted, looping TiVoed soccer games with Brazil always in the lead, teams on each 30" flat panel keyed by their uniform colors to the room itself. In the blue study two Donald Duck cartoons were projected on to mammoth screens posted at opposite walls: the mischievous fowl rescued from the blues by an Aracuan bird in a samba café – dancing, getting mixed into a cocktail, being kicked in all directions from between the flesh and blood legs of a woman working the pedals of a Hammond organ. Keyboards explode: flying ticker tape ribbons. At the drive-in across the room an artist's paintbrush sketched blue Brazilian waterfalls – cascading ejaculations on an otherwise white background.

In the kitchen, three varieties of Brazilian red wine stood uncorked, brought by the Greens. The hors d'oeuvres – ripened Brazilian cheeses, *broa* fennel corn bread and soft *pão de queijo* rolls (the Grays) – were set out on the soapstone-topped center island, and consumed standing up, hands grazing rears, fingers edging shoulders, calves against shins.

Once the churrasco-style meat was grilled, Monsieur White carried a tray of loaded skewers to the dining room table. Madame White followed with the other foods: *coxinha*, chicken-thigh-shaped croquettes; *feijoada*, Rio's traditional black bean and meat stew (the Blacks); *farofa* – a yucca, banana, egg and onion mix – collard greens, rice and beans, *chouriço* sausage, and fried plantains (the Grays).

Everyone took their places – green, black, gray and white dinnerware indicating seating arrangements. Orchids lay horizontally above each Madame's plate. Eight small white envelopes, centered on the dishes, identically stamped:

~ READ ME ~
YOUR BLIND TASTING INSTRUCTIONS

The printed contents were perused with a grin and a blush, then the papers slid into pockets or tucked inside brassieres.

By the time the meal commenced it was a pure bacchanal, fueled by the Blind Tasting intimations. Hands, mouths, tongues, foods – all mixed up – this one feeding that one, the sucking of dripping meats and fingers, stray morsels licked off cheeks, cashmere, wool, silk and crêpe. Eating utensils were hardly touched. It was primitive, nearly pagan. Wine glasses spilling and refilling. Every cock was hard under the mahogany, every pussy ready and drooling.

Dessert eventually landed, a cloud in a decadent haze – coconut flan. The coffee, brewed from dark Brazilian beans purchased on Amazon.com, was drunk slowly, not just for savoring but so everyone could regroup. The evening was not over, the Blind Tasting still to come.

Each Madame selected a bathroom and freshened up on the bidet. Then, arm in arm, they descended the basement stairs, giggling in unison, flushed from the wine and the anticipation of what awaited them.

The windowless underground space functioned as a screening room, draped on all sides with black velvet curtains. It contained blue upholstered seats from a demolished Broadway theater and a carpeted podium, at the edge of which – just for this evening – was a freestanding wall, the meeting's centerpiece. Discovered by Madame White at the flea market, it was an artifact from a dissected carnival, part of a game where balls were pitched into open clown mouths. There were four such faces, each six feet high, painted mural-style across the partially three-dimensional paneled structure. Haywire raffia hair sprouted above ears, red punching bag noses drooped below each pair of wild eyes, and four gaping O mouth cut-outs – several feet above shoe level – were lined with red patent leather cushioned lips, worn and battered by a fifty-year swirling galaxy of balls in motion. A blue velvet curtain framed the unusual flat. Below each silently hysterical jester, distinctly shaped black terrycloth cushions – a circle, triangle, square, and diamond – lay on the floor, stunted tuffets.

On the reverse undecorated side, four heavy metal khaki footstools were planted solidly beneath each portal on the black industrial rubber tiling. A gag – red ball, black strap – sat atop each stool. The Mesdames, as per the instruction envelopes, removed all clothing – tittering nonstop during the unraveling – placing their garments on the dais, but retaining footwear.

Each Madame situated her well-toned rear inside an arbitrarily chosen mouth – like an animal trainer wedging his head into a yawning tiger jaw – and adjusted herself on the padded lips, feet kept on the stool, heels hooked into rungs for leverage. Each Madame took the ball gag and placed it in her mouth, securing the device behind her head. Each Madame waited.

The velvet curtain was drawn, sealing off the clown wall inserted with the four Mesdames – fleshy pegs, corks in holes – their isolated asses hanging in a row from gigantic puffy lips.

The Monsieurs entered and completely undressed as directed, laying clothing over the theater seats. There was to be no talking. Each Monsieur opened a palm-sized purple felt pouch, withdrew an amber glass vial, unscrewed it, and coated his nostril interiors with its contents: essential oil produced from Brazil's finest coffee beans. Spiraled multicolored corded elastic bands emerged next, to be worn somewhere between knee and ankle, Mini-Sharpie markers dangling from attached rings – the color of each writing implement matching the name of the Monsieur to whom it was given; Monsieur White's coil held a pinkie-length Wite-Out correction pen. Finally, each Monsieur took a plastic-wrapped slice from the bag – a cut of mango, papaya, guava or passion fruit – and rolled it in his mouth, a congratulatory cigar. The Monsieurs approached the curtain, stepping randomly on to cushions.

The lights went off. Noises came forth, a soundtrack of the Amazon rainforest: a spectrum of meteorological effects, frogs, monkeys, jaguars, flowing streams, waterfalls, chirping fidgeting insects, hissing snakes, crying macaws, rackety Aracuan tree birds, crickety toucans, vampire bats and other flying creatures.

Aromatherapy units plugged into electrical outlets released a rainforest smell – a pungent mixture of green, orchids, vanilla, cocoa, mango, wood, leaf and musk. The coffee oil neutralized and masked odors; the Mesdames alone could appreciate the heady aromas.

The curtain slowly opened, its mossy fabric lightly brushing bodies on either side.

The Monsieurs felt an aura of heat at crotch level, issuing from the darkness-cloaked wall. Their hands, all eight, almost simultaneously, reached towards the thermal source facing them, as if to unchill by a campfire. Warm toned round flesh stopped the fingers. The Monsieurs realized that they were standing at an altar of asses. Each signed in using his pen, marking X, centered above the proximate hindquarters, where meaty curve became hard spine.

Then, the hands. They fondled, they prodded, they kneaded. The buttocks were smooth, every crevice and pussy uniformly bald. Each Monsieur sampled the sap of the trunk in front of him. Fingers entered fervent wet openings, rear wiggling encouragingly in response. Each Monsieur removed the fruit from his mouth and used it as a pulpy feather, tickling the labia before him, sliding the sweet piece in and out, sucking it for a moment and pushing it back inside, sometimes along with a thumb. Then the mouth, licking the fruit juice off the radiant aperture, teasing its bloated nub with a fingertip. Then the mouth sucking the slice, now mixed with the lubricious female secretions and returning to the pussy – kissing, tonguing, gently nibbling – each Monsieur different but the same.

On the other side of the wall eight knees quivered, mouth gags prevented voices from calling out, from squealing – blocked them from adding to the pleas of the macaws, the screams of the chimpanzees, the chittering of bats.

Four cocks stiffened in the dark, helped by a firm nectar-sticky grasp or two and the drum beat, the thunder, the wind, the entire jungle hum – its acoustical display gradually building in audibility and intensity. Fingers again at each set of parted lips, or caressing the orb of a rump. One digit entered an asshole, to the delight of the identity-unknown recipient, her derrière shivering.

The Monsieurs arrived at the same point concurrently, aiming their saliva-coated cockheads at the welcoming slippery pouts and slowly submerging.

Four cocks, up to the hilt within four pussies, each either unexplored territory or familiar path. It did not matter – it was the thrill of the not-knowing, the maybe, the notion that they could be poking their own Madame or another with whom they've played footsie, stinkfinger, tickle-rump, and Spin-the-Bottle for years.

Clues could not be transmitted to the Mesdames; Monsieur Gray had to refrain from his signature figure eight thrust, lest it be Madame Gray on the receiving end of his carnal movements. But no Monsieur felt limited and each took his time with the fucking – testing and withdrawing, diving in again, deeper, harder and unbridled. The Mesdames, rendered weak by their separate anonymous pleasures, were slumped chests to thighs, heads resting on knees, while vigorously being penetrated by unidentifiable thick anaconda snakes through holes in the wall – each taking a slithering fleshy battering.

The Monsieurs were four oil rigs toiling in blackness, grabbing hips with their perspiring hands, pushing towards the back of the wall. One Monsieur felt as if he were motoring a foreign car that fit like a glove, changing gears as he tracked the curves of the road. The Monsieurs varied and ratcheted their paces, somewhat choreographed by hypnotic rhythms and screeching animals; two divergent in momentum – one plunging very slowly, the other jerky and unleashed, spurred by calls of beasts in the feral night. They could not yell out as that would unmask their identities to each other and the Mesdames into whom they were plowing. This proved quite the challenge, especially for a particular Monsieur. He suppressed Tarzan exclamations and deep jaguar growling as his cock probed tight flesh gripping in reply, an invisible smoke signal.

However, when they came, all four within a short period, as if cued by the low grunts of a howler monkey, goaded and stimulated by each other's body heat and the arousing stirring pops of cocks driving into pussies – the Mesdames pierced on the human skewers nearly fainting from their own ecstasies; whimpering like birds unable to squawk – the Monsieurs yowled one collective indecipherable primal utterance, blending seamlessly with the surrounding untamed yelping. At varied intervals, four molten spouts poured into four pussies, dripping on to the terrycloth cushions as each Monsieur gave his final tremor of emission, the wall shaking and buckling precariously. They slouched, one by one, breathlessly, on the padding beneath, their ammunition shot, regaining a little strength by eating any surviving fruit slices, listening to melodies of birds and streams, their own racing heartbeats adding to the bestial orchestra.

The Amazon rainforest lulled and the velvet curtain closed. The lights rose incrementally from pitch black to a steady duskiness. The Monsieurs and the Mesdames re-attired and gathered their carnival props, perhaps to be used again during another scenario. They rested in the theater seats, scattered among a dozen rows, digesting the activities and recouping their energy. The Monsieurs furtively glanced at the four Mesdames, and vice versa, trying – unsuccessfully – to determine who had been with whom. Adieus were finally bid and the Greens, Blacks, and Grays departed; all Mesdames hanging on to their Monsieurs, all ambulation irregular, everybody spent.

It was only at home that each Monsieur and Madame might learn with whom they had taken their trip around the world. The Madame – a naked reflection in the bathroom mirror – could, with nail polish remover and a cotton ball, rub the X off her lower back. If resisting the temptation to unveil was impossible, she would look at the wad's colored residue. Otherwise, she would throw the unglimpsed lump into the toilet, close the lid and flush, then wash her hands, eyelids shut. If she spotted the family color she could tell her Monsieur that he piloted the airplane taking her on that mile-high Brazilian flight, or she could keep the information secret. She might also dip a finger inside herself and taste mango, papaya, guava or passion fruit, blended with her own juices and semen. Then, she could decide whether to call for her Monsieur, step together into the shower, and suck his fingers or cock before they turned on the hot water.

The next meeting of the Montridge Eight would surely be an interesting one.

Wing Walker

Cheyenne Blue

The conversations go something like this:

"I'm a wing walker," I say, demurely twiddling my glass of Chardonnay.

"Oh?" he says, and his eyes flick over me dismissively, no doubt picturing me in thick overalls wielding an industrial hose of airplane de-icer at DIA. "You don't look the maintenance type."

"I'm not," I say. "I wear a catsuit, not a boilersuit, and I dance on the wing of the plane as it flies along."

That always gets their attention, at the very least a double take, while they decide if I'm serious or not. And if they decide I am, then I have their interest for as long as I want it.

Wing walking goes something like this:

I dress warmly. A layer of wicking thermals because it's colder than the moon out there, with the wind whipping away every thought of warmth. Then the catsuit. It's a patriotic red, white, and blue, a line of stars down the thigh, diagonal stripes over the torso. Patriotism goes down well with the air show crowds. Goggles against the wind, soft slippers on my feet so I don't harm the fabric of the wing.

Bob is our pilot, Buttercup is our plane. Bob is sixty-eight and has a steady hand on the controls. Buttercup is also sixty-eight and she's a Boeing Stearman biplane, a game old girl painted as sunny as her name. Bob and her, they have a long history together. I often think they'll go together in a burst of flame on a hillside. I just hope I'm not on the wing at the time.

We take off from a back strip, away from the crowds. I'm already on the upper wing in my safety harness, securely fastened to the upright struts that protrude from the center of the plane's structure. Surely, you didn't think I'd do this without a harness? Some people used to, but they tended to have short careers.

We circle the air show once, up high. We'll talk a little on the radio. Bob worries how long he can keep doing this. The maintenance on the old girl gets harder every year. Then we get the signal to go and we come in fast and low. I'll be in a pose: arm extended gracefully my long hair streaming behind me like Boadicea the warrior queen. Or Xena the warrior princess – I guess more people have heard of her. One leg cocked up. I'll hold the pose and wave to the crowd as Bob takes us up in a hard spiral. And for the next fifteen minutes or so, Bob will twirl with Buttercup, looping the loop, flying upside down, flipping her from side to side, always within sight of the crowds of course. And me? I'll be up there, posing, slow motion dancing, sometimes a handstand, although Bob has to keep her totally steady for that one, so I only do that when he's been dry for a few days. The wind pummels the breath from my body, and moving a limb is like pushing against cement. The roar of the air and the rumble and creak of the plane beneath my feet fill my head. There's a crowd? I honestly couldn't tell you. It's just me and Buttercup and Bob, flying in our little space-time continuum.

Evenings go something like this:

Me and Bob, in a Motel 6 somewhere, Buttercup in a hangar nearby. We get takeout and sit on one of the double beds, backs against the headboard watching HBO. I trade some of my sweet and sour for Bob's lo-mein, and we wrangle over who ate the most prawn crackers. We compromise on the wine: he likes sweet, I like dry, so as usual we settle on a Riesling, one of those big double bottles and we'll finish the lot.

"You need a man," Bob says, eyes on Sigourney Weaver, her singlet tastefully ripped as she battles aliens.

I grunt. "I can get one anytime I want."

"Not just a one night man," says Bob. He knows about them. He's obligingly asked for another room on a few occasions when I can't go back to their place. "A real man."

"What man can compete with Buttercup?" I ask, adding hastily, "Apart from you."

"I'll find you a man," promises Bob. "One like Sigourney." So far, he hasn't.

Bob and I aren't lovers. There's a forty year age gap. I like men with hair above the neck and none below. Bob likes men who are the reverse of that. We get along like old friends, sharing a room with two beds in each of the cheap motels to save money.

And so our evenings fill the space of a motel room and our mouths and hands follow the predictable routine of takeout and conversations we've had hundreds of times before. I wouldn't change those conversations; I wouldn't change Bob. Only the location of the Motel 6 changes. It teleports itself from Chino to Riverside to Prescott to Pueblo so that it's there when Bob and I fly up in Buttercup to prepare for the next show.

And one day, the conversation goes like this:

"Got you a man," says Bob, reaching over with a fork to snag a pork ball and dunk it in my sauce.

"Can get my own."

"Not that sort of man. Got you a man on the wing tomorrow."

Now my interest is up. Not many men wing walk. It's for the girls; the men are too chicken. Or too heavy. Can't have a 200 lb man moving across the wing. Bob couldn't keep Buttercup steady if that happened.

"Name's Leon. He's a novice but he's keen. Thought we could try out some fancy pants double act."

There's a mild alarm that I'll have to split my cut with this Leon, but I'm intrigued. I've never wing walked with a man. Only girls and there's always an element of competition in that. Whose tits can jut the furthest, whose leg can stay extended the longest, whose hair looks the best backswept and big as we leap lithely from the plane to greet the fans.

"Where'd you find him?"

"Came to the hangar when I was putting Buttercup to bed. We had a bit of a chat."

He must have been convincing. If I had a dollar for every person who says to me, "I did that once" or "I'd love to do what you do", I'd be rich enough to buy Bob his Mexican island staffed by Sigourney Weaver clones in loincloths. With dicks.

Leon is there the next morning. He's lean, feline like his name, small and wiry, the same height as me. He wears some sort of tight pants and a thick clinging fleece. The pants show off his ass pretty well. I think that he's probably gay. I'm wearing an old costume, stuff that is now not good enough for shows. There's a smear of oil across the chest and there's a couple of small holes: one a rip on the thigh where I caught it on the door catch, a small hole in the crotch where a seam gave when I did a handstand.

"Jaye, Leon, Leon, Jaye." Bob does the introductions and I check to see whether he's watching Leon's ass, but he's already turned away to fiddle with Buttercup's struts, so it's up to me and Leon to make conversation.

"When did you last do this?" I ask.

"Year or so ago."

"Where?"

He shrugs. "Mexico. Britain. Australia. Thailand."

Everywhere, it seems, but the States. Nowhere I'd have heard of him.

"Done it with another person before?"

He smiles, showing small white teeth. Both eyeteeth point in slightly. Too poor for orthodontics. That's okay, so was my family. "Yeah. I don't like doing it alone."

Bob's finished fiddling and he produces a second harness. "You'll share the central brace," he says, "one on each side. Ain't had time to put up the other poles. We'll just take Buttercup up and see how you get along together up there."

I hoist up to the lower wing with ease, I do it all the time. When I stand up and look down, Leon's eyes whip away from my legs. Obviously likes women, at least a little.

We attach the harnesses firmly to the central pole, checking to make sure they won't tangle as we move around. It's a wide waist belt with shoulder straps and a slender steel cable that attaches to the pole. That's it. One skinny cable between me and eternity. My long hair is tightly braided and I wear a padded helmet as we're only practicing. No need for glamour this morning. The earpiece of the radio tucks into the side.

Bob turns the prop and Buttercup splutters into life. It's a crisp morning, and my hands are already tingling from the chill, but I don't like to wear gloves, I like to feel Buttercup beneath my palms. I see that Leon is bare palmed too – or maybe he doesn't have gloves. We trundle around to the runway, and Bob revs the engine. Normally, I'd brace myself against the back support as a lever against the wind as we take off – it's harder with two as we have to stand one each side. But then we're up and the ground falls away beneath Buttercup's wings and the lift pushes my feet into the fabric.

Bob's voice comes over the radio. "I'll come around and level off at 500 feet, and fly straight. Then you can do whatever it is you're going to do out there."

Beneath Buttercup's wings, there are corn fields and the yellow flat plains of eastern Colorado. A dry creek, a tangle of cottonwoods, yellowing in the early fall days. The huddle of hangars and huts around the airfield. Bob points her nose to the east and we fly into the slanting sun.

I grasp the support with one hand, lean out star fashion, tacitly encouraging Leon to do the same. He follows and when I glance left, he's arched into the wind, his face ecstatic. I shift to one foot, raise the other leg, point my toe, perform a slow series of poses around the pole. Leon follows a second behind. He's good at this.

"Going about," says Bob over the radio, and Leon nods, prepared to hold his pose through the bank and turn.

I'm the one watching him now, and there's a thrill in watching something so beautiful this close. Watching someone too. He's graceful; more deliberate in his movements than a woman, but no less glorious. With a thrill, I notice the hard lines of his thighs, the curve of his butt, the weight of his calves. And I notice too that in the wind, his suit is pulled tight across his groin, and he's erect. Not simply turgid from effort, but supporting a full on pointing-to-the-right erection. Pointing to me. I glance again. He's not particularly long, but the outline looks thick. He must be really wound up for the cold and the wind not to send him as limp as one of Bob's lo-mein noodles.

Two more passes of the airfield, and then Leon takes the lead. He handstands, as straight and steady as a redwood, his fingers splayed on the wing. He must be confident to try this so soon, with an unknown pilot and plane. Then his legs spread wide, and he holds the pose. Great abs. Another second, and his feet are lightly planted on the wing again.

He flashes me a smile, rests his butt against the pole, jackknifes forward until he's in a cat stretch along the wing. I'm not trying to follow his moves. I'm simply watching him, his body, and trying to ignore the feelings in my cunt. It throbs in time with Buttercup's engine. The throb that tells me to radio Bob to get the hell down out of the sky, so that I can take Leon by the hand and find a quiet corner of the hangar to see if his dick is as delicious as it looks, flattened by his tight pants.

Leon stands. "You try," he mouths, the words whipped away by the wind.

Try what? I've been watching his body in the minutest detail, thinking of golden skin and muscles as hard as Buttercup's seat underneath that god-awful flying gear. I've been thinking of what he'll taste like, all sweat and adrenaline leaking out through his pores, and I haven't been paying attention to his moves.

He smiles. "Put your back against the support," he instructs, this time through the radio.

"Going around again," comes Bob's voice over the radio, and it's Leon who acknowledges him.

Leon waits until Buttercup steadies on her new course. Now we're heading west, toward the Rockies. I can see them, hazy and purple, tipped with caps of new snow.

He's behind me. His fingertips run my body from shoulder to hip. "Good posture." His voice is tinny in my ear through the radio. It sounds strange with him being so close. "Try the cat stretch."

His hands remain at my waist as I jackknife. He's so close to me that I can feel the brush of his groin on my hip. He's still erect.

His hands travel slowly around the contours of my ass, one finger running over the crease of my pants. As bent over as I am, the gusset of my pants is biting into my pussy. The seam is pressing on my clit, and by clenching and releasing my ass these tiny movements bring me higher. I must be red in the face from having my head so low, but I'm not straightening just yet. Beneath my feet, Buttercup flies on, and the rumble from her engine travels up my already heightened nerve pathways as the throbbing builds.

I can't hold the position forever, of course, so I arch out into his graceful cat stretch. His hands fall away from my ass, and the pressure eases between my legs. A temporary reprieve. I'm so horny I just want to bring myself back into reach of his hands.

I stand again, place my hip against the pole and wiggle my ass. As invitations go it's unsubtle, but we can't stay up here forever. Bob will be swinging Buttercup around any second and we'll be heading back to the airstrip. Leon rests against me and I feel the weight of his cock as he dry humps himself, sliding over my shiny suited ass. It's way too cold for him to unzip himself; he'd get frostbite in those delicate swollen tissues. Me, however . . .

His fingers work their way down the seam of my pants, and then, as I hoped he would, they find the hole. It's only a small one, an inch or so of torn seam but it's right over my cunt. My hands tighten on the pole and my breathing is shallow. Buttercup trembles beneath my feet, Bob is humming to himself over the radio, the Rockies are huge and purple and solid in my vision, and my cunt is fiery with need.

Leon slips two fingers into the hole. They brush lightly over my panties and I shudder. Then they scissor and the old thread gives way a little more. Three fingers. And now they brush rhythmically over the gusset. He must realize how wet I am. I grip the pole tightly with both hands and concentrate on his fingers, moving to and fro with deliberate intent.

"Heading back," says Bob over the radio, and there's a dip of Buttercup's wings as he prepares to turn.

Leon's hand twitches; I can sense his withdrawal. He's behind me, slightly stooped to work his fingers over my cunt. But he's also got his harness on and there's no danger. So I close my legs, trapping his hand. My inner thighs are tight and muscled from the wing walking, and he can't get away. He tries again, a tug, but his hand is trapped there as Buttercup banks around and heads back to the airfield.

Bob is still humming a Sousa march, and the sun is now hot on my face. Now that we've straightened out again, there's not long until we'll be on the ground. So I relax my thighs, free his hand, and Leon wiggles his fingers in appreciation. And then he starts to stroke in earnest, getting beneath my panties to caress my lips, and circle my clit with an urgent fingertip.

I'm not sure if the ground is rushing up to meet me because Buttercup is coming in to land or if it's just the thrill and the buildup. But there's a tightness in my chest with the beauty and the glory of it all, and a trembling beneath my feet as Bob throttles back Buttercup's engine. And Leon's fingers are as fiery as the sun that burns my face and my world is tilting, the sky is falling or the ground is rising, and as Buttercup floats down out of the wide white sky, I come, screaming my joy into the wind.

Not a second too soon. Buttercup bumps down on the grass and we're racing along, and Leon whips his hand away – I see his fingers shining with my juices – and we both grip the support tightly, totally unprepared for the landing.

Bob brakes and Buttercup meanders into her turn and taxis back to the hangar. I breathe slowly and deliberately, letting the world straighten itself again. I look over at Leon – my new partner – and smile, and he grins back with all the joy of flight in his eyes. The sun is golden on my face and Buttercup is steady beneath my feet. And here I am, on the wing, there with those that I love the most.

The Dead End Job

Laurence Klavan

They were supposed to be doing something at work, and they were. She was doing something, anyway, talking to him while sitting beside him on super-structured swivel chairs imported at great expense from Finland (or some foreign place) in her office, which had been presented to Isabel as an incentive to take the job – she wouldn't be working in a cubicle, in other words – and which had actually become a boon for them, since it was small enough for them to be close together – "conferring on data" – without arousing suspicions when she did this, when she told him stories about herself to excite him and he touched himself through his jeans or – if he was feeling bold enough – unbuckled and unzipped his pants and touched himself directly.

They had started doing it a few weeks ago during lunch hour when the rest of the office emptied out. She had learned that Martin didn't eat lunch, hardly ate at all, unlike herself, who felt even at twenty-three that she ate too much, even though others thought she was being silly, others found her attractive, Martin did, at any rate, though it took him forever to say so and, come to think of it, maybe he never actually had: he had just moved toward Isabel like an object on a ship's table sliding amidst a storm at sea. Maybe his not eating enough explained more than his – not entirely unappealing – ultra-slimness, it had caused his – how should she say it? – lack of strength in a certain area, something she had discovered during their first date, if you could even call it a date; it had been more, again, a kind of gravitational drift in each other's direction after hours. Though now that she thought of it – as he came forcefully, hearing the most erotic part of her monologue breathed into his ear – he was only weak sexually in certain ways and not in others; in fact, he was incredibly avid when he heard her tales; she might even have called him potent, if potency didn't imply an interaction with another person, though maybe it only meant having the potential of powerfully reproducing, which Martin obviously had, even though he was currently wasting his precious (or was it inexhaustible?) reproductive material in the front flap of his underwear.

They had started doing it at work because they had been so fucking bored. Not that Isabel had expected to be thrilled, exactly collecting data in a company that made security systems – let her get this straight – so that "passive requestors" could strengthen the "trust realms" between "insecure" computers, so that web browsers could better "make requests" of – oh, the whole thing had been so lame to begin with, and so would anybody working in it; but, well, she had needed a job and the industrial park was in driving distance from her apartment (the first she'd ever had, gotten right after graduating college, where she had studied art history, as useless a major as she had been warned it would be), and this was sold to her, too, as another incentive, the short commute, though now in fact she would have preferred a longer ride in the morning, since pressing her foot to the pedal and turning the radio knob were more actions than she performed at work, more of a physical and mental workout, and she was only half-kidding.

Martin had not been her first office mate: Rita had been there to begin with, a nondescript woman of fifty who, to Isabel's amazement, had already worked there for ten years, and who had a heart attack and took early retirement two days after Isabel arrived (Isabel was not the reason, she had been solemnly reassured by her boss, Owen, as if she ever would have imagined that she was; though, in fact, the reassurance actually made her consider it for a second), and Martin arrived soon after, at about half Rita's salary, Isabel assumed.

He was, she immediately noticed, her own age, dark-haired and not unhandsome, though so slight as to seem positively fragile. Isabel had never fantasized sexually about being physically bigger than a man, but in truth she wasn't the most experienced in this area, having gone through college just racking up short relationships with an aspiring and seemingly pot-addicted musician, mostly because they lived on the same hall, and an acting student who had said he was bi-sexual but whom she soon learned was homosexual, or at least would be – he confessed while leaving her for a male stage manager – after his experience with her. Their affair, too, had come about through inertia – they had been at the same cast party and left at the same time, and this, it turned out, was the most they would ever have in common.

Martin and she had quickly formed a tighter bond, one based on incredulity at the fact of their daily tasks, disbelief that they were meant to merely man computers, waiting for data, feeling as suffocated as those at battle stations in wartime submarines but nowhere near as necessary (Martin had said this; he'd been a history major). The two were nearly stunned by the idea of doing this all day, unnerved enough that they couldn't even laugh about it, until, one night on the way home, after they'd each had two beers apiece at a nearby bar, they couldn't stop laughing.

Even here, the torpor of the job had taken its toll, sapped their spirits; they hadn't actively chosen the bar: Martin had just caravanned behind her car until Isabel shrugged, put on her turn signal, and he had followed. In the same sleepwalking way, they had gone to her place afterwards, since he still lived with roommates, one of whom slept out in the open, on the living room couch.

They had watched an animated movie for awhile, one that both had seen several times without even liking. Then, neither being the aggressor, they simply moved closer on the couch like commuters making room for others on a crowded subway car, freeze-framed the film, and got close enough to touch.

Martin's hands had skittered over her like bats, and she had darted her tongue into his mouth, as if trying to reach something under a couch where it had not been vacuumed for years. While each had made the least amount of effort possible, both became aroused – it had been ages for Isabel, after all, and she heard Martin moan in what sounded like agreement when she rubbed his half-erection, her wrist pressed somewhat painfully against the clump of keys in the right front pocket beside it.

Yet by the time she'd returned hopefully from the bathroom – carrying a condom, which she'd taken discreetly from a bowl of free ones in a progressive bookstore downtown – wearing only her panties but still holding against her the T-shirt she'd taken off, self-conscious as ever about her size, she found that Martin was already pulling back on the pants he'd partially yanked down and was reaching again for the remote.

He gave no explanation (later, she understood he'd been too embarrassed or at least too unhappy with himself to speak) and at the moment she blamed herself and then him and then herself again, and sat there feeling strange, still gripping the unwrapped condom with her right hand and the T-shirt with her left, as he began the movie again from the place where they'd stopped it.

While they watched – or while he did, and she stared into a middle distance, wondering if she was blushing (it seemed like it) and, if so, whether if it was from anger or embarrassment or both – without a word or muting the movie, Martin turned and began touching her again, fingering her through the side of her underwear and occasionally moving her T-shirt away to inexpertly but intently suck her nipple. He did it, she thought later, out of guilt and obligation or as a kind of good form and fair play (he was a WASP, after all, he had said so over drinks, though he had gone to school on a scholarship) or from an excitement that (and here she began to feel compassion for him and not contempt) he was unable to fully feel but only witness and acknowledge, the way one smells food that one doesn't actually crave but understands others eating. Whyever he was doing it, he made Isabel come, a bit more intensely than she usually made herself in the evenings, her experience diminished somewhat by the accompanying sound of a song sung by cartoon flounders in the movie, along with which she suspected Martin was quietly humming, though it might have been more of the agreeing-with moaning he had done before.

Afterward, he pulled away, leaving her to readjust her underwear and fully pull on her shirt. The fact that he had even done it, after being impotent (because he lacked strong enough blood circulation or didn't desire her in that way or didn't eat enough – he had only nibbled at the nachos in the bar, while she ate almost all of them – or was, well, ill) somewhat endeared him to her, and she placed an elbow upon his shoulder, as if they were players on a high school soccer team or something, as they watched to the end the movie they still thought mediocre.

As the credits rolled – and Martin finally pressed the mute – Isabel thought she should say something to comfort him, in case he felt at fault.

"I bet you've had more exciting evenings," she said, to take the rap, though she knew – or at least suspected – she was unworthy of such punishment, a tiny residual doubt notwithstanding.

"Oh, hey," Martin said, after a long and tortured pause, direct expression clearly – along with other kinds of human interactions – an ongoing and excruciating trial for him, "it's you who had to . . . I mean, I hadn't been . . ." and that was the best he could do to grab back the ball of blame.

Then there was an even longer pause before, not able to look at her, he asked, "When was the first time you – you did it?" Isabel was surprised, even taken aback, by his inquiry. For a second, she didn't answer and so he took her silence as a rebuke and, "Sorry," he said, "maybe I shouldn't have . . ."

But that he had had the energy to ask her anything, had taken an initiative that wasn't to make up for a failing (as when he'd touched her) or express a negative emotion (as, at work, when he had once "mistakenly" deleted incoming data) so impressed her that she felt obligated to reply, if only to encourage him to continue.

"It was, well, in high school," she said, "at a boy I knew's house."

Slowly, he asked her another question about the encounter (which had been with Bailey Glynn, arts editor of the high school lit mag, the *Long Island Epiphany*), and then another, and each time she answered, because, as she did so, she sensed a commitment from and curiosity in him that she had never seen and did not want to quash, uncomfortable as she was revealing details which up till now had been known only to Bailey and herself.

"He undid my bra, and then we thought we heard his parents pull into the driveway, but it wasn't the case, and, strangely, that seemed to make him harder, and—"

"What did you do then?"

She told him about her first fumbling yet erotic experience with fellatio, distancing herself from the event by pretending to describe a movie she had seen and, accordingly, embellishing it here and there, which both allowed her less unease and increased his avidity, the almost entranced quality of his arousal (his eyes closed, his mouth slightly open) which grew more and more marked as she kept talking.

"And were you excited?"

"So excited."

As she reached the peak of her story, Martin began to undo his pants with great haste, as if he simply could not wait a moment longer. She was surprised by the strength and size of his erection now, as if he were another person, had a whole other body, when she talked to him like this. Before he could touch his penis, she did, and before she could touch it more than once, he came, so loudly and powerfully that he sounded as if he was in pain and had to place a hand on her arm to steady himself, as if he was afraid of what was happening, though this only made her excited and not concerned for him.

Afterward, Martin looked down and saw that his semen had shot the entire length of his bare leg and on to her couch, some of it even hitting the TV remote inches away. He said nothing, just rose to pull one, two, then three tissues from a nearby box and start to fastidiously clean up. Before he had finished, Isabel had tugged his hand toward her, pried the tissues loose from it, and placed it between her legs: he pushed three fingers inside her, and she held his hand there and came again, this time much more deeply and electrically than she had before, than she ever had, she later admitted only to herself.

Each briefly looked in the other's eyes, aware that both were alive in ways that were unknown to other people in the office, and that neither would have known if neither had exposed – sacrificed – something (he pride, she privacy); that both had done things that night and been rewarded, in other words, the opposite of how they spent their time at work. Then they looked away, each secretly knowing what would happen next.

Isabel and Martin didn't discuss or arrange it: speaking to each other was not their strong suit (especially not his). Yet the next day, after staring immobile at information on a screen before pressing a button to distribute it, when no one was passing their door, she quietly asked him what else he wanted to know about her, and he answered her question with another question – "What was the next time you, etc." – and she answered his question with an actual answer, and that made him ask another question, with an urgency he showed about nothing else (had maybe never shown about anything else), and she answered again, his excitement exciting her (her power to excite him exciting her), until he – "nonchalantly" – placed the base of his palm quickly against the large lump that had grown below his belt, and she naughtily brushed it once or twice with her elbow, and ended the exchange, Martin gasping and seeming almost lifted up in the air by the wild rush it afforded him. Then Isabel excused herself and went into the ladies' room where she locked herself in a stall and made herself come, too, which happened almost instantly and left her so sweaty and aromatic that she realized her "natural" deodorant didn't work and probably never had, she just never had known, for she had never tested it with enough effort.

As weeks went on, they got the routine down to a science, knew when to stop if they heard sounds in the hall, when to swivel away from each other, when to start up again. One day, Martin stayed out sick with a cold and called her from home. This was physically easier for her – Isabel only had to eyeball the hall and not physically disengage from him if the coast wasn't clear – yet it took some getting used to, it being more impersonal.

"What did he say about your tits?" he asked, after she had quietly described an event.

"That he liked them."

"That's all?"

"That they were big. That I had nice ones."

"Then what did he do?"

"He kissed around, then licked around, then bit around my nipples. He wouldn't suck them. He was tormenting me."

"Did your nipples get hard?"

"So hard."

"What did you do?"

"I begged him to suck them. And he said I'd have to wait."

"Were you wet?"

"So wet."

"What happened then?"

"He made me promise that I would swallow his come if he sucked my nipples."

"And what did you do?"

"I promised that I would."

"And did you?"

"Yes. Later."

"I really want to hear about that."

There was a brief pause on the other end of the line, as she heard only Martin's slow, slightly cold-congested breathing. Then, "I'll call you back," he said and hung up.

She made up the stories, of course, having long since exhausted her actual experiences, which she had fictionalized in the first place as to make them virtually unrecognizable. She saw herself as a kind of Sheherazade, though only vaguely aware of who that was. When Isabel looked up the name online, she saw that the analogy wasn't perfect but close enough to make her feel connected to an oral tradition, in a line of great raconteurs.

Yet after more weeks, this remained the only connection she could feel. Martin never stopped wanting to hear her "memories" (which she assumed he knew were padded with details picked up from porn films she saw online, actually had researched at home in her idle hours, the sites not being "safe for work", and then made less mechanical and cold when she offered them up as her own) but this remained the extent of their physical relationship. Soon he was not requesting to do it after work any more but only in the office, and didn't reciprocate by touching her (for she, being shyer, refused to have that done in public and still insisted on going to the ladies' room by herself, and then even stopped doing that). Isabel began to feel their actions were fading into another form of passivity, more work, in other words, a new and modern job, the pressing of a penis the same as that of a "send" button, etc.

It was around this time that their boss, Owen, requested her appearance in his office after five.

Isabel had spoken to Owen just two or three times – once when he assured her she hadn't caused Rita's heart attack, once when she rode the elevator with him after only he and not she had carried an umbrella in that morning's thunderstorm and she had tried to laugh off the water literally dripping from her hair and clothes and pooling on the marble floor of the car and he had smiled, politely, seeming, she thought, repelled, and another time she couldn't remember – he hadn't even hired her; it had been an obese woman named Cybil in Human Resources.

So she had been startled when Owen poked his head in her and Martin's office, only a few minutes after Martin had excused himself to clean up in the men's room. Owen had an open and expectant look, as if about to ask if she wanted anything at the store, he was making a run ("I'll fly if you buy," they used to say in college) but that couldn't be it, of course.

When she walked to his office later, it was with trepidation – an instinctive reaction to being summoned by someone in authority, she thought – but she also had a flickering hope that she was about to be fired, though if the cause was her office adventures with Martin, that might turn out to be embarrassing, maybe even featured on the evening news, then splashed all over the internet, where her parents could see it.

When she sat opposite him, though, Owen didn't mention Martin and only wanted her to do some special project on a freelance basis; he would understand if she were too busy.

"Busy?" She was unable to keep a tone of comic disbelief from her voice and immediately sorry about it. "I mean, no, I don't think so. All right. Thank you."

Isabel needed the money, after all – and she tuned out when Owen explained about the mild tax complications that "freelance" would mean, "estimated", or whatever. She concentrated instead on looking at Owen, who was forty-two but whom she thought was either thirty-five or fifty. He had a boyish, snub-nosed face surrounded by graying hair, reminding her of a modern painting in a gilded frame from another century. He didn't meet her eyes as he spoke yet what he said couldn't have been more simple, innocent, and non-incriminating. Was he avoiding something else of which he was ashamed? She didn't know. She had walked in wondering why he'd chosen her and left convinced it could have been her or someone else; maybe he'd just stopped by her office after counting to ten.

When Isabel got home, there was a message on her machine from Martin. In it, he implied an interest in hearing her talk over the phone that night, having apparently enjoyed it when he'd been ill, unlike Isabel, who'd had mixed feelings. Isabel meant to call him back, yet by the time she'd finished the assignment for Owen, it was midnight and too late. She'd completed the task in just one night, despite the "several" Owen had assumed it would take. Since it had been no more interesting than what she did at work – seemed more boring, actually, like spending a vacation in her home – Isabel was surprised by her diligence and went to sleep without comprehending it.

The next day, she politely demurred when Martin nodded suggestively at the empty hall during lunch hour. They had sometimes missed other opportunities – for instance, when they had had to attend day-long, company-wide meetings after which both confessed they had fantasized doing it in front of the entire workforce, which had fueled and made more exciting their next encounter. This was the first time Isabel had actually said or at least shaken her head no, and she could see the disappointment – which was deep – on Martin's face. At day's end, he waited for her to accompany him out, but Isabel simply said she would see him tomorrow.

"I'll call you?" he said, or asked, as if unsure whether he would or would be allowed to by her, it wasn't clear which.

As soon as he was gone, Isabel walked quickly to Owen's office, hoping he hadn't left for the night. She carried the work she had done, which she had printed out and placed neatly in a folder. She could have emailed it to him but wanted to deliver it in person, she didn't know why.

"Well, well," Owen said, impressed, using a way of talking that was older than his youngish face, as if his graying hair were talking or something, Isabel couldn't express it coherently to herself. "Thank you. I had no idea you'd do it so . . ."

Suddenly Owen couldn't finish the sentence – and the final word was almost certainly "fast" or "quickly" – he appeared too appreciative and that made him too emotional. Or was it something else? For whatever reason, his eyes filled with tears.

Standing before his desk, Isabel didn't know what to do. Had she somehow sensed this aspect of Owen – an instability – and complied with the job so quickly out of compassion? She was suddenly unaware of so much, though many things were presenting themselves. She only knew that something had been building in her, begun by her losing interest in – growing to resent really – Martin. Unintentionally, the older man had stepped into the spill of a searchlight Isabel had been shining around, and now she had stopped it; he had her full attention.

"May I close the door?" he asked, still choking up, and Isabel nodded, as if to say, please do.

When he retook his seat, Owen again spoke without looking at her, but occasionally met her eyes and glanced away, testing new waters of trust.

"My wife," he said, "I don't – I don't mean to put her down. She can't help it. I know depression is a disease, that's what the doctors say. I understand that. But she sleeps hours and hours a day – sometimes all day. I bring her books and newspapers – I brought her an easel with an expensive palette, for she used to paint. They all go unused. She's taken every pill invented and none has worked for more than a week. What am I supposed to do? Nothing? That's what it feels like she wants for me to do, not to leave her but to leave her be. How can I? She stays behind a closed door that seems as big as that space monolith in that movie where – oh, of course, you wouldn't know it, you're too young."

The idea of Isabel's age had stopped his confession, returned him to reality, and Owen swiveled to the side, seeming grateful that something had.

Isabel felt a bit offended. She had seen that movie, or at least part of it once, had heard of it, anyway, and besides, he was too young to have seen it originally, either; he wasn't that much older. In any case, she knew that in the only way that mattered, they were the same: Owen was a person going to waste, as she was.

"I do know," she blurted out, and thought she sounded even younger, a child asserting sophistication. It made him smile – mostly with his eyes, if that were possible, as he barely moved his mouth – and that hurt her even more.

Still, her youth meant something to her: Isabel waited for him to speak before continuing the conversation – not because he was her boss, exactly, because what he was going through was something she hadn't experienced, the depth of his despair was something she had never known. Wasn't that worthy of respect or at least silence? This wasn't about her impressing him, after all, though she wanted to, had to force herself not to keep trying, to make him know that she understood him, understood everything, even though she sensed she didn't.

But Owen wouldn't respond, so Isabel had no better idea than to leave. When he saw her start to go, he rose at the same time, actually making a decision, moving toward her as she moved to the door. He was faster than she, because he wanted to get where he was going more.

Owen stood before her, no longer on the verge of tears, as if feeling beyond what tears could tell her. He offered himself as a desperate applicant, without any other options, beyond all embarrassment.

"Please," he said. "Please. Use me."

At first, Isabel didn't know what he meant. Then she realized that she was fighting knowing and did not resist as he came closer, in fact placed her hands at his hips to help. Soon he was near enough to whisper, "Anything you want. All for you. Use me."

As he undressed her, he discouraged her doing anything in return, shaking his head or murmuring "no" when she as much as raised a hand to touch him. She felt she was being prepared – anointed, that was the word – for some ceremony, saw herself in a Roman movie scene, a princess stripped, bathed, and placed naked under robes by female slaves – though, in that case, they would be careful not to caress her, not wishing to offend, they would be killed if they were caught, and, moaning, Owen was stroking and kissing every inch of her he could, after he removed her one good white shirt (which she had feared that morning looked as un-ironed as it was), then her bra, her skirt and, as he placed her with her help upon his – slightly cold – leather couch, her underwear (it had been too warm that morning to wear tights).

Still fully dressed, he moved, a supplicant, down her, and she spread her legs, not sure but daring to assume that's what he wanted. Then he said softly but she was almost sure, "I want to lick the alphabet on your clit," and that's what he did, speaking each letter before he formed it (with surprising efficiency) upon and across her, something she suspected he had seen in a porn film, but a good and imaginative one that she had missed. By the time he licked the three lines for the stems or the arms or whatever you call them of the "E", she came, feeling more naked even than she was, though this was how he'd wanted her, she was only obeying him by allowing him to submit, or something.

Then he lay his head against her thigh, breathing with what seemed relief that he had actually had an effect on anyone, made an impact, that he might be remembered by someone for doing something. She didn't dare to reach down and touch his head (the gray hair of which she now decided she liked, without knowing why), though it was her impulse to at least acknowledge how good he'd made her feel. Soon he had recovered and was undressing himself, moving her gently (again with her subtle assistance) so that she lay beneath him. "So big and beautiful," she thought he whispered though she wasn't positive and couldn't say "what?" because that would be weird, given what was going on, though she was curious, wanted to hear the compliment. She realized he already had a condom, was taking care of everything, was weirdly adept at assisting, her sexual valet in a sense, her "man" as they called it in old comedies about butlers, and the word had so many meanings now, she thought, as he entered her, and she realized she was sort of – babbling – to herself, because she was so nervous and so aroused. As he pushed into her, he knew what she wanted though he hardly knew her; he was catering to her, customizing her account, as it were, her AOL or whatever, in bed. Soon she stopped feeling guilty about giving nothing and decided to go along, for that's what he wanted, to enjoy being on the receiving end, accepting now an action in a way it had never been before.

That he was acting for himself and for her – that he was aware of what effect each push was having, that her pleasure caused his – this was something new. She thought of someone rowing and how the digging of his oar into the ocean moved his boat, rippled the water, and built the muscle in the rower's arm, a seamless situation, and now she was the water or merely made of water, and when he pushed into her, he was, well, not like the oar exactly but like an entire man disappearing into a wave, which was her, or she was made of water, or anyway, she now knew what "so excited" meant and it was different from what she had pretended it meant with Martin, or to put it simply, it now meant something and not nothing, as it had before, when it had been something from a porn film, and bullshit.

"Oh, my God," she said, helplessly, as he pushed particularly hard, and pressed the front of his abdomen (which she noticed was flatter than Martin's, despite his being so much older, fifteen or forty-five years, though she had only briefly glimpsed Martin's soft stomach through his unzipped and partly pulled down pants) against her clitoris, and she thought of a dolphin, as if she was still in an ocean, and how it butted against you or something when it liked you and you swam with it; he (or maybe just his erection) was like a strong and slippery dolphin, rock hard but really responsive, and making that little chirping radar sound, which she now realized was coming from her own open mouth.

"It's good, it's good," she said, and again she hadn't meant to say anything at all.

Then, suddenly, he stopped moving, obviously could move no more without ending everything, which meant that she was on, it was up to her; and instinctively she wrapped around him, from the inside and outside: outside with her arms – and inside she had never known she had such flexibility, like when you realize you can bend a finger back all the way without breaking it, only this was better, had never known that she could be tender with a grown man, not just her baby sister or her old kitty cat Monkey, kissing and kissing them – she was passionate, that's what she was, and why had it been embarrassing to say before now?

Then coming with him felt like (she could not stop comparing things; it made her feel safer to do it, put things in perspective so she wouldn't feel she had entered an environment alien and disorienting – it was still her own life, she had not gone insane, you know?) coming with him felt like that trick where the magician pulls out a tablecloth and all the plates stay put: and she was the tablecloth, the table, and the plates. And he came, too, immediately after, or actually during, though she suspected he'd started a little ahead of her, could feel him doing that pulsing that, of course, came from his heart and had been weaker in her hand when it came from Martin; and Owen's sound was bigger: Martin's was like air going out of a balloon and Owen's was like one bursting, a whole float in, say, the Puerto Rican Day Parade: or he was a terrorist exploding himself along with everything else, and she had made him into one; and that was so exciting that it made her come again, or maybe it was just the end of her first orgasm, an aftershock, like they say there are in earthquakes.

"I can't stop," she said, and perhaps that was another trick, because she wanted it to continue and thought saying that might be the spell to make it so.

Then he placed his lips against her temple, where her hair was wet and slightly stuck to the area above her ear. Would he say he loved her? She didn't think he did; she didn't love him; she didn't fool herself; she wasn't a baby. Maybe she wanted him to say it so she could feel superior, could feel less than he and so more in control.

(She had read once that the young are more powerful in young – old affairs, because, well, they live longer. But what about her uncle's second wife who was twenty years younger and who died first? Who was more powerful then? Her uncle, obviously, who was still alive.) Soon she didn't care about creating distance: she found herself kissing him, too, his cheek, which was not unshaven but getting there, with the night coming on; things were changing, growing all the time, and now she knew it, this was proof.

Her boss had wanted to work for her, and that was what he had done; he had not been lying, been, what was the word, rhetorical: and that made her want to serve him – not serve, that was subordinate and not what she meant – to give to him, to know what he knew, to get pleasure by giving pleasure, to feel the connection or current, the wet finger in the spilled liquid that was then stuck into a socket, only good and shocking, not bad.

She took him into her mouth, even though he protested, weakly, that this was not for him but only for her, tried to insist and sincerely, not coyly, not to get what he pretended not to want. But she wouldn't listen and soon, her breasts intentionally squashed against his leg, she kissed at the gray pubic hairs she had not noticed on him before (and which, for reasons she could not articulate, excited her in a new and discombobulating way), and it was only seconds after she started, sort of forced him to experience it, had hardly moved her mouth on him, was just getting ready to do her stuff, or figure out what stuff would do the trick for him, that he came, and more than melting in her mouth (as crass girls in college called it), seemed to completely disappear, his head tilting back, his eyes closing, his arms laid flat, his hands opening, as if going under in that ocean again – or, better, being pushed off a cliff by coming; it almost scared her: she suddenly knew how lonely he had been and yet he hadn't used it against her but for her, had wanted to deny himself until she wouldn't let him any more (or was the denial his way of getting over the guilt of sleeping with a young girl who was his employee? If he got nothing, in other words, what had he done wrong? He would be a kind of sex saint).

But then she didn't care what was his way to explain it to himself was just glad that she had given him this, given him something – God knows she gave him nothing at the job – and soon he seemed to reappear, to float up to the surface again and exist, and she moved to lie against him, and he buried his face in her sweaty neck, maybe ashamed of how much he had shown of himself, uneasy about how much she knew him now, though she liked knowing him – he knew her, so why not? – secretly wanted to know him more, to know everything, even though she suspected that it would be impossible, would probably never happen, that this was as close as they would ever get, this instant, this afternoon.

Isabel didn't see Owen often after this. Only once did they meet in his house, when his wife was away. While Isabel was there, the door to the bedroom stayed closed, and she could imagine how its dark (was it oak?) wood might have to him a vexing and mysterious power – intergalactic or timeless or whatever it had been in the film – if always in that position. They used a den but mostly stayed in the bathroom, where he washed her slowly in the shower, aroused as he always was by fulfilling a function, being employed, even if the need was one he had created in her, for she did need him now, or wanted him, had had trouble waiting for him, anyway, from the time they entered his home. Otherwise, they met in his office whenever they could, for he had obligations, and – without saying so, without saying much of anything – they both regarded their time together as a gift, could not be greedy for more, just had to be grateful.

Isabel barely spoke to Martin now. Her duties seemed less stultifying, filled as they were with subtext, the numbers on her screen changed into symbols of longing found on another planet or formed in the future and fascinating; but Martin seemed even more frustrated. Isabel could hear him sighing from where he sat, and she believed it was both for her benefit and a genuine expression of dismay. She was sorry for him but not guilty, no matter how much she thought she ought to be.

One dusk, both were alone in the elevator going down, though she usually avoided exiting the building with him. They rode in silence until, a few floors from the lobby, Martin spoke a rare completed sentence.

"I know that you go with him," he said.

Isabel started, and the little bell rang as they hit the ground floor, seeming to underline his remark. She didn't respond, only walked quickly ahead and away from him; but she knew that things were different, had entered a new phase, she could feel it, and he had made it happen.

The next day in the office, Martin kept on talking to her – not even whispering as others went by – in this same clear voice he had either always had or acquired for the occasion, feeling he had no alternative.

"Why don't you tell me about doing it with him?" he said.

Isabel didn't answer, just kept looking as if interested at her screen, though she knew it was absurd to try and fool him in this way.

"I want to hear about you and him," he said, and his voice conveyed at once the sincere needs to please himself and punish her, which was new; before he may have been selfish but not unkind.

Isabel turned to see him, and he didn't avoid her, kept staring at her, as he had been the whole time. Her response was reflexive, though this reflex was also new.

"I won't," she said, and saw him appear shocked, not because she had officially ended something between them, she didn't think, but because he was being denied something obviously available: brand-new information that would no doubt be exciting and could have been given to him easily, as if newspapers were being thrown from a boy's bike on to everybody's lawn but his in the days when that's how people got current events.

As Isabel pushed by him to leave early (being privileged by her association with Owen, she did not need to explain herself), she realized that Martin had always thought her stories were true, and this made her feel differently about him, though in what way she wasn't sure.

For a few days, to Isabel's relief, they sat in virtual silence. Finally, Martin addressed her on their way into a meeting, among a crowd in which it would be hard for her to reply.

"I told her," he said.

"What do you mean?" she was made to whisper back. "Who?"

"His wife. About you and him. I left a message on their machine."

Isabel stopped, bumped by another employee trying to get past. Waiting to be alone with him in the hall, she reached out and grabbed Martin, got hold of his shirt, which she nearly ripped and which he yanked back, annoyed, so she wouldn't. They stood there staring at each other, Isabel nearly shaking with rage both at him and her own inarticulateness; it was as if, with a few words, he had taken everything away.

Martin didn't look triumphant; he seemed shaken, even shocked by her reaction, then grew apologetic and stammered, reverting to his old, unsocialized self.

"I–I–I had to do something," he said, at last: a way to explain.

This was right before the weekend. On Monday, Isabel arrived late, and Martin was already there. He sat faced away, his complexion pale, his chin in his palm, the computer screen before him blank. Was he sick again? she wondered. Or just afraid to acknowledge her?

Soon she noticed a general absence of people around. When she looked out in the hall, many doors were shut, others open to reveal no one and a briefcase or bag hastily, even indifferently tossed in a corner or on a chair. It was like a science fiction film in which a plague breaks out – or a bomb drops – that kills people but not things. She wondered if a meeting had been called without her knowing; but now that she knew Owen, she was always in the loop.

Isabel walked out and, after a few steps, began passing others. All were either heading toward Owen's office or returning from having been there. There was a feeling of people drifting to and from a crime scene or a free outdoor concert at which some were turned away. Isabel could not remember there ever being this kind of purposeful movement in the office, such urgency, concern and curiosity. Had the company been sold? Owen been fired? One woman was in tears. Isabel heard someone say, "I can't believe it," and another, "They found him in his house," and a third, somewhat snottily, "I would have thought it would have been his wife."

Isabel began running through the hall, her feeling of fear in action, and soon was nearly flying. She knew that if Owen's door was closed, it would be bad news – or would it be if his door was open and people were in his office crying the way she was not yet allowing herself to cry?

Now she was running faster than anyone ever should inside, with too much speed to be contained in the office, as if she were about to burst out of it at any instant, and it was true: she would be, in a way, exploded into life by death as soon as she rounded the corner at the end of the hall.

Perfect Timing

Kristina Wright

She should have called before she drove over to the university. Charlotte tapped her nails on the steering wheel as Henry's phone rang. She hoped he wasn't in a meeting. Or teaching a class. She had been so preoccupied with getting her weekly reports finished and getting out of the library that the thought hadn't crossed her mind to make sure he was available.

Finally, after four rings, he answered.

"I'm in the faculty parking lot. Last row by the trees," she said, by way of a greeting. "Can you meet me?"

He sighed, but there was a hint of amusement in his voice. "I'm in the middle of student advisement meetings."

Neither his reluctance nor the overcast sky would deter her. "Can't you take an early lunch break? Please?"

"You make it difficult for me to refuse," he said, his voice low and intimate. She imagined him standing in his office, looking out of the window for her car. "It's hard to think about you down there in the car wearing a dress –"

"Skirt."

"Wearing a skirt, likely with no panties . . ."

"No panties," she acknowledged.

He sighed again, the resigned sound of a man who knew a woman would not be put off. "I'll be there in twenty minutes."

"Hurry. Otherwise, I might have to come up there and seduce you in your office."

"Been there, done that, love," he chuckled. "Probably not the best idea with students coming in and out today."

"Well, then, you should get down here before I'm tempted. I have to get back to the library soon."

"Yes, ma'am," he said, obediently.

Charlotte grinned, triumphant. "I promise I'll make it worth your while."

"You always do."

Charlotte closed her phone and rested her head on the seat. Rain threatened at any moment and the wind whipped the blossoms from the trees and shrubs that ringed the campus, scattering them on the wind like spring snowflakes. Birds chased each other from tree to tree, mating season in full swing despite the inclement weather. A fat raindrop plopped on the windshield and Charlotte glanced toward Henry's gray building, debating whether she should pick him up at the curb. But no, that might draw attention to them and the last thing she wanted was an audience. Thankfully, it was spring break and most of the students and faculty weren't on campus.

"April showers bring May flowers," she whispered as she watched a bushy-tailed brown squirrel pursue another up a tree trunk as raindrops splattered across her field of vision.

She shifted impatiently and pressed the soft fabric of her skirt between her thighs. She was wet already, wet from the anticipation of making love to Henry in the parking lot. She'd had a thirty-minute drive from the library to think about what she would do to him once she got here. It had never really been a question whether he would join her; he had promised that whenever she called, he would come. Quite literally, she mused.

The control made her feel a little giddy with feminine power – but it was the anticipation of having Henry buried inside her in mere moments while the rest of the campus went on about their morning that was an arousing, panty-dampening thought. If she had been wearing panties, that is.

Even sooner than he had promised, Henry slipped into the passenger seat of her car, slightly out of breath from his mad dash through the light rain. Water spots darkened his sage green shirt and his brown hair stood up in wet spikes where he had dragged his fingers through it, accentuating the flecks of silver at his temples. "Ten o'clock in the morning is a bit early for lunch, don't you think?"

"But if I waited until lunchtime, someone would be sure to see us."

"Good point," he said. He leaned over to cup her face in his damp palm and give her a kiss. "And I am getting hungry. It's been weeks since I had your luscious body against me."

Charlotte inched up her skirt to bare an expanse of stocking-clad thigh. "Would you like to see what's on the menu today?"

Henry loosened his tie. "Oh, I think I'll just have the special."

She angled over the gearshift and into his lap. It was no small feat, given the length of her skirt and tight fit of the narrow bucket seat, but within moments she was straddling him, her skirt hiked up around her hips.

"This would be better with me on the bottom," she said. "But I don't think it would work."

Henry slid his hands under her bunched skirt and fingered the lace tops of her sheer black stockings. "You could probably get me to do anything you want right now," he said, stroking the bare skin above the lacy bands of nylon. "You look like the clichéd sexy librarian. Nice touch. Just for me?"

She leaned over and nibbled his neck above his collar, breathing in the spicy scent of his aftershave. "Of course. All for you, darling."

He moved his hand to the juncture of her thighs. She squirmed against him, silently urging him to touch her. "This is my favorite magical spot," he said as his fingers found her wetness. "You're already excited, bad girl. Have you been thinking about me?"

She smirked. If only he knew. Wriggling against his rain-chilled fingers, she gasped, "I could barely keep from touching myself before you got here."

He cupped her pussy in his hand, his thumb stroking her swollen clit in slow, lazy circles. "Really?"

She kissed him, sucking his bottom lip into her mouth. It wasn't the most comfortable position to be in, but she was too aroused to care. "Mmm-hmm."

His fingers delved deeper, parting her silken wetness as his thumb kept moving on her clit. "Well, I'm sorry for keeping you waiting then."

"You're here now," she murmured against his mouth. "That's all that matters to me."

Tangling her fingers in his damp hair, she moved against his hand, showing him the rhythm. He groaned into her mouth as he played with her, driving her to the edge of any rational thought. It would be better if she came while he was inside her, but he was just too good with his hands. Now all she could think about was getting off.

She slid up on his lap a couple of inches to give him some more room, enough so that the top of her head was now above him and her breasts were in his face. With his free hand, he undid the ties of her pale yellow wrap blouse. His mouth found one of her hard nipples through the fabric of her bra and he sucked the tender bit of flesh in the same rhythm he stroked her clit. Charlotte pressed her breast to his mouth, every muscle taut as she clutched the car seat behind his head.

"Oh, oh yes," she moaned as he moved his mouth to the other nipple. He suckled it hard through the fabric until it stood in rigid attention against the fabric. Her bra was wet now with his sucking, but she didn't care. "I can feel that in my pussy."

He murmured his pleasure as he slid a finger inside her. Her skin had warmed his fingers and she moaned softly, eyes closed, giving herself over to the feeling. Her nostrils flared, smelling not only Henry's aftershave now, but also her own arousal. It was an intoxicating scent and, as he pushed a second finger inside her, she felt her body tighten. He slid his fingers in deep, then slowly withdrew them to her opening before pushing inside her once more. He curved them forward, finding her G-spot, and did it again.

The feeling was so intense she nearly told him to stop. But she knew if she could just take it for a few more strokes, he would make her come. So instead of pulling back, she made little thrusting motions with her hips, giving him what he was after. She bit her bottom lip, feeling her orgasm like a knot inside her, slowly loosening. Warmth coursed through her, starting low in her belly and spreading outward.

"Oh god," she whimpered, tightening her pussy around his fingers.

Henry kept up his steady rhythm, using his fingers to coax her toward that elusive orgasm. She went still on him, straining toward inevitable release. As if sensing how close she was, Henry rolled her clit under his thumb as he stroked her sweet spot. She cried out, oblivious to her surroundings, feeling a gush of liquid as her orgasm washed over her.

"Yes, that's it," he murmured against the swell of her breast. "Come for me."

And she did. Wet heat radiated outward from her swollen clit, drowning her in sensations as she rocked her hips on Henry's fingers. She bent her head over him, pressing his hand between their bodies as her body throbbed with her release.

"Yes, yes," Henry whispered. "You are so beautiful when you come."

"Inside me," she managed to gasp as she struggled to undo his belt in the tight confines of the car seat. "I want you inside me. Now!"

Henry withdrew his fingers from her still throbbing pussy and assisted her in her quest. He winced as she dragged his zipper down. "Damn, love, try not to rip it off or it won't be any use to either of us."

A fit of giggles struck her then, the incongruity of the situation striking her as funny. "Oh, don't worry, I always have a spare handy."

"What?"

"Just a joke," she said. "Fuck me."

Aftershocks of her orgasm still rippled through her as Henry finally freed his erection from his trousers and angled it inside her. Suddenly, there was nothing humorous at all about her situation. She gasped, instinctively tilting her hips to accommodate his length. He was all the way inside her and there was no need to go slow because she was already so very wet.

"Oh god," he groaned, giving a short quick thrust. "You feel so damned good."

She pushed back against him, feeling his cock go so deep it almost hurt. She felt full and swollen, as wet as she had ever been. Being on top gave her the control of their rhythm and she went slowly, enjoying the fullness and how she could feel every inch of him gliding inside her. She leaned back in his lap, letting him slide out a bit, then forward, pressing her breasts to his face. He clutched at her hips like a man overboard, seeking solid land.

"Oh, love," he moaned against her breasts. "You're driving me out of my mind."

She'd already had one orgasm, but she could feel a second one building. His fingers had felt nice, but this sensation of engorgement couldn't be caused by anything but his cock. She thrust a little harder against him, her clit rubbing against his pelvic bone. She was so wet and her range of motion was limited, it didn't seem as if there could be enough friction for Henry to reach orgasm. But a few more thrusts and he was gripping her ass in his hands, guiding her faster on his rigid length. She tightened her pussy around him and he sucked in his breath, his cock twitching in instant response.

"Come inside me," she whispered in his ear. "I want to feel you coming deep inside me."

His cock felt impossibly large as she thrust down on him. She could tell he was close to finishing by the way he went still against her. She rotated her hips on him and he all but roared as he started to come, jerking against her so hard she bumped her head on the roof of the car.

She had been so caught up in making him come that she hadn't realized just how close she was to her own orgasm. She kept up those little thrusting motions, dragging her aroused clit over the patch of hair above his cock until she was pushed over the edge into her own climax. She rode him like that until her sensitive clit couldn't take any more.

Collapsing on top of him, her arms hanging down the back of the seat, she gasped and giggled as her pussy clenched around his slowly shrinking erection.

"Holy hell," she whimpered. "Who would have thought doing it in the car would be so hot?"

Her breasts muffled his reply. "No kidding."

Suddenly conscious that they were in the faculty parking lot and the car windows were completely fogged, she reluctantly slid back into her seat. There was so much wetness between her thighs and on his lower stomach, she didn't know who had made a bigger mess. She suspected it was her.

"Hand me my panties," she said. "They're in the glove box."

He chuckled as he handed her the black lace thong. "You're just going to make a mess of them."

"Better them than the back of my skirt," she said ruefully as she shimmied into her panties and smoothed her wrinkled skirt into place. She looked over at Henry sprawled in the car seat with a satisfied smile on his face and his flaccid cock glistening against his pale stomach. He was an even bigger mess than she was and she frowned. "You can't go inside like that."

He looked down. "No mistaking what I've been up to, is there?"

"There should be tissues in there, too," she said.

He fumbled through the glove box until he found the packet of travel tissues and cleaned himself up as best he could. Moments later, shirt tucked in and pants fastened, he still looked like the cat that ate the cream. The noticeable wet spot on the front of his pants didn't help matters at all.

"Don't worry," he said, following the direction of her gaze. "I have a pair of pants in the office."

"Keep extra clothes at work, do you?"

He grinned. "You never know when a beautiful young woman is going to offer herself up in exchange for an A."

"Always prepared." She smiled at him. "You're quite the boy scout."

He stroked a hand through her mussed hair. "You're not bad yourself, love. I'm wiped out."

"Hmm. Well, don't think I'm letting you off the hook that easily," she said with mock sternness. "You never know when I'll be wanting a repeat performance."

"Sounds promising." He retied his tie and adjusted the collar, using the vanity mirror to guide him. "Not that this wasn't a nice surprise, but when can we spend a little more time together?"

"I'll give you a call later." Though she was completely satiated, Charlotte couldn't help but give him a teasing smile. "Tennis tomorrow, maybe? I'll make you sweat to get me into bed."

"I love a challenge," he said, leaning over to press a kiss to her forehead before he slipped out of the car.

She laughed as she watched him sprint across the parking lot. At some point during their lovemaking, the sun had broken through the clouds and the squirrels had returned to their frolicking. She waited until he was gone from sight before she pulled out of the lot and headed back to the library. She was going to need an energy drink before the day was over.

"I need you," Ian growled.

"That's sweet, but I'm going out with the girls tonight," Charlotte said as she drove through the heavy downtown traffic. "Remember?"

"Ah, right, I forgot it was girls' night," Ian said. "I'm on call this weekend, but as long as there isn't a five-alarm fire, maybe we can do something tomorrow."

Charlotte hesitated. "Well, I told Henry I'd play tennis with him tomorrow. I haven't seen him in weeks."

"Fine, fine, far be it for me to come between you and your old professor. How is Grampa, anyway?"

Charlotte found a parking spot on the street and maneuvered into it one-handed. "Don't be mean. Henry is barely fifty and he's in great shape."

"But I want my girl to myself," Ian said. "I guess I'll have you on Sunday."

"You're a darling," Charlotte said, and meant it. "Why don't you stay over tonight? I'll be in late, but I'll wake you when I get home and you can *have* me then."

"Oh, really," Ian's voice reflected his interest. "It's that time, hmm?"

Charlotte checked her lipstick in the vanity mirror and smiled at her reflection. She looked happy. She *was* happy – and hopeful. "Well, yes, but I'd still want you to stay over."

"Uh-huh," Ian said, not sounding at all convinced. "Well, then, have a good time with the girls and hurry home."

Charlotte disconnected and smoothed her skirt before leaving the car. Henry wasn't the only one who kept a change of clothes at work. She now wore a shimmery silver blouse with a red skirt. Red was Terrence's favorite color.

Melissa and Wendy were already waiting at the bar for her inside the trendy bar Fringe. The décor was disco-chic and Charlotte's silver blouse glinted in the light reflected by the mirrored tiles embedded in the walls.

Melissa handed her a dirty martini and leaned in close to be heard over the house music. "I didn't think you were going to make it. Is Ian peeved?"

"Oh no," Charlotte said, scanning the growing crowd in the club. "He's staying over and I promised to wake him up when I get home."

"You've got that man wrapped around your little finger."

Wendy laughed. "He's not the only one." She tilted her head toward the opposite side of the club. "Here comes your little boytoy."

Charlotte followed the direction of her friend's gaze and felt her pulse jump. At six-foot-four, with a body of lean planes and sculpted muscle, Terrence was hardly little – nor was he anyone's boytoy. He was, however, barely out of college, a fact that held more appeal than Charlotte could ever explain. She had met him when he'd come to the library to do research for his senior thesis. He had kept coming back after graduation. He was a lazy, but brilliant, music student with hands that could play her like a finely tuned instrument. As he strolled across the room, oblivious to the predatory looks he was getting from women of all ages, a shiver went up her spine.

"Hey, babe," he whispered in her ear as he pulled her into a tight hug. "Long time no see."

"I suspect you've been staying busy."

"I do all right," he said with a lazy shrug. "But I've missed you."

Wendy and Melissa made themselves scarce, giggling behind their hands as they left the two alone. Terrence knew the effect he had on women, with his exotic features and often insolent expression. It amused him to turn women into quivering, stuttering schoolgirls. Charlotte let him think she could take him or leave him – which she could – and that made her attractive to him.

"Want to get out of here?" There was no subterfuge with Terrence, no hidden agenda. It was one of the things she liked best about him.

"Impatient, sweetie?"

He threw an arm around her shoulders and leaned in. "Impatient to be inside you," he said. "I told you I've missed you."

A naughty thought took hold in her imagination. She took Terrence's hand and pulled him toward a dark hallway. She led him into the women's restroom off the kitchen area where harried kitchen staff put together heavy appetizers to complement the cocktails.

"What are you up to?"

Charlotte closed and locked the restroom door behind him before turning on the light. "What do you think?"

She didn't give him a chance to respond. Pressing him up against the door, she wrapped her arms around his neck and pulled his head down for a fierce kiss. She parted his lips with the tip of her tongue, deepening the kiss with the intention of distracting him from their surroundings. He tasted of tequila and the sharp tang taste reminded her of other things. She knew she had him when she hooked her leg around his hip and rubbed against him. He groaned softly, gripping her ass in his hands as he pulled her up hard against him. She could feel him beginning to stiffen and whimpered low in her throat.

He pulled back, a little breathless from their kissing. "You are wicked."

She fumbled with his belt, laughing softly. "Let me show you just how wicked I can be."

"I really don't think this is a good idea."

Having managed to get his belt unbuckled, Charlotte was not about to stop now. She proceeded to unfasten his trousers, noticing Terrence's cock did not share his doubt about her naughty intentions. His cock was shaped like his beautiful fingers – long and smooth. She felt her own body respond to his arousal and clenched her thighs together.

"Maybe I can change your mind," she said, thankful for her thigh high stockings as she slipped to her knees on the dirty tile floor.

Above her, Terrence's dark eyes went wide. "What are you up to?"

She pulled his cock free from his pants and underwear and kissed the engorged tip. "What does it look like?"

"It looks like you're a very nasty girl."

Wrapping her hand around the length of him, she looked up into his eyes. "Oh, you have no idea."

She held his cock in her hand and licked his shaft from the tip to the base and back again. His sharp intake of breath turned her on, made her want to tease him long and slow. Unfortunately, she knew they didn't have that kind of time before someone came knocking on the door to use the restroom, but that didn't mean she couldn't tease him a little bit.

Looking up at him, she licked the ridge of his cock again. He threw his head back against the door and closed his eyes as she took him inside her mouth, cradling the broad head in the hollow of her tongue. He groaned softly, tangling his fingers in her long dark hair. She didn't move, didn't suck, just held him there in her mouth as she looked up at him. Finally, his eyes opened and he looked down at her, his gaze unfocused.

"Please, babe," he said hoarsely.

That was all she needed. She took him deeper into her mouth, sucking him to the back of her throat before sliding off him. She went back down again, as far as she could, sucking him in rhythm to the muffled throb of the music beyond the door. When he was slick with her saliva, she used her hands to stroke his shaft as she sucked, slow and steady, until he was reflexively pumping into her mouth.

Reaching under his cock, she cupped his velvety balls in one hand. When she gave them a gentle tug, he gasped and bumped his head against the door.

"Oh hell, Char." His fingers clutched at her hair. "You're driving me out of my mind."

She swirled her tongue around the head of his cock, tasting his arousal, before pulling away. Much as she would have liked to finish him with her mouth, that wasn't in her plan tonight. She couldn't help but smile at his grumble of disappointment when she stood up. She stroked his cock as she reached up to kiss him.

"I need you," she said. "Please."

He kissed her hard, thrusting against the palm of her hand. "Anything you want, babe."

A sense of urgency came over her, not only because they were in the public restroom and she could hear voices not far away, but because she ached to feel him inside her. She pulled up her skirt and turned to face the counter. Thrusting her bottom out, she looked at him over her shoulder.

"Fuck me, Terrence. Fuck me hard."

He didn't hesitate. Pulling her cherry red panties to the side, he was balls deep inside her in one smooth motion. She arched her back and whimpered, biting her lip to keep from screaming at the sudden, shocking fullness.

Guiding her hip with one hand, he caught her long hair up in the other hand. She met his lust-filled gaze in the mirror as he pulled her hair hard enough to make her arch her neck. They were both a little out of control now. She knew it and knew the risks – and she didn't care.

"Yes, yes, yes," she gasped as she met his steady thrusts. She closed her eyes, lost in the intense feeling of him deep inside her.

"Open your eyes," he said roughly. "Look at me."

She did as he said, staring at him in the mirror as he drove into her. This was her favorite sexual position, being taken from behind, because his cock hit her G-spot in just the right way to give her mind-blowing orgasms. She liked the feeling of his lean body covering hers, the way he pulled her hair that sent shivers down her spine. The tables were turned now – she wasn't the dominant older woman any longer – she felt feminine and helpless, completely at his mercy. But now, the mirror seemed to add another layer of intimacy to their lovemaking.

She couldn't hide behind her curtain of hair, couldn't escape his dark, knowing gaze as he moved his hand up to tweak her nipple through her flimsy blouse. She tried to tuck her chin against her chest, feeling incredibly vulnerable all of a sudden, but Terrence gave her hair another tug so that she had no choice but to look up.

"Watch me, babe," he said, his voice low as he thrust into her wetness. "Watch me while I'm inside you."

What had started out as a playful, seductive game had become something else. She felt out of control, wanting him to be rougher with her, to pinch her nipples harder, to drive his cock into her until she screamed. She knew they didn't have much time, but she wanted to strip off her clothes and let him fuck her senseless. She gripped the edge of the sink and tried not to cry out as he withdrew his cock to the tip and then slammed into her. Over and over again, bumping against that sensitive spot inside her, he fucked her until she could feel her juices trickling down the insides of her thighs.

She whimpered softly, biting the inside of her mouth because the temptation to scream was almost unbearable. Not that anyone would hear her over the club music, of course. Terrence was silent and stoic, only his heavy-lidded eyes giving away his arousal. He had been so turned on by her going down on him she expected him to finish inside her at any moment, but now he seemed capable of going on like this for hours. If only they had hours.

"I'm not coming until you do," he said, as if reading her mind.

She whimpered again, clenching her pussy around his cock. She wanted to come, but she was distracted by the sound of the voices and music and Terrence's penetrating stare. She closed her eyes once more, feeling like she needed to close off one sense so she could concentrate on what he was doing to her body. She focused on the sensation of his cock gliding into her, the way her body clung to him as he slowly withdrew before pushing back inside. She arched her back a little more, feeling his cock angle down.

"Right there," she gasped.

He thrust into her, faster now, pulling her hair taut until she felt like a bowstring humming with tension. She reached the breaking point as he curved over her, whispering in her ear, "Come for me, babe."

She couldn't help it, she let out a loud, lingering moan as her orgasm washed over her. She opened her eyes, meeting his eyes in the mirror so he could see what he had done to her. He watched her as he continued to fuck her through her orgasm, sweat glistening at his fine-boned temple.

"Yes, oh god," she gasped, feeling as if she were being turned inside out. "Terrence!"

Terrence made a sound low in his throat and went still against her. Her pussy rippled along the length of his engorged cock and, with one hard thrust that elicited another soft moan from her, he was coming, too. Eyes closed, he pumped into her a few times before going still again. He leaned over her back, his damp forehead against her cheek when she turned her head.

"Oh my. That was nice," was all she could manage to say.

She felt, rather than heard, his rumble of laughter. "That's one way to describe it," he said, nipping her earlobe. "You really *are* wicked."

"Yes, I am," she whispered.

Still feeling the lingering tremors of her orgasm, she became acutely aware of their risky position. Reluctantly, she shifted beneath him. His cock slid out of her and she felt empty. Wetness streaked down her inner thighs and she met his gaze in the mirror, smiling contritely.

"I need to clean up," she said. "Think you can sneak out while I make myself presentable?"

Terrence's laugh was pure masculine satisfaction. "You are perfectly presentable. You just look as if you've been well fucked."

She shifted her gaze to her own face and realized he was right. Her hair was mussed and her cheeks were flushed. Her dark red lipstick was smeared and she was fairly certain she'd left some behind on Terrence's cock. Her eyes sparkled in a way that suggested she had a very delicious secret – which she did. She shook her head. "Well, I'll do the best I can."

Terrence straightened his clothes and tucked his still-damp cock back into his trousers. "I don't think it'll be a late night for me. I'm wiped."

"Oh, poor baby," she said. "Every woman in the club will be disappointed to see you go."

Terrence gave her a tired, teasing grin. "I only care about the woman who just came on my cock."

She didn't really believe that, of course, but it was sweet of him to say so. Terrence was still young and wild and unlikely to settle for one woman when he could have three, but he had good manners. "That was lovely, darling."

He listened at the door before turning the lock. "Give me a call, babe. It's been too long and I'd like to do this properly sometime soon."

"I will. Promise."

Charlotte smiled as he slipped out, giving her a rakish wink as he went. She locked the door behind him and met her own smudged eyes in the mirror. "See you in four weeks, darling boy," she whispered as she set about taming her hair back into place. "Maybe."

Charlotte awoke at dawn, naked, and cuddled against Ian's warm, bare chest. She felt a pleasant kind of soreness through her entire body which seemed to radiate from between her thighs. Sighing contentedly, she tucked in close to Ian and breathed in his clean, masculine scent.

Just as she started to drift off again, she felt his hand shift from her hip to between her thighs. She squirmed, thinking he was still asleep by the sound of his steady breathing. Then his fingers began a gentle probing that let her know he was awake – and wanting her.

Silently, she shifted until she was lying on her back, still nestled against his muscular shoulder. He touched her gently, parting the lips of her pussy with his fingers. She wasn't aroused yet, but she knew his soft touches would get her there fast. Sighing, she spread her thighs so he could continue his exploration.

He rested one finger at her opening as he cupped her mound in his warm palm. He gently squeezed her, letting just the tip of his finger slip inside her. She gasped at the dual sensations and pushed her pelvis up to meet his touch.

Sunshine streamed through the half-closed blinds, casting dappled light across their bed and making his reddish blond hair look like spun gold. The quiet was soothing, with only the soft sounds of her sighs and the rustle of the bed linens. Charlotte could feel her thigh muscles tensing in anticipation of his touch and she forced herself to relax and breathe slowly. She had all the time in the world to enjoy this. Neither of them had to go to work, no one was in the next room, there was no pressing need to leave the bedroom until hunger drove them out of bed.

Still, she couldn't help but wiggle against his hand, silently urging him to push his finger deep inside her. He resisted, keeping it just inside her pussy and making small circles. She sighed, impatient for more.

"You got in awfully late last night," he said, his voice still gravelly with sleep. "I missed you."

She could feel his cock, thick and hard, pressing against her hip. She'd been so focused on his gentle, teasing touch, she hadn't noticed he was already fully aroused.

"Sorry. You know how the girls are," she said. "But I missed you, too. You looked so sweet when I got home."

"Why didn't you wake me?" He kissed the top of her head as he continued to stroke her.

She sighed sleepily. "I was so tired by the time I took a shower I just wanted to curl up and go to sleep."

He stroked her pussy gently. "I would have helped you get to sleep."

"This is so much better than sleeping," she whispered, covering his hand with her own. "That feels good."

"Want more?"

She nodded against his shoulder. "Yes, please."

Slowly, he pushed his finger inside her. "You're getting wet."

"Imagine that."

He kept up his slow circles, teasing her with his warm touch. "Naughty girl."

Charlotte hooked her leg over his, spreading herself even wider for his touch. "Oh yes," she said, ending on a sigh as his finger slid deeper. "I think I want more."

He added a second finger inside of her. "Like that?"

She moaned, arching off the bed to take his fingers inside her. "Just like that."

He stroked her slowly, her wetness coating his fingers. She could hear the liquid sounds her pussy made as he stroked her. The noise was as arousing as this slow build up of tension. She squirmed against his hand, eager for more but willing to let him set the pace.

She reached down and fondled his cock just as slowly as he was touching her. He made a soft sound of approval and pushed against her hip. She smiled, sure she could hold out at this languid pace longer than he could.

He apparently didn't want her to think she had the upper hand because he upped the ante by pressing his thumb to her swollen clit. She jumped as if shocked and clamped her thighs around his hand.

Ian chuckled. "I wanted to make sure you were awake."

She harrumphed as she swirled her thumb over the tip of his cock, catching a bead of wetness along the way. "I'm as *awake* as you are, sweetheart."

"Excellent."

His fingers glided into her, curving upward to stroke the inside of her pussy. She was still tender from the previous day, but she was getting wetter as he touched her. A familiar ache began to build inside her and she felt her nipples pucker in response to her growing arousal. Ian's arm was beneath her neck and he reached down to stroke the swell of her breast, the dark edge of her hard nipple. His fingers, callused from years of handling fire equipment, felt rough against her tender flesh. The sensation sent chills through her and she inhaled sharply.

"Mmm, nice," she whispered.

"You're ready for me."

She nodded again. "Oh, yes."

He shifted his arm from under her and moved to kneel between her spread thighs. Lifting her legs over his broad shoulders, she expected him to push his cock into her. He surprised her by cupping her ass in his large hands and raising her up until her pussy was beneath his mouth. Back arched, she stared down between her legs and watched as he licked her swollen clit.

She whimpered at the zing of pleasure that accompanied that one swift stroke. Squirming for more, she was rewarded by his tongue parting the lips of her pussy and swirling around her opening the way his fingers had earlier. She pushed her hips toward his mouth, grasping at his shaggy mop of tousled golden curls, aching to feel his tongue inside her.

He pulled back, teasing her. "You do seem to want me."

"Yes!"

He lowered his mouth between her thighs, the day-old growth of his beard scratching her sensitive thighs. "You smell like heaven. Taste like it, too."

"Lick me!"

Finally, he gave her what she wanted and slid his tongue inside her. She whimpered low in her throat as he lapped at her with the flat of his tongue, drawing her own wetness up over her sensitive clit. She clutched at him, pulling his head into her and rubbing against his mouth shamelessly. Her orgasm was quick and explosive, catching her by surprise. She held his head between her thighs, riding out the long, rolling waves of her climax as he devoured her with his mouth. Then, just when she thought she couldn't take anymore, he lowered her down to the bed and guided his thick cock into her.

With tremors of her orgasm still rippling along the walls of her pussy, he felt huge inside her. She wrapped her legs around his strong back, arching up to meet his slow, deep thrusts. He reached under her to hold her ass, anchoring her to him as he rocked into her. She nibbled his neck, licking the salty moisture from his skin as her whole body quivered against him.

His thigh muscles trembled as he came, still moving so slowly inside her, as her pussy squeezed the length of his shaft. His orgasm seemed to last as long as hers, every short thrust followed by a deep groan. She held him to her, hands soothing the bunched muscles of his back and down to his clenched ass. Finally, he relaxed against her, his solid weight both sensual and comforting.

"Think we did it?" he murmured, tucking his head against her neck.

She stroked his hair, a private smile curving her lips. She was suddenly sleepy again. "Maybe. But the doctor said the more times I make love around ovulation, the more likely I am to get pregnant."

"Give me an hour and I'll see what I can do to increase our chances."

She giggled. "Lovely, but don't forget I'm playing tennis with Henry at ten."

"Hmph. Girls' night out, tennis with Henry. My girlfriend is in high demand." Ian moved off her, pulling her over on her side and into his arms, where she settled with a contented sigh. "At least until you get knocked up. Then you're all mine."

"Exactly the way I want," she said, stretching like a well-fed cat. "Maybe this month is my month."

"Well, if it doesn't happen this time, we'll just have to try again next month," Ian said. "It's all about the timing, right?"

"All in the timing," she agreed.

Double Take

Madeline Moore

Patricia Sheldon was the eldest – by eleven minutes, but that was enough to make her Jeannie's older sister; just as well, for Patricia went first in everything. She walked first, said "Dada" first and was the first to read. Physically they were identical in every way. Nothing but their personalities distinguished one blonde, blue-eyed twin from the other.

Mrs Sheldon dressed them alike from top to toe. They both wore their wavy hair long, tied with identical ribbons. When they were very little they switched beds and giggled when their hoodwinked father kissed Patricia on the head and said, "Goodnight, Jeannie," and then kissed Jean on the head and said, "Goodnight, Patty."

Patty loved volleyball but hated math, so she went to gym class for her sister, who hated volleyball but loved math, and Jeannie went to math class for Patty. This way they maintained high marks in everything and were never absent from a class often enough to raise eyebrows.

Mr and Mrs Sheldon took the twins to the Twin Convention in Twinsburg, Ohio every August. The girls loved the event because just being twins didn't invite attention, so they could vie for it like normal people, and be gratified when they got it. They sang duets in the Twin Talent Show and ate up the applause. The whole family looked forward to it.

They rode the float in the Year 2000 parade. A beautiful blond boy sat down beside Patty on the crowded, slow-moving float. "Hi."

"Hi," said a mirror image of the first boy as he sat beside Jeannie.

"Hi," the girls said, and gulped. Where had these two come from? Heaven?

"We're new," said the first, as if reading their thoughts. "We moved to Oregon this year, from Australia. But *you've* been coming to this Convention for years."

"Uh huh," said Patty. His eyes were green. Green! If there is anything gorgeouser than green eyes and blond hair on a boy, she didn't know what it might be, except green eyes and blond hair on two boys.

"How'd'y'know?" Jeannie asked.

"We looked at the Convention pics online," he said, "and we thought you were the prettiest girls ever."

"Shut up," said his brother, blushing. "We picked you because – you'll never guess—"

"Try and guess our names," interrupted his double.

"I dunno," said Jeannie. She was as tongue-tied as the boy beside her. "Robert and Richard?"

The boys shook their heads. Jeannie twisted her necklace in her hands and shrugged.

"Peter and Paul?" Patty giggled.

The boys kept shaking their heads.

"Thing One and Thing Two?" Jeannie tried.

Gorgeous boy number one stood up. "I'm Gene," he announced. Gorgeous boy number two stood, as well. "I'm Pat," he said. Together, they jumped from the float and disappeared into the crowd.

Jeannie sat, blinking, in the sunlight.

Patty grabbed her hand and croaked, "Oh. My. God."

Pat and Gene's carefully planned introduction was a complete success.

What fun the four children had! What innocent, sun-dappled, group fun they had that year, no twin giving much thought to which twin she or he was talking, swimming, wrestling, laughing, tickling, etc.

On the very night they'd met the boys, Patty whispered to Jeannie, "We're going to marry them."

Jeannie wholeheartedly agreed. Every night they'd whisper into their pillows, "Oh Gene," and "Oh Pat," and then "Oh Pat," and "Oh Gene."

No promises had been made that year, but all four understood that they'd see each other again the following August, and the August after that, and so on.

Eventually, gangly preteen boys greeted awkward preteen girls. The next year, tall teenage twin boys greeted girls with curves. And so on. They were fifteen the summer they paired off for the first time, alternating. The first kiss from Gene, for Patty, was fantastic, but so was the second kiss, from Pat, and the same went for Jeannie.

One might think the two gregarious twins, Patty and Pat, would naturally be more attracted to each other, and the same with the shy Jeannie and Gene, but then, opposites attract too. So, while Patty loved swimming and playing baseball with Pat and Jeannie loved gaming and tech talking with Gene, Jeannie also loved dancing with light-footed Pat, and Patty loved conversing with knowledgeable Gene. All four of them loved singing in the talent show and the duet times two was a big hit. They got tons of applause and attention and they all loved that, together.

A year is a long time for anyone to wait for a lover, but especially for a teenager. It was easier for Jeannie as she was the more patient of the two girls. Patty was *itching* to have sex. Happily, they agreed on one thing – the more experience they brought to their first time with the twin of choice (whoever that might be) the better.

Patty was particularly impatient to be seventeen, because, as anyone knows, a girl who "did it" before seventeen was a 'ho, whereas a girl who was seventeen or older, was not.

Of course they'd been dating for a couple of years by the time they achieved non-' ho status, but they'd held back, which had not been terribly difficult for Jeannie and not totally impossible for Patty. At night, along with their muffled moans of "Oh Gene" and "Oh Pat" each was busy beneath her bedclothes. They weren't shy about trading information or technique, but when it came down to actual self-pleasuring, they made sure one of their iPods was docked and playing, to drown out any ecstatic sounds that might escape their mouths in the heat of the moment.

They saw each other naked all the time and certainly they'd compared hair growth and breast growth and, after that, labia and clits and nipples but they didn't take it any further. They weren't interested *that way* in girls, not even or maybe especially each other. So their exchange of information was mostly verbal, and usually traveled one way, from Patty to Jeannie.

"God, his French kissing was gross," Patty'd say as she and her sister huddled on one of their beds for their customary post-date chats. "Look at these hickeys!" She'd show Jeannie the ring of dark bruises at her neck. "I'll be wearing a turtleneck for a week."

The next week, Jeannie would make a point of Frenching her current boy, just so she could report back to her sister, "He's pretty talented with his tongue." She'd show off her hickey (never more than one) with shy pride.

They were seventeen in August, after, sadly, the convention. In short order, little sister Jeannie was most definitely left behind once more.

"I did it," said Patty, triumphantly. Her face was flushed.

"Tell me," was all Jeannie said.

"We went to Jason's place. His parents were going to be out really late and his bratty little brother was staying at their aunt's. We ate pizza in the rec room, like we always do, only he had a bottle of sparkling wine so we had a glass each, and started watching the Horror Channel."

"Oh Christ!" muttered Jeannie. She couldn't stand scary movies.

"So I was screaming and hiding my face in his shoulder, like always, and we started necking, like always, and he put his hand under my shirt—"

"Like always," said Jeannie.

"Like *sometimes*," corrected Patty. "I pulled away, which surprised him. He was going to say something but I started unbuttoning my blouse. He shut up and watched. I unbuttoned it completely and took it off. Like so." She unbuttoned her blouse slowly, batting her lashes at her sister, and let it slide off her shoulders, revealing a skimpy satin bra.

"My bra!" Jeannie pretended to be scandalized but Patty wasn't fooled.

"I slid one strap down my arm," she said, demonstrating, "and then the other and I reached behind and unsnapped it and took it off."

"God, you're so brave."

"I have great tits. It's a fact."

"Me too."

"Of course," Patty continued. "Jason put his hands on my breasts and gently pushed me back until I was lying on the couch, and then he, he leaned over me and licked my nipples. It was terrific!"

"For how long?"

"I don't know. He went back and forth, and when he was licking one he'd twirl the other one between his fingers. My nipples were hard and pinker than usual."

"They still are," said Jeannie.

"God, you're right," said Patty, glancing down at her chest. "Show me yours."

Jeannie tugged down the neck of her nightie. The sisters appraised each other's chest. Jeannie's nipples were soft and pink, while Patty's were taut, swollen and scarlet.

"Neat," said Jeannie. She released the elastic neckline of her nightie. It sprung back into place. "Go on."

"He took off his shirt and lay on top of me. His skin was hot. He adjusted himself, inside his pants, and then popped the button of my jeans and slid his hand down, under my thong. I was so wet, Twinnie! As soon as his fingers touched my cunt I felt a twinge, almost like a shock, in my clit. I knew right then we were going all the way. I had to have it."

"Wow," said Jeannie. She was so taken by the tale she didn't bother to admonish her sister for her crude vernacular. (Jeannie found the word "pussy" more pleasing.)

"Yeah. I let him take my jeans off and he got between my legs, still in his pants, and started dry-humping me. I swear I could've come but I didn't want to, and I told him so. Of course he thought I was protesting but I said, 'Take me to your room,' and he did. What a kick, moving through the living room, naked, with him in only his unbuttoned pants, the tip of his cock poking out the top. It was like being on a movie set or something. It felt dangerous and exciting, like those moments right before the serial killer leaps out and murders the teenage lovers."

Patty stood up and took off her jeans and panties, then tip-toed around their bedroom, her eyes wide with wonder. "I kept looking, from left to right, even as we went up the stairs. Then we were in his room. Jason dropped his pants. His hard-on was huge."

"How big?"

Patty measured out a span with her hands. "Six and a half, maybe seven. Big enough. I probably went pale at the sight of it. But he was cool, he really was. He put a towel down on the bed, in case I bled, and took a condom from his bedside table, and put it on."

"God, that is *so* cool."

"Oh he'd done it before, that's for sure. I was sitting on the bed, watching, and he came and pushed me back. He bent his knees a bit. I knew he was going to do me, just like that, and I was keen. It was like all the heavy petting we'd done for the last few weeks had just that minute happened and I was totally psyched. I spread my legs a little wider and he slid into me, half-way, then jerked his hips so hard I felt his balls slap against me, just below my cunt."

"Did it hurt?"

"Not much. I liked it."

"Did you bleed?"

"No, but I'm not surprised. I think we both lost our hymens at that Wild West Riding Camp, don't you?"

"Probably." Jeannie nodded gravely. Whatever jealousy she felt about her sister vaulting ahead, experience-wise, was more than equaled by the relief that washed over her with the outpouring of her sister's story. Jeannie liked to go into things informed and once again Patty was a fount of information.

"He went slowly, at first, pushing all the way inside me, then pulling back even slower. He was grinning like I'd never seen him do before, a huge grin, and his eyes were half-closed. He looked the handsomest I've ever seen him, and you know what that means . . ."

"Gene and Pat will be totally to die for."

"Right. Because they are, like, so gorgeous already. But Jason was terrific. We got a rhythm going and he sucked his thumb to make it wet and then diddled my clit until I was crazy, totally crazy! I was trying not to make much noise but he said, 'Go ahead, scream all you want. No one can hear you.'"

Jeannie shivered. "That sounds sort of threatening."

"I know! But he said it in a really soothing way. So it was reassuring and threatening at the same time. I loved it!" Patty's eyes shone. "He kissed my mouth, and my nipples, and he put his thumb in my mouth and I sucked it wet and he put it back on my clit and I started coming. It was fantastic, having something inside me to come against, or, I guess, around. With each contraction it was like I was clamping on to a big hot hard—"

"Prick?" Jeannie offered.

"Cock! And as soon as I began coming, Twinnie, I started yelling, all kinds of stuff, like his name and then 'God' and then 'Fucking Jesus Christ!' I didn't know what I was saying, not really, but it didn't matter, it just felt good, like some of the pressure was coming out of my mouth while the rest of it was being released through my cunt. I dug my nails into his shoulders. He came then, too, but he just groaned, no words or anything. We cuddled. It was good there was a towel on the bed because I'd scratched him so hard with my nails he was bleeding."

"Wow."

"He didn't complain. I think he liked it. We said some sweet things to each other and then we did it again. It was way better than masturbation or dry-humping or anything. You've gotta do it."

"Yeah," muttered Jeannie. "I do. But with who?"

Patty shrugged. "Why not with Jason? He's really good."

Jeannie shrieked. "Aren't you in love with him?"

It was Patty's turn to shriek. "Of course not. I'm in love with Pat. Or maybe Gene."

"Me too," said Jeannie. The girls doubled over with laughter, and then, at the sound of grumpy footsteps approaching, they dove under their covers, one in her nightie and the other naked, and feigned sleep when their dad stuck his head in their door and, unfooled by their angelic faces, grumbled, "Go to sleep."

This was the first time Jeannie and Patty shared a man, but it wasn't to be the last. Patty usually went first, weeding out the duds, and Jeannie always went last, dumping the boys with no tears and an ear deaf to their protests, but since they pretended only one of them was ever with any one boy, neither acquired the bad reputation they both deserved.

The next summer, arriving at the Twin Convention was a big event for the girls. They came without their parents for the first time, and they fully intended to fuck Pat and Gene, as soon as they decided who would be fucking whom. It was Jeannie who insisted they not share the twin blonds of their affection. They discussed it for most of the drive.

"These are our husbands-to-be," Jeannie admonished her sister and, when Patty protested that as such they *ought* to sample both boys each before making up their minds, Jeannie put her foot down. "Absolutely not," she said. "I will always be faithful to my husband."

They both loved Gene and Pat and were sure the twin boys loved them, too, and equally. But choices needed to be made, and soon, as the car was fast approaching Twin City.

Jeannie made the final decision. "It's best you go with Gene and I go with Pat," she said.

Patty was surprised. She'd been sure her sister would go for the quiet one, but Jeannie's reasoning was sound.

"Gene will steady you and Pat will challenge me," she said. "I think that's better for long-term relationships. Also, we're more likely to do stuff together, as we get older, if we share each other's interests."

Patty could see her point, but the biggest reason she agreed to the match was what Jeannie said next.

"This way," said Jeannie, "there will always be a Gene and a Pat and a Pat and a Jean." The symmetry was neat.

Twins greeted twins with customary enthusiasm. In fact, the boys glowed with a new intensity that the girls took for lust. They were disabused of this notion during the opening night barbecue.

The four of them sat at the end of one long table, under the same massive white tent that sheltered the throng of hungry duplicate diners every year. The food was great, as always. But something had definitely shifted.

"We've taken the Celibacy Vow," said Gene.

"Christ!" Patty dropped her fork on her plate.

Jeannie covered Patty's hand with hers. "Go on." Jeannie spoke with admirable calm.

The girls had always known that Pat and Gene were religious. It hadn't mattered, until now, that the boys were and the girls were not.

"It's simple. No sex until marriage." Pat shrugged.

"But . . ." stammered Patty, "we had plans!"

"So do we," said Gene. "We want you to be our first. And our only."

"We hope you want the same," said Pat.

"Oh we do," said Jeannie, quickly, before her sister could betray them with her frankness. Her hand on Patty's tightened. "Now that we're almost eighteen, well, we were hoping it would happen soon."

"It will," said Pat. He knelt by Jeannie's wooden chair. He produced a blue velvet ring box from the pocket of his khaki shorts and opened it, displaying a solitaire diamond, small but not tiny, set in gold. "Jeannie? Will you marry me?"

Gene knelt at Patty's side. He too produced a blue velvet box within which nestled a ring, identical to the one Pat held in his hand. "Patty," said Gene. "Will you marry me?"

"Yes!" the giddy girls replied in unison.

That night, in their room, Patty and Jeannie couldn't sleep, and who could blame them? They'd spent the evening making out like maniacs with their respective fiancés and hadn't said good-night until the wee hours. They fell, exhausted, into their beds, but whenever one managed to doze off, she'd be awakened by the other, shouting, "I can't believe it!"

It hadn't actually occurred to them that the boys might decide between themselves who would marry whom. What luck! And look at the way the diamonds sparkled in the light! The bedside table lamp would be switched on and the sleepy twin would suddenly be wide awake, more than eager to thrust her left hand into the glow from the lamp and admire her sparkling ring, and her sister's sparkling ring, and join in her sister's joy with exclamations of her own.

The two sets of twins announced their engagements at the conclusion of their rendition of "My Heart Will Go On" at the annual

Talent Contest. The crowd went wild. The applause was thundering. An encore was demanded, and since they hadn't prepared one, they sang the same song again, to more deafening applause. They won first prize.

It was a double wedding, of course, in the girls' hometown. They were young for marriage, but neither set of parents could argue the rightness of the union. The girls wore identical dresses, though Patty's was sashed with blue satin and Jeannie's with pink. After all, they didn't want to marry the wrong guys by mistake! The grooms wore matching black tuxedoes but Gene's boutonnière was blue and Pat's was pink. It was a winter wedding, 14 February, in fact. Immediately following the reception, the happy couples boarded a plane for Barbados. Immediately upon disembarking, the happy couples disappeared into their bridal suites, and neither made an appearance the next day, or even the next.

On the third day they emerged, all fucked out and ready for some fun in the sun. The boys wasted no time hitting the surf. The girls stretched out in their deck chairs to chat.

"Do me," said Pat. She held out a bottle of suntan lotion and dropped the straps of her blue bikini.

"Didn't your husband?" Jeannie giggled as she slathered lotion on her sister's shoulders.

"Oh God. Gene's good. Really, really good." Patty sighed contentedly.

"So is Pat," said Jeannie. "What he lacks in experience," she whispered, "he makes up for in enthusiasm. Well worth waiting for."

"Well, mine claims I'm his first but if it's really true, he sure did a lot of research. When we couldn't fuck any more he ate me out until I begged him to stop."

"But you love oral! It's me who gets bored with it," said Jeannie.

"I couldn't stand another orgasm."

Jeannie rolled her eyes. "Did you do anal?"

"Yes, did you?"

"Yes."

The girls had decided since they weren't actually virginal brides, they would remain celibate for the duration of their engagements *and* save their bums for their husbands. In this way they successfully assuaged any guilt they had about their sexual histories.

"And?" Patty cocked her head at her sister.

Jeannie thrust the lotion in her sister's hands. "Do me," she said. She dropped the straps of her pink bikini.

"Tell me! Did you like it?"

"I found it humiliating and degrading," mumbled Jeannie.

"So you loved it."

"Yup." Jeannie giggled.

"I thought it was OK."

"Well, I think it's my favourite," announced Jeannie.

They hooted in unison.

"This is heaven. I wish we could stay here forever." Patty stretched and sighed contentedly.

"I know exactly what you mean," said Jeannie.

All four kids had spent the time from August to February working. In the fall, they'd attend SFU, each couple living on campus in a Student Housing townhouse. It was all arranged. But, once the honeymoon was over, Jeannie would move into Pat's apartment, which was in Oregon, where he worked as a lifeguard. And Patty would move into Gene's apartment, which was in Texas, where he worked as a junior programmer. For the first time in their lives, the girls would be separated.

"Pass me your hat," said Patty, "I forgot mine."

As Jeannie passed her sister her straw hat, their fingertips touched. Jeannie whispered, "Twinnie, I'm scared."

"Sssh," said Patty. "We have ten days left in paradise."

"We've never been apart."

"It's only for a few months."

"A few?" Jeannie's voice squeaked. "Six! Half a year!"

"Christ this sun is hot." Patty dragged a beach towel over her body, up to her chin. "I'm going to sleep."

"Fine. Be in denial. You'll miss me as much as I'll miss you when the time comes."

Jeannie flipped through a magazine for a few minutes, but the sight of her sister peacefully snoozing in the sun was so appealing she soon closed her eyes to join her. Just before she drifted off she pulled a towel over her body, too. The last thing either of them needed was the kind of tropical sunburn that would put an end to honeymoon sex.

Patty was awakened by soft lips pressed to hers. She responded enthusiastically. When a hand slipped under the towel to cup her breast she arched her back, pushing her hot nipple into his hand, cool and wet from the ocean. The kiss deepened. The towel fell.

"Hey!"

Patty opened her eyes to a surprised, red-faced boy in hot pink and black trunks backing away from her.

"Your hat," he sputtered. "The band is pink."

Patty glanced at her sister. Patty's husband Gene, in blue and black trunks, was backing away from Jeannie, who sat up, shocked, and met her sister's eyes.

"Get away from my wife!"

"You get away from my wife!"

The brothers pushed each other, hard, then started wrestling in the sand.

"It's my fault! I borrowed Jeannie's hat!" Patty's heart was pounding in her ears. The situation had to be diffused before tension could threaten the twins' idyllic vacation. That must be why her pulse pounded in her ears, and elsewhere, too. It couldn't be from Pat's kiss. Could it?

"Stop it, you guys!" Jeannie jumped to her feet. "It was an honest mistake. Anyway, we've all kissed before, remember?"

The men ceased wrestling to consider this. They cut a fine sight, their blond hair shining in the sun, their wet bodies, sculpted if not yet tanned, patched in places with glistening white sand.

"True," allowed Pat.

"But we weren't married then," said Gene.

"Yeah," said Pat.

The men resumed wrestling, this time laughing instead of hurling insults.

Patty threw Jeannie's pink-sashed straw hat to her. "I'll try not to forget mine again," she mumbled.

Jeannie couldn't take her eyes off the young men wrestling in the sun. "That would be best," she said. "I think."

The couples settled into a routine of sorts. After an early breakfast the girls would recline on deck chairs close to the surf, where they could tan, chat and watch their men cavort in the sea. In the afternoon they split off, sometimes to their respective suites for siesta and sex, or to take in the sights. They usually congregated with the rest of the hotel guests to watch the sunset, then returned to their rooms to rest and dress for the evening. Cocktails were followed by a buffet dinner, and then they'd dance under the stars or in a disco. After that came long, adventurous nights of passionate lovemaking.

"Gene is the best lover I've ever had," sighed Patty one morning.

"Me too," sighed Jeannie.

They both giggled.

"I mean, Pat is the best lover I've ever had," Jeannie amended.

Another morning, Patty said, "Gene is really hung. I suppose Pat is the same?"

"Should we be talking like this? They *are* our husbands, after all." Jeannie glanced out to sea. It was a windy day and Pat was teaching his brother to surf.

"They can't hear us. Anyway, they probably talk about us."

"You think?"

"No," said Patty. She laughed. "So, is he? Pat? Is he hung?"

"Like a horse," said Jeannie.

Their talk wasn't always so explicit. One morning, Jeannie initiated a conversation of another kind, by saying, "Do you think they're our best lovers because we're in love?"

"It's hard to say. Gene is a very skilled lover, and getting more skilled by the day. He takes lovemaking seriously. Speaking objectively, he's a great fuck."

"But are you? Objective? How can you . . . ?" Jeannie dropped her voice to a whisper, as she always did when she talked about their past. "After all, we've each had the same lovers, for the most part, yet we both insist our husbands are the best."

"Our lovers never noticed when we swapped around. Maybe identical twins are identical in bed," said Patty.

"But we planned it that way. We swapped notes to make sure we didn't give ourselves away. Surely we aren't really the same, sexually?"

"I'm multi-orgasmic."

"Me too."

"Gene can get it up again, and again, and again, in the same day."

"So can Pat."

"He roars when he comes."

"Pat's noisy too."

They fell into a contemplative silence.

"We could always swap hats and find out," suggested Patty with a grin.

"You wouldn't! These are our husbands we're talking about!"

"Of course I wouldn't," said Patty.

"Of course not," said Jeannie. She stood. "I'm going for a swim. I'm hot." As she hot-footed toward the turquoise sea, the sound of her sister's knowing chortle followed her across the sand.

On the last full day of their holiday Pat and Patty went parasailing. Gene and Jeannie watched, hearts in their mouths, as their spouses sailed across the sky like big, colourful bats.

"If he dies, I'll kill him," said Jeannie. "And her."

"Ditto," grumbled Gene. "We can attend their funerals together."
Jeannie grinned. "Deal."

"He always has to show me up," grumbled Gene. "I go scuba
diving, snorkeling and learn to surf so what happens? He has to go
parasailing."

"So? You can parse code like nobody's business. It's just the way
he is. The way they are." Jeannie put her hand on his shoulder. "It's
fine."

"They're coming down," said Gene. His brother and his bride
landed in the sea.

Jeannie didn't realize she was clutching his muscular arm until she
saw her twin and her husband bobbing in the water, laughing and
sputtering. Then she quickly let go.

Most of the rest of that day was taken up with last minute
activities, but the two couples met at sunset for pina coladas and
pictures. Jeannie was quiet, which wasn't unusual, but her sister
was too.

The boys had often been apart, but they were respectful of
the separation anxiety that afflicted their brides. The girls stood,
shoulder to shoulder, as the orange fireball slid down the sky and
drowned in the sea.

"More drinks?" Pat's solution to sadness was spirits. On this
occasion, Gene didn't argue. Both girls nodded.

When their men had gone to get refreshments, wet blue eyes met
wet blue eyes.

"I'm not sure I can do it, be away from you for so long," said
Jeannie.

"Me too."

"We could make a pact—"

"We've already done that, Twinnie. We've done everything we can
to keep what we have. You know that, Jeannie."

"Not everything," said Jeannie. Her eyes twinkled, made extra
bright by unshed tears.

"Hmmm. Tonight's the night, is it?"

"Yes."

"No bra, white thong, white peep toes with kitten heels, pink
chiffon strapless. I'll wear the same, no bra, white thong, white shoes
and blue chiffon strapless. We swap dresses at dinner. Deal?"

"Deal."

And that, as they say, is exactly how the deal went down.

It'd been a while since Jeannie had played at being extraverted Patty, but she hadn't lost her chops. When Gene stripped her of the blue dress she'd exchanged with her twin for her pink one, she remembered to arch her back and pose for him, just as Patty might do. When he peeled off his white tee and dropped his blue shorts to his feet, she saw he was identical to his brother, right to the fair, sparse down on his balls. Certainly, his cock was every bit as impressive and as rock solid as her husband's.

His lips on hers were soft, and his tongue, as it tasted her lips and then her mouth, was luscious and questing, so like Pat's, so familiar, but not Pat's, so different. She was excited, and secretly shamed by how extra wet her pussy was when his tongue slid along her slit, in agonizingly slow strokes, and then dipped inside. He moaned. She felt it more than heard it, a low, deep exhalation that warmed her inside and out.

"I love it when you lick my – um, my cunt," she said.

"Then I'll eat you until you can't come any more," he said.

Inwardly, she groaned at the idea. But as he laved and nibbled and sucked her to one orgasm after another, Jeannie groaned out loud, with gusto.

In the other bridal suite, Pat rolled Patty on to her belly. They were both naked and highly aroused from foreplay.

"I want your ass, Jeannie," he said. "I know how much you love it."

Patty shivered. Who'd have thought her fearful sister would've embraced this dirty act with such gusto. Still, she wasn't about to be found out and so, though anal wasn't *her* favourite, she giggled with delight and parted her legs wider, to welcome him.

She hoped he'd take his time but he lubed his cock and leaned close, rubbing the head up and down her crack until it "caught" at her back entrance.

"You want it?" he asked.

"I want it."

"Tell me."

"I want it." Patty paused, then added, "A lot."

"What do you want? Tell me. You know I like to hear you talk dirty."

"I want your – um – prick in me, in my bum, in deep."

"Me too! I love to do your bum – Jeannie." He leaned in, pushing his way slowly inside her until she was full to the hilt with him.

"Do it," he said. "Do it like you know I like it."

Oops! Jeannie hadn't told her about this. He liked something that her sister did, something special, when he fucked her ass. Damn!

"If you aren't in the mood to do it that way, that's OK."

She was off the hook if she screwed up. Patty'd only had anal sex once with Gene and that had been pretty straightforward, so to speak. But she thought she could guess what her sister might do that was so special. After all, how can a girl do much of anything different when a man's weight is crushing her? What she did for Gene was the only way she could think of. She said, her voice husky, "Lift up, then."

He raised himself on to straight stiff arms and the tips of his toes.

"Are you ready?" she asked.

"Ready!"

Rotating her hips clockwise, she pushed up at him, skewering herself on his rigid flesh until the wet lips of her cunt kissed his dangling balls. She paused, then sank down again, rotating counterclockwise, until only the head of his cock was still trapped inside her.

"Oh fuck!" he groaned. "Fucking fantastic."

She was surprised at the thrill that traveled her body at the sound of his breathless praise. Surprised and inspired. After she'd raised and lowered herself half a dozen times, undulating each time the obscenely split globes of her ass made contact with crotch, his lust seemed to take him over. He pushed her flat and pounded into her, fast and furious. The sex seemed to teeter on the very brink of craziness. Whether it was the taboo nature of the act itself or the depth of the sensations it created, she didn't know, but Patty was seized with a *desperate* need to come. She managed to slide her hand down between her body and the bed and rub her clit so that, a mere moment later, when Pat began to roar and jerk in ecstasy, Patty was ecstatic, too.

The next morning, the girls met in the pool's changing rooms and switched bikinis, so that Jeannie was once more in pink; Patty in blue.

They settled in their customary chairs by the ocean to wait for their men.

Jeannie said, "You were right about your husband." She pouted. "He is better in bed than mine, dammit! Not bigger, mind you, but yes, better. He ate me until I screamed for mercy."

"Funny," said Patty, "because I was about to tell you the same thing. Your Pat is a dynamo, Twinnie. He fucked my ass like there was no tomorrow. It was so exciting! I have to apologize though."

"Why's that?"

"By the time he flipped me over and fucked my cunt – but I called it my pussy, don't worry – I was so out of my mind I raked my nails down his back. He's got marks."

"Oh well, they'll fade. Here they come!"

The girls watched their young husbands approach. Pat wore trunks and a white tee, and Gene was dressed similarly, though, as usual, his trunks had a blue streak on them, while Pat's had a flash of pink. As they neared their wives they stripped off their tees, rolled them into balls, and tossed them to the sand. Together, the boys dashed into the ocean for a final swim before departing the island.

"What the—" Jeannie's grin morphed into an open-mouthed expression of astonishment.

"Oh. My. God." Patty's face mirrored her sister's. For it wasn't Patrick's back that bore the mark of Patty's ardour – it was Gene's.

Which could only mean one thing.

It seemed twins, at least these two pairs of twins, think alike.

The Escape

Jett Zandersen

Her lungs seized as she heard the creak of a floorboard near the door's entrance. The moonlight coming through the French window cast shadows that moved whenever the breeze swept through the muslin curtains – the tendons on her hand contrasted as she froze above the keyboard.

A voice permeated through the tension. "What are you doing here?"

There was no point running. She had tried that a week ago when she awoke from being drugged. The guards had shrugged and chuckled when she jumped out the window and dashed across the lawn, running madly despite the cuts and bruises from the recent struggle. After an hour of darting through thickets and forest, she knew she was trapped on an island. Somewhere. Escape would not be easy.

Letting out her breath, her shoulders slumped and she felt like bursting into tears. She was so close. All she needed was the code to the tunnel that brought supplies from the mainland. And then she'd be free. Another day of what she had already endured would tip her over the edge – and she couldn't give in. There was no point lying either, to the voice in the darkened doorway. The man she knew as "Caspar" could read her mind even when her lips mouthed other words. The lips that he watched as she bit them in concentration when they played chess or poker, supervised by a retinue of guards and the presence of the operation controller, Mr White. Perhaps that's why Caspar had lost the occasional game, if only to grant her some freedoms in the bets he made. If she won, she got a privilege, such as not being handcuffed to the table, or being able to butter bread with a knife. If he won, she would tell Mr White a name or a code. She never gave up her secrets easily though. After a game, Mr White made Caspar leave the room, and when he returned he always had a new bruise, another bandage. But she gave a name.

Even though they all knew it was fake. And then the next day would be another game of chess or poker.

As he walked into the moonlight, she remembered in her dressing gown pocket the iPod she had won back yesterday. Well, won might be a bit wrong. Is it possible to win against exploiting a weakness? Like learning from a dossier that an agent had a broken rib from a mission two weeks prior and then nailing the first blow there so that thereafter he was forever gasping a rasp of breath rather than fighting at full power.

She had been trained in fighting of course, not only with fists and weapons, but with femininity. A look that lingered a little longer, a flash of skin, the gentle stroking against a lengthened neck – anything to see whatever lit up in a captor's eyes. And then a little more skin, a little more stroking until his mind was blanked out by anything else except wanting that primal activity. To fling her down and mate. Or even to think that someone as beautiful as she could ever be interested. And then in a weakened state, she got what she wanted. A key, a name, an escape.

But this time, every trick she had tried was useless, even on one so young and hauntingly handsome. This man, Caspar, was cold. Literally. Two days ago in frustration she had grabbed the glass bishop and lunged forward to stab his hand. But he caught her with his other hand, which felt like a block of ice. She looked at him confused. He took her hand and put it to his cheek, also cold, then to his neck to feel his pulse, so faint and slow she would have thought him in hibernation if not for the glint in his blue eye – an icicle that flashed light in a deep crevasse. He placed her hand back behind her side of the board.

"Your tricks won't work on me."

But then that afternoon before the moon took its turn in the sky, she had heard some music playing down the hallway. She recognized the tracks as from her iPod. When it got to Mozart's "Ruhe sanft, mein holdes Leben", she felt her chest cave in at the isolation of beauty, like the gilded cage she was kept in – an exquisite mansion on a lush forested island in what looked to be the Dalmatian Coast.

The music remained floating in her mind during the latest poker game. After dealing the cards, she had arranged her hand and started humming and swaying a little to the beat from a recent mission at a Berlin nightclub ("Slow", Chemical Brothers remix of Kylie Minogue). She raised the stake and waited for his as-always instant reaction. But this time, he wasn't even looking at his cards, but following with every trace her body made in the space. The way he imagined her soft white skin twisting through the air, her hands so warm touching herself, running her fingers through her hair, the drops of sweat running down her body.

She kept her poker face, not only because she had a straight flush, but because she saw the faintest throb upon his neck underneath the white shirt he wore buttoned up tight. She could see his chest rising higher, the definition of his body, lean and muscular – obviously Mr White's most prized specimen. Were they testing him? Able to resist anything physical, they were testing the ultimate downfall of any man.

Mr White coughed and Caspar shifted instantly: "I'll raise you another Capote novel if you tell me Station Enigma's entry code."

She sniffed and hummed a little more trying to give the air of nonchalance. "No, I want my iPod back."

Mr White came up behind Caspar and whispered in his ear. It would be easy. There were only songs – they had scanned for anything else.

Caspar nodded. They laid their cards down, saw that she had the stronger hand and paused before Caspar left the room. Mr White looked at him severely instead of the usual approving nod, then stamped over and threw the iPod at her.

"We're not done with that name."

"But—"

"He may play to the rules, but I don't . . ."

And that's why when she reached into her pocket later in the moonlight, Caspar had to stifle a gasp at the hand mark left on her wrist, that had been twisted backwards so hard until she screamed so loud that the guard dogs started howling.

She plugged her iPod into the computer to find a song, and he started to walk towards her to stop, but as soon as he heard the music, his feet anchored to the floor. If he got any closer to her, he wasn't sure if . . .

She walked out from behind the desk to be in front of the poker table. Everything was dark except for the moonlight glinting off the polished brass statues and rococo mirrors. The sound of the crickets disappeared as his consciousness diverted to what he had tried shifting from his mind since she was brought here a week ago, still in her jogging gear, eyelashes closed in slumber and peace before the hell began. Not exactly the vindictive assassin he had been led to believe. He had leaned over her, wanting to stroke her thick red hair, to make her wake up so he could see if her eyes were green like in her dossier, but Mr White came in and grabbed his arm.

"No touching. Ever. This is your test."

Back in the games room, she knew that any words spoken would break the spell she had running between the beats and notes. So she closed her eyes like she always did. So she couldn't be reminded of her reality.

As the intro continued, she swayed some more, now twirling the dressing gown tie and letting the silken sleeve slide down so most of her left shoulder and arm were exposed. With the other hand, she dipped her finger in her mouth and then traced delicately over her collarbone, sliding her hand under the gown to touch her breast, raising it up so he could see how the soft flesh tipped up over her fingers.

His mouth dropped open slightly and he could feel moisture gathering above his lips – he licked and tasted salt. The shirt collar against his neck felt like a stricture with his carotid artery throbbing. He knew though enough to stay where he was, and yet he could not walk towards the computer and yank away the iPod. Just once, he wanted to know what it felt like to feel. To react. He was sure he would be strong enough to stop when he needed to.

But oh, when her hand reached down and undid the gown and her gentle swaying shifted her body from exposed to hidden, he had a glimpse of her frame before the light was taken away by the silk. She turned around and both hands reached up to her neck, then to her hair where she undid a ribbon and the hair cascaded out, freshly washed. She reached over to the table and scattered the chips then looked back to see his reaction. A slight nostril flare at the orderliness being messed up, but still he remained, his eyes focused. He was testing himself.

She walked to the other side of the table so it was between them and sat down to remove some cards from the pack, raising an eyebrow for him to join her. His neck was still throbbing but he knew a game would help to take his mind off things, so he walked to the other chair and faced her. Still moving to the music, she let the gown slip down so she was sitting there with only the occasional shadow of curtain to cover her breasts. He looked at the blue veins that criss-crossed her skin and felt his fingers moving in sync as he imagined tracing them, perhaps with his tongue.

She pulled the ribbon from the gown and placed it on the corner of the table. "Well?" She breathed out to pout her lips as she asked.

He shifted his mind back to the cards she was shuffling. "What?"

"Eight-up, five-cards. If I win, you let me go."

"And if I win?"

"You get to do . . . whatever you like."

He paused and breathed in through his nose, feeling the air warm as it drifted into his lungs. "Agreed."

She cut the deck and motioned for him to restack it for her to then deal, revealing a ten of hearts for the deck between them. Picking up her cards, she fiddled with a nearby chip and bit it in her mouth, then leaned forward and pulled the gown away, tossing it over to the side.

He felt all his clothes getting tighter, and he thought about her on the chair, whether she was wet, whether her legs stretched out like long stems ready to wrap around him. When he picked up the ten and put down an ace of spades, she reached for his hand and brought it to her lips. She sucked on his index finger and felt the blood rush to her neck.

He pulled his finger away and traced the outline of her cheekbone. He felt her fingers inch down his hand, letting her creep up to his wrist and feel a pulse both strong and fast. He pulled his hand back slowly and tapped on the cards sternly "Your turn." The track moved to another song.

She bit her lower lip in concentration: "I'm raising the stakes."

She put her cards face down and leaned over the table like a panther prowling in a cage. Holding his gaze, she reached for his cards and put them face down too. Then she reached for his shirt collar and undid the top button. His eyes shifted to the inset of her neck, the line like a swan's where her face met the rest of her exquisite body. His mind flashed with thoughts of slipping his hand in that space and tilting her head so he could feel her warmth on his lips. To thaw out just one time.

While his gaze was shifted, she rolled over the table and on to the edge so her breasts were two inches away from his face, but her legs were crossed. She felt the warm air from his breath tickle her and again she closed her eyes for what she was about to do. She knew she had to be slow, or else he would stop and that would be her last chance. Every move she made had to be plotted like a chess move.

She began by throwing her head back so that her ribs stuck out from beneath her skin and her hard nipples pointed to the ceiling. She could hear his eyelashes fluttering like he was in a deep sleep with his senses overawed. Her hands pressed hard against her body, flexing her muscles so that he could see her strength even after this week of torment. She tightened her hand and pricked her nails into her skin. She knew that some guys got off on that – the infliction of pain. But just as she was about to let the blood run forth, his hand grabbed her and her eyes opened suddenly.

He looked at her, the faintest crinkle of concern crossing his face. His cheekbones cast shadows over his expression and he reached with his other hand to sprawl out her fingers so they were a soft cover instead of a tense claw. She looked at her hand and changed strategy in her mind. *So he's not into that . . . maybe he is into the more vanilla variety.* It was at this point that she realized that her eyes were open. Instead of seeing grizzly stubble and sweating brows thrust in her face and god knows where else, she saw his eyes devouring her, but as if she were a rich chocolate cake, too sweet to be eaten at once, but to be nibbled in small mouthfuls – each lick its own flavour sensation.

Her crossed legs had angled one foot pointing near to his right ear, so she leaned over and started stroking his earlobe with her toe, up and behind his silky thick brown hair. He reached up behind his ear to catch her ankle. He felt the delicate bones and traced up the inside of her calf, then to where her legs crossed over, all sticky from sweat. She held her legs together tightly, but he pushed with both his arms to pry them open, while looking into her eyes. In the periphery of his vision, he saw her thighs glisten with sweat and he let his fingers drift up, slipping. The music's trance ended with the track and they both froze as they heard voices outside the window. It was the guards doing their nightly rounds.

She held her breath, hoping the curtains wouldn't sway and deactivate the screen saver, and that the next track would be delayed. The seconds passed slowly and the guards' voices faded off just as another song began.

At the poker table, they both exhaled at the same time and he pushed her legs together.

That was enough. He looked at where his hands had gripped her thighs and left marks. Horrified, he pushed off from the table to do up his collar, then strode over to the computer.

Just as he was about to yank out the iPod, she tapped on the table, lying across it belly down. "Hey, we haven't finished yet."

He shook his head and shut the screen.

"Scared to lose?"

He looked at her. She was hiding a smirk and her left eyebrow was raised. He walked back over intending to strip the cards away and throw her back into her room and lock the door. But as he got closer, she rolled over so that her hair fell just so, over that space in her neck that he found so exquisite. Like a Rubik's Cube he wondered all the different moves he could make to get his hand in there, a foothold to anything and everything else.

He stood over her, gaze fixed, then he sat down and picked up his cards. "I believe it was your turn," he said, "what is your play?"

She fingered her cards and bit her lower lip, chose a card and leaned towards his face, stroking it along his nose, his cheekbones, his chin – where the faintest hint of stubble was breaking through – and down his Adam's apple, which moved hard against his skin. She placed the jack of clubs in front of them, taking the ace of spades for her hand, then undid his collar again and leaned back in her chair.

He looked back at his dealt hand. He was done for. But never before had he wanted to win so badly. He looked back and forth between her face and his cards. Every time he looked, she was smiling – the same smile he had seen on the second day they played chess and she had made a joke at Mr White's expense – like a toddler who had been sprung finger-painting the white lounge room walls. Oh, she had paid for it later, but that mischief was what kept her going through the punishment.

He reached to swap a card, but her hand stopped him and she pushed his cards face down again and left hers behind. She flicked herself over the edge like a gymnast and came up standing – a perfect goddess statue worthy of gracing the finest garden. She walked behind him and he could feel her breath on his neck as she reached to pull his jacket off. He pulled his arms back and felt her hand trace through his white shirt on to his spine, but the chair back got in the way, so she pushed him gently forward and whispered in his ear. "Stand up."

So he did and she walked around the front until her eyes looked up slightly into his, taking his view completely so he couldn't see her hands. His eyes shifted from hers to push away some hair from in front of her eyes, but she blew it away before he could touch her.

"Close your eyes," she husked.

"No."

She wasn't used to refusal. After all, when eyes are closed the senses are so much more enhanced. Taste more, feel more.

He stifled a smile as her eyebrows flashed confoundedness, like a few days ago when she thought she'd had him lined up for checkmate, only for his knight to take her queen, then it was downhill from there.

Instead he reached behind her, brushing up against the mounds of her breasts – her smell drifting beyond the air and straight to his skin. He placed in her hand the tie from the dressing gown. "Blindfold me."

She felt her lips flush with new warmth and her heart beat faster. *What was his strategy? A faked defensive? A blinded victim-come-villain?* She didn't pause though, feeling each gain she made could easily be lost by another interruption. So she walked behind him and brought the tie around his eyes and knotted it behind his head. She saw him shudder slightly as her fingernails dug lightly into his neck.

The iPod track moved on and he closed his eyes, feeling her presence as she moved in front again and took his hand. He felt her fingers trace the inside of his palm then move up his wrist between his skin and the sleeve. When she got as far as the seams would allow, he felt her move closer; her tongue licking from the base of his hand right up to his elbow.

"You taste good."

He said nothing and stood still. Already though he was feeling his pants get tighter, as before when he had splayed her legs open on the poker table. Then he heard a noise he couldn't figure out; it sounded like two marble chess pieces clacking against each another. Then he understood, just as he heard his shirt tear from the cut she had made with her teeth.

She saw him bite his lip when the tear reached all the way to his left shoulder and she traced the outline of a scar, deep and ragged, stitched badly. She let her lips brush over the raised skin and breathed a kiss.

"Why do you do it?" she whispered in his ear.

He reached for her hand to pull it away from his scar and whispered back in her ear, his hand pressing against the faint scar on the other side of her neck. "Why do *you*?"

She yanked his grasp from her wrist and felt the rage inside her boil over. How dare he question her life? It's not like she had a choice. But then, it seemed neither did he. Both of them were prisoners without any freedom except for the moment.

She tore the front of his shirt and the buttons scattered across the wooden floor. Enough, she thought. And with that, she launched her attack. Her fingers moved against his abdominal muscles that flinched when she lightened her touch. Even he can be ticklish. She walked around his back and pulled the rest of the shirt off, tracing his ribs, kissing them one at a time and she could hear his heart beating like tribal drums. She opened her mouth and scraped her front teeth over his back along his shoulder blades, mocking bites.

⋆ ⋆ ⋆

It wasn't the intentional fondling that was sending him to the edge, but the accidental brush of her breast on his arm, when her foot stepped on his, when her hair tangled on his slight stubble. Beneath the blindfold he felt the sweat gather and pour down his chest as it rose and fell, gulping for enough oxygen to stay standing and in control. Each breath was just more poison – smelling her sweat. When her hand snaked around from behind his back and down the front of his pants he knew that was the point of no return. He could either throw her away and lock her back up, or he could give in for just a little bit longer, to see just how far he could hold out.

She didn't pause – one hand she let creep further into his pants while the other undid his belt buckle and whipped it away in a flash. She put the belt around her neck and tightened it, leaving the end in his hand. While she stepped back to the front, she grabbed the blindfold away and saw his cheeks were flushed.

"Look at me."

He looked at her as she crouched in front of him and unzipped his trousers with one hand while the other gestured for him to tighten the belt around her neck, which he did.

When he looked down at her, he saw himself, rock hard, a slight movement with every heartbeat brought yet more blood and more pressure that he was only just tolerating. She stuck out her tongue, which was red and wet, then licked her lips for moisture. Leaning in, her lips tightened and he had to grip a nearby chair as her warmth met his body, teasing with her tongue as it moved along his shaft. Her movements were slow at first then firm; on the backward stroke she would suck in so that it felt there was no more room, then her hot breath would release him until she inched closer and closer each time, deeper and deeper.

She looked to the chair where his fingernails were tearing at the chintz fabric. Looking up, she saw his head bent back, the sweat rolling over his hard nipples and his Adam's apple dancing as he gasped for more air. She wondered what he was thinking about to stop him from blowing. Usually the man would have by now. Her strategy shifted into the next phase. She stopped on his shaft and instead massaged his balls – kissing, then sucking while her other hand ran up the inside of his thighs.

"*Mon dieu . . .*"

As soon as he said the words he woke up to himself.

Oh no, she's winning. Indeed she was, smiling with those lips that were so twisting him with irrational thoughts beyond the chess moves he was playing in his mind for distraction.

He pulled at the belt to get her to stop and she coughed and fell to the floor, not expecting that he would dare harm the skin he seemed to stare at with such fascination. Immediately her hand rushed to her neck and she loosened the belt.

His eyes were open wide and he looked at his hands, the veins popping out in pressure and heat. His eyes refocused to her, looking at him as if he had cheated at cards. He met her gaze and took the belt and threw it behind him. Enough. His voice *grizzled*.

Her eyes flickered in confusion and hopelessness before sinking to the floor, expecting to be hauled back to her room. Instead she saw him step out of his pants, and his feet approach her. He bent down and brushed her hair away from her neck and launched in to feel his lips on her pulse. It was even better than he imagined. She gasped as he seemed to eat her, then finish with a delicate kiss before he moved down to her left breast and teased it with his finger, licking, kissing then sucking. They were under the table now, on the oriental silk rug that softened their movements, their limbs twisting as they each moved to touch the other.

She would nibble his earlobe, he would reach between her legs. As he thrust his fingers in, she let herself suck in air sharply. She was so wet, she thought he might make her gush, and her muscles tightened around his fingers so that he pulled them out and stroked between her thighs leading up to her chest then to her lips so she could taste herself. She sucked on his fingers and thrust her hips into the air inviting him to taste too. He traced over the scars left by Mr White and kissed each one. She wasn't sure, but she thought she heard a "*désolé*" pass his lips as his forehead sank into the hollow of her belly before his tongue's tip flicked her clitoris in a gentle tickle. She pulled in her abdomen as she tried not to giggle. His tongue then moved down and deep into her, exploring each side.

He looked up at her, wanting to see her arch her back and neck, her fingers grabbing at the edge of the rug, twirling around the tassels like ivy. Now, she was like he had been minutes before. He smiled and let her wetness linger on his lips, down her legs on to her ankles, which he grabbed suddenly and pulled her out from under the table. Her eyes flashed in shock from being taken from the trance he was weaving. He picked her up and put her on his shoulder, then leaned her back down on the poker table, the chips flying.

As she looked up at him, his hair flicked down and hovered in front of his eyelashes. She reached to push his hair way so she could look at him, but he grabbed her wrists and pinned her down. She wriggled and kneed into his ribs. No, this was not her strategy. She had to be on top where she could be in control. To stop and start when she wanted to torment him as long as possible.

He struggled to hold her, their slippery bodies sticking to the chips but he held her there, his cock pressed hard against her leg until she stopped moving and their breathing moved in time. Then she realized. Her cards had been left up, exposing her two pairs: aces and queens and a nine. His cards must have been higher. He was taking his prize. She pushed her cards to the floor in acknowledgment and turned her neck so that the moonlight lay upon her skin.

He released one of her wrists and she left it there, her nipples getting harder. Then he reached to her eyelids and closed them softly while she felt his tongue move to her jawbone, then to her neck and he kissed it and buried his head into the hollow. His body pressed against hers completely, but lightly enough so she could still breathe. As he breathed in through his nose, he smelled her and felt his cock throb harder than ever.

She must have felt it too, because she dangled her fingers down the curve of his back and reached between their legs to stroke him and then finger herself. He took a sharp breath in and rolled her so she was on top, her eyes opened and she looked down at him. His arms were tucked behind his head, his eyes closed and a slight smirk froze upon his face.

She gathered some of her hair and tickled it underneath his nose, then rubbed her cheeks against his stubble before moving her hair on his abs. She waited until this stirred him even more and she kissed his bolt upright cock. As she sucked and kissed, she thrust her hips in time around his leg until he could feel her wetness start to slide over him.

He reached for her arm and then leaned up to pull her face away and bring her close so her eyelashes flicked against him and his gaze said what he wanted.

She shifted her weight and balanced on her knees, hovering over him. Taking a deep breath, she slid slowly on to his shaft, and he leaned back and groaned, eyes shaking beneath his eyelids. She moved side to side at first to adjust, then strained in a slow rhythm. He opened his eyes to see the white-skinned goddess arch her back with every lift and fall, his fingers tracing her ribs and around her nipples. She took his hand and placed his fingers in her mouth where she sucked on them, tasting the sweat. She placed his hand against her neck and opened her eyes and stopped.

He read her thoughts and rolled them over so he was on top. She lifted her legs so that her toes were curled behind his head, pushing him deeper. He felt both warmth and friction and the tantalizing taste like the bitter sweetness of acid chocolate – so soft and yet sharp enough to take his senses beyond. He used the edge of the poker table as leverage to push himself deeper.

She contracted her muscles in time with his thrusts so that he was forever being teased and released.

They continued this, slow then fast – each time he ran to the edge and ran back, until he finally took the leap. Shuddering and twitching, he breathed in deeply through clenched teeth, his hair flicking on to his face and sticking from sweat. After holding himself in mid-air, muscles clenched, he released and collapsed on the table, his limbs a mixture of pins and needles and elastic. His eyes opened and saw her lying there, looking at the ceiling.

She could feel his cum flowing out now that she had relaxed, but she was still gripping the edge of the table in frustration, her white skin moving with every pounded heartbeat. She closed her eyes and then opened them suddenly as she felt his hair brush against her stomach and his fingers trace around her thighs. Again she entered the trance that he had placed her under while they were on the rug, minutes before. But this time he let his tongue and fingers bring her to the point where she forgot to breathe and the release brought light again to her blackout of consciousness.

Her breathing returned and she opened her eyes, staring into space to the outside window at the stars performing for the last encore before the glare of daylight hid them.

He walked over to his pants and put them on, slowly dressing as he looked at her almost-still body from behind, only the faintest rise and fall as she breathed. She heard him walk to the desk, unplug the computer and take out the iPod.

He walked back over to the table and grabbed his cards that were still face down, then took out a pen from his pocket and wrote something on the left most corner before placing it down again. And with one final glance, he walked out of the room and shut the door quietly.

She picked up the cards. He'd had a jack of spades, a pair of eights, the ten of hearts and a king of diamonds. *So she had won after all.*

Between the hearts was a code 07AdV77.

Escape was hers.

Paladins

Robert Buckley

What a shit hole.

The shacks – housekeeping cottages the sign said – were spaced randomly among the tall pines, which prevented any breeze shy of a healthy cyclone from venting them of their aroma of mold and decay. A cloud of gnats and mosquitoes whined in his ears as he stepped out of the trees and on to the dirt drive that led to a clearing reserved for trailer homes and RVs. He paused to light a cigarette in the dark. He didn't smoke; it was all for effect, to look casual, non-threatening.

The only trailer in the lot matched the description of the one they were looking for. He sauntered toward it, eyeing the barrel-bellied man in the bib overalls who warily rose from a lawn chair.

There were children; he counted four. An obese woman in a cotton shift shooed them like a mother sow into the back of the trailer as he approached.

"Evenin'," he shouted to the hulking man.

"How do? Sticky one tonight."

"Brutal. I feel like I'm walking in soup. Makes it awful hard to sleep."

"Sure does. Night like this, a man kinda needs somethin' to . . . help him relax."

"I hear whacha sayin'. But the wife says it's too hot; says it'll take more than the usual to get her interested in working up a sweat."

The man laughed as his belly undulated. "Well, then, whacha think would make her want to get slippery for ya?"

It was his turn to chuckle, wink, and play at being a good ole boy. "Well, sir, she's pretty open-minded."

"Uh-huh. Well, you're a lucky man for having a woman like that. Maybe I have just the – what's that word? – oh, yeah, incentive."

"Oh?"

The man grinned a wide jack-o-lantern leer. Then he said, "Camille? You come out here, hon. I wancha to meet a gentleman."

The girl stepped out of the trailer and around the man. He guessed she was barely five feet three, waifish, bright blond angel hair, and an angel's face.

"You like her?" the man asked.

"Sweet . . . I think the wife and I could have some fun with her."

"She's for sale."

"That so? How much for how long?"

"You misunderstand me, mister. You buy her, she's yours."

"You her poppa?"

"Nah, but she is distant kin. I got plenty of my own to feed. I'll let you have her for a good price."

"To keep?"

"Sure . . . until you want to sell her to someone else. Or, if she's all worn out by then, just leave her someplace. I'll let her go for $500."

He stepped over to the girl and raised her chin in his hand. He held her for a moment, assessed the touch of her skin, and peered into her eyes. "She looks kinda young. What is she? Thirteen?"

"She'll be 14 come September. And, I'll be honest, she ain't no virgin, but she'll do things for you and the missus that won't make you care what the weather's like anytime. Truth is, I've had her myself. You won't get a much tighter, slippery-slidin' pussy and a cocksucking tongue like that little girl got. And don't let her size fool you; she'll keep going 'till you and the missus pass out and then clean ya'll up while you're sleepin'. So, whadya say? Five hundred dollars?"

"Three hundred dollars."

"Four hundred dollars."

"Three-fifty."

"I hate to let her go for that, but we're a bit low on gas and provisions, so I guess you talked me into it, mister. You sure know how to jew a man down."

The fat man chuckled and offered his hand, which was ignored.

He counted out the bills and dropped them into the hammy hand. "Come along, sweetie."

He guided the girl by her shoulder toward his cabin. As they stepped on to the porch and approached the screen door he shouted, "Baby, I'm back . . . with a little treat."

The girl preceded him without hesitation. As the screen door slapped behind him, a brunette came out of the bathroom. She held a formidable syringe.

The girl turned on one heel, her hair shot up toward the ceiling like a hundred streamers; the streamers transformed into ribbons of leaves that lashed at his face like razor grass. As he pushed her away he found his hands clasped around a green stalk, a series of mouths along its length bristling with spike-like teeth. His cheeks stung where the razor-leaves nicked him.

"Spike it!"

The brunette came up behind the creature and pushed the syringe into the stalk. "It won't go in!" she cried.

"Push harder!"

There was a hiss, then the thing shuddered and an ear-splitting shriek made his spine jangle. The thing seemed to wither and rot in his hands. He let it fall.

"Holy shit!" the woman said.

"You let it see the syringe."

"I know; I screwed up. I'm sorry. I was getting it ready just as you came in."

"It's little mistakes like that that'll get you killed . . . or worse."

"I know. Sorry. What the hell was that stuff we injected it with?"

"You didn't get any on your hands, did you?"

"No, I used the whole hazmat get-up. That's why it took me so long. So what the hell was it?"

"Ever hear of Agent Orange?"

"Um, no."

"How old are you?"

"Twenty-five."

"Hmm. Well, it's a pretty powerful defoliant. It'll kill any plant life on contact; it'll kill you too, after a while, if you get it on you."

"What the hell did you say that thing was again?"

"It doesn't have a name, actually. It's called by a dozen or so different things, cane devil, sugar shrieker."

"What about the other kids in that trailer?"

"I'm sure they're human. You see, that lovely couple made a living selling kids, and that's likely what they were intending to do to those others, before they met up with the thing."

"Selling children? To whom, for what?"

"I shouldn't have to draw you a picture. You think this thing we just killed was a monster? That white trash cracker and his sow . . . they're the real fucking monsters. Weak-minded bozos. This thing was running them, probably running them back home to

Louisiana and murdering all the way with those two boobs giving it cover."

"What then – when they got to Louisiana?"

"The legends around this thing say it spawns from the remains of unwanted infants buried in the cane fields. As usual with legends, there's a kernel of truth to them. We've found that they gestate in the ground and live off a living host. Sort of like spiders; they don't kill their prey, they paralyse them and come back to eat them at their leisure while they're alive."

"Yecch!"

"Those kids were on their way to getting planted in some cane field to feed the next generation of these things. Let's hope we put an end to the cycle."

"Sometimes, I'm not sure I can do this job."

"What did you say your name was?"

"For the umpteenth-thousandth time: Rachel!"

"Oh, yeah. Okay, Racey, you clean up here and I'll see to Mr and Mrs Hog Jowls."

"Racey!"

"I'm better at remembering nicknames."

Before she could say anything more the screen door slapped closed and he was gone.

The man at the trailer bolted out of his chair as Locan approached.

"What's the matter, friend? You look surprised to see me."

The man wiped his chin with his palm. "Uh, well, whatsa matter? Didn't she . . . uh . . . ?"

"Oh, yeah, she did pretty much what we expected her to do."

The woman tumbled out of the trailer. She held a hatchet in her hand. "We don't want no trouble, mister." Her voice was like pebbles rattling inside a can.

"Well, Mr and Mrs Lard Ass. You got trouble."

He tugged the revolver from behind his back, leveled it at the man's forehead and fired. He fell back in a wet thud. The woman was about to scream; a second bullet cut it short.

"You say you're peace officers?" The dubious deputy held the IDs under his flashlight.

Another cruiser pulled up behind them. The sheriff emerged, surveyed the scene and growled, "What the hell we got here?"

"Got a call of shots fired from the owner and found two people shot through the head outside the trailer there. Took a .44 Bulldog off him, and a pretty little Beretta off the lady. They say they're law officers."

The sheriff took the IDs from the deputy. "They don't look like any badges I ever seen. What's that say? Palatinus? And the rest, what the heck language is that?"

"I think it's Latin, sir."

"Latin?"

The sheriff spun away from the deputy and strode toward the suspect. His eyes narrowed. "Garreth Locan, that you?"

"Yes, sheriff. I assure you, we are law officers."

"What's this thing here? On your *badge*?"

"That's the papal seal."

"Hey, what? Papal, huh?"

Before he needed to answer, several more cars pulled up, unmarked. Squads of suits emerged and surrounded the deputies.

One approached. "Special Agent Mullens, sheriff, we'll take over from here."

"What? Now we got the Federal B-I pokin' their noses in our jurisdiction? Well, Agent Mullens, I got two bodies and two homicide suspects that ain't going anywhere, 'til I get some answers."

"You couldn't hold them anyway, Sheriff. They have diplomatic immunity."

"Dippo-what?"

"They're traveling under Vatican passports with consul privileges. Now, sheriff, I can't really explain except that sensitive matters of state are involved. We'll take over."

"Well, shee-it!" The sheriff nodded at the deputy who uncuffed the suspects. "Let's get out of here."

As the sheriff's cars rumbled away trailing dust, Mullens turned toward the pair. "Locan, get what you were after?"

"Yes, and what you were after too. There're four young kids in that trailer . . . merchandise."

"The killings? These two responsible, like we figured?" he asked, pointing to the bodies aswarm in a cloud of flies.

"Not directly. The killings were done by what we were after."

"Do I want to know?"

"If you like."

"Never mind. New partner?" Mullens held out his hand to Rachel.

"Yeah, meet Racey McDaniel."

"Racey?" Mullens grinned.

"Rachel," she insisted.

"Well, once you've been nicknamed by Locan, it's like being baptized again; there's no undoing it."

"We'll see."

"Got a message for you, Locan. Didn't come through the usual channels. 'C & C will meet you at the tavern in Oriskany. Three days.' "

"Upstate New York? Well, then, we'd better saddle up. Good to see you, Mullens. Be careful of things that go bump in the night."

"I'm more worried about thing's that go bang in the night."

Rachel hadn't said anything since they'd left Sloane's Hideaway in the Pines. Now they had entered the Interstate and were hurtling north toward a rendezvous in New York that he hadn't seen any need to fill her in on. She thought, after two weeks of traveling and working together, that she deserved a briefing. She hadn't screwed up that much. He never offered much conversation anyway, but now he was dumb as a rock. It irritated her.

"You just shot those people," she said when she couldn't stand the silence any longer.

"Yes . . . yes I did."

"I didn't think that . . . that's not what we're about . . . or is it?"

"We hunt and destroy monsters; I told you, those cracker-ass cretins were worse than the cane devil we killed."

"But they were people."

"So?"

"You killed them in cold blood."

"Hmm."

"I don't think I can do this."

"You said that before, but here you are."

"Not by choice."

"Ha! None of us are. We took the horse by the door."

"Horse?"

"What did you do?" he asked.

"I didn't do anything."

"They don't make you do penance for nothing."

She shrugged and thrust out her lower lip in a petulant pout. "Didn't they tell you?" she demanded.

"Yes, but I'd like to hear it from you. It seems you're a very dangerous young woman."

"I'll tell you, but you have to tell me first; how'd you become a Paladin?"

"I killed a priest."

"I heard there was more to it than that."

"Yeah, well things get exaggerated."

"I heard he was a vampire."

"Not exactly. He just had a disease that brought out the worst in him. See, he was an evil rat-shit bastard anyway. He was a pervert in a Roman collar, but something had happened to him; he'd come across something that infected him. Anyway, he was moved around a lot and then he was assigned to our parish. I was seventeen and my mother would rather we go hungry than miss church."

"Sounds like my mother."

"Uh-huh. So, anyway, right after Father Fred showed up a lot of the little kids in the parish started dying. I remember the state health department coming in and giving us all vaccinations and taking blood and urine and who knows what else. They couldn't figure out what the hell it was; the rest of the city was in a panic wanting to quarantine the neighborhood. Meanwhile, my little sister is getting ready for her first communion. The nuns rounded up all the kids for their first confession, but Mary was scared, so she asked me to come along."

"Something happened?"

"I stayed in the shadows on the other side of the church and kept an eye on her. She goes into the confessional, but a second or two later, Mary steps out and Father Fred opens the door to his stall and brings her in with him. I thought that was odd. A lot of time went by; I got up, walked across the church and headed toward the confessional. Some fat tub of a nun tried to stop me so I tossed her on her ass, and then I flung open the confessional. He'd locked it, but it broke."

"What did you see?"

"Mary was unconscious on his lap. I thought it was some kind of snake; it was his tongue. He tried to retract it. It was longer than my arm. I didn't think about it. I grabbed him by the throat with one hand and drove my fist into his chest with the other. The next thing I know Mary and all the nuns behind me are screaming and I'm holding the prick's heart in my hands squeezing it into mush."

"Your sister?"

"She got sick; she almost died, but after a few weeks she pulled through. And no more kids died after that. I was taken into custody, of course. My mom had a hard time after that, being the mother of a priest killer, after all. The neighbors gave her a lot of shit right up until she died."

"But, didn't they see . . ."

"Nobody saw anything. Or they just ignored what they'd seen. Anyway, a few days later this big hulking monsignor shows up in my cell. He believes my story, but then he shows me the horse by the door and says, take it or leave it. I took it."

"That monsignor, was he a tall black guy with a French accent?"

He laughed. "I thought they'd have retired him by now. So he made a visit to you too."

"Yeah, except he didn't mention anything about a horse."

He shrugged. "Monsignor Hobson."

"Huh?"

"Nothing. Go on with your story."

"I don't know where to start."

"Well, let's see, I expect your family was pretty religious, and pretty strict about it."

"Yeah, but I believed . . . I really believed."

"I'm guessing it was your mother's idea that you enter the convent."

"No . . . it was mine."

"Now, that's surprising."

"Why?"

He looked her up and down. Suddenly she was acutely conscious of her bare legs.

"You don't dress like a nun. Black leather hot pants, black-silk whatever it is – I suppose it would be a blouse if it covered your tummy. Oh, and let's not forget the cleavage-enhancing bra with the lace top showing. Nice legs."

Maybe she had dressed to get his attention, but now he made her feel cheap, and practically naked. He made her feel small, like a little girl. A big daddy figure, he was, but some daddy. She watched him in profile a moment. His face could have been carved out of granite, but his lips were soft, full. And his eyes, darker than brown, but not quite black. A full head of hair, dark, wavy, except for that white flair by his temple.

Finally, she answered, hoping her voice didn't waver. "I didn't think you noticed."

"I'd have to be dead not to notice. So, you went to the convent and it was all your idea."

"Mother was proud."

"Mother? You called your mom 'Mother'?"

She didn't reply.

"Okay, so what happened at the convent?"

"I . . . I fell in love."

"Oh? In a barracks full of women?"

"You must know; they must have told you. I wasn't expecting it. I liked boys . . . I mean, I was attracted to them."

"But you were attracted to girls too."

"That's why I went into the convent."

"Excuse me; you cloistered yourself up with a few hundred women because you were afraid you were attracted to women?"

"Okay, it was stupid. But, I thought . . . you take a vow of chastity. I thought the life would keep me in line."

"Yeah, heard that before. So?"

"So, there was another postulant. Sister Anita. She was so scared. We became friends, and then we came to the notice of Sister Arthur Francis."

"Mother Superior?"

"No, but her second in command. The MS was pretty far gone with senility."

"Power abhors a vacuum."

"She was such a vicious bitch. And a mean butch. She'd been abusing a lot of the young sisters; everyone just looked the other way. Anita and I tried to avoid her whenever we could. I guess, it was because we looked out for each other so much, that it developed into something more."

He nodded but said nothing.

"We couldn't avoid Sister Arthur Francis forever. She could tell what was going on. Then one night she paid a visit to Anita's cell. She made her . . . well, afterward she said Anita would do whatever she wanted or she would make my life a hell."

"Why do you suppose she picked on Anita, instead of you?"

"I don't know."

"Sure you do."

"Maybe, it was because I'd have put up a fight."

"Of course, you were stronger. She was afraid of you."

"I don't know about that, considering what happened."

"I'm listening."

"Anita had been crying all day. I snuck in to see her that night, to comfort her as much as I could. We ended up . . . making love. It must have been a set-up. The bitch had been after her all day; she knew I'd try to go to her that night. Anyway, she came barging in with this . . . it looked like a broom handle. She called us every filthy thing you could think of. Then she starts to undress herself and tells us to lie across the bed. That's when she announces she's going to beat us, and afterward we were both to . . . to . . . pleasure her. That's just how she said it, 'pleasure' her."

"And?"

"The next thing I know Sister Arthur Francis is writhing on the floor screaming, her hands plastered to her eyes. Anita's screaming too, hysterical. The other sisters came running and I got put in a cell by myself. They locked me in. A couple of days later the big black monsignor arrived. He said Sister Arthur Francis had been blinded and I was in a whole lot of trouble. Then he gave me the choice. I agreed, and the next morning we landed in Rome. Took me right through customs. I didn't even have a passport."

"So, you blinded the bitch."

"I don't know how I was supposed to have done that. I was mad, mad out of my mind, angry for what she'd done to Anita. I just remember coming off the bed and going for her."

"You don't remember a flash of blue light?"

"No. But . . . hey, now that you mention it, I remember snatches of conversation between the monsignor and Jacoby."

"Captain Jacoby."

"Yeah, something about a flash of blue. What . . . what does it mean?"

"Don't know. Maybe we'll find out in Oriskany."

What did Oriskany have to do with her? She drew her knees under her chin and clasped her arms around her legs. "I never saw Anita again. I don't know what happened to her."

He said nothing.

She had fallen asleep almost ninety miles back, but now she stirred.

"Hey, can we pull over? My bladder's getting ready to burst."

She said it just as he pulled into a roadside hotel.

"Thank God! A real shower and a clean bed. That cabin made my skin crawl. Two nights in that dump . . . made me afraid I'd pick up some mold infection, or something."

"Wasn't it a hole?" he agreed.

It was almost 2 a.m. The night clerk had been dozing and didn't pay much attention to them as he checked them in. He handed them a key and mumbled something about a complimentary breakfast.

The room was standard, two beds, air conditioned. She began to peel off her clothes, then stopped, cast him a look, and said, "Ooops."

"Take your shower. I can wait," he said.

She nodded, gathered her things and stepped into the bathroom. A few moments later he heard the spray of water and a heartfelt moan of pleasure. He smiled, and then retrieved a document from a valise.

The document was stamped: POR OCULES TUAS SOLUM.

"For your eyes only. Well, no shit."

He frowned as he read the document, then muttered, "Fuck them."

A squeal followed by giggles drew his eyes away from the paper. He slipped it back into the valise and shoved the valise into his bag.

She emerged from the bathroom with an oversized towel wrapped around her. She shivered in the air-conditioned room and pulled it even more tightly.

"Pick your flop," he said and gestured toward the beds. "I'll take a shower while you get dressed for bed . . . that is, if you *do* get dressed for bed."

She smirked and grabbed her bag, plopping down on the bed closest to the door.

Later, he stepped out of the shower and wrapped a large towel around his waist. Its mate was big enough to mostly cover the girl, but not him. He turned the light off before he emerged and made his way to the far bed. She hadn't drawn the curtains and moonlight filled the room, so he could see her form under the bedclothes. He couldn't tell if she was asleep.

But he sensed her eyes on him as he tossed away the towel and then slid naked beneath the sheets. He curled up with his back toward her.

"Locan?"

"Hmm? I thought you were asleep."

"Can't . . . too much going on in my head."

"Better try."

"Do you believe in God?"

"Oh, brother."

"Oh, humor me a little, will you?"

"Do you?"

She was silent for a long time, then, "I used to. Then I didn't; now I'm not so sure. The things I've seen since . . ."

"Since being drafted into the Palatinae? You couldn't have seen that much yet."

"The cane devil. Jesus! How about that?"

"Supernatural creature? Is that how you figure it?"

"Well, yeah."

"So, you figure if there are evil, supernatural monsters in the world, they must have a counterpart – God and his angels and whatever, right? Well, the cane devil is probably a perfectly natural species. It scares the hell out of us because of the legends that have grown up around it. It's likely been around as long as we have . . . mankind that is. Everything we call supernatural is probably just something natural that science hasn't figured out yet."

"Then what about vampires?"

"What about them?"

"How do you explain them?"

"Diseased. They have some malady that makes them crave blood. Just like a diabetic can't make his own insulin, he has to get it by other means. They're pretty pathetic, really, worse than junkies."

"So, there are no true vampires?"

"I didn't say that."

"But . . ."

"Some, the decent sorts, just want to live quiet lives and be left alone. They find ways to keep a low profile."

"Decent sorts?"

"Sure, they can't help being what they are, no more than we can . . ."

"What?"

"Never mind. Go to sleep."

He listened as her feathery breaths became deeper and regular. He got up and retrieved a small penlight from his bag, then approached her bed, bending over her and straining to hear. Satisfied she was fast asleep he gingerly rolled the bedclothes back. She was lying on her stomach, clad in an oversized T-shirt that had bunched up just below her buttocks. His fingers slid beneath the fabric; delicately he lifted the shirt higher, over her round, moonlit globes, then over her hips exposing the small of her back above her tailbone.

He directed the beam to the place flanked by the dimples of Venus.

"Hmm." He rolled the garment back down and reached for the bedclothes. In an instant she came awake and lifted off the bed like a rocket, standing on the bed and bracing her back against the wall.

"What the fuck do you think you're doing?" she demanded.

"Checking out your back."

"You mean my ass!"

"I mean your back. Your ass, well, as lovely as it is, it was not my point of interest."

"Jesus, Locan, if you wanted to . . . I mean, you could have asked."

"To see your back?"

"No! I mean you and me . . . naked."

"Sit down."

She didn't move.

"You don't wear panties to bed, eh?"

She dropped into a sit and bunched her T-shirt at her crotch.

"You have a mark on your back, just above your tailbone."

"Yeah, I have a birthmark, so what?"

"A blue disk; a perfect circle, no irregularities."

"So?"

"Very unusual."

"Yeah, and again, so?"

"I'll tell you in the morning."

"No . . . they told you something about me, didn't they? I knew it; I knew something was up when they partnered me with you out of the blue."

"Don't worry."

"Don't worry . . . this from a guy who put a bullet through two people's brains like he was scratching an itch."

"Fair enough. So, let me say this: I won't hurt you, Racey. Never."

"Then tell me what's going on?"

"Later, after we've slept."

"I can't sleep."

"Trust me?"

"I . . . okay . . . I will . . . just . . ."

"What?"

"Sleep with me . . . if you're here next to me . . . I won't be thinking . . . I won't . . ."

"Okay."

He slid beside her, then he lifted her T-shirt over her head. Instantly his nostrils filled with the scent of skin and just the faintest essence of . . . coconut?

She clasped her arms around his neck and shoulders and rolled on to him.

"Racey?"

"Rachel."

This girl was too soft, too supple, she smelled just too good. Her hair was too lush, too silky, and her lips were just too . . . too . . .

He kissed her and pulled her against his chest. He felt her cushion his cock between her thighs as she trailed kisses down and down until he felt her pubis brush against his cock and her nipples trail down his thighs. Then his cock sprung free again and tapped her under her chin. She responded by taking him into her mouth.

Her tongue snaked along his length, setting off little electrical charges that built rapidly. He was not going to be able to hold back his fluids much longer. He forced himself over on his side, flipping her to the edge. Her lips glistened in the moonlight; her eyes conveyed a question.

He rose on to his knees and clasped her ankles. He straddled them as she rose on to all fours lifting her ass to his face. He positioned himself behind her, took hold of her hips and pressed his cock between the plump folds of her pussy. Then he was inside her, listening to her moan with each thrust. And just below his eyes, the perfect blue disk seemed to pulse.

He felt her shudder, then allowed his fluids to surge out of his cock and flood her cunt. A sparkle caught his eye, like tiny pulses of lightning off her fingernails. Her head was buried in the pillow. He didn't think she had seen them.

They awoke just before they shut down the complimentary breakfast. They were awake, rested, and a little sore.

"Are you going to tell me now?" she said, then downed a glass of orange juice in a single gulp.

"Hungry?"

"Always, after a workout."

"Pretty sassy for a nun."

"I never took my vows."

"Hmm."

"Well?"

"Okay," he said. He put his hands flat on the table and stared at them awhile.

"Yes?" she pressed.

"Jacoby is a little worried about you. Cardinal LeRocque is a lot worried about you. Me, I don't think there's much of a problem."

"Problem? Jesus, why did they put us together? You're not a trainer."

"Okay, I'll tell you. Promise me you'll sit there and not let on, no matter what I say."

"Okay."

"I'm supposed to evaluate you and if this *problem* should manifest itself . . ."

"Yes?"

"I'm supposed to kill you."

She coughed up the remains of a muffin she'd been nibbling on.

"For crissakes, Locan. What the hell problem are they talking about? It's like I'm one of the things they send us out to hunt."

"Hmm. Remember what I told you about the cane devil?"

"I dunno, what?"

"That it was probably some creature that evolved naturally, like you and me, or a lion, or a lizard."

"Yeah, so?"

"Okay, so science pretty much agrees that mankind originated in Africa thousands of years ago. We were a bunch of monkeys' cousins and then we climbed out of the trees and stood up straight, and began this long walk that eventually brought us out of Africa and into the Middle East and Europe and Asia, and all along the journey we kept becoming more and more what we call human today. Following?"

"Yeah, sure."

"Okay, well, somewhere along the line the family split. Some of us followed one path, some followed another . . . I'm talking the evolutionary path now."

"Uh-huh."

"So we have the Neanderthals and then we have the Cro-Magnons, who eventually evolve into us. The Neanderthals, well, looks like they hit a dead end. The point is, the human stalk split."

"Yeah, okay, we survived and they didn't."

"Okay, so what if there were other stalks from the same tree, and they survived and evolved just as we did, but separately . . . but not so separately that you could tell us apart that easily, except for one or two very important differences."

"What . . . differences?"

"Like being born with a blue disk over your ass."

She froze, her eyes narrowed and bored into his.

"Racey?"

"What . . . what are you saying?" Her chin trembled.

"Look, you're a good person, a bright intelligent girl. I won't let anything happen to you, or tell you anything I don't think you can handle. But you're going to have to brace yourself from time to time."

"What the hell am I . . . supposed to be?"

"Oh, I don't know for sure. A hybrid probably. Somewhere back in your family; maybe your great-great-great grandma fell in love with some guy and they had babies with blue dots on their behinds."

"You make it sound so mundane. What am I?"

"I promise you, we're going to find out."

Back on the road they stopped only briefly for a bathroom break and a light meal. He drove on into the night, and would not stop for accommodation until the early morning hours.

"You can't appreciate the size of this country until you've driven across it," he said after a long stretch of silence.

"You should let me drive."

"Yes, I should."

She huffed. Then stretched. "You're a killer," she said, her voice flat.

"So are you."

"Am I? I couldn't kill another human being like . . ."

"Like I did?"

"Yes. Sorry."

"Hmm. You said you were religious."

"Yeah, I guess."

"Did you say you believed in God? I can't remember."

"Yeah, I mean, I believe in something. I just believe there must be something . . . someone."

"Hmm. Well, remember when you were a kid and they taught you that everyone has a soul, and the soul is – what? – a bit of God Himself? The nuns used to say he passed his breath into every baby that was ever born."

"Yeah, I heard that too, at sisters' school."

"Well, I'm not sure about God, but I believe in the soul. I just don't believe everyone has one."

"But . . . that doesn't make any sense."

"No? Look at people, good or bad. The ones with intellect, the ones who have a deep thought, even if it's just once in a while. I think they have souls. But look at the rest. Like that lovely couple we left behind us. Something like that just lives to feed its appetites. And it's not just what we'd consider the scum of the earth. From white trash right on up to the nouveau riche yuppie shithead who's acquired his latest BMW, or yacht or mansion . . . you know the type, they calculate their own worth and everyone else's according to how many things they've accrued. They have no souls, because as insubstantial as a soul might be, it takes a lot to fill the void where it doesn't exist. So they fill it up with things."

"So, what are you saying, that it's okay to kill people like that?"

"I'm saying if it has no soul, it isn't murder when you kill it."

"Did that cane thing have a soul?"

He shrugged. "Maybe. But that was self-defense."

"Maybe you think too much," she said, then yawned.

He pulled into another hotel. A sleepy clerk checked them in. Another room, much like the one in which they spent the night before. This one they entered from a balcony. Outside it began to rain; droplets beat against the window.

They stood together in the darkness by the window. A lightning flash illuminated the courtyard; another caught a naked couple in the room directly across from theirs having sex in their window, a fleeting image of a woman with her breasts pressed against the glass.

He chuckled. "You can't enjoy sex if you don't have a soul."

"Why not?"

"Because if you don't, fucking is just about the fucking, it's just chalking up another pussy or prick, just another fuck to tally on top of the ones you've already had. Just so you can say you had more tail than the other guy."

"And if you have a soul?"

"Well, then it's about . . ."

"Making love?"

"Or . . . something else. In any case, you do it with another person. Some people have sex, and it's no different than if they were masturbating."

"You think too much."

"Let me take a shower at least," she protested weakly after he tossed her on the bed and tugged her shorts and panties off.

"Uh-uh," he said. He knelt and breathed deeply, his nose pressed against her dark pubic patch.

He spread her thighs apart. She didn't resist.

Then his tongue laved her swelling vulva. Her own tongue slipped along her lips as his licking became more determined.

He kissed and sucked; he also stroked her clit with the tip of his nose. Each time she felt like she would levitate off the bed. His lips sealed to her pussy as his tongue probed the walls of her cunt and she grabbed handfuls of bedclothes in her fists. Tongue, lips, nose – his fingers stroked her pubic hair – he used them all like a master conductor creating a piece of music, and she was singing the aria. She came with a shudder and a squeal and lightning flashed like it was inside the room and blue fireflies danced in her eyes.

It was an exhausting orgasm; she wanted to lie still forever and let it just drain away. But he turned her over and lifted her ass.

"Please . . ." she mewed, knowing it was futile, knowing that he was going to take her from behind again.

"I hate nuns," he said as he plunged his cock into her. "I never thought I'd enjoy fucking one."

"Unngh! I told you – owwww – I never took my vows."

"No, you're a nun, and I'm doggy-fucking your nunsensical brains out. Hear me, Sister Racey Pink-snatch?"

"Oh my God!"

"Convent slut! I'll make you do more than say your rosary on your knees."

"God!" she gasped. "You bastard . . . fucking . . . fuck me . . . geeesh . . . I can't . . . coming again!"

She almost bucked him off the bed. His cock slipped out trailing an arc of semen.

Afterward, they took a shower together and toweled each other off. Then they fell naked into bed.

As she slid into slumber, Rachel whispered, "I have a soul."

"I know."

She was barely more than half his age, he thought, as his mind crested a wave of coddling comfort on its way to slumber. He liked the way she nestled in his arms; he liked screwing her from behind. He never should have let it get this far. He didn't care.

Now his thoughts veered off on to other avenues, taking him for a ride toward the inchoate realm of dreams. He was a child listening to his mother's mother, sitting rapt as she spun stories about his great-grand uncle, the Civil War hero, the sniper with a sixth sense. Then a worm bored into his dream, corkscrewing out of the darkness. His eyes snapped open and he bolted up in bed. A woman outside the window, standing on the balcony, held a pistol in a combat grip. It was aimed right at him.

He reached for his revolver as metal knocked against his temple.

"Move and you're dead," the voice said. Another knock against his skull, he could tell that it was the barrel of a gun hitting him.

"Who the fuck are you?"

Another knock to his scalp, this one opened a wound.

Movement in his peripheral vision caused his eyes to slide sideways away from the voice. It moved along the wall like a shadow.

"Where's the bitch?" the voice demanded.

"Huh? Bitch?"

Then the window exploded into a thousand shards, a blue flash, like an electrical arc illuminated the room. The voice in his ear became a scream. Locan knocked the gun away and rolled out of bed taking his assailant by the lapels, and slamming his head against the wall. He cocked his arm and sent his fist crashing into the man's face. His nose and teeth crumbled. Locan cocked his arm again and drove his fist into the face, now wet and pulpy, again. The man seized, then he went limp. He stood and spun around. Rachel stood outside on the balcony naked. He ran to the door and stepped outside. A woman's body hung backward over the railing, its head dangling by a strip of flesh.

Rachel stood trembling. Her face and breasts painted with blood.

Somewhere a woman screamed. People began to pour out of doors and on to the balcony.

"Shit!"

He grabbed Rachel's arm and pushed her back into their room. He guided her to the bathroom where he grabbed face cloths to wash away the gore.

"I . . . I don't know what happened. I just woke up; I knew they were there, I just knew they were there. I saw her holding the gun on you; I don't know why she didn't see me."

"You'd gone dark."

"What? Dark?"

"It's like becoming invisible, but you aren't really. You blend into the shadows."

"It was like . . . like . . ."

"What?"

"Like back in the convent. I can't remember."

There was a pounding at the door. "Police . . . get your hands up."

"We aren't dressed."

"Get your asses where we can see them or you'll be dressed for the undertaker."

The officers grabbed their wrists and spun them around.

"Can she have a blanket?" Locan asked.

"Shut up!"

Outside pulses of blue and red lights turned the place into a party club. Locan and Rachel were made to sit on the bed. Finally, one of the cops tossed some blankets over them.

More cops arrived, as well as the coroner.

The one who appeared to be the lead investigator stared at the IDs one of the officers handed him. He leaned toward another plainclothes cop. "Look at these. Vatican passports . . . diplomatic passports. What the hell are these, badges?" He stepped over to Locan while Rachel was taken to be interrogated in another room. "This your name? Garreth Locan?"

"Yes."

"Who the fuck are these dead people?"

"I have no idea. They broke in."

Outside someone yelled, "Careful how you move that body; her head's going to fall off."

"Did you do that?" the detective asked, gesturing back toward the voice.

"No."

"Who did?"

"Can't tell you . . ."

"Sergeant."

"Very well, sergeant."

"It looks like you were expecting trouble," he said, holding up his and Rachel's pistols.

"They were never fired."

The sergeant shook his head. Another cop approached him and handed him a cell phone.

"Yeah, did you run those IDs? Christ, they're legitimate? We can't even hold these people? It's a fucking massacre here. What? Mullens? Yeah, hang on."

He uncuffed Locan and handed him the phone.

"Yes?"

"For Christ's fucking sake, what's with you two?"

"Mullens . . . do you have any idea who the hell these people are?"

"They used to be a husband and wife hit team. Do you believe in coincidences?"

"Not really."

"They were hunting down the runaway wife of one of the biggest money launderers on the West Coast. We were too, trying to get to the lovelorn couple before they did. They were contracted to kill her and the boyfriend. We'd just located the couple at the Quality Inn about a half mile from where you're staying. Then all hell broke loose. Seems you and your partner are the victims of mistaken identity; although, the way things turned out, maybe you weren't the victims.

"Anyway, the couple we got here, the guy looks a lot like you, and the wife, well, she's blonde but she was traveling as a brunette."

"You've explained things to the local constabulary then?"

"Yeah, you're free to go, but I gotta tell you, Rome's been in touch. They're mightily put out that you haven't been maintaining a low profile; in fact, they're pissed. They want you and your partner back there the day before yesterday."

"Thanks, they'll have to wait."

"For crying out loud, try not to kill anyone for a while, will you?"

"You know me, turn the other cheek."

"Shit. Get outta there."

They were allowed to dress and take their belongings. A police car escorted them back to the Interstate.

Rachel sat still, her legs drawn up as she gnawed on the knuckles of one hand.

"Hey, cut that out, will you? You'll draw blood."

"I killed her didn't I? They were the couple we saw making love in the window."

"Were they?"

"You know they were. Did they have souls?"

"Doesn't matter – self defense."

"God, it was horrible, but why can't I remember? Going dark?"

"Yes, a pretty useful talent in our line of work."

"Stop! Just tell me what's happening to me. I was dead asleep and I woke right up. I knew they were there before I even knew I was awake."

"Sometimes your senses will become acutely heightened."

"Sometimes?"

"For instance, when you've just had really good sex."

"Cripes."

"Or whenever you feel threatened, or angry . . . or even happy."

"When are you going to tell me what's happening to me . . . what I am?"

"Soon, Racey. Very soon."

"Rachel," she insisted, though her chin trembled and a tear spilled over her cheek.

"I promise you."

He could feel Rome breathing down his neck; they wanted an answer or a result. And, if he didn't check in soon, they'd send someone after them. Not another pair of Paladins, but a pair of blockhead Swiss Guards who'd follow their orders without reservation – like a pair of Nazis.

They checked into a hotel in Utica, cleaned up and then started out for the village of Oriskany.

They sat in the car outside the tavern for a while.

"I think we'll have some answers for you, maybe more than you were hoping for," he said. "The thing is, you need to hold yourself together, no matter what they tell you."

"Who?"

"C'mon."

They entered the tavern and he took her hand and paused. He nodded toward a couple at a corner table.

The man was tall. Rachel could tell even though he was sitting. Black hair flecked and streaked with silver. She wondered at his age, but couldn't put a number to it.

The woman was long and lean, a cowl of the blackest hair draping her shoulders. She wore a deep blue satin blouse, black leather mini skirt and nearly knee-high boots. Her legs crossed under the table, her thighs pale in the shadow. They were so long, Rachel guessed she had to be six feet tall or more.

She squeezed Locan's hand.

"The man's name is Connor," he told her. "He's been on the Paladins' hit list since there were Paladins. I could shoot him right now and walk away – no questions asked. I'd probably even get some half-assed decoration from the Pope."

"Then why . . . ?

"I never would, but even if I wanted to, they haven't invented a bullet fast enough."

"But . . . what is he?"

"A species unto himself."

"The woman . . . she's striking."

"Wait until you see her up close. Her name is Clare."

Locan took Rachel's arm and guided them to the couple's table. Connor rose to greet them. He was taller than Locan, but he had the same, dark fathomless eyes.

"Locan, good to see you again," he said. His voice was lightly accented, but Rachel couldn't place it. "And this lovely lady?"

"This is . . . Rachel . . . Rachel McDaniel."

Rachel turned a bemused glance at Locan as Connor took her hand and kissed it lightly. A tingle ran up her arm.

"Clare?" Connor nodded toward his companion.

Clare extended her hand; Rachel took it in hers. This time more than a tingle coursed up her arm. Tiny sparks, like a company of blue fireflies danced around her wrist and marched toward her elbow. She released her hand and looked into Clare's eyes. They shone pale blue, like backlit arctic ice. Rachel shivered.

Clare smiled.

"Remember." Locan bent to her ear. "Hold it together."

"Rachel?" Connor said. "Hasn't Locan rechristened you with a nickname?"

"Racey," she answered.

"Racey!" Connor laughed. "Of course."

A waitress in a white dirndl dress asked for their order.

"The steaks here are splendid," Connor said. "Shall we order, once and all around?"

Locan nodded. Rachel assented.

"Very good." Connor smiled at the waitress. "Make mine very rare."

"Bloody rare," Clare added. The waitress, shaken, retreated a step when she noticed Clare's eyes.

"Um, medium, please," Rachel said.

"Medium well for me, dear." Locan nodded.

Rachel tried not to stare at Clare, but her eyes were mesmerizing. Clare looked right back, a smile, or perhaps a sneer curling her lips.

"Your accent," Rachel asked, her voice suddenly timid. "Are you French?"

"Breton."

"Oh."

"So, Locan," Connor said, lifting a glass of dark red wine to his lips. "How's the fiend-hunting business treating you?"

"So far, so good. And the benefits . . . out of this world."

"Ah yes, traveling in the company of charming young women." He nodded toward Rachel. "Seems to me you normally worked alone."

Locan nodded and smiled. "Maybe they think I'm getting too old for the job and I need someone to watch out for me."

"Old? You'll excuse me of course, old is a concept I have trouble grasping."

The men laughed. An invisible nod passed between them, an inside joke Rachel was not privy to.

"And Rome?" Connor asked. "Still fervent about their crusades."

"Fervent . . . fervent to a fault."

"I miss Rome," Connor mused, swirling his wine in the glass. "I used to know a girl there, the youngest sister of senator . . . oh, the name escapes me. A sweet girl . . ."

Rachel's head turned slowly toward Clare, the source of a low frequency rumble that grew louder as Connor spoke.

Was she growling? God, Rachel thought, she *is* growling.

The waitress returned with the steaks, putting a period to Connor's story of the girl in Rome.

Dinner conversations continued, just normal small talk that Connor would punctuate with a historical anecdote.

After dinner, Connor ordered a round of dessert liqueurs. Rachel sensed an intimacy, as if a veil of shadow had been drawn around their table.

"Rachel," Connor said. His voice was deep, calming. "Locan has asked my assistance and I cannot refuse because I owe him a debt that cannot be repaid in one lifetime. But even if I did not, I am glad to help, that is, Clare and I are glad to help . . . you, to understand."

"Yes?"

"Do you believe in God?"

"I . . . Where have I heard that before?"

Connor smiled. "It doesn't matter, whether you believe in God or Mr Darwin. But let's keep this simple. The human family tree came into being; it split off into various branches. Some withered, others thrived. So now we have the human species as we know it, ostensibly alone, but what if that species is not alone; it has . . . cousins it is not even aware of.

"Let's say God has stepped away from his masterpiece, the 'paragon of animals', and sees that as masterful as it is, it is not perfect, it has flaws."

"Yes?" Rachel had no idea where this was going, but she loved listening to his voice.

"So, he creates this companion species, not to supersede homo sapiens, but to . . . take out the garbage, as it were."

"I'm not sure I understand."

"That's all right, you'll reach your own conclusions soon enough. The thing you need to understand now is that both these branches of man could, and have interbred from time to time. Rarely, due to circumstances that are rooted deep in history, but such unions have occurred."

Rachel began to tremble, sensing an impending epiphany she wasn't certain she wanted to experience.

"Clare," Connor said. "Rachel looks like she could use a bit of fresh air."

Clare stood. Rachel thought she would keep going up and up. Clare took her hand and drew her on to her feet, but she still towered over Rachel.

"Come on, *petite soeur.*"

Locan and Connor watched the ladies leave.

"You care for her very much," Connor said. "A dangerous thing to care for one so much, in your line of work."

"I know."

Connor raised his glass. "You're a good and noble man, my friend."

"I hope she goes easy on her," Locan said.

"She'll open up a new world for her."

"Yeah . . . I just hope she's up for it."

Connor laughed. "She looks tough enough to me."

Outside a clear twilight sky cast the first stars over the heavens.

"Follow me," Clare said.

"Where?"

"Across the road, to the edge of the forest."

Rachel complied, her eyes captured by the sway of Clare's hips, and her pale, sculpted thighs. Women's thighs excited Rachel, in all their shapes and textures. Clare's were smooth, muscular, strong. Rachel thought about touching them, even kissing them. A tickle began to swirl in her belly.

They crossed the road and Clare stepped into the trees.

"Do you smell them?" she asked Rachel.

"Smell? Who?"

"Give free rein to your senses. There now, smell them . . . beer, sweat, sour breath, bowel stink?"

Rachel filled her nostrils and nearly retched. The clean smell of pine vanished; she felt like she was standing in a very dirty men's room.

"What the . . ."

"I don't like them," Clare said.

"Them?"

"People . . . I've seen the worst of them. But . . . Connor . . . he's shown me many have worth, they can even be noble."

"Oh."

"These swine are only here to do harm. Shall we have our fun with them?"

"I . . . I don't know . . ."

"You've shifted?"

Rachel shook her head. "Shifted?"

"It's frightening at first, when you don't control it, and it comes over you all of a sudden," Clare said. "Like the first time you pass blood."

Rachel said nothing; her mind was astir with questions she couldn't form into words.

"You were in the convent," Clare said. "So was I, a long time ago." Then she grinned. "You may want to leave your clothes here. We can return for them later."

"Leave my clothes?" Rachel asked.

"I go through so many clothes. They don't survive the shift. It can get . . . expensive."

Clare began to unbutton her blouse, and then she turned her back to Rachel and shrugged it off her shoulders. Her bra instantly fell beside it.

Her skirt was already set low on her hips. Rachel watched her, dumb as the trees, as Clare shook it off her hips. There, above her tailbone, a perfect blue disk.

Clare turned. "Well?"

Rachel stripped, quickly, clumsily.

Clare held out her hand. "Come along, little sister."

Rachel took her hand and the night turned into a sea of blue light.

She was running, bounding through the forest, a step behind a sleek black animal, its silky coat streaming as they traversed clearings, streams and columns of pines. Even the stars passed by in a blur. The sheer sense of speed was exhilarating. Then she realized . . . she was running on all fours. She could hear Clare clearly communicating a change in direction . . . not as a voice, but as pure thought. Her senses had never been so keen, she processed a cascade of aromas and sounds, heard a mouse rustle in its nest, a pair of night birds mate on a branch yards away, and felt the wind as it rushed past. And she could see into the darkness.

They were close. Clare had told her. The stink of the men became stronger. Ahead of them a creature moaned in fear and despair. Flashlights marred the dark. They had chased a black bear up a tree and were throwing things at it, trying to get it to fall. Some wielded bats and swigged from cans.

It was all a blur of screams as they tore into their company, doing no real harm other than hurtling into their bodies and knocking their legs out from underneath them.

Rachel bowled one of them over and now she stood, stock still, a rage pulsing in her core. The man looked into her eyes and screamed, "Oh, Jesus! Please!"

There was a snarl, ferocious, announcing the arrival of hell itself. It was Rachel, baring her fangs. Then the scent of urine stung her nostrils. The man had pissed himself and passed out.

Clare called her to withdraw. The bear jumped from the tree and bolted into the woods. The other men had scattered screaming, all but the one who fainted beneath Rachel's fierce gaze.

This is all so . . . wonderful, Rachel thought.

Connor and Locan stood at the edge of the pines staring at two piles of ladies' clothing.

"They shouldn't be much longer," Connor said, and clapped Locan on the shoulder.

Several yards up the road, two men stumbled out of the trees and on to the roadway. One tripped, and then he tripped again.

"Get your ass up and let's get outta here!" his companion demanded.

"Jesus . . . Jesus-Jesus-Jesus . . . what the fuck were they? Did you see Harry? I think one of 'em got him. Should we go back for him?"

"Fuck that! Harry's on his own. I'm never going back there again."

"Jesus . . . what the hell . . . they were wolves . . . they were wolves, man! There ain't supposed to be no fucking wolves around here."

"Shut up! Let's get outta here. And if Harry don't show up, we know nothin', right?"

"Shit! Poor Harry."

"Fuck Harry."

The two hurried past Connor and Locan, wheezing, trying to run stiff-legged from exertion. They didn't notice them standing just inside the trees. Connor grinned as they passed.

Minutes later an effusion of blue luminescence illuminated the forest, and then another. Clare and Rachel, naked, stepped out of the trees. Connor had brought a cape that he placed around Clare's shoulders.

Locan awkwardly retrieved Rachel's skirt and sweater and held them out to her, but she stood unabashed. He thought her eyes sparkled.

"It was so incredible, Locan. My God . . . it was so incredible."

He nodded. "C'mon, better get you dressed."

"Huh? Oh, yeah."

They returned to the tavern and seated themselves at a quiet booth by the bar.

"My mother loved a man," Clare said, staring into the glass of clear amber liquid in her hand. "I am his child. I think, Rachel, that perhaps your grandmother, or great-grandmother loved such a man . . . perhaps the same man." She sipped from her glass. Rachel thought a veil of melancholy shaded her face.

"Your . . . abilities," Connor said. "very rarely pass down through the male line, and when it has, it has not ended well. As for you, Rachel, I would guess at puberty a restlessness overtook you. But I suspect you were raised in a disciplined family and that helped you suppress it. Still, were there times you wanted to tear your clothes off and go running into the night?"

"Yes . . . I did try to suppress it. I tried to suppress . . . a lot of different feelings."

"You can control your shifts," Clare said. "Your spirit is strong. You wanted to tear that filthy slob to pieces tonight, didn't you?"

"Uh . . . yes. I never felt such pure, righteous . . ."

"Lethal?" Connor said.

"Yes, lethal rage. It was . . . intoxicating."

Clare chuckled. "Just be careful what you eat."

"Huh? Eat?"

"I think," Connor said, "you've had more than enough placed on your plate for one evening, Rachel. Your questions will be answered, they'll all be revealed. Decisions will need to be made, however. A long life awaits you."

"How long?"

He shrugged. "I can't say."

He stood, and Clare stood with him. He took Rachel's hand and kissed it, then Clare bent down and kissed her cheek.

"*Bonne chance*, little sister."

Locan and Rachel remained.

"He said I'd live a long time, Locan."

"Uh-huh."

"Locan . . . how old is Connor?"

"Well . . . I'm not so sure. That debt he says he owes me. Seems an ancestor of mine, a Paladin, caught him napping one evening after a long pursuit. Had him cold. But, for whatever reason, he let him live. Just stuck his sword into the ground and they had themselves a nice chat, like a couple of gents."

"His sword? When was this?"

"I dunno, around 800 I guess. Connor's tangled with Roman legions . . ."

"Roman?"

"Uh, yeah."

"And Clare?"

"Oh, Clare's just a baby."

Her eyes pressed him for an answer.

"Okay, she was born late in the sixteenth, maybe early seventeenth century."

"Jesus, Locan. Are they . . . immortal?"

"Connor says no, but he has no idea how long he'll live. They *can* be killed, so . . ."

"So what?"

"Nothing . . . just don't get reckless."

"Oh my God . . . Locan."

"I know it's a lot to dump on you all of a sudden. The main thing is, I need to convince Rome that you're not a threat."

"Why . . . Why are they hunting them?"

"I don't know. Fear, mistrust . . . history."

Rachel tossed back her drink. "They kill . . . don't they?"

"Not anyone you'd miss," Locan replied. "Like Connor said, they take out the garbage."

Rachel frowned and squeezed his hand.

"C'mon kid, let's get out of here."

She had lain in his arms about an hour, but he could tell she was awake. The poor kid, he thought. What a pile of brick to be dumped on one girl.

Then she stirred and climbed on top of him, nestling his cock between her thighs. It didn't take long for him to stiffen. She raised her hips and sheathed him with her warm, slick cunt. No words, just a swivel of her hips and a steady grind that increased in intensity. He just laid back and let her fuck him, let her take control. A roiling began in his balls; he didn't want to release until she reached her climax.

He watched as her deep red nipples swirled in circles with each swivel of her body.

"Oh, God . . . Locan!"

Blue sparks danced around her shoulders and a flight of blue fireflies flittered around the bed.

"Racey! Sweetie, be careful!"

"It's okay . . . I'm . . . in . . . control . . ."

Locan closed his eyes. "Oh, Jesus!"

Rachel shuddered; she'd soaked him. Blue electricity sparkled all around them, and then subsided.

She bent over, her breasts flattened against his chest. "Yum," she cooed. "I want to eat you up."

He traced his fingertips over her back, all was smooth, soft.

"Whacha looking for . . . fur?"

"Um . . ."

"It's okay. I'm in control."

"You can say that again."

"But . . ."

"But what?"

"I thought you liked doggie sex."

"Jesus, Racey."

"I just want to lick you all over."

"Yeah . . . sure . . . ohhhh . . . down, girl."

He closed his eyes and surrendered to ecstasy.

She giggled.

Cardinal LeRocque hesitated a moment before he placed his hand on Rachel's head and pronounced the final benediction as she was inducted into the company of the Palatinae. She looked up at him and smiled like a little girl who'd just received her first communion.

Jacoby stood with Locan. A dwarf, the top of his head barely reached Locan's elbow.

"It took some time," Jacoby said, "reassuring the cardinal."

"Thanks."

"I said you said she was okay, so she was okay with me."

"Thanks again."

"You lied, I lied."

"She'll be one of the best," Locan said.

"I know that. But we both know what she is; she does too, I see. Well, her abilities will no doubt prove useful."

"No doubt."

"You fucked her, didn't you?"

"Captain!"

"What the hell were you thinking?"

"I . . . I guess . . . it's a lonely life, captain."

"Well . . . I can't blame you; but I won't condone it. It was a blockhead thing to do. It seems to have turned out all right, but . . . it was a damned dangerous thing to do."

"Yes sir."

"Well, go congratulate her. It'll be your last chance."

Rachel ran into Locan's embrace. "Thanks . . . for everything. We . . ."

"There can't be any more 'we', Racey. They won't let us stay together. In fact, they'll try to arrange it so we never cross paths again."

She pressed her forehead to his chest. "I can't imagine hunting monsters without you, Locan."

"You'll be fine. I know you'll be able to take on anything out there, except maybe a pooka."

"A pooka."

"A mischievous entity that gets into your head and makes you do embarrassing and humiliating things. There's no defense, you just gotta let it get tired of you and move on. There was a guy . . ."

"Shhh."

She clasped his head in her hands, stood on her toes and kissed his mouth, a wet, lingering kiss.

Ducks

Elizabeth Coldwell

That morning, I had almost thrown the ducks away. For six months, they had been sitting on the desk at the side of my Mac computer, on a three-inch mirrored square, beaks touching, just as Frances had proscribed. She had bought me the little wooden ducks in a shop in Covent Garden; they were good Feng Shui, she had told me as I had unwrapped them from their tissue paper covering, and if I put them in the correct place, they would bring a man into my life.

Frances was a sucker for all that kind of stuff: good luck charms; the *I Ching*; the horoscope column in the *Daily Express*; the gypsy fortune teller on Brighton Pier who'd allegedly read the palm of Kylie Minogue. She'd wandered round my flat, periodically consulting a book on Feng Shui, before telling me that having the dressing table mirror facing my bed would disrupt my sex life and the reason I was single was because the relationship corner of my home was down the toilet. Physically down the toilet. If she hadn't been my best and oldest friend, I would have laughed. The reason I was single had nothing to do with badly placed mirrors and toilets: it was because since Tim had dumped me for his PA, nine months earlier, I had thrown myself completely into my work. It killed the pain, but spending most of your day photographing toast racks and standard lamps for interior design magazines didn't give you a lot of opportunity to meet men. Admittedly, I did have an occasional sideline taking shots of male models for the sort of publication you wouldn't let your granny read, but most of the men I photographed were either so vain or so dim they made a standard lamp seem a more attractive option.

So the ducks might as well go, for all the good they were doing. I'd reached down and picked up the drake, with its green and blue painted plumage and its beady little eye, and I'd held it over the waste paper basket. And then I'd remembered that Frances was coming over on Saturday night; I was cooking spaghetti carbonara and she was bringing the latest Brad Pitt film, courtesy of her local video shop. She loved to poke round the flat while I was busy in the kitchen, much as she always denied it, and she would notice instantly that the ducks had gone. I put the drake back in position, cosying up to his dowdy-looking mate, and decided I would dispose of them on Sunday.

I was in the kitchen, making myself a cup of coffee, when the phone rang. It was Izzy Russell, the art editor of *Your New Home*, one of the magazines which employed me on a regular basis.

She sounded breathless, slightly panicky, and I thought for a moment she was going to tell me my latest job had been canceled. "Hi, Lauren, just to let you know we're having a small problem."

"Nothing too serious, I hope," I replied, thinking of the possible hole in my bank balance and the bills which were due at the end of the month.

"No, it's just that I'm supposed to be sending you over the props for the tea table shoot, and we've gone way over our courier budget for the month. So one of the boys in the art department has agreed to bring you everything, as you're on his route home. I hope that's okay. Expect him about six."

Crisis apparently averted, I went to retrieve my coffee mug from the kitchen, and turned my attention to my e-mail inbox. A couple of wannabe models had sent jpeg images of themselves, in answer to an ad I had placed online, and I gave them the once-over. One was a skinny, street urchin type, all gelled hair and sneering attitude. He looked barely old enough to be posing, and I decided to leave him for the gay magazines, whose readers had a decided taste for what appeared to be jailbait which I definitely didn't share. The other had sent an illiterate e-mail and a couple of shots of nothing more than his erect dick, fat, pale and out of focus. I sighed, and deleted them. It was a while since I'd done a nude photo-shoot, and I had a sudden hankering to photograph flesh and blood, rather than bone china, but until a suitable model presented himself, I would have to stick to the commission Izzy had chosen to give me.

The entryphone buzzed, and I realized it was a little after six o'clock. I went to answer it. A deep, Northern voice enquired, "Lauren Lynn? I'm here with the stuff from *Your New Home*."

"Brilliant," I said. "Bring it up. I'm on the second floor."

I stood at the open door to my flat, watching him struggle with the heavy rucksack he was carrying. I ushered him inside and helped him ease the thick straps off his shoulders so we could gently lower the rucksack to the floor.

"I'll tell you, I was terrified of someone bumping into me on the Tube and breaking something," he said, as he unzipped the big compartment at the top and started lifting out cups, plates and a teapot, all packaged in layers of bubble wrap. I watched him as he worked, unconsciously studying him with a photographer's eye. Early twenties, tall and broad, with short, spiky dark hair, sleepy azure eyes and a dimple in one cheek which was revealed when he smiled. Which was often. It was a warm day outside, and that, coupled with the weight of the rucksack, had caused him to sweat; I could smell it slightly, but it was a spicy, sexy smell that was making its presence felt down low in my belly. He was cute, and fit, but the way he was dressed, in a tight, faded indigo T-shirt and baggy combat pants, suggested he didn't seem to care too much about his appearance – or the effect it was having on me.

"Do you have to rush straight home, or can I get you a beer?" I asked. "I mean, you've been kind enough to bring all this over . . ."

"Yeah, that'd be great, thanks," he said, and I went to hunt a couple of cans of ice-cold lager from the fridge. When I came back into the living room, he was standing in front of what had once been the chimney breast, looking at the photograph I keep hanging there. It's an arty, black-and-white shot of a well-muscled man, his face in shadow, wearing nothing but a pair of torn denims. The fly is open enough to show the beginnings of his pubic bush, and his hand is reaching in to cradle his cock. Nothing is explicit; everything implied.

"That's some photo you've got there," he said, taking one of the cans from me. "Is it a Mapplethorpe?"

I shook my head, surprised by his knowledge of erotic photography. "Thanks for the compliment, but no. I took it."

"Seriously? It's fantastic," he enthused. "Don't get me wrong, I don't have a thing about other men or anything, but if I did, it would more than likely turn me on."

"I do quite a bit of that sort of work." I took a swig from my drink, hoping the lager would cool the fire that was being stoked in me, but standing next to Izzy's gorgeous errand boy was having entirely the opposite effect. "Well, to be honest, not as much as I'd like. I do sets for *Dare* magazine now and again."

"That's the porn magazine for women, isn't it? I met a guy at a party who used to be their designer. He told me some pretty wild stories about the stuff they print."

"It's good fun," I replied, kicking off my shoes and curling up on the settee, "but they don't buy many black-and-white sets, which is a shame. I'd love to take some photos for them which really concentrated on the muscles in a man's body; emphasize how they move, and the power they contain." I noticed him raise the can to his lips again, and saw the way his biceps pressed against the taut cotton of his T-shirt. "Don't take this the wrong way, but you have really good muscles in your arm. Do you work out at all?"

He shook his head. "I play football on Sunday mornings, and I'm helping a mate renovate his flat at the moment. That's pretty physical work, but I've never been in a gym in my life." He drained his can. "What are you saying, that you reckon I'm worth photographing?"

I reckoned far more than that, but I just smiled. "I think you have good muscles. It's a start."

"But I thought you use professional models?"

"Not always. To tell you the truth, I don't always like using professionals. A lot of them are a pain in the arse. They think they're doing me a favor by turning up for a shoot, they whinge, they whine and they have these terribly possessive girlfriends who want to claw my eyes out for daring to look at their man naked. So I put adverts in places, and I get guys who've never modeled before, but they have great bodies and they have this natural, unspoilt air about them. I've even shot guys I've met in the street before now." A memory swam into my mind: a bloke I'd seen in a coffee shop on Regent Street, impossibly tall, Viking fair. He'd been a Danish student, disbelieving at first when I'd pressed my card into his hand, then flattered, and grateful for the money the shoot would bring. The photos had been among the best I'd taken, and *Dare* had used them as their centrefold. I sensed in the man sitting before me the same potential.

"So say I was modeling for you, how would you shoot me?" he asked.

"In the bedroom," I replied without hesitation, the image forming in my mind so vivid I could almost touch it. "I'd have you lying in the crumpled sheets, looking like you'd just had the best sex of your life." I could see it now: his limbs spread languidly on the bed, the rucked-up sheet nothing more than a strip of fabric across his groin, soon to be pulled away to reveal his hard cock in all its glory . . .

"Sounds good," he said. "Why don't we go for it?"

I gaped at him. "Are you serious?"

The dimple appeared in his cheek. "Why not? Ever since that designer told me what he did, I've had a fantasy about posing for some sexy photographs. This seems like the perfect chance."

If he was up for it, who was I to argue? I had been bemoaning the lack of suitable models less than an hour earlier, and now one had pitched up in my living room. "I'll need a couple of minutes to set things up. There's another can in the fridge if you want it," I told him. My camera was sitting in the spare bedroom, which I had converted into my darkroom when I'd bought the flat. I went to hunt it out, together with a couple of lamps which would create the dramatic lighting I needed for the shots I had in mind.

The bedroom was less messy than it could have been, considering; having set up the lights to my satisfaction, I bundled up the duvet and shoved it out of the way beneath the bed, replacing it with a freshly laundered white bedsheet. I was moving various personal items off the bedside table when I became aware of a shadow behind me, and realized my model had come into the room. I hoped he hadn't seen me bundling the slim, white vibrator which had passed for my sex life since Tim had left into the drawer.

If he had, he said nothing, just glanced round the impromptu set I'd created. "So how do you want me?" he asked.

So badly my pussy is throbbing just thinking about it, I thought, but I was determined to keep this professional. "Take your trousers off," I said matter-of-factly. "I'll start with some of you in just your T-shirt and underwear. I take it you are wearing underwear?" When he just looked at me, I continued, "You wouldn't be the first who wasn't . . ."

He was, as I discovered when he casually slipped off his trainers, socks and combat pants: little black briefs that clung to the contours of his cock and balls. I picked up my light meter and took a reading, then ordered him on to the bed. "Right, lie on your back," I told him. "Raise one knee and let your legs fall apart slightly. That's great . . ."

When sportsmen have a great match, they talk about being in "the zone"; that moment when they can't fail to hit the ball, when they feel almost incapable of making a mistake. Sometimes when I'm wielding the camera, it's just the same, and it felt that way now. My instincts had been right; he was a natural model, with no shyness or inhibition. When I asked him to cradle himself through his underwear, he did it without embarrassment, and I could have sworn he was giving himself a couple of sly rubs through the fabric, helping to raise his cock from its slumbers.

The camera clicked away as he stripped out of his T-shirt, displaying a chest that was firm and hairless. His nipples were hard, and I wondered just how much of a kick he was getting out of posing for me. I would know soon enough.

"Okay, let's get you out of those pants," I said. "Peel them down very slowly, like you're teasing me. I just want to see a glimpse of your pubes."

He did as I asked, hooking his thumbs into the waistband and pulling them away from his hipbones. When he finally eased them down and off on my request, it was to reveal a half-hard cock, thick and already impressive. Even though the bedroom window was open, letting in the traffic noises which reminded me the everyday world was still moving past outside, it suddenly felt stiflingly warm in the room. Not only that, but my jeans seemed to be a size too tight, the seam pressing into the crease between my legs so that every movement I made put a subtle, aching pressure on my clitoris.

"Let's do a few with the sheet round you," I suggested. "Just drape it over your legs, like you've kicked it off in your sleep."

He wrapped the sheet loosely around the lower half of his body, and then I arranged it to my satisfaction, pulling it away so it was barely covering his muscular left thigh. My fingers brushed his warm flesh as I did, and I shivered slightly at the contact. I couldn't remember the last time a man had affected me so powerfully.

I grabbed my camera again, and directed him through the sequence of shots I wanted, taking some close-ups of the sheet where it was molded to the outline of his cock, then finally asking him to pull the sheet away entirely so I could photograph him naked. He was completely uninhibited as he grasped his hardening dick and played with it languidly till it stiffened fully, rising up towards his belly button. These were shots the magazines in Britain could never use, but I was no longer thinking about a potential market for these photos. Now, it was all about having a beautiful man lying on my bed, erect and unmistakably ready for sex. My pussy was hot, the pulse between my legs beating too hard for me to ignore. And then the roll of film ran out.

"Okay, all done," I said. "You can get dressed now, if you want."

"I don't want," he said, catching hold of my arm and guiding me to sit on the bed beside him. "I mean, what I am going to do about this?" He gestured to his cock, still hard and bobbing slightly as he moved.

"Well, if it's a problem, normally the model goes into the bathroom and sorts himself out," I replied, trying to sound as though this happened all the time. Usually, they just collected their fee and left.

"Doesn't the photographer ever give them a hand?" he asked with what I could have sworn was a hopeful tone in his voice.

"Not if they don't want to get a reputation for being unprofessional," I told him.

"Not even if the model were to ask nicely?" He looked at me with such a devilish expression in those blue eyes that my pussy clenched in a powerful spasm.

I knew I shouldn't be doing it, that it went against the professionalism which was such an important part of my job, but I couldn't help myself. I reached out and circled his cock with my fingers, feeling the hot, hard length of him. His sigh of pleasure was barely audible as I stroked him gently.

He rolled back, pulling me on to the mattress with him, and we began to kiss, his mouth soft and tasting faintly of spearmint. It felt strange to be still fully dressed while he was naked, but if I thought that gave me the upper hand in matters, I was proved wrong. Suddenly, he climbed over me, and the weight of his body pressed me down as he straddled my chest. My hand barely broke its rhythm on his shaft, even when he pulled my T-shirt out of my jeans and started cupping and squeezing my breasts through my bra. I wriggled beneath him, using the seam of my jeans to give my overheating pussy the stimulation it craved.

Now it was his mouth that explored my tits, his tongue dampening the nylon of my bra and flicking over my nipples. "Take it off," I urged him, wanting to feel his lips against my bare skin.

My T-shirt and bra were stripped off me without ceremony and, as he suckled my bare breasts, my hand continued to wank his cock. We were both panting heavily by now, and drops of sweat glistened on his torso.

I guided his hand down to the fly of my jeans, hoping he would take the hint. I was pretty sure he knew exactly what I wanted, but he seemed determined to make me beg. "Please . . ." I murmured, pressing my crotch against his fingers, and I was rewarded with the rasp of my zip being pulled down.

Between us, we started hauling my jeans and panties down, but when they reached my ankles he pushed me back to the mattress, leaving me effectively hobbled by the tangle of denim and white cotton. It felt strange to have my movements restrained as his fingers began to explore the soft, wet flesh of my sex, but I gave myself up to the feeling. I had let go of his cock and lay submissively as he circled my clit with a lazy fingertip. I was blossoming, opening up under his touch, readying myself for the moment when the thick head of his cock breached the entrance to my pussy, and yet somewhere at the back of my brain a little voice nagged at me.

"Condoms," I muttered. "In the bedside cabinet." If he found the vibrator now, I didn't really care. An image flashed through my mind of him using it on me, sliding its buzzing length deep into my cunt, or even using it to explore my tight, virgin arse.

He was straddling me now, his dick sheathed in translucent latex, and I parted my legs as widely as the knot of clothing around my ankles would let me. Slowly, he nudged into me, and I moaned as the thickness of him stretched me wide. And then he was moving, rocking his hips back and forth, and I was moving with him, finding his rhythm and matching it with one of my own. If the traffic was still moving on the road outside, or the breeze still stirring the curtains, I was no longer aware of it: the world had shrunk to the size of this bed, and the only noises I heard were those we were making as we hurried towards our orgasm, our breathing fast and ragged, our sweat-slick bodies sliding together.

His mouth met mine again, and we were still kissing fiercely as I began to come, the blood singing in my ears and my pussy clutching at his hot, solid cock. He groaned, low in his throat, and, with one last thrust, harder than anything which had gone before, he, too, climaxed. He held still for a moment, and then he slumped against me, spent.

We rolled apart, so he could peel off the condom and I could finally free myself from my tangled-up jeans, and then he wrapped his arms around me and I cuddled against him, still not quite able to believe what I'd just done. I didn't fuck men I'd only met a couple of hours earlier; it was so out of character for me.

Of course, when I told Frances what had happened, she would put it all down to her stupid Feng Shui ducks, but I knew things didn't work out like that in real life. Far Eastern superstition hadn't brought this man into my life; if anything had, it was Izzy Russell's overspending.

"By the way," I said, "this is going to sound stupid, but Izzy didn't actually tell me your name."

"It's Aiden," he told me, that sexy smile dimpling his cheek again. "Aiden Drake."

A Cruel Heartless Bitch

Severin Rossetti

The cruel heartless bitch, she fucked the arse off him, she tore at his flesh as she used him and left him a dry husk of a person, like an empty purse without so much as a penny in it, a body without a soul, a man without an aim.

He should have heeded the warning, read the portents, seen the signs. But then yes . . . he *did* see the signs.

The bar was in that "city" part of the city where Brian had business, a place where men such as himself, in sober suits and with busy schedules, went for lunch or for a couple of quick drinks after work before catching their trains back out to the suburbs. Its ceilings were low, there were just two rooms decorated with much dark wood and polished brass, and squeezed as it was between two banks, with floor upon floor of offices bearing down on it, it seemed like an afterthought, like a vestige of some past time when commerce was a less hectic thing.

Though it was barely midday Brian had already had two lengthy meetings, was left with an hour to kill before the next one, so thought he would call in for a drink and a sandwich.

The place had the beery smell he expected, of hops and polish, maybe faint traces of the previous night's excesses, and the gleaming pumps offered an interesting selection of ales. Any sampling of them would have to wait until he had conducted the last of his meetings, though, he was far too professional to meet a client with beer on his breath, and so he took his place at the bar, waited while the only other customer was served, then asked for a tonic water.

"Ice and lemon?"

She was at the far end of the bar, where her other customer was slouched silently on a stool, and as she turned to face Brian the first thing he noted was her lack of make-up, quickly followed by the realization that she had no need of any. In the tawny light of that bar, where brass and glass and polished wood cast so many reflections, her pale complexion seemed as perfect as well-worn marble, as if she was a sculpture which had been caressed by legions of admirers. She was as soberly dressed as any of the pub's clientele might be, wore a dark pin-striped jacket and trousers which were sharply creased, a grey silk polo neck beneath against which hung a slender string of black pearls which glinted as they caught the light, drawing the eye to her full breasts.

"Well? Ice and lemon with the tonic?"

She had moved the length of the bar, set Brian's drink before him, he had not been aware of the staccato tap of her heels approaching so nodded quickly, said, "Yes please. And maybe a sandwich?"

"We have ham and cheese or cheese and ham," she told him, dropping a slice of lemon and a cube of ice into his glass.

"That will be fine, thanks."

"Which?" she asked, and when he looked into her eyes, expecting to find some trace of humour, he saw none, just her cold unsmiling gaze.

"Ham and cheese will be okay," he hurriedly said.

He was served, he paid, and she retreated to her station at the far end of the bar. As he chewed on his sandwich Brian noticed the brass plaques which were fixed above the bar, the sort that were common to many pubs, each bearing some motto or legend. He scanned them distractedly, expecting them to be of the usual "you don't have to be crazy to work here" kind, but instead he saw them to be refreshingly more original.

"I take my desires for reality because I believe in the reality of my desires," read one.

"To make a fetish potent outside its cult is precisely the function of the aesthetic," said another.

And perhaps most amusing of all: "I may be a cruel heartless bitch . . . but at least I'm good at it."

Amusing? Perhaps that was the wrong choice of word, for he had yet to recognize any humour in his hostess, either in her manner or the set of her lips. She went efficiently about her business but he had yet to see her smile or have anything pleasant to say to any of her customers.

Perhaps he was intrigued then, rather than amused, as he read the motto again: "I may be a cruel heartless bitch . . . but at least I'm good at it."

"Pretentious piffle," Brian heard, the words spoken in slurred tones, and turned to see the pub's first customer at his shoulder. "Pay no heed, take no notice, it's all a load of bullshit and will fuck up your mind."

And with that he was gone, lurching towards the door, shoulders hunched and shuffling, as if his feet were shackled together or his nuts were in a knot. Brian watched him leave, then turned to the landlady with a wry smile on his face, expecting her to share his amusement and maybe give some explanation of the man's eccentricity.

She was dealing with another customer though, serving him with what Brian now took to be her customary cold and efficient way.

She *may* well have been the "cruel heartless bitch" of the legend above the bar.

Other meetings were conducted, Brian's afternoon was busy, but as well as he had planned his visit there were still matters left pending. Fortunately he had anticipated this, that nothing ever goes to plan, had had the foresight to pack an overnight bag and so checked into a hotel.

It was one of those Travelodges which could have been anywhere, clean and comfortable enough but each room the same and totally devoid of character. He showered then, changed, went back out but found himself in a city which was much like any other.

There was the drawback of travelling so much, of conducting business in so many different places, that ultimately everywhere seemed much like everywhere else.

But then he remembered the tiny little pub which seemed somehow apart from the world around it, found it easily and entered.

"A pint of 'Speckled Hen' please," he said, as casually as if he were a regular in the place.

"Ice and lemon in that?"

It was the same woman as before, dressed as before, as if still expecting her sober suited clientele though it was now a little too late for them.

"No ice or lemon thanks, I'll just take it as it comes," Brian said, a grin on his face as he realized that she remembered him, thinking that now that the business of the day had finished – the place was as empty as it had been before, just two other customers in opposite corners of the room – she might be a little more forthcoming in her conversation.

"No ice or lemon then," was all she said, though, pulling his pint and setting it before him, then going to the far end of the bar where there was no one to distract her.

He sipped his beer and then drank more deeply, ordered another when he had drained that first one, and then a third.

Perhaps it was the beer that had him grinning when she came to serve him, and she found his smile engaging, or perhaps it was the slackness of the custom which had her bored. Whatever the reason, this time she did not return to her usual spot at the far end of the bar but stood almost facing Brian, just a little to one side.

"A nice place," he said of the pub, to make conversation. "There's just you works here?"

"I have staff when there's a need," she replied. "Lunchtime through to early evening. Times like this, and when you were here before, I can cope alone."

So the pub was hers, she was employer rather than employee, and already his mind was working, running through a number of scenarios.

"And later on?" he ventured.

"There is no 'later on', there isn't the custom to keep the place open once the office workers have gone home."

"So then it's home for you too?" he supposed. "And where might that be?"

"Why do you ask?" she wanted to know.

"No special reason." He shrugged. "Just . . . You know . . ."

Just thinking that she might like to go for a meal . . . and . . . you know . . .

"I have a house, a home," she told him. "And there's a small flat in the basement for those times when I need to stay over."

"In that case, I wonder if—?" Brian began, but before he could make his suggestion one of the other two customers was leaving, bidding her goodbye, and the second was at the far end of the bar, wanting her attention.

Cursing inwardly as she walked away, Brian swallowed a mouthful of beer, leaving just an inch in the bottom of his glass, and crossed the room to the "gents".

As he emptied his bladder of the beer he had drunk he felt his cock heavy in his hand, not erect but getting there. When he washed his hands beneath the tap he felt his cheeks burning, saw in the mirror how flushed they were and splashed them with cold water.

Christ how he wanted that woman behind the bar!

Behind the bar, on the floor . . . anywhere!

When he came out of the toilet he saw immediately that the bar was darker than before, that the curtains had been pulled across the windows and the door shut.

In the gloom her pale flesh was more radiant than ever as she stood beside the door, a bunch of keys dangling from the index finger of her left hand.

"I'm about to lock up for the night," she told him.

"And me?" Brian wondered, less quietly than he had intended.

"Yes, and lock up *you* too," she said.

"Pardon?" He smiled.

"I saw you looking at my mottoes before," she said, her eyes glancing up to the brass plaques above his head. "The 'cruel heartless bitch' . . . that's me. So now it's up to you, you have thirty seconds to decide."

Her hand lifted slowly, raising the keys to the door and, as Brian smiled and leisurely drank down the last of his beer, she shot across one bolt, a second, a third, then turned key after key in a succession of locks.

As she turned and came back towards him her hips swaying delightfully, he saw the first trace of a smile on her colourless lips and reached out a hand to her.

"It's decided, then," she said, at the same time that she rapped him hard across the knuckles with the heavy bunch of keys.

"Shit!" he swore, clutching one hand in the other as she moved past him, behind the bar and towards a door.

"A cruel heartless bitch," she reminded him, "but at least I'm good at it." And as she disappeared through the door she said, "This way, if you have the courage."

When Brian had soothed the stinging in his knuckles, shaken his hand to chase away the pain, he clenched that hand into a fist and followed. Beyond the door she had passed through was a staircase, dark, and from the bowels of the building there came a strong smell of beer. As he descended the stairs he felt the walls rough on either side, the floor bare stone beneath his feet as he reached the bottom.

A basement flat, was it? Or a cellar?

Sure enough, to one side, in a darkened room, he could make out kegs and barrels of beer, bottles of gas and crates of empties. To the other side a door was slightly ajar, a crack of light escaping to point the way.

Cautiously he pushed this open, stepped through.

She was standing in the centre of the room, her legs spread wide, the bunch of keys she held resting lightly against her thigh, shining like a weapon against the dark material of her trousers. She had removed her jacket and the polo neck she wore was sleeveless, cut high at the shoulders to leave bare arms which he could see were firm and muscled.

"So many keys, for just the one door? Didn't you wonder?" she asked, a gentle twist of the wrist making the keys chime against each other, and her head turned slowly to the left, to the right, inviting Brian to take in his surroundings.

This room at least had some rugs to make its bare stone floor more comfortable, hangings hid the naked brick of the walls, and in one corner was a large bed which seemed inviting enough.

But such other more disturbing "furnishings" there were that he was momentarily lost for words!

What he first took to be a child's cot beside the bed he saw to be more like a cage, enclosed not just on its four sides but also on top, and apparently constructed of cold steel rather than polished wood; a large upholstered stool might have been unremarkable if it had not been for the shackles fixed to each of its four legs; a large wooden chair as grand as a throne was so intricately carved that it could surely not afford a comfortable seat, and hung with all manner of straps and chains and restraints.

These were everywhere, in fact, fastened not just to each item of furniture but also hanging from the walls, the low ceiling, even curled up on the floor, fixed there by stout bolts driven through the rugs, into the stone.

And everywhere, too, the padlocks of assorted sizes, as many and as varied as the keys she held in her hand.

"So, where shall I have you first?" she wondered, coming slowly towards him, and when he took a step back she grinned humourlessly. "Oh come on, don't be shy," she coaxed. "I told you, I may be a cruel heartless bitch, but at least I'm good at it."

"Look, this really wasn't what I had in mind," Brian said, still backing away from her.

"No, I can guess just what you had in mind," she said, and there was something mesmerizing about her voice, her cold gaze, that as he thought he was backing towards the door he found himself moving instead in a lazy arc, as if they were two wrestlers circling each other in the ring.

Then his retreat was blocked as wood dug into his calves, her face came within inches of his and she grinned.

"Ah! So it's to the heartless bitch's throne?" she said, her body bumping into his, knocking him off balance and toppling him arse first into the large chair.

Though the seat was smooth, and contoured to fit his buttocks, the back was uncomfortable, its intricate carvings making it feel as though there were sculpted polished breasts digging into his shoulder blades, male genitals pressing against the base of his spine, stubby cocks and polished balls coming at him from every side.

Before he could even shift his body, though, let alone try to rise, she had moved closer again, raised one knee and brought it forward on to the seat, pressing it painfully into his groin.

"Be still, trust me, don't resist, because if you do I will crush your balls as easily as if they were ripe plums," she threatened, her breath fragrant in his face, her body rising on that one knee which drove between his thighs.

Her hands came up, moved out, one still holding that bunch of keys with which she had rapped his knuckles, and her bare biceps flexed as she took his wrists and lifted his arms above his head.

The key barely made a sound in the oiled locks as his hands were fixed there.

The strap around his chest she fastened with a buckle, as she did the one about his belly and those which held his thighs in place.

The restraints which kept his ankles fixed to the feet of the chair, were secured by more locks and keys and now she seemed satisfied, tossing the bunch of keys on the bed behind her as she stepped back to consider her handiwork.

"Delightful! Just perfect!" she decided, her gaze travelling the length of Brian's body, from the hands which were tied above and behind him to the ankles which were fixed below. "But a little too overdressed for what I have in mind."

She turned, crossed the room, her step first silent across the rugs, then ringing out on the bare stone floor between them, and though he tried to turn his head to follow her movement he found himself unable to. His hands fastened behind his head made things difficult enough, but then the slightest movement to left or right brought his face to the wings of the chair where further carvings kept him pinned . . . more polished unyielding breasts, cocks large and small like wooden dildoes which might puncture his cheeks, representations of testicles as hard as lacquered walnuts.

Brian could only wait, then, try to follow the sound of her movement across the room, his eyes flicking anxiously from side to side.

When she finally came back into his field of vision he was startled to see the knife in her hand, a glistening kitchen knife with a wickedly broad blade.

"Don't look so worried! I'm not about to chop your balls off!" she laughed, now with genuine humour as she noted his alarm, and as she squatted down before him she proceeded to run the sharp blade through his shirt, his trousers, reducing his clothes to shreds. "And please don't look so violated," she added, as he felt the blunt edge of the steel cold against his skin. "They're only clothes, trappings, a disguise to hide behind. I'm sure you can afford to replace them, should you feel the need of new, should you feel the need to leave."

Feel the need to leave? Was there any possibility he might not want to? It seemed a ludicrous notion, that he might not be away at the first opportunity after the way this heartless bitch had treated him, but as she peeled away the ribbons she had made of his clothes he looked down with shame to see that his cock was erect.

Erect, protruding, weeping from the tip.

"See?" she said, standing. "I told you that this cruel heartless bitch was good at what she did. And if you think *that* is hard," she added, with a dismissive nod at his cock, "then you ain't seen nothing yet!"

In the brief seconds it took for him to blink, she was gone, he heard her step first soft and then sharp again, as she moved across the room from rug to stone to rug again, bruised his face against the sculpted wings of her "throne" and chafed his arms against the bonds which held him as he tried to follow her, searching for her perfume, straining for her warmth.

Her body seemed cold when she came back before him, naked but for the dark silk stockings which gripped her thighs, pinching the pale flesh, the slender heels which had rung against the stone floor, the skimpy black bra and the silky knickers which covered her genitals.

"So, now that we're both comfortable, how do you think a cruel heartless bitch would treat a man in your position?" she wondered, swaying a little on her heels, hugging herself like a younger girl surrendering to a teenage fantasy. "What *would* the bitch do with the man?" she asked, and when Brian was slow to reply she snapped, "Answer me!"

Despite his reaction he pretended to be cool, shrugged as best his bonds would permit and said, "Since she has him tied, she would probably beat him, but I told you—"

"You're not into that." She nodded, stepping forward so that she stood between his thighs. "But no, the bitch is cruel and heartless because she gives the man what he *doesn't* want, what he doesn't expect," she said, leaning forward, resting her hands on the chair to either side, so that her breasts were just tantalizing inches above his face, her bare midriff just inches away from his mouth.

Her perfume was sweet enough to mask the beery smell of the cellar, the warmth of her naked flesh made it seem thick and cloying, and, as Brian's eyes closed and his body involuntarily strained to savour it better, so her back arched and she moved just out of his reach.

She chuckled, a low rasp in the back of the throat like a man enjoying a dirty joke, said, "See? That is cruel and heartless. That is the bitch."

He permitted himself seconds more of picturing, behind closed eyes, what it was that he wanted, what it was that he hoped for, then opened them to see her grinning down at him.

One hand trailed down his cheek and across his chest, the sharp colourless nails scratching lightly over his belly.

"Now expecting. . . what?" she asked, feeling his body tense, and brought her hand quickly away, knowing that it had been his cock expecting the sensation of her fingers around it. "Oh no, not that, not yet," she told him, with a sorry shake of the head, though in her choice of words – not yet – he sensed some promise.•

For the moment, though, it seemed that his predicament was amusement enough for her, her own body entertainment enough, for as her eyes drank him in, relishing the way his arms strained, the way the straps bit into his flesh, so she ran her hands across her body, caressing every inch of it, cupping her breasts and squeezing them, pinching the nipples through the thin fabric of her bra, slipping down across her flat belly to her groin.

When she made a claw of her fingers and dug them between her thighs, as if there was an itch there which needed to be eased, Brian saw the silk of her knickers moulded against her genitals, could make out the swollen labia almost pouting beneath. With her index finger she forced the material inside, ran that finger up and down so that he could almost believe he heard the rasp of silk against skin.

"I am wet, they are wet," she told him, one hand tugging the knickers down over her thighs while she covered herself with the other, for a moment discordantly demure, like some figure in a painting by Botticelli.

Then, with a graceful dip at the knees, she stepped out of them, scooped them up and came back towards him.

"Smell, taste how wet they are," she invited, offering them to him, and his head came forward to meet them, caught their pungent perfume as they were wiped across his face.

Then they were dropped into his lap, where they fell on his aching cock, and for all that the material was light and sheer they seemed like an agonizing weight bearing down on his erection.

If her hand, if *any* hand, were to close on his cock now he would come in an instant. Of this much he was sure. But he was just as sure that this was not a thing the heartless bitch would permit.

Not yet.

As she made a slow pirouette before him, turning her back to him, he just caught sight of a bared breast in profile as she removed her bra, was denied a full view of it as plump pale buttocks filled his field of vision, her slender waist and the soft indentation of her spine, the firm thighs pinched by the black silk stockings.

"Kiss," she ordered, her hands on the arms of the chair to support herself as she moved between his spread legs, lowering herself so that she was so close he couldn't possibly refuse.

Brian touched his lips almost reverently against one buttock, then the other, felt her press harder against him so that his lips parted and his tongue licked against her warm salty flesh.

"With more intimacy," she insisted, her hips swaying and lazily rotating so that his face was sucked into the crack between her buttocks, his nose pressed against her arse, his tongue lapping beneath it.

"Ah! Oh yes! That's nice!" she sighed, her body churning against him, and slowly, as if her arms could no longer bear her weight, she lowered herself into his lap so that his tongue ran from her buttocks and along her spine.

When she was finally settled Brian's face was crushed against her back, his mouth mashed between her shoulder blades and his cock caught between her thighs, her weight bearing down on it as it fought to spring up free and erect.

"What would you do for an orgasm?" she asked, resting so heavily on him that he might have replaced the chair which supported them both, actually become that chair, become nothing more than a fixture, a furnishing, something to be used by her.

He gasped as he felt her buttocks against his belly, the silk of her thighs closing on his cock, the discarded knickers still draped over it causing him such exquisite agony.

His incoherent reply gave her the opportunity to rephrase her question, there was an added pressure to his cock, her fingers compressing it through the silk which swathed it as she said, "No, scratch that, rather let me ask—"

"Anything!" he gasped again.

"– rather let me ask what *must* you do for an orgasm?"

Her body writhed against him, not fiercely enough to make him come yet, just enticingly enough to draw an inspired answer from him.

"Make *you* have an orgasm first?" he guessed.

"Close," she said, her body stiffening a little, "but no one *makes* this cruel bitch do anything."

"Encourage you to have an orgasm then?" he said.

"Good boy! You're learning!" she congratulated him, her body relaxing again, and while one hand rested lightly against his cock, sustaining his erection, the other one crept away, her sighs giving him a clue as to where.

It was Brian she was using – as a toy, a tool, a support or whatever – but it was herself that she was pleasuring. That free hand was between her thighs, he knew, strumming her clitoris, parting the lips of her sopping cunt where he longed to bury his aching cock, dipping finger after finger inside until her whole fist was dripping.

Perhaps her wrist was aching, perhaps she wanted to tantalize him further . . . whatever the reason, she switched hands, the teasing one leaving his cock to delve between her thighs and the other lifting, pulling her hair aside so his lips could kiss her slender neck, then working their way behind her head and between their bodies so he could taste her excitement.

Her wet fingers forced themselves between his lips and he sucked on them, knowing that this was what she wanted of him, that this was the only way he could give her the orgasm she demanded. His mouth fastened on them, his tongue lapped at them, she writhed so much that his body was bruised by hers, squashed between her firm flesh and the sculpted hardness of the wooden seat.

Then, with a sigh which was like the last gasp of a dying person, her head fell forward.

"Oh fuck!" she sobbed, her back bowed before him to finally allow him some air, rocking in his lap and nodding her head, saying, "Yes! Yes! Oh fuck!"

The shudders which shook her body slowly subsided, her breathing became slow and deep and Brian found his matching it, as if he shared her satisfaction.

But of course he didn't, his cock was rock hard and as red as a piece of rare meat, burning beneath the knickers which were still draped over it.

She could guess at his discomfort, could not help but be aware of the effect she had on him, and with a tantalizing slowness she uncovered him, drew the soft silk along the length of his erection before letting the knickers fall to the floor.

His cock sprang upright as she lifted from his lap, jutting out in something like a salute as she turned to face him.

"He wants to come?" she supposed, an unnecessary remark in the circumstances, addressing Brian's cock rather than him as she nudged it with her knee, bringing a gasp of delight from him. "Yes? He does?"

"If my hands were free—" he said hoarsely, offering a threat, a promise.

"Yes? If your hands were free. . . what?" she asked, but he had no need to answer, she knew what he had in mind.

She was the cruel heartless bitch, though, as she had boasted.

"I will free every other part of you, but not your hands," she told him, walking around him, behind him, running her fingers across his face and through his hair.

He felt her hands on his, unlocking the shackles which had them fastened behind his head, but his freedom was short-lived, for immediately cuffs snapped on his wrists had them bound together before him.

"I will now release your other restraints," she said, coming back around to face him. "You could run then, you could be uncooperative, but where could you go in this state? You understand?"

Brian nodded meekly. "Yes."

"Or you could do as I say and perhaps be rewarded with the satisfaction you need."

"Please, yes," he whispered.

She smiled, and he read nothing in that smile other than pleasure at his compliance, she crouched before him and began to remove the straps from his chest and waist, his arms and thighs and feet.

"This way," she said, rising and drawing him with her, tugging on the chain which linked his wrists to coax him to his feet.

She led him across the room, from that chair which had been so uncomfortable to the bed which seemed so inviting. Only a foot or so away from the soft mattress, though, she gave a harsh tug on his cuffs, turned him from it towards the cage which he had mistaken for a cot.

"No! Not there?" he said, as she raised the top.

"If you want your orgasm you'll step inside!" she barked at him. "It's your choice! In or not?"

The tips of her fingers lightly brushing his balls left him with no option but to comply and obediently Brian stepped inside the cold steel cage.

"On your back, hands above your head," she directed him, and he squeezed himself into its narrow confines as best he could, his knees raised since it was too cramped to take his full length.

As the top fell on the cage with an ominous clang she threaded a chain through it and the cuffs, locking his hands in place as before.

"Don't want you playing with yourself, do we?" she chuckled. "Your orgasm is my privilege and mine alone. Now, so I can get to that aching cock of yours will you please oblige me by spreading your legs a little wider?"

His knees chafed the top of the cage as he stretched his feet out as far as he could and he felt leather circle his ankles, heard the click of more locks fastening them to each corner of the cage.

"There, all done," she said, standing, and as he craned his head to follow her he saw her climbing on to the bed.

"But—!"

"But what?" she chuckled, sprawling out among the soft sheets and plump pillows, her white body stark against the midnight blue of the bedding. "Didn't I tell you I was a cruel heartless bitch?" she reminded him, one foot dangling over the side of the bed, working its way through the bars of the cage to brush his face.

And very good at it, Brian was coming to learn.

She slept before he did, her situation more comfortable, her state more satisfied, but would wake at intervals throughout the night – usually when Brian felt that he might at last find some sleep himself – and resume caressing him with her foot, maintaining his restlessness, a time or two getting out of bed to squat beside his cage, working her hand between the bars to fondle his cock or caress his balls.

Her body was so close then, but denied him by the steel bars which separated them, and as much as he wanted to bury his face between her breasts, kiss her flat belly or feel her strong arms enfold him, all he could do was press his cheeks against the cage to show her how much he needed these things.

Whatever hour of the morning it was when she finally released him he was unable to say, there was only one long narrow window high on the wall in that basement room and a heavy velvet curtain covered it. In any case her treatment of him throughout the night, the repeated deprivation of sleep, had made any notion of time too confused.

Whatever the hour, finally Brian's hands were freed and the lid of the cage lifted, his feet released from their restraints and a hand offered him, helping him to rise.

His limbs ached from being held immobile for so long and he rose like an arthritic old man, flexing his muscles to try to bring some feeling back to them, stood unsteadily on tottering feet as he stepped out of the cage.

Stumbling, he fell into her arms and, though it was more support than an embrace which she offered him, it felt so wonderful, a warmth and a comfort such as he had never known in the arms of a woman.

Slowly she turned him, as if they were dancing, backed him towards the bed and let him fall on to it.

However many hours before, when he had first set eyes on that woman, Brian had pictured himself fucking her like a stallion, rutting like a wild beast, pounding away on her body beneath him. Now all he could do was lay there and gaze up at her as she lifted first one knee and then the other on to the bed, straddling him.

One hand circled his cock, as she lowered herself on to him, and he thought he might come just to feel her touch.

"Don't you dare!" she cautioned, reading the thoughts which had his eyes rolling behind closed lids. "Don't you dare come!" she said, taking him inside her, the lips of her cunt still soft and moist, as if all her dreams had been wet ones.

Her weight settled on him, her cunt flexed to grip him firmly, and when she was satisfied that he was deep enough inside her she began to rise and fall on top of him. Her movements were slow at first, as if her intention was to make him harder still, but then she picked up the tempo, driving harder, faster, her hands on his chest as much to keep him pinned as to support herself.

Her eyes were closed, she made no sound, her mouth set in a grimace as she concentrated on her own pleasure; he might have been nothing more than a wanking machine as far as she was concerned.

Then the instant before he might have been about to come, as if she could read his body's responses so well, her eyes snapped open and flashed at him, she rose on her knees and froze, carefully withdrawing his cock from her cunt.

"No, no, no," she said softly, climbing from the bed, her fingers clamping around his balls as if this was the surest way of preventing his ejaculation.

She tugged, painfully enough to bring a cry from him, insistently enough that he was brought to his feet, drawn after her and across the room to the stool.

"Face down over it," she told him, and he knelt before the stool, stretched across it, feeling the leather padding warm against his belly as straps of less supple leather bound his thighs to two of its legs.

His cuffed hands hung over the other side, his head between them, his cock like a pendulum swinging free between his legs.

A slap across the buttocks told him to be still, a light caress across them promised rewards if he obeyed, and so he kept his head down, seeing nothing more than the rug before his face, his knuckles grazing it, the polished steel which linked his cuffed wrists.

Then her bare feet came into view, as erotic as they had been when in high heels, the pale skin contrasted by the dark red lacquer of the nails.

"Look," she said, and when he found it difficult to lift his head her fingers clenched in his hair, tilting his face up.

In her free hand she held a rubber dildo, one end long and curved like a scimitar, the other thick and stubby. As he watched, as her grip on his hair insisted he watch, she worked this shorter end into her cunt, first stroking it back and forth against her wet lips to lubricate it, then screwing it deep inside.

"Kiss," she said, her hips thrusting forward to offer it to his mouth when she felt it was seated firmly enough.

Pouting his lips, Brian touched them to its wicked bulb, seeing her labia swollen around its root where it was buried inside her.

"Now lick, for if it is not to cause you too much pain it needs to be moister," she continued, pressing the weapon against his lips until they parted.

His tongue licked at the rubber until it was forced aside as she bucked her hips again, inserting an inch of the thing inside him, then another inch, until he was choking on it, salivating over it.

"Good enough, I think," she decided, finally withdrawing it, and in the brief moment he was allowed to catch his breath she had moved around and behind him, was on her knees and pressing it against his arse.

"No! Please don't!" he begged, on feeling that first contact, but her body bearing down on him, her breasts flattened against his chest would allow him no escape.

"You expect pity from a cruel heartless bitch? Silly man!" she laughed.

There was no subtlety about the way she inserted the dildo into his arse, she simply forced it forward, slowly but with determination, not seeming to care whether it entered him or rended him in two.

Fortunately it filled him rather than ripped him, though this in itself was still painful enough, inch after inch entering him until he knew – and she guessed – that he could take no more.

"Enough?" she asked.

"Enough!" he answered, his reply little more than a sob.

"Then now you will feel what it is to be fucked by a cruel heartless bitch," she promised, pulling back a little and then pressing forward once more, back again and then forward, her movements short and shallow at first but then becoming more extreme until she was not so much pressing into him as thrusting into him, her hips slapping against his buttocks.

His body rocked against the stool, it was only her body pinning his that kept the thing upright on its four legs, and as excruciating as the pain was he marvelled that his erection sustained itself, his rigid cock straining against the underside of the stool.

One of her hands worked its way down to grip him, to squeeze him, her nails dug into him and then her fist formed itself around the swollen gland, encouraging his ejaculation at the same time that she seemed intent on preventing it.

"Yes? No? Which?" she laughed, her lips to his ear, and his body was wracked with both pain and delight, the dildo torturing his arse as it stretched him cruelly, her grip on his cock so abrasive that it burned, so exciting that it made his balls ache.

He screamed then, closed his eyes as he forced the ejaculation which she was fighting to contain, spitting it out so fiercely that it spurted between the fingers of her clenched fist.

Never mind that she might make him lick those fingers clean, take a cane to him as punishment or slap his balls with the flat of her hand until they smarted.

For that single orgasm he was willing to give the cruel heartless bitch anything.

*   *   *

Business took Brian back to that city some two months later, his contacts were established and his meetings conducted more quickly on this occasion so that he made the time to return to that pub with the brass plaques above the bar.

She smiled at him sadly, and then more sadly still as he drank pint after pint of her beer; he stayed there from mid afternoon, when the place was as busy as she said it could be, until early evening when it was as quiet as he remembered it.

His last memory, as he returned to his hotel, was of a man seated at the bar where he had once sat, gazing up at those brass plaques, his lips were moving silently as he took in the portentous legend – "I may be a cruel heartless bitch".

Brian was aware of her following him along the bar, the heavy bunch of keys in her hand, and so he paused to rest his hand lightly on the man's shoulder.

"Pretentious piffle, take no notice, it will only fuck up your mind," Brian told him, his words a little slurred, and with shoulders hunched he shuffled from the pub, as if his feet were shackled together and his nuts in a knot.

Pierced

Alison Tyler

"I want to get my clit pierced."

She stared down at the marred counter rather than up into his dark eyes. "My clitoris," she stammered after. Maybe "clit" was too colloquial. What was the proper way to ask for what she wanted? She quickly scanned the walls of the tattoo parlor/piercing studio, landing on an image of an impish Devil Girl with a spiked tail stuffed violently up the ass of an innocent-looking Angel Girl. Maybe "clit" was okay.

"You're not ready."

When she looked at his face, she saw that he was grinning – the lines deepening around his eyes. He liked her. She could tell. She'd guessed that when he'd pierced her ear, his breath on her skin so she could feel the heat. The flash of pain had been over in a second – far too quickly – the whole experience taking less than ten minutes from the time she handed him her neatly folded cash to when she walked out the door on to the glittery grit of Melrose Avenue.

Afterwards, she'd spent hours sitting on the fire escape of her apartment, touching the silver hoop in the middle of her right ear, twirling the metal, holding it. She had the usual ear piercings from when she was a teenager, but this one, high up on her ear, felt different. Somehow the new hoop there had made her life the tiniest bit less lonely.

Weeks had passed before she'd had the nerve to go back. She was a good girl, after all, with a respectable job and a decent salary. She wore sensible clothes, low-heeled pumps, suitable for work in an accounting office on the Miracle Mile. Piercing/tattoo studios weren't places her friends visited, or discussed, or fantasized about. Nor were the boys who worked there. Tattooed boys who made her heart race. She requested nipple piercings next, standing in front of the counter wearing a white T-shirt and a white bra, chinos from

Talbots, glossy brown penny loafers. He gave her a hard look this time, as if he didn't believe what she'd said. Not someone as normal – or in her mind, boring – as she was. Embarrassingly normal. The freckles on her pale skin. The sleek dark hair that would not hold a curl. Slim-hipped body. Hardly any curves.

"You're sure?" he'd asked once he'd taken her into the private room, and she had tried to look brave as she removed her shirt and sat down, flinching when the sticky plastic coating on the chair met her skin.

Her breasts were extremely sensitive. Wearing the right – or wrong – bra would create such pleasurable friction she could almost climax. So when he rolled her dark pink nipples between his gloved fingers, she'd had to stifle a moan. Her eyes were closed the whole time. If she stared at him, she might say something. Something she'd regret? Perhaps.

Something she wished she'd said now?

When he'd told her to prepare herself, she'd licked her bottom lip, sucking it into her mouth, something she did when she was scared.

"You're sure?" he'd asked again, right before sliding the needle through, and she'd simply said, "Yes. Please."

For a month, a solid month after her nipples had healed, she'd been able to make herself come by tugging on the sterling rings adorning her tits. Just a little tug to start, working harder, imagining him pulling them with his mouth, biting into her. On weekends, she'd started wearing tight T-shirts without bras, loving the way her decorated breasts looked beneath the stretchy fabric. Yet soon the ache started up again. That and the loneliness.

Her belly button was next. She didn't have to get naked this time. She lifted her shirt, let him see her nearly concave stomach. His breath there made her clench her thighs together under her knee-length plaid skirt.

"Breathe, baby."

She looked down at him, startled. Had he called her baby?

But he didn't repeat the word. Didn't act as if he'd said anything unusual at all. She wondered if he understood the big picture – they were working down her body in a silver-studded game of musical parts. If he did, he kept quiet, professional in every sense. She watched his head bent over her, and thought of telling him that at night, she envisioned him fucking her asshole, the gloves, the lube. The tears that would streak her face when he thrust in deep.

He'd only touched her with gloves so far, and somehow they existed in her fantasies. Every last one.

There weren't many places left. She could have gone with her nether lips. But why wait? She was going to have her clit done, and she knew exactly how it would feel. She'd done the research online, understood the procedure.

How many times had she imagined watching him slip on the rubber gloves? Smelling that sweet sickly scent of antiseptic. The sensation of him touching her through that barrier, coaxing her clit to attention before slipping on the clamp.

"Not your clit," he said, looking at her. "The lips first."

Her eyes widened as he slid a photo album forward. Here were close-up shots of women, bejeweled parts on display, and she blushed immediately, even though she'd been fantasizing about this moment endlessly. Each time she went to the studio, she'd meant to ask for this, but had failed herself again and again. What else would she have to pierce to make him understand?

"The clit's extreme," he said.

But she knew, she wanted to say. She knew what it would be like: the needle. The slow thrust forward. The pain shot with ribbons of pleasure. She was going to come when he did it.

"You're not ready."

She hadn't been expecting this. The customer was always right, after all. She had the money. She had the nerve. But then she realized – her clit would be the finale. The end game, and she nodded – fine, let him decide. He led her back to the private room once more, and this time, for the first time, he seemed to really see her.

The door was shut. He came forward, slid his hands up under her skirt, pulled down her simple white panties. Her throat was tight. He turned her sideways, unzipped the skirt, let the fabric fall. Now she was half naked, and that felt wrong. He understood, pulled the T-shirt up over her head. This was better. Totally naked, with her silver-ringed tits on display, her belly button decorated, her body so pale and pretty. Jesus, pretty. For the first time ever, that's how she felt.

He sat her in the chair, spread her thighs, handed her a mirror. "Like this," he said, "we could pierce you here," and she trembled all over. "Or here." The shivers wouldn't stop. Her teeth were chattering. She couldn't speak.

"You have to hold still."

She looked at him, her eyes wide, breath hitching. And then he bent forward and licked the ring on her right breast, then the one on her left. He kissed his way down, pausing to tug on the barbell adorning her belly button. Fucking god, he was – he was kissing her. Licking her. His soft hair tickled her naked skin. She shifted her hips, lifted her hips. He was there, between her legs, spreading open her lips, kissing between.

"You're not ready for your clit," he said again, looking up at her. "I'll tell you when you're ready. We'll do it together."

"Yes," she said. "Fine," she said. Whatever he wanted, was what she wanted to say. As long as he would keep touching her. But he didn't. He stood back up, got the instruments.

"Hold still," he told her, as he had every time. There was no stiller than what she was like right now. Her breath was frozen. Her heart raced. He pierced her just as he'd said. Not her clit. Not yet. She sucked in her breath when she looked down her body. Shaved sex. Beautiful ring right there at the top.

"We'll get to your clit," he assured her once more. Now, he pinched her between his thumb and fingers, stroked his gloved thumb over her swollen clit so she closed her eyes and leaned back in the chair.

"And it's going to hurt," he said, and she squeezed her eyes shut even tighter – because he was talking to her the way he spoke to her in her fantasies. He was saying the things nobody ever had said out loud. "Because that's what you need, isn't it?"

"Yeah," she managed, a rush of breath, hardly an answer.

"But you need so much more. You need a collar here." One gloved hand went to her throat, pressing once against her. "And you need a bowl of water on the floor by the bed, where you can lap it at night if you're thirsty."

"Oh, fuck," she whispered, and there were tears in her eyes now, tears spilling.

"It's been so scary, hasn't it? All those thoughts in your head, and nobody to tell them to. Nobody to listen. You've been so lonely."

Like he had been there, with her, in her nearly empty apartment. Sat at her side on the fire escape. Looked out into a city of millions of people and been all by herself. And then he bent down and licked her in a circle, a circle within a circle, and she came. Vibrant. Colors behind her shut lids. Like every orgasm she'd had thinking of him, thrusting his gloved fingers up inside her, fucking her ass with two fingers overlapped while he sucked hard on her clit. She came in shudders, in waves, and then fell back, limp in the chair. But even as she came, understanding flooded through her.

Somewhere inside, she'd pierced him.

The Tinkling of Tiny Silver Bells

M. Christian

Jasmine died two years ago. She showed up three weeks ago. Should have expected it, knowing Jasmine as well as I did.

I didn't know she was back, not really, for almost a week. Stomping around my little Long Beach bungalow, the one she had called my shell, I caught glimpses of faint reds, gold, of the hazy glow of sunlight through baggy tie-dyes, and of God's Eyes turning in the windows. They were just there enough so I knew I saw something, but was always a part, always a fragment of that something. Same with smells: incense, patchouli oil, pot, cheap wine, and that simple lemon perfume. Same with sounds, walking from the little kitchenette into the living room I would catch the slap of leather sandals on the hardwood floors, the opening clap of *Stairway*, and that tiny sound, that special sound that would always mean bells on toes. Jasmine.

She had outlasted the ghost of the sixties by a few years, Jasmine had. Even though she'd been born in '71, she was a spirit of the Merry Pranksters, of Airplane, of the Summer of Love, acid, pot, Fat Freddy's Cat, the Stones, and tie-dyes.

It wasn't easy being a flower child in the age of the World Wide Web, ecstasy, coke, NIN, Courtney Love and body piercings, but Jasmine pulled it off. She drifted with a smile on her face, and those fucking bells on her toes, through life – hitching rides with only good people, taking only the best drugs, being friends with only good people. She was a ghost of the sixties, a spirit of the Haight and the Diggers.

Now she was just a spirit.

I never could figure out how she could exist. She was fascinating in the same way a Mary Keene painting (admit it, you've seen them – big eyed children) can be: innocence distilled to the point of being surreal. Jasmine could hitchhike with Jeffrey Dahmer and get out alive, and with some money to help her on her way. Deep down, though, I knew her luck couldn't last. Whatever is out there hates the lucky and the innocent.

If there was a sin in Jasmine, in her perfect fortune, this unblinking good luck, it was that it didn't leave much room for depth or brains. Jasmine was a spirit who walked slowly through life, letting it bump her this way and that. Never ask her to meet you anywhere, never make plans around her. Jasmine was pot and incense and a soft, warm body that fit so comfortably in your arms, but she wasn't someone you could count on. No one who knew her said it, but we all knew it was true – and having her turn up two years after we all put her to rest in the Long Beach Municipal Cemetery proved it. She was late for her own funeral.

I can't really remember the first time I met Jasmine. Maybe it was that party to celebrate Rosie getting her first gig at the Red Room. Maybe it was that picnic that Robert and Steve threw down at the remains of the old Pike. Maybe she had just shown up on my doorstep like she always seemed to, jingling her tiny silver bells and lazily sweeping her tie-dye skirt back and forth. No place to sleep that night and Roger Corn was always up, awake, and willing to take her in.

God knew what we had in common, save we . . . fit somehow. We didn't talk music (Airplane! NIN! Joplin! Love!) or books (Kesey! Coupland!) or anything else for that matter (You're always so damned happy! What do you have to feel sad about?), we just fucked and played and took our respective drugs (Coffee and weed! H and pot!). A spirit of the 1960s and one hack writer making his bread and butter writing porn, *True Detective Stories*, and articles on how to get your cat to use the toilet. We just seemed to go together somehow. We tolerated each other because we liked to fuck and kiss each other. Relationships can be based on worse things.

When I got that call, Rosie so calm and collected, I was sort of ready for it. Jasmine always did what you expected her to, if you understood her, so when the phone rang and Rosie said that Jasmine had "passed on" I knew almost exactly how, where and why.

The funeral was sparse and sad for the little spirit – just the four of us. We had all pitched in to get the coffin. It was a colorful affair, you had to give it that: Rosie in a gaudy color-blast of a red sequined gown and boa, Robert in his own retro seventies platforms and polyester, Steve with his beads and a (where the fuck did he score that?) Nehru jacket. I wore something aside from black. It was hard to find, but I managed to score a brilliant red shirt from a friend of mine. In many cultures – my shitty education not enough to tell me exactly where and who – red is the color for the dead.

Two years later she was paying me a visit.

The first time I realized that something was going on I was scared shitless. I was washing my coffee cup (my lucky one), high a wee bit from this shitty Mexican that Rosie had scored for me, and I felt someone behind me. Thinking it was Montezuma's revenge acting through the weed I shrugged it off. Then the someone put their arms around my waist and hugged my little pot belly. I screamed, dropped my cup (*Java is the Spirit of Creativity*) into shards of ceramic, jumped into my Docs and ran over to Steve and Robert's.

You'd think that OD'ing on H in Rosie's apartment would be enough to keep a girlfriend down.

After a day or so Rosie had convinced me that it was just lack of sleep, too many sips from my favorite mug, and a sudden flash of missing Jasmine. Rose said she felt her own late ex touch her sometimes – when she was in just the right mood. Of course there are differences between a dyke who'd gone off a bridge on her Harley and Jasmine the flower child overdoing the nostalgia just a bit.

Back in my place I kept seeing those flashes of Jasmine's colors, smelling her smell, and hearing her bells. And sometimes, just before drifting off at three a.m. I'd feel her body warmth – just the heat of her at first, you understand, slip into bed with me.

Then, about two weeks after that first touch in the kitchen, I was coming from the living room into the kitchen, empty new mug in hand (*Coffee is the Last Refuge of the Sleepy*), straight for my Saint Coffee machine and there she was: sandals, tie-dyed drawstring pants, simple white cotton shirt, scarf tied over her head. She was just there, at the kitchen counter, reading the paper, as I'd seen her a million times: joint burning in one hand, twirling a few strands of her blond hair in the other, chewing her lips at some newspaper headline or another and – while she'd never actually said it – you could still hear her thoughts clear and distinct: *Why don't people get along?* Like she had on many mornings, as she had countless times.

And there she was again, after two years cold in the ground.

Then she wasn't. She was there for about as much time as it takes to blink and think, for a panicked second, *Is that really her?*

That was the first time. There were quickly others.

Jasmine liked to get in the bath tub with me when I was practicing my Death Trance Meditations. I like to sit in warm water with the lights off and think about myself in terms of flesh, blood, bone, hair and where all those pieces could end up, say, in a million years. You can get into some profound thoughts, laying in the dark, in the water, like that. And it can really mess with your head when the door would crash open and this demented hippie chick, all bounce and giggle, would come storming in jingling her tiny silver bells to pull off her balloon pants and squat herself down on the john to take a piss. We used to fight about it, especially when I didn't even know she was in the house. You can imagine the shock she made after she was dead.

Mornings were Jasmine's favorite time of day. If I'd let her she would go on and on about the opening of the day, with the accompaniment of birds singing and the soft applause of butterflies. She would wax cliché about the possibilities "dawning" (and giggling at the pun) with the new day and wonder how many adventures she'd have by sunset.

I am a Creature of the Night. I run from the burning rays of the sun and seek solstice in the cool darkness of my shell. But, still, I would always get up on a cheery blast furnace of a morning and be happy as a clam – especially when Jasmine treated me to one of her early bird special blowjobs. She liked that word, "blowjob" – said it sounded cute. And, boy, was Jasmine skilled in its performance. Just the right amount of tongue, suction, lips, wet, dry, hands. She used to wake me up with soft kisses along my leg to let me know she was there and what she was up to. Then the kisses would run up to my stomach. A hand carefully placed over my cock and balls would warm them and add some sensation. When her mouth did finally touch my cock, it was after those soft, soft hands had stroked, teased, tickled and coaxed me into a painfully intense hard-on. Then the mouth. Then the real ride.

Mornings haven't been the same since she died. The sun must be a little brighter, stronger now. But then that one morning came. I was sleeping off my usual late-night writing stint (with a celebration of a new one finished: *I was a Teenage Trailer Park Slut*) when I got this amazing hard-on. I was so zonked that I really can't tell you if it was because of Jasmine or just because I was remembering my past with her, but there it was: long (no brag, but seven inches), strong and mighty. It was a mechanic's cock, a soldier's cock, a fuckin' basketball player's cock (okay, one of the white ones). I was proud of my cock, pleased with it that morning. With a hard-on like that, even hack writers can go out and become president (if you know the right people).

Then Jasmine started to work on it. Dear dead Jasmine. Maybe because of my half-zonked condition, maybe because I just missed those lips, that throat, but I didn't do what I should have done: run screaming into that intense morning. But I didn't and dear dead Jasmine started to really get down and suck at my cock.

Death did not diminish her knowledge of blowjobs, it seemed. She was all of Jasmine rolled into that one cock-sucking. I could, in fact, squint and see her as I had seen her on all those mornings: her firm, slightly heavy body folded over, her face concentrating at my cock, with her right hand between her legs as she humped herself along with her sucking.

God, I could feel every inch of Jasmine – even if I couldn't see her. I could feel her tongue playing with the ridges and corona of my head, I could feel her lips play over my skin and veins, I could feel her throat – hot and firm – as I grazed it during her sucking. When I came, it was so good it hurt real bad, and my come shot into an invisible mouth and vanished into ectoplasmic nothingness just as real live Jasmine had liked to swallow it.

Other people would have run – to their pastors, to the cops (why?), to some science guys with a gizmo to exorcise the latent spectral energies, or to their priests (who would rattle their beads and speak some Latin). But most folks don't consider themselves a Child of the Night, groove on gloom, or hate any color save pitch black. Besides, Jasmine had been a sweet girl (tinkle, tinkle) and one motherfuckin' hot lay.

The fact that she was dead and haunting me didn't really seem to bother me at the time.

Jasmine was great for surprises. She liked to catch you unawares and get caught unawares herself. I can't remember how many times I'd "caught" Jasmine in the living room, or on the toilet, in my bed, rubbing one of her little, soft fingers up and down on her little moist slit. She was like a little kid in that, her body and other people's used to give her so much pleasure. Death didn't even slow her down.

Listening to the newest Lycia CD, all moan, cemeteries, statues, clouds, rain, and mourners, I would get the strong impression of flowers, macramé, pot and the distinct sound of the tiny silver bells on toes jingling merrily away and look next to me to see Jasmine, half there and half not, not quite developed, not quite visible, legs spread wide, fingers gently rubbing up and down on her gumdrop-sized clit.

She became, over those weeks, to be more and more in my life. More so than she had when she was alive. Flesh and blood Jasmine used to come over maybe, tops, three times a week. Then I wouldn't see her for months. Once a year passed before I walked in to see her dancing, naked, in my living room, the air thick with Mexican greenbud. But now that she had passed on, time seemed different to her. I would expect to feel or feel this spirit of Morrison, of Cream, of Sergeant Pepper at least once a day. Dancing in the living room, reading the Sunday paper in the kitchen, masturbating on the toilet, spooning with me in bed.

Bad? No, not at all. I felt special that of all the people she lived with, had fucked, had fought with, this one grungy hack writer living in a cheap-ass bungalow in Long Beach was the one she wanted to spend eternity with.

But there started to be other times, too. I would walk from the kitchen into the living room, coffee cup in hand, straight for my Mac with visions of *Truck Stop Bimbos* running through my head like a pneumatic chorus line, and I would see her, standing by the window looking at something only the ghostly Jasmine could see. What bothered me more than anything was that Jasmine, alive, never really had an interest in the traffic on Oleander Street. Jasmine wasn't just an echo drilled into me and my cheap-ass stucco walls. Something of the real Jasmine was here with the spectral one. Something that was missing something.

It became pretty obvious when she started to get . . . . distracted by things. Right in the middle of one hot and nasty morning blowjob, her ghost would stop right in the middle (*coitus spectoralus*) and I would get the definite impression that she was looking out that window again like she was trying to remember something that she had forgotten.

Rosie, my only expert on dead relations coming back to cop a feel, got real quiet as she poured my Darjeeling tea, then said: "When Bolo left this world –" Rosie's ex who tried to jump her Harley from the Queen Mary to Catalina "– she came back to visit me a couple of times. It was like she just wanted to say good-bye in a way she couldn't when she was living. When she had done that, she just faded away."

"Yeah, but I don't get the vibe that Jas is here for a reason. It's like she just sort of moved back in."

Rosie stirred her tea with a chiming that reminded me way too much of Jasmine's tiny silver bells. "I got the impression from Bolo that she knew where she was going and that she was just stopping by. Remember, we are dealing with Jasmine, here. She could have gotten lost."

Great, a girl who could get lost in a Safeway had taken the wrong turn between death and the afterlife and was now trapped in my house.

It got worse soon after. The sex was still there, but now it was . . . sad. The one thing the flesh and blood Jasmine wasn't was sad. The best way to get rid of her, in fact, was to get depressed: she'd vanish like pot smoke to find someone more cheerful. I've always had a hard time putting on a happy face, the one reason why Jasmine and I never stayed together for too long. Now, though, it looked like she was stuck in my dark little bungalow. Trapped.

And it was making her sad. It wasn't something she was used to, getting sad, and it was hitting her hard.

I heard her cry one day. I was hard at work on something for a porno mag specializing in dirty buttholes "and the guys who love to lick them" when I heard this weird sound. A sort of choking, wet sound. I hadn't heard it before.

I found her next to my bed, curled into a partially invisible fetal position. Jasmine was crying. It was that heaving, nauseous kind of crying, the kind you do when your cat gets run over, when you know you've taken way too much of the wrong kind of shit, when you're lost and know you can never find your way back.

I'm not a very altruistic kinda guy. I don't really know where it comes from, or doesn't: I just really don't give a flying fuck for a lot of folks. Yeah, I'll take Steve to the hospital when his T cells are low, or hold Rosie when she thinks too much of Bolo, but I don't really see those things are being good. Good is, like, helping fucking orphans or something, or giving change to the smelly crackhead who hangs out, or passes out, at the Laundromat. I don't have that kind of temperament.

I really didn't care that much about Jasmine. Yeah I'd bail her out when she got busted for forgetting her purse and eating up a storm at some diner. Yeah, I'd give her whatever I had in my checking account when she really needed it. Yeah, I'd always let her in, no matter what was going on in my life. But she was just a pal, and a really good lay. I honestly didn't think of her in any other terms.

But then she was dead, and crying in my bedroom.

I could guess the cause. Bolo was a dyke who always knew where she was going and how exactly to get there. She was an iron-plated mean mother who knew what the score was – despite her profound depressions and mood swings. Jasmine was flowers and pot and the Beatles. She could get lost walking from the bathroom into the bedroom.

It wasn't all that hard, once I made the decision to do it. One phone call, to Rosie. Then into the bathroom.

I hadn't done my Death Trance since she had manifested herself those two weeks ago. It was just too much of a temptation for her and the shock of her walking in had been way too much when she was flesh and blood. Since she was a ghost – well, I don't really want to see if I'm cardiac prone.

Had trouble sleeping a few years back. I was lucky enough to have health insurance at the time, so was able to see a doc who could actually give me pills. I had only taken one – the fuckers were so strong that I stopped taking them and simply started staying up late.

I took five and lay down in the warm water.

We are nothing but matter. We are nothing but the flesh that hangs on our bones, the blood that gushes through our meat. Bach took shits, Aristotle got piss hard-ons, Mother Theresa the runs, Ghandi really liked enemas, Lincoln got wind. We are animals that have learned to walk upright, that have trained themselves to use the next best thing to fishing with termites with a stick: the nuclear bomb.

I didn't have to think long. About the time I was drawing analogies between Sartre and seals that know how to play "Lady of Spain" on car horns, I was interrupted by a tiny sound, the sound of cheap Mexican toe rings chiming their tinny, cheap tones: the tinkling of tiny silver bells. Then the sound of Jasmine pissing into the toilet.

But this time it didn't sound mischievous, it sounded sad.

The pills had started to take effect, I braced my feet against the tub so I wouldn't drown and whispered, as loud as I could (which was just loud enough for the dead to hear), "Follow me."

I don't know what she saw, but I started to hallucinate pretty badly. Either the pills, or I had really started to fade, myself – I don't know. I was in the kitchen, full and real and solid, looking out of my window. The sun was bright, so bright that I had to close my eyes against the brightness – but for some reason it reached right through my eyelids and right into my brain. I realized then that it couldn't be the sun – for at least the obvious reason that sun never came in that window, anyway.

No tunnel, no saints (or sinners, either), just that bright light. I felt myself start to come apart, like the flesh I had always talked about, thought about in my trances, was starting to unravel and decompose around me, leaving just a lightweight fragment of Roger Corn left.

It wasn't a pull or an enticement, it was just a direction that I was walking myself to.

Jasmine. Somewhere I thought that, and reached back into my apartment for her, but I couldn't seem to find her. I looked in the bathroom (I looked so silly laying there in the tub, mouth hanging open), the living room, all the closets, the kitchen . . . everywhere. No Jasmine. Not even her ghost.

Then that sound. Her sound. Cheap bells on her toes and a smile on her face. I found her masturbating in the bedroom, chubby legs wide and open, finger dancing on her clit. Typical. I smiled and took her hand and pulled her towards me, into me –

– and then pushed her away, into the brightness.

The cops and firemen busted down my bathroom door about that time. I don't remember much after save the sound of their tools smashing my interior door to cheap splinters. I probably don't want to remember being naked in front of all those macho public servants, having a tube run down my throat and having all that guck and pills poured out. Rosie had come through, with perfect timing.

No repercussions, no real ones at any rate: what's another botched suicide, after all? At least I had accomplished something with this one: a spectral repercussion.

She's gone. You'd expect that. Gone wherever magical little Deadheads go when they OD. She's with Janice now, with Morrison and Lennon – in a place where the seventies never happened and where everyone gets along.

And, yeah, I hear those damned happy bells now and again.

Simon Says

Alice Gray

Everything is set, my choice. The meeting place, the dining (*if we get that far*), the final destination. I'm grateful for the condensation on the whiskey glass cupped in my hands. It hides the fact that my palms are sweating worse than the ice.

I'm also grateful for the easy, warm glow the alcohol has given me. That's why I showed up forty minutes early. Who wouldn't need a little shot of courage? It's two on one, their turf. I want to see them before they see me.

The last few drops of Red Label still burn my throat when I spot them coming in, ten minutes early. They look like an ordinary couple, out for an intimate drink after they've been apart for an entire day, separated by ordinary obligations. But I know better.

I know why they are really here. It's exciting, this secret knowledge.

A smile I can't contain spreads across my cheeks. A quick wave gets their attention and earns me two smiles in return.

"Ronnie!" She squeals my name and slides around the long curve of the booth to throw her arms around me.

Her scent sets off tiny detonations across my skin. "Ava!"

We press awkward, unsatisfying kisses against each other's cheeks before disentangling.

He slides up next to me on the other side, trapping me between them. His lips are warm and in control when he kisses my cheek.

"Simon." I encourage his contact, placing a firm hand to his cheek. After all, he's part of the deal. The stiff bristle of his short beard crackles under my palm and tingles against my face for an instant before I let go.

The skinny bitch of a waitress who's ignored me since I arrived shows up with surprising speed.

"Can I get y'all somethin' ta drink?" She snaps her gum and makes big eyes at Simon.

He laces his fingers together and leans across the table on his forearms. "Jameson neat, all around."

A quick glance at Ava tells me she finds Simon's effect on the waitress as funny as I do. The waitress doesn't seem to notice; she only has eyes for Simon. With an exaggerated turn, she bounces off toward the cocktail station.

"Ronnie." Simon turns his attention my way and takes my hand in both of his. "How was your flight?"

"The flight was as good as you could expect for someone who hates to fly."

Ava squeezes closer to me and lays her head on my shoulder. "I hate flying, too. Simon says it's because I'm a control freak."

Panic flashes through me in warm rush. Things are moving too fast.

"Here you go." The waitress deals out three cheap cardboard coasters with a matching trifecta of drinks. "Twenty-four dollars."

Simon slides a sinuous arm around his back to reach for his wallet. The plastic card snaps against the laminated tabletop. "Start a tab."

The waitress's resin nails click when she peels his card up. "Of course." She gives him a mischievous smile before twirling away.

Pent-up excitement flows like an ocean current under us.

Simon holds up his glass. "A toast. To new friends."

Ava and I hurry to raise our drinks. The clink of glass on glass is lost in the buzz of conversation around us. Some of the liquid spills over my hand, warm and cool at the same time. There is nothing cool about the whiskey as it runs down my throat.

Simon slams his glass to the tabletop and swipes his thumb across his lips. "Damn, that's good."

His eyes are quicksilver in the dim light. I always pictured him with eyes as black as coal. It's unsettling. Another reminder that I don't really know these people I've traveled so far to see. A second round of drinks and the conversation flows like liquid gold, engaging, stimulating. Hands begin to wander under the table. My fingers on hers, hers on mine. She traces light circles against my palm, sending shivers rippling up my arm.

The night's entertainment takes the stage. Their appearance draws the focus of the audience forward. Anticipation spreads through the crowd. The drummer begins a low, steady beat. Guitars, languid and rhythmic, pour out the hypnotic notes of roots reggae.

Ava squeezes my hand. She shifts until her lips are an inch from my ear. "Dance with me, Ronnie."

I finish my drink and follow her. There is no handholding as Ava and I thread our way forward. The dance floor is filling with other couples looking for hot fun on a cold autumn night. All I can see is the way her skirt rides the curves of her backside with each step. The whiskey has done its job, leaving a volatile trail of desire.

It's a small club, intimate, but there are few enough people tonight that we have our own universe within the mass of hot bodies. A universe with a perfect view, just for him, so he can watch as we spiral toward each other, toward ignition.

Music fills the room, leaving no escape. The rhythm has invaded her, washing her in an ethereal splendor. So beautiful, her hips swaying in languid figure eights, lips parted, eyes burning into mine.

I know they are a package deal. In order to have Ava, I must share her with Simon. He's attractive enough but she is the reason I came so far.

I reach for the swell of her hips. Her warmth seeps through the thin material of her skirt into my hands. We move together, alone in the sea of bodies. Her hips, my hands, our only contact points, still separated by a searing gap of space. She covers my hands with hers, pressing them harder against her hips, taking control. Each sway brings her closer to me until our bodies touch at last.

She feels so good. Her breasts against mine, our bellies touching, her body so like my own. And, there is nothing left in the universe but the live wire that is her.

"Veronica." The sound of my name is lost in the music but I don't need to hear her tone to understand her.

I twine my fingers with hers, squeezing, using the leverage to guide her mouth to mine. She parts her lips in anticipation. So soft. She tastes of smoky vanilla.

Trailing small kisses, I nip and suckle her slender throat. With bold hands, she cups my breasts through my clothing, capturing my nipples between her thumb and forefinger. The pressure borders on painful and draws a moan from deep within me. Time and place lose all meaning.

I seek her warm, inviting mouth wanting to devour the sounds of her arousal. The skin between her thighs is smooth, her panties silken and taut under my fingers. Her moan vibrates down my throat and rumbles in my chest. She rocks, pleasing herself against my hand.

An insistent tapping on my shoulder breaks the spell. It's a man in a sharp suit wearing an unhappy, somber expression. Ava and I scramble apart, guilty like children caught with hands in a cookie jar.

"Excuse me, ladies. I'm going to have to ask you to take your party elsewhere. Sorry. Club policy."

One glance at Ava and we're both giggling.

"That's an unfortunate policy," Ava says. "You'd probably make more money tonight if we were allowed to stay." She casts a glance around the club, pointing out the fact that there are plenty of people watching us instead of the band.

I'm still giggling when Ava takes my hand and pulls me away.

Simon sits where we left him, a satisfied smile on his face. Before we can take our seats, he slides out of the booth. "I already settled our bill. Shall we?"

No dinner tonight. There are other things on the menu.

We make the trip to my hotel with no contact between us. Conversation is limited to what is necessary to reach our destination. Instead of serving as a damper, this limited contact, this self-restraint heightens the anticipation.

In the elevator, I wonder what the gentleman who has the good fortune of sharing this ride with us is thinking. The tension is so high that I'm almost surprised when the elevator doors don't blow off their tracks and spill us all to the plush carpeting in the hallway.

I pause in front of my door, plastic key card in my hand poised before the small red eye of the electronic lock. I decided a long time ago to give myself to them. This is it. The point of no return. Theoretically, I've had the option of backing out at any time. I know once we go inside my room, there is no turning back.

With a quick push, the smooth plastic glides home releasing the lock with a quiet snick and the red eye goes green. A small electric spark arcs between my fingers and the cool metal door handle.

I step into the room, holding the door open for them. First him, followed by her. When she passes by, I reach out and take her hand, keeping her close. The door swings shut and I can't wait any longer.

With an urgent kiss, I pin her against the door. I need to feel her again the way we were on the dance floor. Her mouth. Her nipples. The soft skin of her belly. I can't get enough. The smell of her hair. The soft sighs of her breath against my skin.

Her hand slides between my thighs. She slips her fingers under the edge of my panties and pushes into me.

Through the haze of excitement, I hear a faint jingling from Simon's direction and think he has had enough of sitting quietly to the side. I imagine that he is undoing his belt buckle and pants so that he can begin to stroke himself. I am so wrong. He rises from his chair and comes to where I have her pinned against the door.

With the front of his body, he traps me between them. The hard length of his cock sits high on my back.

"Hold still." He whispers his command in my ear.

I try to obey but she's fucking me with her fingers and kissing me, making it impossible to keep from moving.

Some unspoken signal passes between them. She breaks away from my mouth and uses her free hand to gather my hair off my shoulders. He slides a sleek leather collar around my neck. The buckle jingles again as his practiced fingers make quick work of the fastening.

"Bound by collar rules, Veronica." His words are low and hot in my ear.

She hasn't let up on me. I'm so close to coming that I know my legs won't hold me up if they release me from their embrace.

"Rule number one. You have to ask permission to come. If you come without permission—"

"Please, please, oh please . . ." Already they have me begging, fighting with everything I have not to break the rules before I even know what the rules are.

He backs off me a little and reaches around to cover her hand with his. "Naughty girl. Don't interrupt me when I'm speaking to you." He makes Ava stop. "You don't have permission to come, yet."

My orgasm threatens to steal over me when he draws her fingers out of me. My head is too heavy. I rest my forehead on her shoulder and draw long, ragged breaths.

"Rule number one is only for coming quietly. Rule number two. You need special permission to come loudly."

I nod to let him know I understand.

"Rule number three is to obey me when I say 'Simon says'. Understand?"

"Yes."

"Good. You will be punished for any rule that is broken."

Cold air rushes across my back when he takes a step back. It helps to clear my head.

"Simon says, undress, Ronnie. Everything but your panties and your shoes."

I step away from Ava. She still has her back against the door, arms at her sides with her palms pushing flat against the door behind her. Her breasts rise and fall with her own excited breath.

I try to be quick because I don't know if there is a time limit but my fingers are shaking. I have to slow down. When the buttons are all undone, I slip my arms out of the blouse and let it flutter to the floor. My bra is next. The black lace falls away, exposing my breasts to the cold air. My nipples sting as they contract. Skirt. I tug the small zipper down, hook my fingers into the waistband, and slide it over my hips until it puddles around my feet. Stepping out of it, I kick it aside. I'm left in nothing but my silky black thong, my heels and my new collar.

"Good girl." His words hold encouragement. He moves closer, holding something out to me. Her collar. "Put it on her."

I grasp it in both hands and reach toward her neck. Her eyes are on fire as she lifts her hair up, baring her throat. There are small red marks on her pale skin, marks I left there earlier with my teeth. I circle her neck with the thick leather, fumbling a little before securing the buckle.

He moves impossibly fast, one long arm around my waist, pulling me back, back, back until he is seated in the soft wing chair with me draped over his thighs, like a –

"Naughty girl," he says.

I cry out from the sting of his hand. A spanking, my first of the night.

Smack!

"I didn't say 'Simon says'."

Smack! Smack!

My skin heats up where his hand is certainly leaving a trail of bright red marks against my pale flesh. Each blow fades from pain to hot tingling pleasure. The spanking over, he helps me up.

"Now, Simon says undress her, same as you." He takes his seat, watching to make sure I carry out his orders.

At last, my chance to see her undressed, to feel her smooth skin against mine, touch her unencumbered by the confines of her clothing. I kiss her once and take her hand. I want to undress her in full view of him, away from the door. She follows as I lead her within arm's reach of the spanking chair where he sits.

Holding her face, I press my mouth to hers. Her hands settle over my hips. Dipping a quick tongue into her mouth, I trail the kiss along her jaw. One kiss above her collar under her chin. One kiss below in the hollow of her throat. A kiss for each metal stud buried in the leather. She shivers under my touch, her fingers digging into my hips. The sound she makes has me burning inside, barely in control.

Taking the hem of her shirt, I lift it up. My hands trace her curves as I help her get it over her head. She wears no bra. Her skin is so pale, her nipples a sweet pink. She turns her head to watch him.

I lean in, stroking her bare back, and take her small perfect nipple into my mouth, sucking it, grazing it with my teeth. Her breath speeds up. She tangles her fingers in my hair and guides my mouth to her other nipple.

The small buttons marching down the back of her skirt come undone in my fingers. Squatting before her, I balance on my high heels and slide the tube of material down her legs with deliberate slowness. The muscles in her thighs tremble. She rocks her hips forward when I place a light kiss on her belly, just below her navel.

Her skirt drops to the carpet. She kicks it aside and widens her stance. I look at her face long enough to see desire burning behind her eyes before burying my face in her damp lacy crotch. Her smell, her taste, fills my mouth and nose. She moans and her grip on my hair turns painful.

A burst of excited energy jumps from her to me, firing across all my nerves. I part my lips and rub them in a light circle across the plump swollen front of her panties. She swears softly when I nip at the tight knot of her clit through the material. Her salty tang intensifies. A flood of wetness, my own, dampens my thong.

I'm ready, so ready for her to be out of her panties so I can make her come. Hooking my fingers into the material on either side of her hips, I yank them down. I want her naked. Exposed.

"Uh oh, Veronica . . ." He leans forward in his chair and reaches out to cover my hand with his, keeping me from getting her panties off. "You broke Rule number 3. I told you to undress her, same as you. Shoes. And panties. Left on." He pulls me away from her, slow this time.

"Climb on to my lap, naughty girl."

Fear and excitement combine, making me dizzy as I settle across his lap. My muscles grow tense waiting for the spanking. He's dragging it out this time. I flinch each time he caresses my ass, expecting the sting of his slap instead of tenderness.

Smack! Smack! Smack! Smack! Smack!

Each blow brings a new flood of pain and pleasure. The urge to come is almost impossible to stop. I dig my teeth into my lip and concentrate on keeping quiet this time. As before, he helps me up when the spanking is over. I stand still, waiting for him to tell me what he wants from me.

He sits, considering his next move, and rises from the spanking chair.

"Lay down on the bed on your back," he says to Ava.

She has her panties back in place and moves quickly to obey him. He follows her, placing her where he wants her. I stay where I am, watching them.

He glances at me. "Come here and stand still. Simon says."

I step up beside him.

She lies before us on the bed, her legs dangling over the edge, waiting for my touch while I listen for his instructions.

He leashes her collar to the headboard before bending between her legs to ease her panties off. With a lover's gentle touch, he decorates her thighs with thick leather cuffs. A silver chain links the cuffs together, leaving her just enough slack to spread her legs.

With his tongue and fingers, he teases her for a moment.

Watching them elicits a groan from me. Her hips rise off the bed to meet his touch. Jealousy flashes its heat across my skin even as he moves away from her to me. He kisses me for the first time, tasting of Ava.

I want to touch him but I don't dare. Not yet.

"Do you want to see her come, Veronica?" he asks.

"God, yes."

He is rough in his handling of me as he jostles me into place between her legs. The soft skin of her inner thighs presses hot against the outside of mine. It's a tight connection, constrained by the length of chain.

He slithers around me and pulls first my right wrist, then my left, behind my back. The material he binds my wrists with feels like warm velvet. When the knots are secure, he pulls me against him. His excitement over this grown-up version of a child's game is plain to feel.

"Ready, Veronica?"

"Yes." Caught up in my own excitement, it comes out as a low whisper.

"Simon says, down on the floor, on your knees."

I drop to my knees on the thick carpeting. More jingling. His hands reach around my throat, a short length of chain with clips at each end grasped in his fingers. He clips one end to the center link binding her thighs and the other end to the ring imbedded in my collar.

"Beautiful," he says.

He stands, admiring his work for just a moment before starting to take pictures. When he is satisfied, he sets the camera aside. Kneeling behind me, he reaches around either side of my body to stroke her skin above the cuffs.

"Simon says, show me. Show me what you can do with your mouth and your tongue. Make her come loudly." He thrusts himself against me, encouraging me toward her while his fingers raise thin red lines on her pale skin.

Pushing back into him, the chain tethered to my collar goes taut with a metallic chink. She likes being made to wait, likes being teased on the edge for as long as possible. I don't know if I can wait that long.

I kiss her thigh before opening my mouth to lick a wet path from her inner thigh to her outer, just above the edge of the cuff. Her breath comes in fast, excited little noises. I switch paths, working my tongue up, letting the chain between us grow slack. She jumps a little as the chain settles against her pussy. As much as I want to taste her and lick her and feel her come in my mouth, I hold back, pulling the chain tight again so that I can do the same to her other thigh. Her whole body vibrates. She moans, louder and longer this time.

He leans his weight forward, pinning my bound arms between us, urging me on. Time has run out, there's nowhere left to go but forward. I trace my lips across her smooth, bare skin for the first time. She hisses and jerks. A warm trickle runs down the curve of her thigh. I want to hear her begging to come. Using only the faintest touch, I kiss my way toward her clit, stopping just short. She moans and rocks her whole body toward me, straining for contact.

He stands and begins undressing. When he has everything off, he kneels behind me and leans against me once again.

"You're so good with her," he whispers. "Simon says, make us both come, Veronica." He shifts on to his knees and slides his cock against my bound hands. "Make us both come."

Without letting up on her, I grip his cock so he can fuck my hands.

He reaches forward, his fingers digging into her thighs while he thrusts. Every time he buries his cock in the tight well of my fists, it forces my mouth harder against her. He helps me fuck her this way, all on the same rhythm. So close, she is so close. All it takes is my tongue finally flashing across her clit to set her off.

She begs for permission to come loudly. He swells in my hands at the sound of her words.

Before he can even finish granting her permission, I feel her climax flow through her body, hear her loud cries of release, taste her orgasm. He comes right behind her, spraying hot jets across my back.

She goes quiet first, laying limp on the soft bed. He rests his weight against me, his breathing deep and controlled. After a couple of minutes, he backs off me.

"It's your turn, Veronica. We're both going to make you come. Simon says."

Rain and the Library

Kris Saknussemm

The thing about research is that it's so much more fun with two. And the thing about a library is that it's like a superstore for people who love books and secret, seemingly random knowledge that suddenly gets found, as if part of a quest. So, I was excited about you helping me dig up a very hard to find book in the main files.

On the surface, it was a legitimate, innocent venture. Two smart people, who wanted to spend time together, doing something productive. It wasn't something suspicious. The shortness of your skirt? That was just part of the play. There's no harm in a young sexy woman teasing an older man. It's a sign of affection and respect. Part of the game. And if he really does get a furious hard-on for her, and that thirst in the mouth, as if for a stem of rye grass when he was walking home from school as a lonely kid, when demons started appearing and people died or wished they had, that's a good thing.

Besides, it was raining very hard and you couldn't have predicted that. Spring thunderstorm. Black licorice and ozone smell. It would be good to get inside the library. Where it was dry. And where our minds wouldn't wander.

I'd come a long way to find an original of a very old book called *The Trials of Great Men Accused of Magic*, which as it turned out, was to be found down in the lower basement, down in a very quiet labyrinth of books arranged on very high shelves. It was a lovely bonus that the only library in the US to have a genuine, undamaged copy was at least a little close to where you live.

It gave us the excuse of not doing what I wanted to do straight up – and take you to some lost Magic Fingers motel or some resort along the coast where people in uniform bring the rum to your room and discreetly turn away. This was going to be work.

I couldn't help but notice the shortness of the skirt though. And I knew instantly, in some animal way, that you weren't wearing panties.

Which made me think all kinds of thoughts as we descended to the basement. Do I kiss her? Do I fondle her? Or do I just let things run their course? Do I behave?

The basement was silent, a veritable maze of old, unlooked-at books filled with who knows what. I was intrigued, however, to see a ladder of a particular kind resting against one of the shelves. I'd often dreamed of having just such a ladder, in the private library of my brownstone on the Upper West Side of New York (of course!). It was very tall, neatly made of individually dowelled rungs, with hooked ends at the top and lubricated wheels at the bottom.

The curious thing about such a ladder, however, is that its very ingenuity undermines its function. You would think that it would allow a single person to scurry up to its full height and pluck out a book from even a very high shelf. And so it does, they do. But with a catch. Someone must brace the ladder, because the freedom made possible by the wheels is offset by the fact that the wheels can turn in their brackets – the ladder's height making it too heavy for the wheels to only move in one direction, the designer of such things having apparently decided it was easier to find a person to "mind" the ladder rather than to help move the ladder.

I think you were inclined to climb up it just for the fun of it – or to see my reaction. But as it turns out (and don't things have an interesting way of turning out, when you start off properly?), the book we were looking for was supposedly on the top shelf where the ladder was.

So, you being young and spry (and wearing a very short skirt), were selected as our ambassador to the heights. And while you were rummaging around trying to find the book in question, batting away the dust and dead moths, you came upon another volume called *The Chains of Desire*. It was on the very top shelf, near where the other book should've been. It looked old and the spine was broken, but the original making was clearly of a very high standard. You couldn't resist having a look, having climbed up to the top of the ladder and blown away a cloud of dust to boot. And you couldn't help thinking that whatever page you opened up to would mean something. A special stop on the journey. A clue in the treasure hunt. Balanced on the top step of the ladder, you opened to a scene. And, to your surprise, this is what you saw . . . you see it now . . . and will never quite forget it.

The picture is sumptuously illustrated and deeply obscene. It shows a man, naked and tautly muscled, wearing a glistening metal mask in the shape of a bull's head – like the suggestion of a minotaur. There is something evil and yet inviting about the beast face … something forbidden and perverse … and yet proud, noble, even tragic. You can't quite bring the impression into focus, for there are other things to consider. Like the height of the ladder.

And the size of his penis. While the rest of his body is that of a human male, the organ is that of a bull – or a monster. So swollen and erect it seems to be like another creature … making an angle with his rippled abdomen that reminds you of the cleft between the first thick branch and the trunk that made a favorite tree easy to climb when you were a little girl. But this is no room for little girls. All innocence has been swept away in this private world … with the sight of the shining cock head, sculpted like some kind of medieval battering ram.

And then there is the room. It is richly appointed, like something from eighteenth-century France, the curtains not quite drawn, with a hint of rain on the leadlight pane. So, this moment too, that you've just stumbled upon is another afternoon of rain and possibility. Lust. Perhaps things unleashed. Another piece of the puzzle.

Before the bull-man lies a naked woman, porcelain white of flesh, but coated with a fine sheen of perspiration and fragrance – spread wide on an amethyst and black sheeted bed of silk with fat tasseled pillows, like a giant version of a pearl butterfly she had made for her at great expense by a blind jeweler who died when it was finished and she only bothered to wear once.

She has the air of grotesque wealth and depravity, the kind that is only shown in secrecy. Her legs are parted fully, so that you can see how neatly she has been shaved by a serving girl, how smooth her thighs are, her clitoris unusually large, bulbing up from under its hood of skin in monstrous mimicry of the minotaur's giant phallus. Her whole sex is gaping, like an overbloomed rose torn apart in a single swift gesture by strong hands. You can see all the way inside her … all the way to the words she wants to say … her mouth open like a second ravenous, meat-eating flower.

There is a blood-red sleep mask in her right hand – you can't tell if she's just removed it or longs to put it on, confronted as she is by the monster – the wall-splitting girth of him poised before her. Does she feel horror and fear … or insane longing?

Beside her, on the floor by the bed, is another woman, also naked, much younger, and even though you can't see her face, you realize she is much more beautiful. Perhaps she is the serving girl who has done the immaculate shaving and grooming . . . plumped the pillows, misted the room with aromatic spray.

You can tell the younger woman has a very different bearing than the woman on the bed, even though her position argues against this. She is bent over, with her hands tied with black velvet behind her back . . . her ass curving up like . . . like the ass the older woman wished she had. It is round and rude, and yet exquisitely shaped, so that even in its intense lewdness, there is some sheltered modesty. Completely exposed. Flaunted. The skin is the same color as the inside of a snow apple, the kind that only come into season very suddenly and then are gone. So sweet it's like tiny crystals of sugar have been ladled into full cream . . . and yet savory too . . . a confliction of tastes . . . a flavored ice treat and a chunk of just shot game, cooked hot and fast on spit-burst charcoal. A perfect ass, bent over in total supplication . . . the skin and curve of the young girl, the flow into her lower back and up the spine, all suggestive of that hint of divinity the ancients used to claim lay hidden for all to see in the white meat within a single walnut.

This delicacy intrigues you, and saddens you. For the girl too is neatly groomed, so that her tender pussy lips are visible between her legs, as pink as a shellfish, but thick and tactile, like a puckered fig.

There are other things in the room. Objects of disturbing implications. Hairbrushes that look too sharp, too big. A kind of chair seemingly made of bones – and iron. A draped veil that looks more like a net to catch something in. Paper masks hang from long hooks in the shape of hard penises. Masks of distorted faces, some animal-like . . . goats, pigs, wolves. Some like faces of the damned. Swirled and cracked . . . or bloated and leering.

You begin to realize that this is not a single scene, but a ritual you are witnessing . . . something which has happened before. More details emerge then. The wood and leather crop that lies beside the bed . . . just fallen from the hand of the older woman perhaps.

You notice a faint but still cruel line of blush across the full rounded cheek of the younger woman's buttocks that you hadn't seen before. And you see that the light reflects off the minotaur's mask in a strange way that hadn't earlier caught your eye – the stack and line of his carved body and the massive organ having distracted you.

He is not staring at the woman on the bed, eager to ream her – to plunge inside her and thrust her inside out. He is mindful of the girl on the floor. The serving girl with the ass made by God's own artisan.

And then you understand the terrible truth of the picture.

This is not the minotaur's game. The mask can never be removed. It is fixed to his head forever, like a kind of cage. He is a slave, wanted only for his virility. He is but another implement in the room . . . and the servant girl with the voluptuous ass and tender other mouth of young female succulence . . . she is what has been used to entice him . . . to bring up the blood and thicken his root. She is the one he wants . . . and can never have . . .

All this of course, has been taken in very quickly in real time. Meanwhile, I have been fixated on a picture myself.

Perched on the tall ladder, your skirt falls in such a way, that by standing behind the ladder I can not only glimpse, but luxuriantly examine, the curve of your ass. If I move forward, slipping between the ladder and the shelf, I can look up and see your pussy just above me . . . and more than that. Stopped still in mid air above me, I am close enough to catch your scent . . .

Like Italy . . .

The way the canals and markets of Venice smelled to me when I came down out of the chalk-blue frigid-faced passport thumbing police-ridden Balkans, broke and hungry, so sick with fever and bronchitis I saw huge candelabra before my eyes at midday and all the pigeons in St Mark's Square were like angels . . . and people I didn't know offered me food and wine instead of clubs and jails.

Like the mirror tidepools of Apollo Bay, each volcanic indentation of seawater a miniature miracle world of writhing, watchful life.

Like slivers of spring onions hissing in a pan of Spanish olive oil in a Chelsea flat at 2 a.m., the police still mopping up the murder down on the street below.

Like saltwater taffy and ozone when the thunder rolled in over the roller coaster in Santa Cruz long ago when I thought it was cool to carry a switchblade, and I drove a Dodge Charger with baby shoes hanging from the mirror, the same baby blue as another girl's eyes, that I'd bought with money working in the lettuce fields where no one spoke English.

Like summer. The kind you never really have, but only dream about, and later, pretend that you remember – that you can hold on to.

And then it occurs to me – having often wanted to own just such a ladder, and a huge climbing matrix of books – and always having dreamed of such a vantage point – that the trick to these kinds of ladders is that they can be readjusted. From the ground, even with someone up on the highest rung, the wheels allow it to be readjusted, to be ratcheted down a shelf – which strangely has the effect of making things more precarious for the person on the ladder, not less. With the center of gravity neatly engineered to be in my control, you are suddenly out of balance – lower to the ground, but still too far to safely reach. You have to lean more into the cage of the ladder, clinging to it to maintain balance. What a good joke, you think.

But it isn't a joke. You're stuck, like someone in a hammock strung too high. You would have to not only jump, but to roll first – and if you did, the ladder would give way from the shelf and so would collapse. It takes but a moment for you to fully appreciate the physics involved. You can only come down the ladder if I let you. Until then, you are there, balanced, needing both your hands to retain equilibrium.

I, on the other hand, unlike the minotaur man (who retains his vividness in your mind ... with his fearsome appendage and awful mask) am now free to do whatever I like. If I make use of the stool down the aisle of books, which has been made available to those who want to browse the lower shelves, I'm exactly the right height to do many things. If I stand on it and poke my head through the square of neatly dowelled wood to the front, I can lift your skirt and gaze without concern at your femaleness. I can breathe over your vulva. I can tongue your thighs. I can bury my face in your pussy and smear myself into it like devouring a ripe, slit-open mango. There's nothing you can do. You can't loose a hand to guide me, stop me, or stroke yourself – or you'll tumble to the floor.

If I want to suck your clit like a single pea from a freshly snapped pod, I can. If I want to duck behind the ladder, part your cheeks and lick your asshole, I can do that too. You've really gotten yourself into a bit of a muddle. And you laugh at that at first ... and sigh ... because of course, why would you want to fall to the floor when such things are happening?

But here's the thing. When you really are trapped between the ceiling and the floor ... when you no longer have any control or power over what happens ... when your clit can be mercilessly teased, your butthole not only rimmed but greedily sucked ... you begin to find the edges in yourself. Once, twice ... again ... and again ... you come right up to the brink of climax. The nastiness ... the frankness ... the sheer reality of what's happening begins to drive you into another state. All your mechanisms for showing or hiding your reactions are gone. It's undeniable when you're about to come . . . and the frustration is scentable when the stimulation stops. A deep mouthful of haunch . . . a pulling back of your lips with lips. The fire of it moves from your cunt – and suddenly you want to shout the word "Cunt!" at the top of your voice in the silent, civilized world of the library – up into your belly and then your breasts – your nipples so hard now they feel soft and precious – like raindrops . . .

Which makes you think of the hint of rain in the picture in the book that is still so close you can smell its old pages. And the long forgotten rain outside – which world? You can see the girl naked on the floor with her ass offered, the monster in his prison head, the exaggerated penis jutting forward. You think you are ready for the beast creature now. To not simply be entered, but to be split apart . . . exploded and remade. You want more than anything to be fucked. To be fucked asunder.

But you are not ready yet. It takes more time still. More rain outside, in the world beyond the ladder and the library. You must be taken again and again to the precipice . . . until you are annoyed, angry. Until your body starts to cramp on the rungs. Until you are ready to jump, so that you can fondle and even mash yourself, and find relief.

You find yourself becoming vicious. The teasing is more than you can take. You are becoming the words the woman on the bed in the picture was about to say. You must have a fucking orgasm now . . . the way sometimes you have to piss and shit – to eat. You cannot last another minute. You hate me. You want my mouth, you want my cock. You want to be safe on the floor. You want to cry. You want the minotaur man to pound you open and put you back together.

And then you hear a sound you've never heard before.

In the stately silence of the library basement, with only the vague hum of the electrical infrastructure behind the walls, and the muffled sky sluicing down outside, you hear the soft steady wet of your own desire falling like secret, intimate rain, striking the floor. You have never been so soaked and open . . . or suspended from a height great enough to hear that private precipitation.

That sound frees you. To beg. Not just plead. Not just moaning in play. But to really beg – to be fucked. The way someone in serious pain begs for morphine. A total loss and surrender of all dignity and shame.

Only when I hear that telltale timbre in the voice, do I lower the ladder. Lift you off. Plant you on all fours and lift up your sopping skirt.

Then, with your ass arched up, which in your mind is just like the beautiful younger woman in the picture book, I do fuck you. I slice you like a fig. I smash myself into you, balls slapping up under you, your asshole still glistening from my saliva. In a dead quiet aisle of dusty forgotten books I fuck you like a man released from a cage.

It's wet and messy – squishy and loud. I slap your ass. I crush the meat of it in my hands as I pull you into me, pushing more of myself deeper, so that you get the whole man and not only the cock, fucking you until the monster in us both is pooled and fluorescent on the floor . . . whole rows of books toppled and gaping open for the first time in years, as if in sympathy and release, gobs and jets of me, splashes and flecks of you on the tired linoleum – wrinkling a little, it seems, like hard dead earth after a sudden heavy rain.

And fallen on the floor in the mingledness of us . . . is the very book we were looking for, a ladder and a lifetime before.

We found it.

Park Larks

C. Margery Kempe

"I can't believe you've never been to the secret garden!" Alice said, hands on her hips to show her disapproval of his ignorance. Charley shrugged vaguely, but she wasn't about to let him get away with it. "You were born in London, Charley."

"I have hay fever," he whined, hoping she would change the subject soon. His thoughts were on getting her back to his flat for a little adventuring before the night was much older. Drink up, he silently wished. "I don't play weekend rugger, but I've walked through the park a million times. It's just the shortest distance to Camden Town. I'm always sneezing by the time I get to the zoo, though."

"It's supposed to be nice tomorrow. We're going to go," Alice said decisively, pointing an accusing finger at him. "You're going to like it. I'll make sure of it."

Charley grinned. There was no use arguing with Alice when she made her mind up. It was one of the things he found most appealing about her. She threw herself into any activity with a verve and vivacity that he found bracing, so unlike his own torpor.

The next afternoon they met for lunch. Alice informed him right away that she had taken the afternoon off, and while Charley was reluctant to do the same, he had a feeling she would not let him commit to any less. He had come to enjoy the way she wrapped him around her finger. He also enjoyed the sight of her in that thin green shift dress, its light fabric barely concealing her flesh. The green seemed to be important for her scheme, but he was more interested in the clear lack of a brassiere. His hands itched to caress her breasts, where her tiny nipples already taunted him.

"All right, to the park," she ordered him as they stepped out from Baker Street station hand in hand. Crossing into the green they saw the usual gaggle of lunchtime idlers and omnipresent tourists feeding the coots and swans with bread, candy bars and popcorn.

They turned to the right and headed for the rose garden where a profusion of blooms greeted their eyes and ears with a barrage of sensory delights. Most of the blooms were barely more than buds, but the scent was pervasive. Of course, Charley felt a sneeze coming on almost immediately.

Alice, however, walked determinedly through the fragrant bushes without looking to the left or the right. Crossing the inner circle, Charley was surprised to see a gateway he had never once noticed and the long tunnel of a passageway he had never walked down. At the curved end, they stepped out into what looked like a private garden.

"It used to be part of that house," Alice explained, pointing to the rather surprising little manor that lay at the end of a long expanse of green stretching from the little circle into which they had first emerged. "They fell on hard times and had to sell it off. Now it's public, although not everyone seems to know about it." The calla lilies were in bloom and waved in the hot breeze. Spring was rapidly giving way to summer and the lazy buzz of bees filled the air. It seemed an ideal setting to promote indolence.

There were people here and there, sprawled on the grass or stalking among the flowers. Alice took his hand and led him away from the house back through the circle and toward another little nook. Here there were some benches, a sort of sculpture and lots of bigger bushes. They headed for the bench in the middle. A bloke who looked like some kind of banker was reading a *Financial Times* on the left bench and a pair of elderly ladies were on the other.

"This is the place," Alice said with finality.

"For what?" Charley asked.

Alice smiled that dirty girl grin he knew so well. Oh my, he thought.

"But there are people here," Charley said as Alice's hand caressed his thigh.

She giggled. "Yes, of course, but they'll get embarrassed and go away if we start some earnest canoodling."

Charley frowned, hoping she knew he was feeling highly dubious about this adventure. "What if they're tourists? Tourists won't be embarrassed by public displays of affection. Especially Spanish tourists," he added, although he wasn't quite sure what prompted him to say that. A buried memory?

"Tourists don't come back here. They're over in the rose gardens. Kiss me." She reached up and pulled on his shoulders until he wrapped his arms around her neck and met her lips in a kiss that quickly went from a mere meeting to opening wide, thrusting his tongue between her teeth, fucking her mouth the way she loved. Alice sucked his tongue, which persuaded his knob to rise to the occasion, too, tightening the front of his trousers. Oh Christ, Charley thought, are we really going to do this? He couldn't tell if he was more frightened or aroused.

Charley heard the man at the next bench refold his paper with a good bit of rattling, as if to remind them of his presence. He was cheerfully ignored. Charley pulled Alice over so she was straddling his lap while they continued the dance of their tongues and his fingers began making circles up and down her back, reminding him that she was wearing no brassiere beneath her light summer shift.

Off to the side, there came more paper rattling. Charley glanced over to see the man with his face buried deep in the folds of his *Times* as if he could make them go away by wishing. It only made Charley think of how he'd like to be burying his face between Alice's legs for a feast of his own. His erection lay solid beneath Alice's hot pressure as she leaned in as close as possible to him. It was hard to remember ever being quite this excited before.

He stole a glance to his left and found that the elderly ladies had already departed, doubtless wagging their heads at the shocking brazenness of the youth of today. Or maybe, Charley thought as Alice rubbed her hardened nipples against his chest, maybe the two old women were grinning, remembering their own fearless adventures from youth. Perhaps they came here to reminisce, he considered, maybe in another time they too had come here with lovers, far from the prying eyes of parents and elders. Like a clicking kinetoscope, images of fumbling lovers shedding period costumes filled his imagination and Charley raised his hands and buried them in Alice's hair, aching to bury himself inside her, in that warm wet cunt that always welcomed him, clutching hungrily at his thickness.

Alice broke the kiss long enough to look over her shoulder toward their neighbour on the benches. The man continued to stare into the depths of his paper, stubborn to the last. Alice shifted around so that she was sitting across Charley's lap, her back to the reader, her arse planted between his thighs. She moved Charley's hand around to cup her small breast and moaned aloud, leaning back into his other arm. Charley let his eyes dart toward the man on the bench who seemed rigidly still, as if anger had frozen him like a statue. Charley leaned in to bite Alice's neck, his thumb flipping across her popped nipple and she moaned happily again, squirming in his lap with tantalizing nearness, her heat adding to his own. His cock seemed to swell even further.

It was too much for the man. With a sudden explosion of noise, he wadded up the newspaper, stuffed it in his carrier bag and muttered under his breath as he strode off with a stomping step that was wasted on the soft ground.

They were alone.

"Quick now," Alice said huskily, her eyes bright with desire. She hopped off his lap and led him by the hand into the tangle of plants behind the bench. It wasn't much cover, Charley thought, suddenly worried. There was another building visible through the bower. Would someone see them?

But Alice was already reaching under her dress to slip off her knickers, tossing them into her bag without another thought and standing legs apart, looking at him with a wicked grin. Charley felt a whimper rise to his throat, but reached down to unzip his trousers. He couldn't quite resist looking over his shoulder, but they were alone so far.

"Lie down," Alice told him. Charley opened his mouth to complain, but closed it again. Alice would come first, as usual. But she would come again. Charley grinned and lay down, slipping his trousers down around his knees as he did so. His prick sprang up eagerly, ready for action. Alice smiled. "Now that's the way to do it."

She stepped over him and lowered herself with agonizing slowness, reaching down to guide his cock inside her. Alice paused, swirling around the tip in leisurely circles until he wanted to scream, when all at once she slid the rest of the way down and he groaned happily to feel himself squeeze tightly inside her – that hot, slick, welcoming, warm home.

Charley reached up to fondle her tits, groping through her thin dress as Alice bit her lip in concentration, lifting herself up before sinking back down with a sigh. Charley had forgotten about his fears, about the openness of this place, the tickle of the grass against his bum and the sneeze that threatened to build in his nasal passages. All his attention fixed on Alice's slow rise and fall, and the way his prick wanted to explode inside her warm walls.

Out of the corner of his eye, Charley suddenly saw a young girl, maybe fifteen, who had come up the path and then frozen when she saw them. To his surprise, she did not turn and flee, but tried to hide herself behind one of the larger bushes, crouching behind it to conceal herself as she peeked through the branches. While he had felt himself wilt a tad when he spotted her, the girl's veiled view gave him a sudden surge of power. He let his hands slip to Alice's hips, guiding her movements to a slightly faster pace as he sensed their breaths hastening in union.

Alice reached up to caress her breasts, head thrown back, mouth open. "Charley, I think I'm coming, oh yes, I'm coming! Faster now, harder! Come on, Charley!" Her movements became manic, grinding into his pelvis as he sought to match her rhythm, but she was crying aloud, her cunt spasming wildly around his cock as she came, still holding her tits tightly.

Charley couldn't bear it any more and swiftly rolled over on top of the very surprised Alice, who laughed out loud. Breathing raggedly, Charley practically growled as he thrust her legs up over his shoulders and buried himself inside her as deeply as he could. Alice's eyes rolled up as she moaned happily in time with his thrusts. Charley thought his too-white bum must look a sight to that teen's eyes but he no longer cared, instead panting as his balls slapped against Alice audibly and finally, after what seemed like forever, he could feel himself coming – it seemed to be rising up from his toes – shooting inside Alice's quivering quim and feeling like roaring aloud to the whole of the city to trumpet the wonderful sensation of it all.

He plastered Alice's face with kisses after releasing her legs. She reached for her bag and fished out a handful of tissues, intent on cleaning them up for a hasty exit. Alice rubbed her crotch with pleasurable vigour and stroked his semi-hard cock with the bedraggled tissues. Charley grinned ruefully. He could be ready to go in another few minutes, he thought with surprise.

But they would do well to skedaddle, Charley admitted, clambering to his feet and pulling his pants up. The teen voyeur had departed as far as he could tell. No one yet had come to replace her.

"Let's go to the toilets in the rose garden," Alice said, taking his hand as they ran laughing back down the corridor. The people they passed must have thought they were drunk or mad, although they doubtless left a whiff of sex in their wake.

As he washed his hands in the gents, Charley couldn't keep himself from grinning. He had seen the raised eyebrow the American had given him after glancing at his grass-stained knees while they stood at the urinals. Rather than embarrassed, Charley felt quite good. In fact, he was hard again just thinking about it. At least he was until he started sneezing. No doubt his hay fever was going to linger, but it was worth it.

Alice hadn't come out so he stood whistling idly outside the ladies. "Charley, that you?" He turned to see Alice's face framed at the door. "C'mere." She beckoned with her hand.

Charley grinned. Yes, definitely worth taking the afternoon off, he thought, as he walked up to the door to the ladies with a quick backward glance. He was already unzipping his trousers as Alice leaped up and wrapped her legs around him. "More," she whispered in his ear. Charley would have no trouble complying.

She Gleeked Me

O'Neil De Noux

A woman in a form-fitting blue dress tapped down her sunglasses and peered over the top to gleek me. I tapped my own sunglasses down and gleeked her right back, checking her out. Had to admit, the neighbourhood was looking up, attracting women like that particular long-legged red-head to the Arabesque Café, corner of Barracks and Burgundy Streets, caddie-corner from Cabrini Playground.

We were both seated at outside tables. She had her dress hiked above her knees, a few inches above her knees. She put her coffee cup down, uncrossed her legs and began pulling the stocking on her right leg up, all the way up to her garter belt. I caught a flash of white panty as she refastened the stocking. She spread her right leg and pulled up the stocking on her left leg, giving me a full view of the front of her panties. Things like this didn't happen often enough for my taste and I was not the kind of fella who would look away. If I had a camera I'd have a permanent image.

Miss Long-legs got up, smoothed her dress down and came straight to my table. She put a hand on her hip, looked down and gleeked me again, showing me green eyes, before saying, "You're the detective, aren't you? From down the street?"

I folded my newspaper, stood and extended my right hand. "Lucien Caye, at your service."

"Of course you are." Her handshake was delicate and brief. In her heels, she was as tall as me, six feet. I caught a whiff of perfume. My Sin. "Mind if I sit?"

Like I'd *mind*.

"Not one bit," I said, pulling out one of the small metal chairs for her. She sat and slipped her sunglasses into her purse. I called to Maria who flipped a white towel over her shoulder as she came out of the café. "I'd like another Turkish," I told Maria, then asked my guest what she'd like.

"The same."

"The same for Miss, uh . . . uh . . ."

"Grey. Alice Grey." She leaned forward, conspiratorially. "Grey with an 'e', like the English."

Maria strolled off.

"You know the waitress by her first name?"

"Maria?" I tucked my sunglasses into my shirt pocket. "She's married to Alfonse the cook. I've been coming here a lot lately."

Alice put her elbow on the small table, resting her chin in her upturned palm. "Didn't think you were ever going to notice me the way you were reading that newspaper so carefully."

I'd been reading about the aftermath of last Friday's hurricane, 19 September 1947, a date we'll not soon forget. The eye of the storm blew right over the city. It hit neighbouring Jefferson Parish far worse than here. New Orleans International Airport, as they now fancifully called Moisant Field, had wind gusts up to 112 mph and floodwater two feet deep, six feet in other parts of Jefferson. We had no flooding here in the French Quarter, thank God, but there was a call out for the dire need for tidal protection levees along Lake Pontchartrain.

"I spotted you rounding the corner," I said, "watched you walk up and sit. It took you nine sips to finish your coffee."

She smiled and those dark green eyes seemed to twinkle at me. She reached over and picked up the paper. "So what's news?"

"The hurricane."

"Isn't that India?" She pointed to the front page.

There was a picture of Lord Mountbatten standing behind a microphone in his white uniform. Caption beneath explained he was declaring India and Pakistan's independence from Great Britain. That was a month ago, 15 August to be exact. Sometimes the newspaper was more "olds" than "news".

"So there was a hurricane here last week?" She had a mid-west accent.

Maria came out with our Turkish coffees and I scooped in three sugars. Alice took six. The coffee was hot and strong.

"You just get into town," I said.

"Two days ago. And I've been looking for you." As so many women are wont to do. Ha.

We each took a sip of coffee before she went on. "I want to hire you to investigate my uncle's murder. The police have come up with nothing."

She took another sip of coffee and didn't seem all too flustered about her uncle's murder, so I suggested, "Why don't we finish our coffee and go down to my office and you can tell me all about it?"

"Never thought you'd ask."

As she drank her coffee, I noted the diamond ring on her right ring finger, the ruby ring on her left ring finger and matching earrings. Was that an emerald brooch pinned to her dress? The bracelet on her left wrist was covered with diamonds. Lady was crazy to walk around this neighborhood with all that ice.

My office in Suite 1B, 909 Barracks Street, was right below my apartment, Suite 2B. The landlady only recently started calling them suites instead of apartments in an attempt to dress up the place. The two-storey building at the corner of Barracks and Dauphine Streets was in better shape than most of the buildings in that portion of the lower Quarter, its wrought-iron lacework balcony wrapping around the building's corner overlooked Cabrini Playground.

The interior walls had been removed from my office, except for the bathroom. A small kitchen occupied the far portion of the wide room. I had an oversized sofa against the wall next to the door and a large desk, which I'd bought at an estate sale. Like me, it was a little beat up, but served its purpose. For some reason most of the people who sat in the two chairs in front of my desk chose the one on the right, as did Alice Grey. I dropped the paper and my sunglasses on my desk and went around to the captain's chair I'd got at the same estate sale.

"So," I said after taking out my fountain pen and note pad, "your uncle was murdered?"

"He was a cab driver for Yellow Cab. Four months ago he stopped to pick up two young men on a street called Rampart, according to his log, and was taking them to a street called Gentilly. His cab was found by your park named after John James Audubon. He was slumped on the seat with a bullet in his head."

She put her elbow up on the desk, chin in palm again. "Is that park near the street called Gentilly?"

"Not even close. I guess the killers just dumped the car there."

"Is it a bad area?"

"Audubon Park? Just the opposite. It's uptown, lots of mansions, universities and the zoo."

She nodded.

"He wrote his fares were 'young men' in his log book?"

She got up and went to one of the windows facing the playground and started toying with the Venetian blinds. "The police," she said over her shoulder, "should have all this information."

"You talked to the police?"

"No." She looked over at the sofa then moved to me, circling the desk and climbing into my lap as I turned to her. Now this happened to me a lot. That's why I'd moved my desk away from the wall to give myself room for this. Yeah. Right. I'd moved my desk from the back wall to cover a gouge in the hardwood floor.

She gave me a long stare, bent forward and brushed her lips across mine, both our eyes open, watching each other. She grinned, closed her eyes and gave me a good, lingering kiss. Her tongue touched mine and my dick throbbed. The weight of her breasts pressed against me and the kiss continued. When she pulled back, we were both breathing heavily. She took my hand and led me to the sofa. I had to interrupt the action to fetch a little rubberized protection from a desk drawer. I went to close the Venetian blinds and Alice called out, "Leave them open."

She lay on the sofa and said, "Strip for me, baby." Which is something I would normally ask a woman, but I'm half-French and half-Spanish, with too many male hormones to argue with a pretty woman who wanted me naked. No, I did not dance around, put on a show. But I didn't rush either. I tried to act cool although I was simmering. My dick was up like a flag-pole and just as hard and she licked her lips when she saw it.

"My turn," she said, getting up. "Unzip me."

I unzipped the back of her dress, sat and watched. She put on quite a show, wiggling out of her dress, moving to the windows to undo her bra. She dropped it, just as she'd dropped her dress, turned and came back. Her breasts were C-cup, with small nipples, nice and pointed already, and light pink areolae. She stepped out of her high-heels, put her right foot up on the sofa and undid her right stocking.

"Be a good boy and pull it down for me, honey."

I was staring at those breasts as I obliged, trailing my fingers down her long, smooth leg. The left leg was next and, with the front of her panties right in my face, I kissed her silky crotch, feeling her pubic hair beneath.

She dropped the garter belt, put her hands behind her head, arching her back. I reached up and lightly traced my fingers up to her breasts, caressing them, rolling my index fingers around her nipples. I drew my hands to her panties and pushed them down slowly, kissing her stomach, belly button. Her bush was soft and a darker shade of red.

She shoved me back, stepped out of her panties and went down on her knees. She kissed my thighs on her way to my dick. Her tongue flicked its tip and it throbbed in response. She kissed her way down to my balls, kissed each and licked her way back up to the tip.

Miss Alice Grey pulled the hair away from her face with one hand, grabbed my dick with the other and sank her mouth on it. I felt her tongue moving back and forth as her head worked up and down.

Jesus Christ! I pumped back, fucked her mouth for a full minute, before she got up, sat on the sofa, turned and wrapped those incredibly long legs around me. I stared at her open pussy, moist already. I kissed her inner thighs, kissed her silky bush, kissed her thighs again as she writhed, slowly grinding her hips in anticipation.

My tongue brushed her pussy lips and she gasped. I licked and her grinding turned to gyrating. I worked at it and she responded, bucking me, gasping, making mewing sounds, then crying louder.

"What . . . are . . . you . . . humming?"

I pulled away, said, "The French national anthem. Makes my tongue vibrate better." I kissed her pussy. "You know we Frenchmen invented this manoeuvre."

Between gasps, she manage to giggle. "You . . . may have . . . invented . . . the French kiss. But the Indians . . . discovered eating pussy." Her hips gyrated in anticipation.

I pulled back. "Indians? Which tribe? Cherokee? Sioux? Was it the Mohicans, before they got wiped out?"

She laughed. "India – Indians."

"Really?" I pretended to be thinking about it.

She yanked my hair, bringing my face back to her crotch, grumbling, "Put your tongue to better use."

I did and continued until she bucked wildly, her legs squeezing my head, actually hurting my ears. She came and continued bucking.

"Rubber!" She panted.

I donned one and she reached down, pulled my dick to her pussy and I sank into her. She cried louder, let me pump her three times before she got into the rhythm and we moved in unison, her pussy milking me. I stopped, pressing my dick as far in as possible, then began the plunging again.

This woman knew how to fuck, knew how to squeeze the pleasure and held nothing back.

"More," she cried. "More. More!"

"That's all there is."

She gasped, raised me high. Like riding a bucking bronco. I came in long spurts, jamming my dick into her until we both collapsed. I took the rubber to the bathroom, came back and climbed next to her. She was a hugger and it was nice. Very nice.

So I got to know Alice Grey in a biblical sense. Lying next to her after, the ceiling fans cooling our sweaty bodies, I wondered what that phrase meant exactly – "in a biblical sense". I supposed it's in the Bible. The nuns in grammar school never mentioned it, neither did the brothers at Holy Cross High School. I made a mental note to check out the King James version I had somewhere around the office. I remembered there was a lot of "begots" in the Bible, like Abraham begot Joshua and Socrates begot Hercules. Maybe, when they did it and there was no baby, since they didn't beget anything, they simply knew each other "in a biblical sense". Anyway, that's how my mind works after sex. An old girlfriend used to get up and start cleaning the place, dusting, running the vacuum, a ball of energy after sex.

After freshening up in the bathroom, Alice took her hair brush across the room to the windows facing Barracks Street. I was still on the sofa. She stood there, brushing her hair, her fine ass facing me.

She waved at someone outside. "I've interrupted a sporting event," she said.

"Baseball or football?" The boys were out in Cabrini Playground, as usual.

"Football. Kid just made a home run. The other boys are watching me."

"Not much of a sports fan are you?"

"What?"

"A home run in football?"

She turned and brought that fine body back. "Only sport I know much about is the sport of screwing."

I watched her dress. Not as much fun. I pulled on my jockeys and pants before heading back to my desk. I didn't want to mention money at that precise moment, but I needed to know how to get a hold of my new client.

"I'll get a hold of you," she said and waltzed out.

On my way to police headquarters later, I thought about that oversized sofa, which sure came in handy. It was a Monlezun, an extra-wide davenport, special made in Sioux City, Iowa. Best of the best, or so I've been told. I'd gotten it a few months back when a tenant from one of the rear apartments beat feet and the landlady asked if I could help move some of his stuff out for a new tenant. She said I could have any of the furniture. That's also where I got the two chairs in front of my desk.

I really didn't expect Detective-Lieutenant Frenchy Capdeville to be in, but he was and waved me into his office as I entered the Detective Bureau.

"What's up, pretty baby?" he said as he fired up a cigarette. There was already one simmering in the ashtray atop his grey metal, government-issue desk. I remained in the doorway of his small office. He held up the evening paper and said, "I'm reading about a black widow."

"Spider?" He knew I hated spiders.

"No, not like your black widow." He chuckled and started a coughing fit. "I'm talkin' . . . about a . . . woman." The coughing took over and I waited for him to recover.

"My" black widow crawled across my office floor one afternoon while Frenchy was visiting. Black witch was just strolling along, big as life. I grabbed my revolver but Frenchy beat me to it, stepping on it and telling me. "You can't shoot a spider with a .357 magnum."

"Wanna bet?" I'd meant it.

He laughed then and now, holding up the paper. "This black widow's a redhead. Killed her husband, a bank president husband up in Canada and absconded with a million dollars." He started coughing again.

Redhead? Naw. What were the chances?

Frenchy was a sergeant when I first met him, my rookie year at the Third Precinct, what they teasingly call the French Quarter police. That was a good eight years and one world war ago. By the time I got back from Europe, he was a lieutenant and I had a purple heart, a silver star and a scar from the German sniper who almost took me out at Monte Cassino.

"A redhead sent me," I said when he'd finished coughing. "About her uncle, a Yellow Cab driver found in Audubon Park four months ago. Signal thirty." NOPD lingo for a homicide.

Frenchy, who looked too much like Zorro, with his curly black hair, pencil-thin moustache and flat Cajun nose, bobbed his thick eyebrows at me and said, "Cab driver?"

I gave him the low-down on Alice Grey's story. He listened patiently, sucking on his cig.

"First," he said when I stuck my head outside for a breath of semi-fresh air, "there's no dead cab driver. It's not something we'd miss around here. And second, how many times I gotta tell you? You're a private investigator, not a detective. You handle adultery cases, we solve murders." He gave me that smart-ass grin.

"Sam Spade solved murders, Marlowe and Mike Hammer too."

"Fiction. This is real life, my boy."

"Yeah." Like I forgot.

"Then again," he said, "methinks your new client's been weaving a little fiction your way."

Weaving, like a spider, right?

The evening paper had more about the hurricane, how we should build levees along the lakefront and the outfall canals, like the Mississippi River levee. Hell, why not? Give people something to do around here. They'd need more drainage pumps, that's for sure. Most of Metairie in Jefferson Parish was still under water.

The headline was actually about India, describing it as a killing ground. Apparently vicious fighting had broken out between Hindus and Moslems over the last week, particularly in the Punjab borderland between India and Pakistan. Over 100,000 dead. Religious strife. I remember reading about the Thirty Years War, Catholics versus Protestants in Europe. Don't remember how many, but a lotta Christians died there. Maybe I should get a set of encyclopedias.

I checked out the black widow story. The Canadian woman was believed to be in the US now, Las Vegas or Reno, according to the paper. It described her as a redhead, thirty-nine years old, who went by several names – Elizabeth Evans, Edie Evans, Ellie Evans. Alice Grey might be my client's real name, but she wasn't pushing forty. Then again, you never knew.

I looked at the Monlezun and had to grin.

Eight a.m. sharp, just as I started in on my second Turkish coffee at the Arabesque, Alice Grey strolled up the banquette – what we call sidewalks in New Orleans because they serve as banks when the streets flooded, which happened often. She wore another form-fitting dress, this one yellow, and matching high heels. Maria brought her a Turkish coffee before Alice arrived and stood towering over me. She gleeked me again and said, "I owe you an apology."

"About your fictitious uncle, right?"

She sat and poured six sugars into her coffee, took off her sunglasses and said, "My father's missing."

OK. I handled missing person cases all the time. I was just recovering from a wandering daughter case that broke my heart, but that's another story. I took out my notepad and Parker t-ball jotter ballpoint and said, "What's your father's name?"

Alice's story went like this – her father, a Presbyterian minister from Westhope, North Dakota, left Alice and her mother a year ago. At first the police suspected foul play because Jonathan Grey hadn't left Westhope, except for occasional visits to Bismarck, since he'd returned from the Chicago Seminary where he was ordained in 1911. Two weeks ago, Alice's mother got a Bourbon Street postcard with an exotic dancer on the front. Postmarked New Orleans, the wandering minister said he was sorry he'd left so abruptly, but he'd found a better life and to not worry about him. No, Alice hadn't brought the postcard.

Bourbon Street, that narrowed it – over two miles of the scummiest dives, strip clubs, clip-joints, heroin dens, reefer houses, whorehouses, you name it. I told Alice that and she grew pale for a second and said, "Then you'd better get started."

"I'll need a description of your father and a picture."

She withdrew a three-inch square, grainy, unfocused picture, probably taken with a Brownie camera, of a man and a woman standing in front of a white wooden house. All they needed was a pitchfork to be that painting of the bald guy and homely woman, I don't remember the name or the artist. Jonathan Grey was sixty-two, stood five nine, with a thin build.

"I'm going to need a retainer from you, too. A hundred dollars. I charge thirty a day, plus mileage and expenses."

She put her sunglasses back on and withdrew two crisp c-notes, passing them to me. "Two hundred," she said, "it may take a while." She picked up her coffee and took a sip. I rubbed the backside of the bills on a napkin and some of the ink rubbed off, which meant the bills were probably genuine. Ink on counterfeit bills dried completely.

"Now what was all that guk about a dead uncle?" I asked.

She just winked at me.

We parted company after draining our coffees. She pecked me on the cheek and waved down a passing Yellow cab, gleeking me from the back seat as the cab pulled away on Burgundy.

That was Saturday, 27 September. On Sunday evening, as a driving rainstorm slammed fat raindrops against my building, forked lightning dancing over the roofs of the Quarter, thunder shaking the building, I stood in my apartment and peered out of the French doors that opened to the balcony. I watched the street flood. My doorbell rang and I hit the buzzer, went out on the landing to watch Alice come through the building front door with two large suitcases and stand there dripping.

"I'll get a towel," I called down to her. By the time I came back out on the landing, she was halfway up the stairs hauling those suitcases. I went down, handed her the towel and took the suitcases, nice Samsonite luggage.

"They're waterproof," she said, "so's my purse. But I'm not."

I brought the suitcases into my apartment while she dripped out in the hall. Hair soaked, lipstick smudged, eyeliner dripping down her cheeks, her tight black dress was pressed even tighter to her slim body. She gave me a coy look as a puddle formed on the carpet beneath her feet and said, "I owe you another apology."

"Don't tell me. Your father's not missing?"

"He's been dead ten years."

The agony of the last thirty-six hours flashed through my mind, like snapshots from a horror flick – burly bartenders glaring at me, bouncers telling me to get lost, buxom strippers peeling off gaudy costumes, reefer maniacs hiccupping as they sucked in smoke while I showed them the grainy, out-of-focus Brownie picture, not to mention a long line of prostitutes painted like – forget it. My feet ached and I'd even worn the reddish-brown oxfords with the rubber soles I'd picked up on my wandering daughter case, but that's another story.

Alice ran the towel through her hair and looked like a maniacal Medusa now. She wiped her face and ran the towel down her body before tossing it to me. She turned and said, "Unzip me."

I suggested we step into my apartment. She said, "You want a puddle in your apartment?" So I unzipped her and she kicked off her heels, stripped right there in the hall, handing me her dress, half-slip, garter belt, stockings, bra and panties. I passed her the towel again and she dried off.

My neighbour across the hall took that moment to peek out. John Stanford was an eighty-one-year-old Englishman, a very nice gentleman who often gave me history lessons and took a keen interest in my love life. Alice turned to him as she finished wiping off and tossed the towel over her shoulder to me to give Stanford a better view, some full frontal nudity.

"Enjoying the view, sir?"

"Oh, yes. Quite."

She turned, rolled her hips at him on her way into my apartment.

Stanford grinned at me and said, "It's always a pleasure, old chum. What? Ho?"

I went into my apartment, closed the door as Alice lay on the sofa. She gave me a wink and said, "You gonna offer a girl a drink, or what?"

She took her bourbon on the rocks. I opted for a cold Miller High-Life. The rain slapped the windows, lightning danced over the rooftops, thunder rumbled and I sat in my easy chair watching a naked woman sip my bourbon. OK, not completely naked with all that jewellery around her neck, wrist and several fingers, not to mention earrings.

"I want you to take me to Rio," she said.

"De Janeiro?"

"Is there another Rio? I need protection and I'll pay you ten thousand dollars, American, to sail with me on a Brazilian ship, tomorrow night. Get me to Rio and you can come back, if you want. I need a bodyguard."

I looked at her body and said, "You're telling me?"

We did it again, this time on my bed. It was her fault. I was a goner as soon as I unzipped that dress, so don't blame me. Women used me a lot. Bless their souls.

Alice Grey was a fairly predatory lover, reaching for the pleasure, knowing she was giving it back. She kissed hard and fucked hard, bouncing me like a toy atop her. Coitus brought out her strength. She was louder this time and cursed. My first girlfriend did a similar thing. Elvira wasn't as predatory, a good Catholic girl, but she could curse.

Alice started with "Fuck me!"

"That's what I'm doing." Here's a lesson for men. When they start cursing, you're not supposed to respond. Just let them vent. Alice pinched me hard, so I shut up.

"I want dick! Fuck! Screw me! Fuck my pussy! Inside! Fucking harder! Slam your balls! Dick! Dick! Fuck me!"

I obliged, like an obedient boy.

Lying in bed after, Alice curled against me, a light rain tapping against the bedroom windows, I tried to figure her out. I'd been too busy wrestling with her body to wrestle with the idea she might be a lunatic. When she woke, I planned to question her. I mean, what the hell was all this, sending me on wild goose chases and now *Rio de Janeiro*? Then again, ten grand was ten grand and I'd be holed up on a ship with that body.

I thought of the black widow. Not the spider but the woman in the paper. Red-headed woman from Canada. I'd looked up Westhope on the map. It was only about five miles from the Canadian border. What if it was the woman curled in my arms? How did she put it – "ten thousand dollars, American"? What other dollars could we be talking about? Canadian dollars, maybe?

Disentangling myself from Alice, I climbed into a pair of shorts and checked her luggage. Locked. I went out to her purse, which she'd left on my Formica kitchen table. The contents hadn't gotten wet and I found a set of keys with two Samsonite keys, a compact, two lipsticks, a small make-up case, a wallet with an Ontario driver's licence bearing a Toronto address in her name, a library card for the Toronto City Public Library, nine one hundred dollar bills, six fifties, two twenties and nine ones, all American money, and two bank books from Swiss banks – Banca Arras in Geneva and Suisse-Maximilien Bank in Zurich – with no amounts listed, just coded numbers. I also found two first class steamship tickets for the SS *Jozinda*, destination Rio, and a nickel-plated .25 calibre Para-Ordnance semi-automatic pistol with plastic grips.

"Para-Ordnance is the only gun manufacturer in Canada," Alice said as she eased into the kitchen. She folded her arms beneath her breasts. "You've found me out."

"You're the black widow?"

"Black widow? No, silly. I'm Canadian. That's why I need you to sneak me aboard the *Jozinda*. I don't have a passport or visa."

I re-stuffed her purse, except for the automatic, and sat at the table. She came and sat across from me and slowly repacked her purse.

"What about your uncle and your missing father? What the hell was that all about?"

"I wanted to see if you were up to it. Obviously I liked your looks, your moves in the sack, but could you take instructions? You tried. That's all I needed to know."

What did I say earlier? Lunatic.

The doorbell made us both jump. Two o'clock in the morning. Couldn't be good news.

I hit the buzzer, went into the hall to look down as Frenchy led two skinny guys up the steps. They came straight in, the strangers spotting Alice and pushing past me for her, one declaring, "You're under arrest in the name of the King."

Alice put her hands on her hips. Frenchy almost swallowed his cigarette as he gawked at my naked guest.

I asked Frenchy, "What King?"

"King George VI," said the skinnier of the two strangers.

"The King of England?"

"And Canada," he said, "the entire Commonwealth, in case you're interested."

Frenchy blew out a long trail of cigarette smoke. "These are Royal Canadian Mounted Police."

"So, where are the red coats?" I quipped.

"I went over this with you before. These are real detectives." Frenchy smirked but he wasn't looking at me. He was checking out Alice's body parts. I wanted to flick the cigarette out of his mouth but I'd only probably burn my finger.

"Actually we're inspectors."

What they weren't doing, however, was inspecting Alice. They did not seem to even notice she was naked as they glanced around the room. What were they looking for? Canadians? What did I expect?

I couldn't think of one thing a Canadian ever did. OK, they were at Normandy. Juno Beach. Under British command, they did well.

"Wait!" I called out. "The black widow? I've been canoodling with a black widow?"

The skinnier Mountie gave me a pained look, moved his gaze to Frenchy and said, "What is your friend blabbering about?"

"He hates spiders."

The second Mountie said, "What's *canoodling*?"

"It means screwing," said John Stanford, now standing in my apartment door. He smiled at Alice and added, "You are looking quite fetching with your hair all fly-away."

The skinnier Mountie took a step toward Alice and declared, "Prudence Francine Greyson, you are charged with embezzlement, grand larceny and unlawful flight to avoid prosecution."

Prudence? No wonder she used Alice as an alias.

The other Mountie asked me, "Did she bring luggage?"

I pointed to the bedroom. "The keys are in her purse."

Alice came over to me, her eyes wet now. "You turned me in?"

She moved to Stanford, pressed her face against his shoulder and began to cry.

She was good. My old friend wrapped his arms around her as the skinnier Mountie dug the keys from Alice-Prudence's purse and went into the bedroom. He came right out with the suitcases, laid them on the sofa and started unlocking them while his partner started taking the jewellery off Alice, beginning with the necklace.

I asked Frenchy, "Could you give me a hint as to what the hell's going on?"

He smirked again. "International cooperation of law enforcement officers. You should be taking notes."

Besides clothes, and there were a lot of clothes, the inspectors discovered six small bags bound with drawstrings in the suitcases. One bag contained loose diamonds, one rubies, one emeralds, one contained gold jewellery adorned with diamonds, rubies and emeralds, one contained platinum jewellery, equally adorned, and the last bag contained what the Mounties explained were semi-precious stones – garnets, jade, amethyst, opals and blue lapis lazuli streaked with stripes of gold.

Frenchy put a friendly hand on my shoulder. "You see, your new client-slash-girlfriend absconded with most of the family jewels. Greyson Jewellers of Toronto. Canada's largest jewellery dealer. Her father owns it."

"How'd you put all this together?"

"It's real detective work. Wouldn't interest you."

"Humour me."

Frenchy went to the kitchen sink, rubbed out his cigarette and fired up a fresh one. "You mentioned a red-headed client who'd sent you on a wild goose chase. They came in with a warrant for a red-headed diamond thief."

"That's it?"

He actually winked at me.

"You failed to mention," said the skinnier Mountie, "we've been one step behind her for two months and traced her to your Jung Hotel."

"Yeah," Frenchy admitted. "Georgie Crane tipped us. Said he'd recommended you to her when she asked about a private investigator." Crane had been my sergeant when I was a rookie patrolman at the Third Precinct. He'd retired and moved on to the Jung Hotel as its hotel dick.

Prudence Francine Greyson, alias Alice Grey, had stopped whimpering, but was still pressed against Stanford. I watched his wrinkled hands slowly descend from Alice-Prudence's back to her hips to her ass, which he squeezed.

She pulled back, brushed her lips across his, said, "Would you like to feel my tits before they take me away."

"That would be magnificent." The old man caressed her breasts.

"Enough of that!" the second Mountie said. "Why isn't this woman clothed?" About time he noticed.

"I don't allow women to wear clothes in my apartment," I said.

The Mountie seemed even more confused, said, "Awfully irregular."

"You'll need to dress her," the second Mountie told *me*.

"I only undress them. You'll have to dress her. There's plenty of clothes over there."

The skinnier Mountie pulled Alice-Prudence from Stanford's hands and we watched the two Mounties dress her. She didn't cooperate too much, but Mounties are hard workers and managed.

When the Mounties were ready to take her and the suitcases away, I passed Frenchy the nickel-plated .25 calibre Para-Ordnance semi-automatic pistol with plastic grips, which I'd been holding in the palm of my left hand. "Y'all might want to take her purse too. Besides money, there are bank books from two Swiss banks and steamship tickets for the SS *Jozinda*, destination Rio. And I have two c-notes downstairs she paid me."

"Keep 'em," said Frenchy. "You earned 'em."

Frenchy grabbed a suitcase while the skinnier Mountie picked up the second one and the other Mountie took the purse and Alice, now handcuffed behind her back. Alice stopped next to me and smiled weakly, "We almost made it, didn't we?"

She'd put on fresh lipstick before she'd come out of the bedroom. I hated to mess it up, but what the hell? I kissed her and she kissed back. I told her I'd never forget her. Her eyes suddenly filled and she sucked in a deep breath before looking away. Man, she was good. I was kidding.

Frenchy shook his head, asked the Mounties, "How much is that reward?"

The skinnier Mountie said, "It would amount to ten thousand dollars, American."

"And we all know," Frenchy went on, "cops can't collect reward money." He blew smoke in my face. "Since you're not the real police, you actually qualify."

I felt my heart stammering in my chest. As I dressed, I came to my senses and figured this was the best practical joke Frenchy had ever played on me. Reward, right? I'd be thankful if they let me go after I gave my statement.

The certified cheque arrived from the Ottawa branch of the Bank of England three weeks later in the amount of £5,000 sterling. British money. The real stuff. I called my bank right away and the exchange rate meant I held well over $10,000, American. I stared at the Monlezun for a long moment, a smile creeping across my face with the memory of the long-legged wench. Ten grand and I didn't even have to go to Rio.

And that was how I, Lucien Caye, private investigator, solved my first international caper. Well, almost solved. And, to think, it all started with a gleek.

Slut

Charlotte Stein

I couldn't put a name to him at first. I'm not used to using a name like that for boys. But he is none the less: slut.

He isn't a slut in the same way that some guys are – players and bounders and cads. The word "slut" doesn't quite seem to apply to them. But it applies to him, when we're in the stationery cupboard together.

We're in there, and he smiles his little sly slut's smile at me. At the time I didn't know what that smile meant, but I did soon after. I did when he turned around and bent over as though to reach for something on a low shelf, and his bum very obviously pressed into the front of my skirt.

Not even the front of my skirt. Into my groin. Definitely against my groin. He even had to kind of crouch to do it, because he's very tall. But he managed it none the less, and I felt those firm buttocks push into the place where my pussy is.

He did it like a woman urging her bottom back for a man's cock. He did it like an animal seeking a mounting. I had no idea how he expected me to mount him, but after the initial shock that's what I thought of anyway.

I've never wished so fiercely that I had a cock. A big fat cock that I could have plunged into his tight little arsehole – made him beg for it, made him whimper and whine and twist on me.

It occurred to me later on that he was gay and some kind of fascination with me had gripped him. Perhaps he felt that I was a rather mannish woman, perfect for trying out straightness.

But that misconception didn't last long.

It stopped when I caught him looking down my top. It stopped even more when I deliberately leaned forwards and let him see further, and he couldn't even contain his little sigh of satisfaction.

He didn't even look embarrassed when I flicked my gaze to his face, and finally, finally, his eyes drew up and away from my tits to meet mine. I think he tried to contain that sly slut's smile of his, but other than that he did nothing.

Because sluts never do anything about getting caught, being a slut.

He became even more flagrant when I ogled him openly and lewdly. I caught him changing in his cubicle – just his shirt, nothing more – and instead of walking away and giving him his privacy, I stood there and ogled him. I did it like a challenge. I drew my gaze over his long lean torso, the slow slide down into his narrow hips, his thickly broad shoulders and his skin, oh, his lovely pale milk skin.

I didn't apologize for it; I didn't let myself be nervous. I imagined what it must be like to be a man, if he were the woman. His sluttishness would make me confident, horny, unabashed. Why shouldn't I look, if he delights in it?

And he did delight in it. Far from stopping, he had worked his vest oh so slowly up, up over his thick chest, fingers skimming his gorgeous skin as though wanting them to be my fingers, burning dark eyes never leaving mine.

Right at the very last moment he had bitten his lip, and dropped his gaze.

I think I loved him, for that.

He does more things that I love him for. Many more things. Many more things that my pussy loves him for. He becomes a clit-tease, a filthy little temptress, pushing on my nerves and my restraint.

Surely he knows. Surely he knows that soon, I won't have any.

When in a board meeting, an important meeting that he is only present at to take minutes in his silly too-big handwriting, I know that he looks. I can feel his eyes ever returning to me, waiting for me to look back. Sluts are only satisfied when you look back. He wants my attention on him, confirming his attractiveness. Making him sure that what he has worn that day pleases and excites me.

And it does. I have no idea how he knew, but I have a thing for men in V-neck jumpers. Buttoned up like a female relic from the eighteenth century, tie knotted too tight for comfort, material clinging in a way that suggests that the wearer is not aware it is clinging. No one who wears V-neck jumpers could be aware that they're in something clingy.

Except for him. He obviously designed it that way: the perfect trap for my desire.

But clearly, he isn't satisfied with the effect just yet. It isn't quite enough for me to occasionally admire his shoulders, or to wonder what it would be like to hook my finger into the loop of his tie and lead him around the office like a dog. That dog who wanted me to mount it, back in the stationery cupboard.

No. He has to go one step further. He has to push it. He has to lean back in those thankfully smooth and soundless meeting room chairs, stretching his glorious body out for my delectation. He has to take his pen, and pat it lightly against his full lower lip. That lower lip I want to bite.

Even worse, he then decides to part those biteable lips, and just ever so slightly nudge the pen inside. I see his perfect white teeth bite down – not hard enough to leave any sort of mark, but not lightly, either. The perfect biting strength for, say, a nipple. And then maybe his tongue could . . . oh yes. Just flicker against the thing in his mouth. And maybe he could then . . .

Suck.

I watch his cheeks hollow, just a little, just enough to put a person in mind of a little boy sucking on a lollipop, rather than anything lewd. But, of course, it's lewd to me. It's lewd because I know what he is and what it means, the tease.

Because that's what he's doing, really. He's teasing me with his perfectly cut features and his broad shoulders and his limpid eyes and his sucking mouth. He probably thinks I won't do a thing about any of it, because how could such a lovely creature as him be interested in me?

But he's a fool. I would say he's playing with fire, but fire has nothing on my libido.

When the meeting ends, I line my voice with calm cool iron and say to him: "Can I see you in my office, Brad?"

Of course he has a name like Brad. Something wholesome and cute. If he were a girl, he'd be called Candy.

"Of course, Ms Layton," he replies, and oh the devil pushes just the right hint of bemusement into his voice. Why, he has no idea what I might want with *him*. He is only a little insignificant peon. What on *earth* could he have done wrong?

I am going to show you what you have done wrong, Brad.

I hear him lolloping after me. He's very tall and near gangly, despite the bulk of his chest and shoulders. I suppose that's why I don't feel intimidated by his size, though I accept that there are other reasons.

It's hard to be intimidated by a floozy.

Even though I think he wants me to be intimidated. I think he wants me to be in awe of his sexual power, in thrall to him. I should be hypnotized and tormented by his behaviour and the way he looks. Big boss woman Ms Layton brought low? We'll see.

Once we're inside the safety of my office, I close the door behind us. I lock it. He jerks a little when I do, but it's too late for him to be surprised and innocent. Now he's going to have to pay the piper.

"Have I . . . ?" he starts to say, but I think something in my expression stops him.

"Yes. You've done something very wrong. Very wrong indeed."

His face falls – and he does it well, too. It hardly looks put on at all. "I'm so sorry, Ms Layton," he says. "How can I make it up?"

Again, it's all very convincing. He's a clever boy.

"Bend over that desk, and write on the notepad I have there exactly what you've done wrong, and how you expect to resolve the matter."

He hesitates for the barest of moments. I see his tongue touch his upper teeth.

And then he does exactly what I've asked.

He presents his rump to me perfectly, just like in the stationery cupboard, and then he takes up my best pen and starts scribbling with it. Each time he scribbles, his bottom wiggles just a little bit.

It's delightful. It's begging for my hand. I don't know why he makes that little shocked sound, when I whack my palm against that begging flesh.

"Hoh!" he gasps. But he doesn't stop writing. He doesn't even turn around. It's the third slap he looks back at me on, and I see his eyes so naked and his cheeks flushed and that mouth hanging open. Shock and sex and hunger all stirred up together.

"Eyes front," I tell him. "While I punish you."

"Is this how you punish all your staff?" he asks, so I reach around and unbuckle his belt. Clearly he needs something more severe, and he doesn't deny it. He doesn't even go to stop my hand or ask again if I do this with all staff, he just moans and whispers something I can't hear.

"Louder," I say, so he shouts out with a break in the middle:

"I can't believe this is happening!"

"What did you think would happen, tease?"

"I—" he starts to say, but then I yank his Calvin Kleins down to meet the trousers that are now around his ankles, and he groans for me some more.

He has stopped writing altogether now. The pen is still clutched in his hand, however, though that doesn't last long. Once his underpants hit the floor so does the pen, and, though I can't see, I know exactly what he's doing: jerking off.

His thighs butt against the desk. His hips roll. I hear that slick clicking of a hand shuttling up and down a stiff cock, and he must know I can, too. But he doesn't stop. Not even when I slap his bare buttocks hard enough to leave a mark.

Instead he gasps: "I'm going to come all over the nice neat writing I've just done for you."

"Bad slut," I tell him, and slap right over the handprint I've just made.

Unfortunately, this only makes him groan and fuck himself harder. I actually think he's really going to come that quickly; I can see his bum cheeks clenching and he's making far too much noise and soon he's babbling: "God, I'm sorry, I'm sorry, I need to come so bad, God, I've been thinking about your tits all afternoon."

I yank on his arm and get his hand away from his cock as punishment. He squirms with frustration, but doesn't try to start it up with his other hand, as though he were just waiting for me to stop him and a show of stopping him is enough.

"All afternoon?"

"Yeeessss," he whines, and I want to turn him around so much. I want to see his gorgeous face all crumpled with impatience and lust, and then I want to watch him tug his cock until it gleams.

"Is this something you've done before?"

Oddly, I feel like a doctor. It isn't a terrible feeling by any means.

"What? Think about . . . your tits . . . or jerk off at work?"

That last bit comes out in a rush, and sets me glowing. Oh, to think of him doing himself in one of the stalls or in his cubicle under his desk! My clit twinges in sympathy.

"Usually I . . . Usually I have to . . . you know. Because I've been thinking about you."

"What do you think about me doing?"

"I catch you. I catch you playing with yourself. Playing with your nipples with your shirt open and your skirt up."

Oh Jesus, that's nice. I've done it before, too, in my office. With the door locked, of course, but sometimes I'm daring enough to leave the blinds open, hoping that some beefy window cleaner will chance by and see me as lewd as can be, legs spread open, fingers strumming my clit to a great big juicy orgasm.

I need to come so bad now that I can feel my clit straining against the material of my panties, and I'm wet enough to feel it when I move. Maybe I'll make him watch while I bring myself off with that little buzzing dildo I keep in my bag. Maybe I'll make him lick my clit with his hands tied behind his back so that he can't do himself. Maybe I'll let him fuck me over the desk, great handfuls of my tits in his big hands, some window cleaner watching with his cock in his fist.

Oh the possibilities are endless, when you've got a slut on your hands.

"You like my tits and my nipples, huh?"

"Yes," he gusts out.

I circle the desk, slowly, leaving his sore arse and all that shameful need to not look him in the face behind. My legs almost buckle when I get a look at him – firm, endlessly curving prick as red and glistening as you please, shirt tails flapping, face flushed and slack. He looks like he could devour just about anyone right now. I could probably bring in Margot from accounting, and have him hump her over my couch.

"Would you like to see them now?"

"Seriously? Jesus, yes."

I think it's the most sincere I've ever heard any man sound. I don't think he knows how to be anything but, though I suppose that's what sluts are really made of – honesty. He cannot be anything but honest about his own desires.

So I reward him by unbuttoning my shirt. He answers me by breathing hard and going for his cock again, but I tell him no. No, the price he has to pay for the sight of my breasts is keeping his hands by his sides.

It delights me that when I tell him this, he closes his eyes and clenches his teeth, but still obeys. The hands at his sides become fists – I hadn't realized how much fun sluts were to play with. Do men do this all the time? Make them beg and plead and clench their teeth?

What fun.

I slide my shirt all the way off, and then unfasten the front clasp of my bra. His eyes have completely forgone my face but I can't blame him. I'm too flattered to blame him – he looks like he's about to see God.

My sensitive nipples brush the lace of the cups as I peel the material away, but the soft sigh of my pleasure is freely given when he sighs too.

"Are you turned on?" he moans – I think more because my nipples are so small and tight than because I sighed. "Does it turn you on, screwing around with me like this?"

"You know, I think it does," I say.

His eyes shutter closed again for the briefest moment. "Can I jerk off?"

"Not yet."

"Please. Please. I think I'm gonna burst."

"You'll live. Now, I want you to come here, and play with my tits. Do you think you can do that?"

I don't think he can do it fast enough. He almost trips over his own trousers getting to me, and then his hands lunge at my breasts as though magnetized.

I slap them. He says sorry. But even when he's saying it he can't stop ogling them. I suppose they're nice breasts – firm and full, nipples spiking upwards, skin as soft and fair as his – but even so. I just hadn't realized, in between all of his teasing and cheekiness, that he might be so horny for me.

"Lick your fingers, first," I tell him, and he does so real quick without any kind of teasing show. But then he waits, he waits, and that's even better. "Now gently pinch and stroke them."

He's not a bad boy at all; I was wrong. He's very, very good. He licks and strokes and thumbs my nipples, sometimes lightly pinching, other times just circling, ever slick and smooth. The ache from those tight tips soon transfers itself to my swollen clit and my empty, creaming pussy, but I squeeze my thighs together against it.

"Suck them," I say, and he immediately falls to it, licking and sucking and mouthing until I'm shivering with pleasure. I even let out an "Oh yes, just like that," and he groans into the flesh of my breast.

It makes it so that I can't wait any longer. I slip my knickers down while he's still licking and playing with my breasts, and then I pull away briefly to sit on the desk, legs spread. The cool air feels wonderful against my heated cunt, my stiff bud, but, God, his mouth would feel so much better.

I don't even have to order him, either. He pushes up my skirt immediately, exposing my slick spread sex to his gaze.

"You've done that to me, tease," I say, and part my sex lips with two fingers to give him a better view. My clit stands out proud and coated in my own arousal, and I can't resist stroking it, lightly. "What are you going to do about it?"

He drops to his knees, immediately. I am reminded of someone about to die and praying to God to deliver him, and I have to say, I don't mind that at all. He can pray all he wants at the altar of my pussy.

He hesitates before he leans forwards, but all that does is remind me how little he has hesitated so far. Not even at the lines I made him write. Not even at the spanking. But then again, you can't exactly hesitate when you've rubbed your bottom into someone's groin. It's like a game of chicken, and no one wants to be the one who puts their foot on the brake first.

I wonder where my brake would have been, if I hadn't decided to punish him. Would I have let him keep pushing me, going further and further – how far would he have gone?

Dirty pictures in my inbox, I think. Naughty emails and memos and oh, I should have let this game go on longer. I miss what I never got to see – him jerking off, just for me.

But now he's licking at me, fingering me, fucking me with his mouth and hands and I can't complain. He laves his tongue over my clit roughly at first, but soon more softly, more teasing, more exploratory.

Occasionally he replaces his flickering tongue with two fingers, scissoring around my clit and rubbing while he laps and mouths at the entrance to my pussy. The back and forth is maddening, but the caress of his tongue around every part of me sends slivers of sensation up my spine and back again. He coaxes out sensitive places I didn't know I had, ever eager.

It's the eagerness that makes him good, really. But then he has to be – good, I mean. He probably services women all the time.

Finally I give in and order him to bring me off, tugging him up by the thick hair at the nape of his neck so that his tongue can work my clit. Hearing my urgency, he laps quickly, pushing two thick fingers inside me and twisting them as he does.

It's too much. My body seizes and my clit swells against his tongue, fresh liquid spilling over his fingers as I orgasm with a fistful of his hair clenched in my hand and my back arching. I grunt like an animal and tell him mindlessly: "Yes, I'm coming, I'm coming." Mindlessly because of course he can't fail to realize what's happening. He moans and pants against my slippery flesh, doing his best to draw every last drop of pleasure from me, before I finally push him away.

He sprawls back, cock now so stiff and angry looking that I actually feel bad, for a moment. Even if he is a dirty tease, that can't be comfortable. He actually seems to have leaked pre-come all the way down his shaft, and I can see his hands clenching and unclenching at his sides.

When I stop leaning back on my hands – relishing the slow dissipation of everything he has just given me – and move towards him, his cock jerks. He jerks. There is heat high up on his perfect pale cheeks, now, and soft dark tendrils of his hair cling to his temples. He looks like a livewire, juddering with too much electricity. He wants me to cut it in two, and let the snapping sizzling power out.

Which I will do.

I feel as though I'm prowling towards him. I am flushed and full up and he lies prostrate before me, back on his elbows, shoulders jutting forwards, lips parted. He tosses his head and his cute little sweeping fringe is out of his eyes. Sometimes they're puppy-dog and sometimes they're sultry and right now they're burning black and deep.

"That was very good, Brad," I say and he smiles – not quite that sly smile, but one that says he knows. He knows he's good at worshipping pussy. He even replies in a delightful sort of confirmation, plain and as sincere as he had seemed before: "I love pussy."

I stand astride his near-spread thighs, and look down into his upturned face.

"Tell me how you love it," I say, and when he speaks it's in tumbling, never halting, barely sentences.

"I love licking it and tasting it and smothering my face in all that hot wetness – your clit, too, I love your clit when it jumps against my tongue and when you squirm, I love it when you squirm, Ms Layton, I love it that you're at my mercy at the same time that you're not."

"I hear that's why girls like giving guys blow-jobs, Brad," I say, but he doesn't flinch. He doesn't look embarrassed.

"Is that why you like giving blow-jobs, Ms Layton?" he asks, but I don't think he really expects an answer. I think he's amused, but his amusement doesn't anger me. It angers me even less when he tells me: "I don't care about what I am or what you think of me. This is what I like, and I don't care if you think it's the wrong way around."

I wonder how many people have told him before now that he's the wrong way around. I wonder if they told him so because of how terrifying he is. His power over me is terrifying. I've locked the door and spanked him and made him write lines and had him lick my pussy, and all without him telling me to – not even a little bit.

I wonder if he's made other girls do things like this, hypnotized them into dominating him with just the power of his good looks and his boyish appeal and his teasing.

I sink to my knees astride him, his bobbing cock occasionally patting between my legs when he stirs or it jerks. He lets me push his jumper up over his head, and then his shirt too, but I leave the loop of his tie around his neck.

It makes a handy leash, to wrap around my fist and use to pull his mouth up to mine.

The groan he pushes into me echoes through my body, tying me up in knots once more and making me thrust my tongue into his mouth. He responds eagerly – I'm sure eagerness is all he knows – stirring his own tongue wetly against mine, letting his mouth fall slack as I force myself over him.

He tastes like me. I've never tasted me before. Not like this, anyway. I taste sweet, so sweet, as sweet as sweat on the back of the strapping young man you hired to mow the lawn.

One of his hands leaves the carpet and grasps me at the small of my back, urging me forwards, urging me harder down on him. His cock finds its way underneath my ruffled up skirt, and the more he pulls at me the more flesh it makes contact with, until finally I feel the soft-hard slick head of it split my slit, and rub up roughly against my over-sensitized clit.

I don't stop it happening. Instead I reach between our bodies and press his cock right into the seam of my sex, feeling the lips there close around it almost as my wet hole would. When I lean forwards and rise up just a little, the fit is almost perfect, and I rock my clit against the sensitive underside of him.

He bucks up against me, now shamelessly moaning into my mouth. I rub him against my flesh, striking just the right amount of pressure to eventually bring myself off – not that he's going to last that long. He's trembling, and when I reach down with my free hand and cup and massage his drawn-up tight balls and the soft moist place just behind, he lunges up hard against me and draws his mouth away from mine.

"Oh God make me come, Ms Layton," he pants against my jaw, my cheek, everywhere leaving wet trails and hot breath. "Ah yes, rub me there."

I do. I have to prove, after all, that I'm as good as he is.

"Wait," I tell him. "Wait. I want you to come in my mouth."

He likes that. He likes that, oh yes, he does. He lets his head fall back and the column of his throat presents itself to me, stark and strong, ready to be bitten. I had a boyfriend once who loved nothing better than to bite me, to mark me, to leave little circles all over my body. And I liked it too. I have always liked the sensation of teeth sinking in.

But this is the first time I've wanted to sink my teeth into someone else. Not just *wanted* to, but *craved* it. I want to mark all that perfect pale flesh, to scatter myself all over him in nips and bites, and see what I used to look like, reflected in his midnight eyes. Shuddering, shivering, beneath another person. Pulled taut against nearly pain.

I want to teach him more about what nearly pain is. Of course I'm sure he knows already. I'm sure he knows a lot of things already, horny and gorgeous as he is. But he's also delightful enough to pretend for me, I know.

I bite him just at that place where his throat meets his shoulder. That little cup made for my teeth. And then he gasps and hisses and that meaty pressure satisfies my teeth – that lovely tensing and releasing feeling that I've only ever felt with my own hand pressed to my mouth, something buzzing between my thighs.

"Please," he begs me, with his hand in my hair. "Please."

But I know he doesn't mean *please stop biting*. In fact, he presses my face harder into his throat, and sighs when I'm done leaving my little mark.

He rubs his fingers through the wetness I leave there, an expression much like wonder on his face. Wonder that's mostly a show, just for me.

But a little red pattern can't hold his attention – faux or otherwise – for long. He cocks an eyebrow at me, head still turned to one side, fingers still on the bite mark. Now, I suppose, should be the time when the tables will be turned, if he wasn't the wrong way around.

Instead he goes with: "What do I have to do to have you?"

He really shouldn't give me such possibilities. I don't think I'm a very nice person when I get possibilities. Maybe that's why all my other boyfriends liked to tie me up. Maybe that's why I liked to be tied up.

Maybe that's why I'm suddenly not as sated as I was before. My teeth and gums hum with the memory of his flesh. My clit swells against his trying-to-rock prick.

"Tell me a story," I say. "Tell me the hottest story you can think of, and don't come all the way through it."

A shadow of bashfulness falls over his face. He looks rueful, humble. I want to eat a slice of him.

"I was never a very good storyteller."

"Try. And while you're trying, you can dress for the occasion. If, of course, I allow the occasion to come about."

I stand, leaving his cock wet and bereft of the enclosing warmth of my pussy. He groans, but in no other way protests. He takes the condom I retrieve from my purse without a word. Sticks his tongue into the corner of his mouth as though concentrating hard – whether on rolling the latex down or inventing a story, I have no idea.

But I want to eat a slice of that, too.

"Hottest story . . ." he says, and it sounds almost as though *he's* toying with *me*. Except for the up and down quaver in his voice, of course. "Hottest story . . ."

I retrieve my knickers from the floor.

"You know, I'm completely satisfied, Brad," I say, even though that's now a complete lie. He looks absolutely incredible stood there, mostly naked. Tie around his neck, pants still kind of around his ankles, condom-clad cock trembling. I've never wanted anyone to fuck me more, and more than just once, too.

I'm unlikely to be giving him up any time soon. I do so hope he's prepared.

"No – no, wait. No, give me a chance. I've got one." He actually looks panicked. I don't think he's prepared at all.

"Okay, okay. So there's this woman, right?"

"I see," I sigh, and hop back up on to the desk. I cross my legs, knickers still dangling from one finger. Bored bored bored – only, you know, wet enough to ruin my mouse pad at the same time.

"And she's a real tease. She's the biggest horniest tease there is. And she has all these little minions at her beck and call, and they just have to watch as she stalks around in her tiny tight skirts and her blouses that show off all her cleavage."

"Does she have nice cleavage, Brad?"

"Gorgeous cleavage. Her tits are like . . . They're like . . . moons."

I'd laugh, if it were not for the enthusiasm he packs into this . . . "story". He's practically spluttering with it. And it's obvious that he's getting off on it in some way, too, because his stiff prick is now almost touching his belly.

"And there's this one guy . . . this one guy she loves to torment more than the others. She loves to stand real close to him so he can smell her perfume right down to his cock. She likes to bend over him and show him everything she's got. She likes to lick her lips and get his mind stuffed full of how it'd look sucking on him.

He can hardly think straight and keeps doing things wrong because everywhere she's there, begging for him to just . . . fill her mouth and her pussy and her . . ."

"Yes, Brad?"

". . . her ass."

There are so many things that I don't mind about Brad, this story included, but I think I like the little swallow he does after "ass", the best.

"I bet you'd like to do one after the other, wouldn't you, Brad?"

He swallows again, harder this time. Takes a calming breath. "If I say the wrong thing, am I gonna get cut off?" he asks, so plaintively that I actually *can't* stop myself laughing, this time.

"I tell you what, Brad. Why don't you start with my mouth, and we'll see how far you get."

"I think about right here," he says, half-amused with himself, half-tremulous.

I laugh again, and reach for him. He does not come to me easily. Now that his finger's on the trigger and there's so much on offer, he's reluctant to start.

"You know, I can usually go forever."

"What's different about now?" I ask, as I slither off my desk and down, down his body until I'm on my knees. He looks gargantuan from down here.

"You," he whispers, before I run my tongue along the rubber-clad underside of his cock. It should taste bitter, I suppose, but it doesn't at all.

"Keep talking, Brad," I say, between licks. "What happens next?"

"Next she . . . Oh! Next . . . Jesus . . . she . . . she decides I need to be punished, for all the things I've been doing wrong . . . no don't. Don't suck me. Not yet – don't!"

I squeeze the base of his shaft and cock a look up at him.

"You're doing *really* well, Brad," I say, and he tries to fumble on with his story.

"I . . . uh . . . where was I?"

"You were about to get her on your desk and fuck her with your big prick."

"I don't think I got to that part yet."

"Yes you did, Brad," I say, as I stand up and lead him by the cock to my waiting pussy.

I go to hop back up on my desk, but now that story-time's done, he grabs me around the waist – just two big hands, practically swallowing me – and picks me up. Sets me back down and barely waits for me to steady myself or cling to him or anything. Just yanks me forwards with his hands on my ass, and shoves in.

I think I shout. It sounds very high-pitched and too loud. He apologizes when my hands clamp on to his shoulders, but then just falls to rutting against me, grasping my ass cheeks and tugging hard when it's not enough for him.

He feels too fabulous, too hard against the soft sweet place inside me – I can't stop myself from rippling my pussy over his stiff flesh. He groans in protest when I do, but that just starts the cycle up all over again: he groans, I spark with pleasure, my pussy shimmies and shivers, he groans again.

Until, finally: "I'm gonna come – damn. Damn. I wanted to fuck your ass."

"Then do it," I say, cool as you please while my insides boil and my pussy creams and I wonder what, exactly, the wrong way around actually is.

I didn't think it was a thick hard cock skimming and slipping through all the juice that's made its way between the cheeks of my arse. I didn't think it was him saying: "I don't think –"

Before my clenching arsehole gives way to his cock. But maybe it is, because now I'm getting fucked in the ass on my desk in the middle of a workday, and any second someone's going to knock on the door, and I'll have to answer full of cock. Stretched and fucked and the dirtiest I can be.

Though in all honesty, I think I can be dirtier. I wonder if he'd like me to fuck *his* ass.

"Jesus Christ, you're choking me," he gasps, but he doesn't stop jerking against me and clasping my spread thighs and running all his little "uhs" together.

"You can't come until I do, Brad," I say, but that's too cruel even for the person I'm being now.

Even so, he obeys. He presses the heel of his palm to my straining clit and makes me come without me even knowing what does it. His trembling does it. The way he bites his lip and can't control his jerking hips. The way he moans: "I'm gonna go, I'm gonna – I can't stop, oh man, oh man –"

It's always the sights and sounds of someone else, that set me off. And I *do* set off. I shake with it. I clasp his hand to my pussy, I clasp him inside me. I moan loud enough for everyone to hear – even worse, I moan his name. He wrings it out of me, all these great surges of sensation. It's like being washed in orgasms.

And then it's all done, and he collapses over me on my desk. The desk where I once responded to an invitation from the prime minister.

"Behave yourself in future, Brad," I tell him. "No one likes a tease."

I have to say, it's somewhat disconcerting to see the flash of purest confusion cross his perfect open features. He looks almost stupidly baffled, like a cartoon character of a real boy. But he pauses, and considers, and finally tries to formulate words.

"I . . ." he begins, then takes a step backwards, back towards safety. Though he doesn't look unsafe, exactly. He smiles faintly, as he leaves, settling on acquiescence that seems as pleased as much as it is confused: "All right," he says. "All right, Ms Layton."

I don't know what to make of that. I don't know what he means by "all right", and I have even less of a clue about what he was going to say after that first halting "I".

But then I look down on the piece of paper he half-filled for his punishment, and see that he has written, over and over in his silly too-big handwriting:

"I have no idea. I have no idea. I have no idea."

Reunion

Lisabet Sarai

Three years since I last saw him, and now his plane is late. I perch on the edge of the chair across from the American Airlines desk where he told me to meet him, tension winding me tighter with every moment.

It's always like this. My chest aches. It's difficult to breathe. My nipples are as taut and swollen as if he already had them wrapped in elastic bands. I try not to be distracted by the stickiness between my bare thighs. I glance at the arrivals screen. His flight has just landed. Ten minutes, fifteen at most, before I can expect him. I fill my lungs deliberately and try to slow my racing pulse.

I hover between joy and terror. It has been so long, too long. What will he think of me, the strands of gray in my hair, the new wrinkles? What will he ask of me? Will I be able to give him what he needs? I remember other reunions, too few, too short. No time for more than a few kisses, a few playful swats on my bared butt. I remember lying on his lap in Golden Gate Park, my skirt flipped up around my waist. I can precisely recreate my shame and my excitement. I recall slouching down in the front seat of his car in a dark, sweltering parking garage, while he unbuttoned my blouse and dabbled his fingers in my cunt, naming me as his slut. A few hours every few years is all we manage, a country and my marriage separating us even as our history and our fantasies draw us together.

Today will be different. I've booked us a hotel room, in this city where neither of us live. We have the entire day. My husband waits for me at home, while I wait here in the airport for my master.

I don't call him that to his face. He'd mock me, his voice bitter. "If I were your master, I'd simply order to you leave him and come to me, and you would." He doesn't give me that order, although I suspect that he's tempted. He refrains, out of respect for me and my choices, or maybe in fear that his power over me is not as great as he would like to imagine. He spares us both, and I'm grateful, though now, waiting, burning to see him again, I almost wish that he'd put me to that ultimate test and take away the awful yearning that I feel when we're apart.

Every one of my senses is on alert, yet he manages to surprise me. I'm looking toward the gates. He comes from the other direction and calls to me softly. "Sarah."

I start and then laugh nervously. When I stand up, my bag tumbles off my lap to the floor, toys clattering inside. "You're here!" I feel clumsy, silly, stupid, but when he bends to kiss me, everything but the joy disappears. I'm flooded with it, gasping, overwhelmed.

In his limbs I feel his pitiless strength. His lips, though, are gentle, questioning. Am I still his? I melt, open my mouth and my mind to him. Does he sense the answer? Sometimes I am certain that he reads my thoughts. He laughs ironically and calls me suggestible. I don't know what to believe, which suits him perfectly. He wants me a bit off-balance.

I struggle to act normal, as if I were just meeting an old friend. "How was your flight? Did you have trouble with your connections? What about your baggage? Is that the only jacket you have? October here can be kind of chilly . . ."

"Hush," he says, laying a blunt finger upon my lips. "Don't chatter. Take me to the hotel."

We take public transit to the city center. The desk clerk eyes us curiously when we register, an odd couple, me so petite and my master so tall, checking into a hotel room at ten-thirty in the morning. I blush as the clerk hands back my credit card. "Have a nice stay," he says, and I'm sure that I catch something conspiratorial in his tone. However, my master is already pulling me towards the elevator; I don't have time to worry about what other people think.

This hotel is more than a hundred years old. I selected it deliberately, hoping that it might offer some Victorian style, but the room is fairly ordinary – no four-poster bed, no fireplace, no curtain fastenings that might serve double duty as attachment points for bonds.

There is, however, a fine wing-back chair next to the window, with a footstool. My master tosses his backpack in the corner and settles himself into the chair. He grins at me, and butterflies swoop through my stomach. "Well, Sarah. Alone at last."

I stand on the other side of the room, the bed between us, clutching my bag. What I really want to do is to rush over and kneel at his feet.

I can't move, though. It seems as though I'm in a dream, rooted to the spot. Hardly surprising. I've dreamed about this meeting for months.

How shall we start, then? Should I strip? The last time we were in a hotel room together, years ago, he bound me to the desk chair with my stockings. The time before, he unscrewed the post from the fake colonial bed and fucked me with it until my screams brought the hotel management knocking on the door. But that was in another life, before I misread my master's heart and chose a different partner.

"So, what do you have in your bag?" he asks finally, after watching me squirm for long moments.

"I have the corset." I'd purchased it for myself, thinking to please him, knowing that there was no way he would ever buy me one.

"Good. And the other things that I told you to bring?"

"I have the ruler, the rope, the alligator clips, and the timer." I remove the items one by one, arraying them on the bed for his inspection. Without announcing it, I take out a package of condoms and place it on the bedside table. His eyebrows arch in a silent question, but he just nods.

"I'm sorry, but I couldn't find a rug beater, or the switches. It's too late in the year; the trees are too brittle. Anyway, I wouldn't have been able to carry them . . ."

"No excuses!" He sounds stern but I can see a smile twitching at the corner of his full lips. "I'm sure that you know better than to disobey me. We'll see about your punishment later."

He settles back in the chair, crossing one leg over the other. "Right now, I want to see you in your corset."

I carefully extract the gorgeous black satin garment from its tissue paper wrapping. My master looks relaxed, but I know he's not missing any detail as I pull my jersey over my head and attack the buttons at my waist. Of course I'm not wearing a bra. My nipples feel hot, as if illuminated by a spotlight. They seem to scream "Look at me, see how stiff I am."

My rayon skirt pools around my ankles and then I'm naked in front of him for the first time in nearly two decades. His eyes widen but he doesn't say a word.

"Why don't you close your eyes while I put it on? It's rather an awkward process. And I want you to get the full effect."

"You can't hide anything from me, Sarah," he says, but still, he turns to look out the window while I struggle with the clasps and laces.

My fingers don't work at all, I'm so nervous. I know he's getting impatient, yet I can't seem to reach the last hooks. I suck in my stomach, worried that I've gained weight and I won't be able to fasten the thing, but, finally, I manage.

The boned curves press into my flesh. I move a bit stiffly, my breathing shallow so that I don't burst open the hooks. The corset elevates and separates my breasts; they spill lushly over the top of the garment. Meanwhile, I can feel my bare buttocks bulbing out behind.

"Okay – I'm ready."

My master leans forward, eager, his smile baring sharp white teeth. "Very nice. Come over here."

Stumbling a bit in my high heels, I circle the bed and stand in front of him.

"Very nice indeed. Walk around for me, Sarah. Let's see more of your tits and your ass."

His mocking, lecherous tone thrills me. I'm terribly embarrassed, but I love showing off for him, and he knows it. My pussy swells and moistens. My nipples harden further, so painfully sensitive that one touch might send me into orgasm. He doesn't touch me, though. He just watches, while I strut back and forth in front of him, swinging my hips.

I notice the seaweed scent, rising from between my dampened thighs. I'm close enough to him. I know he can smell it too. I don't dare to look at his face. Instead I hold my head high as he taught me, imagining that I'm wearing the collar he once promised me.

I feel his hot eyes ranging over my body, and I rejoice, knowing that I please him, that he's as aroused as I am. And all at once I'm awed by the power of our complementary fantasies. I want him to watch me; he has flown 3,000 miles to do just that. He nourishes all my perverse notions, rewarding me for being the outrageous slut that I secretly am, the submissive, devoted wanton that he recognized in me, long years ago.

"Bend over," he says, his voice gruff with lust. I know exactly what he wants. I stand with my back to him, between the chair and the ottoman. I bend at the waist, presenting my ass to his gaze, holding the stool for support. He leans closer, but for a long time he still doesn't touch me.

His gaze traces paths across my bare skin. I swear I can tell when his eyes linger on the pale globes, or probe more deeply into the shadows between them. This inspection excites me beyond belief.

I know that he'll touch me, sooner or later. I think that I'll die if he doesn't do it soon.

Still, I'm not prepared when he slaps one cheek with his open palm. "Ow!"

"You are such a nasty little girl! I had forgotten. But now I remember (slap) just how kinky and twisted you really are." He gives me three more spanks in quick succession, and I'm wailing out loud. At the same time, I'm hoping that he doesn't stop.

Of course he does, knowing how to stoke my fires with frustration, but only for a moment. "Across my knees, Sarah." The armchair is perfect for a spanking, and once again my spirit soars, as he lays into me, landing one ferocious blow after another on my tender butt. I'm where I belong, and both of us know it.

My butt is burning like it's been barbecued. It's starting to hurt enough to interfere with the pleasure. I wonder if he still has that uncanny sense of my limits that he used to demonstrate. Just as the thought crosses my mind, he whispers in my ear. "I'll bet anything that you're soaking wet, Sarah." Without waiting for a reply, he thrusts three fat fingers deep into me. The fires race from my ass to my cunt and back. I come hard, grinding down on his hand, wanting him deeper, always deeper.

Afterwards, he strokes my hair and plants little kisses on my ravaged ass. As for me, I'm content to just lie across his lap, glowing inside and out from his attentions. His erection pokes through his slacks and into my belly. He doesn't make any moves to release his cock, and I don't dare do so myself.

He's restless, though, aware as I am of the minutes ticking away. "Go get the ruler," he tells me. It amuses him to have me supply the instruments of my own torment.

"Oh no, please, I'm too sore! Please, wait a while till I recover."

He ruffles my hair. "Okay, the rope then. Then I want you on your back on the bed. Legs wide, knees up to your shoulders."

I'm not sure that I'm still flexible enough to comply with his orders, but I manage. He loops the soft cotton rope around one thigh. "Sit up." I struggle to raise my back off the bed, and he slips the rope underneath, around my torso, then winds it around my other thigh. I'm now roped open, my cunt lips spread wide. It's an incredibly vulnerable position. I love it.

"Grab your ankles." When I do, he circles my wrist and ankle on the left and then the right, binding them together on each side. He finishes up on my left side with a neat bow.

His light mood has fled. He's concentrated, serious. A sparkle of fear dazzles me. What will he do, now that I'm totally helpless?

"How's that? Any pain, or numbness?"

I wiggle my fingers and toes, then shake my head.

"Good. Now take a look at yourself."

I hadn't realized that there was a mirror at the foot of the bed. It's difficult to raise my head enough to regard my reflection, but it's worth it. In all the filthy pictures and videos he has sent me, I've rarely seen something so obscene. My thighs and belly are pale as marble contrasted with the black satin of the corset. My labia, emerging from the damp tangle of my pubic hair, are purple and puffy. They are stretched wide, open, and I can see a wet cavern between them, pulsing and quivering. I can't see my clit, but I can feel it, hard, insistent, crying out for his attention.

He zips open his backpack and pulls out a plastic bag. "I thought I should bring some supplies of my own." What does he have? I wonder, simultaneously worried and aroused. He replies as if I'd asked the question aloud. "Just a few clothes pins and elastic bands." He hovers over me, searching my face. "Are you ready?"

I nod, then yell as he fastens a plastic clothes pin to one of my pussy lips. It bites into my flesh. Sharp pain ricochets through my sex. Each echo modulates subtly in the direction of pleasure. I feel liquid trickling from my cleft on to the bedspread. Then he ramps up the pain again by clipping a symmetrical pin opposite the first.

"You know I'm a frugal guy. Why bother paying for toys when there are so many ordinary household items that can be pressed into kinky service? Shall I add a third clothes pin on your clit, Sarah?"

The pain is already overwhelming, though muddied with pleasure. He's giving me the chance to choose. I don't really want more pain, but I want, I need, to please him. There's so much time to make up for.

"If you want," I whisper. "Whatever you want." My clit throbs, trembles, anticipating new agony. But I'm so aroused by now that the third pin hardly hurts. It just turns up the volume on the pleasure.

My master sweeps a fingertip through the opened folds of flesh in front of him, ending with a flick to the plastic pin fastened to my core. I moan and writhe, though I can hardly move, trussed up as I am. "You looks so sexy, Sarah. I've got to get some pictures."

He leaves me stranded on the bed, open and aching, while he gets his camera. The shutter clicks quietly as he captures me from a variety of angles. "These will keep me company, after you've gone." I'm so embarrassed I think that I'll die, but at the same I can't wait to see the photos. "Maybe I'll put these up on the Internet."

"No, you wouldn't . . ."

"Are you sure?" I'm not, not 100 per cent. He has a contrary streak that's a bit scary. "Or maybe I should email them to *him*." My master has actually met my husband, briefly, but he refuses to say David's name.

"No, don't, please . . ." David knows, intellectually, that I'm interested in BDSM, but I think he'd find these photos, this reality, pretty difficult to face.

My master leans over and brushes his lips across mine. "Don't worry. I think I want to keep these treasures all to myself." This brief intimacy is enough to set me shuddering, teetering on the edge of another orgasm.

He sees, and laughs. "Don't come yet, little one. I've got some new sensations for you."

He kneels on the bed between my splayed thighs, and I hope against hope that he'll simply pull out his cock and fuck me. But instead he grabs one of the elastic bands and starts snapping it hard against my inner thighs. The rubber stings the tender skin there; I notice that dampness seems to make the sensation stronger. The pain is not extreme, but it wakens the bite of the clothes pins.

"The elastic leaves little red marks," he tells me. "I'll bet you'll still have them tomorrow."

There is no tomorrow. There is only now. I'm tingling all over, balanced between pleasure and pain, wanting him as I've never wanted anything else.

"Please . . ." I moan. "Please, Eric, touch me . . ."

"Poor little Sarah," he says. "My poor horny little slave." He wriggles one of the clothes pins on my labia, and I scream at the fresh rush of pain. He pulls roughly at the one attached to my clit. I tumble into a loud, frenzied climax, my body jerking like a helpless puppet as jolt after jolt of ecstasy hits me.

I regain my senses. I'm drenched with sweat. The bedspread underneath me is sodden. My master is smiling at me, looking pleased with himself. Love surges in me; tears tickle the corners of my eyes. I want to let him know what he does to me, how much I need him, how grateful I am.

"Feeling better now?"

I nod weakly. "Thank you . . ." The words I want to say suddenly seem silly, mushy. He'll just mock me the way he so often does. I lie silent as he removes the clothes pins. I still feel the ghost of their bite. He begins to untie me, the stops.

"I'm hungry. How about some lunch?"

Maybe lunch would be a good idea, a chance to take a few deep breaths, reduce the intensity. "There's a nice sushi place around the corner that we used to go to . . ." I tend to avoid using David's name under these circumstances, too.

"Oh, I don't want to waste our time by going out. I'll just order room service."

"But . . ." He withers my objections with a masterful look. Before long he's on the phone, ordering a hamburger and French fries and an ice tea. "What do you want, Sarah?"

I'm not hungry. I'm aching and stiff and a bit sad. "Oh, I don't know. Do they have tuna sandwiches?"

"One tuna sandwich coming up." He conveys the information to the person at the other end of the phone, then hangs up. "Ten minutes, they say."

"That's fast! So, can you untie me now?"

"No, I don't think that I want to do that just yet. I'd like the room service waiter to have the chance to appreciate you."

"No! Please, no." The thought is as horrifying as it is arousing.

"Are you refusing me, Sarah? After all these years, are you going to disappoint me?"

No, not that. I've disappointed him so many times. Broken so many promises, as we both know. This time, today, I want more than anything to please him.

"No – it's okay. If that's what you want."

He sits down next to me, gently brushes my hair away from my face. "Good girl. You're mine, aren't you, Sarah? Mine to use as I please?"

The old thrill races through my trussed up body. This is what I crave, to be owned, to be cherished. "Yes," I say, so soft that he has to lean close to hear. "I'm yours." And at that moment, as he kisses me, I believe what I am saying with all my heart.

The doorbell shocks us both. "Hush, be still now," he says as he gets up. "Just a moment," he calls to the waiter. He raises the corner of the bedspread and flips it over me, hiding my bound form. Then he goes to the door.

The waiter looks barely twenty, rangy with tousled blond hair. He can't help staring at the strange, shrouded lump that is my body as Eric signs the check. "Is your wife all right?" he asks.

"My wife couldn't be better," Eric replies. I hear an edge in his voice that the waiter probably misses. "We're just playing a little game."

"Hide and seek?"

Eric tries hard not to laugh. "Not exactly . . . There you go. Thank you."

"Sure thing. Have a nice lunch."

"Oh, we will."

I'm laughing too, in relief and in joy at being alone again. I should have known that he wouldn't risk exposing me that way. Then I think of some of our past encounters, and I'm not so sure.

"I'm always torn," says Eric as he works at undoing my bonds. "Between showing the world what a delicious slut you are, and keeping you all to myself."

I stretch out my legs and groan at the stiffness.

"Sorry to keep you tied up so long. Maybe I got a bit carried away."

"I'm out of shape. Not used to this stuff anymore."

"I'll get you whipped into shape in no time." He hands me my sandwich with a grin. "Here. You've got to keep your strength up.

"You know, it was so hard to decide what to take with me this time. I thought about bringing my laptop and some recent videos. We could watch them together – there's nobody I can really share that sort of kinky stuff with except you. But then I thought we wouldn't have the time . . . One idea I had was to make a ginger fig for you – you know, a little present after not seeing you for so long. I'd love to see how you react to a spicy plug of raw ginger up your ass. But then I realized that it would dry out on the trip, wouldn't be effective . . ."

He talks on between bites of his hamburger. I'm content just to sit here in his presence, my sex still humming from my orgasms, listening to my master, face to face with him at last.

After a while, though, both his food and his conversation run out, and we're there, looking at each other, wondering what comes next.

"I want to see you naked," I say finally.

"Well, I want to try out that wooden ruler." So he does, and of course, I like it. I've always been willing to let him experiment on my body. It turns me on like nothing else, to put myself in his hands, to let him investigate the effects of various implements, positions and techniques. Sometimes the sensations are pleasurable. Even if they're not, giving myself to him sends me flying. When we're apart I miss his voice, his hands, his humor, his intelligence, but most of all I miss the roller-coaster thrill of his taking control and his outrageous sexual imagination.

By mid-afternoon my buttocks are criss-crossed with scarlet streaks and I've shaken through two more climaxes. He seems pleased with himself. Still, he must be frustrated. Certainly there has been a bulge in his trousers ever since my first spanking.

We're stretched out together on the bed. I've taken off the corset. He's still fully clothed. Tentatively I reach out and stroke his erection. "Aren't you uncomfortable? Don't you want to come?"

"I'm putting it off as long as I can. When I come once, that's usually it for quite a while."

I remember in the early days of our relationship, how he'd jack off all over my bound body and be ready to fuck me twenty minutes later.

He reads my thoughts. "Yeah, well, I was a lot younger then. So were you."

"Eric . . . what can I do for you?"

He sighs. "You're here. You let me touch you, bind you, beat you. You come for me."

"Is that really enough?"

"Maybe it has to be enough."

"No – you deserve more, Eric."

The bitterness in his laugh wounds me. "I don't even have the right to that much. But if you insist, Sarah, you can suck me." He is already unbuckling his pants.

"Oh, yes!" I'm jubilant, eager to give him even a fraction of the pleasure he has evoked in me. I understand that my submission satisfies him in ways that are deeper than a physical orgasm. But I want him to enjoy the physical side as well.

He sits up in the bed, propped against the headboard. I kneel between his spread thighs. His cock is pale with pulsing purple veins. The skin is stretched so tight, I'm sure that he'll burst the instant that I take him into my mouth.

I'm a bit reticent. None of our previous reunions has included anything like this. I begin by licking him gently, flicking the tip of my tongue across his slit, massaging the bulb, soaking him with my saliva. He tastes salty and a bit sour, unfamiliar. The strangeness makes me see and wonder at how comfortable we are together, generally, despite our long separations.

Soon I am sucking hard, taking his full length down my throat. He's mostly passive, letting me do the work. Only his cock, jumping or twitching in response to my tongue, tells me how he's feeling. Aside from an occasional grunt or moan, he's quiet. Mostly, there's just the squelch of my wet mouth on his smooth flesh.

I want him to pump, to thrust, to yell, to flood my mouth with his bitter spunk. I suck on and on, my jaws beginning to ache, feeling terribly inadequate that I can't give my master one good orgasm after he's made me come so many times. I reach out to him with my thoughts, begging him to relax, to trust me, to give himself to me.

And all at once, as if in answer, he quickens. He starts to jerk his cock back and forth between my lips. He arches his back, slamming his rod against my palate, using all the strength of his massive body to stimulate himself. I'm gagging, almost choking, but I don't care. He's finally close. I can feel the fluid pumping up the length of him, pulsing, swelling, and I hold my breath, praying for his release.

When he howls, when his come fills my mouth and flows down my chin, I give thanks for his benediction.

We doze for a while in each other's arms. It has been so long, too long. I often dream of him, of us together, of a time like this. Comfort and peace in the wake of passion, complementary desires satisfied. Two sexual outlaws, offering sanctuary to one another.

The rays of the sun slant in, gilding the wing-back chair. It's nearly evening. Soon we'll need to rise. We'll shower together, then I'll put on the bra and panties that I brought, to make myself outwardly respectable. He'll come with me to the station, kiss me tenderly goodbye, and put me on the bus for the two hour voyage back to my home and my husband. I'll spend those hours feeling my master's marks, reliving these few magic hours.

My master will stay in this room tonight. After all, it's already paid for. It will still smell of my cunt and his come.

My husband will greet my bus. He'll kiss me. He won't ask questions. I'll have dinner with him, feeling guilty and awkward, but grateful for his unselfish acceptance of something he doesn't understand.

Later, there will be poems and post-mortems. My master and I will discuss, via email, all the things we didn't do. The alligator clips. The unopened package of condoms.

And we'll dream of the next time outside time, our next reunion.

An Inverted Heart.
Glowing Ruby Red

Marissa Moon

I'm staring at an inverted heart. A perfect peach. Ripe for the plucking. My husband's bottom is small, firm and round. His legs would make many a woman jealous and I wonder if any of his squash partners have ever commented on his smooth hairless limbs or the lack of pubic hair. Despite a taste for slinky lingerie he's still a fit sexually active red-blooded male, not one of those prancing ninnies who desire nothing but cross-dressed humiliation and the chance to kiss Madame's feet. Not that there's anything wrong with that . . . (Sissies!)

He's aroused but apprehensive. Kneeling over a flogging trestle in tarty fishnets and red frilly knickers, hand behind his back, face in profile on the leather headrest. I like to see his reactions as he is punished. He's aroused, already anxious to be inside me but he knows he must first face the ordeal of fire.

The chamber is lit with red candles, perfumed with rose oil and the twelve red roses he bought me are close at hand. I like to rub the thorns over his ruby red bottom as a final reminder of what happens to naughty boys.

Our Valentine's Day ritual always starts with him presenting me with a gift, this year a delicious black and red leather heart-shaped spanking paddle, which will soon tan his taut white rump as red as the surface of his thoughtful gift. Black and red, the colours of fetishism. Or should it be purple and black? Well, a careful Top shouldn't leave bruises. Not after a slow gentle warm-up. But I feel more like a pagan priestess today. I may have to be cruel to be kind. He is gagged, with a pair of my recently worn knickers. Every now and again I rub a finger inside my shaved pussy and dab the moisture under his nose. He groans, eager to snuff up my scent. We have agreed that forgetting to research my Valentine's Day lecture is a serious offence, heinous enough to merit a punishment spanking. I had been asked to address the London Ladies Munch. And I wasn't expecting to chip my nail varnish surfing around the net scaring up information. That's his job. As he well knows. Although the London Ladies wouldn't want much of a lecture, as it gets in the way of champagne-fuelled gossip and the highly enjoyable character assassination of any ladies not present. I stand back and start to rehearse my speech.

"Some believe the Bible prohibits the symbol of the heart, since it is associated with the pagan observance of Valentine's Day."

Four hard smacks get my boy's full attention. I take the paddle, press it to his lips. He kisses it, reverently, knowing it symbolizes my dominance over him.

"Others think the heart should be purified on this day. And some, including myself, believe the inverted heart represents a soundly smacked bottom." I use the paddle to underline these words.

It's harder than I thought to get a satisfying smacking sound from the leather implement. Maybe I need to swing it harder, lower down on the sweet spot. Well, we have plenty of time to practise. He wriggles and mewls all the same, always a pleasant sight and sound. But I want more. I have better luck with three hefty open-palmed smacks, which draw a muted protest.

"There's no better way to purify the heart than to deal with its fleshy counterpart. Your impudent, little rump." Three more very hard smacks elicit some twists and turns. Cuter than kittens at Christmas. His lean little bum is luscious, almost demanding you smack it. I stroke his hair, breathing over his face and into his mouth, rubbing my hand inside his slinky knickers to check he is rock hard. He moans harder as my fingertips brush over his anus. He is yearning to be penetrated, while fearful of which implement might enter his most secret place. Kissing him passionately, I press a purple butt plug into his mouth. He sucks at it busily, my darling demonstrating just what an eager little tart he is. He will be needing that busy little tongue later when I am queening him, rocking back and forth on his face. I take the plug, the width of three bunched fingers, lube him up and press it in his bottom. I pull his panties back up and give his rump a maternal pat. He's squirming with pleasure as we kiss, slowly and lovingly, still hungry for each other after all this time.

When we started it was all about him. I was apparently privileged to watch a preening narcissist get in touch with his feminine side, a female persona whose appeal eluded me. While it was occasionally fun I could only see it as a waste of a perfectly manly man. While he would once have been thrilled to tart around in lingerie, imagining himself to be as alluring as his beautiful Mistress he is now all too aware that these pleasures must be paid for. I'm breathing deeply, drunk on power and wondering how far I can go this time.

Domme, do no harm. A simple mantra I recite whenever the spirit of vengeance threatens to claim me. It would be all too easy to tan his hide till the tears ran down his face, over the leather headrest and on to our thick dungeon carpet. (Note to self. Push his boundaries. Soon.) But today is about love.

"Valentine's day didn't used to be childishly sentimental – a cutesy, vomitous exchange of newspaper greetings and cards. 'Ickle Susie loves her big Poppa Bear.' Hearts and chocolates. It used to be Roman women yearning to have their bare flesh whipped by strips of cow hide."

I abandon the paddle for my hand and soon hear a satisfying smack ring out. It sounds so good I give him two sets of six. I remove my panties from his mouth. I wish to hear his cries of distress as clearly as possible.

"Drunken lust-crazed maidens fighting each other for the honour of being flogged with leather whips. Pert white buttocks striped red, cries of initial outrage becoming urgent pleas for more. Heat from glowing bottoms spreading to nearby erogenous zones."

The smacks ring out, colouring his bottom a darker red.

"Ow! Please! Mistress! Not so hard!"

"How else will you learn?"

He knows better than to argue.

"Romance!" I signal the change of subject with a hefty slap across both cheeks, then gently scratching the reddened surface with my fingernails. I run my hands up and down the insides of his legs, then tease his cock and balls. Slowly and carefully I peel the panties down, freeing his stiff manhood, which is yearning to be inside me. For which ultimate pleasure he will have to wait. I am as moist as he is hard. Were I not such a scrupulous avoider of the vulgar I would say we are both "gagging for it".

"Romance is the only fetish sanctioned by society. The glue that keeps workers chained to their mortgages."

I put my index finger to the base of the butt plug and wriggle it slowly, enjoying the look of pure dumb pleasure on his face. I keep up the finger fucking as I sift through my thoughts on Valentine's Day.

"The original Valentine was a priest who married couples in secret after the Emperor Claudius made marriage illegal. I suppose that's one way of bringing back the romance to these mutual slavery contracts. Make it illegal."

I give him another two sets of six slaps. He's finding it harder to stay in place.

"Keep still! Or I'll cane you. And you wouldn't want that, would you, my lad?"

Decorum is restored. If one can use that word of a man kneeling to offer up his bare bottom for punishment and penetration. I stroke his warmed flesh, keeping him yearning for my touch.

"Some anthropologists think two years is the limit for chemical attraction, for a union to last any longer each party must make an effort."

Two more sets of six slaps and I can hear a whinier note in his voice. Good. I'm getting through to him.

"Perhaps female domination is the answer to marriages that have gone stale.

"That's female domination in the sexual sense as opposed to the usual henpecking. Women can be powerful and capricious while men can be as slutty as they like, becoming the sex slaves they were always designed to be."

I pick up the paddle and start to cook his flesh, ignoring his pitiful protests.

"These cute little buns of yours are going to glow like red hot coals." Three of the best and brightest accompany those words. I find the spot that gives the best whacking sound, although it's still not as resonant as my hand. Keeping the whacks coming on the same spot has him moaning hard.

"Please, Mistress! Ow! Please . . . I can't . . . OWWW!"

Time to give the little lamb a rest. That certainly is a most attractive shade of crimson.

I crouch down and slip my fingers into his mouth, watching the cute little slut suckle eagerly. He's still moaning, deep in his trance. Time to give his prostate another workout. I jiggle the butt plug up and down till he looks like the proverbial cat with the cream. I do spoil him. You should always spoil the one you love.

"For what are we without love? Heretics like Gore Vidal restrict themselves to casual sex, refusing to believe in Cupid's darts. Having said that, even the suave and sophisticated Mr Vidal spent his life with a platonic partner – probably just to have someone to tell him how great he was everyday. That's writers for you. Almost as needy, and deluded, as the average *X Factor* contestant."

I pour some rose-scented water over his bottom, which will make him feel the remainder of his spanking more keenly. I settle into a steady rhythm of loud, hefty smacks, putting my arm around his waist as he starts trying to avoid the blows.

"Take your punishment, my boy. Or it's the cane for you."

Instant acquiescence. He is so well trained. I keep the spanks coming, opening his cheeks to get right into the crease, right on top of that butt plug he loves so much.

That brings soft sighs of pleasure. All very well but I take more pleasure from hearing his reaction to the next flurry of sharp smacks.

"To keep or rekindle the passion in a long-term partnership try giving something which will become a fetish – 'an object that is believed to have magical or spiritual powers'."

Which is how I think of my canes come to think of it. I pick one up and swish it through the air.

"But Mistress . . ."

"Silence!"

Well, it's a woman's privilege to change her mind. The pause lengthens, redolent with his fear and my passion.

"A fetish object can be any reminder of shared passion – love letters, cinema tickets, cute little dildos, scented lubes. Knickers and stockings are perennial favourites but don't let him keep too many intimate trophies. Or he'll be straying into Hannibal Lecter territory."

Just as he's enjoying his little break I give him three quick hard swipes, as close together as I can manage. Which makes him howl.

I stroke it better or as better as a soundly spanked and beaten bum can be.

"There, there."

I kiss him on both cheeks before unleashing two hard strokes. His eyes screw up tightly as he tries not to whimper. The next stroke gets him right on top of his legs. He'll feel that whenever he sits down for the next few days. Saving the best till last I step back and give him one from the shoulder. They're harder to control but luckily it catches him right across the centre of his crimson cheeks. He yelps in pain, his hips swaying from side to side, his breathing now well out of control.

"Please! Mistress! No more!"

I look at his bottom, beaten deepest, darkest red, striped by the cane. He's panting, on the verge of tears.

"Have you been thoroughly punished, my dear?"

"Yes, Mistress." Ooh, it's good to hear him gasping. On the verge of tears.

"You may rub your bottom."

He grasps his burning cheeks and rubs furiously, his agonized face a perfect picture.

"On your back, boy!"

He lays himself down, grimacing as his well-beaten bottom hits the carpet. As usual it has been vacuumed to within an inch of its life by my love. I hitch up my robe to mount his face, treasuring his deep groan of satisfaction. Which soon turns to a frenzied moaning as he licks and nuzzles me front and back. Very soon I'm floating off on clouds of pure pleasure. Eventually, having gorged myself to my heart's content, I take him into my mouth. If I could talk I might finish off with this: "Valentine died in AD 269. Which more or less commands you to wrap yourselves around your lover in a 69 position." I pump his shaft as he gets close. I don't swallow his hot, salty seed. But only because it's one of the best anti-wrinkle creams Mother Nature has gifted us. I rub it around my eyes and forehead then cuddle my boy close. I wonder whether I'll give the London Ladies the secrets of my special face pack. Maybe I'll keep it to myself. They don't deserve it. You can't love *everybody*. . . . as told to Mark Ramsden.

Strippers

Greg Jenkins

If my mouth had swung open any wider, my chin would've bounced off the macadam parking lot where I stood stunned and weak-kneed, teetering with my two plastic bags of groceries. The girl in the window above me was sinfully young and achingly beautiful and artlessly sensuous in her movements. (And she was moving, I noticed.) A lambent angel in the gray evening sky.

She was also, I noticed, as close to being naked as any young man would've dared to wish for.

It was a Thursday in early summer, the dusk misty and warm. I'd just finished buying my usual quota of uninspired staples at the Superfresh – cereal, tuna fish, TV dinners – and I was headed to the far, dim corner of the lot where I'd parked my pickup. I never parked close to my destination; I liked to walk, and I especially liked to walk when my head was loaded with chemicals, as it usually was in those days. My job got me high. I stripped furniture for a living, and all day long I breathed fumes that put the world on a tilt, and made me feel sad when I shouldn't, and caused me to think that my sinuses – and even the inside of my skull – were coated with a thin, shimmery layer of silver or frost or one on top of the other.

When I drew near my truck, a pink light came on above me, and it shot through my fuzzy mind that this – the sudden wash of pinkness – might be another effect of the methylene chloride. But then I looked up and saw a large lilac bush, heavy with thick white flowers, and behind it a wooden apartment house, and above the white-tipped lilac, two stories up, a casement window glowing softly with a warm pink light. In a moment, the girl stepped to the window. She was wearing only a low-scooped bra and thong panties – white or possibly pink. Not a stitch more that I could see. As I stared up at her, she began to move, to stroll back and forth with a kind of slow, languid, musical rhythm. Sometimes she'd turn away from me, and that's when I saw she was wearing a thong.

"God up in heaven," I whispered.

It never occurred to me that what I was doing might be wrong – or that what she was doing might be wrong. I was caught up in the moment, and while it lasted, nothing else seemed to matter.

At first I didn't think she was aware of me, but then I began to suspect differently. Her graceful movements – the strolling, the strutting – began now to evolve into something else. Into dancing. Very gradually and subtly, she'd begun to dance, swaying and stretching and undulating in the window. Her movements were slow and controlled, yet they were passionate too, especially when her long auburn hair swept across her full breasts, and her slender hands, as if of their own volition, passed down over those same breasts, to her taut belly, to her lush thighs, and then lovingly back up again. She kept at it for five or ten minutes, maybe more, and then suddenly the light cut out, and the window was dark.

Her performance had clearly been aimed at pleasing her one-man audience, and I could've mused that she was simply following in the grand tradition of Gypsy Rose Lee, Blaze Starr, Lily St Cyr – the great exotic dancers of the modern era. But at the time no such musings came to me.

"Good God up in heaven," I whispered.

Eventually I noticed that I'd set my grocery bags down on the macadam. Without enthusiasm, I picked them up and carried them to my truck.

"You're missing some spots," my boss said sharply. "Look here." He'd turned the chair completely upside down to expose the shoddiness of my work. "And look here," he said, his probing finger finding still more flecks of dull blue paint.

I was skeptical. My nostrils felt clogged with ice-cold silver. "You really think anybody's gonna turn that chair upside down and look up in there?" I said.

"Damn straight they will." He was pretty fired up. His face was a bright, patchy red, and when he spoke the word "straight", a bubbly strand of spit flew from his teeth. "This here's a ball-and-claw-foot dining chair, a hundred years old! Mahogany! Folks are gonna study every square inch of this thing."

I studied my boss, though I didn't particularly want to. His name was Calvin Pickering, "Mr Pickering" to me, and he was the proprietor of Auntie's Antiques. He was a sight to behold, a tall spidery man in his forties, old enough to be my father, with protuberant eyes and bucking incisors that kept his mouth slightly open all the time. Because of the problem with his eyes and mouth, he always appeared mildly surprised, as if he could never quite accept what life was forcing him to see or hear at a given moment. He was essentially bald, but he made it his sorry habit to comb a few remaining hairs from the area of one jug ear up over his pate to the other jug ear. The effect was at once disturbing and funny. Watching him, I vowed right then that if I ever started losing my hair, I'd shave my head clean, or, like that Japanese writer Mishima, have someone decapitate me before I ever resorted to a comb-over.

Mr Pickering wondered out loud in a tone that approached despair why I hadn't used a putty knife any better than I had, and I wondered to myself why I was working for somebody like Calvin Pickering in a place called Auntie's Antiques. To this point in my life I'd accomplished only what was minimally expected of me, which was almost nothing. My family and friends had done little to distinguish themselves (they all drank a lot, they all had broken relationships or none, they all worked menial jobs or didn't work at all), and my example was no more stellar. But Auntie's Antiques? Was this where I truly belonged? Even the name of the place annoyed me, called up oppressive images of perfumed and prunelike old dowagers, clustered together in some ancient drawing room, murmuring inanely about sewing or flowers or recipes for apple crumb cake. Why not Larry's Liquors? I asked myself, if we're going to be alliterative, or Hootie's Harleys, or Bob's Big Boy, or—

"Just what the hell kinda stripper you wanna be?" Mr Pickering demanded of me. "Huh? A first-class stripper that takes it off smooth and gorgeous the way you're supposed to? Or a stripper that can't strip?"

Truth is, I was beginning to think I didn't want to be a stripper period, but I didn't figure that answer would've lifted my boss's spirits.

A few days later, when I made another trip to the Superfresh, I saw the girl again. This time, of course, I was watching for her. Once again it was summery twilight; a sprinkle of lightning bugs winked at me, and in the distance I could hear the sounds of a small-town baseball game: the postmodern plink of an aluminum bat, the collective shout of a crowd. As before, I was lugging a couple of bags of groceries to the far recesses of the parking lot. I noted that the girl's house was one of three that faced me from the opposite side of a narrow street adjacent to the lot. All three houses were dark and quiet; no one seemed to be stirring.

Then the pink light came on, and the girl was in the window. (Had she been watching for me as well?) Like last time, she was clad in a skimpy bra and panties, neither of which provided more than technical coverage. They were a rich, devil's-food-cake black on this occasion, and she had a sheer black scarf around her lovely neck. Soon she began to move, to dance, and I became conscious of my heart, which began thumping against the walls of my chest as if it wanted to escape.

She'd evidently been practicing, because her dancing was more advanced than before, more stylized. She did things, for example, with the scarf, flicking it this way and that, drawing it across her golden skin, even working it back and forth between her thighs, against her crotch. She appeared to be listening to music, and I wondered what song it might be. Or maybe there was no music, just a self-generated rhythm that flowed inside the dancer and nowhere else. More than before, I tried to glimpse her face, which wasn't easy since the window's rectangle tended to limit my view to just the center portions of her curvy body. But now and then I did spy her face and was struck not so much by its youthful, understated beauty as by its look of pure and innocent rapture. Her eyes were half-closed and her lips parted; she seemed lost within herself, or perhaps outside herself, and blissfully happy. Yet I was certain she was also aware of me.

Toward the end of the show, she stripped off her bra and danced topless, her round, uptilted breasts gently heaving. Then the window went dark.

My own chest was heaving as much as hers. For a long while I stood there at the edge of the dim lot wanting to do something but not knowing what I should do, exactly. I considered erupting into a raucous round of clapping and whooping but was afraid I might draw more attention from the neighbors than from the girl, and unfriendly attention at that. I weighed walking over and knocking on her door but wasn't sure if this response would be welcome either. (Was she alone in there?) I had no precedent for how to act in this situation, and the chemicals in my head were clouding my thinking, feeding my doubt. So I continued to just stand and stare up silently at the dark window. In the end, I picked up my bags, carried them to my truck and drove away.

Not surprisingly, I began dropping by the Superfresh several evenings a week whether I needed groceries or not. I'd always arrive at the same time, about eight o'clock, and I'd always park in the same location; I wanted to be consistent. I also made it a point to go into the store and buy something, however trivial: a pack of Juicy Fruit, a roll of Tums, a carton of Winstons. Buying something allowed me to tell myself that I was there for a legitimate, defensible purpose and not just to watch some delightfully misguided babe dancing and stripping – or stripping and dancing – in a window.

But I knew the real reason I was hanging around that parking lot, and I'd bet hard cash the girl did too.

Sometimes she'd put in an appearance, and sometimes she wouldn't. (Mondays and Thursdays, I discovered, were the most reliable nights.) On the nights she didn't show, I'd feel foolish and confused. I'd mope outside my truck in the gathering gloom, smoke a few cigarettes and ask myself a whole succession of harsh, prosecutorial questions. How could I justify, for instance, being a furniture stripper, especially since the job paid dirt and I didn't even care about furniture? What was that methylene chloride doing to my brain? Why hadn't I gone to college? Why hadn't I moved on to a real city at least, with real opportunities and amenities? Most of all, as the minutes collected on me like the bumps on a rash, I wondered what kind of moron would spend his evening loitering in an ill-lit parking lot outside an empty supermarket waiting for nothing. One time, in a burst of frustration, I flung a roll of Tums about fifty yards into the dark, an act which itself made my stomach hurt.

Of course, on the nights the girl did appear, all this negativity went somewhere else. Life was good. I could temporarily forget who, what and where I was, and I could abandon myself to what was happening within the four borders of that pink-glowing window.

For me, the experience wasn't sexual, or wasn't primarily sexual. It was more about having a peek into an alternate universe – about seeing something that logically shouldn't be occurring but was. The experience spoke of alien possibilities, of fabulous new dreams and vistas that were dancing, just as the girl was dancing, in plain view before me, but ever so slightly out of my reach.

As I often brooded about myself, I likewise puzzled over the girl. Who was she? What was her name? And what did she do besides entertain me? Was she a secretary? A nurse? Maybe she was a student at the community college. I didn't see her as an up-and-coming executive; she was too young, for one thing, and her general demeanor didn't hint of one who was bent on crashing through some corporate glass ceiling. Petersburg was a small town, and I was positive that plenty of people knew her, or knew of her at any rate. But at the same time I was wary about asking around.

One night I was gaping up at her, murmuring wistfully to myself, when suddenly a male voice spoke up from just beside me. "Man, that's something, ain't it?" the voice said, and I almost collapsed in fright. Was it a cop? Worse, was it the dancer's boyfriend? Her husband?

I turned and saw a dumpy-looking guy about my own age wearing a Mighty Ducks baseball cap and a dark, wispy goatee that looked as if he'd inadvertently smudged his mouth and chin with soot. His draft-drinker's belly filled his T-shirt to capacity and beyond, and the stalklike legs that sprouted from his Bermuda shorts seemed overmatched by the weight they were assigned to support. He was whomping on a chew of tobacco. I immediately concluded that this was no cop, and no boyfriend or husband either.

"It really is," I said, and let my eyes trail back to the window.

"She do this often?"

"Fairly often. Yes, she does."

We said nothing more till the performance ended, and even then we didn't gab too much.

"Well!" he offered, a minute or so after the light had gone out.

"There you are," I said.

I guess we were both still trying to process the lingering, dazzling image of the girl's grand finale: a prolonged shimmy move that caused her bare breasts to quiver back and forth rapidly and hypnotically. It was the kind of vision a man might carry with him for decades, one that could easily survive auto accidents, stock market crashes and the loss of close family members, one that could heat the imagination deep into old age and debility.

The guy stuck out his hand. "Hal Sprague," he said.

"Jimmy Long."

We shook hands and went our ways.

Soon enough, though, I got used to meeting Hal beneath the window; like me, he was hooked. It turned out he was a pretty solid guy – worked for the railroad, had a house on the river and a German shepherd named Creampuff. Loved to bowl, loved to fish. Sometimes we'd arrive early and shoot the breeze for a while. I told him I was a furniture stripper, and he didn't react much to this disclosure one way or the other. "We all got bills to pay," he said.

Before long, in fact, other guys started to take in the shows with us. Two or three at first. Then seven or eight, ten or twelve. Maybe Hal spread the word about what was happening, or maybe the others had simply noticed us standing there at the edge of the parking lot staring up at something moving in a pink window; maybe they wanted to find out what the attraction was. Some of the guys would have groceries with them and some wouldn't. Most of them, I learned, were single. By and large, they were straight shooters, regular people. Fred McElroy was a mailman; Del Snider was a truck driver with the paper mill. I remembered Del from several weeks before when he'd brought me a rolltop desk, medium oak, to be stripped. They all came shambling over in their rumpled T-shirts and loose-fitting jeans or shorts and gazed up at the girl in the window with the same profound awe one might evince in peering up at some fantastic extraterrestrial craft that'd fixed itself in the evening sky, slowly rotating with a play of eerie pink light.

In all honesty, I didn't mind the company. Certainly I had no personal claim on the girl, and I rather enjoyed sharing my discovery with others. We'd show up early and have some ripsnorting bull sessions: sports, movies, politics, the economy. It was really quite pleasant. Some of the guys took to bringing snacks from the Superfresh. Doritos chips, salted peanuts, chicken wings, Coke and Yoohoo – that sort of thing. Two or three times Hal brought his gas grill and cooked us all some hotdogs and hamburgers. Funny how food always tastes better when it's cooked outdoors. I'd have three hotdogs and then three Tums, one per dog, and wash them down with a bottle of Lipton's iced tea.

But when the girl took her place in the window (and even before; we could usually sense when the moment was at hand), a hush would descend on us. It was as if we were in church and the sermon was about to begin. Once she got going, wending her way through a routine that was never the same twice and never less than riveting, someone might occasionally let go with a soft grunt of approval or a stifled cry of delight, but mostly we kept ourselves in check. More often than he should've, Boomer Nazelrod, a cattle farmer who was prone to drink, would holler out: "Lookit them ta-ta's! Lord, Lord!" but he always said it in a wholesome way, I'd argue, never in a vulgar way. When she finished dancing, our applause would be sincere but not boisterous.

The shows went on like that for weeks, and then abruptly they ceased, all at once. No warning, no explanation. A half-dozen evenings in a row we congregated beneath the window with our snacks and banter, our hopes and shortcomings, but nothing happened up above. The window stayed dark.

Maybe she was sick, we speculated. Or maybe she'd moved away. Maybe the man in her life – surely she had a man – had learned of what she was doing and put a stop to it. Maybe the police had gotten wind of the burlesque shows and shut them down. As with so many facets of the world's business, we just didn't know. I recalled that in her last performance, the girl had stripped down absolutely to the buff, the only time I'd seen her do so. A lot of impressed fingers dropped a lot of food that evening. Had the nudity been her way of saying not just goodnight but goodbye? Had it been the glorious capstone to what she meant as her farewell performance?

Well, as I say, we didn't know. Didn't know her name or anything about her, other than she was easy to look at and wasn't opposed to stripping in a public window – or up till now she hadn't been. The scant knowledge I had of her left me feeling somewhat guilty, though I couldn't have explained why.

I told Hal that he and I should get together sometime under different circumstances – go bowling or fishing or maybe just sip a few cold ones – but I doubted we ever would. And, as it happened, we never did. The other guys I'd hung out with all seemed to vanish as well, and on the rare occasions when I bumped into one, we found we had little to say to each other. After a while, my trips to the Superfresh shrank away to what they'd been before the advent of the girl. I went there only when I needed groceries. If I thought about it, I'd glance up at the window, which nowadays was always dark, but mostly I didn't. I felt sad that a special epoch in my life had ended, but I wouldn't have traded it for the moon or the stars or all the antiques in the world.

Speaking of antiques, I recall with singular clarity the last time I saw my boss, Mr Pickering. Or, to put it more accurately, I recall the last time he put his bulging eyes on me.

The quality of my relationship with the boss tended to parallel the quality of my stripping, and, by mid-summer, both were in breathtaking decline – the sort of decline you get when you drive a car headlong off a cliff. On this particular afternoon he'd turned a table made of tiger maple upside down – he was a great one for turning things upside down – and was registering dismay at my handicraft.

"You've scratched the wood!" he said, letting his mouth dangle open about an inch wider than usual.

"I wanted to make sure I got all the paint off," I said.

"My God, you got all the paint off and half the wood!"

I tried to explain to him that when people used the table, they'd have it right-side up and wouldn't be able to see the scratches underneath, but he never did give this type of argument much credit.

"You can't strip!" he said from his kneeling position next to the table. His tone was one of both outrage and sorrow, but mainly outrage. "You cannot to save yourself strip!"

Right about then two of our better customers, Mrs Deffinbaugh and Mrs Seilhamer, came wandering back into the stripping room, I guess to see what the commotion was about. I noticed them all right, permed hair and pressed outfits, but even their presence couldn't dissuade me from doing what I'd already started to do. My pent-up frustration with life, the chemicals singing in my head, and my own poor judgment had blended together into a perfect storm of misbehavior.

"I can so strip," I said. "Check it out."

And I began to glide through the room, swinging my butt, pouting and vamping. I imagined myself moving to the throbbing, brassy sound of that timeless classic "The Stripper". My hand went to my goggles, which were strapped around my sweaty forehead, ripped them off, whirled them repeatedly overhead and tossed them at Mr Pickering. They missed him but horseshoed around one of the table's upright legs, spun once and clattered down. Next I took off my rubber gloves, inch by inch, fondled them a bit and cast them aside. I never stopped moving; I'd seen this done before. Still in full strut, I removed my toolbelt, flipped it this way and that and dropped it at the ladies' feet. Popeyed, they both sat back against the edge of a shipping crate and watched me intently.

Mr Pickering stood up. He was watching me too, his permanent look of surprise more focused than I'd ever seen it. "James?" he said.

But I couldn't be stopped. I took off my workboots and socks and flung each in a different direction. I was wearing one-piece denim coveralls, and my hand found the zipper and tugged it down, lower and lower. When I got the zipper to waist-level, I stood straight and let my coveralls fall to the dirty floor in a heap. The ladies gasped audibly, and Mr Pickering looked as if he wanted to say "James" again but couldn't summon the strength. I was wearing nothing now but a pair of paisley boxer shorts – not the most powerful effect, I'll grant – and I meant to shed those as well. So I sashayed around the room twice more, tossing my arms, tossing my head, and pranced into the restroom. Out of sight, I yanked down my shorts, chucked them back into the stripping room and hung my naked leg out the doorway.

A moment passed, and Mrs Deffinbaugh said in a scattered, winded voice: "Well!"

Another moment passed, and Mrs Seilhamer put in: "There you are."

I waited to hear Mr Pickering's comment, but he never said a word. He didn't have to.

One evening a week or two later I was pushing my shopping cart through the Superfresh lost in thought. My former job was just a fading memory at this stage, and I was concentrating more on what lay ahead for me. I was venturing back to school in the fall, and not the community college either; I'd been accepted into the state university two hours away. The chemicals had left my head – I felt natural again – and I was thinking more clearly than I had in ages.

I was rolling along toward the meat section when suddenly wham! – my cart collided with one being pushed by a young woman. I said excuse me, though it was my impression that neither of us had been watching where we were headed. She had shoulder-length auburn hair and warm brown eyes that said nice things to me just in the way they blinked. She was wearing a pink tank top and tight denim shorts, and something about her hair, her golden arms, the way those shorts molded themselves to her hips . . . She looked like someone I'd known years before, and she was staring at me in the same hesitant, quizzical way.

She said: "You're one of the guys in the parking lot."

Astonished, I took a step backward to have a better look at her. She seemed shorter, more petite, from this angle. "You're the –" I didn't know what to call her "– the girl in the window. The dancer."

"Lisa Broadwater," she said, and offered her hand.

"Jimmy Long." Like her eyes, her hand was warm. "I haven't . . . seen you lately."

"I quit." She shrugged. "Retired. It was fun for a while, but you can't build a life on stripping in a window."

I nodded. It occurred to me that you couldn't build a life on watching someone strip in a window either.

"What you did was artistic," I said. "Communal." I fumbled along at some length trying to convey my notion that there'd been more going on with her dancing than met the eye, but I don't know if she took my meaning.

She said she was going back to school to become a veterinarian. "I want to help sick little animals," she said.

I told her I was going back to school myself.

"To study what?" she asked.

"I don't know." At the time, I really didn't know, and it was fun just pondering the savory menu. "Something worthwhile."

The moment had come for me to strip away my inhibitions – to get down to the naked wood. In this regard, I was more capable than some people would've believed. She gave me her phone number, and in the days ahead we'd get together again, more than once. But the important part of what would happen between us had already happened, and that was enough.

Hands on her cart, she tossed her hair in a way that made my blood jump. "It was nice seeing you," she said.

I watched her as she pushed the cart up the aisle. "It was nice seeing you," I said.

Only When it Rains

Rose B. Thorny

Why it happens only when it rains, I have no idea.

Well, that isn't totally accurate. I have a few thoughts on it, but it doesn't really matter. I don't actually care, and no one else would understand, so it's of no consequence.

In the winter, when it snows, it doesn't feel the same at all. Perhaps, because it is just too cold and cold is invasive, cruelly invasive. Or perhaps, because, in the snow, I would leave behind footprints, evidence, and my mind has made that adjustment to facilitate self-preservation.

In the winter, I like to closet myself. Push the doors tight against the gusting winds and freezing draughts, frame the windows in heavy drapes so I may observe the drifting white fall of chiffon snow without actually feeling its frigid caress, watch the sweep of wind-driven flurries, and listen to the crystalline glissandos of sleet against the glass, without suffering the needles of icy pain piercing my skin.

In the winter, I like to build a fire in the wood stove and kneel before it to warm my hands.

I like crumpling the old news and tossing it on to the blackened, ash-stuccoed iron grate and building little pyres of kindling over it. I arrange them, just so, tiny wooden structures, like frail stick houses that a huffing, puffing big, bad wolf might blow down without a second thought. What a silly tale; fire is so much more effective, so effortless by comparison, and so much more gratifying.

I grasp the box of wooden matches in one hand. Sometimes, I think of them as lucifers, a name by which they're still known, the reason for such a name being apparent to anyone familiar with brimstone, black magic and the fires of hell. God and his minions – or are they cohorts? – are delightfully inventive in their destructive tortures. They know how to create and feed the punishing flames.

The match rasping against the encrusted side of the box offers a gritty, satisfying sound and the flaring tip excites me.

I gasp every time kindling ignites.

I peer into the flames, grip the poker and jab at the dry fuel. It pops and snaps. I imagine piles of brittle old bones being crushed underfoot in some ancient, cavernous crypt. As the inferno expands, waves of heat envelop me. The fire crackles with the intensity of ravenous, snapping jaws and I'm mesmerized by the darting orange and yellow tongues licking at the hapless wood, devouring it. The little house is in ruins, but the fire is alive, searching.

I feed it. Showers of sparks explode; a beast straining to free itself, to gorge on fare more sumptuous and juicier than dead wood.

When the blaze is roaring, when I have it controlled and contained within that iron prison, I stand and turn my back to it. Can I trust it not to consume me?

I slip off the clothing covering my legs, let the garments fall and rest around my feet. The heat assaults my buttocks, seeks ingress, and I close my eyes, inhale deeply, and contemplate what I do once winter is past, when the rains come.

In the winter, in my house, the urge to venture forth and indulge does not overcome me. Oh, it's there. I cannot deny that. It's alive, I can feel it, but quiescent, germinating. The anticipation builds and I let it.

I think about my bliss and the heat radiates. My gut clenches, tingles. The frisson spreads lower and I get hot between my legs. Hot and wet.

My house is old, the oldest one in the neighbourhood. I bought it years ago with a small inheritance and some insurance money, the only silver lining, some people said, of a tragic dark cloud that deprived a young woman of her only remaining family. It sits on a rise at the end of a cul-de-sac, an old Victorian looking down on a clutter of mismatched post-war bungalows; a stoic dowager standing apart from its youthful kin.

And when it rains, only when it rains, does the wealth of those houses present itself to be plundered.

Once winter has passed, I study the sky. I watch for the storm clouds.

Thin April drizzle won't do. A soft rain is too transparent and most people do not find it unpleasant to don their raincoats and rain boots and open their umbrellas to walk in an April shower. In fact, they welcome it, that harbinger of flowers, those splashes of colour bursting from the neat gardens framed in manicured lawns.

It is not the light spring rainfall I await.

I bide my time, until the sultry, charged air of ponderous summer heat pulses and swells as a fecund belly, then births the relentless deluge of a thunderstorm. The rumbling stirs my blood and the bolts of lightning explode in my brain, tearing me open, even as they rip the sky apart, exposing my innards to the elements. This is what I wait for throughout the crisp brilliance of autumn, the glacial chill of winter, the fresh vibrancy of spring. I wait for the cloudburst and the torrents, the terrifying power of Thor himself, that drives even the bravest of ordinary souls indoors.

I am not ordinary.

But the time must be right, too. Mornings and afternoons are not the right time. Too many people rushing about trading whatever it is they have to offer in payment for their lives. They look like so many staccato raindrops stampeding across the pavement. And there are way too many children running back and forth, stomping in puddles, laughing and shouting and making more noise than the heavy raindrops beating a tattoo on my tin roof. Even during a daytime storm, there is too much light for me to indulge myself. Even in an ominous daytime storm, there is not enough darkness for me to watch the keepers of all those other hearths.

Only when it rains at dusk and in the night do I allow myself the pleasure of making sport of their imagined safety. I wait until they're all ensconced in their little dwellings, their tidy little homes, with the frilly curtains and the polished hardwood floors; their little stick houses.

Many people favour the easy-to-spot yellow raincoats, the colour of sunshine and daffodils and fresh lemons. Others prefer the pretty paisleys and popular multi-hued geometric designs. I choose black, of course. Black doesn't reflect the sweeping beams of random late headlights turning into driveways.

If the conditions are just right – which is what they are this evening – if the summer storm is such that the heat of the day is not dissipated by the sheets of rain, I wear little, if anything, under the slicker.

I am not without humour.

Barefoot, I slip into my tall, black rain boots and stand before the full length mirror in the foyer. I perch the wide-brimmed rain hat atop my head and, otherwise naked, strike the cheesecake poses that made Bettie Page a hot chick. I am not a hot chick and that is obvious, even to me, but that doesn't mean I don't drink in my own reflection. I poise one hand on the hat and place the other on one hip, bend one knee and thrust my pelvis forward. I make a face and stick out my tongue and giggle, sounding quite girlish, though it has been a long time since anyone has thought of me as a girl.

I'm not sure that they think of me very much, at all, and that suits me just fine.

To everyone in this little suburb, I'm that just past middle-aged spinster, who works at the library and lives alone in the old house at the dead end. At work, I'm quiet and pleasant and just stern enough to have earned some respect and obedience from the children, yet not frighten them unduly. It wouldn't do to frighten the children. At work, I'm friendly and even-tempered enough to encourage trust.

At home, I smile and wave at my neighbours and chat with them when our paths cross. I've practised being as ordinary as possible when I'm with other people. It's advantageous to be thought of as ordinary. If the Christmas cards I find in my mailbox, during that festive season, are any indication, I'm not considered some kind of pariah, which is just as well, of course.

The children aren't afraid of me, but neither do I go out of my way to encourage their friendship. It is the one thing I find difficult to do; feign excessive amity towards children. I'm sure of many things, but I'm uncertain if, despite those wide-eyed, supposedly innocent stares, they detect the animosity behind my indulgent smiles. I've seen the way they study me, as they would some curious object, the purpose of which they are unsure. There is no real indication that it would harm them, but it's an unknown, so they can't be certain. I don't allow them to look into me with any intensity. Children see things with a clarity unobscured by guile. And there are things that children should *not* see. When they stare at me, I avert my eyes.

I really don't like children very much, noisy, spoiled little creatures that whine and cry, when they don't get their way, and prance about as if the world, indeed, the whole solar system, revolves around them, as if the rules, *my* rules, don't apply to them.

At the library, they obey the library rules, no doubt because the head librarian, Mr Janus, is commanding and enforces them and has been known to eject the unruly.

I've never ejected anyone. It serves my purpose not to be thought of as mean or frightening.

At home, there is no Mr Janus to back me up and the children obviously do not take me as seriously as they take him. Of course, he's a man and they afford him that additional deference, because they think he is somehow superior to me. They've been taught that it's a man's world; that, Queen Elizabeth notwithstanding, men rule. They all believe that Mr Janus's status as *male*, bestows upon him some inherent respect, as if possession of some thickened, generally floppy piece of flesh hanging between one's legs is a definitive measure of worth. They don't know the things about Mr Janus that I do.

Mr Janus doesn't like thunderstorms any more than the rest of the people in my sphere do. I've visited him often enough to learn things about him, too. The children and their parents wouldn't be quite so respectful of Mr Janus if I shared my knowledge of his habits. I keep that to myself, however. It's enough for me that *I* know.

I resist marching out of my house and confronting the youngsters, when they encroach on my unkempt lawn. I may be harmless and ordinary to them, but I'm sure my yard is something of an extraordinary, even eccentric, sticking point with the neighbours, who offer to cut the lawn for me, when the grass grows beyond what they believe is proper, and I let them. If they want to do the weeding, that's fine with me, too. Free labour; why not? But I think it is that very non-conformity of the landscape which attracts the children. I refrain from chastising them for trespassing, thereby not appearing to be a mean old crone, and they can't resist the lure of the wilderness, pretending to be explorers in the untamed frontier masquerading as my yard. Much as they annoy me, though, I don't really blame them for being wilful and disobedient. One of my mother's favourite sayings, repeated frequently, right up to her untimely demise, summed it up: *As the twig is bent, so grows the tree.* I concur. It's their parents' fault.

And it's their parents who interest me.

I shrug into my long raincoat and snap the fasteners shut. There's a finality to the sound, a shotgun slide locking into position. I'm ready to hunt.

I have my favourite stands, of course. Some prey are just so much more attractive than others.

There is no sound but the storm; rain splashing on the leaves and the pavement, drumming on trash can lids, thrumming in hollow cadence on the carport roofs. The deep timpani of thunder rolling back and forth over the distant hills, punctuated by the occasional cymbal crash when a bolt of lightning hits close to home. Oh, yes, much closer to home than anyone might think.

Psychoanalysis is very much in vogue these days, along with a plethora of psychiatrists, who attempt to find explanations for everything. They have to know the reasons, all the whys and wherefores. They want everything to be neat and predictable. They believe that when someone, such as I, gets caught, it's because, deep down, such people *want* to be caught. Because they want everyone to know how brilliant they are, or because they truly desire to be helped and "cured" of whatever it is that compels them to do what they do. The psychoanalysts believe they have it all figured out.

Needless to say, they're full of shit. I don't want to get caught. I'm having way too much fun. Of course, I *am* brilliant, but I prove it every time I *don't* get caught. And I have no desire to be "cured", because I'm not ill. People such as I only get caught if they get sloppy. And I'm not sloppy. Others, who do get caught, aren't like me at all.

Earlier, as soon as I saw the thunderheads roiling, building upwards, further and further, climbing towards the stratosphere, I mulled over who would be first on my list if the conditions permitted an evening sojourn. I chose the Barkers. If time allows, if the storm lasts, and I have the energy, I'll move on to the Johnsons.

I have to admit that the Barkers are my favourite prey, possibly because they are the exception to my parent rule. They don't have children yet, and they've provided hours of uninterrupted pleasure – children can ruin the perfect moments – but also the most frightening moment, the one time I almost was discovered.

I was in no way culpable for that. It was not sloppiness on my part, nor any desire to be apprehended. It was raccoons getting into the trash, knocking over the galvanized cans and making a din, clearly distinguishable during the lull between thunder claps. Gerald Barker rushed out the back door to see what the commotion was. I ducked and froze below the window and it was the storm that protected me, for the lashing rain was relentless. He looked neither right nor left, his only goal to shoo away the marauders and return to the house. If he'd checked for other possible intruders, it is almost certain he would have spotted me.

Perhaps, that's the reason Gerald and Pamela Barker *are* my favourites, because of the danger that was attached to that incident. Perhaps a part of me craves that extra surge of adrenaline and there is a hope it might recur. It was so exciting I almost didn't have to stay any longer than that, but it was not quite enough, and I remained till they and I were done. Admittedly, though, the moment had passed and that time, I had been almost more aroused by the near discovery of my indulgence than the consummation of their lust.

As close a call as that was, however, I'm too clever to be caught and, by morning, the rain will have washed away any trace of my presence.

I think it's ironic that Pamela Doggett married someone whose last name is Barker.

She's lovely, really; almost perfect. I'll give credit where credit is due. Shapely and just the right average height, though in high heels, she's easily five foot seven, or eight; warm, honey blond hair that she still ties up in a pony tail. She was a cheerleader and still looks like one; a healthy glow radiating beneath her peaches and cream complexion. Her face is flawless according to popular standards. On someone like Pammy, as all, except I, call her, a dark mole isn't considered a flaw; it's a beauty mark. Not by me of course. I don't think it's lovely at all. I may be the only one who sees it for the imperfection it is.

But perfect or flawed, single or married, Pamela Barker, née Doggett, is a bitch.

Gerald Barker is home already, of course. He's always on time, occasionally even early. And why not, when he has such a gorgeous, fuckable bitch waiting at home for him?

Their side kitchen window, in the lee of the prevailing wind, is wet, but open just enough to let in whatever cool air the storm might provide. It also allows me to catch at least some of what they may have to say to each other. Additionally, this window, and the one above their sink is blocked from sight of the next house over and the one behind them, by a tall, thick thuja hedge, which makes it so much easier for them to indulge their carnal urges someplace other than in the bedroom. And that makes it more interesting for me. Bedrooms tend to become boring and, too often, people dim the lights in their bedrooms, or turn them off altogether. Even in the hot weather, some hide under the sheets, ruining the show. I don't want just sound, which is often drowned out by the thunder and rain anyway. I wouldn't go to the movies then sit there with my eyes closed, would I?

But that is always part of the anticipation. What will they do and where will it happen? How much will they give me?

Pamela and Gerry – I've called him Gerry, ever since I stamped his first library book – have obviously finished dinner. Gerry is nowhere in sight. Pamela is standing by the sink washing the dishes.

It looks so idyllic. She's June Cleaver without Wally and the Beaver. The runnels on the pane distort the image. It's like watching a television screen when there's an atmospheric disturbance and the image wavers.

Generally, when the subject arises, I tell people I don't watch television, and while that may not be completely true, I'm sure I don't watch the shows in the way other people do. I don't laugh at those so-called comedies, wherein the parents are making cute little quips to each other and the children are mischievous, but adorable, and by the time the closing credits roll, another crisis has been averted and everyone in the supposedly perfect family ends up laughing at their own foibles, which makes them appear to be even more perfect in their acceptance of life's little trials. What fools they are, almost as foolish as the people who watch and believe those flickering images to be a blueprint for real life. The children grin like fresh-faced, sugar-cookie cherubs – little demons if the truth were known – and the bits of fatherly wisdom and motherly advice make me want to puke.

When I watch those shows, I feel both incensed and vindicated. The hypocrisy of them is evident, if only to me. Others are so naive; stupid, in fact. I see the filth behind the façade.

This is better than black and white television, though. And much better than the ghastly new colour sets. Those are hideous. This is what colour television *should* be like.

The kitchen is all white and green and yellow, clean and cheerful. And Pamela blends right in. It's as if she is part of a well-appointed set upon which the costume and set designers collaborated. And she knows it. Her very posture reveals how highly she thinks of herself, the snotty bitch.

Her house dress is pale yellow, a fall of watery sunshine. It pinches her waist and flares over her hips. The strings of the starched mint green apron are tied in a neat, wide bow. The air is still hot and humid, but she's wearing nylons and I can just see the pair of white sandals with wedge heels, not very high this evening. A bright green satin ribbon adorns her pony tail. She looks like a starlet in a dish soap commercial. She has adjusted the radio dial and I catch errant strains of some pop music station. Pamela sways her ass back and forth to the rock and roll.

She's a slut.

I wonder, when she finally gets pregnant, if she'll undergo that ersatz transformation, the one from slut to Madonna.

That excites me. Not the possibility of her becoming that sainted illusion – that's just a myth – but just saying the word "pregnant", inside my head, instead of using the coy euphemisms, "in the family way", or "expecting".

It's exciting because it means sweet little Pammy, the butter-wouldn't-melt-in-her-mouth girl next door, will prove to be just another knocked up whore, and everyone will know it. It will be visible proof that her wholesome, handsome husband, at some point, spread her creamy white cheerleader thighs, shoved his cock inside her, and fucked her, the same way he'd fuck any other cheap slut. Madonna, my ass.

Pamela stacks another plate in the dish rack, but the sound of it is obscured by the rain pelting my hat. A few drops find their way inside the back of my collar. I don't move to alter my position, lest any motion be detected, but I shiver involuntarily as the stream dribbles between my shoulder blades and down my spine to the furrow flanked by my buttocks. I clench the muscles embracing that delicious trickle.

Come on, Gerry. Where the fuck are you? Your little bitch is waiting for you. Can't you see her wiggling her rump, just begging for it?

Speak of the devil, as my mother used to say, and he's sure to appear. She never banked on me; I only had to *think* his name and there he is.

Gerry Barker looks the part of a handsome devil. He is as dark as his little wife is fair. His curly black hair is neatly trimmed and sets off his bronzed skin. I know his parents. His father is tall, pale, and blue-eyed, the result of forebears who hailed from somewhere in England, but his mother's people originated in the Mediterranean area. Obviously, her genes had the biggest impact on his colouring, but he inherited his father's height. He grins, white, even teeth flashing.

He is no fallen angel. Ordinary mortals produced a god.

I remember, in the library, watching the high school girls swarming around him like giggling gnats. Oh, they were hot for him. I could see it in their hungry, glittering eyes and on their blushing cheeks, virgins who wanted nothing more than to have him draw their first blood.

And now, here he is standing in the doorway of Pamela's spic and span kitchen, the kitchen that's all clean and scrubbed and shiny, just like her. Except there's always dirt somewhere, isn't there? Just because you can't see it, doesn't mean it isn't there?

The garbage sits out of sight under the sink, but it still smells. The floor tiles appear to be spotless, but look closer and you'll always find grit and grime in the crack along the toe kick. Even little Miss Sparkling Clean Pammy can't vacuum well enough to get all the dirt. And, what muck's in the trap of that drain, Pamela, that dark hole under the fresh scent of Joy?

Gerry knows.

He's watching Pamela, who is as unaware of his presence as they both are of mine. So much for sensing the love of your life even ten feet away. She never was too bright. I don't know what he saw in her, beyond the luscious body and perky Sandra Dee looks.

Even through the watery distortion I can see his eyes gleam. I can feel what he's thinking. It's stronger than the electrical charges of the lightning flashes. Oh, yes, this storm is bringing out the very best in Gerry. I chose well tonight.

He's still wearing his work slacks, but the belt is unbuckled and the ends are hanging on either side of his zipped fly. The sleeves of his white shirt are rolled part way up his muscular forearms, and the front is unbuttoned, revealing the dark hair on his tanned chest.

In a few short strides he is behind Pamela, grabbing her around the waist. She jumps and screams then laughs and wiggles against him. I can hear her exclamation over the drumming of the rain and my heart.

"You crazy nut, you scared me half to death."

I can't hear him, but I can see that he mutters something close to her ear as he pulls her tighter against him. Her *mmmmmm* is theatrically loud, as if she's doing it for an audience. There is no way she can know I'm standing here, yet she does it in the same way that a clique of school girls laughs louder, amongst themselves, when they want to make it clear to the outcast that she's missing out on all the fun. I saw her do that, she and her gaggle of silly-goose friends, trying to impress Gerry and his pals, all the while taking sidelong glances at the outsider, who never had a prayer of being one of them.

I watched and listened, from deep in the stacks, while Mr Janus gave them a proper tongue-lashing and told them, right in front of the boys, to leave *this moment*.

Mr Janus is a stuffy, old fart, albeit a perverted one, who hasn't had the decency to retire or die, so that I may become head librarian, but in that moment, I silently applauded him, even though I found the outsider – a mousy, otherwise non-descript girl, who spent hours regularly poring over medical texts – quite repulsive. She deserved to be ridiculed for being such a weak, submissive little worm, but Pamela and her friends deserved, to a much greater degree, the humiliation of being thrown out of the library with the boys as witnesses to the deed.

She put on a front of laughing at Mr Janus, too, but left as he directed. Her laugh hasn't changed.

Whether Gerry finds it attractive, or not, I don't know, and I don't really care. He finds her desirable and that's why I'm here.

Is the storm passing, though? The rumbling grows distant and the rain lets up enough that I can hear them talking. Please, no! If it stops, I'll have to leave before they're done, before *he's* done. It isn't any good unless the rain is washing over me.

"Hey, Pammy, want your ass warmed?"

She squeals a sophomoric imitation of the Big Bopper succumbing to the charms of his Chantilly lay. "Oh, baby, you *knoooooow* what I like."

The dishwater will be left to cool.

Gerry swings Pamela away from the sink and bends her forwards over the mint green Formica top of the kitchen table, rucking up her dress. Even though she doesn't say another word, I know she asks for this. I know it, not just because I've seen them do this before, but because she's not wearing underpants, just a white garter belt to hold up her nylons. She wanted this to happen. Her chubby ass cheeks are practically quivering.

The bitch always looks so prim and wholesome, squeaky clean, but Gerry knows what she is, and so do I. I sometimes wonder if he knew *before* they were married. If he did, that was probably the reason he married her, in the first place. If he didn't, then he got the bonus of his life with a filthy little slut like her.

He pushes her shoulders down. She's resting on elbows and forearms, which are pressed in close to her. Gerry wedges the hem of her dress between her arms and her torso, then tucks her slip under the waistband of the raised dress so it won't slide down.

"Stay right where you are, little girl. Daddy has some business with you."

Pamela whimpers, again as if she's on a stage, or in front of a camera. Phony cunt.

She's not facing my way and I'm just as glad of that. I'm not afraid she'll see me. The kitchen is brightly lit and all either of them would see, should they attempt to peer out the window into the murk, especially in their now distracted state, is their own reflections. No, I simply don't want to look at her face while Gerry's working her over. I don't want to see her eyes squeezed shut, her gaping maw groaning out animal sounds. I don't want to see Pamela's lovely, though slightly imperfect, visage contorted in lust ignited by Gerry's attentions.

I do want to look at Gerry's face, though. Even through the distortion of the droplets on the glass, his face is handsome. He bares his teeth, again, in a ravenous smile. The rain has intensified again and thunder rolls around this suburban enclave as a predator might circle its helpless victim.

He speaks to Pamela, but the rumbling drowns out most of what he says. I catch only, ". . . just what you deserve," as he pulls his belt out of the loops.

Oh, yesss. Yes, Gerry, she deserves whatever you're going to give her. Go on. Do it. Do it!

He grabs his belt by the buckle and pulls on it, sliding it out of the loops. My heart, already thumping wildly, feels as if it is going to rupture, when he doubles the strap and gives himself a couple of test slaps across his palm. I stifle a groan at the sight and sound of the leather striking his hand.

Pamela moans and begs. "Please, oh, please, don't hurt me." I'd almost believe her, but for the silly giggle that threatens to spoil the mood. Not one of us buys the act for a second.

But what's Gerry's plan tonight? There's something extra in his eyes tonight. Something I've never seen before. They've only done this twice before, for my benefit, and he seemed in a hurry to get it done; heat up her ass fast then fuck her. Something's different tonight.

He caresses her bottom with the leather, teases her cunt with the looped end, and kneads one cheek with his free hand, then pinches her. She squeals and he laughs. Still holding the straps against her cunt lips, he smacks her bottom, as one would a horse, then his hand darts up to her pony tail and he grabs it, yanking her head up and back.

Now I can see her face from the side and she's grimacing. This is new and I can barely contain myself.

Yes, Gerry. Make her wince. Do it!

"You my little pony?"

"Yes, yes," she whines and scrunches up her face as he pulls harder.

"Show me."

Tugging against his grip she shakes her head up and down, just as a horse would.

"Come on, little pony, you can do better than that." He slaps her ass again and I unsnap the fasteners of my raincoat.

Pamela shakes her head again then stamps her foot.

"I can't hear you."

They won't be paying attention to anything but what they're doing, and I pull my coat open. I back away just enough to let the rain wet my exposed skin and the first drops striking my nipples harden them.

Pamela stamps her foot again then neighs in a remarkably horse-like fashion. I almost laugh out loud; a bitch that whinnies instead of barking.

Still grasping her hair, but grinning, Gerry moves to the side and raises the belt.

"Does my little pony need a good whipping? Does she?"

I'm already breathing hard through my open mouth and my hand darts to my own cunt. The hair is wet from the rain, but it was already slick and slippery from the fluids leaking out of me. I rub my clitoris while Pamela, the pony bitch, nods her head and stamps her foot.

Gerry strikes her ass with the belt, lightly at first, and she doesn't move very much. I'm wiggling more than she is.

Come on, Gerry. Harder. Whip her harder. Hurt her. The bitch deserves it.

And it's as if he's gleaned the message telepathically, because he increases the intensity. Her ass is reddening and Pamela starts shifting from one foot to the other, trying to avoid the strap, an impossibility of which she must be aware.

Don't let her get away. Make her take it. Whip her harder. Come on. Harder. The filthy slut-cunt-pony-bitch has it coming.

Pamela's prancing now, stamping her prim white sandals. Her flesh is quivering and bright red. Even from here, I can see the raised welts. I'm quivering, too, inside and out. I can barely control my hand, the muscles are so tense, cramping.

She starts sobbing. The horse whinny is replaced by desperate whining pleas.

"Oh, stop, stop, stop. Please, Gerry. Stop the whipping. Gimme me the other."

Come on, Gerry. Now, now. Hit her hard! Fuck her!

He gives her two more vicious whacks, lays the belt on her back and lets go of her pony tail. He moves so fast, unzipping his pants and letting them fall. His white underpants are bright against his olive skin, but he yanks them down freeing his cock. My God, it's huge, bigger than I've ever seen it. And hard, so hard. The veins are bulging, and the head is purple and shiny, wet for sure.

The rain is drenching me and the lightning flashes, and, a moment later, the crack of thunder splits the night.

Fuck her, Gerry. Fuck the bitch. Take her down. Take her down.

I'm working myself faster and faster, harder. I'm on the edge. I feel myself getting closer.

Gerry's cock is bobbing against Pamela's ass. He grabs the belt with both hands and loops it in front of her face, forces her mouth open. She pretends to struggle against it, but grips it between her teeth. He holds the belt behind her head with one hand, pulling hard, and grabs his huge brown cock with the other, rubs the head of it against her dripping, swollen cunt then rams it into her.

She bellows, and he just pushes hard into her, one, two, three strokes and he's in her up to his balls.

He's going to take her down and make her beg. The bitch is going to come. Not so prim and proper now. Not cool any more, the hot, filthy cunt.

Now, now, now! Fuck her, Gerry.

He's pounding into her and the table shifts. She reaches out to the sides and grips the edges, groaning and gasping against the leather bit, gurgling unintelligibly. "Ga-ga-ga-ga-ga!" Her spasms are uncontrollable. The pony bitch is broken, humbled.

Gerry thrusts once more, hard, his face contorting as he grinds out a scream between clenched teeth.

The rain washes over me and the wave of my orgasm grips me. I've never come so hard, but I'm standing outside myself. I don't recognize the sound coming out of me. I'm not even aware that I'm making the sound out loud, until, abruptly, the tableau shatters.

Gerry turns towards the window looking right where I'm standing and hollers, "What the fuck?"

He releases the belt and reaches down to pull up his drawers and trousers. I back away, still rocking from my climax, but suddenly grown cold. I glance up just as a bolt of lightning sears the night and blinds me. The *crack* is almost immediate. So close, so close. It's struck something nearby.

"What, Gerry, what?" Pamela's screaming. She has no idea what's happening.

"Fucking pervert. There's a guy out there, a fucking perv."

It can't be. I can't be caught. I won't be.

Pamela's babbling. "Oh, no. No-no-no. Oh, God. Did he see? Oh, my God. Oh, shit."

By the time Gerry gets to the window, I've wrapped my slicker around me and dashed down the walk between the house and hedge. The splashes of light are still burned into my retinas, the way a flashbulb leaves a white imprint. I run and stumble, going down on one knee and pain knifes into my leg. My palms scrape the gritty concrete sidewalk. I crawl scrambling to my feet again, tripping and staggering towards the street. I can't think and just race into the streaming sheets of rain illuminated by streetlights. I hear a door slam. He's giving chase. He's going to catch me. He mustn't catch me. Can I outrun him? No chance. He's half my age and an athlete. I just run. I have to get away from him.

I race towards the wooded park where all the mothers bring their children in the light of day. I can lose him there. I sprint between the trees into a particularly dense copse. He won't find me there.

Gerry Barker bawls through the pouring rain and murk. "You fucking pervert. I catch you, you're dead."

But I'm hidden now. There's no way he can find me. The storm is protecting me. The storm always protects me.

My heart isn't thudding any more, but I'm still shivering. Wrapped in my thick chenille robe and huddling in my favourite easy chair, I've tried to warm myself. A half-filled snifter of brandy sits close to hand on the end table. It was full when I started it. Even so, I'm still chilled. The shaking won't stop. The fear feels like ants crawling all over me and worms wriggling inside my gut.

I go over the scene again and again, a stuck record playing the words over and over.

You fucking pervert. I catch you, you're dead.

I waited in the woods until I was sure Gerry had given up and gone back home, back to his slut-bitch. It was her fault. She made him so hot he couldn't control himself. And when he gets that way, I can't stop myself. I want her to get what she has coming to her.

But tonight was different. I've never felt it so intensely. The storm was perfect. The scene was perfect, best ever. But it was too much for me tonight. I got carried away. I've never done that before; made noise. I've always managed to remain silent, dead silent.

But he couldn't have seen me clearly. Not my face, or else the police would already have been here pounding on my door, and I'd be under arrest.

If Gerry knew who it was, I wouldn't be sitting here wondering how this could have happened.

But I can't take the chance anymore. Now they know. Now they know someone watches them. They'll be cautious. They won't let themselves be seen any more and they'll be looking out from now on. Will they tell their neighbours to be on the lookout, too, or just keep quiet about it? I can't be certain. Supposing they lie in wait, set a trap?

Fuck them. They've spoiled it. They've spoiled it all.

And Gerry calling me a pervert. Fucking bastard. He always was a snotty prick. Thought he was so cool just because he was good-looking and the girls threw themselves at him. Stupid bitches.

And now he's worse, the prick. And calling *me* a pervert. What about him? Him and sweet, prim little Pammy? He was the one getting a hard-on whipping his wife's fat ass. And her pretending she's some trained pony, dancing around and shoving her cunt at him.

Not exactly Ward and June Cleaver, now, are they? All that fresh-faced innocence they show the world is a lie, a filthy lie. Pamela all wide-eyed and honey-blond sweet, and she's nothing more than a whore parading her wares for that cocksucker, Gerry. I'd feel sorry for him, except he isn't worth it. I was wrong thinking he was special. He's the pervert, not me.

I take another sip of brandy.

The rain has tapered off. My window is open. I can hear everything dripping; there's no other sound, now, except a few crickets chirping, and a dog barks in the distance. The calm after the storm. A light breeze wafts in like a sigh in the wake of a tumultuous orgasm.

I start feeling comfortable in the glow of the single lamp beside me. The storm has passed and I'm feeling more in control again. But everything's changed now. It won't be safe any more. They've ruined it. Gerry and Pamela Barker, Mr and Mrs Perfect Suburbanite in their neat little stick house, have spoiled all my fun.

Or have they?

The wood stove is cold, dormant for the summer. I stand up and go over to the bookcase against the wall and retrieve the box of matches then sink back down into my chair.

I slide the cover open and extract one lucifer. The rasp of it against the box arouses me and the head igniting makes me catch my breath. The brandy helps, but this? A tide of warmth surges inside me, as I stare into the flame transfixed, until it threatens to singe my fingers and I blow it out.

I toss it into an empty candy dish by the lamp then strike another. One by one, I light the matches, clench the muscles in my cunt each time, savour the throbbing then blow it out, until there is little pile of blackened sticks in the dish. Little charred stick houses.

Canvas Back

Craig J. Sorensen

I love Ollie's Bargain Outlet. I don't go there with anything specific in mind, but I never know what I'll find. Still, when I needed a Chilton's manual for my twenty-year-old Swiss cheese Chevy Suburban I found one for two bucks.

They live up to their motto at Ollie's. *Good stuff. Cheap.*

Before I start sounding like a commercial, let me explain.

It was long after my red period. I was working big, deep gallery wrap canvases in bold colors. I was obsessed with an abstracted form that implied the motion of tall grass in a field on a windy day. I called it, rather pretentiously, my wheat period. My current high-relief impasto technique and taste for pricey Sennelier oil paints left little of my limited funds for anything else. It might have more aptly been called my ramen noodle period.

But every man has his limits. For the third morning in a row I'd woken up with a gouge in my ass from the spring that stretched through the cover of the fleabag queen bed I'd found two studios before. I was finally pissed enough to do something about it.

Enter Ollie's. I decided to give it a shot. Maybe they'd have a queen mattress in my price range. Luckily they did.

"Can I get some help with it?"

"Pick up for customer." The pimple-faced teen's voice echoed in distorted strains through the cavernous space. He pulled back from the microphone and looked out into the store. "Little Leeny will help you."

Little Leeny was neither. She stood around six feet tall and had atlas shoulders. But her face was sort of pudgy and girlish with skinny lips atop a deep chin. Her eyes matched the dark sapphire posts through her left nostril and her long earlobes. She bound her bright red hair tight atop her skull so it splashed like a red gerbera daisy from its bright green band. She didn't linger like the other employees though business was slow. She worked like a woman who had known how to go hungry.

Leeny didn't say a word as I pointed out my new mattress. Her Secret powder fresh deodorant mingled with sweat and Irish Spring soap as she set it on the flat cart.

"Let me help you with that," I said as the wheels fell silent by the back of my Suburban.

"I got it, hon." Her voice was high and girlish. She tossed the mattress in like a throw pillow. She gave me a strangely sweet smile that seduced me to smile back.

"Fuck." My voice came back in a long echo. "Fuck!" My most recent painting was a true piece of shit. I'd known it all along, but I worked on like it would somehow resolve itself. It didn't. "Goddamn it!" I rubbed my fingers hard into my scalp.

I had a new mattress, but little else. I was out of canvases. I had a sale coming in another week, and just enough crap in the improvised kitchen I had set up at the end of the large main room for sustenance. The side effect of less important pursuits like buying mattresses and food was that sometimes there wasn't enough left to do the important thing. Paint.

I started rifling through my stash of finished paintings in the hope that a blank canvas was mixed in. In the musty storeroom, I unearthed the remnants of my red period, back when I used pastels and large, toothy papers. Back then I obsessed with the figure and a classic technique. I smiled as I recalled the pleasure of having a model in front of me as soft waves of Technicolor dust rippled down the paper.

Little Leeny popped into my head. The nametag said "Colleen". She wore loose navy coveralls and scuffed steel-toed boots. Her long hands sported chipped cherry red polish on stubby nails that punctuated long, strong hands. I figured her to be in her mid twenties. What skin I could see was porcelain pale, smooth with a satin shimmer.

Strong but girlish, sturdy but fair, contrasting eyes and hair. I still had a big box of pastels and a small stack of paper stashed somewhere. I decided to revive my red period.

Little Leeny grinned skeptically. "Are you serious? You want to paint me?"

"For real." I forced one side of my mouth to curl into a neo realistic smile.

"How much?"

"Ten bucks an hour."

"How many hours?"

"I dunno. At least three or four."

Leeny's eyes lifted up to the Spartan roof of Ollie's. "This is a joke, right?"

"I don't joke much."

"Oh? How 'bout fifteen bucks an hour."

Up to this point I had assumed Little Leeny wasn't terribly intelligent. I realized how wrong I was as I measured the depth of her eyes. "How about twelve."

"What the hell, you've got a deal. Where and when?" She shook my hand like a longshoreman.

As I recited directions, she pondered. "Near that old furniture factory?"

"In the old furniture factory."

One of her red eyebrows lifted high.

"I forgot to ask one question. When do I get paid?" Leeny pushed away from the door jamb as I opened up.

I measured my response. "Well – that's another matter. I'm selling a piece in another week, so I'll have the money then."

"Nothing up front?" She started to turn away. Her tight jeans framed a perfectly rounded butt.

"Wait, wait." I went to the old bright blue cabinets I had found in an alley near a demolished house. I forced my stash drawer open and found my last drops of "emergency cash": a ten and a five. "Fifteen now, the rest when I get paid? It's going to be at least eight hours, so at the end that'll be –" I started to calculate.

"Eighty-one bucks. One question. Why me?"

"You're interesting. Your skin is amazing."

As Leeny laughed her steamy breath vaporized. She shrugged, pulled her hand from the pocket of her cracked vintage leather flight jacket and took the two bills. She stuffed them in her jeans then blew in her hands. "Am I going to end up looking like something from a Picasso?" She scanned my wheat period paintings.

"I do realistic works too. You won't have both eyes on one side of your nose."

"Makes no difference to me. It's your dime." Leeny continued inside. She made a pretty O with her lips and blew as if to see if her breath was still visible. It wasn't but she poked her finger in the trailing breeze of wintergreen anyway. "If you want me in anything less than a coat, you'll have to warm it up in here."

"This is about as warm as it gets in the winter, but you'll be sitting under the lights." I pointed to the spot in the middle of the factory, which was illuminated like a spotlight on a dark stage. Leeny's mouth slowly curled to a frown. She finally shrugged and took off her coat.

"Shit." I focused on her left arm. "I fuckin' hate tattoos."

Dad's '88 Buick hissed and I jumped out. The bump on my head had not yet begun to rise, but I could feel it coming. That didn't bother me. The sound softly decayed, and I looked up and down the country road. There was a house a half-mile or so back. I walked slowly toward it, and paused from time to time to kick larger rocks along the way.

The suspicious man inside stood with his arms folded while I used the phone in the entryway. On the wall was a gallery of Navy photos. I scanned from them to the crudely rendered tattoos on his forearms. On one was an anchor. On the other was a nude woman drafted in thick, tasteless lines. It was much too crude to be a portrait. It was more symbolic, like the anchor. I finished the call and waited.

It was probably only ten minutes but it seemed like two hours, as I anticipated what I would receive when I got home. Dad was going through his black and blue period and had been for as long as I could recall. "Scott, this is going to hurt me more than it's going to hurt you," was his mantra. On this occasion he would be right. He broke two bones in his hand.

But before he drove me home for the inevitable, Dad paused to admire the gallery of Navy ships. The ex-sailor eyed Dad's upper arm. Dad proudly pulled his sleeve up to reveal a dark green and red dragon tattoo.

"That's a beauty." The sailor grinned.

Dad smiled, but his eyes glared at me. "Thanks."

Leeny shrugged. Her hand disappeared in her pocket and she pulled out the ten. "I'll keep the five for my trouble." Her coat gave the soft groan of hardened old leather as one arm disappeared inside it. I looked at that sturdy but very feminine body and her pale skin. That hair and those eyes. Damn.

"No, wait."

She turned back and waited. I nodded softly, and she set the coat back down on a rusty Samsonite chair. I pointed to the brightly lit chaise longue. It was my models' favorite platform back in the day.

It had a pristine carved frame and its richly padded sangria red velvet covering was comfortable enough to sleep on. I was glad I'd decided not to sell it for noodles during one of my many "I'd eat cockroaches" periods.

Leeny kicked off her ratty tennis shoes and looked at the black fabric draped all around the chaise. She reached her hand under the lights, testing their warmth like the shallow end of a pool. She nodded then unbuttoned her jeans and let them fall. She hooked a prehensile big toe in one belt loop and ably tossed the jeans to the seat of the Samsonite. She peeled her tank top and tossed it atop the jeans. There was no hesitation to her stripping. There was a crude art to how she moved.

Unlike her left arm with the realistic bright red long stem rose that extended from elbow to shoulder, her right arm was bare. Contrasting the rose was a bright green and purple dragon who came into full view as her pale blue bra fell. He curled around on her broad back. The serrations of her spine were worked impressively into the dragon's form. She removed her panties displaying the bottom of the dragon's tail, which curled like a fishhook around the curve of her butt. "How do you want me?"

"Huh?" My eyes fixed on the bright golden Jaguar that stalked in tall bright green grasses, perfectly fitted to the outside of her strong right thigh.

"How do you want me?"

"Tattoos like that must cost a mint."

"No, they were free. How do you want me?"

"Free?"

"Thought you hated tattoos."

"I do. Just go ahead and lie on your back. Cross your left leg over. No, turn your shoulders a bit more. Face toward me." It wasn't the best pose, but I had the damned tattoos obscured.

I sat on the old red barstool with the duct tape patch and pinned the first paper to a piece of ply in the jaws of my old easel. I took account of my soft pastel sticks carefully organized in their foam beds in shallow wooden trays.

She settled into the awkward position as if she were taking a nap.

I started drawing, and time stood still. She was so at ease as I filled in the outlines. Her small breasts and muscular stomach were so fair. Her nipples drew me to a stick of ruby red. Her hair made me tumble through cadmium yellow, red ochre and carmine. My left hand gathered the sticks between thumb and forefinger, then paused in passing to blend colors while my right skidded out fresh, bright streaks.

"I have to work in the morning." Her voice broke my trance.

It was after 2 a.m. "Oh shit. Is that the time?" My sandy hands and clothes were smudged in Leeny's colors.

"Yup." She didn't move until I nodded. "Mind if I look?"

"It's still pretty rough, but go ahead."

She tilted her head as she put on her panties. "S'okay."

"You'll come back, right?"

"Yup."

Leeny was good to her word. Slowly, I introduced her tattoos into the paintings.

When I got paid for my dwindling stock of wheat period paintings, I gave her what I could. Twenty here, fifty there. It could not have equaled the hours she was there, but I'd lost track. She never really pressed.

Leeny was far and away the best model I'd ever worked with. She could hold a position for hours and never complained.

One night, while she sat on a black barstool with her back to me and I tried to capture her dragon, she told a story. "I met this up and coming tattoo artist in college, and he thought my skin was perfect. He wanted to tattoo me. I told him I couldn't afford it. He said he just wanted to work on my skin to add me to his portfolio. That's how I got the tats for free."

Turned out this tattoo artist became a maestro of his media. Even I knew his name.

My eyes settled on the unadorned flesh on her right butt cheek. Perfect skin indeed. "Well, that solves one."

"One?" Her shoulder length hair hung free, still as Red Rocks.

"One mystery. Now tell me why you work at Ollie's."

"No mystery there. I love to work with my back. I like to lift things, use my muscles."

"So go to a gym. It's obvious you could get another job."

"I don't want another job. When I do, I'll get one."

The next position I had her hold was back on the chaise. It was a bit provocative, and gave me a perfect view of the vibrant red hair between her legs. Her vagina was particularly beautiful, with an inviting pucker that was wonderfully complex to paint. Her eyes locked on my crotch as I reached in my pants and lined my sudden hard-on up along the zipper, as if that might provide some camouflage. She opened her legs a bit more and rested her hand on the crease of her groin.

I'd only gone to bed with models twice before. Some artists claim not to be affected, but it had an undeniable Samson and Delilah effect on me. Perhaps it was the release of tension, succumbing to the inferior sense of touch, or simply a mutant synapse in my brain that sapped the creative flow.

Leeny grinned. "Ever paint in the nude?"

"What?

"You heard me."

"Uh, yeah, on occasion."

"With a model?"

"Well, no." My chest throbbed and I took a deep breath.

"Go for it." Her eyes were locked in mine. They drifted approvingly down my chest and took in the bulge. "Do it."

I moved slowly at first, taking off my socks and shirt. I drew a deep breath then stripped off my jeans and underwear. She smiled as my boner popped free. I tried to cover, but I've always painted with both hands.

I fought my urge to join Leeny on the chaise. I continued to paint, my cock fitfully softened and hardened. I managed, somehow, to keep to my easel for the rest of the session.

At the next session, Leeny would not take off a garment until I had matched her, and again I painted her with artist and model in the nude. I finished the painting I was working on, and directed her to a new position on the chaise. For the first time, she just couldn't seem to get it right.

I approached.

I touched her hip to turn her. She was like steel wrapped in silk. The almost cool blue tone of her flesh belied the radiant heat that poured from her. She smiled at me then let her mouth open just a little as she resisted my physical adjustment of her pose. I couldn't help but taste. Her breath was laced with piquant, sweet cinnamon. She pushed her tongue deep inside my mouth, and the gold orb through her tongue plowed my taste buds. Leeny's hot fingers squeezed my stiff rod almost too hard. I deluded myself that I might have some self-control left.

She spread her strong thighs. "Taste me."

"Oh God, yes." I knelt between her legs and traced up and down her opening slowly, then cradled her clit. Leeny's moans grew as she anchored her arms to the top of the chaise and ground her hips to my face. I pushed my tongue in her. She was delectable inside. Not perfumed, real and a bit meaty. My voice was muffled in her crotch, a series of incoherent exclamations of the beauty while I combed her fiery pubic hair with my thumbs.

She waved insistently for me to climb her. I rushed my cash stash drawer and found a strip of rubbers and tore one packet open. Leeny made a wide O with her mouth and positioned the curled rubber on it. She slowly covered the tip then down the shaft. She retreated, tracing her steps with post in her tongue tracing the thick bottom vein.

She laid back and spread her body again. "Give it to me, Scott."

Some cunts kiss. Some cunts stroke and some caress. Leeny's swallowed greedily. I drew my fingers along the lines of the rose tattoo, then the jaguar as I savored her ripples. I focused on the artistry of her adornment to hold the floodwaters behind the feeble dam. Yes, they were tattoos, but the artist was a master.

I told myself that a sensation of this depth could only lead to even finer paintings of Leeny. She turned me over and straddled me. She read my responses masterfully and stopped the powerful swinging of her hips each time my orgasm came close to resolution.

She pulled off of me, then turned over on all fours and patted her pussy in an invitation. I entered her from behind and traced the colorful dragon with my index finger. Leeny's girlish voice became louder. Choral gasps and moans reverberated through the cavernous room. She screamed an orgasm and her pussy gripped me. I exploded a desperate shot toward Leeny's womb, only to be repelled by the rubber. I collapsed on to her back, as if an iron trying to affect transfer of her dragon tattoo.

Leeny's strong limbs supported my weight like a suspension bridge.

Despite my rationalizations as we made love, we were never the same. I spent nine sheets of paper trying. I began to miss the smell of oil paints. For some reason I never could execute a good portrait with the brush.

Leeny and I became cordial, then quiet. There came a time when she simply stopped coming by, and I stopped going to Ollie's.

On a late spring day, I could no longer resist the mysteries of my favorite store or a glimpse of my favorite model. I wandered the aisles taking in the new stock. I paused at strategic points to see if I could spot Leeny. I just needed to hear her voice, maybe smell her fading deodorant, honest sweat and cheap shampoo.

I finally took a couple of books and a bottle of Habanero sauce to the register. "Is Leeny off today?"

"Leeny?" The stale cigarette scented older woman said.

"Colleen."

"No idea." She rang up the next book.

The kid at the service desk called over his shoulder. "Little Leeny quit last month."

"Where'd she go?"

He shrugged without looking back.

It became evident that my wheat period had passed its twilight. It was time to stop naming things. I resisted the urge to try to paint dragons, roses or jaguars, but there was no denying their shapes and colors infused themselves on the abstracted forms I now painted.

One late summer day the UPS truck showed up just in time. I was finishing my last canvas. My heart hammered when the edge of a woman's tattooed thigh poked through the open door. A brightly colored Jaguar stalked in the grasses.

Leeny grinned as she easily hefted two large boxes to my door. "Hiya, Scott."

"Let me help you," I said.

"Got it covered, hon." She set the boxes down inside the hot building. She tilted her head and looked at my right thigh. She wiped her brow on her wrist then reached for the cuff of my shorts. A strong women's jaguar-adorned thigh came into view. Leeny pulled the fabric up further to expose a nude red-haired woman on a black stool. Her back displayed a dragon. Her arm, turned out slightly, hinted at the top of a rose. "I thought you hated tattoos."

"I do, but I got a good deal. When I showed the artist the portrait I wanted him to work from, he said he'd do it free if he could keep the painting, even though he's a big name in the business."

She grinned. "Good stuff cheap."

"Look, I feel bad, Leeny. I can't have paid you all I owe you."

"I've been the canvas and I've been the model. Now I'm the inspiration. Paid in full." She stroked my stubble coated chin softly then gave my cheek a firm pat. She turned around and her daisy hair bounded as she trotted to the big brown van to drive to her next delivery.

The Witch of Jerome Avenue

Tsaurah Litzky

Yesterday morning I went off to art school at the Brooklyn Museum but our teacher felt sick and sent us home. I was disappointed. I loved drawing the magical objects in the museum's collection, the kachina dolls and pharaohs' crowns.

It was my mother's idea that I go to art school. She signed me up when she saw me doodling in the margins of my school notebooks. She made me the pink brocade shoulder bag that I use to carry my art supplies.

When I got off the bus at our corner I realized I could still catch the Saturday matinée with free popcorn at the Valentino Cinema on Avenue L. It was *East of Eden* starring my heartthrob, James Dean. My mother and little brother Seymour weren't home. They were at a science fair at Utrecht High School where my brother had won some kind of prize. His revolting interest in the earthworms he dug up from the swampy marshes near our house had paid off. Maybe my father was home and would go to the movies with me. I love going places with my handsome father.

Women were always looking at him and I wondered if sometimes they thought I was his date. When we go to the movies, he always buys two Hershey bars with almonds but gives me the almonds from his because he knows how much I like them. On the way home he likes to talk about my opinion of the movie. He tells me I have a very smart, insightful mind.

Our gray Plymouth Fury was in the driveway, an encouraging sign. I went in the side door that led to our finished basement. I thought he'd be down there reading the newspapers in his big leather chair.

My father was in the basement but he wasn't reading newspapers and he was not alone. He was leaning over the studio couch, his pants down to his thighs. What happened to his underwear? There was a woman beneath him and she wasn't wearing clothes. He was moving up and down on top of her and she was letting out silly little squeals like my brother's pet hamster, Eisenhower.

I knew exactly what they were doing. My parents had a book, *Love Without Fear*, that they kept in the drawer of my father's bedside table. I used to read it when I was alone in the house. I knew all the illustrations by heart.

The woman had such big boobs they spread out on either side of her like yeasty white dough. I could see my father's scrotum, pink as a chicken neck, bouncing up and down below his ass as he moved. He bent his head; started to kiss her chest. Her nipple was exposed; a sloppy brown stain like a coffee spill, but that didn't stop him from taking it into his mouth.

Then I saw her face. She had an ugly little snout for a nose. Bright orange lipstick was smeared all over her mouth and chin. She looked like a clown. My father started pounding into her harder and harder; I stood on the bottom step, as if rooted, unable to tear my eyes away from the horrid scene.

I felt a quickening between my legs where I was cleft. The tiny button that was there, which *Love Without Fear* called a clitoris, began to twitch. My insides were heaving and churning. I felt sick.

I made myself go back up the stairs and outside. A few doors down from our house a brand-new, pink and white Oldsmobile was parked. I'd never seen it on our block before. I knew this was the evil chariot that had brought the clown to our house.

I ran down to Seaview Avenue, the border between the development of split-level houses where we lived and the fields beyond. I went out through the bulrushes into the swamps, way beyond Canarsie Pier until I found the spot I was looking for. It was a deep dip in the sand surrounded by rocks and tall reeds a little distance from the Belt Parkway. I had gone here with Morty Rothman three times to make out. I crouched between the rocks crying and throwing up. After a while I went home.

The Oldsmobile was gone from its spot and our car was gone too. The door was locked so I let myself in with my key and went up to my bedroom. I lay down on my belly, unzipped my jeans and put my fingers inside the crotch of my panties. This was the position I liked best when I wanted to comfort myself. I put three fingers into my slit; my mother likes to call it a lily. I pretended I was wearing a pharaoh's crown and Morty Rothman was my body slave. He was rubbing baby oil all over me and between my legs. He saved my clitoris for last. I came twice, then I dozed off.

I heard my mother and brother talking downstairs. I got up and found my mother in the kitchen washing dishes; my brother was watching the TV in the living room. When I told her what I saw in the basement, she staggered to the kitchen table and fell into one of the chairs still holding the soapy sponge in her hand.

She sat quiet for a long time. Her face was pale. I thought maybe I didn't do the right thing but then she told me she loved me very much. She said I should go and watch _The Gong Show_ with my brother. That evening, my father didn't come home for supper.

In the middle of the night terrible yelling woke me up. My mother and father were having a big fight. I put my thumbs in my ears and my pillow over my head but I could still hear them.

This next morning when I woke up my mother told me we were going on an adventure, a visit to my Aunt Zippy in the Bronx. She sent my brother to spend the day at his friend Bruce's house.

When we got on the train at Utica Avenue, my mother started to tell me about Aunt Zippy. I only knew her from weddings and Bar Mitzvahs. She was an old lady who wore velvet dresses and funny hats on special occasions. Even though she was bent over and had wrinkles on her face the men buzzed around her. She danced every dance.

My mother told me that Aunt Zippy's full name was Zipporah. She was a witch, a real witch with potions and spells. She'd studied with the most famous witch in Lithuania, Hepzibah the Hebrew. Aunt Zippy came to America long, long ago before people were riding around in cars.

On the day she arrived in New York she was standing on a street corner trying to hail a livery carriage. She had the address of a Witches Association in Rego Park, Queens. A distinguished gentleman in an elegant carriage pulled by two snow white horses drove up and offered to take her anywhere she would like to go. It was Diamond Jim Brady. He was captivated by her ravishing looks and brilliant wit and helped her set up shop in the top floor of the Woolworth building. She was quickly successful, drawing her customers from the cream of New York society. The Great Houdini came to drink champagne with her after his magical feats. Boss Tweed, with whom she had a passionate affair, was among her many admirers. Powerful men among her acquaintances helped her make some good investments in real estate.

Then she fell in love with a musician, a saxophone player she met at a speakeasy named Slim Fats. I knew what a speakeasy was because I had seen *Public Enemy Number One*. She soon found out Slim Fats was already deeply in love with someone else: his sister. All Aunt Zippy's spells and incantations were not strong enough to break that tie.

When Slim Fats left her, she went out of her mind and was sick for a long, long time. Boss Tweed arranged for a special maid to be with her night and day and bathe her in milk. Houdini visited and fed her creampuffs with his magician's hands.

Eventually Zippy recovered, only to find she had lost her powers as witches do when they fall in love. After a miserable year of doing nothing but crossword puzzles, one of her powers came back, that of clairvoyance. She wanted to return to work right away and help women who like her had suffered disappointments in love.

She moved out of Manhattan to one of her properties, a tenement on Jerome Avenue high on top of a hill in the Bronx. Once again, Aunt Zippy took the top floor with its many windows because a witch must be able to see the nighttime sky, the moon and the stars. A few phone calls were all it took and soon she was back in business, women clients only. Gradually, Aunt Zippy regained the ability to do simple spells, but she knew that never again could she change herself into a tiny fairy the size of a thumb or fly through the night riding one of the hounds of hell.

Two huge, battered stone lions stood guard at the door to Aunt Zippy's building. We ascended six flights of stairs to stand in front of a heavy steel door.

The door was flung open before my mother even had a chance to knock. There was Aunt Zippy. She was wearing a tall, black pointy hat and a long filmy red negligée. Beneath the flimsy fabric of her negligée I could make out the top of her low cut black brassiere. Aunt Zippy had amazing cleavage.

"Darlings," she cried out. As she stood on tiptoe to embrace my mother who was only five feet two, I saw that Aunt Zippy's eyes were yellow, smoldering like the eyes of the tigers in the zoo. She kissed me on both cheeks, then took my head in her hands.

"You resemble your mother," she said, "but you have a beauty of your own. You have the face of a poet."

Did she know about the secret notebook I kept under my mattress already half-filled with poems?

A black dog the size of a collie but without a collie's pointed muzzle stood behind her. I didn't like dogs and drew back.

"He's not a dog," Aunt Zippy said. "He's a cat, Morris, my long time companion. He will never harm you." She led us down a long hallway, lined with photos of her with many different women. There was a picture of Aunt Zippy seated with Greta Garbo on a park bench. Another picture showed Aunt Zippy drinking cocktails with Mae West at a long bar and another showed her sitting in a rowboat with Eleanor Roosevelt on a calm lake. There was also a photo of Aunt Zippy shaking hands with Golda Meir.

We entered a light airy room with a high ceiling. Curtains of crystal beads hung in front of the high windows, sending shining reflections of sparkling light on the white walls. A modern white sofa stood in the center of the room, flanked by matching armchairs.

The only testament to Aunt Zippy's profession was a gleaming skull on top of the pine coffee table in front of the sofa. The contemporary decor surprised me.

"Just because I'm a witch," Aunt Zippy said, "is no reason for me to succumb to conventional thinking about my vocation. I've already lived a hundred and ten years. Maybe I'll live a hundred more. Why should I spend my time in some dismal dump filled with bats? Like they say, it isn't over until the fat lady sings."

My mother giggled. "Right," she said, smiling.

Aunt Zippy snapped her fingers and three glasses filled with ruby liquid materialized on the coffee table. She picked up one of the glasses and handed it to me.

"Enjoy this wine," she said, "A glass of wine a day will keep the worry wrinkles away. Your mother and I will be back shortly."

My mother nodded at me encouragingly as she and Aunt Zippy each picked up a glass. They vanished through a door decorated with black roses that had appeared in a corner of the room.

Morris didn't follow them. He spread out under the coffee table and regarded me lugubriously. I had never tasted wine before. I took a sniff. It smelled like raspberries and Vicks Cough Syrup. When I tasted it I found it had a much stronger zing. I closed my eyes and listened to Morris purr softly somewhere below me. He seemed to be humming the first few bars of "Earth Angel", my favorite song.

Morty Rothman and I danced to it when we met at the party celebrating my friend Cora Sue's sixteenth birthday. That was the first time I felt a boy's bone grow hard and press against me through my clothes. He nuzzled my neck and stuck his tongue in my ear, another first. It was warm and wet and I liked it.

"Sorry to disturb you," Aunt Zippy said. "We need you to do something; pull a hair out of Morris's tail? It won't hurt him, he's used to it. We need a hair from a black cat's tail. Only a virgin can pull the hair out and you are the only virgin here so it's up to you." Already I could refuse Aunt Zippy nothing. Morris swung his tail up on the couch next to me. I gingerly took a single long strand between my thumb and index finger and yanked. It slid out easily. I handed it to Aunt Zippy. "Thanks," she said and vanished again.

When my aunt and my mother came back into the room, my mother was wearing a small purple velvet pouch on a ribbon around her neck. I watched her tuck it beneath the collar of her red polka dot dress. "Oh, I need to go to the toilet," she said. She turned and went back behind the black rose door.

Aunt Zippy sat down beside me. She put her feet up on Morris as if he was a footstool. "First, I want to give you my phone number. Call me any time," she said. She handed me a white card with a number in gothic lettering. "Second, I want to tell you something. Your true love will have blue-green eyes." I was puzzled. Morty Rothman's eyes were a flat brown like a Hershey bar. "But, but . . ." I started to object. "No buts about it," Aunt Zippy cut in. "Now, promise me you'll remember what I told you."

"I promise," I said.

My father didn't say anything to me about me telling my mother. For the next few days no one said much of anything around our house.

Wednesday afternoon Morty Rothman sat down next to me on the bus riding home from our high school. "How's about we go to our spot today?" he asked. "I have a surprise for you. I know you'll like it." I was feeling sad and maybe the surprise would cheer me up. He was unusually chivalrous walking through the swamp. He carried my book bag, something he never did before. When we got there, he even took off his Levi jacket and spread it out for me to sit on. Then he pulled something out of the back pocket of his pants, a red rubbery thing that he stuck on the middle finger of his hand. It had a lot of little spines all over it like a caterpillar. The top was cut off and the tip of Morty's finger poked through.

"This is a French tickler," he said. "I put it on my thing and then I put my thing inside you. You'll love it." He wiggled the tickler finger at me. It looked disgusting.

"If you let me do it, it will mean we are going steady." I noticed for the first time how small and squinty his eyes were, like the eyes of a pig. So far I had let him put a finger in me, only a finger. "I won't come inside you," he went on. "I promise."

I heard Aunt Zippy's voice talking in my head. "*Liar, liar, pants on fire*," she said. I knew she was right. "No, Morty," I told him. "No, I won't do it, no way."

His face got all tight and angry. "What have you been doing all this time, stringing me along?" He almost spit at me. "You little bitch, you will do it."

He jumped on top of me, pushing my body down with an arm against my chest. "Bitch," he repeated and slapped me across the face. He slapped me again. I felt myself growing smaller and smaller, thinner and thinner as I changed into one of those gray sand lizards that lived in the swamp. I slipped out from under his arm and scurried away through the reeds.

He didn't try to follow me. As I moved towards Seaview Avenue I found myself growing larger and larger, changing back into myself.

When I got to our house, I stood outside to catch my breath. I was so lucky I escaped.

A few days later I was sitting at the kitchen table doing my homework. I looked out the window and I saw the red seltzer truck pull up and double park. Mr Fleishman, the seltzer man, was here for his weekly visit. My mother was down in her sewing room in the basement. She let him in through the side door.

When they came up into the kitchen, it was not fat Mr Fleishman with his potbelly walking behind her carrying the wooden box of seltzer and sodas on his shoulder. It was a slim, wiry man who looked like an older James Dean. He even had his hair slicked back in the same style. He put the box down on the floor and straightened up.

"I'm Fleishman's nephew Spike," he told us. "My uncle had to have a hernia operation so I'm filling in. Your usual? Three seltzers, three cream sodas?"

My mother nodded and he put the bottles on the kitchen counter. Then he grinned at me. "You must have got your pretty face from your beautiful mother," he said.

"Stop with the fresh remarks," my mother told him.

"Just being truthful," he answered. "Say, did you grow up in Brooklyn?" he went on. "You sure don't have the accent."

To my surprise, she gave him a big smile. "I was raised in Manhattan," my mother said, "East Ninth Street and Avenue A."

"What a coincidence," he replied. "I grew up two blocks away."

Within five minutes, I was exiled to the basement to finish my homework and they were drinking coffee and eating my mother's raisin marble cake at the kitchen table. Before he left to complete his rounds, he gave us two complimentary bottles of cherry soda.

The next day when I came home from school, the seltzer truck was outside and Spike and my mother were in the back yard. They were on their hands and knees in the little garden she had planted there, heads close together over the tomato plants. He was gone before the time my father got home.

The night after that, my mother didn't make any dinner preparations because Spike arrived at five-thirty to take us out. We played miniature golf, two rounds, on Ditmas Avenue. Seymour won both times. After that, Spike took us to a fancy Chinese restaurant on Flatbush Avenue, all red and gold inside. The fortune in my fortune cookie said *Go with the flow*. On the way back, Spike stopped at Carvel Custard and bought me and Seymour hot fudge sundaes. My mother said she couldn't eat another thing. We were sitting in the cab of the truck outside our house finishing our ice cream when my father came up the block. He was staggering from side to side like he was drunk.

When he saw us he ran up to the truck and yelled through the open window, "Get out of there, get out of there, right now."

"Drive away," my mother told Spike, but he didn't start the engine. Instead, he got out and walked around the cab of the truck to face my father.

"She doesn't want to get out," he said. "Why should she?" he added calmly.

"I'll knock your dirty block off," my father yelled at him, balling his big hands into fists. He was six inches taller than Spike at least and maybe thirty pounds heavier.

He swung a wide right at Spike's head and missed.

"You asked for it," Spike said. He crouched low, dancing from side to side on the balls of his feet. Then, with a lightning one-two punch he socked my father in the chin.

My father fell back on the sidewalk all curled up like a baby. Spike climbed back in the truck and we drove off. He turned up Seaview Avenue.

"Why don't you and the kids spend the night at my place, Ruthie?" he asked my mother.

We drove a few more blocks before she answered. "No," she said. "It's not right. I should try to work things out with him. He's my husband."

Spike sighed. When he pulled up in front of our house, he and my mother kissed. Then he kissed my brother and me and drove away.

My father was sitting in the kitchen with the lights out, his head in his hands. My mother told us to go upstairs and go to sleep.

Sometime in the night I head the sound of the bedsprings squealing in my parents bedroom. It was a sound I hadn't heard for a long time. I wondered if my mother was the one on top, riding him, but I didn't want to get up to see if maybe they had left the door open and I could get a peek.

Summer vacation came and my mother and father had fully reconciled. The bedsprings were squeaking almost every night. Mr Fleishman was back on the seltzer truck. When I asked him about Spike, he said Spike was traveling. I hardly ever thought of Morty Rothman now I didn't have to see him every day at school. By the end of the term he was openly going with Vivian Smolar. Rumor had it she bleached the hair between her legs the same platinum color she dyed the hair on her head. I was sure she let him use the French tickler.

On my brother's eleventh birthday my mother asked me to go with him to the pet store. She had so much sewing to do for her customers she couldn't take him. She was buying him his first big snake for his birthday. He could keep it in an aquarium under his bed. She gave me twenty dollars to spend.

The Jungle Pet Store on Rockaway Parkway had a cage of monkeys in one window and a cage of brightly colored tropical birds in the other. Our arrival occasioned so much cawing and squawking I almost expected a bare-chested Tarzan to be standing behind the counter.

Instead it was a tall skinny guy in a white T-shirt with short red hair and freckles. One step closer and I could see his eyes were blue-green like the ocean at Coney Island. A big smile opened up inside me. We just stood there looking at each other until Seymour pulled at my arm.

"My snake, my snake," Seymour said, then he addressed the proprietor. "I want to see the snakes, sir."

"We have the best snakes in Brooklyn," the guy said. "Come this way." As he moved out from behind the counter, I noticed the big bulge between his legs under his tight jeans. He saw me looking and I felt my face turning red. "And you don't have to call me sir," he added, "my name is Larry."

He led us past a pen of puppies and a wall of tropical fish to a long, low tank at the back of the room.

"Wow," said Seymour, looking down at the squirming, undulating mass. "What are the different kinds?"

"Those light green ones are your common variety garter snake," Larry told him. "We also have Montana black horn noses, domesticated South American anacondas, and one rare purple ribbon snake from Peru."

"I'll take the purple one, he's the most special," Seymour said.

"Good choice," Larry told him. He leaned over and deftly grabbed the purple snake, putting one hand behind its head and the other in the middle of its back. He lifted the wiggling creature and carried it back to the counter. He deposited it in a big plastic bag with little holes in it and knotted it at the top.

Seymour was so happy he jumped up and down.

"That will be $25.99." Larry said "I won't charge you tax."

"Oh, oh," I said, "my mother only gave me twenty dollars."

"That's okay," he answered. "You can have the snake for twenty dollars. My father owns the store."

"Thanks so much," I told him. We looked at each other again. I could feel my eyelashes curling.

He started to speak, stuttered, "Er, er, er . . ." His face turned red. Finally he got out the words. "Would you like to go out sometime?"

Larry and I have dated all summer. It is like a dream. We talk about everything. He thinks my poems are wonderful. He wants to be a writer too. His interest is science fiction. He wants to write about intergalactic space travel and machines that can think. He says one day there will be such things. He likes the movies as much as I do and he likes taking long walks in the marshes.

I never showed him the spot I went to with Morty Rothman. Larry and I have found our own spot, further out along Jamaica Bay near a clump of ailanthus trees.

We do a lot of things. We undress each other and kiss everywhere. He sucks my nipples and I suck his. He showed me how to do this, how to nurse and nibble there. His nipples taste like salty peanuts and I cannot get enough of them. He kisses between my legs, finds my clitoris and sucks it like he does my nipple. He pushes his tongue down inside me, flicks it in and out. He says he has the tongue of a snake. I take his prick in my hand. That is what he has taught me to call it. He says "prick" is not a dirty word and that the word "fuck" isn't dirty either. He likes it when I say *fuck me, fuck me* and that is what he does between my legs with his tongue while I rub my fingers up and down on his prick until we both come. We want to do more. We want to go all the way. Larry says we have to plan it on a Sunday when the pet store is closed and we have the whole afternoon. We decide on the next Sunday

I call Aunt Zippy and tell her I am going to give my maidenhead to Larry Petchnick in a few days. I tell her he is my true love with blue-green eyes. She says she knows and it's about time. "Will it hurt very much?" I ask. "Maybe," is her answer, "but sometimes pain is the gateway to the greatest pleasure. You will understand this more when you are older." Before I hang up she says, "Wear a blue ribbon in your hair and the day will be fair." I tell her, "Thank you, Aunt Zippy," and I hang up.

On Sunday we walk to our special spot holding hands. Larry has the plaid blanket from his bed around his neck. I have a bright blue ribbon woven through the braid in my hair.

Larry has a Trojan, the same kind of condom my father keeps in his bed table drawer, in his jeans pocket so we will be safe.

When we get to our spot, he puts the blanket down. We undress each other and then sit down.

I'm scared. I know that once I give up my maidenhead, I will be grown-up, a real woman. I can't go back to being a girl again. I will be crossing a great divide with a question mark on the other side. I wonder if I should break the silence between us by telling him I love him.

Before I can get the words out he grabs me in both arms and we join in a kiss. He starts to fuck my mouth with his tongue and I take his prick in my hand. What a big, purple prick my Larry has, so swollen it fills my palm.

I guide it between my legs and he is lying on top of me. He licks my neck, my shoulder. He puts his hand over my breasts, stroking, caressing. He is slow and tender at first but then he gets rough, pulling my nipples, pinching them. I like this even more, waves of wanting spread out into every part of my body. His prick is so hot and heavy against my skin; I think it will break through. Larry puts his hands on my breasts in such a way so that my nipples rest between his wedding-ring fingers and his fuck-you fingers. Slowly he squeezes the fingers together and lifts his hand pulling the rest of my breast up, up, up. My body turns inside out and I become a giant pulsing vacuum wanting him. I am delirious. My head thrashes from side to side and I hear myself say, "Fuck me, fuck me." I don't want his tongue now. I must have his prick.

"Yes, yes," Larry says, as he rises and gets the condom from his jeans pocket. He sits cross-legged as he tears it open and slides it on, sheathing his prick in white. He kisses me again, a soft little kiss, my last kiss as a virgin.

I am lying on my back. I spread my legs for him; open them wide into a "V". He positions himself above me, leaning himself on his elbows to spare me his full weight. I know it is supposed to hurt but I am not prepared for the sharp slice of pain as my maidenhead rips open.

"Am I hurting you too much?" he asks. I find myself taking long, deep breaths.

"It's okay," I tell him. He takes it slow and soon it doesn't hurt much anymore. As he moves inside me, his pelvis rubs against my mound; it is as if he is rubbing my clitoris, sending sweet thrills down. I am getting wetter and wetter, going with him, lifting my hips up, pulling him deeper in. We go faster and faster, our bodies building a fire that gets hotter and hotter. Then it happens, the heat between us grows and grows. Our insides melt together and we come in a way we have never come before. I feel the way a shooting star looks as it streaks across the sky.

I thought I would hear music like in the romance novels my mother likes to read. I don't hear any music, not even a violin. Larry is still inside me but his prick is getting smaller.

He kisses my eyes, pulls out of me and rolls over on his back. He pulls the Trojan off and puts it in the sand. With his T-shirt he gently wipes between my legs.

"Is there a lot of blood?" I ask. "Nah," he answers, "hardly any." But when he puts the shirt back on, there is a long red stripe across the front.

"See," he tells me, "I'm wearing your brand. Want to go for pizza?"

"Sure," I say.

When I get home the family has already finished dinner. My mother is clearing the table.

"You hungry?" she asks. "No," I tell her. "I ate pizza with Larry." She takes a good, long look at me. "All right," she says but her expression changes. I can't read her.

That night I am too tired to watch *The Ed Sullivan Show* with my family. I climb into bed and fall asleep right away. When I wake up, the first rays of faint morning light are rising in the dark sky outside my window. I want to see the sky turn orange. I get up and stand in front of the window. When I look down into our back yard I see my mother kneeling barefoot in her nightgown digging a hole next to the tomato plants. She takes the purple pouch on the purple ribbon off over her neck and drops it in. I watch her bury it, carefully tapping the earth down with both hands.

Once More Beneath the Exit Sign

Stephen Elliott

On the fourth day together we broke up. We had planned this for a while. Not the breakup, but the four days. Her husband wanted to spend a week with her over Christmas in Chicago, get her out of the Bay Area, and so she wanted to spend four days with me when they returned. That was the deal they worked out.

We had been dating for over five months and her marriage was falling apart. Eden was in one of those open marriages, the kind where you see other people, the kind everybody says doesn't work. Except her husband didn't see other people. Which was fine because they had different desires but then I came along and we fell in love and in the nine years she'd been with her husband she had never fallen in love with someone else. Her husband told her he felt ripped off. She told me he hated me but I didn't think it was my responsibility. It was the situation that was killing him. I was incidental. Anyway, I had my own problems.

We spent almost the entire four days in bed and when we broke up there were condoms on the floor, latex gloves covered in lube, a rattan cane flecked with blood. There was rope spread under the desk and near the closet and attached to the bedframe. There was a roller box full of clamps and clothes pins and collars and wrist cuffs and a gas mask and leather hood pulled from under the bed so we had to step over it when we got up to go to the bathroom. There was a strap-on dildo and holster sitting on top of a box of photographs next to the door, a purple silicone butt-plug near the radiator.

Love is a hard thing to explain. I didn't mean to fall in love with a married woman. I had successfully not fallen in love so many times that when Eden told me she was married I didn't even flinch. We were in a café and she was wearing all black. It was the first time we met. She mentioned her husband, said he was away for a couple of days. "I tell him everything," she said. "I told him we were meeting for coffee." She wanted to be sure I understood that he was her primary, that I could never be first in her life.

Two and a half weeks later I was sitting on her kitchen floor while she prepared dinner – slicing eggplants, soaking them in salt and transferring them to the stove. The flames licked the bottom of the pot and I was careful not to move. I didn't want to get in the way. She leaned down and took my face in her hands.

"Look at me," she said. "I love you."

"I love you too," I replied.

The breakup didn't come from nowhere. I had lost my mind in the week she was in Chicago. I called friends I hadn't seen in years just so I could tell them my story: that I was in love with a married woman and I slept with her once a week and the other six nights I slept alone. My thoughts were consumed with her and I couldn't do my work. My savings were nearly depleted. I lost my adjunct position at the University when I failed to show up for two classes. I saw her two other days each week during the day while her husband was at work and on days we spent apart we spoke for an hour on the phone. Sometimes I saw her on the weekend as well and we went dancing and she came back to my house to sleep over an extra time. I told my friends I saw her more than her husband did, as if that counted for something.

They said, "Get rid of her."

I said, "What if it's me? What if I'm not capable of love?" And what I meant was that I was thirty-four years old and I had never been in a serious relationship in my entire life. I had never been in love. I had minimal contact with my family. There was no one in the world who depended on me in any way.

Before we broke up she told me the story of meeting her husband. They had been neighbors in the Haight District. It was the neighborhood that had been the capital of free love and counter culture forty years ago before succumbing to drug addiction and excess and is now populated with fashion boutiques and street hustlers, junkies sticking themselves against the frosted windows and smearing their open sores on the meter in front of a bar shaped like a spaceship. The worst of the rich and poor.

She had a boyfriend and lived with him downstairs and her would-be husband lived upstairs with his wife. They rarely spoke, instead she spoke with the wife and he spoke with the boyfriend. But years later he was divorced from his wife and Eden was no longer with her boyfriend and he called and asked would she like to go see a band. He'd fathered a child since the last time they met.

He didn't try anything that first date, because he's a gentleman, with his short dark hair and innocent face. He's tall and thin, straight shouldered and from a good family with a good name. He works in a brokerage, wears a suit to work and a black leather jacket. He asked her on a second date and then asked what her deal was. She explained that she was seeing someone, this guy. But the guy had moved to Seattle. So now they were still together but she was seeing other people as well. She said she liked seeing other people. She didn't believe in only seeing one person anymore, in constraining her love, not fulfilling her desires. She was never going to be monogamous again; she had tried and it made her unhappy. This was Northern California, a woman's body was her own and people didn't have to abide by the old rules if they didn't want to. He asked if he could be one of those other people she was seeing and she said yes and six months later they were living together and then they were married and she became a mother to his son.

We had almost broken up on our first of four days. I had arrived to pick her up at her house badly damaged and trying to hide it. Why was I so sad? I thought it was the holidays. Christmas is my least favorite day of the year. And my girlfriend had been gone, unreachable, away with her husband. And we'd had a fight before she left. And my friends were also out of town. But maybe I'm just a sad person. I make decisions assuming that I'm probably going to kill myself anyway. It's just a matter of time. That's my big secret.

Christmas was over; it was cold and the streets were wet. It was eight in the morning and I was on time but not early because her husband left for work at 7.30 a.m. and he and I had already run into each other too many times. They owned a house in Berkeley, a small ranch house built in the backyard of a larger house. Their bedroom was different from mine, dominated by a king size bed with a short space between two large dressers. Her husband's laundry sat in a small pile in the corner and I waited there while Eden showered.

She had been miserable in Chicago where the streets were so cold and her feet hurt from walking the city. She said they'd been to the library and the museum, the Art Institute, and Clark and Division. They'd taken a train to Addison and seen Wrigley Field. I was from

Chicago and I held my tongue because I thought they had missed everything.

Later that day, in my room which is just a yellow space I rent in someone else's apartment and is filled with everything I own in the whole world because I own so little, before the box full of sex toys was all the way out from under the bed and maybe there was just one or two gloves on the floor, she told me she didn't think it could work. And we broke up. But then she changed her mind. In the morning she broke up with me again, and again changed her mind. We never left the bed.

I told a joke about Arabs sending threatening email in order to get the federal government to come out and dig up their yard for them.

On the third day we didn't break up. She caned me, then tied me spread eagle to the bed and got on top of me. "Don't come," she said. And then we laid in bed talking about how much we loved each other and the various things we had done together. It was a list that included Nashville and honky-tonk bars and packed lunch on cliffs overlooking the San Francisco Bay. We'd been to readings and parades and movies and shopped for organic produce at an Asian grocery in Berkeley. We always held hands. We'd been dancing and we danced together well. We spent hours on the phone agreeing on the political issues of the day. Beneath it was this: we were sexually compatible. She liked to hurt people and I liked to be hurt. She liked it when I cried and I wanted to cry all the time.

She turned me over and tied my arms forward and my legs spread and a rope around my ankles and thighs to keep my knees bent and greased her strap-on and slid it inside of me and fucked me violently. "I'm not going to go easy," she said. "I want to hear you."

When we were done she said, "I did all the things you like today."

"You did," I told her. She asked me why I thought she did these things and I said because she loved me and I told her I loved her too.

We went out that night. The only time in four days we left the bed. But not for long. We went to a noodle house with small round tables and I looked at other couples on dates or just eating dinner. Everyone was in pairs; no one was eating alone. There were couples who had just met, trying to impress each other, still a long way from that moment of truth, still hiding their core, afraid of what the other might think when he or she saw them whole. Older couples were there, people who had been together many years and stopped talking altogether. Each person in each couple was unique with their special needs. I wondered what those needs were and if they were being met. A famous analyst was once asked, "What would you call an interpersonal relationship where infantile wishes, and defenses against those wishes, get expressed in such a way that the persons within that relationship don't see each other for what they objectively are but, rather, view each other in terms of their infantile needs and their infantile conflicts? What would you call that?" He replied, "I'd call that life."*

From the noodle house we went to a bar. There were people I knew at the bar and they were playing darts. One of them was moving to France. "I'll be gone six months," he told me. He was going to finish a novel he'd been working on for years. I didn't want to know about it. I thought the bar was cold and empty and there was too much open space.

Then on the fourth day we broke up for real.

It was 1.40 in the afternoon and the curtains were open. We could see my neighbor sitting at a computer in a square of light on the fourth floor of the large apartment building across the street. She asked if I remembered when we first got together and she told me how she was territorial and jealous and I had said I could be monogamous to her. She told me she was consumed with jealousy. It wasn't a matter of me seeing other women, she was burning with the idea that I might desire them, which I didn't deny. She had never felt this kind of jealousy before.

I told her I didn't know what I wanted because I had never been in a relationship like this. I didn't know what it would do to me. I didn't tell her that I was in free-fall. I didn't say what I thought, which was that this was about other things. That we both wanted our lives back and we had run our course together and there was nowhere left to go. I wanted to write and she wanted to save her marriage and I wanted to find someone who would love me all the time even though I doubted I would. Even though I knew deep inside that being with her part time and sharing her was more than I would ever get full time with someone else. But we had stopped growing. Everything had stopped. We were stuck and there was nowhere for us and there was no acceptable change. She wasn't going to leave her husband and the depression that lifted when we met had returned and engulfed me and was getting worse.

Our four days was two hours and twenty minutes from ending. She was meeting her husband at Union Square. They were going

---

* *Psychoanalysis: The Impossible Profession* by Janet Malcolm

to go shopping, and then maybe see a movie. It was New Year's Eve tomorrow and she wanted to get groceries so on New Year's Day she could have a traditional breakfast with fish and rice, friends invited over to start the new year correctly. Earlier in our relationship she mentioned that she hoped we could get to where I could come over for New Year's and be comfortable with her husband and he with me. But we never got to that point. I never fully joined her harem with her husband who has stayed true to his wife these nine years while she went through a parade of men looking to see if it was possible to love two men at the same time and finally deciding on me. Maybe it was the sex. We fucked like animals. She rarely had sex with her husband. He wasn't into the kinky things we were into. He hadn't grown up eroticizing his childhood trauma the way I had. And he had married a sadist.

We had two hours and twenty minutes and she said she couldn't do it and I agreed. Then I waited a heartbeat and I said, "So we're breaking up?" And this time I knew it was true because I started to cry and she grabbed me closely and I buried my face inside her hair.

"I can't leave you."

"I don't want to be without you," I said.

"Then don't be."

But five minutes later I asked what was going to happen and she said we were done and I nodded my head. Still we stayed in bed and I pressed my lips against hers, placed my hand on her ass, ran my palm over the contours of her backside to the top of her legs. I kissed her deeply and cried more.

"Don't cry," she said. I'd cried in front of her so many times over five months. At first I had been embarrassed but then I realized she liked it so I cried freely. I was shocked by my own propensity for tears. I never knew I had so many of them and they were so close to the surface. I would cry when she was hitting me and she wouldn't even stop. She would beat me the whole way through until the tears were gone and I relaxed again and I came back to her. She said she wanted to provide a space for that little boy inside of me. But now she didn't want me to cry anymore and I tried to put the tears back into wherever they came from and I succeeded and then they came again and then they stopped.

Still I knew I was making my own decision. There were things I could say to keep it going and I wasn't saying them. I was once again jumping from a burning building, abandoning what seemed like an unsustainable situation, something I had been doing since I ran from home when I was thirteen, moving out to the streets of Chicago. I never went back. I never did. I've been running away my entire life.

I reached into that tub next to the bed and grabbed a condom from a paper bag. I fucked her hard and fast and in a way unlike I had ever fucked her before. She began to scream and then her own tears came, drenching her face until she resembled a mermaid. This was our due. We were breaking up and we were entitled to this sex and we were going to have it. I slammed into her with everything I had. It was like fucking in a storm. I gripped her legs, the flesh of her thighs. I sniffed at her neck. "C'mon," I said, and she screamed and shook with orgasms. Then we rolled over and she was on top of me with her fingers in my hair and one hand on my throat. We were still fucking. She pinched my nipple hard, she reached down between my legs. It didn't matter. I wasn't going to come.

"I want to come," I said.

"OK," she whispered.

"I can't come inside you."

She got off me. We were running out of time. I lay next to her and masturbated quickly and came into the rubber. She pulled the rubber off me, tying a knot in one swift motion, pulling the end with her thumb and forefinger, striding across the room while I watched the naked triangle of her legs tapering into her ankles.

She tried to call her husband. She didn't want to meet him downtown, she wanted to meet him at home. But he had already left the bank.

"I have to shower," she said.

"He's your husband," I told her. "You don't need to shower for him. He's seen you dirty before."

"I'm not showering for him," she said. "I'm showering for myself."

I followed her into the bathroom. My shower is small, barely room for the two of us. We used the chocolate scented soap she bought me. She was always buying me fancy soaps. This one was composed of dark brown and white blocks and thin lines and the bar separated into its parts while we were scrubbing.

"I have to go," she said.

"I can't walk you to the train," I told her. "I don't want to break down at the station."

I got dressed while she dressed. I pulled on my jeans and an undershirt and a T-shirt. I laced up my gym shoes.

"Why are you getting dressed if you're not walking me to the train station?" she asked.

"I don't know," I said.

It was raining and I offered her my umbrella. I lose my umbrellas so I never buy expensive ones. The umbrella cost six dollars. I considered giving her my necklace but I knew she wouldn't wear it. She turned down the umbrella. She was going to get wet. We moved toward the door of my room. She was wearing her long blue wool coat.

"Don't go," I said suddenly. I didn't even know where it came from and my hand was in the pocket of her coat and her hand was along my neck and the back of my head. I could have turned into an animal, a dinosaur. I could have grown a giant tail and swung it and broken the windows and the table legs and smashed the bed to pieces.

"Walk me out," she said.

I walked her downstairs, out the front to the entryway to the building. I lit her cigarette on the steps. We kept having one more kiss. She was going to be very late to meet her husband. But he would probably be relieved, his ordeal was over. He would make rules next time, communicate better, draw lines in the sand. There would be no sleep-over nights with the next boyfriend. No boys in the house when he came home. But for the foreseeable future he would have to hear about me and comfort his wife while she romanticized our love and cried in his arms.

You concentrate on your time alone, you never think about how hard it is to be in bed with someone else, thinking about you, she said once.

She opened the gate and stepped onto the sidewalk and the rain hit her immediately. It blew horizontally in sharp little beads. I ran down the stairs and grabbed the gate and watched her walk to the corner. I waited for her to turn around. She never looked back. She crossed south and then the light changed and she walked east in front of the housing projects toward the station and the train, which would take her home.

Plasticity

Salome Wilde

I was one of those children that always had something in my mouth. The tit first, of course, though I'd happily chew the nipples of bottles even when they were empty, also fingers, pacifiers, toys, or food. As I grew, so did my repertoire: knuckles, the pad of my thumb, earpieces of eyeglasses, key fobs, pussy, cock. I wouldn't call myself indiscriminate – I know what I'm sucking, licking, and chewing on when I'm sucking, licking, and chewing on it; but I'm rarely empty-mouthed. And when I am? I'm wishing my mouth was full.

Mood doesn't temper the fixation, though it can alter the objects of choice. Good nervous energy – the kind that inspires me to take new risks, work harder, explore self or world in fresh directions – makes me eat. Starting a new piece of writing, for instance, means food. Baby carrots are great: I like to hold them between my back teeth and press down, suck them, then hold the end with my hand and scrape my teeth like a grater over and over and eat them in shredded layers, finally snapping the twig at the end and crunching the little core. Such ornate pleasures, however, do not keep me from wolfing down Dreamsicles (yes, I chew on the wooden stick afterwards until it begins to soften and splinter) and digging into pot-pies with equal aplomb.

Bad energy is when I most delve into non-food orality. Painful break-ups from relationships I never should have entered in the first place have left me with an apartment full of eraserless pencils and nails chewed down to the nub. At such times, I tend to live on coffee and Fresca and my breath has got to be smelled to be believed, I hear.

My most recent casualty of the heart wasn't even worthy of the nail biting and stomach aches I devoted to it. Believe me, you don't even *want* the details. Suffice it to say, I moved him in with me from across the country with no job prospects after only a brief and predictably trite internet affair, and he spent six months sponging off me and giving me guilt about talking to my mother too much on the phone.

But I cannot loathe him too much because the break-up did give me more than just a room full of crunched up bendy straws. As I busily threw out any evidence whatsoever of his existence around the apartment, I found myself shifting into an unexpected and unfamiliar cleaning frenzy. I'm not the neat-freak type – that's anal, not oral, right? So, I am throwing out his geeky Inuyasha T-shirt that was left on the closet floor (and ok, I confess it, before I trashed it I put it over my face and smelled it one last time), and I see this shoebox in the back corner I hadn't opened in years. I knew what was in it before I even opened it, and somehow I felt all shivery and excited with anticipation anyway.

I brought it over to the couch, pausing to pet Miss Lemon (my greedy, sofa-hogging equally oral fat cat – the only one who does not judge me for my messy, foolish life). I sat down with it on my lap and carefully raised the dusty lid. And there she was: Western Fun Barbie, circa 1990. Her hat was missing and the fringe on her pink jacket with enormous padded shoulders was unraveling. Her hair was the precise kind of frizzy mess Barbie hair always is after a week or two, when you've styled and bunched and combed and ignored it. Her boots are gone. But her feet . . . oh her feet. So perfect, with their pristine insoles and ridiculous arches. I remember viscerally how I longed to bite them off when I'd play with her. Oh, that rubbery plastic of her feet: so juicy and perfect to snap off with hungry child-teeth. But I forbore, with this doll alone – entirely because I had chomped the toes off all the others and my parents swore that I would never get another Barbie if I dared dismember this one. So I satisfied myself with chewing and sucking on all her boots until they were unwearable and let the temptation of her footed perfection drive me deliciously mad.

And now, here she was again. Just as enticing and flawless in her sexist version of beauty and comical pink and purple pseudo-Western style as ever. I laughed as I looked her over, and decided I had nothing better to do than indulge in that wonderful pastime of undress-and-dress. I removed the jacket and skirt, undid the Velcro on the little blouse beneath, and soon she was naked, her pointy breasts hard, her waist twisty, her pink smile absurd, and her legs so long and juicy they made my mouth water. And then, yes, I put them in my mouth and suckled.

I let my tongue lap and flick like I was sucking cock. Licked between the legs like delving between long, thick labia. Fought hard against the desire to let her slip almost out so I could touch then chew those precious feet. Such temptation and now no reason not to give in. But instead I teased myself, and Barbie, by sucking her legs and just enjoying the feel of her phallic length in my mouth.

And then I heard a whimper. My own pleasure, of course, at having something in my mouth to suck. Something inanimate so I did not have to worry about his rejection. Something female so it wouldn't make me think of him. Something cocklike so it would make me think of him. So, of course I would enjoy it, and make little enjoying sounds.

But after a few contented moments, the whimpering grew louder, and it was so entirely clear that it was *not* mine. I pulled the doll from my mouth and looked around the room in that insane way you do when you think you're suddenly in a horror movie and if you snap your head around fast enough you'll spot the ghost of the class president who killed herself in high school. Or, in this case, the whoever-it-was who was making little high-pitched erotic noises while watching me suck Barbie's legs. When that didn't work, I looked at Miss Lemon, who was curled in a sweet little feline ball with her tail covering her nose, obviously uninterested in either Barbie-sucking or little erotic noises from nowhere.

I gave a mental shrug and thought about doing more cleaning or maybe writing or chatting online or forcing myself to eat something. But then Barbie's legs were just all I wanted in my mouth right then, so back in she went. I really devoted myself this time, thinking about how it would be to have a lover who truly appreciated my devotion to all things oral, who would constantly command me to suck their genitals and nipples and asshole and tongue as well as their fingers and toes and ears and belly and whatever else struck my fancy. Why did I keep ending up with idiot women who only liked penetration (and tongues didn't count) and moronic men who passively accepted blow jobs only until they were hard and ready to fuck?

The whimpering noise started again. This time louder. And damned if the more I sucked the louder it got. I didn't take her out of my mouth this time but still whipped my head around to see what could be making the noise. But when I slipped my tongue up hard between those creamy tender plastic thighs, the pitch raised and I realized, without a doubt, that it was Barbie herself who was moaning.

I pulled her from between my lips, fast, and looked at her absurdly smiling face. It did not move. I expected it to, frankly, because if she could moan I was in the Twilight Zone and she should be blinking and her mouth moving, too. Funny how once you go there, you just go all the way. But she was not moving and the sound stopped. Then, of course, I had to experiment. Into my mouth went her legs again and the whimpers began again. Out of my mouth and silence reigned. Entirely insane, sure, but I wasn't thinking about the break-up at all now.

An idea suddenly came to me: spread those legs and make Barbie come. But damn, Barbie's legs do not spread! I had never realized this – or perhaps I had, for Western Fun Barbie came with a horse (long ago lost or given to Goodwill) and no way could she ride it, except maybe sorta sidesaddle. Right now, though, I wanted to lick Barbie's pussy, or the flat plastic patch that substituted for it. So I took her out of my mouth again and scissored her into the splits (so limber in some ways, so rigid in others), and licked and lapped at the space between her leg joints. The whimpers became a whine then, inspiring me to lick faster and faster, devoted entirely to my task and feeling like a feminist goddess giving Barbie what she has deserved all along for her suffering in an impossibly shaped body. It fed me, too, and I grew wet then wetter as I labored, until at last the whine stuttered to a ghostly "Ohhhhhhhhhhhhhhhhhhhhhhh" and I knew my doll was coming for me, just me; and I was giving it to her just the way she wanted it.

When her orgasm noise stopped, she was not silent, however. She started making little puppy noises, like there was more she wanted, but I could not understand them. I kept licking, but the sounds did not change in timbre or volume. I put her legs back together and put them in my mouth again, but still the same urgent little sounds. I put her down in my lap for a moment because my pussy was wet and I needed to adjust my panties, and then her vocalizations grew more intense. Barbie wanted me.

Who was I to keep the girl from getting exactly what she wanted? I removed my underwear, spread my legs (excuse me, Miss Lemon, don't mind my splayed thigh in your face), and teased my clit with those lovely feet. Barbie made a high humming noise now, and it brought the delights of battery-powered vibes to mind. My frizzy-haired girl teased and played and danced on my pussy. I pressed her toes down the cleft of inner labia and back up again. Around and over, firm little plastic roaming my slick flesh until we were both whimpering together as she brought me to climax.

Now she's my constant companion, sitting on my desk as I write, on my kitchen counter while I cook, in my bathroom when I go. She sleeps on the pillow where the ex's head rested. She never hogs the covers, she loves the way I suck, and she's always hard for me. Oh, and even when I'm tempted to bite the toes that feed me? Barbie always forgives.

The Spanking Machine

Rachel Kramer Bussel

What's a girl to do when she longs to get spanked by a powerful hand, but can never seem to find a man who'll commit? As a high-powered publicist to celebrities, I'm a bit too butch for most men. Maybe it's the short blonde hair (do gentleman only prefer generous yellow curls or long straight glossy pale tresses?), or the sharp New York sense of humor, or the fact that I make close to half a million dollars a year. Maybe it's that I don't tolerate fools, even ones who know where to land a smack. They might do for a night, but that's about it. The others say they want a woman who's a handful, but really that's the quality they look for in a pair of tits; they're not looking for a full-fledged actual woman, one with thoughts and opinions.

At forty-five, I can't just prowl the bars, and the fetish clubs are a little too intense for me. I want a man who both loves me and loves to make me beg and moan, but until I find him (if I ever find him), I ask again, what's a kinky girl to do to satisfy her urge to be smacked, spanked, and struck with force? Well, she could go gay, but having a live-in girlfriend isn't really my thing, much as I love to strap one on now and then or fondle a gorgeous pair of breasts. I believe women can deliver spankings as powerful as those from men – I've felt plenty of 'em – but that wasn't what I was looking for on a permanent basis. I could hire a professional, or likely even hire myself out, a slutty, spankable bottom for hire (in disguise – I do have a reputation to protect), but to me, playing with a partner is only fun if you're both into each other. What if I wound up with someone I couldn't stand; would I lower my standards, not to mention my drawers, for a man who repulsed me simply so I could get the paddling I craved?

There were too many variables in human nature for me to rely on it for my daily quota of spanking, as I'd learned over many long years of kinky deprivation. So, for my pleasure, I've taken my fondness for sex toys to a whole new level. You see, more than any other fetish, more than sweet kisses or a hard cock pounding me or anything else, I love to get spanked. Hard. I like to get spanked so firmly that my ass tingles for days on end, so it's hard to sit down, so I have to think about my bottom every moment of the day. I'm greedy about my spankings; I crave them in a way that's tough for most of the partners I've had to keep up with. Only the kinkiest of souls have managed to give me exactly what I wanted, and they often got tired of keeping up with my increasingly naughty need for degradation.

So as a modern, liberated woman, I decided to take a particularly American approach to the problem, and buy my pleasure in the form of a spanking machine. If that sounds ridiculous, go online and Google those words; you'll find several models suited to various needs. The more I researched, the more excited I became. After all, I had a collection of powerful vibrators to fuck myself with when there was no one else around (and sometimes even when there was), so why couldn't a mechanical device help me get my ass-smacking on?

I opted for the Robospanker, because it offered the most intense, hard spanking. I loved the fact that it wouldn't let up until I told it to, giving me the chance to top from below, which is what I tend to do anyway. Spanking is one of those activities that you just can't provide for yourself, even with your own hand. So I was willing to set the scene, as long as the machine did the work of making me whimper, making my ass burn, making my pussy throb in the way that only a good spanking can do.

For a moment, as my finger hovered over the purchase now button, I had my doubts. It might be 2009, but what would a new lover say if he came over and saw that this machine was his competition? Men are squeamish enough about vibrators, even the battery-operated kind, and this wasn't the kind of toy I could shove into any drawer or closet, and since I live in Manhattan, I don't exactly have much by way of storage space. I pictured the scene: a stud and I hot to trot, then he sees this contraption. I could say it was an exercise bench, I supposed. And then I slipped my fingers into my frilly white panties, and pictured my olive-colored ass turned a dusky rose, making the contrast against these very same panties even more intense. Tears sprang to my eyes as I tried to recall when I'd last gotten spanked. Oh yes, Raphael; he'd gotten tired of my constant lateness and hurled me across his lap, ripped my fishnets and panties, and pounded my bottom with his hand until I banged against the floor with my fists, until I almost couldn't take it anymore, flirting on the edge of giving up. My cunt danced with excitement as I recalled his anger, and I pressed the button, setting the transaction in motion. Of course, a machine wasn't going to get angry with me, but that part I could supply for myself.

Waiting for it was like having a long-distance lover and pining for his arrival. Every day without it felt shallow and empty to the point that even my clients noticed. "Claire, I think you need to get laid," one of the most famous actresses in the world said to me and I knew she was right; she just didn't know how right. The day the machine was set to arrive, I called in sick and waited anxiously. I couldn't risk my new master being misdelivered or, heaven forbid, the doorman peering too closely at the box and wondering what exactly it contained. Even though I'm sure the neighbors in my upscale high-rise have heard plenty of moaning, yelling, and spanking coming from behind my door, I've never out and out admitted that I'm the girl in 12D who likes to get spanked, who likes to role-play, who lets her lovers use and abuse all her orifices after a good, hard smackdown; who loves to wince the next day as she sits down in her skirt suits, wondering if the men who sit across from her at meetings or lunches, the reporters who press her for details, know exactly what's caused the expression on her face. What I do inside the confines of my well-upholstered apartment is my business.

For the special day, I wore my favorite jeans and a loose white top, leaving the pearly buttons undone to the center of my bra. I went online and read story after story of naughty girls who needed to be spanked. Some of them horrified me; I mean, I'm a middle-aged businesswoman, and I was getting off on the idea of girls half my age getting paddled by their former teachers right after they'd graduated? Well, yes, I was. All those pretty young things in their schoolgirl skirts made me long to be eighteen or nineteen again, innocent and carefree. How I'd wasted my early years, content to do it in the dark, under the covers, missionary or, if I was lucky, on top.

Marco hadn't even let me suck his cock, telling me that such behavior was unbecoming of a young lady like myself. Of course, when he wasn't around, I'd spent copious solo masturbation time fantasizing about a man who didn't give a shit what was ladylike or even what I would be into; he'd take from me exactly what he needed, pulling my hair, slapping my ass, and "forcing" me to suck his cock. Those fantasies got me through countless boring classes, solo expeditions, and even a few sessions with Marco.

And now, perhaps, I was simply doing what I was destined to do: take the spanking that rightly belonged to me. That's right; this was all about empowerment. I jolted in my seat, feeling heat rising to my cheeks as my doorbell rang, and wondering if I had a just-been-fucked flush on my skin. I buttoned my jeans back up and gave myself a once-over in the mirror, then raced to the door and flung it open. It should say a lot that I barely glanced at the muscular young man before me. He looked like a college student; way too young for me, but that had never stopped me before.

"Good afternoon, ma'am," he said, almost killing my sex buzz. "Where shall I put this?" I'd pondered and pondered that question, but had opted for the only real space I had available: my living room. The bedroom would've been more discreet, but it also would've swallowed it. Besides, I live alone and I have the right to get off in any room I damn well please. I'd certainly spent plenty of nights sprawled on my couch with my vibrator pressed against my clit while watching a dirty movie.

I watched him put the box down, then wipe his brow with a handkerchief. "Would you like something to drink?" I asked, more out of rote politeness than any real desire to delay him. I wasn't looking to seduce him, or even flirt, which was new for me; usually men like him were a challenge to me, a pleasant distraction from the rush of my daily business dealings.

But I'd just plunked down a very healthy amount of cash for something that would distract me any time I wanted, so when he asked for a beer, I just smiled and went to get it. I took one for myself as well, cracking them open and feeling the wetness in my panties as I walked back to him. "Feel free to sit down," I said, my fingers itching to open the box but willing myself to wait.

"Do you need any . . . help?" he asked. It was only when the red splotches sprang up on his cheeks that I realized he might have a clue as to the contents of my very special box.

"What kind of help did you have in mind?"

I wasn't embarrassed, though I was surprised that my secret had somehow been revealed. I truly hoped the company was discreet enough to leave the word *spanking* off their packaging. "Well, I just . . . it was pretty heavy, and maybe you need some help assembling . . . whatever's inside." He turned his mouth to the rim of his beer bottle and sucked hard, avoiding my eyes.

"Do you have some special expertise in assembling . . . machinery?" I asked, making sure he noticed my eyes drop from his face to his crotch.

"Not special, exactly, but I'm handy," he said after another long sip from the bottle.

"Handy. Hmm ... well, maybe you can be of service," I said, draining my own bottle, then walking over to the box. I slipped my Swiss army knife out of my pocket and neatly sliced through the box. He stood and walked over to me and I felt that familiar electricity crackle between us, the kind where all you have to be is one person in a room with another and suddenly, no matter their age or sex or anything else, your body reacts in a way that means you want to fuck this person as soon as possible. I would've groaned, but I was too intent on getting my machine set up.

He didn't speak then, just put his hands on the box and slid it away so the spanking machine was revealed, although it didn't quite look like the BDSM fantasy sex toy of my dreams so much as it really did appear to be an exercise bench. When all the parts were on my living room floor, I just stared at it. It really was going to be up to me to take the reins, to top from below, because the machine wasn't going to start itself!

"Do you need any help ... ma'am?" he asked tentatively. Even though he wasn't my type – too short, and not take-charge enough to light my subby soul on fire – I paused for a moment as I wondered whether I did, in fact, want his help; want him to watch me bend over, orchestrate my own submission to a machine made for just such a purpose. Ultimately, I declined, putting a tip in his hand and giving him what I hoped was a mysterious smile. I like to think that he had an inkling what my machine was all about, and went home and jerked off to the image of me getting my bottom smacked again and again.

But I had more important things to worry about. This behemoth in my modest living room was, effectively, my new lover. I had to name him – and yes, it had to be a him. I stroked my hands over the metal, then the spanking implement, the one that would presumably hit me hard enough to make me see stars, the good kind, that would smack every bit of doubt or confusion or depression out of me and leave me simply tingling. I settled on "Hulk", a beefy, macho name, one that no real man would ever possess. I planned to have a long relationship with Hulk and I worried that if I named him, say, Jerry, I'd someday meet a man with the same name and my fantasies would get muddled.

So I put Madonna on the stereo, opened a bottle of wine, spread out the instructions and started assembling. The process didn't take long, but I was nervous about making everything right. There's nothing worse than being primed for a spanking and then not getting it. After an hour of screwing pieces into place, I had to admit that Hulk looked exactly like he had on the website and in the brochure. I got naked, dropping my clothes on the floor, simply because I could. I changed the CD so that "Hanky sPanky" was playing. Then I settled myself upon Hulk, my bare pussy meeting the leather of the cushion as my breasts mashed against the upper part of the seat.

I kissed Hulk for good measure, then secured my arms into the slots for them, a simulacrum of bondage since I could, of course, escape. Then, holding the remote control in my hand, I pressed it, and down came the mechanical arm to smack my right cheek. "Yes," I hissed to myself, as the familiar feel of being spanked echoed through my body. It didn't matter that the only human involved in the process was me. I love submission, yes, but I also love the pure physical joy of getting spanked good and hard, and I had started out not at the lowest level, but one of the middle settings.

I squirmed excitedly as Hulk's next blow landed. I shut my eyes and cleared my mind as best I could. The smacks continued at a steady clip, and soon I was lost in the same sweet spanking sensations I'd been craving. It didn't matter that they weren't coming from a human hand; in a way, it was even better, because unless I'm with someone truly wicked, in the back of my mind there's often that niggling concern that they're getting bored or their hand is stinging or they'll be expecting something from me. All the Hulk expected was my bare bottom. I kissed the seat and spread my legs, relishing the wetness as I turned the dial to get the machine to spank me harder.

It really kicked into gear and I whimpered, the pain shooting through my lower half. I held on tight, lifting my ass slightly to make the whacks come even faster. While of course the machine could never rival a human in disciplinary tactics, it seemed to make up for it with the stern, even whacks it doled out. Yes, I had the ultimate power to stop it, but I didn't want to. It was like the machine was testing me, and I was testing the machine; who would win? I wanted to hold out as long as possible, at least, until I couldn't anymore.

As I let myself go to the highest level of spanking, where the whacks came so fast and furious it was like one continuous smack, I started to go to another place, as if I were looking down on myself. I wasn't sobbing or whining or begging; I became one with the machine. I plunged my fingers into my pussy with one hand, shifting around so my entire broad bottom could get its spanking fix. When I came, my fingers were drenched, and when I finally got it together to press stop, the world seemed quiet, like it had stopped entirely in the time it took me to get spanked. I cleaned off the machine, then examined my butt; indeed, its normally pale skin was marked by pink lines and an overall reddish tone. Even better, all that misplaced sexual energy that had been churning through me, looking for a proper kinky outlet, had found it. I felt at peace, truly satisfied, even though I hoped to someday be able to share my machine with a lover.

I plan to write to the company that makes my spanking machine praising them, and suggesting some additions for future models. I hope that with advances in technology, new versions will be able to speak to the user and tell her what a naughty girl she's been, along with reading her body temperature and movements and sensing when she needs a stronger spanking, even if she's not quite ready to request it. For now, though, I have a daily date with my spanking machine. I usually use it in the morning, when others are going to the gym to use other, slightly more masochistic machines. I walk out of my building with a grin that has everything to do with my blushing bottom and being able to afford the best spankings money can buy.

Raw

Adam Berlin

I craved raw fish. And like an addict, from the first time I ate perfect
sushi, carefully cut, colorfully presented, dark soy sauce, green
wasabi and white rice highlighting the delicate pink and pale and
red fish flesh, I was smitten. It was like love. All of my money went
to eating sushi. I worked and I went out to eat. I worked to go out to
eat. I ate sushi until I was full and then I rested and ate more sushi
until I was beyond full. Unlike other foods, the craving was back
the next day and, as I plodded through my nine-to-five, I dreamed
of sushi, all kinds of sushi. Plain sushi and sushi rolls, simple rolls
wrapped in seaweed and inside-out rolls rolled in sesame or roe,
maki tuna and yellowtail and salmon and eel and combination rolls,
exotic, innovative rolls. And the more sushi I ate, the better the sushi
needed to be. A ten-dollar hand of blackjack becomes dull with time
and so the player bets twenty-five dollars and then a hundred dollars
a hand and when he wins, he bets more, thousands of dollars just to
keep the high going. A gambler who bets six figures a hand is called
a whale. Fish and addiction. The addiction of fish.

The first time I fell in love was at Nobu. I was there with a first date
who had a reservation, made a month before. She'd just broken up with
her boyfriend and to exact revenge she went to Nobu without him. I'd
met her at a bar the night before, and she'd invited me out. I'd always
liked food. The New York City social life is defined by food, meals out at
name restaurants the measure of cool. So we went to Nobu after drinking
at a nearby bar, and to keep our buzz going, to keep concentration from
cutting into the high, we'd asked the waitress to order for us. This was
no diner waitress pushing the daily leftover special. At Nobu everything
was fresh and so the waitress had suggested this cut and that cut of fish
and, drunk, we'd taken all of her suggestions.

After the miso soup that tasted of faraway seas, after the creamy-
spicy shrimp tempura, one of the best dishes I'd ever eaten, after the

delicately glazed cod, the sushi appeared. When I hadn't been staring into my date's eyes, which I already knew were good enough to stare at drunk but not sober, I'd been watching the sushi chefs work. Our table was close enough to distinguish the different widths of the knife blades. There were two wiry men, who cut the raw fish in fast, crisp gestures, and one man, tall for a Japanese man, with the thickness of an athlete grown-up. The muscles under his white chef's suit looked menacingly solid and his face was strong and impenetrable, a block of a face that enforced the inscrutable stereotype. He cut the sushi like it was a show, but a show for himself, his gestures economical. After each cut he'd wipe his knife with a hint of flourish, and when he placed the flat plates of sushi on the counter for the waitstaff to pick up, he would nod, once, for himself. I was drunk so I thought I could hear the sound he wasn't speaking, the internal sound he made each time he nodded his head. Haiii. Like a karate movie, fist through a board.

The platter was set on our table. It was a piece of art. The different colored rolls were beautifully arranged, each with a mosaic inside, flecks of green and orange highlighting the more subtle fish colors, the fanned tail of a shrimp emerging from the center of a large roll as if beckoning us to eat. And we ate. The hot wasabi and salty soy sobered me and my sushi-drunk was better than any alcohol high. I ate beyond full. I couldn't get enough of the raw fish. If I'd been fucking instead of eating, and I would not have traded those Nobu rolls for anything, not anything, my cock would have been ripped raw. When we left the restaurant, me walking chivalrously behind my date who'd insisted on paying since, she desperately said, I'd made her forget her ex completely, I made eye-contact with the thick sushi chef. He nodded once for me and I nodded once for him.

I had no type. I had fucked them all, every age and race and ethnicity, from every continent, and not because I was playing Around the World. It just happened that way. I think most thirty-seven-year-olds, if they were still single and enjoyed the single life that was New York City, would have been around the world several times. But when I saw her, walking out of Sushi Samba just before I was walking in, I stopped. Nothing made me stop when sushi was the destination, but she did. My sushi could wait an extra minute even if I had spent the day in my cubicle dreaming of Brazilian fusion rolls. She was beautiful, but there are many beautiful women in New York City. She wasn't the most beautiful woman I had ever seen, not at all. Her eyes were a little too close together and her nose was a little wide and her body, while thin and fit, did not have the long, lean minx-quality that was as close to a type as I came. But her mouth was perfect. Her lips were the color of the best cut of tuna, rich and red and moist-looking and, seeing her lips, I couldn't help but think about what her other lips looked like. I pictured her. I pictured myself in her. My cock inside two perfectly cut, sushi-colored lips. I had to stop. And I had to talk. I wasn't even drunk, but I was drunk with wanting her and so, standing there on the crowded side of Seventh Avenue, I forced myself to block out the noise and block out my need for fusion rolls served with three flavors of dipping sauce, and I looked in her eyes instead of her mouth.

"You," I said, simple and clean, one-word raw.

She didn't say anything. But her eyes were clear and she didn't move her eyes.

"Even if you're full, even if you're stuffed, come back inside with me and let me buy you one more roll," I said.

Her lips parted in a smile. Her teeth were white, white as rice, highlighting the healthy pinkness of her un-lipsticked lips. She knew her lips were beautiful, that they needed no enhancement. But she didn't know, I didn't think, that her lips looked good enough to eat.

"I'm with a friend," she said. "He's just using the bathroom."

"A friend?"

"Yes." Her voice was playful. Maybe she'd been drinking sake and the whole world looked fun. "A friend."

"A friend, or a boring date you just realized is only worthy of being a friend?"

"Well done," she said.

I took my business card and put it in her hand. "Call me," I said. "You have to call me. We'll go out for sushi. We'll go out for the best sushi we can find."

"I love sushi," she said and her smile was up-to-something. Her eyes were alive.

"I love it too."

"Well then," she said.

"Tomorrow," I said. "Call me. I think your friend is coming out of the restaurant right now so hide my card and call me tomorrow and we'll eat sushi together tomorrow night."

I was right. It was her friend. He came over to her and took her arm, tentatively, and she let him, but I wasn't really watching him.

I was watching her and, like magic, my card disappeared into her hand.

I went into Sushi Samba, sat alone at the sushi bar, ordered a full plate of spicy tuna and yellowtail and fusion rolls. I watched the sushi chefs work. It was a performance the way they rolled, cut, separated, displayed the sushi on colorful plates. I took my chopsticks from their paper holder, moved one stick against the other, wood on wood, like making a fire.

I picked her up at her door. I was never this chivalrous, good-looking enough to simply hold a door once in a while without ever having to pay for a cab, but she was not just another woman. Her mouth, when she came out of her midtown office building, was as I remembered. Her lips were almost more perfect. The perfect thickness, the perfect color. The perfect texture, I guessed. I had already kissed her in my head, had already bitten down on her lower lip, had already tasted the salt of her blood, like the salt of the sea. I forced my lips away from her mouth and gave her a polite kiss on her cheek, but let my lips stay there for a moment so she'd know I more than liked her. I'd made reservations at Haru on the Upper West Side. Nobu had been booked solid and I didn't want to spend hours drinking cocktails at a nearby bar until a table at Nobu Next Door could be secured. Bond Street was booked. Blue Ribbon Sushi was booked. I wasn't the only one who lusted sushi.

Haru was not great, but it was good, and some nights it was very good, and that's where we went. On the taxi ride up, we made small talk, ran through abbreviated versions of our biographies. She knew it was just talk and I knew it was just talk so after a while we stopped talking background and just talked, punching and counter-punching like we'd known each other for a long time. The cab pulled in front of Haru and I reached for my wallet. While I handed the driver the bill, I looked at her lips.

Haru was crowded, but I had a reservation and they gave us a nice corner table in the back where we could sit next to each other and have a view of the other diners and of the sushi chefs rolling and cutting.

"I love sushi," I said.

"I love sushi too," she said.

"Why?"

She looked at me and smiled. It was an impossible question.

You can look up love in the dictionary and the definition is meaningless. Sushi's definition would be even further from the truth, a simple noun defined as simple raw fish, but the woman in front of me knew it was more, knew the word didn't come close to what sushi was, and I could see her thinking, really thinking about the why, and then I could see her forming her answer. I admired how she thought before she spoke and I watched her mouth move, just slightly, as she went from one thought to the next to the revision of the thought into words before she spoke.

"Sushi is pure. It tastes pure, tastes like it should go into your body, and it looks pure. They're perfect cuts of fish, as if they could be stacked one on top of the other. When I eat a lot of sushi I picture it in my stomach, the pieces stacked one on top of the other. And then I picture my body taking the pieces into it, one perfect piece at a time, the fish flesh making my blood red and my flesh pink and my skin smooth and my heart strong and alive. That's why I love it. It's pure. It's the perfect food."

"When it's perfect, it's as perfect as anything in the world," I said.

The sushi came. The raw flesh glistened so wetly it could have been alive. I had read of such sushi. A master chef would take a fish from a tank, cut off a strip of flesh, throw the fish back in the water and the fish would swim, while the chef prepared the sushi.

We ate quietly. There was no need to dilute the experience with talk and she seemed to know this. Her lips were as perfect as sushi and I pictured the pieces of fish stacking up in my stomach and then another picture came to me. Her lips. Not her lip lips, but the lips hidden by the tablecloth that shielded her lap. I pictured a piece of those lips stacked in my stomach and I felt a rush go through me, more intense than the greatest craving. I put my chopsticks down and looked at her and I nodded my head, like the thick-muscled sushi chef at Nobu.

"I want to take you to Nobu one day."

"There are sushi places better than Nobu," she said.

"I know. But Nobu was my first and I want to take you there."

"Why did you stop me last night?"

"I had to."

"You didn't have to. How did you know I wasn't dating a jealous man who would hurt you if he saw you giving me your card."

I lifted my arm, made a muscle, asked her to feel it.

"So you would have hurt him."

"I don't fight," I said.

She moved her hand over my forearm. "That's the muscle of a hoodlum," she said.

"I was born with it."

"You have hoodlum in your blood."

"I have sushi in my blood. Or it will be in my blood. First I have to stack it in my stomach."

"That's the image I have," she said and picked up a piece of yellowtail scallion roll, dipped it in the soy and wasabi, moved it into her mouth.

"It's a perfect image. Can you keep stacking?"

"I can stack sushi all night," she said and there was no hint of sarcasm in her voice.

"Then we will."

I called over the waiter and ordered more. More and more. I watched the waiter move to the sushi bar, place the order. The chefs started cutting.

I took her to my place. I never took them back to my place, preferred the option of making a speedy bolt in that limbo-moment between drunk and hungover, but I wanted her in my place. I didn't want to know where she lived or how she lived. I didn't want to know anything about her. It felt more pure that way. I just wanted to know her, know her lips, know how they felt. I had kissed her in the cab. Her lip lips were perfect and I tested her immediately, kissed her and kissed her and then I pressed my teeth into her lower lip and she took it without a flinch of protest and I pressed harder and she took it and I grew bone hard. I tasted the salt of blood and stopped biting. I kissed her lips gently. The cab stopped. I took her hand, took her up to my bedroom, undressed her on my bed.

I liked to keep the lights on. A friend of mine, a hunter himself but not a lover of sushi, was the same way. We loved to see it, spread it. We always joked how we would be happiest to go to bed with a miner's hat on our heads, the attached flashlight providing the perfect beam of light to look deep. It was all about the mystery for us. We weren't tit men. We weren't ass men or leg men or feet men or eye men. We were cunt men. It was all about the slit of skin, the pink flesh, the mystery, which, we knew, we'd never fully see no matter how bright the light.

But I kept the light on and her lip lips had not lied. Her cunt was perfect. She had waxed so I could see its perfect definition, its perfect symmetry. I put a finger inside her and opened the two lips, the color of perfect sushi. I worked another finger in and opened her more and then I put my cock inside her and did what I did best, listened to her, put my head in her head and listened to what would get her there, sensing the tide and then moving to it, closer and closer, picturing the beginning of her orgasm like a small wave, just starting, still far from shore.

And that's what I said in her ear, that's what I said in all of their ears, but none of them had ever felt perfect. I worked for her, talked to her about the wave, about the growing wave, moved to the growing wave, and the wave started to gather water, started to gather strength, the salt water starting to foam, and I moved to it, harder to it, faster to it, talking to her the whole time, making her picture the wave, making her realize I was the only man who could truly fuck her, the wave getting bigger, her voice starting to take over my voice, and I fucked her and fucked her until the wave peaked, was right there, too high to fold in on itself, too high to go back, too high. It was going to crash.

"Let it crash," I said.

"Yes," she said.

"Let it crash all the way. Let it all go. All of it."

"Yes," she said.

"Go," I said.

The wave crashed. I lifted myself up, straightened my arms, looked down at her lips, perfect lips, sushi-perfect. I felt the wave start in myself and kept my eyes right there, right there.

For a full month, every Saturday night, we met and ate sushi and fucked. Each time in bed I went further and further. I pressed my finger hard into her palm, moved my finger up her wrist, up her forearm, hard, harder, streaking her skin red, and I listened. I listened to her sound, listened to hear if it was pain or pleasure. I pressed harder each time and the sound was the same sound she always made, only louder. Pleasure. I took her nipple between my thumb and forefinger and squeezed until my fingers cramped, and the sound was pleasure. I took a knife from the kitchen, moved it along the inside of her thigh, then back, back and forth, pressing in harder every time and finally I cut the skin, a thin line that didn't really bleed and would heal in a moment and the sound was pleasure. She took it and then she took me and I came into her, my sushi-fed sperm shooting forward, strong and strong and strong.

I waited outside Nobu. I knew the kitchen closed at midnight, but I didn't know how long the sushi chefs took to close their station. There were knives to be wiped clean, counters to be scrubbed, fish to be wrapped, uniforms to be put into the laundry, hands to be washed. I pictured what they had to do. It passed the time. I wondered if I would even bother washing my hands, or if I would keep the fish smell on me at all times. I watched the diners coming out of Nobu, glowing from fish and sake. They were different from steak eaters. Steak eaters looked slow. Too full, they were more interested in sleeping than fucking. The sushi-eaters were full of life, their blood fortified, the stacked fish in their stomachs providing energy, not sucking energy the way meat did, pulling blood into the stomach so that the rest of the organs, the rest of the muscles grew fatigued.

The last people came out, two couples, together, laughing and glowing. Each couple walked hand in hand, energy in their steps, moving fast into the lit darkness of New York City.

The sushi chef came out.

He was shorter than he looked behind the sushi bar, but his muscles were as thick, his arms bunched up under a T-shirt, his neck mighty, his broad face hard. He was done performing and his brutality seemed more quiet, more dangerous.

"Excuse me," I said.

He turned to me. He looked at me. He didn't say a word. He didn't nod.

"I always admire you when you work," I said. "And I wanted to know, what's the trick to cutting perfect sushi?"

"The trick?"

"Maybe that's the wrong word. What's the technique?"

"A technique takes years to perfect."

"I don't have years," I said.

"Are you dying?" he said.

"No. But I have to know."

I looked the sushi chef in his hard eyes, made my eyes just as hard, like before a fight, when you put everything away, all life away, like you could fight to the death because your eyes are already there. I had the same nervous feeling going. I was alive and dead at the same time. Nine times out of ten the other guy backed down, but there was no back-down in the sushi chef.

"A sharp knife," he said.

I waited.

"The sharpest knife," he said. "I brought my knife from Japan when I came here as a young man."

"What else?"

"You must commit to the cut. You must never hesitate once you start the cut."

"Never hesitate," I repeated.

This time the sushi chef waited. His eyes were more open now, taking me in, letting me take him in.

"I want to cut a piece," I said. "I feel like I'll fully appreciate eating sushi if I know what it's like to cut the fish."

"You already appreciate sushi."

"How do you know?"

"When I'm working, I see everything around me. I have seen you in Nobu many times. Every time I see the pleasure in your face."

"I love sushi," I said.

"Haiii," he said and smiled. He nodded his head once for me and started to walk away.

"Wait," I said and he stopped. "I need your knife," I said. "Just for one night. I promise I'll return it to you tomorrow. I'll be here as soon as you start your shift. I'll be here before you start your shift. I promise."

"Do you know how to use a knife?"

"You commit to the cut. You never hesitate."

The sushi chef looked at me. I let him into my eyes. The sushi chef turned, walked into Nobu, came out one minute later with a leather case. He handed the case to me. "I start my shift at four. Exactly at four."

The sushi chef walked away and I stood there for a moment, leather case in hand, the knife inside. Then I opened up my cell phone and made the call.

I met her downstairs and paid for the cab. I treated her like a princess. I'd never believed in princesses, too jaded to see the fairy tale in anyone, but when I thought of her, thought of her in the world outside my bed, I pictured her as a fish princess, swimming through the crowds of New York City, raising herself above the people for a playful moment before diving back down. And when she was with me, I pictured her coming up for air all the way, the most beautiful fish princess, but unlike a fish, whose colors were most vivid underwater, she was perfect on land, most perfect spread out on my bed. And I felt perfect too. Inside her was where I was supposed to be. Inside me was where she was supposed to be.

She kissed me hard. I kissed her hard back, bit into her lip.

"Where are we going?" she said.

Whenever we met, we ate sushi first. Pieces and pieces of sushi and then, nourished, we would be ready.

"We're eating in," I said.

"In?"

"I already ordered. Lobster tempura rolls. Inside-out maki rolls. Yellowtail and tuna rolls. One eel roll for you. And one roll with nothing in it."

"An empty roll?"

"For me."

She smiled and I smiled. I took her hand and walked her into my building, up to my apartment, into my bedroom. I undressed her and spread her out on my bed.

I kissed her lip lips, and moved my tongue down, between her breasts, over her stomach, around the inside of her thighs, circling, and then I spread her lips apart and tasted her, fresh and salty, licked her and listened to her rhythm until she was almost there, right at the line, the line that separated coming and not coming, as impossible to measure as the line between sky and ocean on the horizon, and that thin. I kept her there, kept her there until the door buzzer rang and I took my head from between her legs. She kept moving herself forward, fucking an imaginary me.

"Sushi," she said.

"Sushi," I said and went to the door, stood by it, waited for the Japanese delivery man to ring the bell. The bell rang and I paid the man, took the bag, went into the bedroom. I'd bought a flat, aqua blue platter and I put it on the bed. I unpacked the sushi and arranged the rolls on the platter, the eel roll closer to her mouth, the empty roll, just inside-out rice with a hole in the middle, closer to me. I took the leather case and put it by the bed. I moved my head between her legs and took her to the line once more and then I lifted my head and told her to wait.

I loved the sound she made and she was making it.

I put myself inside her and started to move.

I took a piece of the eel roll, dipped it in the soy sauce and wasabi, fed it to her, her lips holding my finger for a moment, her tongue licking a final drop of soy from my skin. She made the sound. She loved sushi.

I fed her the whole roll, all six pieces, and while I fed her I fucked her and I brought her right there, but I didn't let her come. She wanted to. She wanted to after the first piece and she wanted to more with the second piece and up and up, all six pieces stacking up in her stomach, feeding her. I put my head next to her head, my mouth to her ear, and I whispered what I wanted. I moved inside her and told her exactly what I wanted to do and she didn't flinch, just like she never flinched. It would be the smallest piece, the smallest smallest piece, and it would feed me, become a part of me, the most romantic thing I would ever do if she would let me do it and I moved in her and moved in her and the only sound she made was the sound she made.

I lifted myself off her and picked up the leather case. I'd already pictured what I would do so many times, so many times since the first time I'd been between her perfect lips.

I opened the leather case. I took out the knife.

It was the sharpest knife I'd ever seen. I'd read of Ninja swords, how the artisans melted the steel, folded and refolded it, over and over until it could cut a man's hair in two, lengthwise. This knife was not a weapon. But I pictured an artisan folding the steel, testing it on a raw piece of fish, cutting the slightest sliver, perfect. That was all I wanted. The slightest sliver. To be inside of her and have her inside of me, fortifying me, making her mine. It had always been just an expression. Your cunt is mine. I said it in their ears when I was fucking them, making them come, but with her, her perfect lips, her love of sushi, I wanted her cunt to be mine. I wanted to commit to more than the words. I wanted to commit to the cut.

She looked at the knife. I had cut her before, and she had taken it. I pressed the cool steel against her belly and moved my cock inside of her. She made her sound.

"It's a sushi knife," I said, my voice becoming a whisper, as if this blade, this work of art that turned raw fish into works of art, was too sacred to talk about too loudly.

"I know," she said.

"It's from Nobu."

"Nobu," she whispered back. "Where you had your first sushi." She remembered everything.

"The sushi chef gave it to me."

"Does he know why you want to use it?" She was breathing heavy.

"Do you know why?" I whispered.

"Of course. I knew before you told me. And I trust you enough to let you."

"How did you know?"

"When we met, you weren't just talking. You gave me your card, you took me for sushi, you take me for sushi every night, and you whisper things in my ear. I listen. I listen between the words. You make me feel good and this will make you feel good."

"You won't even feel it."

"I want to feel it a little."

"Just a little."

"And then we'll say good bye," she said.

"You do listen between the words," I said.

"The words stack up," she whispered and I moved inside of her, to get her to that place again.

When she was there, when she was on that edge, I opened her up, took a piece of her lip and pulled it taut. The flesh was perfect pink. I pressed the knife's fine edge against her lip and committed to the cut.

One. Two.

It was just a sliver, the smallest sliver, a tiny V of raw, live flesh.

A drop of blood formed, bubbled and then popped into a thin line of red. I took her flesh and put it into the empty roll. I did not need soy sauce or wasabi. I wanted this pure. I put the roll in my mouth and held its flavor there and I fucked her for me. She was making her sound and I fucked her harder and I didn't have to tell her to go over now, she knew the words and between the words, all the words, all the meals, all the nights stacked up.

She started to come and I let myself come and right at that moment, me inside of her, her inside of me, I swallowed the roll.

Perfect.

She kept pressing against me. I lifted myself up so I could look down at her. At her perfect lips.

I was the master sushi chef, the story come to life. I had taken a piece of the fish and then I had let the fish go. This fish would keep swimming. I had nothing else to take and so nothing else to give and this fish, my fish, uninjured, just missing a small perfect piece stacked inside me, would swim and swim, her colors vivid, human-vivid, swimming and swimming out of the water where she belonged.

Careful What You Wish For

D. L. King

"I've been thinking about sharing you with another woman; does that idea make your cock stand up and take notice? Oh, I see that it has definite possibilities."

Greg lay restrained by his wrists and ankles to the head and footboard. He was also blindfolded and gagged but he could hear just fine. His wife's words created a zing from his ears, straight to his balls, making his cock shudder. He'd found, aside from moans and groans when he was in this state, he could communicate his thoughts and emotions quite clearly through his cock, and Eagle-eyed Audrey always caught them.

Greg had been telling Audrey for months how he'd love to submit to her while her girl friends watched, or maybe even joined in. It seemed she'd finally taken the bait and he was going to get his fantasy.

"I have a friend, Moira, who thinks you're just adorable."

Greg smiled around the gag and a little more drool ran down the side of his face.

Audrey slowly inserted a well-lubed, gloved finger into his ass to the accompaniment of his sigh and moan. "And her boy is really quite special. He's about ten years younger than you and works as a personal trainer. I've been thinking that I wouldn't mind a bit handing you over to her and swinging with Ian. That would be fun, wouldn't it?"

Greg's eyes flew open inside his blindfold. No, no, no, this was supposed to be about him and other women. Audrey wasn't supposed to be with another guy. He made some appropriate noises and, even though the anal attention he was receiving was certainly arousing, he felt his cock begin to wilt.

"Oh, what's the matter, baby? Not what you had in mind?" She continued with her gentle massage until he was nice and hard again before applying a cock ring to keep him that way. "You know, my darling, Moira's also ten years younger than me, and very attractive. You could do worse.

"They have an open relationship and go to various swinging functions and play parties. Anyway, I've invited Moira over to meet you and get to know you a little better before making up her mind. She should be here any minute."

Audrey unbuckled Greg's gag to a quiet whine. After he licked his lips and worked his mouth, the first words out of his mouth were, "Today? Right now? Both of them?"

"Yes – and no, just Moira. She wanted to get a sense of what you're like to play with before committing. She saw you when you came to pick me up after the book club meeting last week and thought you were sexy, but she wanted to watch you in action, or at least, in flagrante, before making a decision."

"But . . ."

"Oh, there's the door. I'll just go and get that, shall I?"

Audrey stood up at the sound of the doorbell and, as she started to leave the bedroom, Greg turned his head to the sound of her footsteps and again said, "But . . ."

He heard the door open and the sound of Audrey and another woman talking and laughing and couldn't help but squirm in his restraints. He'd been fantasizing about submitting to another, severe woman, while Audrey stood by – or submitting to Audrey while another dominant woman – or maybe even *women* – watched but now it would be for real. He was getting more and more agitated and nervous. What if she didn't like him? What if she was too extreme? What if she wasn't extreme enough? What if she thought he wasn't worth her time? What if *he* didn't like *her*?

He heard footsteps coming towards the bedroom and decided fantasy and reality colliding, while he lay naked and bound, was a bit on the anxiety-producing side.

"Oh, this is very nice. I like what you've done with him. But that's kind of a sad little cock, isn't it?"

"No, actually, he has quite a nice cock. I think he's just nervous."

Audrey's words washed over him like a calming balm and he began to swell with pride.

"Ah, that's better. Yes, I see what you mean."

Greg felt a hand wrap around his growing member as his blindfold was removed. It took a minute for his eyes to adjust to the light but as soon as he could see again, he saw her. She was pretty, but not beautiful – not the way Audrey was beautiful. She looked like an

Irish stereotype: red hair, green eyes, white skin, freckles, but it was the black leather dress she was wearing that got his attention.

She stroked his erection and stared him in the eye. "You're a pretty little boy, aren't you?" she asked. She picked up a black leather bag from the floor and set it on the bed, between his spread legs. Opening the bag without breaking eye contact with him, she reached in and brought out a red riding crop. "Would you like to play with me, Greg?"

Audrey drifted to the head of the bed. She sat down next to him and began a light caress of his nipples. As they reacted to her touch, he turned his head to look at her and smile before feeling an intense stinging on the inside of his right thigh. His head immediately snapped back to watching Moira. Even though he was no longer gagged, he had grown used to not speaking unless required to do so.

"I asked you a question, boy."

He sucked in air and gasped. "Yes, ma'am."

"Boys are so easily distracted, aren't they?"

Audrey pinched one of his nipples hard and he gasped, turning again to look at her before he felt the rhythmic stroke of Moira's crop on the inside of his thighs. She alternated sides, and he was sure there wasn't a square millimetre of flesh that wasn't cherry red by the time she stopped. Audrey played sensuously with the top of his body, caressing his nipples, playing with his ears and kissing him, while his lower body was being punished. It was almost complete sensory overload.

As if with a silent agreement, they both stopped touching him at the same time. His cock bobbed and twitched as he panted and gasped.

"Oh yes, he'll do. You've seen Ian. What do you think, want to swing?"

"Totally," Audrey replied. "How about Saturday night at Franco's? About seven o'clock?"

"That place on Elm? Great; we'll be there." Moira made her way to the head of the bed and kissed Greg on the cheek. "I'm looking forward to it," she said, winking at him. She turned and, with a no-nonsense motion, sent the crop into the depths of her bag, snapped it shut and walked out the door, followed by Audrey. Greg couldn't help wondering just what else she had hidden in there.

His wife came back, after showing Moira out, and set to unfastening him from his restraints. "Well, that's enough excitement for you today! You should save some of that energy for Saturday; it's only three days away, you know."

"Are you sure this is right? You sure you really want to do this? I was only talking about a little scene with one of your girlfriends watching or something."

"Yes, baby, I'm sure."

"So, you're talking about sex and everything?"

"Well, yes, of course. I mean, I guess we could just switch off and play, but I thought it would be fun to really swing. Why, you're not attracted to Moira?"

Greg just stared at her for a moment, not sure of the proper response. How do you tell your wife you're hot for someone else? It's not like he wasn't still hot for Audrey – he adored Audrey and was turned on by just thinking about her at least ten times a day. But Moira was exciting. And actually, the thought of Audrey playing with and fucking another man was also kind of exciting. Hoping he wasn't digging his own grave, he said, "Well, yeah, I guess I am. Is that OK?"

"Of course it's OK; that's the whole point."

"So you're not mad or anything?"

"Don't be silly. That's why I arranged this."

After three days of almost constant arousal, Greg found himself handing the car keys to the valet at Franco's. Audrey had picked out his clothes – a royal blue silk shirt and black wool pleated trousers, a black sport jacket and no tie. The shirt contrasted beautifully with his dark hair and set off his blue eyes to best advantage. Audrey looked amazing in a black raw silk pencil skirt and a white silk blouse with silver cuff links. The skirt fell just below her knees and the blouse fell open almost to the middle of her chest. Her honey-colored hair had been slicked back in a tight chignon at the nape of her neck. She was devastating.

She patted his ass and gave it a little squeeze when she met her at the front door to the restaurant. "Ready?"

Butterflies were swept into a hurricane in his stomach and bees buzzed in his balls as he nodded his head and opened the door for her. As they walked in, he glanced towards the bar but didn't see Moira. The fluttering subsided a bit until Audrey gave their name to the maître d', who nodded and said, "Yes, madam, your party is waiting for you at the table. This way please."

Just as Greg recognized Moira, seated at a three-quarter banquette, her blond and suntanned companion stood for Audrey as they approached. Ian looked like a kid, but a pretty impressive kid. He had tousled hair that looked like he'd just gotten out of bed and a trimly muscled chest, tapering to a small waist, all shown off by the fitted green sweater he was wearing. Audrey had said ten years younger, which put him at about twenty-nine. God, had he ever looked that good? His wife's eyes were sparkling.

"Why don't you sit here, by me," Moira said, patting the booth next to her. Her hair fell in waves, past her shoulders. Greg couldn't see past her waist, but she was wearing a softly gathered black halter-top, which appeared to be silk. As she turned to him and smiled he caught a glimpse of her nipples poking against the fabric and his butterflies woke up again.

The two couples shared a light dinner, accompanied by a nice champagne. Audrey ordered for them both, as did Moira for Ian. They ate lightly, so as not to be too full for the activities ahead and Audrey plied Greg with enough wine to help loosen him up.

Throughout dinner, Moira touched or caressed Greg's thigh for emphasis or attention and, as the evening wore on, he began to feel more and more comfortable with the whole idea. The butterflies were still there, but they seemed more like excited butterflies, rather than nervous butterflies.

Greg wondered if Audrey was touching Ian in the same way. Ian didn't seem the least bit nervous, but then he and Moira did this all the time. Well, maybe not *all* the time, but often enough. He wondered whose idea it had been; had Ian said the same thing about wanting other women to watch Moira dominate him? But, evidently, it worked to both their satisfaction. He was beginning to feel more and more comfortable with the idea and more aroused at the prospect of not only playing with another woman, but having sex with her as well.

When the check came, he reached for it, but Moira placed her hand over his. "No, let's let tonight be my treat." As she placed her credit card on the tray, she leaned over to him and spoke directly into his ear. "I'll exact payment from you later." As they got up to leave, it was quite obvious that her words had produced the desired effect. Sheepishly glancing at Ian, Greg noticed that he was in the same state.

Realizing he was slightly light-headed, Greg asked Audrey to drive. Moira and Ian arrived shortly after they did. Moira brought the same black leather bag from three days ago in with her. Once inside the house, Audrey ordered Greg to strip. Moira followed suit, telling Ian to take everything off and leave his clothes neatly folded by the couch.

Being naked in front of another woman gave Greg an immediate hard on. This was a completely new situation for him and he looked over at Ian. The man was essentially hairless. Greg couldn't tell whether his chest was naturally bare or had been waxed but he knew Ian's genitals had been shaved – or possibly waxed – as he was completely bare. He was so exposed that Greg felt embarrassed to look. He felt a hand on his chest and turned to see Moira studying him. She put her arm around his neck and licked, then kissed, one of his nipples. As it crinkled from the attention, she reached up and placed a gentle kiss on his mouth. He turned to see what Audrey was doing, but Moira brought his face back to her and kissed him much more deeply. The arm around his neck moved down to the middle of his back and she lightly ran her free hand down his side, causing goosebumps to form and his nipples to stiffen even more.

"Pick up my bag and show me to the guest room, Greg."

As he picked up the bag, he looked to Audrey, but she was already ushering a naked Ian towards their bedroom. Unsure of what to do with himself, he picked up the bag and looked to Moira before heading off after Audrey and Ian. Halfway down the hall, he stopped at a door. "This is the guest room, ma'am."

"You can call me Moira, after all, we're all friends here, aren't we? I think you're a little nervous, but there's nothing to be afraid of. Audrey and I have had several discussions and I know your limits. And, well, you know how to have sex, so I'm sure we'll have a fine time."

"You and Audrey have had several discussions?"

"Yes."

"About me?"

"Yes."

"And swinging?"

"Yes, of course. What's the matter, don't you think your wife listens to you? Now, I want you bent over the side of the bed, face down, that's right."

"But she didn't say *anything* to me about this. Nothing."

"Well, that's fine. Now put your head back down on the bed. You have such a lovely ass." She stroked his bottom gently. "Are you saying you don't want to do this?"

"No. I'm just saying . . . She never said anything to me. That's all." Greg felt a hard smack to his bottom and jumped just a bit.

"Ah, that's nice. Your skin colors right away." She peppered his bottom with hard spanks until her hand became almost as tender as his red behind, before pulling a few lengths of rope from her bag. "Now, let's see, how had Audrey fixed you to the bed before? Oh yes, of course. Turn over on your back now, Greg, in the middle of the bed, and spread your legs for me, that's right."

She fastened his ankles and wrists to the bedposts and stepped back to survey her handiwork. She unzipped her black leather pants and slipped them off, then her halter top. Leaving only her black thong on, she stood otherwise nude before Greg. He couldn't take his eyes from her creamy breasts and their small pink nipples. Noticing where his attention was centered, she cupped her breasts and kneaded them, pushing them up and offering them to him. Although his ass was on fire, his cock stood proudly.

"Is this what you want?" she asked, showing him her breasts. "Well, maybe as a reward – later." Reaching into her bag, she pulled out several items, showed them to him and laid them down on the bed. Among them was the same red crop she'd used on him days before, as well as a pair of gloves, some condoms and a bottle of lube. When she'd finished laying everything out, they heard a loud yelp from the master bedroom.

"There now, that's what I like to hear. Audrey says you like anal penetration. That's good. Maybe next time I can really fuck you. Today I'll just explore you with my fingers. But first, let's see about getting your front to match your rear."

Greg was still back at the yelp. He wondered what his wife had done to Ian to make him yelp like that. He'd sort of forgotten where he was and it wasn't until the crop hit his nipple and his own yelp brought him back to the present.

Moira rained smacks on his chest and both nipples until he was completely tenderized, then she went to work on his thighs again. Once his body was tingling and vibrating with sensation, she began to gently explore his anus, first just teasing the outside of his sphincter, then letting her gloved finger dip in and out while she played with his balls.

Greg had been hard for quite a while and the deeper Moira explored inside him, the tighter his balls became. When Greg pleaded with her to finally let him fuck her, she was ready for him. Kneeling between his legs, she'd been keeping close tabs on his arousal and already had the condom out when he begged. She rolled the condom down his cock and while he was fastened, spread wide for her, she removed her thong and settled herself on top of him, slowly impaling herself on his length.

He groaned his appreciation and began to rock his pelvis with the little mobility afforded him. Moira leaned forward and lay across his chest, stopping his motion. "Now Greg, you stay still; I'll do the work." She bit one of his nipples and gripped his cock tightly inside her until he squeaked. Easing up on him, she sat back and let her body rhythmically milk him until she felt him begin to shake.

"Don't you dare come. I'm not finished with you," she said.

"Please, Moira, I don't think I can last much longer."

Moira leaned forward enough to allow the base of his cock to rub against her clit as she bounced up and down on him to the music of his groans. "You just wait till I tell you. I know you know better than to come before me.

Her motion became more and more frantic until finally, in the middle of a stroke, she froze with his cock half in and half out of her. Greg could feel the vibration start in her body and transfer itself to his cock. Her orgasm broke over both of them like a storm and, somewhere in the middle of it, Greg came with a roar.

Once Moira relaxed, she rolled away from Greg and said, "I don't remember telling you to come."

"Sorry, Moira, I couldn't help it."

"I guess next time I'll have to deal with that."

Put back together and dressed, they made their way into the living room to find Audrey and Ian already there, sitting on the couch, talking.

"This is one sexy husband you have here," Moira said.

"Yours too," Audrey replied.

"We have this little club of couples into more than just swinging," Moira said. "We get together at each other's house about once a month. I thought you and Greg might like to join us. I think you'd fit in perfectly and I know you'd like the other couples in our kinky swing club."

Audrey looked at Greg and he grinned.

"Well, you think about it and let me know. I'll call you tomorrow, but now I think I need to get Ian home. Boys! They just come and go, don't they? I think yours needs to be put to bed too."

Greg could feel his eyes wanting to close, but got up to walk the other couple to the door, with Audrey. After they said their goodbyes and Greg closed the door, he put his arms around Audrey's waist and said, "Well, what did you think?"

"I think I'd like to see *your* privates shaved," she said, giving him a playful swat on the ass. "I'm exhausted! Let's go to bed."

The Communion of Blood and Semen

Maxim Jakubowski

On a day like this, I held her tight.

On a day like this, she put her head on my shoulder, said nothing but almost purred. It felt good. It felt right. She was wrapped up in layers of clothing, like in a cocoon as she sheltered herself from the daylight on this day like no other. My gift wrapped impossible fuck.

The sky was blue, not a cloud in sight and a chilly wind channelled its way down the city streets, insidiously digging its way through the fabric of our coats, freezing the bones all the way deep under the skin.

Her hands reached for mine. "Your skin is so warm," she said.

Hers was as cold as ice.

Had always been.

Her eyes were shielded from the brightness by dark glasses. I'd never known her without the glasses, even at night. Maybe that's what first actually caught my attention about her. I'd always felt that people who wear shades in all and inappropriate circumstances were pretentious, poseurs or worse. She'd been the exception.

A yellow cab drew up on McDougall, responding to my arm signal.

"JFK," I said as we bundled into the car. We had no luggage.

We'd met in Manhattan. On, of all places, Craigslist, the Internet Sargasso of obscene desire, barter, thievery, fakery and false identities. I was travelling on business and feeling lonely, as endless New York nights stretched on forever as both jet lag and the repeated assault of bittersweet memories combined fiendishly to keep me awake most of the night with my hand not far away from my cock. Caressing myself aimlessly as I recalled the walk down from Washington Square to Ground Zero with Gina, and the rubber stamp embossed with the words "I Love You" I'd bought along the way on a gift shop on Broadway: tendrils of lust rising through the thick trunk of my awakening cock. Remembering a night at the Gershwin Hotel where I'd, in a spirit of mad improvisation, crushed a few raspberries and pushed the pulp inwards with two fingers up the cunt of the New Zealand woman I'd picked up a few days before at Newark Airport, and then followed the fragrant fruit with a square of chocolate which quickly melted in the furnace of her innards before I finally lapped it all up with my tongue before we fucked: my cock now becoming half hard and just that bit longer and sending a hundred volts of sexual electricity all the way through my groin. The apartment a few blocks up from Columbus Circle where I'd mounted Pamela, the wife of an experimental Armenian jazz musician, and breached her sphincter quite roughly as Bruce Springsteen's "Candy's Room" from the *Darkness on the Edge of Town* album punctuated our rhythmic thrusts on the record player: by this memory I was hard again, at last.

But there was no point evoking other New York memories, of women, of bodies, of heartbreak: jerking myself off at three in the morning in a hotel bed would, I knew all too well, bring me no relief. It would not banish the thoughts, the images, the faces and cunts (every single one so different, so unique I could lose myself in a whole novel of genital descriptions, a journey through craters, gashes, crevices and infinite deeps of soft, ridged alluring flesh . . .). I needed reality, a body, eyes looking into mine as I caressed her skin, the smell of tobacco or food on her breath, the fragrance of a woman's sweat, the beating of heart deep inside.

So, I'd placed an ad online under Casual Encounters: "Visiting English Writer Seeks Companionship and Tenderness". Within a few hours there were three responses: Sarah just wanted to exchange mails about books but was reluctant to meet; Becky, who worked in a museum in Brooklyn, joined me for a sushi in Greenwich Village the next day but was too young and thick-waisted and just kept on talking about her college boyfriend; and Carmilla. Of course, I'd read LeFanu and the name and its vampiric allegiance appealed. There was a sense of danger about her. "I am available," she said, and the smile on her jpg spoke of sensuality and a curious sense of destiny. "If you enjoy taking risks."

"I'd not enjoy life if there were no risks to face. Risk brings you alive," I replied in my e-mail.

Little did I know.

We met.

She was even better than in the photo.

Her eyes like pools of black soot.

It was night. A small bar near Bleecker Street.

Within minutes I knew I had to have her.

I was surprised by the dry coldness of her flesh when I soon undressed her – we had wasted little time on preliminaries or undue conversation; somehow an exchange of meaningful glances, signals and silences had been enough to confirm that the No Strings Attached encounter we had both been seeking was going to happen right there and then that same night. But she sheltered quickly within my embrace and my external warmth migrated across the maddeningly smooth landscape of her flesh and spread its comforting tendrils. The scarlet lipstick that illuminated her features soon stained my lips and my own skin. Her small, hard breasts with night dark nipples sharp as blunt razors were grazing my chest, and even with the hotel room's main light off the delta of her cunt was like a deep primeval forest shining like a beacon in the heart of the darkness that surrounded us. We fucked. As soon as I was inside of her, I knew this was where I had always aspired to live, sheathed within her tightness, sliding effortlessly against the ribbed texture of her damp walls. Our mouths savagely vacuumed the contents of the other's lungs in unholy communion. I came quickly. Exhaled. But her cunt still gripped my cock like a vise and would not allow it to go soft. She arched her back under me.

"Do me again," she asked me.

I shifted, the tip of my penis now moving against her cervix. The coldness inside her drew me in even further. Her nails scratched my back and the pain felt good. It all felt good.

It was primitive, no doubt the way our ancestors first mated in deep forests under a pockmarked moon. It was right. It made us both feel so abominably alive.

Later, she took me inside her mouth, licking the primordial soup we had jointly created and which I had already tasted with relish after I'd gone down on her and savoured our combined and now intermingled fluids and secretions. As I expected we were a totally perfect cocktail even if at first my tongue delving into her had drawn back from the unaccustomed coolness of her insides, even after the repeated and frantic sex we had enjoyed. Her own tongue was at first as cold as ice but it only served to conserve my hardness. She licked and nibbled and allowed her teeth to teasingly draw sharp, hard lines against my aching, bulbous and purple head.

"I want to bite you," she remarked, her voice flat, neither in jest nor in lust.

"Somehow, I don't think I'd even mind," I responded with a smile.

I was hoping my joke would make her laugh, but instead when I looked down at her face, there between my thighs, her red lips still voraciously sucking on my cock, I noticed a single tear running down her cheek.

I chose not to comment.

Finally, we exhausted ourselves. We were both raw, aching in all the right places, coated with a patina of sweat and God knows what else and we must have fallen asleep simultaneously.

When I woke up some hours later, it must have been daylight outside, but the curtains were drawn. She was sitting on the opposite edge of the bed, with her back to me. The shape of her naked body was like a knife stabbing my heart: she was so fucking beautiful, every pale curve silhouetted against the muted light trying to enter the room was like a symphony of harmony, balance and grace. From the fall of her dark straight hair against her elegant shoulders, the shadow of her delicate breasts, the arch of her vertebrae straining gently against the skin, the faint down in the small of her back, the upper moon of her white ass; every body part reminded me of other women I had known, loved and pined for, Gina's ass, Kathryn's breasts, Aida's hair . . . But here they all came together in perfect harmony. My heart skipped a beat and my cock hardened yet again.

She heard me move and turned her face towards me. Her shoulders swivelled and I saw that her nipples were still as pointy and hard and aroused. And she had put her dark glasses on again.

We ordered breakfast with room service. There was no way we were leaving that bed and I guessed anyone looking at us that morning would have read every visible sign of debauchery and excess all over the two of us like an open page. She only wanted fruit juice. I also had a bagel with salmon and cream cheese. I was famished from our exertions.

"Aren't you hungry?" I queried.

Her eyes looked down at the mess that were the sheets in which we'd drowned our lust. "No."

There was a finality in her tone.

Soon after we pushed the breakfast tray on to the hotel room floor and she lowered her head towards my lap and again took my cock inside her mouth. The coldness and the fire returned. An uncanny duo of emotions and feelings.

Later, "Have you met many other guys this way through the Internet?"

"A few . . . It's the only way I can satisfy that hunger inside, you see," she remarked matter of fact, in no way apologetic.

"I think I understand," I said.

And so the next few days went on. In a whirlpool of madness, flesh rubbing against flesh, mouths drowning in the thin air from which we'd sucked all the oxygen in our frenzy of desire, body parts inflamed, stretched obscenely. We drew the worst out of each other, as if never before had we even skirted those dark borders of absolute need. We had no shame, no limits. I fisted her, hurt her even, but she begged me to push harder, further. She squatted over my spent body and urinated over me as I rubbed the cool ambrosia that stemmed from her innards all over my skin. Had she asked, I would have drunk from her cunt lips.

I don't know when we crossed the frontier from which there is no going back. Possibly the day I was scheduled to fly back to Europe and blithely missed my flight.

The more we stayed together, tested the very limits of our bodies, the more we knew we could never part. We now inhabited another world.

She scratched me badly one morning. Not deliberately. It was in fact surprising that the inherent violence in our movements, our coupling, had not caused more damage before. Sprains, bruises, cuts. The blood welled over my shoulder blade. Her sad features turned somehow even paler than usual as she watched the solitary drops of blood she had summoned lazily slide down over my chest like dark pearls.

"I feel like licking you," she said quietly.

"I wouldn't mind," I remarked. "Maybe the right way to celebrate our unholy union . . ."

"No," she said. "I would want you even more if I did."

She despatched me to the bathroom to clean up. But her eyes said something else.

Another morning, I cut myself shaving and again the look that spread across her features was an unsteady blend of hunger and utter despair.

She walked towards me with all the burdens of world weighing down her steps. Stopped just an inch away from me. Watching the minute flecks of blood on my chin. Her mouth opened. Her eyes clouded.

It's right then it all finally came together.

Her unnatural pallor.

The ambiguous clues she had unwittingly provided me with.

The ever present dark glasses and nocturnal life.

The origins of her name.

Why I never saw her eating food.

I asked her.

And she told me her story.

The tale of a beautiful vampire adrift in the confused life of a world in which she could never belong truly. How she survived. How sex could sometimes act as a substitute for the blood lust that kept her alive. But was never enough.

I'd read the innumerable books; heard of the countless legends.

"And if I allowed you to taste my blood, bite me . . . what would happen?" I asked her.

"You know," she said.

Yes I knew. I would die. But awaken anew as a monster. Another freak who could only survive the madness by feeding on the blood of others. As she had done for centuries.

But I loved her now. Of that I had no doubt. And I wanted us to stay together. Forever.

Now we had met, now we had come as one, neither of us could ever bear the loneliness of being apart again.

"I will," I said.

I maxxed my credit cards and we took a flight to Venice.

Our hotel is a converted palazzo and from our windows we have a half glimpse of the Grand Canal and further upstream the stillness of the lagoon. Maybe I'm too much of a romantic, but I wanted it to happen in a place like this.

On a day like this I have asked her to kill me so I can live forever and roam the land of death with her until the end of time, both now renegades, lovers in the blood, vampires.

The Woman in his Room

Saskia Walker

Luke had a woman in his room.

I could hear the familiar sound of his voice – gravely and seductive – as it filtered out of the partly open bedroom door. I paused on the landing and listened. There was music playing in the background, something sensual and rhythmic. Then I heard the woman's laughter, and something inside me altered.

The small part of me that was still immature balked because it was some other woman, and not me. But the part of me that was a young woman who was becoming more deeply aware of her own sexuality – the part that had been stimulated by my exposure to Luke in our home – responded altogether differently.

Desire, and the sure knowledge of my own needs, flamed inside me. The crush I had been nurturing for Luke changed. It wasn't an ethereal emotion cloaked in sighs of longing and wistful glances anymore. It was hardcore lust. And I liked it.

I liked this feeling of being a woman who had physical needs that were more powerful than her daydreams. I could just as easily be that woman in Luke's room. I wanted to be that woman, it was as simple as that.

I'd wanted Luke since the day he had moved in, three weeks earlier. I doubt my father would have let his business partner stay over after his wife threw him out had he known that I would develop an obsession with him. Dad thought I was far too busy at college. Too busy to notice a man like Luke? No way.

"You've met Luke, haven't you, Karen?" my dad had said when Luke walked into our house that first night, a suit carrier flung casually over one shoulder, an overnight bag in the other hand. I remember being glued to the spot, thinking that I'd surely have remembered him if I'd met him before. Apparently I had, briefly. Four years earlier. I guess I'd been different then. I'd been fifteen and a tomboy. Now I was at college, and my focus was on the adult world, with all its risks and discoveries.

Luke had set down the bag he held and put his hand out to me. "You've grown up," he said under his breath and looked at me with an appraising stare that made me feel hot all over.

I managed to put my hand in his. He held it tightly, drawing me closer in against him. I looked up into his wickedly suggestive eyes, and it made my pussy clench.

My mother disapproved of him. *Why had his wife thrown him out?* she demanded of my dad, when Luke was out of the house. Dad wouldn't answer. I made up my own reasons, fantasies that featured me in a starring role. Maybe he left his wife for a hot younger woman, me. The truth was that Luke moving in had made something shift in my world. He was a man, a real man. Sex with him wouldn't be like the fumbling bad sex I'd had with a guy I met at college. As soon as I saw Luke, I knew that it wouldn't feel like that, not with him. Sex would be exciting, maybe even kinky. The idea of it fascinated me.

Luke wasn't what you'd call handsome, but he was attractive in a bad boy sort of a way. Tall and leanly muscled, his body suggested athletic vigor. His features were craggy, his hair cut close to his head. He had a maverick quality about him that appealed to the dark side of my imagination. At night I'd lie in my bed and imagine there was no wall between our rooms and that I could reach out and touch his body. I'd imagine him responding. He'd climb over me and screw me into the bed, teaching me what it was like to be fucked by a real man.

During the day when he was out I would go into his room and touch his things. Sometimes I even lay down on his bed. I would close my eyes and breath him in, getting high on the smell of his body and his expensive cologne, the experience building up a frenzy of longing inside me. What if he walked in and found me there? The idea of being caught by him made it even worse. Sometimes I'd push my hand inside my jeans and press my panties into the seam of my pussy, massaging my clit for relief.

Then my parents went away for a fortnight, leaving me in Luke's care. Oh, the irony. If only they had known how much the idea of it excited me.

It was our first night alone, and I had been thinking about him all evening, barely aware of the blockbuster movie I'd gone to see with my friends. I wanted to get home, to see if Luke was there.

But now he had a woman in there with him, and that woman wasn't me.

I was intensely curious, and it struck me that I was getting hot just thinking about him having sex, even if it wasn't me he was having it with. The push-pull reaction of the unexpected situation had me on edge. Torn, I glanced at my bedroom door. He probably thought I was in there, asleep. Like a good girl. I looked back at his doorway and saw a shadow move across the room beyond.

His shadow.

I couldn't walk away.

Luckily I hadn't switched the landing light on. I was glad of the darkness, glad that I was standing in the gloom and that his door was open and I could see into his room. I'd had a couple of beers earlier. That probably helped, too. I stepped farther along the landing, until I could see him.

He had his shirt off. I'd seen him seminaked before, in the kitchen in the mornings. He'd have a towel round his waist, his body still damp and gleaming from the shower. I managed to muster up an early morning conversation so I could watch him pouring out coffee, stirring in three teaspoons of sugar as he chatted to me easily, watching me all the while. Watching me in a way that made my body feel womanly and alive. That's what he'd done to me; he'd made me feel alive. And although I remember saying something in response to his early morning conversations, it wasn't what I was thinking. What I was thinking was X-rated. I wanted him to bend me over the breakfast bar and introduce me to real sex.

The woman was sitting back on his bed, and he had his knees pressed against hers. As I watched, he bent over her and pushed her silky red dress up along her thigh, exposing her panties. Craning my neck, I could see that they were very small, a narrow strip of sheer black fabric. Luke stroked the front of them, and when he did her hips moved on the bed, rocking and lifting under his touch.

My pussy ached to be stroked that way. My pulse was racing. Would he strip? Would I see him naked, as I longed to do?

He spoke to her in a low voice. I couldn't hear what he said. Then he straightened up and she also moved, into an upright sitting position. The light was obscured and before I knew what was happening the door opened wide and Luke's shape filled the frame, a dark silhouette against the light behind him.

My hand went to my throat, but there was no time to try to escape.

"Well, hello," he said. He didn't sound surprised. Did he know I'd been there, watching?

"I was at the cinema, just got back." I could hear my own breathlessness. The light was behind him, but I could see that his fly was open, the belt on his jeans dangling suggestively down his thigh.

"I knew you were out here, Karen," he said more quietly. "I heard you come in. I was waiting for you to get back."

I stared at him in stunned silence. He knew I was here. He knew . . . he knew I wanted to go into his room and be with him, that was what he was insinuating. I could hear it in his tone. Did he know I'd already been in there, on his bed? I could feel my face growing hot.

He pushed the door wide open. The woman was sitting on the bed looking in my direction with a curious expression. Perhaps it mirrored my own. Even from here I could see she was pretty. She had jet black hair and a smile hovered around her ruby painted lips.

"Come in, join the party," Luke said. The casual remark was powerfully suggestive. It went right through me, thrilling every ounce of me. He lifted his hand. He was holding a glass, and I heard ice chink as he shifted it from side to side invitingly. "You know you want to."

I did want to. That's the moment I addressed what was inside me, what I was becoming – a woman who could be proactive about her desires. I had a choice, but I knew what I wanted, and he'd invited me closer to it. I stepped past him and into the room, my entire skin racing.

Tension beaded up my spine when I heard him close the door. He stood at my back. I had to force myself to breathe, telling myself over and over to chill.

The woman sitting on the bed ran her fingers through her hair as she looked me over, her body moving in time with the music. "You're even prettier than Luke said you were."

She knew about me? That was when it hit home. He had planned this; he'd told her about me. Should I be annoyed? I looked at her more closely. She was maybe a couple of years older than me but she had an edge, a self-assured confidence I knew I didn't have, but wanted.

She patted the bed beside her, and when I sat down, she lifted a tumbler from the floor and offered it to me.

Luke followed and stood close by, at the foot of the bed. When I glanced his way, I got an eyeful of bare chest and open fly. Just what I wanted. The only part I wasn't sure about was the other woman.

"I'm Lisa," she said. "I'm glad you came to play with us . . ."

She was flirting with me.

I didn't think it was possible for my temperature to rise any more than it already had, but it did. *Okay.* We were going to "play", and I didn't think she was referring to a card game. She was looking at me as if she were deciding which item of my clothing to take off first. Luke, half undressed already, smiled down at us. I was getting the gist of the setup now. He wanted two women. As long as one of them was me, I figured I could roll with it.

But the way she was looking at me . . . that did weird things to me. She was very sexy. I found I wanted her to flirt with me some more. I swigged heavily from the glass. It was whiskey. The potent liquid washed over my tongue and, when I swallowed, the hit was just what I needed. "Thanks," I said as I handed the glass back, and tried to look as relaxed as she did. Crossing my legs, I rested one hand on the surface of the bed.

Luke smiled down at me, approvingly. I had to take a deep breath to stop myself from grinning like an idiot. Jesus, this was really happening. All I could think was: *Thank god for the whiskey.*

The woman, Lisa, sprawled easily on to the bed beside me. When she got settled she reached over and ran her hand down the length of my hair. I stared at her, and when she paused with her fingers close against my neck, I smiled. She moved lower, touching my breasts briefly through my T-shirt, before wrapping her arm around my waist and drawing me closer to her.

I rolled on to the bed next to her and she kissed me full on the mouth. I was stunned, and stiffened. I'd never kissed another woman before then. But then I melted, because she was all soft and yet full on, at the same time. I felt the urge to answer her, and I kissed her back.

Oh, how delicious that was. For a moment I almost forgot that Luke was there. Almost. When I looked back, he had a gleam in his eyes and the bulge at his groin was larger. Between my thighs I was aching with longing and with him looming over the pair of us I felt the urge to be wild, to explore. I pushed my hand into Lisa's silky hair, and drew her in for another sweet kiss.

"Oh yeah, you're delicious," she said approvingly as we drew apart, pushing me over on to my back. She laughed gleefully, and it was infectious.

I bit my lip, but couldn't contain a giggle.

"You're really horny, aren't you?" She pulled my T-shirt up over my breasts and off, as she asked the question, then squeezed my nipples through my bra.

"I don't suppose there's any point in denying it," I responded, another laugh escaping my mouth when she shoved my bra to one side to tug on my nipple.

Before I knew what was happening, she had my sandals off, and my jeans undone. She wrenched them down my hips. Playfully, she lifted my panties and put her hand underneath them, touching my pussy. She watched my face for my reactions. My breath was captured in my chest. I glanced at Luke, who was looming close by. He looked as if he was about to pounce. I couldn't predict what was going to happen next, and that thrilled me.

When I didn't resist her, Lisa pulled the panties off of me as well. Luke looked me up and down. I lifted my arm and drew it over my face, closing my eyes, unable to watch him staring down at me when Lisa moved between my thighs.

I'm doing this with a woman, and Luke is watching. I felt slightly crazy, lack of control and sheer horniness sending me dizzy with pleasure. And then I felt her mouth close over my clit, and every nerve ending in my body roared approval.

Her tongue moved with purpose, tracing a pattern up and down over my clit, driving me mad. Her hands were locked around the top of my legs, her thumbs stroking the sensitive skin on the inside of my thighs in time with the movements of her clever tongue. This was alien to me, to have a woman service me, but it felt so fucking good and I didn't want her to stop. My head rolled from side to side on the bed, and I cried out loud, unable to keep it inside. "Oh, oh fuck, it's so good."

She knew just what to do, and when I was thoroughly wound up, she nudged at my clit with the tip of her tongue until I came, my body writhing as I spasmed and fluid ran down between my buttocks.

She rose up to her knees on the bed, and then she pulled her dress off in one long slow move. She was naked beneath, aside from that tiny G-string that barely covered her shaved pussy. She was sleek and lissome. Her breasts were small and pert, nipples hard and dark. Tossing her hair back, she looked down at me. "Fuck her now, Luke. She's so ready."

My face burned up, but she was right, boy, was she right. I shot a glance at him to see his reaction to her comment. He nodded at me when he saw me looking his way, and when he did, I clenched inside, my gaze automatically dropping to his groin. He undid the final two buttons on his fly. His cock jutted out from his hips, hard and ready. Holding it in an easy grip, he reached into his pocket with his free hand and pulled out a condom packet.

My hands were shaking, I knew they were, and I pressed them down on to the bed to keep them steady. I couldn't stop myself. He really did mean to use the condom on me. I stared at him rolling the rubber on to the hard shaft of his cock.

Lisa had moved to one side and was watching expectantly.

I could scarcely believe it. The surprise must have been there on my face, because Lisa chuckled softly and reached in to kiss me again, easing me back down the bed. When I was flat against it, her hands roved over my breasts, and then she captured one nipple between finger and thumb, tweaking it. As I glanced down, I saw that her other hand was in between her thighs, where she was stroking herself.

"I like to watch, it makes me hot," she whispered. She flashed her eyes at me, and then her mouth closed over my other nipple, her teeth grazing it.

Tension ratcheted through me. My eyes closed, my legs falling open, and then I felt the weight of him, right there between my thighs, his hard erection pushing against me.

"Ready for me?" he asked, when my eyes flashed open and I looked at him. He was lifting my buttocks in his hands, maneuvering me into position, his cock already easing inside.

I managed to nod. I was so slick from Lisa's attention that he claimed me in one easy thrust, the head of his cock wedging up against my cervix. I moaned aloud and my body closed around him, gripping his hardness in relief. Pleasure rolled through me when he drew back and then thrust again.

Lisa was sucking hard on my breast and the pleasure arced through me to my core, where Luke was riding me hard, massaging the very quick of me with his cock. My orgasm was coming fast. I panted, hard. I reached out, gripped on to his arm when wave after wave of pleasure hit me.

"Oh yes," he said, and thrust deep, staying there, while his cock jerked, sending an aftershock of pleasure through my sensitive cervix that made me cry out.

It took a full minute for me to catch my breath.

Lisa was snuggled up against my side, and she kissed my shoulder affectionately when Luke went the bathroom.

"What about you?" I said, without thinking, brushing her hair out of her eyes.

"I'll get mine." She smiled. "Don't you worry about that." She winked at me.

"How you doing?" Luke asked as he rejoined us, lying on the opposite side of me to Lisa. He cupped my buttock with one hand as he asked the question, and smiled that wicked smile of his.

A breathless laugh escaped me. He knew just how well I was doing.

"Good, I'm doing good." I returned his smile, and then glanced over my shoulder at Lisa to include her. She made me curious. That hadn't gone away.

"I meant to tell you," Luke added, "I'll be moving out when your parents get back."

My hands tightened on his shoulder, and my smile faded. I didn't want hear that.

He squeezed my buttock tighter. "You'll have to come round and visit me in my new apartment."

I nodded, quickly.

"Both of you," he added.

At my back, Lisa chuckled softly. I felt her breath on my shoulder. Soft, seductive, and warm. She moved to spoon me, her hand stroking my side affectionately. I had her – so alluringly feminine – on one side of me, and Luke on the other – hard, hot, demanding, and all man. Something joyous and liberated in me reveled in the decadence of it, the blatant mutual pleasure.

"I'm up for it," Lisa said, as she clambered over me, pushing Luke down on the bed and straddling his hips. "What about now. Ready for more?"

"Too right." He reached for the bedside table and grabbed a box of condoms. When he did, she winked at me again.

Could I watch him with her? A small residual doubt ticked inside me, but I couldn't look away when she grabbed a condom packet off him, opened it, and rolled it on to the stiff shaft of his cock. Mounting him, she put her hands on her hips, circling on the head of his cock. The crown pressed into her slit, and I watched, mesmerized, as it eased up inside her, splitting her pussy open before my eyes.

The sight was so hot that my hand went to my clit, and I thrummed it as I watched her riding him. A moment later Luke reached out to me, pulled me closer, and kissed me, thrusting his tongue into my mouth. The doubts inside of me slipped away. I was being introduced to a world of sensuality and erotic possibility.

And I was ready, ready for all of it.

Kiss My Ass

Jax Baynard

Whenever someone aggravates me I say, "She needs to get fucked up the ass." Or he. It's a gender-neutral designation. They have to enjoy it. That's key. Otherwise it's just this traumatic thing that happened to you. But if you enjoyed it, you have to look at yourself in the mirror and admit that you are a person who got fucked up the ass and liked it. My husband thinks this is Machiavellian. I think it could have world-changing ramifications.

Of course, I never particularly wanted to myself. I told my husband early on, when I started to get the feeling he might be a keeper, that I thought of my anus as an exit not an entrance. What if anal was his absolute favorite thing in the whole world? If it's going to be a deal-breaker, you want to know sooner than later. But lately I'd been feeling edgy, like I wanted something different. With two bodies, there are only so many variations, and I wanted a new one.

"Want to have sex?" I asked my husband.

"Maybe." He didn't look up. He had assumed his favorite position: kicked back in his chair, feet on the desk, laptop across his thighs, trying to best his own high score at Spider Solitaire.

"Okay," I said from the bed, where I was reading. "Let's figure out all the places you could put your cock."

"The usual?" He still hadn't looked up.

"Nope. Guess again." His gaze slid speculatively to my mouth. "Assume I need that for talking." That only left one orifice. He's good at math.

The feet came off the desk, the front legs of the chair hit the floor, and the laptop snapped shut with a metallic little click. "Let's clarify," he said, coming to stand at the end of the bed. "You want me to fuck you up the ass?"

"Got it in one," I said, stroking my cunt lightly under my dress.

He hitched his jeans up, then settled his hands on his hips and gave me the look that means I'm haring off after something and he's not quite following. "I thought that was off limits."

"Not today. There's a special: Buy One, Get One Free. Interested?"

He was, avid curiosity being difficult to disguise. I could see it in other parts of his anatomy as well. He popped his button-fly jeans open. "Roll over," he said.

"Okay," I said, "but you have to make sure I like it. That's the deal."

He threw up his hands. "Oh sure. No pressure." Then he grinned. "Don't worry, honey. I'll rise to the occasion."

I stripped off my dress and he got rid of his clothes. He knelt between my legs, massaging my buttocks. Then he spread my cheeks. There was a lengthy silence. What? I was thinking. Hemorrhoids? The Heartbreak of Psoriasis? "What are you doing?" I finally asked.

"Looking," he said.

"That doing something for you?"

"I'm thinking about putting my cock in it," he said. "So, yeah, I guess it's doing something for me."

When he put it like that, it started to do a little something for me, too.

"I'm also thinking we're going to need some lubricant," he added matter-of-factly.

I didn't have any. Usually, I make more than enough for both of us the old-fashioned way. "As long as it's not WD-40, I don't care."

"Hang on." He got off the bed. When you live with someone for nine years, you know how they think. If you don't, you haven't been paying attention. I could see him in my mind's eye, walking naked into the kitchen, opening the cabinet next to the fridge, assessing our common household foodstuffs for their lubricative potential. Please just not the Crisco, I prayed. He padded back into the bedroom, and I could tell from the first whiff what it was. The coconut oil melted at first touch, and he slathered it liberally everywhere – my inner cheeks, my anus, down to my cunt which, in another minute or two, wasn't going to need any help in that department. "You smell like the beach, honey," he said happily.

"Yeah, well, just don't get any sand in there."

He didn't laugh. He was busy running his finger back and forth over my anus and around and around it in little circles. It felt surprisingly good. New location, same nerve endings. He slipped the tip of one finger inside and I jumped and tightened around it.

"That didn't hurt," he said. It wasn't really a question. His voice had changed, gone lower and hoarser. He slid his finger all the way in and I had to stifle a moan. Play hard to get, I thought. That was my MO here. He took his finger out. "This feels . . . small." The next thing he put on it was his mouth, and I did moan then. I hadn't imagined it would feel that good. On a scale of relativity: less sensitive than my clit, more sensitive than my G-spot. He swirled his tongue around and made little stabbing motions into the center of it. I let one hand drift towards my clit.

"Oh, no you don't," he said, catching me. "I know you. You'll come and then you won't want me to do this anymore."

I thought about it. "That might be true." I giggled.

"Ha ha," he said, and got up again. He returned with two silk neckties and tied my wrists to the headboard, which – conveniently for him – has little wooden knobs running across the top of it.

I glared at him, but let him do it. "The special is for ass-fucking, not bondage," I said.

"You said two-for-one," he reminded me glibly.

"I meant two orifices (two orifi? I wondered irrelevantly), not two activities."

"There's only one activity going on here," he said definitely. The bed dipped under his weight. "My cock in your ass. Although," he said thoughtfully, "I think you need to relax a little." I heard the bedside table drawer slide open and shut and he settled behind me with my vibrating G-spot finder. "This one goes to eleven," he said, in a perfect imitation of Nigel Tufnel in *This is Spinal Tap*, and wriggled it gently into position. He went back to tonguing my anus, alternating with a finger.

It was like being fucked backwards. I love my G-spot finder. To have it purring away on the spot is a pleasure in itself – more diffuse than clitoral stimulation, but just as good in its own way. I'd often wished I could have the G-spot vibrating and Neil fucking me at the same time, and now suddenly I'd gotten my wish. "Ready?" he asked, and I realized I'd actually forgotten the cock part.

"I want to see it," I demanded. "Your cock. I want to see it."

"Too late for that," he said thickly. He leaned forward. I could feel his thighs, keeping mine spread. He braced himself with one arm near my left hip and with the other he reached under me. He didn't so much rub my clit as grasp it between his thumb and forefinger and sort of manipulate it. Not enough to make me come, just enough to drive me crazy and distract me from what he was doing with his cock. My husband is on the big side of average. Around six inches, I think. I've never measured it, but I've eyeballed it plenty of times. With the G-spot vibrations and his fingers working on my clit, he probably could have driven a 2×4 in there and I wouldn't have objected, but in case you're wondering, in your ass, Average feels Really Big.

I kept forgetting to breathe, I was so swamped in pleasure. But once he got his cock all the way in, he took his fingers away. "Neil," I said warningly.

"Give me a minute," he said. "I need both hands."

He was gentle with his thrusting. Gentle enough that I encouraged him by pushing back against him at the top of every thrust. The only problem was that with my hips tilted back and my hands tied, I couldn't get enough purchase to rub my clit on the bedspread. Fingers would be better, but any port in a storm, right? I wasn't going to be picky. And he was going to come soon; I could feel it in the way he was moving.

"Neil," I said loudly, in what I hoped was a menacing tone, "if you don't touch my clit this instant, you will never, ever, ever fuck me up the ass again."

He didn't say anything, and he didn't slow down, but one hand inched its way between my body and the bed, so I could drag my clit across the heel of his palm. It was a shrieking relief. With everything going on everywhere else, the sensation wasn't so pin-pointed as usual, which made me go a little crazy. I was harder on it than I usually am. Neil went haywire at the end, shoving hard on one long, deep thrust before going rigid, but I didn't care because my nervous system was in a riot of its own. Neil pulled out, and we collapsed together in a sweaty heap, breathing like a herd of bison.

"That was incredible," was the first thing Neil said as he untied me.

"Thank you," I murmured.

"I was talking about my part," he said. "You were good, too, though." I elbowed him in the ribs. "What's funny?" he asked, noticing my Mona Lisa smile.

I felt a little sore and very replete. "I was only thinking," I said, "that when I look at myself in the mirror, I'll be one of those people who will have to say, 'I got fucked up the ass, and I liked it.' "

Ladies Go First

Alex Gross

I'd been in Chicago for three days on business, and this was my last night. After dinner I wandered into the hotel lounge just on the off-chance of finding someone. There was a big crowd, but it didn't take me long before I spotted her. Her eyes were like a beacon as they zeroed in on me as well. She had long black hair and was about five inches shorter than me. She was leaning against the bar, her vibrant figure arching slightly outward, projecting both rough defiance and soft welcome. Her butt also had a thrust to it, and she had prominent breasts for a short girl. She was wearing a very brief mini, and her long, lovely legs were shooting out akimbo in every direction.

Our eyes were locked together as I approached her, wordlessly motioning her to join me in a booth. We sat down, our eyes still joined, and our words came fast and easily. She too was in town on business, and we would be flying back to opposite coasts the next morning. We both confessed to being married, even to loving our partners, but we agreed that we sometimes longed for more.

It was as though we instantly recognized each other. She held herself a bit aloof, she was breezy and bossy, just like a few other girls I've known. She saw herself as the brightest girl in the office, someone not everyone could get to know.

I came on fairly strong with her, just to let her know I could be bossy too. She smiled, and I think we both realized something was likely to happen. We started talking a bit too fast, then we laughed and slowed down a bit. We felt as if we had known each other far longer, and it hit us that we had been handed the perfect opportunity. It wasn't hard persuading her to come to my room.

In the elevator, I put my arm around her, and she let her body fold against mine. I couldn't help congratulating myself that now by my early thirties I had finally learned how to handle women. I liked them best when they were assertive, it meant they were also likely to be passionate in bed. I knew that their bossiness could melt away when I began to lick them where it mattered.

I felt sure I knew how things would go. I would undress her and let her take all the time she wanted until she was fully pleasured. And as she came down from her ecstasy, I would mount her lovingly from behind and take a long, long time riding her. Half an hour doggie-style, maybe even longer, an hour would be better, before I sought out my own pleasure. I'd spend the night with her and take her that way a few more times, maybe once the tight and narrow way for a change. In the morning I'd just give her a slap on the butt and say so long. Mornings like that were the best.

Back in the real world I was a bit less competent. My fingers were almost useless as I fumbled with the key to my room. But she was patient.

"Hey, what's your name?" I quipped to hide my clumsiness.

"Does it matter?" she replied. She was right, and we both chuckled.

Once we were inside, the rest of the world vanished, and we simply threw ourselves at each other. She dropped her handbag, and we embraced passionately for at least five minutes until we almost collapsed together.

She finally broke the clinch and pushed me away. Then she grabbed her handbag and took out her cell phone, which she decisively turned off. I did the same with mine as she retreated into the bathroom. I began to remove some of my clothes, and when she came out she was wearing little more than her underwear.

We wrapped ourselves together again and began edging in the obvious direction. With her back to the bed, I knelt down before her, plunging my face into her red thong. I kept my lips there for a long time before I pulled the thong to one side with my teeth. I loved what I saw there, and I moved my lips even more deeply between her legs.

She moaned and pressed me further in. Then she sat down on the bed, spreading her legs, and drew my face still further within her. She moaned again and seized my shoulders to pull me up on to the bed. I obliged, landing on top of her, as I tried to keep my face wedged between her legs.

But she pulled my head away and made me sit up and look directly at her. She spoke to me in her bossiest voice. But I could also hear her pleading with me.

She really wanted me, I could tell she was just as aroused as I was. She was just afraid what she said might turn me off.

"Listen," she said urgently, "I need to confess. I'm a little bit kinky. Please be patient with me. Let me do it my way first, and then I'll let you do it any way you want."

My agenda precisely. How could I object? "Of course," I replied.

I was almost gloating inside. It was just what I wanted. I sensed I was only a few minutes away from riding her butt.

"You absolutely promise?" she asked.

"Sure, you're the boss. In fact, let me call you Bossetta."

She smiled happily. I'd given her just what she wanted, and my mild mockery went right past her.

We took off our last garments, and she put her handbag next to the bed. Then she jumped right on top of me, sitting high on my chest, and pressed down hard. She felt heavier than I had imagined and was bristling with energy. For a moment I actually thought she was trying to pin me in wrestling. Then she did something unexpected.

She reached down into her handbag and pulled out a tube. She opened it and squeezed some kind of gel on to her palm. Before I knew it, she was smearing it all over my face, on my cheeks and chin, my nose, even my forehead. No girl had ever done this to me before, and I almost started to panic. But then I realized that what she was spreading on my face was nothing but lube.

I still didn't fully get it, but I must have somehow sensed her intention, and it occurred to me that I was in for quite a night. "Listen, you're not going to . . ."

"Don't worry, I promise, it won't hurt . . ."

I could scarcely believe what was coming down towards me. I saw it first from afar, then closer, and at last just a few inches above me. It was the very best view of a lady's jewels I'd ever been treated to, and suddenly it wasn't just a view any more. There it all was – outer lips, inner lips, the whole works, spread out over everything below my eyes.

"Oh, I want to do it this way so much, I know I'm really going to enjoy this," she gushed at me from above. I couldn't believe how excited she was. She was no longer the least bit bossy, she sounded like a passionate kitten. She gazed down at me with incandescent eyes. "And I know for sure, you're really going to love it too." She sounded almost obsessed.

This was all totally new to me, though I had to admit she now had my full attention. It all felt a bit scary, but she seemed to know just what she was doing. Anyway, I had given her my word, and I didn't want to chicken out now. I'd just let her go ahead, I figured, and it wouldn't be long before I turned her over and enjoyed her my way.

I wasn't sure what to expect. She was both passionate and abrupt, it was almost like an attack.

And yet it was also soft and comforting. Even her pressure on my face felt strangely soothing. It was a unique feeling, completely unfamiliar, ranging between hard and soft. I didn't entirely dislike it, so I didn't complain.

I suddenly realized there was no way I could complain anyway. Her crotch totally covered my mouth and my nose, I could make little more than animal noises. Once again I felt panic looming up, but I fought it away. After all, I reasoned, this was nothing more than upside down muff-diving. Except it was her muff that was diving into my face. This was cunnilingus on steroids . . .

It all happened so fast that I still didn't fully grasp what she was doing. At first I had thought it was merely some kind of massage or perhaps a gymnastic drill that would soon merge with what I thought of as regular love-making. But the growing frequency and urgency of her moans soon left me in little doubt of her ultimate aim.

Let me do her justice. She was sliding and gliding and riding over my face with a remarkable degree of skill. Yes, there were moments when she was thrusting down on to me with a great deal of force. But there were also times when she moved so delicately that she was just barely grazing my features, almost like an angel, gently caressing my nose and mouth with her tender parts. She had all the control and confidence of an artist, and this gave me confidence too.

As aggressive and as strange as I found her, I did not for even a moment consider trying to stop her. And even if I had, her wiry strength and the sheer joy she exhibited would probably have made it impossible.

I suddenly realized that I was letting her do all the work, that I ought to do my part with my tongue. So I started to lick her . . .

"Don't do that!" she ordered.

This made no sense, so I continued. She came to a complete halt.

"I told you, don't do that!"

"Why not?"

"Because I don't want your tongue to lick my pussy lips. I want my pussy lips to lick your face."

God, she was weird! But I was in no position to argue, so I obeyed her. It suddenly hit me that from her point of view, I wasn't possessing her at all, she was possessing me. It was an odd feeling.

Her mood quickly passed. I looked up at her and found myself astounded at how remarkably lovely she looked from this perspective. And how powerful as well.

I realized that I had never looked at a woman from this precise angle before. Ranging up from where she held my face, her hips zoomed out past her midriff into the broad thrust of her breasts, which looked even larger and more formidable when seen from below. Sometimes she would move forward, blocking my view with her belly, and now and then she would slide decisively upward, shading my eyes in an almost total blackout.

But as she rode me and drove both her pressure and her softness over me, I was able to look up and intermittently see her face, even glimpse her expression, And I sometimes found her own eyes gazing back at me to gauge my own reactions. Not all the time, just occasionally – most of the time she was entirely caught up in her own pleasure.

She looked so eager, so totally intent on her goal. But I also sensed a touch of anxiety. A chance for perfect ecstasy lay before her, but she also had to pay attention to her every move if she were to reach it.

At least now and then she carefully looked down and scrutinized me, as though she wanted to know exactly how I was taking it. Yes, she was well aware that I was there, that I was technically her lover, I could even tell that she felt some kind of tenderness for me.

But I could also tell that she saw me mainly as a tool, an implement she needed to reach the highest level of pleasure. Almost as a necessary evil. At one point she came close to admitting it.

"Oh . . . I own you . . ." she sighed.

And in a flash I realized that this girl was actually taking my cherry in a realm of sensuality I had never known before. I had no choice but to trust her and be grateful to her for taking the trouble. I also had no choice but to believe that this new domain was entirely real. All the intensity and passion of sexuality were present, all the excitement and tension of a fully mounted couple. All the pressure of body against body, the rhythmic strokes and lunges, the sense of looming fulfillment.

There were only two differences: I was the one being mounted, and all of this passionate energy was being channeled directly into my face.

And I suddenly became a bit concerned too, not totally sure of my feelings. No one had ever made love to me like this before. What she was doing was truly intense and totally personal, but also somehow distant, almost as if it were happening to another person . . .

It was as though she were following an accepted routine with definite rules as she alternated strokes and lunges and teasing motions with her most precious parts. I found myself wondering if she might actually be counting her strokes according to some exotic and unknowable formula. Now and then she made gentle moaning and yelping sounds, as though she were marking the end of one phase and the beginning of another.

During the time when I was able to discern her eyes clearly – during that time at least there was no way I could miss them – they seemed to be eating me alive. I could almost see them even during those longer periods when my vision was blurred or totally blocked by her motions. Her gaze so completely possessed me that I kept longing for her eyes to reappear and gaze down upon me again.

Most of the time her inner lips were perfectly centered on my nose, perched on the sides of my nostrils, and yet I felt no real pain or shortness of breath, at least none that I was aware of. Both her scent and her taste were positively intoxicating, sweet and musky together, so powerful that I began to wonder if she was somehow using it to hypnotize me.

Sometimes she would transfer her orifice upwards on to the rest of my face, all the way from my chin to my forehead, totally covering my eyes. But for the most part she zeroed in on my nose, making smaller motions up and down, or from side to side. Or she would indulge in multiple mini-bounces, slightly painful though they caused no real harm.

Once again, I began to wonder if her goal was to entrance me with these rhythms. Or to make me feel faint by limiting the air I could breathe. But then suddenly I would see her eyes again – as soon as I looked into them, I felt almost infinite comfort and reassurance.

This whole sequence of motions and rhythms went on for some time, I can't say exactly how long, but I wouldn't be surprised if it lasted half an hour.

At length I found myself growing a bit impatient. And to my surprise I realized that she felt the same way.

"Something's missing," she said abruptly and rose up from me. I wondered if I should try to escape from her now, but I had promised her she could do it her way first. And one of the few rules of love is that lovers' promises should be kept. Besides, I did not want to escape.

She immediately turned around and sat back down on my face from the other direction. Whatever she was looking for she now seemed to find, as she ground herself even more deeply into my features. I now found my nose implanted in her rosebud and my chin dividing her lips. She rocked back and forth repeatedly between rosebud and lips, nose and chin. Now the aroma was even muskier, though still not unpleasant. But what precisely was she trying to do to me?

From this position her hands were free to fondle my cock, and she had begun to do so. She wasn't too gentle about it either, at first pulling and tugging the shaft in various directions and finally dealing it some hard, audible slaps. But at least I could tell that it was, if not yet at its hardest, usefully erect. This too was just a stage for her, it didn't last too long, at most a few minutes.

"That's it!" she shouted, and she turned herself around again on top of me, coming back to her former position. She drew back from my face briefly and picked up her lube tube again.

"Now I've got it!" I think I heard her mutter. But I wasn't sure – it could just as easily have been "Now I've got you."

She pressed more gel on to her hand and straightway rubbed it down into my face. Then she pressed out another palmful and stretched her right arm out behind her. I felt her hand clasping my cock and distributing the gel there as well. To achieve this her balance now veered slightly to the right, a posture her strength and agility allowed her to achieve with grace and elegance.

"Here we go!" she concluded. Her pussy engulfed my face again, and I simultaneously felt her hand begin to fondle my cock. Fondle isn't quite the word, she was also busy slapping it from side to side. But she finally settled for encircling the shaft with her fingers and sliding them up and down and around. I smiled inwardly. I was pretty sure she wouldn't have much luck with this, as I prided myself on my ability to resist ejaculation.

This is silly, I thought, she can't possibly mean to come in my face and make me shoot my load at the same time. There's no way she can do that.

But Bossetta was oblivious to my reasoning; she was beginning to tap into a wisdom far beyond my own. She began to set down a rhythm that ran from her hand to her crotch and back again. She was working to realize her ultimate goal, and nothing could stop her.

It was from this point onward that things became rather strange for me, and I wondered again if shortness of breath and her commanding tempo had combined to distort my view of reality.

It was not a total hallucination, I was aware that the hotel room was still there around us, but everything else suggested that we were somewhere on a mountain top together with a temple in the background, and that she was a goddess who was somehow both consuming and nourishing my spirit. Except that she was a goddess who was also a demon with tentacles, and two of her tentacles were concentrated on possessing both my face and my cock. Her aroma became ever more alluring and irresistible, and I could tell from the clasp of her hand that my cock had grown larger and harder than ever before, both in length and girth.

This added to my confusion, since I couldn't imagine how she had done it. It was as though she had dug inside of me through some secret gateway and taken over part of my body. I was also still hoping to mount her from behind afterwards, and I wanted nothing to detract from my prowess when the time came.

There are orgasms, and then there are orgasms. The most usual kinds are the ones that after a certain period of stroking and love-making you yourself have. They work fine, though they are expectable and to some extent unexceptional. And then there are the other orgasms, the ones you don't have, the ones that suddenly sneak up and have *you*. This was one of those orgasms.

I was totally in the power of this goddess-demon who showed no sign of relenting or relinquishing her control over me. If anything, her passion had grown even stronger, and I felt the warning signs from between my legs as her massage grew ever more powerful.

I did my best to chant internally a Taoist formula I'd learned from a Taiji master. It was aimed at stopping the flow of sperm, but in this case it didn't seem to help at all. I suddenly felt as if there were two of me, one my normal self, but another full identity inhabiting my penis.

I personally was doing my best to hold back my seed, but then suddenly that other version of me inside my penis felt himself overwhelmed and thrown into violent eruption. These two identities were writhing and pulsating and spasming together, and the combined force passed from my penis into me and up through my body and into my face, where it effortlessly passed over into my goddess-demon-tormentor. Bossetta was perfectly aware of how I felt and simply let my crisis run its course, as that other part of me spewed gobs of my manhood on to her back.

She waited until my final vibrations had settled and then summoned her own forces, which soon more than equaled mine.

She set herself in cataclysmic motion, bouncing almost chaotically and coming down on me even more heavily than before. It was as if she had entered into her own climactic battle with whatever goddess ruled over her. She rubbed, she ground, she groped all over my face, finally settling on my chin. Then her complexion reddened, and a change came over her. At last she simply moved back and forth three or four times, and my face was awash with her juices, thick, sweet, and musky. I quickly swallowed those closest to my mouth and felt her hand come down to gather some for herself.

I reached behind her back and brought back some of my own fluids and fed them to both of us. For a short while we were like innocent hedonists feasting on love's ambrosia.

During that time there was total peace and understanding between us.

Bossetta moved back on to my shoulders, and when it was all finally over, she looked down at me and summed up our situation from her point of view. "You are my conquest."

She sounded both arrogant and sincere, as though she really meant it. I simply nodded in agreement. To make her point even more obvious, she moved her haunches forward again, and our two sets of lips met in a perpendicular kiss. Yes, it was a sensuous kiss, but it was also a delicate kiss of greeting and recognition.

"My conquest . . ." she repeated.

I couldn't deny that she had a point, one that I was in no position to dispute. She had made prolonged and passionate love to me in a manner I had never known before. At a time entirely of her own choosing, she had forced from me the strongest and wildest orgasm I have ever lived through, tempting me beyond my most ecstatic dreams.

It was almost as if she had ripped it out of me, and I was still reeling now that it was over. I felt so totally sated that I wondered how long it would take before I could show her my way of making love as well. And she had totally confirmed her conquest with a long, powerful orgasm of her own that still covered my features. Its power was still alive in both of us. Yes, I still wanted to take her from behind, but I knew it would have to wait a while. After all, the evening was young. I felt perfectly happy with everything that had happened between us and bore no trace of resentment.

Her skills were simply too undeniable to allow any anger, and her everyday reality was beyond all doubting. We had enjoyed a kind of contest together, and the results were clear. I had come in with my game plan, she had come in with hers, and there could not be the slightest doubt that her game plan had totally demolished mine.

I couldn't believe what we had just done together. But the evidence was all too palpably present, after our kiss her whole set of lips was still settled over my mouth and chin.

Gradually we separated and began to fondle each other more calmly. I kissed her gently all around her body, and we tasted each other's juices a second time.

In between these moist exchanges we gazed at each other in joy and disbelief, amazed at how much we had experienced together. We started to giggle uncontrollably and would break one embrace only to begin another. This degenerated into a mock wrestling match, which, ever the gentleman, I let her end by pinning me down on the bed.

"Okay, we've done it my way," she volunteered. "You just go ahead – take me any way you want."

It almost sounded like a dare, as if she challenged me to equal her in her passion and inventiveness.

We wrestled around for a long time before we looked at the clock and found it was already two in the morning. She mentioned something about having to be up early the next morning.

"Look, I don't feel sleepy," I said.

"I don't either," she replied, "but we've got to get some rest."

During this time all of her bossiness had disappeared. She was so totally sated that she felt no need for it. And she treated me as though I were some kind of furry animal she truly loved for helping her to be so happy.

We wrestled and fooled around for most of another hour, with neither of us feeling aroused enough for another round of sex. After all, we had both mightily exerted ourselves.

But we weren't ready for sleep either – we were much too excited for that. And I still harbored my own desire, though my body gave me no sign this was possible.

At length we made ourselves lie down, as we tried to force ourselves asleep, but that didn't work either.

"Look," she said in the midst of laughter, "I know a way to make us fall asleep."

I dared her to show me.

Once more she jumped on top and this time it was her breasts she brought to bear on my face. She pressed down and kept on pressing, until I thought I would pass out. But suddenly she changed tactics, and I felt sudden hard blows against my face, waking me back up again.

This time she was no longer suffocating me but pummeling my face with her breasts. They were more than heavy enough, and I knew that if she went on too long, she might well knock me out. I felt this was a cruel way of sending me to sleep, but before I could object, she changed tactics again and began to use her breasts in the way women best employ them, to massage and soothe and comfort my face.

This time I felt she had it just right, but before I could doze off, she went back to smothering me again. And then to pummeling, and finally back to comforting. She even started over a third time – smothering, pummeling, comforting, and, as she reached the comfort stage, I thought it must be over as we were both by now truly tired.

I was just about to doze off, but to my surprise, she started in on a fourth round of smothering. It didn't last long – it ended when I felt her erupt into a sharp shudder that left us both a bit shaken. Now at last we were both truly ready to sleep and, as we curled up in each other's arms, I couldn't help wondering if that shudder of hers had been some other kind of orgasm, one I had never seen before.

"Hey, you really do own me . . ." I remember muttering just before I dozed off.

When two lovers sleep through the night together, all kinds of things can go on that they may not recall the next morning. I remember them pretty clearly, simply because this entire encounter was so remarkable in so many ways. I know that we remained cuddled together all night long and that even though we needed our sleep, our bodies were still wildly attracted to each other.

Of course there were also dreams, reminiscences of our recent passion, at least once reenacting the precise sequence of her movements that decisively defeated me. Even today in my mind's eye I can recall that series of strokes, twists, and fingerwork that turned my lower body into a human juice machine.

All night long our arms and legs remained linked and our faces were often touching. Most clearly I remember that the head of my cock spent almost the entire night right inside the vestibule of her passage. And sometimes it tried to peek further in, only to be gently prodded away.

After all, we needed our sleep more than passion. But I recall for a certainty that during that night, though we did not make love again, we were as close as lovers ever can be.

On one occasion, about an hour before dawn, I almost woke because I was getting hard, but this time she resisted even more fervently. Once again sleep trumped sex. And I also remember thinking, Oh, well, nail her in the morning, just as I fell off again.

It was she who woke me that morning with the noise of a TV news program. As soon as she saw me moving, she turned it off. I had trouble focusing my eyes, but I could see that she was standing stark naked by the TV, and just as desirable as ever.

I think I was still half-dozing, while she rattled on in the background about how she had to have breakfast with another girl from her firm before they both flew back to LA together. This meant she would have to return to her room and change clothes, because she couldn't possibly come to breakfast looking the way she had in the bar last night. I was still sleep-logged and couldn't absorb it all.

"Please don't go," I blurted out.

"I'm not going anywhere," she replied, coming right up to the bed. "I have no intention of going. I'm not leaving until I've taken you again . . ."

She wasn't joking at all. She stood next to me, right above me, and her voice was at its bossiest. In one motion she jumped back into bed and landed on top of me again. Needless to say I began to wake up, but she had taken me by surprise, and there was no way I could stop her from what she was already doing.

Out came her lube tube, squish went a large glob all over my face, and there it was again, looming downward towards my nose, irresistible but maybe just slightly menacing, her whole passionate center throbbing as it moved to engulf me. She had fully and truly mounted me again, and when I looked up I saw how useless any resistance would be.

This time, she didn't even ask my permission. She simply took charge of me as though I were her property. I felt a bit resentful, since this meant any hopes I had of taking her were null and void.

I found it infuriating . . . well, not quite. As soon as her vulva settled on my face and began its teasing massage, all my objections fell away, and I happily settled into her enticing rhythm. She was busy humping away at my nose and chin as though they belonged to her.

Well, after all, I reasoned, she had once again taken me fair and square, if a bit unexpectedly. I had to give her credit for that. She had allowed me several hours to do things my way, and I had done nothing. She had every right to take command again.

Then it suddenly hit me what she was doing, and a touch of resentment came back to the fore.

This was nothing else but the classic finale to a one-night stand: the early morning good-bye fuck. Except it was her pussy fucking my face again instead of the way I really wanted.

Once again her taste and smell were overpowering, and she had me perfectly pinned beneath her. Her rhythm was positively enticing, and I realized that I was for the second time succumbing to the sheer force of her sensuality. There was no doubt that her mood towards me had changed. Yesterday I was an interesting experiment for her. Today I was just meat. She had somehow downgraded me from her favorite sexual partner to little more than a slut. And at least some part of me seemed to be accepting this role. This time she didn't bother with any explanations or apologies. She was in complete control, and she knew it.

She was coming down on me even harder than the first time, and she was cutting off my breath even more completely. I could feel her juices coursing within her, and I knew she could let them loose on me at any moment. Amazingly, it hit me that I actually felt eager to receive them. But I also soon realized that she was taking her time, that she wanted to make our final encounter last as long as possible, mainly for her, incidentally for me.

She now said something aloud that confirmed this perfectly: "Oh, I'm having you, I'm taking you, I'm using you . . .'

In any contest there are times when the loser begins to identify – or at least sympathize – with his winning opponent. After all, that opponent is doing precisely what the loser would like to be doing to the winner. It must have been this, or perhaps it was just everything added together – her taste and scent, my reduced ability to breathe, her pressure upon me – that sent me off once again into a fantasy world.

Except I didn't believe it was fantasy. I was suddenly certain that I had become one with her, that I could hear her thoughts as she had her way with me, that I was actually inside her head listening to those thoughts . . . And I was absolutely certain they went something like this . . .

". . . Oh, now I've really got him, this is just fabulous, he's so easy to take, and I'm handling him just right, he's totally my prey, my absolute victim, he's never been made love to like this, he's never come this close to a girl's pussy before, the poor bastard . . . he just doesn't know how to deal with it . . . anyway I'm the one who's helping him, who's busy deflowering him … And I'm really being quite gentle about it, I'm doing my very best to make it all perfect for him, I mean, sure, I'm going to let it all shoot loose soon, but only when I'm good and ready … oh my god, I'm getting too close, gotta pull back, it almost got me too excited … can't let that happen … build it up slowly again … yes, that's it … WOW! I am really using this guy, but I don't feel the least bit guilty about it … should I feel guilty? hell, no! … he's loving every minute of it … it's the best time he's ever had in his life … so I'm going to just go on using him … I'm even raping him a little, I jumped him before he was ready, maybe I even raped his cock yesterday, but what the hell, what's the point of knowing how to do all this if I can't use it to fuck a guy's brains out … anyway he's happy I'm raping him, just look how much he's enjoying it … oh god, I'm coming too close again … oh, that feels so GOOD! … oh yeah … what the hell, gotta do it some time, HERE WE GO … ! ! !"

And at that exact point her whole body started to vibrate, her sexual regions began to churn and contract and release. She had so totally taken over my mind that I was cheering her on. It seemed nothing less than glorious when she lunged at me with all her force five or six times, and my face was once again drenched with her fluids …

She rocked back and forth over my face a number of times before she finally came to rest. She pulled herself back to glance down at me, but this time there was no real ceremony. She had taken me, just as she had promised she would, and that was that. She playfully tweaked my nose with her fingers and arose from me with a "mission accomplished" air.

"Hey, you are one great piece of face. I've got to take a shower." She uttered both sentences in the same tone of voice. And she again mentioned having to meet her office colleague for breakfast before flying home.

She went into the bathroom, and I heard her turn on the shower.

For the first time since last night I was actually alone in the room, and this seemed to prompt all the misgivings I had been hiding, even from myself. Yes, she was truly gifted as a lover, I reflected. And yes, over the last ten hours she had shown me a whole new domain of sexuality, one I had never known existed. And yes, it was utterly genuine, as intense as any sexual pleasure I had ever enjoyed. I would certainly want to go on enjoying such pleasure in the future. And this is where I foresaw a real problem …

Now that our encounter was almost over, I found myself wondering how on earth I would ever be able to enjoy this kind of loving again. And with whom. This was a remarkably new way of enjoying sex, something I knew I would never be able to achieve with my wife. There was no way I could hope to teach her, I wouldn't even know where to begin.

How could I ever find another girl like Bossetta? If I wanted to go on making love like this, I would have to bring about some important changes in my lifestyle, perhaps frequenting darkened East Village haunts or posting suggestive ads on weird websites. But if I did this, I wondered how long my marriage would survive . . .

I was also still unhappy that I had not been able to finish our session the way I wanted. In our short remaining time, how could I ever convey to her my deepest desire? That I needed to see her before me on her hands and knees, her bottom arching high as the clouds, while I gleefully rammed her buttocks into the sunset.

There had to be a way I could do this. Hell, now I was really getting angry! She promised me I could do it my way. And then she jumped me in the morning before I was ready! Damn it, she has to keep her word!

But how could I persuade her? Calling me her conquest was an understatement – she'd scored several direct hits and totally demolished me. She'd taken the lead at every point, claiming my face twice and ravishing my cock, not to mention her strange assault with her breasts. But she had clearly broken the rules, she had gone too far. What I had trouble understanding was why I found so much of what she had done positively exciting and all of it remarkable.

But she still owes me something, I concluded, she has to do it my way too! Anyway, there's no reason any of this has to end now. We can stay a whole other day, even two more days if we feel like it, I could call in sick, and so could she, we could change flights . . . no, this doesn't have to end now at all!

I got out of bed and went to the bathroom door. It was open just a crack, and I could see her form behind the glazed wall of the shower. Should I just go in now and tell her? No, it would be more polite to wait until she came out. In later days I would have reason to regret this decision, I would even become almost certain that if only I had gone into the shower and accosted her naked, it would all have ended differently. When she finally came out, I realized in a flash that I didn't have a chance.

She was dressed again as she had been the night before, her complexion was flushed with all the pleasures she had enjoyed, and she looked more beautiful than ever. Her breasts jutted out jauntily in one direction, her butt in another. She was agleam with sheer desirability, and I could hardly believe I had held her sweating and straining above me just a few minutes earlier. What I most wanted was to go back to that lounge and pick her up and start the whole night all over again.

"Hey," she gushed, "we had a good time, didn't we . . . ?"

"Listen," I started, but the words would not come. I felt like a naked peasant approaching the lady of the manor in all her finery.

"Wow, make sure you wash your face. It's a real mess," she said with a touch of pride.

But there was no way I could hide it, I had to go on, and I tried to make a fresh start . . .

"Wait . . . stop!" I shouted. "You've got to stay . . . I want *more* . . ." I reached for her. She saw my erection, and under her gaze I could feel it begin to dwindle.

"Listen, I really don't need this," was all she replied. And she turned towards the door.

There was no hope left. She was simply in her own world. She was even ending it on her terms. She was making it amply clear to me. I truly was her total conquest, and she didn't take prisoners.

Once again she made me feel like nothing so much as a used, messy, vanquished peasant. I heard my voice, almost as though it were not mine, calling out for one last favor, imploring her . . .

"At least tell me your name, give me something to remember you by . . ."

"Okay, I'll give you something. Just remember this. I did you. You didn't do me. And we both enjoyed it. That's all that matters."

She picked up her handbag and headed for the door. Her face was flushed with joy and triumph. I followed her and sought out her eyes, and these at least she granted me.

She gave me one last puckery little kiss. I will never forget what she did next.

She reached down and slapped me hard on my bare ass. Just to make sure I got the message, she slapped my butt even harder again, this time with a resounding thwack. Her bossy expression was at its bossiest, but I thought I caught just the slightest glint of compassion in her eyes.

Then she opened the door and walked out of my life forever.

Calendar Girl

Angela Caperton

Desi Palladino couldn't take her eyes off April 1958.

The calendar hung on the wall of Stu Gilbert's tiny office at the back of the garage, where Desi brought him coffee and helped keep the books. There were calendars in the garage too, most of them with drawn or painted girls, prettier than any real woman could ever be, but the calendar on the wall of Stu's office was the only one with photographs of real girls, one for each month of the year.

"Whatcha lookin' at, Desi?" Stu bustled through the open door, wiping his hands on a greasy rag. Stu Gilbert was pushing fifty, stocky, almost bald, but he smiled like a naughty twelve-year-old.

Desi's cheeks burned. "Nothing," she mumbled. "Checking the delivery date for the parts you ordered last week."

Stu chuckled. "She's somethin', ain't she?" He sighed and brushed his fingers over April's bare stomach.

"I thought it was against the law to show ... I mean ..." Desi's mouth turned desert dry.

"I figure somebody screwed up," Stu said.

Miss April's ash blonde hair framed a plump face with ivory skin and pouty lips. Desi wished she had hair that color and the complexion to go with it. Her own hair fell in heavy black waves where it refused to curl over shoulders of pale olive, the gift of her father's Sicilian blood. The calendar girl's breasts curved in gentle slopes, pink-tipped and perfect, and her torso, where Stu's finger twitched wistfully, looked firm, with just a hint of flesh around her stomach, then flattening down to a triangle of pale curls with the shadow of a line at its center.

"I have to go, Stu," Desi said, rising to ease past him and the scent of gasoline and tobacco he carried.

He laughed as she reached the door. "If it bothers you, kid," he chuckled, "I can skip to May."

But he didn't take April down, and every day, all month long, Desi worked two or three hours in Stu's office, looking at the girl on the calendar, her mind turning over and over as she thought of the real person, the girl in that picture, somewhere. She looks so happy. No, more than happy, Desi thought. She looked joyous.

At the front of the calendar Desi read the address where it was printed, on Stafford Street in San Francisco.

Somewhere out in California, a pretty blonde girl had stripped herself bare before a man, as open to him as a bride to her husband, sinful and brave, and so very beautiful and he had caught her exuberant beauty with his camera. Desi thought about her constantly, trying to imagine what April's life must be like, how she had been caught in that moment, wondering if she had really been as happy as she looked.

Stu didn't mention the calendar again, not directly, but she saw his eyes when he looked at April and heard the catch in his breath. No man had ever breathed for Desi like that, though plenty of them had tried to get their hands in her blouse. Some days, just walking through the garage could be a gauntlet. Desi never, not for a single second of every working day, forgot she was the only antelope in a plain of lions.

For the most part, the guys in the shop weren't slobs or creeps. She might have dated Bobby Dridger or Jeff Culhane if they'd asked her properly, but they were the nice boys who always changed into clean shirts at the end of a greasy day and too shy even to flirt.

On the morning of 1 May 1958, Desi clocked in early and carefully removed April from the calendar above Stu's desk, revealing May, a redhead as beautiful as April, but far less alluring. Desi carefully placed April in an envelope and hid her on a shelf between two ledgers.

Of course Stu's first words when he arrived were, "Where's April?"

Desi pretended she didn't hear him and Stu, God bless him, didn't ask her again.

All through that spring, sometimes when she was alone in her room at home, Desi stripped her clothes off and imagined posing. She would have died if Mom or Dad had ever caught her at it. She'd not been seen naked by either of them since she was six. Even her doctor had only seen her bra-covered chest.

Only the girls in her high school gym class had seen Desi naked. Desi remembered her terror but also the excitement as she rushed through the shower hardly daring to look at the other girls, hoping for invisibility, but also realizing many of the other girls raced just as she did. Her gaze trembled and darted on the others to see if they looked at her. She felt embarrassment at being seen, like Adam and Eve ashamed of their nakedness.

Now, Desi wondered if Adam and Eve had been excited as well as ashamed.

Sizing herself up in her mirror, Desi thought she compared favorably to April. Her breasts were bigger, with little dark nipples instead of pink points, and her waist was tight and curved, sexily, she thought, above the swell of her hips. From the back, her bottom was high and firm, rounded and symmetrical as a perfect olive, golden where the sun had never touched her. But what held her eye and tempted her fingers was the patch of silky fur that covered her treasure – Mom's name for her pussy.

A real girl, Desi thought, and slipped her fingers through the satiny moss, but a goddess too, sacred to men, naked and made to be worshipped.

Sometimes she stopped but other days, the thoughts were too much and she reached deeper, across the rough, sweet spot into the heat of her treasure, wet, sometimes dripping, desperate for a touch, or, even better, to be seen.

Closing her eyes, before the fire burned her alive, Desi sometimes imagined the girl in the mirror was April.

Desi usually arrived at the shop before anyone else. Stu trusted her with the books – she kept them better than he did. She took calls, handled the payroll, made coffee, and chatted with customers. Some days were slow, especially in the morning. During lulls she would wander to the shelf and draw the envelope from between the two ledgers where she had hidden it, slip it open with nervous fingers and stare, growing wet under her cotton panties.

One Tuesday in late May, she had just put the envelope back between the ledgers and turned toward the doorway. Bobby Dridger stood not two feet behind her and her ragged breath lodged in her chest.

"She's really pretty, ain't she?"

Bobby looked a little like Buddy Holly with muscles. He had tawny, straight hair that he combed back in a wave and he wore black-framed glasses.

His question vibrated the air between them a long time before Desi nodded.

Bobby reached past her and took the envelope from its hiding place. Smiling, he shook April out and held her. April stared up at them, open, no secrets among the three of them.

Heat rolled off Bobby like the purr of a lion in Africa. He smelled like musk and gasoline.

"This is good stuff. It's the light makes the difference." He drew a line with his grease-stained finger, not quite touching the photo, along the curve of April's breast and Desi saw what he meant, the light emerging under Bobby's black, ragged nail.

He looked at Desi, and then back at the picture and lightly touched it, right in the middle of April's treasure. "Somebody missed this," he said, much as he might have pronounced a carburetor dead. "They ought to've airbrushed this."

"What's airbrushed?" Desi asked in a whisper.

"It's a retouch they do on these girls," he said, clearly pleased she had asked the question. "It's why none of them other girls have p— why they don't show hair down there. Come here." The small office shrank to a tiny matchbox. She only took two steps before she stopped, her breast almost touching Bobby's arm. She breathed his breath when he turned and smiled and ran his finger down May's belly, the dark half moon of his nail skirting the top of the smooth, hairless labia. "See?"

Bobby held April out and grinned. Desi took the page from him, her cheeks burning.

"Desi," Bobby said, nervous, and hopeful. "I sure would like to take your picture."

"Just sit still, Desi. Relax." Bobby lifted her chin and brushed a wisp of hair from her dark mane so it hung to her eyebrow. She wore a crisp white shirt and a navy blue skirt. He shot against a background of azaleas, their blooms thin and pale at the season's end.

Bright in a clear sky, the sun had just begun to gather shadows as it settled over the town. Bobby said it gave her an aura. In his yellow linen shirt and black chinos, he looked like a college boy.

"Put your arm up behind under hair, baby. Look just to my right." He stepped behind the tripod, snapping several shots as she raised her arm, aware that it made her breasts stand out against the white shirt. The straps and lace of her bra must show, she thought. *What if I wasn't wearing a bra?* Her nipples stiffened.

"Perfect, Desi. Don't even breathe, baby."

The sun's light kissed along the edge of her cheek and the nape of her neck, and pulsed between her legs. Disobedient, she turned her head the tiniest bit and smiled at Bobby, hoping her eyes and the flush she felt in her cheeks conveyed how much she wanted him.

He looked a long moment, then disappeared behind the shutter with a steady click, click, click.

When he showed her the pictures the next day, Desi stared at the girl painted in vivid colors, hardly believing it was her.

"Baby, you're amazing," Bobby said. "There's a dozen shots in here I could sell."

She leafed through the pictures. "Who'd buy them?" she asked as her treasure hummed.

"I don't know. Glamour mags? *Popular Photography*? You're a natural, baby. The light loves you."

She thought about April, out in California.

"Desi." Bobby rubbed his chin. "You know what a camera club is?"

She shook her head.

"Like it sounds. A bunch of shutterbugs who get together every few weeks. We share lights and lenses and we pool our dough for a model and sometimes a studio."

"So?" she started, and then she felt herself blush as she understood what he was asking.

Bobby picked her up at ten Saturday morning. She'd done as he said, and wore pretty clothes – a calf-length, pleated red skirt and a pale pink linen blouse, nearly white and nearly sheer. Beneath the blouse, she wore a silvery-grey camisole and beneath that her lightest weight white bra. Her mother hounded her to wear girdles, but Desi liked her full hips so she left the girdle at home, opting for plain white cotton panties and a garter belt the same color as the camisole. She settled on dark red lipstick and subtle lashes, and, at the last minute, she rolled on her darkest stockings, real silk in rich, charcoal gray.

"It's ten bucks an hour up front," Bobby told her. "But then, if the guys like you, they tip you. There's no funny stuff, baby. These guys are serious. They ain't creeps."

"It's very exciting," Desi answered, feeling a little awkward and foolish, so nervous her treasure had almost soaked her panties.

"Today's shoot is at Ike Bentley's place, which is cool. Bentley's got cash. He has a permanent studio and when we use it, sometimes he springs for costumes and props. I told him about you so this ought to be fun."

Mr Bentley's house sat on a big lot with a view of Lee's Lake. A young man with a trim moustache answered the door and grinned at Bobby.

"Hey, Charlie, this is Desi," Bobby said as he patted the man on the shoulder.

"I figured." Charlie took her hand into his warm, muscular one and shook it lightly. "You're even prettier than Bobby said." He held her hand a little longer and looked her over with what she guessed was a photographer's eye.

She walked down a parquet hall to a sun-flooded room with a ceiling mostly of glass. Along one side of the big room, she glimpsed richly colored curtains, furniture, and tall flood lamps, but Charlie steered her to the men on the other side. Four of them waited among a forest of tripods.

Bobby made the introductions. Mr Bentley, handsome for a man of his years; Gus, older too, and quiet, but he had a nice smile. Doug Spencer, dark-eyed and lean; Desi remembered him from his tenure at the garage the summer before. Wetness began to seep between her legs. Before she could squirm, Bobby introduced her to Dr Barlow. Dr Barlow, the most eligible young man in town – in spite of his wedding ring.

Six men, some strangers, others familiar. She smiled at them, feeling the light in her eyes, the shine in her lips, the look she had seen on the beautiful girl in Bobby's pictures. She held the tether of allure for a long moment until Mr Bentley said, "Perhaps we should get started."

Bentley barked directions, and Charlie moved lights and props and opened shutters and curtains. She wondered if Charlie was like a butler. A look around the room told her that Mr Bentley might be that rich.

"We'll start over here." Bobby took her lightly by the arm. Her skin sensitive, suddenly thin enough to tear, burned beneath his fingers. He led her to a white wooden chair by a table where a bowl bloomed with roses. "Sit down," he said.

Charlie adjusted the window shutters and Desi blinked against the wash of golden sunlight.

"Now, just do what they tell you," Bobby said with a wink and stepped behind his camera.

The room rustled and clanked as the tripod forest moved. The intensity of the men's concentration as they adjusted knobs, focused, changed lenses and filters added to the warm butterflies fluttering in her core.

What would they tell her to do?

"Get her the roses first," Mr Bentley said and Charlie picked her a bouquet from the bowl, eight perfect red roses that he presented with a bow and a grin.

"Hold them," Mr Bentley ordered, "just at your breast and inhale them."

She did exactly as he said, gathering the silky flowers against her pale blouse, breathing them, the sweetness a cloud in the morning, her vision misty against the white windows, the shapes of the men in the light. She smiled, full-breathed, and her breasts pushed out in sharp peaks.

Click, click went the cameras and after awhile, she exhaled, though air still felt shallow in her chest, a thin pool where her pounding heart swam.

"All right," Bentley said. "Unbutton the top three buttons of your blouse."

"Yes, sir," Desi said, trying to find Bobby in the glare. She laid the roses in her lap and smiled at the cameras, her fingers at the buttons.

Click, click.

"Hmm," Mr Bentley said, and Desi hated the note of disapproval she heard in his voice. "That's not going to work as long as you are wearing a brassiere. Do you mind removing it?" He pointed to a changing screen near the colorful furnishings on the other side of the room.

Charlie appeared like a genie to take the roses and she stood and walked to the screen, her breath faster and the line between her legs sodden and dripping. Desi paused beside the screen, looking at the lurid curtains and the sofa, like something in a sultan's harem. She thought of the Arabian Nights and the woman who kept herself alive by telling stories, by enchanting a man with her talents.

She thought of April and her nipples tightened.

She shed her blouse, camisole and bra without hesitation, and before she put the blouse back on, she looked at the costumes on hangers behind the screen. Some of the shining fantasies were no bigger than her hand, and her nipples grew as hard as marbles as she imagined herself in glossy black and white, shining patches of satin. She stole a glimpse of herself in the mirror, unable to look directly at her image, the rising curves with dark rigid tips, and her face that of the woman in Bobby's photos.

She slipped on the sheer blouse and buttoned it to the place Mr Bentley had asked for, aware of every place the linen touched her, its cling no more than mist, but intense as a warm finger. She stepped from behind the screen, her blood pulsing in her ears, her throat, and her treasure. Almost giddy, she walked toward the men and their cameras.

As she approached the chair, she understood at once that everything had changed. She smelled something in the room, a scent, sharp and tangy, exhilarating and new. She heard their breath, as ragged as her own, but with a primal edge.

Every one of them watched the bounce of her breasts.

She sat and gathered the roses, leaned forward so that the revealed cream of her chest emerged from the linen, her dark nipples harder yet in clinging, translucent pink, her lips parted in a smile, a promise.

The clicking almost deafened her.

"You are everything Bobby said, my dear." Mr Bentley took the roses from her this time. He put his hands lightly on her shoulders and his fingertips kneaded lightly through the blouse. He held her gaze, the unspoken question as clear as a shout. She answered it with a nod. He knelt, his gray eyes intense on hers, not looking down to where his fingers worked at the last four buttons, not until he had finished and stood up so that she could open the blouse and drop it in a whisper to the floor.

Click.

She picked up the roses, spread them in a fan over her breasts, not covering herself at all, letting the red flowers brush the most sensitive spots just below the nipples. The men watched her, rapt, their cameras silent.

She grew still in the moment, the pulse in her treasure and the blazing heat just under her skin demanding obedience.

She saw the intense shapes against the rising light of the morning sun and tried to find Bobby among them. Paint me, she thought to him. Paint me with light.

Raising a finger to her lips, she wet it to dripping, then touched her right nipple, slick and shining, catching the sun like the sweat of its luminescent desire.

Gus groaned. Click, click.

"Wait," Bobby said, stepping between her and the cameras. She became a goddess under his gaze and his hands felt divine where he touched her shoulders while he turned her slightly in the chair, so that her breast stood in sharp silhouette. He took the roses and selected one, the darkest of the dozen, and rested the cool bloom against her nipple. "Hold it there," he said. Bentley nodded his approval as Bobby stepped back.

She imagined each of the men in turn as an absent lover whose memory had come upon her like a ghost, wistful, vulnerable, the red flesh of the rose the spirit of distant lips, kissing the brown tip of her breast.

"Beautiful," Bentley breathed.

Hundreds of clicks filled the room. They shot her with the roses, without the roses, standing, sitting, her body arched into the light. Her nipples softened only to harden again as Bentley or Bobby posed her, and she felt their arousal as each new seduction unfolded.

Somewhat to Desi's disappointment, no one asked her to remove her skirt.

"We're losing the morning light," Doug Spencer said after awhile.

"Time to move to the seraglio," Mr Bentley laughed. "Would you like some wine or a drink, Desi?"

She picked up her blouse and draped it around her shoulders, a thin vein of self-consciousness creeping into her when the cameras no longer courted their queen. She was glad, but also a little sorry, when Charlie brought her a robe. Smiling, still slick between her legs, her voice trembled slightly as she nodded to Mr Bentley. "A little wine, maybe?"

Most of the men had a Collins, though Mr Bentley took straight Scotch. They talked about the photos, about film and lenses, things Desi knew nothing about, but they talked to her too, including her in their discussion of the poses, what they saw through their lenses, what they hoped to capture. Her. She. Light made solid on glossy paper for unknown – and known – eyes to see. She sat among them, her breasts still, for all purposes, bare, their gazes easier on her now, though she still saw the heat in their eyes, the anticipation of whatever lay ahead, and she shared that anticipation with them, loving the threads of communion and impulse.

The wine was sweet and barely chilled. Desi had only had wine a few times, at weddings and parties, but she remembered how much she liked it, how the warmth moved under her skin.

When the drinks had been mostly consumed, Charlie helped everyone move their tripods and gear across the room to the Oriental divan at the center of the bank of lamps.

"We'll spend the rest of the afternoon here, Desi," Mr Bentley said. "I bet you have a good imagination. Our theme will be a night in a harem. Is that all right with you?"

"Sure." She smiled.

"Good. You will want to undress completely. We want all the costumes to look authentic. Are you ready?"

"What should I wear first?" she asked as she started toward the screen. Her head spun a little with the wine and the heat that had collected between her legs.

"Any of the costumes you wish."

Behind the screen, she dropped the robe and her nipples stiffened instantly. She examined the costumes and picked one with a short red jacket and a pair of ballooning ebon pants. She grinned as her hands unfastened her skirt and dropped it beside the robe, unsnapped the garter as if she broke chains, and rolled the stockings down her shapely legs.

She felt them on the other side of the screen, six men, all waiting for her. She slid her soaked white panties down her legs. All through the morning while the men had been shooting her she'd watched them and felt their desire, saw their erections – some more than others. She knew what men had between their legs – she had seen statues and paintings – but this was different. Statues and paintings were tastefully flaccid, not stiff enough to snap a photo.

As she posed for these men, they had all grown hard watching her, wanting her, just as she needed them to see her and to want her. Never, even in her imagination, had anything felt so good, so purely ecstatic.

She peeled away the wet panties and reveled for a moment in anticipation of their worship, and then she pulled on the harem pants and slipped on the halter that might as well have been made of spun glass.

When she stepped in front of them, the wine's heat spread all through her legs and up her spine. Pleasure she had known in dreams and a few times when she had touched herself, manifested magically before them, before the wide eyes of lenses.

They posed her on the divan, chastely at first, but then more wanton, sprawled in opiate abandon, her jacket open and then gone altogether.

"Change," Mr Bentley commanded and she obeyed, wearing a bra made of golden chains and a belt and breechcloth that barely covered her pleasure. When she took off the bra and only a scrap of silk covered her, Doug Spencer's pants looked like they might split open.

Charlie wore a costume too, a harem guard, they said, and he looked good in what there was of it. He posed with her, his stomach and chest bare and hard with muscles. Mostly he posed behind her, but sometimes he stood over her while she sat at his feet. Every time he touched her, she thought she might come.

All the time, the other five men clicked intently, spellbound as she was, their cameras touching her, chasing the light along her curves, fondling her breasts and bringing the nipples to explosive sensitive peaks, molding the tight curve of her thighs and hips. She turned before them, showing her bare bottom, aware that if she bent only a little, they would see the spread lips of her treasure.

But she kept that from them.

Then, late in the afternoon, the light beyond the windows ruby and gold, she wore the last costume, a tattered white shift that left her breasts and almost all of her legs bare. Charlie had stripped down to a single band of white cloth, the idea being that she and he were slaves together to a wicked sultan.

"Now, Desi," Mr Bentley said, his voice warm and breathless, "take off the dress."

She did not hesitate, her heart trilling with power and excitement, but she held them in the infinite compliance of her motion, not pulling it over her head but letting the thin straps fall from her shoulders and the fabric pool around her waist, standing to roll it over her hips and down.

With a little gesture of submissive flirtation, Desi stepped quickly out of the white cotton and dropped it, finally naked before them.

The light on her treasure thrilled her, their eyes, their desire, pulsed through her sex. She welcomed them, wanted them, soared into an ecstasy that their eyes would drink, their cameras record. Charlie's hands rested on her hips as ripples of pleasure flowed from her treasure, through her core, her heart, her fingers and toes, and she came right there, immortal on their film.

Scheherazade. That was who she was. The servant of these men and their mistress, and the thousand and one tales had only begun to be told.

"Oh, baby!" Bobby exclaimed to her in the car on the way home. "That was the best. You're incredible."

"I liked it," Desi laughed, drunk beyond the wine. "I liked it a lot."

Mr Bentley, his gaze hot and flashing, had handed her a $100 tip. Dr Barlow gave her 50 and the other men pooled another 100. They wanted her to come back, but Desi didn't commit. Another idea bloomed in her soul.

"Bobby?" she asked. "You ever been to San Francisco?"

"Once," he said. "Why?"

"We could go out there," she said, resting her hand on his thigh as the car rumbled down the lane leading away from Bentley's house. "I could be a model and you could be my photographer."

"That's . . ." he started to say and then he laughed. "Why not? You're amazing and you make me amazing. Those pictures I took the other day – they're the best I've taken – well, until today."

"Bobby," she said, her hand running up his thigh. "I watched you today. You weren't like the others." She stroked the line of his penis under his pants and he stirred, but only a little.

They rode in silence for a few minutes.

"Baby," he said. She heard the serious sound of his voice as he hunted for words. "When them other guys shoot you, they want to make love to you. When I do, it's 'cause I see how beautiful you are and I want to *be* you. You dig?"

Her gut tightened at the candid confession, but now, after this day, she understood and it was all right with her, maybe better than all right. Certain kinds of jealousy would never be an issue between them.

"Bobby, I've never felt so beautiful," she said, resting her head on his shoulder. "And I want to go to California with you."

Stu Gilbert turned the envelope in his hands, his brow furrowing at the postmark: Oakland, California. He tore the paper and smiled his naughty twelve-year-old smile.

Four months into 1959 and somebody had sent him a calendar worth hanging in his office. He leafed through it, regretting that he had missed January, February, and March, figuring he at least owed them a look.

When he flipped the page to April, he stopped breathing.

Desi! His Desi smiled back at him without a stitch on her, every bump on her pretty nipples sharp and clear as if painted with God's own hand. She winked at him. His smile split his face as he admired her mink bush and her legs spread just a little to show perfect pussy lips.

Stu's boner didn't go down till he made it to the john and jacked the toilet full of cream. He came back to his office and reverently, like a priest with a cross, hung the calendar over his desk, where it was a shrine for the rest of the month, to every one of the mechanics and the parts guys and half the customers. Stu grinned wickedly watching some of the women blush, but they couldn't take their eyes off her.

When the month ended, Stu very carefully tore the page from the calendar and put it with April 1958, in a folder he had found between the ledgers.

He scratched his neck as he wandered toward the john, his cock rubbing against his trousers, the image of Desi's snatch vivid in his mind.

April 1958 was pretty. April 1959 was the sexiest thing he'd ever seen.

What the hell would 1960 bring?

The Hamper Affair

Mel Bosworth

"Why do you still do it, Harry?"

Harry had been caught again, this time with his cock penetrating a swirl of wet panties. Laura stood looking on, jug of detergent hanging limply at her side.

"I'm sorry?"

Laura stormed off. She knew as well as Harry that he wasn't sorry. He'd been fucking the laundry for years. Her footfalls in the kitchen came fast and loud, but Harry would be damned if he didn't finish. He was still a man with principles, no matter the work or fetish. With a few sudsy pumps, he emptied his load into the wad of fabric, then tossed it back into the machine.

Laura wasn't in the kitchen by the time he made it upstairs, his belt loose and dangling.

"Laura?"

Since the children had gone, the need for discretion had dissipated as far as Harry was concerned. Laura might not agree, but she'd grown cold ever since menopause, which in turn fueled Harry's thread lust.

"Fuck it," he said to himself.

Harry looked out the window. Laura's car was absent from the driveway, the space offering a loud, prophetic echo of things to come. Shaking his head, he noticed his neighbor, Marla Johnson, hanging laundry on the clothesline.

With his belt already undone, getting his pants off was a snap. He jacked himself dry on to the window pane while watching her shake and clip, shake and clip, soppy jeans and white brassieres, her fingers well versed, her lipstick red. When Harry was spent, he slunk off to the bedroom and lay down, thoughts of stretched socks and ratty nylon ushering him to a peaceful mid-morning slumber.

★　　★　　★

"Wake up, Harry. I'm leaving you."

It was past noon, and Laura stood at the foot of the bed clutching a suitcase. Harry flopped around, cock caught in a soiled pillowcase, balls tucked into the sleeve of a T-shirt.

Laura looked away as he gathered himself.

"Where are you going?"

"I'm going to stay with Heather for now. I'll be gone for two weeks, Harry. I don't want to see even a trace of you when I get back."

Harry sat up, absently pawing a pair of boxer briefs. He brought them to his nose, and sniffed. His cock stirred, rose, then whapped against his naked stomach. Laura's face twisted like a sheet in a tornado.

"This is exactly what I'm talking about, Harry. You and your fetish. It's taken over. I thought I could handle it, I thought I might one day be a part of it, but you're not interested in me anymore. You're only interested in fucking baseball caps and fleece jackets."

"I never really got into baseball caps, Laura."

Harry's attempt to defend himself only incited Laura's rage. She swung the suitcase wildly, the hard nubs on the bottom grazing Harry's forehead. He fell back, a girlish scream slipping from his lips. Laura laughed.

"You're such a bitch, Harry. If only the children could see you now."

"I'm having dinner with Cody tomorrow night," said Harry, suddenly remembering. He'd planned the dinner with his son the week before, immediately after he and Laura had come from the steakhouse. The tablecloths there were green, and rough like a seasoned whore. Laura had pretended not to notice him curling an edge around his pole. However, when he came, he came hard, and the table shook, inviting the curious eyes of patrons and waitstaff. Laura had nearly choked on her ribeye then, but Harry was too bent in his swoon to notice.

"Good," she said. "You can explain to him that we're separated. I'll tell Heather."

"Separated?" asked Harry. "You don't want a divorce?"

Truth be told, nothing less than divorce was what Harry had expected, and the fact that he was okay with this notion made the idea of a separation a bit of a disappointment. It's not that he didn't love Laura anymore, but he just . . .

"No," sighed Laura. "I don't want a divorce. Not yet." Then her face went slack, eyes drooping. "But look at yourself, Harry. You fuck our dirty laundry. You fuck our clean laundry. Why? Have you become so disinterested in sex with a real person that you'd rather roll around with a shit-stained towel?"

The image made Harry's rod pulse, and Laura shook her head disgustedly.

"Never mind," she said. "Don't answer that."

She leaned toward the door, and Harry could tell she was waiting for something, but what, he wasn't sure.

"I'm sorry?" he offered, but the words immediately fell flat, both knowing they were devoid of sincerity. Harry just wasn't ready.

Laura cried, but she cried proudly, still strong and feminine.

"It's not all my fault," said Harry, and Laura hardened like dried mud on sweatpants.

"What the fuck do you mean, Harry, it's not all your fault?"

Harry recognized the tactlessness of his words, and melted. "I'm sorry," he repeated, this time with real emotion. "But ever since your 'change', Laura, you've grown distant. And I know I've had my . . . fetish for years, but . . ."

"But nothing, Harry. I've tried to enter into your world, I really have. Remember when I wore the same panties for a week? I asked if you wanted to play libertine? No, of course you don't remember. You were too busy humping the mattress cover to notice me. And I know I'm still sexy. Men hit on me all the time. But . . ." Laura took a step toward Harry. ". . . I still love you." Then she took a step back. "But you don't see that anymore."

Harry put his face in his hands, trying to ignore the scent of flowery detergent. "Laura," he began, an exasperated breath filling and then leaving his lungs. "It's . . ."

But Laura was gone. Again.

Harry wept into the blankets for a time, thinking of all the years he and Laura had shared, all their joys and laughter. Then he grew hungry and thought about the steakhouse, then the tablecloths. He simply couldn't wait to have dinner with Cody. "Cody? It's Pop. Can we push that dinner to tonight? I've got some news."

"Elastic pants, Dad? Really? Is that what you're wearing?"

Harry had opted for elastic pants for two reasons: they were comfortable, and they were practical.

If caught in a pinch, he could tuck away his meat hammer without anyone being the wiser, especially his bright-eyed son, Cody.

"I'm old," said Harry. "I can wear what I want. Am I embarrassing you?"

"No, you're embarrassing yourself. You've done it for years. I suppose I should be used to it by now."

Cody had always been a good boy, and Harry's unspoken favorite. It was not that he didn't enjoy Heather's company, but as she grew older, she began to take on the less desirable aspects of her mother, namely that she didn't enjoy his fabric fetish. It probably didn't help matters that she'd walked in on him plunging her prom dress two days before the prom. And it certainly didn't help matters that he'd finished himself off instead of stopping, and that Heather had stood watching, mortified. It was at times like those that Harry questioned his stubborn fortitude, but it was a fleeting hesitancy in commitment that had never merited a change of behavior.

"Turn away!" he'd barked to his pimpled and plump teenage daughter. She'd burst into tears as she got an eyeful of her father's furry ass squeezing and shaking. She'd refused the replacement dress he bought her, instead looking to her mother for support and, well . . . sanity. Their relationship became strained from then on. The only gifts he was allowed to give her were books. He made sure to line her shelves.

Cody looked over the menu. "How's Mom?"

"Your mother? She's fine, I guess."

"What does that mean?"

"What?"

Harry's distraction had already begun. His wrinkled penis was out and flirting with the overhang of green tablecloth, teasing it as one would an old lover. Cody sat up straight, and leaned in.

"What are you doing, Dad?"

Mr Ding Dong went back under wraps, the elastic waistband snapping loudly.

"What? Me? Nothing, Cody. Tell me about you. How's work?"

"Work is fine."

Cody's interest in his father's subterranean activities at the table had been piqued, and his eyes were narrowed and probing. Like his sister, he too had had his share of jarring experiences with the old man, but unlike his fairer sibling, he could empathize, somewhat. After all, he was a producer in the adult entertainment industry, a career choice Harry had applauded, and Laura had merely accepted.

"What news did you want to tell me, Dad?"

Harry squirmed in his seat, rattled. He called for a moment by raising his hand, then took a drink of water. "Your mother and I are separated," he blurted.

"What? When?"

"As of today. She's staying with your sister for two weeks. I have to get out of the house while she's away."

Cody sat back, shoulders slumping. "But . . . why?" Then his eyes flickered with knowing, and became angry. "Wait. Don't tell me why. I already know. You're un-fucking-believable, Dad."

"That's what they say."

"That's what who says? Who would say that? The clothes at the Laundromat? Are you dating a trophy pair of silk panties now?"

As Harry moved to point an irate finger at his son, he inadvertently knocked over a glass of water. The cool liquid seeped into the green tablecloth, conjuring images of bikini beauties washing cars, or young lovers fucking in the surf, or . . . a wet, green tablecloth.

Harry's patience and control suddenly met an abrupt and bitter end. Leaping from the booth, he ripped the cloth from the table, then sprinted toward the bathroom, leaving befuddled patrons, staff, and son in his panting wake.

Once inside the stall, he had trouble getting his pants down. Despite the easy access the elastic offered, his raging erection had become a nuisance, an uncooperative child, thickly hindering the lowering of his britches. Not to be outdone by his manhood, Harry tore the sides of his pants to free himself, then laughed maniacally as the garment pooled around his ankles.

"My cock!" he exclaimed. "My whore!"

Harry cradled the tablecloth like a dancing partner and, as he bent deeply in a convoluted dip of reverence and passion, the sheer joy of this union, as well as the rush of myriad broken mores, fired his cock with girth and life. Even his speech became antiquated, a cry to older times, a cry to the ageless libertine within, a cry of gluttonous whimsy.

"I shall now fuck thee, my luscious, whorish damsel!"

Then a cautious knock met the door of the stall, followed by an equally guarded voice. "Dad? You need to come out. We need to leave. If you don't, they're going to call the police."

"But lo!" boomed Harry. "A true test of my will and resolve! I shall not be denied!"

"Um, Dad? You will be denied, or you will leave in handcuffs. The manager is here with me, and she's not happy."

Cody stooped to peer under the door. Harry looked down at his son's face. Initially confounded by the sadness it possessed, Harry's torrent of hedonist confusion thinned as he studied the boy's pained blue eyes and helpless lips. The boy resembled his mother in the cheekbones and chin, and for a calm moment, Harry could actually see himself, see what he was doing. Never before had he viewed himself in this way, never before had he witnessed himself mirrored on the face of his own flesh and blood. The portrait was crippling, and the green tablecloth slid from his hands.

"I've lost control," he whispered.

"I know, Dad. Come with me. Let me help you."

The rush of sobriety came quickly and candidly, and Harry blubbered like an infant. "I'm so sorry, my boy. What an embarrassment I have become."

"It's okay, Dad. Just pull your pants up and let's leave. The manager has agreed not to phone the police. They know your wife just died."

"My what? Laura is dead? Tell me it's not so!"

Cody, still crouched, turned his head and winked up at his father. However, Harry, in his weakened state, missed the signal and crumbled to the floor. The toilet paper holder popped on his way down, spilling sheets and sheets of tissue.

"My Laura," he wailed. "My poor, poor Laura."

He flailed in the toilet tissue, then, struck with the oddities of grief, he began funneling it around his head. Once he'd successfully mummied himself, he pushed his tongue through the whiteness, and wagged pink, bawling. His hulkish erection settled on the tile, a broken soldier too long at war . . . with nothing.

Cody worked himself under the door and into the stall. Hooking his father under the armpits, he pulled him to his feet. "We have to go, Dad." Then, hushed, "Mom is okay. I just told the manager that so they don't report this as some sort of sex crime."

Harry's limp body jolted with life, and he embraced Cody. "My boy!" he said, mouth filling with frayed edges of toilet tissue. "My boy! I love you, my boy!"

The manager tapped an anxious shoe just beyond the door. "Is everything okay in there? I'm sorry about your wife, sir. But you understand, we can't have outbursts like this at the restaurant."

"I understand," spat Harry, ejecting gummy white balls on to Cody's cheeks. "I understand that some things are best kept behind closed doors."

Then Harry laughed, blind behind the toilet tissue, limp cock rubbing against the belly of his only son.

Cody helped his father unravel, then, discovering that the old man's pants had been rendered useless, he worked out a deal with the manager in which a few bills were passed. Harry walked out of the restaurant with his face hidden on his son's shoulder. He walked past the slack-jawed staff and the snickering patrons, his gait broken, yet strangely proud. The tail of the green tablecloth, which had been fashioned into a makeshift skirt, swooshed elegantly behind him.

"So, you're like . . . Cody's father?"

"I am," said Harry.

Harry sat on the chair while the woman strutted and bounced around the room. She was tall and thick, tits squeezing out of a bra two sizes too small. She was the result of good breeding. Harry wondered what her folks must have looked like when they made her. "Where are you from?" he asked.

"Texas."

She danced to a halt in front of Harry, then, curling her arms behind her back, she unclasped the bra. The straps trickled from her shoulders and down her arms, twin cups falling and displaying hard nipples and soft, soft skin. Harry wasted no time yanking his cock from his shorts. The woman grinned.

"Now listen, honey, Cody told me that you're not to touch me, and I'm not to touch you. Can we handle that?"

"Yes, ma'am."

Harry snapped at the bra as she dangled it in front of his face. His hands wrestled the socks from his feet.

"Give them here," she said.

Harry began balling them, but she asked him to stop.

"Leave them long, sugar," she cooed. Then she giggled and licked her lips.

"Why have I never met anyone like you?" asked Harry.

"Because you never looked," she said. She flicked her wrist, and the bra crashed on to Harry's face. Then she pulled down her panties, string-thin and black. Her pussy was clean and swollen, and when she kicked up a leg to wedge her heel on to the back of the chair, it threw enough heat to warm Harry's nose. He closed his eyes and inhaled.

"You smell so good," he said.

The woman smiled as she wiggled her hands into Harry's socks. "You should smell my panties, you little bitch."

Harry leaned forward to retrieve them, fingers greedy.

"Watch your face now, sugar," she warned. "Don't you touch this hot snatch of mine. You know the rules."

Harry took care to avoid contact, his face curling with great deftness along the length of her toned thighs, his eyes never once losing sight of her pussy. Gripping the panties, he leaned back, and sighed.

"You okay, sugar?" she asked.

"Never better."

"Good," she said, hips rocking, pink lips inches from his face. "Let's do some work."

She pulled Harry's socks to her elbows, fabric groaning. Wearing the socks like filthy gloves, she began petting her pussy, at first with one hand, then two. The flow of her movements gave the garments grace, and Harry's horn surged upward, straining dangerously close to her oiled thighs.

"Put my panties in your mouth," she moaned, head back, eyes fluttering wildly behind closed lids. Harry did as he was told.

"You fucking bitch," he said, sucking the panties, tasting, biting, chewing. He knotted the bra around the base of his cock, trapping the blood, engorging the organ, creating a bottled symphony of power and come. "You've helped me to be a man again," he said.

"Shut up, bitch."

"You've helped my family in ways you don't even know."

"Shut up, cunt," she snapped.

Her hands moved sensually, slowly, then quickly like a woodsman learning to love a tree. Her covered fingers were the tools, her pussy the soft cherry. She kept busy, pressing her clitoris and spreading the folds. Harry's leathery mitt cranked his cock forcefully, the clips of the bra chafing his balls. Their respective trees teetered, then picked up momentum. She fell as Harry fell.

"Bitch," they muttered in unison.

Her mouth opened, then locked. A trapped scream bled out in a staccato chirp. "Uh. Uh. Uh. Ah. Ah. Ah."

Harry spat out the panties, then wrung them around the head of his cock, bulbous and purple, true royalty once more, a rising Colonel. "You whore!"

"Oh, sugar!"

Her leg bucked, and the chair rocked back. She tried to quell the gush with her hands, but the spray was determined, and those juices that didn't immediately saturate the dirty sock-gloves covered Harry's face.

"B-b-bitch!" he stuttered, himself a victim of orgasmic eruption, the seed discharging from his weapon like double-ought shot. Globs of gooey man-love stuck to the smoothed crease behind her extended leg, the place where thigh meets ass, the place where lips dote, and fingers lose themselves. When the crack and splinter of the fallen trees had settled, the woman dressed herself in a robe and then stretched out on a velvet couch. Harry tied his shoes, lips fixed in a permanent grin.

Cody had told his father to wear a suit. After he'd parked the car in front of the home of his slightly estranged but always loving daughter, Harry stepped on to the sidewalk wearing his finest three-piece.

"Laura!" He waved.

Laura stood on the porch flanked by the children. Cody held his father in a steadying gaze. Heather, making no effort to mask her disgust, stared off in the distance. Laura, fresh from the beauty salon and wearing a green dress professionally stitched from the infamous tablecloth at her son's request, stood tall and open, eyes kind, if not a bit weary.

"It's great to see everyone together," said Harry, moving to embrace the children. Cody stepped up and accepted the arms of his father.

Heather slid to the side and nodded. "Hey, Dad."

"Hello, Heather. Is Rita here?"

"No." Heather frowned. "She's at a rally. I should be there too."

Harry had forgotten that his daughter's lover was extremely active in the lesbian/feminist movement. Now that he'd had time to reflect, after years of being clouded, he wondered if Heather might've liked the cock a bit more if she hadn't caught him plowing her prom dress way back when. Not that it mattered much to him, he wasn't averse to his daughter's lesbian lifestyle, but he simply wondered now if things would've been different if he hadn't been so selfish. He leaned in and kissed her cheek before she had time to pull away.

"Okay, Dad. That's enough."

Lastly, Harry turned to Laura, beautiful Laura who he'd neglected for far too long. With full eyes, blue and penitent, he knelt at her feet. "I'm so sorry, my dear Laura. I've been so lost in my fetish that I've forgotten just how beautiful you are."

"Do we have to be here for this?" asked Heather.

Cody shushed her.

Harry kissed the top of Laura's hand. "Our son has helped me, Laura. Our beautiful son. And you too, Heather. Your presence here today means the world to me."

"Sure, Dad. Whatever you say."

Harry's eyes climbed the curves of Laura's body, then nestled in her shaking smile. "I love you, Laura. I always have, and always will."

"I love you too, Harry," she said, hot tears breaking the crest of her cheekbones. "And I want to be a part of your world. I want you to fuck me in this dress. I want you to fuck this dress after you fuck me. I want us to fuck each other while the whore you see fucks herself with our clothes. I want us to be whole again."

Harry buried his face in Laura's crotch, allowing himself to smell her cunt, still vital after all this time. That it was cloaked in the rough fabric of the green tablecloth made the experience even sweeter. The onetime bane of his existence had now, at last, become his boon.

The Lady and the Unicorn

C. Sanchez-Garcia

Consider the handiwork of God;
who can straighten what He has made crooked?

Ecclesiastes 7:13

Blood has a range of taste, as scent has a range of aromas. Blood has a high level taste and an under taste. It is a blending of elements like music. This is also the way of scent. The under aroma tells you there is a trail and betrays to you the direction. If the scent becomes fresher you are following the creature that produced it, so you must use the under scent to know which direction is older and which is newer. It is as though the air were filled with singing voices and you are picking out from the choir the sound of a single voice. The high scent will tell you the individual, the condition of the individual, if it is injured or sick, horny or filled with fear. It will tell you how to catch him, where he is likely to run to. To acquire the high scent the animal, or myself, must pause to commune with the air and pay attention. Close the eyes. Hold the nose still and just so. Let the night air speak. It is the same with the deep taste of blood, except that scent is on the move, and if you are tasting the blood – well. It is no longer on the move.

I have survived so long by being aloof, as any hunter does. We do not love or hate that which we hunt. The wolf does not hate the deer. The deer does not feel sorry for itself. An endless life of repetition is borne only by solitude and indifference. Love and eternity do not go well together, the way people think. Love is meant to die. Your love will die too. One must be alone and apart to bear eternity without sentimentality or self pity. With nothing new, one must be cruel sometimes to relieve the boredom. To love is to feel the full burden of your damnation. It is a marvelous and mortal wound. When one pierces this shield of emptiness, it is a disaster.

I had been safe in my pose as a fatal little marionette holding forth the sulky lure of lust but feeling none, until *kuschelbaer* imbued me with love and his life, knowing me for what I am, and taking me. Like the wizard in the story he has bestowed on me a heart. Now this abandoned heart has put me on his scent, a hellhound hunting him down to keep his promise to make of me a real girl.

He left me during the day in a trail of strewn clothes and broken dishes all through our little house. And other things also, which he left behind and I have brought with me in a little gym bag I carry in my hand as I walk down the dirt road following his scent. Because of what is carried in this bag, I know he loves me still. He could not have left behind a sweeter valentine.

I have followed his scent for two nights. If it were not for the delay of the daytime, I would have had him already. I want to give him his bag. I want to talk about the things that are upsetting him so. This is not a chase that I enjoy, it is of necessity. My love is building in me like madness. It will explode into something terrible if it is not released.

Walking at night in the country, alone, down dark dirt roads, close to the pure land like those midnight forests of my old Germany, there is always the smell of smoke over everything. It is so much as that place where I lived as a pink young girl in the sun, that if a cuckoo bird should call from the trees I think my wicked heart would break into a thousand grieving stars. But I have his scent held fast. There is a bit of my own scent mixed with it from the year of lovely nights I rolled in his arms, and I would know it and follow it anywhere.

The scent is bright enough to say I've found him. I will see him tonight. He is hiding from me just over there, up the road there in the damnedest place. It is a tent.

Not any old tent, it is very big. At first, as I came up to it, I thought it might be a little circus such as I remember when I was a girl. It is filled with people and there is music too and the people are dancing around and singing. Now I see it, a brave banner has been painted and hung facing the highway: "Temple of God Holy Ghost Faith Revival".

Oh, how stupid.

He knows me better than this, why has he come to this place? Is he religious now? Conscience bothering you, honey? Your little unholy ghost out here knows how to get your mind off that, lover, if you give me half a chance.

He knows me so well, he knows churches hold no terrors for me. No, I have never feared the cross; I suppose it is the same for others like me, I don't really know. You may ask, why would one fear a crucifix or any such toy? I will tell you. It is not the thing itself, it is the ghost. The ghosts of the past that remind you of what you were and make you want to run away and grieve for yourself and what is lost and how you have stained your hands. After so many years, I am a holocaust. A massacre. It might be the same with a crucifix I suppose, or the bottom of a cup of tea in some childhood home. The cross only reminds such as me of the great question that hangs always over my head like a sword. If a creature such as me is possible, what else is possible? A soul?

I don't want to go in, I can't stand crowds, this he knows at least. I've been hanging back by the trees, smelling the forest air and it is hard to stay here also, because my need to be with him, to touch him and to feed on his touch is so unbearable.

Shall I go in? The reek of people is so strong, I can barely pick him out, but he's in there all right. Front row and left, or close to it. I think . . . I think I smell . . . yes. He's wearing his New York Yankees jacket I got for him. Darling!

It is hard to come from the cool dark to the bright electric lights and all the noisy people waving their arms and shouting. I don't understand; what made him come here? He must tell me before this is over. There are chairs in the last row and I put my bag on one and I'm about to sit and wait when I smell something interesting. An animal smell, it reminds me of soft cheese. I pause over my wooden folding chair and sniff the air, trying to pin it down but the air is riot with odors. This smell. It is an old smell, from my childhood, I should know this smell, what can it be? And there, a few seats away I see where it comes from. There is this girl, yes. And there is a new baby she has, yes. But she is feeding it, feeding it from her own breast. It sucks life from her. I have not seen this sight I think since my days in the sun. A girl with a baby at her breast. She's not a healthy girl to be sure, you can tell by the quality of her high smell, and she is thin and pale. A wind or an illness could knock her over. Or a bit of bad luck, such as I. Such a person, I think her blood will be thin and have a bitter under taste of old disappointments. It will be unsatisfying. Garbage blood. But with all the noise around her and the shouting and singing, she is an island of peace, a Madonna with her baby at her nipple, hidden modestly by a soft little blanket. I cannot take my eyes from her.

This baby, how long will he live? His bright, watery eyes, his musky scent of neglect, in a few years she will be beating him half to death, this girl. I feel sad for him, which is a strange thing for me, to feel sad for someone. I am filled with this feeling I have no name for, but I feel terribly sad for this girl and her kid who have no future.

The baby slips off her long brown nipple, the blanket drops a little and I see the young men looking sideways, leaning in, trying to catch a peek. She takes the blanket and covers him but it is too late now. Our eyes have met. She sees the hunger in me, and not for blood. I see the thing in her also; I know when a person wants to die. I know it instantly, because it is my business to know such a one, a sick animal as wolves might cut out from a herd. She wanted to, once. But not anymore.

The baby is now looking at me too. Hello, baby.

Taking up my little bag I come over and stand above them, looking down. The baby looks like he wants to sleep in her arms, and the noise doesn't bother him at all. He is such a calm and peaceful little thing. Will he then be brave when he grows up? He smells not very clean, no. But in spite of everything, he has a sad beauty, like a fallen king. You're a pretty little boy, aren't you, now? He has little flaky things in his scalp and he is not fresh because she's not washing him properly, is she? No. He deserves better than what life has given him. Lazy girl, now if this were my baby I would give him a good scrub in the evening first thing after rising and put oil on his head and . . . and . . . what?

Oh now it begins. Now it begins, all the sticky stupid things. I will grab my man and drag him out of here by his dick if I have to. I won't stay another minute.

Yes – but see him!

"Oh he's sweet. Look at him. May I see? Is anyone sitting here?"

"Go ahead." She nods at the chair. I put down my bag and look again at the smelly little thing in her arms. Oh, this stupid woman. This good child should be kept better, beginning with his bath. He will grow up to be stupid like the people here.

"May I hold him a moment? Please?" He is already half asleep and she wraps the blanket around him and offers him to me. As gently as a butterfly I take him and hold him to me.

Instantly, he goes crazy. He is looking at my face and wailing. Whatever he is seeing in me, it's terrifying the little shit out of his mind. Now, good God, the skinny *frau* is staring at me too. He has seen nothing yet of the world, but he is wild at the sight of me. How does he know? Is he already so wise?

Now he is just howling and kicking, absolutely inconsolable. It hurts me. I can't believe this little turd, without enough in him for a snack, has the power to hurt me. But he does. The sight of him makes memories bubble in me. Already she is holding out her arms and looking at me strangely. "I don't understand, he likes people, he never acts like that."

What do you mean by that? I want to ask her, demand of her – what do you mean by that? She has him now, oh yes, brave girl, she has rescued him from the evil *nosferatu* bitch, is that what she thinks? Is it? He is crying still. Christ. Let me wring his neck or something, to shut him up.

But the wailing little thing has Daniel's eyes. Oh, oh – but see him! The poor scared little boy. Beautiful boy! There you are – I stretch out a finger to touch his face but she pulls him close to her, protecting her cub from she knows not what. Could we? Is it possible, and if it were, our boy might be wonderful, and maybe have my good silver hair and Daniel's big shoulders. I would wash his soft hair in the evening and keep him very clean and sweet smelling, and I would tell the old stories to him . . . and . . . stop.

No. No more of that. Daniel has been stuffing his stiffy up in me every night and letting loose for a year and there is no such baby. No, no, no, it would have happened if so. But I am thinking. My womb is dead, it is a ghost's womb, I am thinking. But Daniel, he is not like other men, I am thinking. His cum feeds me better than any blood. Neither of us knows why it is so. If he can be so different, so special from other men, what else can he do? Doctors, they are very clever these days. They can do miracles.

No. Stop that.

She is trying to console him, he will not stop crying for anything and now she is shaking him – you're shaking him too hard – not like that! Don't hurt him! My hands, they're reaching for him and I stop myself instead.

I didn't come here to moon over somebody's little shit pie. Let her shake him to death, it doesn't matter. What the fuck is this place doing to me? I'm getting out. I don't want to be here anymore. Where is he?

Without saying goodbye, I pick up my little bag and move away down the row towards the far end to reach the aisle. Standing on toes I peer over the crowd, searching but I can't see him. A crowd of people have come into the tent behind me and I'm boxed in. This whole thing is getting out of control.

I'm scanning over the crowd for him, and there is a hand on my shoulder.

"Delia?"

A heavy black woman is turning me around and has a huge smile on her face. "Is it you, honey?"

I don't know what she wants and I shake my head and try to step away to get her goddamned hand off of me, but she steps towards me. "Oh I'm sorry," she says, "I thought you were my god daughter Delia. Oh, you look like her, just like her!"

This woman is so happy to see me, and then there is a fat man behind her and she's shouting to him, "Doesn't she look just like Delia?"

"Shit, she does. She got that real platinum hair for sure."

The woman yanks me towards her and before I can stop she has me in a hug. My face is pressed into her neck and I'm smelling her hair and the odor of her sweat and she is clapping me on the back calling me things. The man is there and she passes me to him like a child and he's all over me too and he's hugging me, covering my face with his smell until my nose goes dead.

"Naw, she don' look like Delia." He holds me at arm's length and peers at my face. "Just got her hair's all."

"Ain't she got beautiful hair, ain't she?" The woman is pawing her blood-fat fingers at my head and stroking it and she's so happy. "Oh, I do love me that silver hair she got." Other people are crowding me now and the hunter in me smells a trap. At any moment will come the silver bladed knife and my eyes are darting, searching the crowd, trying to pick out who it will be, some gypsy, some special person who will have serious eyes, but I can't pick it out.

"Bless you child!" An old white lady who came with them grabs my arm with white gloved hands and shakes it and my eyes are darting side to side – my other arm raised to ward off the attack I know is coming. How will they do it to me? If one grabs my other arm, do I dare kill them before I have rescued Daniel? "Don't she look like Delia?" yells the black woman again.

"Oh not at all, lands no," says the old lady holding my arm, "but Delia's older, ya' all see can't you, this here's only a young girl."

The black woman smiles in my face. "Welcome to the revival. This here's our Holy Ghost church. We got the Holy Ghost all night! You'll have a blessed evening. I'm Ruby."

Someone behind me, I try to spin around, but the old woman has me in her bony hands – I see it all now, their plan and suddenly there is a face of a young man close to mine. He has managed to creep up behind me, which never happens. My free hand rises to strike out his eyes before the weapon is in me but there is no hatred in him, he is truly happy to see me. His empty hand is out. "Welcome to our Holy Ghost revival. I'm Brother Edward."

"Howdy doody," I mumble, and touch his hand. I don't know what else to do.

"Now don't she look like Delia?"

"Got that hair," he says.

I like the fact they keep going on about my hair. It is really very nice hair, silver blonde, almost white. You don't see people with this hair much anymore. I wonder where this poor Delia is, maybe the lost lamb of the family. I look past them at the girl with the baby. The wretched thing is sitting by herself with her reeking infant. She is looking at me and I feel a burst of pride because she sees I can be loved too, do you see? I am popular! I have admirers, here they are, and look at so many people who are happy to see me. Not like you. She looks away, wounded. Good.

The little band starts up again and everyone around is clapping and singing along.

"Who you here with?" hollers the jolly fat man.

The old woman has let go of me and I point over the crowd. "My boyfriend is over there."

"Sit with us," says Brother Edward and shakes the back of a chair at me. Well, I guess. I like the music. It's like the rock and roll. I stand in front of the chair and put down my little gym bag and clap along, trying to fit in until the right time.

When the song is over, a man in a cheap black suit steps forward to the lectern. His face is shining in the electric lights and his suit, which someone should iron for him, is stained with sweat as he raises his arms. He yells "Are you ready for your blessing tonight?"

Everybody cheers and jumps.

"I feel an anointing!" he yells, waving his arms and closing his eyes.

I turn to Ruby. "What is *'anna-noiten'*?"

"Now what is that? What's that little old sound you got?"

" 'Anna-noiten'?"

"Where you from, darlin'?" says the old white lady with the gloves.

"Germany."

"Germany!" hollers Ruby.

"I feel an anointing tonight," yells the preacher man, "there is someone here with a broken heart. There is a stranger here and the Holy Spirit is anointing me to reach out to this person with a broken heart."

A girl is moving towards him, walking with a cane until he puts his hands on her and closes his eyes and shouts in something that sounds like a make believe language. I have been around for quite some time, and in the business of things I now speak four languages besides also my proper *Deutsch*. But this crazy language he thinks he has, it sounds like sheep going baabaabaabaa.

The girl drops the cane and raises her hands to heaven, crying. Is she supposed to be cured of something? Everyone shouts "Amen!" and "Hallelujah!" and I am shouting it too, surprised at myself, but getting into the spirit of the thing. It's very nice, this silly tent church. It's not so stuffy, like the Catholic Church. It's like a happy party with music. I think I like it. Maybe no one wants to kill me after all. But I will be careful.

I am still trying to get my nose back, snorting and wiggling it. I don't see Daniel anymore and I am too ruined to smell him out in this aromatic labyrinth. "I was a stranger and you took me in." The preacher man starts it all up again. "And the Lord said when you take the least of these in you take me in. Hallelujah! Blessed are the broken in spirit for they will be comforted. Hallelujah! I feel the spirit moving and the Holy Spirit has put it on my heart what to speak to you tonight, of the broken heart. The broken heart. The stranger with a broken heart – hallelujah! – the homeless with a broken heart – hallelujah! – the parent with a broken heart, the child with a broken heart – hallelujah! – to speak to you – hallelujah! – baa babaabbahey! – of the enemy hidden among us."

Oh no. I see it now. A trap. It's been a long time since this happened to me. I came here only for one person, I didn't plan to hurt these people but I will have to. I see the best escape, over there where the tables will slow them down, unable to surround me, forcing them to come at me one by one. The first kill will be the most important. They will be underestimating me because of my small size and delicate beauty. All but one. Let them think I'm weak as long as possible, feeling out the hidden leader. He will be the one with the angry eyes, who does not stink of fear. He will be their strength, so his death must be precise, vicious and ghastly, a big show to take the heart out of them. Take out his eyes, then his breath, then I will tear him to pieces at will for them to see. It will put the mob into a panic, buying me time to make the woods. Once there, we are in my arena and I can play in the shadows, picking them off.

Did Daniel betray me to them? *Et tu kuschelbaer?* No, he would not do that. And if he did, I would not want to go on anymore.

"I am speaking—" he says in a hushed voice, whimpering with emotion as though he were trying to force himself to tears "—of the enemy among you who wants you to have a broken heart, who wants to bring you down, who wants you to feel abandoned, who wants you to have no hope, who wants to separate you from God. The enemy wants you to have a broken heart. I want to magnify the Lord tonight, somebody! Somebody help me! Somebody help me magnify the Lord. Somebody tell me amen!"

"Amen!" everybody yells in one voice.

"Amen!" I yell too, watching them carefully. They are not watching me. Maybe it is okay.

"We're on our way to Heaven, and you don't need a map, and you don't need a GPS, and you don't need the Internet, you only need Jesus – hallelujah! – and a broken heart. You need it, you need the broken heart, and our Lord – our Lord he had a broken heart – hallelujah! – and he was on the Cross and his heart was broken and he was abandoned and he cried out 'Why have you forsaken me?' and-and-and—"

I do believe he is going to cry or something. He is certainly working himself up to frenzy. I am watching the faces of those around me, smelling them a little better now, trying to feel what they feel, and though they are much excited, there is no anger anywhere. They are very happy, these people.

"—and he was crying out to his heavenly father and hallelujah! – and crying out from the scriptures, abbabablelujaheyahey – let me read you, let me read you, let me read you from the Word of God; amen!"

"Amen!" yells everyone and I do too. I am beginning to feel happy, and there he is! The blue satin jacket with the silly top hat and baseball bat on the back. I see him second row left, where I smelled him before. Does he know I'm here? Already all my body is starving for him and wanting him. I want his hands on me, I want him deep inside me all the way, to have him all to myself. I want to see how his eyes again become so wide when I show him my breasts. My little bag and I will surprise him tonight, but I must cut him off before he gets away with whoever brought him here. He must leave with no one but me.

"Here—" yells the preacher in that whimpering broken voice, ready to explode "—here is the word of God." In his hand, a badly beaten old Bible. "I want to read to you, I feel a great anointing tonight to read to you from the book of Psalms. I want you to hear about the broken heart. In the Book of Psalms, Psalm 137 – listen here, here's what it says, it says, 'By the rivers of Babylon, there we sat down, yeah, there we wept, when we remembered Zion.' The children of Israel – they had the broken heart. They sat by the waters of Babylon – and yeah – they wept for all that had been lost and taken away from them! Hallelujah. Hallelujah. They had the broken heart, and cried out to their Heavenly Father to comfort them."

Look at him. The waters of Babylon. Talking in voices like a sheep. The man is trying to work himself into tears like a little boy who is afraid of a spanking.

"And here – oh, listen with me, can I get an anointing?"

"Amen!" yells the happy mob. "Amen, brother!" I yell too, and Ruby is happy for me, and gives me a hug which makes me happy.

"—Now listen to me. Jesus was on the Cross, and he wept and he had the broken heart, he had the broken heart for you – yes, you! For me, for us sinners. Look! Look right here! Oh look here in the twenty-second Psalm." He slaps it with a bang.

"Read it!" yells Ruby, almost in my ear and the mob is yelling "Read it!" and "Tell it!"

"Get it said!" I yell and people around me cheer. Maybe Daniel has heard my voice. Maybe he will come to me by himself.

He turns it to a place he has marked and holds it up for everyone to see. "Psalm Twenty-two – My God! My God! Labbabab-bachsathenthie! Hallelujah!"

I hate when he does that. It sounds so stupid. Who does he think he is fooling with that phony language?

" 'Why hast thou forsaken me? Why art thou so far' – why Lord? Why? 'Why art thou so far from helping me and from the words of my roaring?' Why Lord are you so far from my broken heart?"

I hate to say it, it is humiliating to admit, but he is kind of getting to me. This talk about the broken heart. That is my heart he is talking about.

"Read it!" I scream, loud enough for Daniel to hear. "Get it said!"

"Amen, sister!" yells Eddie and whaps me on the back. I like it.

" 'Oh my God, I cry in the day time, but thou hearest not, and in the night season and am not silent. But thou art holy, O thou that inhabitest the praises of Israel. They cried unto thee and were delivered. They trusted in thee and were not confounded.' The Lord wants you – all you with a broken heart – to trust in him. All you who weep by the waters of Babylon, the Lord wants to dry your tears. Look what else it says here, look – look here – and God does not lie, it says, 'But I am a worm and no man, a reproach of men and despised of the people. All they that see me laugh me to scorn and shoot out the lip—' "

There he goes. He's starting to make himself cry now.

" '—they shake the head – they shake the head—' " (now he shakes his head for us) " '– saying he trusted on the Lord!' " Okay, now he is jumping up and down and tears are on his face, and see there, Ruby and her husband – they are jumping too. I begin jumping up and down together with them, glancing over the crowd to get a glimpse of my man. I take care to see I don't jump too high so as not to seem creepy to everyone.

" 'He trusted on the Lord that he would deliver him; let him deliver him, seeing he delighted in him.' They were laughing at Jesus, and Jesus was alone – hah! And he was on the Cross – hah! And they laughed at him – hah! Saying, 'Let him come down from the Cross' and Jesus' heart was broken. He had the broken heart. The heart of the stranger and he was a stranger among us, amen! Amen! Amen!"

Everybody is going crazy and yelling, "Amen!" and jumping all about everywhere like fleas. Now I hear it, many of them are speaking now to make themselves crazy in the silly words that sound like a language. Baa baa baa. Baa baa baa. I am the wolf surrounded by sheep going baa baa baa.

Sheep! You sheep going bababba – I can kill any of you. I can do it! What do you know about God or death or evil? Dumb bastards. Dumb fucking bastards. I can kill you! One or all at once. What a fat neck sweaty Ruby has. I'm not evil! This was done to me, I didn't ask for it! I'm probably a saint compared to some of you. I should kill someone here just to show you the devil's face. Stupid fucking sheep!

"Say what?" says Eddie, looking at me funny.

I imagine Eddie the way he would look with his eyes gouged out by my fingers. I imagine his body floating in a swamp like the French farmer I tortured all night until dawn, long ago in his own garlic field. Fucking black bastard! I can kill you nigger sheep! *Swarzen!*

. . . what in the world . . . ?

These people. I have killed so many just like them. Some of them, like Ruby, I made them suffer and I did it just for fun.

I hold my hands in front of me, these fingers, the things they've done. They cannot guess at the person standing next to them. I glance up at the old white granny with the funny white gloves. Her brittle bones. Once alone, an easy kill. Old blood is like old wine.

But what would her grandchildren say?

"If the bank has got a hold of you, and it's got your house, and it's got your car and it – it has broken your heart, the Lord wants to heal you. If your boyfriend or your husband has left you, or your wife has left you, the Lord wants to heal you. If-if-if-if you had some drugs in the past, and-and-and you're burning up for drugs, but you say to yourself 'this is not God' and your heart is broken and you're alone, somebody help me, God wants to heal your broken heart. 'I may tell all my bones' the Bible says right here, 'I may tell all my bones, they look and they stare at me, they part my garments among them and cast lots—' "

"Shut up!" I murmur at him. "Stupid bastard! With your fucking fake language! You don't know anything about the Devil. Not like me! I'll bite your dick off in pieces and play with your guts!"

Ruby looks at me shocked, no one else seems to have heard. A gob of pink foam drops from my lips to the floor. I give her a look and she moves away from me.

" 'Be thou not far from me' – hallelujah! – 'Oh, Lord, Oh my strength, haste thee to help me—' "

"Shut up! I'll fucking kill you!" I yell again, this time for real. "I'll cut your dick off and fuck your skull with it!" Eddie has been standing next to me with his hands in the air as though being arrested, weeping his little heart out and going babababa. But he stops and looks at me shocked. "What do you think you're looking at, you big nigger bastard? Are you looking at my tits? Do you want to fuck me?" I yell at him, holding out my breasts. "You buck nigger bastard? Is that it? I'm the devil! I'm the demon! I can tear your throat out and not give a fucking damn about any of you! I'm the devil!"

He's staring at me, but no one seems to notice yet.

I fling my hands up over my ears.

"Stop!" I am turning in circles now with my arms over my head. "Go away!"

" 'Deliver my soul O Lord,' " says the preacher man, " 'deliver my soul from the sword—' "

"Get away from me! I'll hurt you. I've killed so many people. More than everybody! I want blood! So much blood! So many people!"

" '– and my darling from the power of the dog. Save me from the lion's mouth—' "

All around me! I see them – their faces. I know them. Their faces! I've killed so many. They're all around me, people who hate me. And they should hate me, I am a monster. I am loathsome. Daniel will never want to touch me. I will never be loved!

"–'save me from the lion's mouth oh Lord, for thou hast heard me from the horns of the Unicorns!' "

"Love me!" I am swinging wildly at the air, trying to get at their heads. "Love me you stupid fucks!" I grab someone's hair. "I've killed so many people!"

"– The Lord has called all with the broken heart, he has called you even from the very horns of the Unicorns."

"Unicorns!" I scream, not knowing what I'm saying anymore.

I'm tearing out my hair, clawing at my eyes. I can't see! My feet trip over something and I fall blind on my head.

"– The Bible says 'thou hast heard me from the horns of the Unicorns!' Call out to Jesus!"

"Jesus!" I am wild now, kicking, snatching blindly, biting at my own hands, swallowing my own blood, trying to tear the meat off my bones so I will never be able to hurt anyone ever again. I must die! I'm drowning in stolen blood. "Blood! Love me! Pray! Pray for me. Oh God – somebody pray for me!"

Above me the mob is screaming my name. Thrashing around on my back, crashing against chairs and snatching at the air, trying to tear my own skin off of me and claw the eyes out of my head. The demon is inside of me! I must tear myself open and get the demon out! There is not so much pain now, but I know I need to die. I scrabble over the floor, trying to get at my bag. "I'm the devil's blood bitch! I'll kill you all!" A man reaches for me and I lash out scratching his face. Blood! His blood on my nails. I stick my fingers in my mouth and drool. There is so much blood on my hands, such as I never knew, and I'm going to die now with all of it to pay. I'm clawing at the gym bag, trying to tear it open with my teeth. "Kill me! Somebody kill me!" Waving the gym bag in the air. "For God's sake somebody kill me!" I am screaming like an animal.

Words. Words. The air is filled with words. Soft words.

Light. The air is filled with light. Soft light. It's so quiet and peace is coming to me. Is this true death at last? My body is shaking and my clothes are torn. I can see. But the faces around me, looking down over me, are Ruby and the others, fearful and concerned. Hands to mouths, lips moving in prayer, hands held out over me as if hoping to call down some magic power. The preacher is standing above me.

"I cast thee out!"

He wants me to go?

"In the name of our Lord, who has given us power over demons and devils – I cast thee out of this girl in the name of Jesus Christ."

He has cast the demon out of me? But I thought I was the demon.

"In the name of Jesus Christ – be gone!" The people are looking at him, hanging on his words, his countenance.

I'm searching the faces surrounding me and there is no hatred. How is it I'm alive? These people, they know nothing of me. These are not the ones I killed, but only Ruby and the others. I search the crowd for Daniel's face, but he isn't here, and everything feels different.

I roll on to my knees, searching inside, wanting to believe in miracles, oh – I have faith. No one has faith like the damned. But I feel different, there is no hatred. I don't want to hurt anyone.

I have been wrong. I have been healed. It was not me. All along it was not me, and I'm only a girl who the devil has possessed and played a terrible trick on for all these many years and endless nights. It was not me, no it was never me killed those people, it was the demon possessing me and am I free now?

Sitting up now, looking at my hands, only the hands of an innocent girl who has been abused in a nightmare. Is it over?

The preacher is looking in my face and sees no evil there. He is relieved and joyful, and why not? He has seen a miracle. "Do you accept Jesus as your Lord and Savior?" he says.

"Yes," I say. "I think I do." It sounds stupid the way I say it.

"On your knees. On your knees, child, and pray with me. Confess that you are a sinner."

"Oh sir, I am a sinner. You have not met such a sinner as me."

"Do you accept Christ Jesus as your personal Lord and savior?"

"I do. *I do*!" My heart is overflowing. I will be one of these people. It can all be different now. I will have friends! I will go out at night, together with all my friends. We'll have fun and harm no one. I have forgotten what it is to have a friend.

He reaches out and hugs me, and I hug him, burying my face in his shoulder. But something disturbs me. I am smelling too many things. Am I really so different now?

As he lets go of me, Ruby is on her knees and hugging me. And then other people too. Everybody is hugging me and crying for me and holding me tight, and they are so happy and I have made them happy. I love them. I love them all. They love me. I am forgiven of my crimes. Jesus has forgiven me and I want to be with my new friends here.

Their hands are all over me, rejoicing over me. I am one of them. That is the miracle, that I can be one of them, even someone like me.

I am ordinary. Amen.

I must find *kuschelbaer*, I must tell him the good thing that has happened. I want him to see me and be proud of me, and we can be together now. We will have a baby too and be a family like any family. I will get a job in the Wal-Mart store.

I don't see him in the crowd standing around me. He has either fled or doesn't know all this hubbub is over a person he knows. I scramble to my feet and feel terribly weak and even hungry. Hungry. What do I eat? What is it my body really wants? If I eat food, will I be sick in front of these people? Will they see me despair and weep blood tears? I run through my feelings, touching and searching inside to see who it is, who is the real me, and who is doing this searching and what is it I am looking for? What is the urge I am feeling, what does it want? Blood? Food? I am a shadow standing at the edge of a dark shore.

Where is he? Peering over the heads of the crowd, looking for his shiny blue jacket. He must be outside. But the people, suddenly they are all over me. Ruby is hugging me. Her husband, people from everywhere – see them! They're weeping for me. Some of them, hands up in prayer, praising God, praising Jesus and I want to praise Jesus too and find some way, I don't know how yet, some good work to do to show him I'm not a sinner anymore and he has invested his miracle wisely.

It frightens me to think, what shall I do? To be only human? When Jesus healed the lepers, did they feel this way, did they have to learn how not to go about being sick and shunned anymore? Did they have to learn how to be only healthy men just like anyone? When Jesus raised Lazarus from the dead, was he like me? Did he have to learn how to inhabit the world again and to forget what he had learned from death?

I want to see Daniel. It is the only thing I know for sure. I move away from the crowd and they begin the clapping and the music and the jumping as the preacher returns to his little pulpit, mission accomplished. I want to pray but I don't know how. I only know how to curse God. I don't know how to talk to Him.

Outside the air is cool and damp and filled with forest smells, but I can't tell which nose is smelling them. What I scent, do others scent it as I do? Or am I still smelling with the demon's nose?

"Wait!"

Running to me from the tent, it's Eddie and he has my bag. "You left this."

He puts it in my hand, beaming with happiness for me. He's proud of me.

"Thanks."

"Man that was sure something tonight," Eddie says.

"Yes," I say. "I'm very glad I came here." Suddenly I remember and I feel terrible. I take his hand in mine. "Eddie, my good friend. I'm sorry I said those bad things to you. I didn't mean them. Do you know that?"

"I know."

"You must tell Ruby for me, I didn't mean those bad words and that you and I are good friends."

"She knows. You coming back in? Want to pray together?"

"Soon. I want to say hello to someone."

Daniel is over there, by the tree line and he is watching me. I don't know how I know this, what senses are telling me this, if it is some ordinary thing anyone would know or if I am still as I was. I could ask Eddie if he knows Daniel is over there, but I'm afraid of what he will say. He shakes my hand, Brother Eddie does, and then scampers back in and is lost in the crowd and the noise.

What are you thinking, my love? I know you're there, watching me from the shadows as I once watched you on a country road one night, the night I almost killed you. The night you got to me.

There he is.

The tent light only reaches a little way. He is standing at the tree line and he's waiting for me to come to him. I hold up the bag in my hand for him to see. I want to snuffle the air to see what he is feeling, but that's not possible anymore, is it? Is it? And if the night air should speak to me of him, what does it mean? Am I not cured? Am I not now the good ghost of the girl before who was the evil ghost of the good girl before her? Do I dare to draw a breath?

I must be mortal. I must make myself mortal, by living without tricks. Of course the final trick will be when the sun rises. There will be no fooling the sun. Walking down the hill, past the light, into the dark and still I see him clearly which I think is not as it should be. I might ignore my nose, but I can't make my eyes pretend to be blind. I come up to him. "Hi, Daniel," I say, feeling shy and stupid all of a sudden, as though we had never embraced. "I'm back."

His eyes are intense as my own, defiant. Had the crowd attacked me, I would have picked this face as the leader, with his lidded intense eyes.

His eyes are filled with his sense of violation, and an immense loneliness. His loneliness is the price of loving me in my natural solitude, the lamb loving the tiger. I had thought once to meet his family, but realized I could not. There was room in my world safe only for him and no more. Beyond that my heart could not stretch. But that was before I was saved.

"You found me," he says. Before I can answer: "What just happened in there?"

"Did you see everything?"

"Yeah. Were you just fooling everybody? Was it real?"

"My love, it was real. I went a little crazy, but I accepted the Jesus Christ now. I'm not evil anymore."

"You went totally bat shit in there. I thought you were going to start attacking people. I thought you might go after me next. You knew I was there."

"I came here to bring you home."

"I was about to flag you down, get you to go after me and maybe spare the other people, but then you fell on the floor and went into a fit. What the hell happened to you in there?"

"It's all right now, listen to me. Daniel. I'm your ordinary girl now. The evil thing inside, it's gone. I feel different. The preacher man, he healed me. Jesus has healed me."

He looks at me suspiciously. He wants to search my face, but does he see in the dark the way I can see him? Does he see my face so clearly?

"Why did you come to this place?" I say.

"It's nothing complicated." he says. "I'm staying with Aunt Tilly. She's born again and wanted me to come here with her. That's all it is. I didn't want to stay at her place alone." He is keeping his distance from me. "Are you sure you're all right?"

I move in close to him, touching him again – and oh the joy to feel him against me, the heat of him – still holding my bag, but stepping close enough for my breasts to aggressively brush up against him. I'm trying to get him to put his arms around me, but he steps back and I feel his fear. "Why?" I say.

"I got to know if you're all right."

"No – why did you not want to be there, alone? You were afraid."

He looks down, ashamed. And afraid.

"Why, my love? Why were you afraid?"

"I thought you might be looking for me."

"Of course I was looking for you," I say soft and slow, feeling the bag in my hand grow heavy. "Why would I not look for you? Why would you not want me to find you alone? I'm still your woman. Don't you want to be alone with me?"

"I thought . . ." He is really sweating it now. It is miserable to see. "I thought you'd be pissed."

Whispering. "Why would I be pissed? Hmn. Now, let me think."

He only looks at me with those angry frightened eyes, and I wish I were blind. This is not the Daniel I came to find.

"Why would I be pissed, *kuschelbaer*?" He is looking at the bag now. He knows. "Oh, I wanted to give you these. Look what I found beside my little bed." I put the bag on the ground, unzip it and reach in. One in each hand, I show him. A hammer in one hand, I show him. A sharpened piece of wooden broom handle in the other, I show him. I hold them out to him. "Is this why I would be pissed at you? You think?"

"Dammit, Nixie!"

I thrust them out to him. "What are these? *What are these?*"

He turns away. He can't look at me, but I am trembling now. I can't stop myself or what I feel. "What is this?" I shake them at him. I stamp my feet. I know I'm ruining everything, and I can't help it. I love him so terribly I want to bite his nose. "Is it a sexy new game you want to play? You can dress up and be the fearless hunter Mr Van Helsing, *jah*? And I will be sexy little Miss Lucy, in my nightgown in my toy coffin, and you will climb in with the hammer and the stake, yes? – and we will play and do the rinky-tink together and have some fun, yes? Would you like to maybe do that now? Now is a good time. Let's play Van Helsing—"

"Shut up! Shut up!"

Now he is almost crying and I am almost crying too. I shake them at him, screaming, "*What were you thinking?*" I hate this, to be cruel to him. I'm hurting him, but it's the only way to know where things stand. I try to calm myself and remember what it really means, finding there the hammer and the stake discarded beside my bed. "You couldn't do it, could you?"

"I couldn't do it. God help me, I couldn't do it."

I hate myself for doing this, but this is the road I must lead him down, until he is tame again. "Why?" Softly I speak, because I would be his lover again and he is almost mine. "Why not?"

He shakes his head.

"I want to hear it. Please say it. Say for it for me, please. Why couldn't you kill me in my sleep?"

"Because I couldn't. I love you. God forgive me."

"Why God forgive you? What's wrong with being in love with me?"

"You know why. Don't act innocent."

I shove the hammer and stake at his chest but he won't take them and steps away, blundering backwards. "Why don't you kill me now? Right here?"

"I can't! But somebody should."

Oh this hurts. I didn't expect that he would say it.

"Why somebody?"

"*Nordchen*, I love you with all my soul and I always will. But. But, you need . . . That is. Somebody needs . . . You need to be put down."

"Put down?" To hear it said that way. It shocks me. "Why put down? I'm not some mad dog, Daniel."

"Jesus, Nixie—"

"Stop! Don't say his name in vain."

"Oh now, now you're getting all religious on me, is that it? It's not that simple, honey."

"Why is it not that simple! Have faith in me. I love you. Love me!"

"I do."

"I'm saved, Daniel. I'm saved by the blood of Jesus. The holy man has removed the demon from me, did you see it? I'm just a girl now like any girl. We can have a baby. I want a baby for you. We will have a home. My sins, all my sins, they're forgiven. We'll begin again. Make a baby with me."

"I don't think it works like that, sweet pea," he says. The fear in him is changing to rage, and I can't help but smell it. He's getting out of my control. "Tell me something. And damn you, tell me the truth."

I know already what it is.

"There's this thing on the TV news," he says.

"No!" I say. "Don't you keep bringing that up again."

"You listen to this. Four bodies behind the railroad yard."

"No!"

"They were torn to little pieces. Jesus."

"Shut up!"

"No fucking heads! Does that mean anything to you? No heads."

"So?" It is all I can do now not to throw the hammer and wood at him and run away crying like a little girl.

"Last week I found you with blood all over you."

"So?"

"Blood all over you?"

"I told you already – I told you. It was pig's blood."

"Pig's blood? Four guys, ripped to fucking little pieces. Somebody saw you. They're calling you 'The Ripper'." Now he's pulling at his hair. "Oh God. Oh God," he says. "Pig's blood! Pig's blood?"

"*They were pigs!*" What's the use.

"Jesus! Nixie! Je-zus!"

Feebly I hold out the hammer and stake. "So do it if that's what you want. You were afraid I'd be pissed at you, and maybe pull your head off. Is that what you think of me? I won't fight you. Where do you want me to lie down?"

"No!" He is in agony. Sweet prince. "I can't. I won't. I can't stand the thought of hurting you."

"You've already hurt me. Your eyes have hurt me."

I thought I knew him, but he is going right to pieces. Yet I feel his growing excitement. There is yet a part of him, not a very nice part that likes this, that a creature who could do such terrible things could love him also. It is unnatural, but it has bound him to the old me.

Since he will not come to me, I go to him, catch him, struggling, and hold him tight to me. "I understand," I whisper in his ear. "And you were right before. But it's different now. We have many ordinary days ahead of us, you'll see. I'm not that person. I'm just your girl now. I'm washed in the blood of Jesus Christ." Now his arms are around me too and for the first time I feel his desire for me. It's not enough to love him. I must have him too. I want to arouse him. I want him to want to fuck me. More than anything I want him to stay with me.

I throw the things down on the ground and wrap myself around him, licking at his neck and he shivers and does not pull away. I whisper in his ear, "We have only each other." I loosen my hold and drop to my knees. I am going to do something new for him, what women do, but what I have never done for him. On my knees I unfasten his old belt. Open. The zipper down. Both hands – take – tug and all down, and there he is – there he is and I have missed him and longed for him so.

I have it in my mouth, warm, surprised and stiffening between my lips, struggling in my hand like a warm bird. I have never done this for him, and it is a thrill to do this. I have done this in the past to relax the prey only, until the fatal moment they close their eyes in pleasure.

But this is real. This is sincere, because it is my Daniel in my mouth and I am his woman and his love and I would do this, and anything, to have him back and he must know this truly.

Sucking him hard, feeling him swell. His belly muscles tense and now his hands are on the back of my head, and his fingers in my hair. I have him. We are together again, and I have won.

He pushes me off of him. But in this moment, when he might scold me and run back to the place where the people are, his clothes are coming off. He is hungry for me. I have won.

I pull away my jacket, drop it by the old pine tree. I pull off my T-shirt and throw it on the ground, standing with my fists at my side, daring him, waiting for him to undress the rest of me. Already he is nude, his sex standing up hard as nails for me. He seizes the straps of my bra and pulls it up and over violently, snapping the little buckle off into the grass. My breasts fall free, and his eyes – does he see as I do? His eyes are on me. I am an ordinary girl, only a woman, but his eyes claim me. I am his woman.

Off with my jeans and then all the rest, pulling and taking me forcefully. His lips on my face, his hands smoothing over my breasts, spinning me roughly in his arms and pressing me backwards against his chest while his rough forearms hug me hard from behind, palms hoisting my breasts, pulling me fiercely to him. His fingers pinching my nipples so that I have to crouch down from the pleasure as fierce as pain. "Pig's blood," he whispers in my ear and drags me down roughly to the ground.

I feel such doubt now. His words frighten me. I am not that demon, but only a clumsy relic, an ignorant Hessian girl who doesn't even know how to drive a car. Maybe he was the right person for me before as I was, but maybe that has changed too. Maybe he is wrong now that I'm not evil anymore. Maybe he is a man who must love an evil thing to be excited, and I am only a girl like any other girl he might have for himself. I will not be bound by death and dark anymore. Will we still want each other?

He will be the sacrifice of my liberation from sin. I am alive. I might have anyone too, but I want him. I must fight for him.

Laying on my back, like every woman has from the beginning of days. My man laying on top of me, dropping his weight on me, kissing me and moving his palms over my chest, burying his face in my neck. He meanly nips my neck. He has never done this before. It hurts a little, not so fun. Why did he do that? I want to ask him, but he is sliding down my belly, hands slipping under my breasts from underneath their swell, hoisting them up as he breathes in my curled hairs, exploring my netherlands with his lips. I am lost in him. I don't want him to stop. If he were to kill me now in my happiness, I would let him.

Lips on my cunt, lapping, tongue poking and provoking. Everywhere jolts and gushes. My knees rise to show my surrender more to him and he pushes them down. We are musicians reading each other. I feel him down there working at me, listening and feeling for my response and I moan for him. He works harder, good boy! Do! Do! I listen to him too, with my bones and skin.

This is not as before. It is not about feeding anymore. This is how men and women make love. I had been a virgin until now. We had had pleasure, but it was about the evil, we did not make love like this. My clit is in his lips and I have never felt him do these things before. He has been given his taste of freedom too, and he chose me. Is he now then mine? Is it not so? He teases my clit with his tongue and I press my cunt at him. A fog of gratitude. I'm afraid to move or distract or frighten him. Is this what women feel? Does Ruby's husband do this for her?

He pauses and stops. Just when I'm about to ask what is wrong he pokes his tongue deep into me and I shriek with a sudden thrill of pleasure.

He is breathing from the nostrils, puffing from the mouth, tickling the short hairs of my cunt, my thighs tense and rise and he presses them down again, running the flat of his tongue over my clit. "Unh!" My voice, pushing hard against his lips, wanting what he is doing. I grunt. I ripple. I am a pig wallowing against his lips, vibrating in the pleasure. "What are you doing?" I whisper. A deep shudder and a wild gathering thrill as if bees are flying under my skin. "Daniel!" A shout, as though he were breaking something. "What are you doing to me!" Squeezing his face with my thighs, rising, pressing my thighs down again, my belly down. He is in command. There is a huge pink ocean inside my loins. I feel huge and swollen and soaked and in his thrall.

I could feel the excitement coming together inside me, gathering like rain. It was not only the sex, I wanted him. I had never felt this way. It was not about feeding. I wanted all of him, his devotion forever. I wanted to belong to him, like his shoes belonged to him. I want him to be vulnerable to me and for us to own each other again.

My body is moving by itself and there is a wall inside me I want to pass. I am struggling with myself to let go, to surrender, to truly surrender to him as I only pretended to do with so many others, suckers sucked dry, and left for dead. I don't want to remember them now! This moment belongs to me – to me! I am a child learning to feel in a new way.

My nails in his back, his hair, his ears, his tongue rasping flat against my yawning sex. I would do anything for him at this moment – would die if he asked me too. If he took up the stake I would hammer it home with my own hands to make him want me more.

Clasping his cheeks between my legs and keeping him lest he ever run away again. The pleasure pools in me everywhere, rising and falling and I feel my heart, and it is beating! There is a heart in me and it lives. Does he feel it? If I reach down between my thighs and grab him by the ears and draw him up and press his ear between my breasts will he hear it, and know Jesus has done this for me, and his own faith in me has done this for me by keeping me with him – by making me want this moment – and it belongs to him as I belong to him body and soul, my ordinary little soul? I will do it.

And so I do. Lifting up, his eyes looking up at me, questioning, seeing my drunken smile. My hands take his ears like pitcher handles and I pull him up protesting, and my tingling pussy protesting too. I want him inside me when I come, and the night is passing too fast. I put his head on my chest, press his ear in the valley between my breasts where I feel the fast beat thumping. He hears it too and his eyes are wide. He looks up at me in wonder. He hears a miracle down there in the depths of me. I sigh for him and he hears me breathe.

"Come inside," I whisper. "I don't need to be put down anymore."

I wish he would say something, to reassure me, but instead he gets right to business. It makes me a little angry, he wants to fuck, but I am not that demon, I am a proper woman now and he should make love to me instead. It should be more now that I have a heart beating in my breast. He should understand.

I had been killed a virgin. I had never really fucked this way before, as only a woman and a man. This is that rarest thing for me – a new experience. To make love and feel what a woman feels. To conjure in him the wanting, the groaning desire for more and more of me until there is nothing in the world for him but me in this moment. I want to open and bloom for him.

Hard, soft head of his cock so warm, insinuating, knocking at the door of me. The head of his cock pressing between the lips below feels so good, I want to scold him for being in such a hurry. But the thing is in and it is moving. Going in, knocking against the last skin of my virginity that will never be renewed again.

Ow! – oh . . . Fear. It is so fearful to be pierced, knowing it will not come again. It is so right. Inside. Inside me. More! Stay. Stay there forever.

His belly slapping, slapping down, his weight on top of me, panting, his breath in my ear, his hand behind my head, clutching hard my hair, and his other hand under me, squeezing my ass. My hips pushing up, shuddering, to welcome his thrusts. He knows. He would not dare to put his face, his neck so close to my teeth before, but he knows and he is making love to a woman now, not a white evil mannequin. He believes. His body and his manly way with me tell me he believes there is no danger in me now and I am a woman and I am his woman.

He stops moving, hanging. I am tormented and suddenly he bangs at me hard, as though his body were a cudgel. "Unh!" he yells. "Unh!" I receive him. He hovers over me, holding himself up by his palms and feet so that nothing touches but his cock inside me. "Nuh!" He lets himself down hard and bangs me with his whole body and I feel it all, his slick cock, his belly, the pine needles sticking in the skin of my back. I feel all of it. His cock is the stake, his belly the hammer and I am slain and in bliss.

"Please," I whisper.

"Unh!" Again, the stake thrusts and the hammer of his belly strikes with my legs splayed wide. He hovers over me, his face just inches from mine, smiling, looking into my eyes and I am the one hypnotized by him. I am his slave and in this moment I would do anything for him. I would do anything to make him want me more. His eyes staring fearlessly into mine. My young white American boy. He would never kill me now. I remember – I remember now, this is how babies are made. Now that I am ordinary, will we have a baby tonight? We will be a real family like any family and he will mow the lawn for me and I will taste the food I cook for him.

"Ah!"

I take his thrusts which are coming hard, angry, fierce. In a rhythm with a tormenting pause at the end of each blow, just long enough to make me yearn for the next. Strengthening. Yielding. Impatient. Amnesiac. Deep. Hard. More! Do it! Don't stop. Do it to me! Faster. Together. Confused. Astonished. Harder! Do it!

His hand behind my head – Unh! – in my ear, gripping hard my hair, pulling my head back, baring my throat as I have done, breathing, his mouth open in pleasure, biting my skin, hurting me, whispering. "It feels so good. You fuck. I missed you. You cunt. You little scary cunt. You scary little fuck. Unh!" Hammer and stake. Pounding me hard into the good night earth. My cries like song birds from my mouth to his ear.

Twisting tremors, the sea boiling, rising up in my loins – Leviathan rising – "*Kuschelbaer!*"

It is different. It feels so different, to come this way. To feel what woman feels at that moment, dying at every second. I am no demon. I don't need to be put down.

I am much changed. I was a virgin when I died. He tore me tonight. Do I bleed? Suddenly I have to know. Everything depends on it. If I am a girl, surely I must bleed down there, a simple girl on her wedding night. Again! I want to feel this again!

"Unh! You scary little blood sucking fuck!" His breathing racing, his heart beating against the skin of my breast. Heart beating against heart.

I sneak my hand down there, my right hand. I reach inside my leg, my right leg. Wetness there, I gather on my fingertips.

"Nixie! Nixie!"

I raise my hand to my nose. Blood. I know the smell. My blood. My blood is on my fingers. I have blood.

Do I dare to taste it? Is it blasphemy?

"Nixie! Ohmygod I love you! Ahh!"

Jets. Jets from his cock inside me. Love. His body goes stiff, rises above me; trembling in every little bone. His neck stretched over my ear, shaking with his pleasure.

I taste my fingers.

It is my blood. My own. It is bitter, and it is mine. I feel it rising in me. His lips. His tongue in my ear, licking, biting me, moaning with his relief. I want to bite him. To bite him! I long to bite him! The waves of pleasure rise again, bursting, blotting out everything. My teeth. My teeth. Deep. Taking it in, all in, sucking. Greedy. Blood in my mouth.

Whose blood is in my mouth? *There should not be blood in my mouth!*

Oh no. Oh God no. I am saved. It cannot be. It cannot. God would not let it happen.

NO!

I'm saved. Jesus saved me. He did. *We had a deal!*

He is lying on top of me, all limp and vacant and hollow. He has left me again. Where will I chase him to now? I slip my teeth, now familiar and long, from his skin and a small angry trail of blood follows after. I can barely move, the fading pleasure in my hips, turning bitter, the feeling of the blood within. I roll to the side and tumble the carcass off of me.

Kuschelbaer . . . no. I bury my face in his cold belly and scream my agony into his skin.

Oh God. You should have killed me instead. You should have killed me. If only you had killed me instead when you could have. I'm so alone. I feel so confused. I can't think, everything is happening too fast. Who am I? Am I supposed to be the girl or the demon? I should be dancing somewhere, am I late? Why am I naked? Where is my baby? Will the Unicorn come and call my name? Why can't I live on the moon?

Come back to me. Why are there no tears? I want my tears. There should be tears for him.

My . . . my big snuggly bear, *kuschelbaer*, don't leave me again. Oh no, oh no, oh no . . . dance with me.

I want to kill something. Kill it slowly. I want to feel my teeth in something and hear it cry and beg to God for its life. Jesus! Lying bastard Jesus!

Blood.

Over by the trees, further down the river, the whisper of blood is on the air. Under the smell is a bright feeling of pain. There is pain and there is blood and there is an emotion I can't understand anymore.

Walking through the high grass of the field between tree groves along the river bank. The bright moonlight on my skin. Without love or hope of love, I am exactly who I am meant to be. I am transforming. I am becoming glorious. The whore of Babylon riding the beast. When people see me they shall worship me. The grasshoppers jumping away from me as I pass. High above, crows are crying for me, poor black angels. The night air leading me. I am home again. Somewhere God is shaking His fist at me.

Baaa baaa baaa.

Weil ich Jesu Schaflein bin . . . Freu' ich mich nur immerhin . . .

I am Jesus's little lamb. *Ich Jesu Schaflein bin.*

Baaa baaa baaa. Hop hop hop.

I am Jesus's little lamb chop.

Baa baa baa. Chop chop chop.

Blood scent coming from those trees beside the water. But there is this funny sound. I lower my head and listen carefully and there is a slap . . . slap . . . slap . . . not of skin on skin, but something else. And the sea smell of tears. Now I move like the hunter. I am the Angel that withers hope. I am Death become woman. Cry you crows! Cry for little *Nordchen*. Here he is, here in the trees, I see him.

He is sitting back in the shadows under a tree. His skin is bare, naked like me. The smell of the blood on his back and on his shoulder, is shaped in streaks, cuts and welts. He is on his knees and he is whispering in the silly baaa baaa baaa language and his arm moves, crossing his chest. His hand rises – slap! Leather cords across his back. Blood on steel balls. Is it Jesus whipping himself? If this is Jesus I'll punish him for lying to me.

He is hurting himself. I've seen these things before. But it is only the preacher man. In the grass near his knee, the bitter smell of blood on steel again. That must be a knife. Yes, on his bare thighs there is a row of cuts. As I move in close behind him a man smell, the smell of his cum. It's different from the smell of Daniel, drying sticky on my thighs. But there is no woman here, only himself. I remember sometimes meeting men like this in the past. Angry, dangerous men. They are fun to kill.

"Hallelujah . . . Oh my Lord Jesus, deliver me . . . Abba abba hey yeah . . . yeah, reprove me, oh my Lord. Reprove my flesh from lust . . . Abba Eloi Adonai . . ."

His eyes are closed and he doesn't see as I reach down and pick up his knife. His blood is on the blade. I lick the blade and taste his blood which is already a little stale. This is a lonely tasting man.

If it had been any man but this one, I would have his head dripping from a tree by now to comfort me. But I am curious about him and I am terribly confused and I want to kill every creature in the world so that I can be alone but there so many things that must be killed and . . . and . . . and he must tell me why I am not saved anymore which I think might have become a good thing and God has abandoned me instead and I must keep killing people now and . . . and . . . and – why?

I shut the blade and let him hear the sound so he will notice me. At the sound, he turns suddenly and stinks of shame. He is looking at me wide eyed, but he can't see me the way I can see him. There is a bloody lash in his hand, and his legs and belly are covered in sweet smelling cuts. I want to tear him into food for owls and crows. But I want to lick his body and weep in his lap. I feel so confused.

"Who's there?"

"Help me, sir." I step around into the small patch of moonlight between the tree shadows and let him look at me. His knees are apart and his sex is erect and making the man smell.

He throws down the little whip, glances down at the grass where the knife was. I hide my hand behind my back. "Where . . ." He looks up, fearful. He sees me in the light, small pale, big breasted and nude. "What are you?" He jumps to his feet, stumbling backwards. "What are you? Who sent you here?"

"I smelled your blood." As I say that, there is a new puff of fear from him, and his wounds bleed a little faster. The smell is confusing me and filling me with light and my head with noise. The winds of the Holy Ghost are roaring in my ears. Above me enraged angels are descending blowing trumpets. "Why did you do that?" I point at his wounds.

"Who sent you? God? Satan? Why are you like that?" Pointing at my nakedness. "Are you tempting me? Jesus has forgiven me for what happened in the motel."

I want to cry. I want to kill. I want to die. I don't know what I want. "Why are you like that?" I wave at his bloody cuts and welts. "Are you trying to tempt me?"

"I know you. You were the girl with the devil."

"I know you," I say. "I'm the girl with the devil." I begin clawing at my face. I want to tear the flesh off my skull and show him my grinning skull, but he steps forward and takes my hands away from me.

"What happened to you?" he says.

I'm still holding his knife, hidden in my hand. I should maybe give it to him, I think. But not yet. "When you die, sir, what will happen to you?"

"What is your name? Tell me your name."

"Nixie."

"You want to know what will happen when we die? Where will you spend eternity, Nixie? Where?"

"In Hell."

"No, Nixie, no. You're saved by the blood of Jesus—"

"No!" I yell at him. "I'm going to Hell. No matter what." My shoulders are shaking and my head is bowed. His arms are around me and he draws me close. "Where will you go when you die?"

"Heaven," he says. His hands pass gently down my back and he holds me tighter. "When Jesus shouts and the rapture comes I'll go straight up to Heaven to be with Jesus. Won't you?"

"No."

"Haven't you accepted Jesus as your savior?" His hands are moving gently down my arms to my waist. I can hear his heart now, which I could not hear before.

"I tried." His hand is lifting my breast.

"Then you'll be with the Lord, together with me. You'll be in Heaven, Nixie. You will be with me together in Heaven as Jesus promised."

Now his other hand is at my other breast, touching me. His man smell is strong. "But, I want to be with Daniel." I feel so confused. Then I remember the blood. "Why did you do that to yourself?"

"Jesus has forgiven us of all our past sins, do you believe me, Nixie? And the Lord forgives us our future sins even before they're done. Do you trust me, Nixie? Even if we be weak in the eyes of God, we are forgiven by grace alone. Do you believe that?"

"No . . ." I whisper. "I don't."

"I'm not perfect, Nixie." His fingers move over my nipples. "What we're doing, this will be our secret. Do you trust me?"

"No . . ." I whisper. "I don't." Gently, I push him away from me.

He raises his arm, points his finger and says, "Get thee behind me!"

"Get thee behind me?"

"Satan!" He shakes his hand at me. And points again. "Get thee behind me, demon! I cast thee out in the name of Jesus Christ."

I fall on my knees. I spread my arms wide for the devil to leave me.

The preacher man comes towards me, stands in front of me, towering down imperiously. His cock is in my face and it's bobbing with his heart beat. "I command you . . ." he sighs. "Obey me. Obey me. Adonai – abbba laba elehu abba. Abba."

I am waiting for the devil to leave me. For the peace to come and heal me and make me a good girl for Daniel again so he will come back to me, and the angry angels beating me with their lightning will leave me alone. Alone! Alone! I close my eyes and wait for the miracle.

I feel something soft and hot brush my lips. The angels go away. I open my eyes and his cock is in my face. Pray. Pray for me.

Prey. Prey for me.

Overhead the stars are falling and the moon is turning as red as blood. The earth is crawling with dumb bastards. The night sky is ripped in two with thunder revealed to me. I am the Dragon of God. I am the Wrath of God made rampant. I am the one true way. I am Death made perfect. The prey is not perfect. I will make him perfect.

I stand up slowly, silently so as not to startle him. With one hand I soothe the stiff penis, to relax the prey. I feel him become languid. The prey has closed his eyes and is moving his cock inside my fist. I've seen it all before so many times. It's all so tedious. The prey is ready now. I flip the knife open and the smell of the prey's blood fills my head. "Abbbaaa . . . Adonai . . . adaonai . . . hallelujah . . ." he whispers.

My hand lets go of his cock, strikes out and grabs his throat. The prey's eyes pop open. "I am not possessed by a demon." I lean in and scream at his face, "*I am the demon!*"

I squeeze. His lying tongue that tricked me into killing my Daniel pops out. A swift cut with the knife and his tongue falls in the grass. This is a good little knife. Now he won't trick me with lies.

"*Du!*" I say to the prey in my Holy Ghost language. "*Du sollst den verdammten keine falschen Hoffnungen machen!*" He is beating at my hands, and his struggle excites me more and more. The sound of his heart pounding in my ears fills the sky and the dancing trees. Crows – cry for him! Where is his God now? The blood running down his gullet is strangling him.

"You are going to Heaven, *jah*? Do you think? First you must share a moment with me in Hell." He's trying to shout and cannot. I slip the knife up and inside his left rib and in a fast high motion run the blade along his rib bone, slashing the diaphragm. Now he can't draw a breath or cry out. It's nothing. It's an old trick.

I will not have his blood. That is not the message he will carry to God for me when he trudges to the gates of his Heaven. No. I have had the blood of the most sacred lamb, which I swore I would never touch, and there is no one worthy to mix with the blood of my *kuschelbaer*. I will not drink again. Ever. I didn't know this until now. I only just thought of it. I hear the man wheeze and bend over.

God has a message for me. What can it be? God must explain to me why I feel so confused. I will read the future!

The prey swats at me with his limp hands. I ignore him and push the blade sideways into his belly now and cut straight upwards, avoiding the tough belly muscles which are too much work for the little knife to saw through. Red and blue intestines puff out like balloons. There is this tough membrane that covers them and you must cut through this membrane and free them – like so, and then pull them out – like so. But gently so that he does not die and escape Hell with me.

Now I let him fall. Boom.

I watch him crawl for a while crying and dragging himself. His guts are getting all sticky dirty in the dry pine needles. I think he is trying to hide behind the tree. There is no hurry, it takes some time to die this way. Come here, sir. What a bad evening you are having. Well, I am having a bad evening also. I grab his ankle and pull him backwards and his guts are covered with pine needles now like a bakery treat. I look at his entrails, watch his convulsions as he flops his arms. I pull apart some of his intestines, looking for patterns. I want to read them, I want to see my fortune in them as Grandmamma did, but she didn't teach me how. I wish she were here to help. He slaps his hand at me. Slaps at his guts, maybe trying to gather them back in. I pull the ropy, sticky things apart a little, trying to peer at what is beneath, looking for some hope in the future, and his back arches as though with pleasure and he makes a sucking sound with his lips. I think there is something there. There is a message there, how do I read it? Oh this man! He just won't lie still.

I punch him hard in the face to make him behave. I sit on his chest.

What are you seeing, sir? Only some naked girl? Or are you seeing my absence of humanity, do you think I am not like you at all? Are you proud you are not like me and you're bound for the Heaven and I for the Hell; do you think you're superior to me because God loves you more, do you? Do you see poor lost *Nordchen* in me at all anymore, or only a devil? Do you see the real me? Tell me, who is she?

He will not answer me. Do you see, Daniel, it is only a pig's blood on my hands. I don't lie. It's all going rotten and I can't stop it. I'm so confused. Do you feel there is any hope for me, sir? He will not answer me, he is so useless. I take my knife and cut off his lips and now he looks like a clown. Stupid man. Stupid useless man. Do you like that?

I turn the knife around and knock out his front teeth with the butt of it, but it makes me feel even more confused.

Don't you see, sir?

I would have found you anywhere you went. We belong together.

Suddenly I am filled with rage, a blind and bloody rage towards this man and his God. I cannot remember my name I am so filled with hate for this person. Where are my tears!

Two fast chops with the knife in the neck and I let the fountains spray over me. I stab him over and over in his face and his eyes and his mouth and his neck and his chest. Ah! Ah! Ah! Like tenderizing a beef roast – oh God!

Oh God. I never made a pot roast for my man.

Oh my love, forgive your *Nordchen*. You would have loved my *sauerbraten*. You would have.

I want my tears. Why are there no tears? Give me my tears!

I shower in his warm blood. The useless prey did not know how to cut himself good with this knife – but I do! The smell of the blood fills my senses and I want to kill every living thing in all the world one by one.

I want everything to stop and be quiet. I'm so confused. The stars are falling. I want to be alone! What if the people find me here – leave me alone! Time to think about the years all gone, all lost. But I hear the echo of voices drifting through the trees, are they the people? Is it the Unicorn come to call for me? No – I don't think. Do ghosts smell? I don't know. Why? Why don't they all fade away? Leave me alone. Alone! Alone! Alone! Why don't they leave me alone?

"Harold?" A young woman's voice, high and thin. "Harold? Are you over here? Are you done?" She is coming, waving a flashlight.

She comes close and she is carrying something wrapped in her arms in a blanket. I stand up to greet her and to be polite to her. I've seen this girl. "Harold . . . ?" The flashlight shines in my eyes. "So – *you're that whore he's been fucking!*"

She swings the flashlight at my face and I dance back from it. She can't move well because of something in her arms that smells like Harzer cheese. We are alone. I show her the knife, but the flashlight is shining on my body and she sees my glory. I am the dragon. I am the lamb of salvation, washed in the blood of a fool. I spread my arms wide and I feel them turning into huge feathered wings to sweep me up to Heaven to be with *kuschelbaer*. She sees the prey and her scream stops in her throat. "What happened?"

Why do people ask stupid things? I am filled with the Holy Ghost but she is not looking at me, she asks stupid things instead of worshiping my glory. I must speak in her language so she can understand instead of using the Holy Ghost language. I point the knife at her commanding as I did before to the prey. "Thou shalt not give false hope to the damned!"

She starts to scream, really screaming now. The blanket in her arms slips away – and I see him – it is the baby boy. This woman, I know her! The baby looks at me, he sees me. His eyes! He should not be looking at me that way. His eyes fill me with terror. The horror of it sweeps over me. It is unbearable!

"Love me," I plead to the baby, my voice cracking, backing away from him in fear and shame. "Please love me too." I look down. Somehow I am covered in blood. So much blood. He must not look upon me!

The baby opens his mouth as he sees the blood of his father drenched all over me. His toothless grin. He laughs at me. A gurgling, bubbling sound like someone drowning in their blood. I know that sound so well!

I throw my arm up over my face. Don't laugh at your daddy's blood! Don't look at me! I can't stand it. The mother screams, far away the shouting of voices. Under the scream all I can hear is the terrifying gurgling laughter of the little boy I will never ever have. I am melting.

Throwing down the knife. Get away! The baby, the drowning laugh – get him away from me! Help me! Blood! Blood, little baby! So much blood!

Jumping into the river to flee from his laughing eyes. Down. Down. The dark water, so dark even my eyes can't see. The deep cold water and my mind is clearer.

Down deep in the water, I push my feet in the sand and feel the cold flow against my bare skin. The solitude calms me. What was I doing just now? For a moment I'm not sure where I am. Everything is a coffin dream. I want to see Daniel. It's the only thing I know. Climbing up out of the water, thrashing through the tall thick weeds, the riverbank is slippery and hard to climb, but I must see Daniel. I'm so tired. I wish I could really become a bat. Or a wolf would be nice. I wish I could do those things and not be a woman ever again. All around me there are animals watching me. I don't want to see people ever again. Up river where I was, the woman is crying and still screaming like crazy and now another woman is screaming with her. I remember everything, but it is fuzzy. Well, now I guess they have found him. A new smell, of sour food. Strong men are vomiting.

There he is. So still. So vacant. He is all inside me now, but I would give my useless pointless life a thousand times to put my broken doll back together again. On the other side the sun is rising over the trees, like a hot silver blade in the high clouds. It will be light soon. It is humiliating to hide from it in defeat. I want to make my stand here and curse at it until it burns me up or until I can blot it out. I don't want to go on anymore but maybe not just yet. I want to hold him in my arms as I rest. I want to be with him longer, both dead together, each in our way.

Shaking water from my hair, drawing away a strand from my eyes. I dress myself again in my torn clothes, and it reminds me of the mornings before, dressing myself after the love, his eyes eating me up, his cock rising back a bit, offering me a little more. The good dawn time when he would pull me back down on to him and undress me again, grabbing each other and laughing like children.

Oh the little baby.

Soon the people will come looking for me. I will carry him with me into the water and we'll wait out the day in the bottom of the river. I will hold him tight to me until there is nothing left of him. Oh, but see him. I will never see him again as he is now. Let me hold him a while. See, how he looks at peace. We had to sleep apart in the day, because I might kill him by accident in my sleep. But see – it happens anyway.

So ist Das Leben . . . It's just the way it goes. In the end, we are only what we are.

I dress him now too, like the little boy we might have had. Wake up! Wake up! Time to get up, sleepy head! Must get you ready for school, here's a nice sandwich and an apple for you, and one more for your teacher too, all in a bag and a kiss goodbye at the bus stop that will embarrass you in front of your little friends. Goodbye sweetie, goodbye!

Now. Now here they come. I have my tears. And is this how you make of me a real girl, *kuschelbaer* – to make me cry? Was it the best you could think to do?

Sit now *nordchen*, by the waters of Babylon and weep.